Fiona Walker lives in Worcestersh... children plus an assortment of horses and dogs. Visit Fiona's website at www.fionawalker.com.

THE LOVE LETTER

Fiona Walker

SPHERE

First published in Great Britain as a paperback original in 2012 by Sphere
Reprinted 2012 (twice)

A CIP catalogue record for this book
is available from the British Library.

ISBN 978-0-7515-4789-4

Typeset in Plantin by M Rules
Printed and bound in Great Britain by
Clays Ltd, St Ives plc

Papers used by Sphere are from well-managed forests
and other responsible sources.

 MIX
Paper from
responsible sources
FSC® C104740

Sphere
An imprint of
Little, Brown Book Group
100 Victoria Embankment
London EC4Y 0DY

An Hachette UK Company
www.hachette.co.uk

www.littlebrown.co.uk

For the Boddington Bon Vivant, the flame-haired Freudian and the High Peaks academic, whose kinship and company is such a joy, and who enjoyed the 'real' Spywood; with love and gratitude.

Prologue

From: Kelly
  To: Allegra North
  Re: PFEF Finland

Dear Allegra,
Thank you for forwarding the Finnish edition of *Ptolemy Finch and the Emerald Falcon* for Gordon; I will mark one for his attention.
Kind regards,
Kelly

From: Gordon Lapis
  To: Allegra North
  Re: PFEF Finland

Allegra,
Kelly has just put this in front of me and once again I am astonished by the liberties taken in translation. I have been working my way through it with the aid of BabelFish and a Finnish dictionary and see that in Chapter 5 when Ptolemy suffers a reaction to the sting from the dune wasp, Purple tells him 'your dick is swollen'. Later, in Chapter 18, when Rushlore asks Ptolemy where his sidekick is, he replies 'I had sex with Purple yesterday'. I know the Finnish are liberal sorts, but I will remind you that this is a children's book.
GL

From: Allegra North
To: Gordon Lapis
Cc: Kelly
Re: PFEP Finland

Dear Gordon,

I believe that in Finnish the phrase for 'swollen tongue' is very close to 'swollen dick' and there may be a small typo, which we trust will not affect the reading pleasure of your many Finnish fans. Similarly, I am told that 'I saw her yesterday' only requires a missing umlaut to become a far more intimate statement. Again, I'm certain it won't affect readers' enjoyment.
Regards,
Allegra

From: Gordon Lapis
To: Allegra North
Re: PFEF Finland

Allegra,

It's essential that Ptolemy remains asexual. Perhaps this is why in Chapter 21 of the Finnish version, when he and Purple are sitting on the clifftop above the Sea of Sand, he says 'I am a parasite'? Parasites reproduce asexually, so no doubt you will reply assuring me that I should be grateful to my Finnish translator.
GL
P.s. I cannot get through to Conrad. Where is he?

Dear Gordon,

I gather 'iloinen' (happy) and 'loinen' (parasite) are easily muddled, but of course I will take this up with your Finnish publisher as a matter of urgency.

May I take this opportunity to apologise profusely on behalf of Conrad, myself and all at Fellows Howlett for any distress this is causing you.

Conrad is out of the office all day, I'm afraid, and not contactable on his BlackBerry. I haven't seen him since yesterday, but I will make sure he's apprised of this.

Regards,

Allegra

Allegra,

Is that 'seen him' with or without an umlaut?

GL

P.s. Please do not always cc our correspondence to Kelly; displacement activities like re-translating translations are an author's secret vice, and my assistant is my guilty conscience.

Gordon,

Nothing umlautish about Conrad, as you know.

As secret vices go, I believe teaching yourself Finnish is deeply noble. I have heard back from your publisher in Helsinki who reassures me that the translation is perfect and that BabelFish is leading us both astray. I trust that makes you feel parasitic.

Allegra

Indeed, my tongue is swollen with delight. I think Conrad has a great deal of the lout about his accent. In diacritic terms, I am regrettably grave.
With apologies for antagonism,
GL

No apology needed.
A
P.s. I'm acute.

Fellows Howlett has an imposter in its midst; a sense of humour is surely against company policy. I believe you are also a fan of detective fiction?
GL

It's my dream to discover a bestselling crime writer from the agency's slush pile.
A

What future would you suggest for a Finnish detective named Iloinen Loinen?
GL

A name change. While you were quite right to insist 'Ptolemy with a silent P' could be loved and understood by the public, Iloinen Loinen is never likely to be big in Japan.
A
P.s. Scandinavian detectives are very last year.

And what do you predict will be big in Japan, Allegra?

A young, gutsy female detective from west London; you can feature popular tourist attractions interspersed with violence, murder and Knightsbridge department stores. Think rumpled, blonde, big smile, kind heart. Incredibly sharp, witty and courageous.

I take it the grizzled, hard-drinking man with a broken marriage is also 'last year', along with monochrome landscape of high rises, dingy pubs, back alleys and sex workers . . . ?

That's still a good formula. How about a double act? She = rumpled and feisty; he = grizzled and boozy. Mismatches are always a hit; readers will love the sexual chemistry.

I'll remind you that sexual chemistry is not within my literary canon.

Untrue! Ptolemy Finch always makes me v hot under the collar when chatting to Purple on clifftops. You totally understand the secret of building sexual tension over soooo long it makes your readers ache.

You must moderate these urges if you are to remain as my research assistant. You must also stop discussing our communications with Conrad, in or out of work.
I shall call my detective duo Julie Ocean and Jimmy Jimee. Their relationship will be entirely professional, a concept you will need to use your undeniably vivid imagination to grasp.
GL
P.s. Please forward IM+ name and keep an open line at all times.

Is IM+ name like porn star name (first pet and street name)?
Gopher Kew.
A

From: Kelly
  To: Allegra North
  Cc: Gordon Lapis; Conrad Knight
  Re: From Gordon Lapis

Dear Allegra,
Gordon asks that you stop sending emails direct to him because he is working on a new project entitled *The Girl with the Parasite Ache* all afternoon. You can direct any further emails via my address as usual.
Kind regards
Kelly

From: Conrad Knight
To: Allegra
Re: Gordon

Legs,

DO NOT encourage Gordon to write detective fiction; we have enough problems keeping him focused on Ptolemy. You must remain professional. Think 'Reveal'.

It has been brought to my attention by Human Resources that your personal mobile phone is inadequate for your enhanced professional role. Fellows Howlett are therefore providing you with a company cell-phone which will be carefully monitored for use. Do not play games on it.

Conrad

P.s. Book our usual table for dinner.

Booked! A xxx

P.s. We don't have an HR department, do we . . . ?

Chapter 1

'Breathe *in*, Legs!'

Allegra North breathed in deeply as her sister hauled at the corset laces in the satin bodice. As her waist narrowed, her chest expanded and her white bra rose out of the square Elizabethan cleavage and burst through the delicate lace bib like airbags popping through a car windscreen.

'I knew you should have put on the whalebone basque.' Ros's reddened face appeared over her sister's shoulder as Legs crammed the offending spheres back in and peered down at the broken stitching.

'I can't believe you thought this would fit me. You were only a size eight when you married. We all remember the raw fish diet; you were sucking Smints all the way up the aisle.'

'But it was worth it,' Ros sighed, glancing down to her size fourteen curves before gazing wistfully at her sister's reflection in the mirror ahead of them. 'I love this dress.'

Legs also regarded the huge meringue that she was now uncomfortably sporting, modelled on the Ditchley portrait of Elizabeth I. It had never been to her taste, especially the high lace ruff and wired collar which she'd secretly thought made her sister look like Cruella de Vil posing as a butterfly when Ros had married Will twelve years earlier. But it was undoubtedly a spectacular creation, meticulously hand-embroidered. Now, carefully released from the plastic cocoon in which it had been resting on the back of the spare room door for over a decade, it had just been lowered onto Allegra with the reverie of a queen's coronation robes being fitted to a maid to enable a royal escape from treachery. She was at least a dress size too large and six inches too tall for the made-to-measure creation, and her familiar pink-cheeked outdoors complexion looked faintly ridiculous peering into the mirror above such delicate stitch-work and intricate detail. She fingered one of the embroidered flowers, seeded with pearls, which had been a labour of love for the designers who'd attached two hundred of them ready for The Big Day.

Ros swatted her hand away from the precious little four-petal motif and then reached behind her sister to tuck the corset laces into the skirt waist.

'I so love this dress.' She sighed again as she began buttoning up the lace panel over the stays. 'I'd always hoped you might want to wear it when you and Francis . . .' She stopped herself, face ducking out of sight behind the huge ruff. 'You do look beautiful in it.'

Rosalind's wedding day had been a no-holds-Bard Elizabethan extravaganza. Despite marrying into one of London's oldest Catholic families whose heritage dated back to before the Reformation, she'd somehow pulled it off. If they could have feasted on roast swan, Legs knew her sister would have ordered it. The occasion had been spectacular, theatrical and fun, as so much surrounding Ros had been in those days. A vivacious, clever musician still studying at the Royal Academy, Ros had been playing harpsichord in the foyer of the Barbican when Will Herbert first spotted her, her energy and passion causing him to miss the play he was supposed to be reviewing for *Time Out* and ask her for a drink instead. A year later, they were married at Brompton Oratory and Allegra and Ros's father Dorian had literally sold the family furniture to pay for it, some of the best pieces he'd collected over the years suddenly finding themselves relocated from the family's tall, Victorian Kew townhouse to his Richmond antiques shop in what he had tactfully referred to at the time as a 'much-needed declutter'.

The dress Legs was now sporting had cost Dorian a matching pair of George III Sheraton armchairs and a marble-topped Louis XV bombé and had been just as awkward to fit in the back of a vintage Rolls Royce.

Still only nineteen at the time, Ros had been a radiantly happy bride, her conversion to Catholicism as all-consuming as her love for Will. That day, bursting with joy, the new Mrs Herbert performed in public for the last time. As a personal gift bestowed from wife to husband alongside the wedding list dinner service, silverware and crystal from their guests, Ros insisted that she must give up her musical training and dedicate herself to becoming a homemaker.

To bridesmaid Legs, poised to begin studying for her A levels amid dreams of globe-trotting and career-building, such devotion to domesticity had been anathema and she'd dived out of the way when the skilfully tossed pomander bouquet had flown in her direction. But Ros firmly believed that the holy trinity of happiness lay between the altar, the kitchen sink and the font.

Within weeks, she'd fallen pregnant amid frantic nesting in the Fulham flat the newlyweds shared. When Nico was two, the family moved to a Regency villa in Ealing, meaning that Will forfeited his dreams of freelancing while writing a novel, and instead let the Herbert family pull one of their many old school ties to secure him a well-paid editorship of a worthy but dull financial journal which bored him rigid but paid the monthly mortgage interest. Once Nico started school, Ros took on private piano tuition to help ends meet, but the money and the marriage wore increasingly thin, and that Elizabethan feast which had united writer and musician seemed a world apart as husband and wife slowly became affection-starved enemies under the same roof.

The cherished wedding dress had remained in the house long after Will's tenancy ended. Five years earlier, he'd run away with the part-time nanny (and tenant of their ground floor flat), struggling scriptwriter Daisy, this betrayal made more awkward still by the fact that Daisy was a family friend who had been thick as thieves with Allegra since childhood. After a brief spell of utter disbelief followed by inconsolable fury, Ros had retreated into martyrdom, a state in which she still existed, refusing to acknowledge the second life her son now had with his father and his half-siblings.

These days, Will and Daisy lived in glorious chaos in Somerset with two more children and a third on the way, their rural idyll funded by Daisy's runaway sitcom success *Slap Dash*. Although Will picked up occasional freelance work in between cooking, childcare and chicken rearing, this house-husband role was a cause of much criticism from Ros, who thought he'd 'wimped out'. His income barely covered the maintenance, and finances remained the biggest clash-point between the sparring ex-spouses – and they were the reason Ros had decided to clamp her younger sister in the dream dress today.

'I knew it would suit you perfectly,' she sighed, on tiptoes again and looking over Legs' shoulder, their matching dark grey eyes lined up, Ros's features sharper and framed with hair the colour of cinnamon roast coffee beans cut into a neat urchin bob like a principal boy, making Legs resemble a rather blousy Cinderella by contrast, with smudges of last night's mascara beneath her wide eyes and her cloud of wild blonde hair on end, showing too much dark root.

'It's a bit short.' Legs peered at her flip-flopped feet poking out, complete with the three star tattoos on the left ankle she now regretted getting during her first term at university. Francis had made such a fuss when he saw them. At the time she'd been rebelliously unapologetic, but now she hated them, their zig-zag blue permanence a perpetual reminder of her unofficial catchphrase, that if you live for the moment, you also have to live with the consequence.

She'd been determined not to think about Francis, but now that she did, his face appeared beside hers in the mirror, seeing her in a wedding dress, blue eyes softening with pride, blonde hair swept back from that fallen-angel face. He'd make the most debonair of bridegrooms, so tall and handsome and charming. Ever since they'd first got together as two dare-playing teenagers who'd agreed to practise their kissing techniques on each other, she'd been fantasising about their wedding, remodelling it in her mind as the years passed. At first, it had been a sparkling Cinderella dress and a horse-drawn carriage; in her later teens the plan had changed to rock and roll Chelsea Registry Office and clubbing around London all night; then when they travelled together after university, she'd fallen for exotic white sand beaches, sarongs, sandals and simplicity. A decade after their first kiss, Francis had made the fantasy real by popping the question in the tiny Ladbroke Grove flat they shared together, both by then carving careers in publishing. Together, they had planned a simple ceremony in the chapel at Farcombe within earshot of the Celtic Sea off the North Devon coast in which they had swum together since childhood, the gulls calling above the cliff walks they'd known all their lives and the coves they'd spent so long exploring. In the evening, they planned to host a huge party in the main hall, Francis's childhood holiday home, with his father playing the bassoon and Ros the piano, other musician friends joining in, the arts-festival crowd adding eccentricity and colour, their school and university friends, the families that knew one another so well, village pub the Book Inn running the bar and the locals from Eascombe and Fargoe invited, all hell-bent on enjoying the celebration of the decade. It would be a party never to forget, and it was several years in the planning, with the couple's families eagerly adding their input, including the offer of the dreaded Ditchley dress.

Legs looked at her reflection again, the dress totally unsuited to her, its corset now so tightly laced that her waist was freakishly pinched above the farthingale and her face was turning red. She looked like a wild poppy drooping in a square jewelled vase.

Yet there was something about wearing a wedding dress that suspended her customary sardonic streak and forced a wellspring of sentiment through her protective shield. Just for a moment she let herself imagine the past year had not happened and that she was getting married after all. The thought made her giddy.

'I was the happiest I've ever felt in my life when I wore this dress.' Ros had tears in her eyes. 'It makes you feel ethereal, doesn't it?'

'It's not too late to change your mind about it, you know,' Legs said kindly, reminding herself that any ethereal, giddy feelings were due to lack of oxygen. She was growing increasingly light-headed because she couldn't breathe properly.

'Nonsense! The photographer is waiting and we must press on. I'm needed at the abbey to help arrange the altar flowers. What are you going to do about your hair?'

'What's wrong with it?

'You can't leave it like that.' Ros reached into a drawer of her dressing table. 'It's hanging all over the ruff – here!' She scraped her sister's uncombed blonde hair into a topknot and anchored it so tightly with a jewelled scrunchy that Legs winced at the impromptu Essex facelift. 'Much better. You can go into the garden for pictures I think. You'll have to bend your knees so those flip-flops don't show.' She turned to march from the room, calling 'Nicholas! Nicho*las*! We're ready for you!'

Lagging behind and still fighting for breath, Legs picked up her new mobile phone to check whether Conrad had texted yet to say whether he'd make it. He hadn't. Gordon Lapis, meanwhile, had sent several emails very early that morning, complaining about the Portuguese translation of *Emerald Falcon* and asking her what Julie Ocean's typical breakfast routine might be.

When Conrad had insisted that the company fund the newest, whizziest iPhone for his PA – quite unprecedented at Fellows Howlett, where one got to take home an office laptop about as often as a school guinea pig and at least one director had yet to go digital at all – Legs had excitedly assumed this meant that he wanted a hotline to her at all times. She now realised that he just wanted to get the agency's most awkward author, Gordon Lapis, off his back and onto hers.

She tucked it into her sleeve and followed her sister along the landing.

Predictably, there was no answer from the room at the far end of the corridor covered with 'keep out' signs.

14

Ros knocked hard. 'Nicholas!' She always pronounced the last two syllables of her son's name 'alas', as though he was something to regret. He'd recently announced that he would answer only to 'Nico', a fact his mother chose to completely ignore.

'I need you to come and take photos of Legs in the garden,' she insisted.

At the mention of his aunt's name, Nico unlocked his door and peered out, only one suspicious green eye visible behind a small chink in the heavy brown fringe. Then he reached up to sweep his locks aside and gape at the Ditchley replica.

'Wow. That's badass. Is that fancy dress?'

Legs laughed, which was a mistake as her boobs burst up through the lace neckline again, like two lifebuoys bobbing over a wave.

Ros gave the ten-year-old a withering look and gritted her teeth. '*This* is the dress in which I married your father, Nicholas. Aunt Legs is modelling it so we can put it on eBay because the bridegroom now pays a pittance in alimony and I can't afford your schooling without selling things.'

'I'm on a full scholarship,' Nico pointed out flatly, eyes glazing over as they always did when his mother started bad-mouthing his father in front of him.

'That takes no account for all the extras.' She waved her hand dismissively and started marching towards the head of the stairs. 'Now I'll leave you two at it because I'm already late. Nicholas, you're needed for choir at ten-thirty; the ceremony's at quarter to eleven. Jamie's mother will call for you when they walk past. Be sure to wash your hands.' She marched off, face set hard as it so often was when she spoke about Will, more so today because of the shock of seeing her wedding dress and remembering the hopes and joy that had surrounded the happiest day of her life.

Nico stood in his doorway watching her retreat, his father's big fawn eyes blinking from his face, accustomed to his mother's spikiness, that abrupt, no-nonsense tone she used at all times, and at stressful times most of all. Then he eyed his aunt again.

'That really is some frock.'

'You've never seen it?'

'I sort of remember seeing it in a picture once, but Mum threw away all the wedding photographs when Dad left us. I bet she looked amazing.'

'She did. Granny North still has some pictures I think.'

'Was it a good day?'

She nodded. 'I was a bridesmaid; we all got to wear red velvet brocade and funny headdresses like nurses' hats. It was jolly hot, like today. Take my tip and wear the latest Arsenal strip when you get hitched.'

Nico closed one eye. 'Nah, I'm never going to get married. I don't like girls much.'

Legs shot him a sympathetic look and he dived back into his room for his high tech camera.

Aside from singing and football, Nico's greatest talent was photography, something Legs privately guessed he was far more passionate about than the choral practice his mother encouraged him to do each day.

'I know it's not quite *Vogue*,' she apologised as they trailed downstairs. 'But it's a start.'

'I want to be a sports photographer,' he reminded her.

'Sure.' She smiled encouragingly. 'Capture the Gunners winning the Treble.'

'Too right.' He bounded past and led the way downstairs and out through the open plan kitchen to the pretty walled garden that stretched behind the west London townhouse, currently bursting with its best midsummer finery, the dahlias and zinnias waving vast lollipop heads of red and pink from the borders, buddleia and rambling roses bobbing overhead, lavender and sweetpeas crowding fragrantly around the trunks of the fruit trees.

It might have appeared perfect wedding weather through the window, with the striped green lawns dancing with sunlight, but in fact it was blowing a gale. Stepping onto the decking, Legs almost

16

took off as her skirts inverted, revealing a skeleton farthingale and her bare thighs.

'DO NOT take a photograph!' she ordered from inside several layers of silk and damask as she fought the skirts back down, knowing that the temptation for a ten-year-old to capture the moment would probably be too great. The shot could be used as blackmail for years to come, although she supposed at least her face was covered in pearl-studded cream silk. But those legs would be unmistakeable in the family. They were legend.

Being called Allegra was always going to lead to one nickname, particularly fitting given how distinctive her legs actually were. Yet this nickname hadn't been bestowed on Legs as a result of her possessing long, slender lower limbs up to her armpits; quite the reverse. From toddlerdom on, her legs had always been like tree-trunks, despite her otherwise slim frame. She did her best to hide them at all times, and had learned all means of cunning tactics to emphasise her good points while playing down the sturdy girders that ran from hip to ankle like two ungainly termite mounds. The maxi dress was her best friend, along with boyfriend jeans and wide-legged trousers. Elizabethan petticoats flying around her head revealing nothing but her M&S tanga, however, was not a good look.

Having fought the skirts back down, Legs adjusted the uncomfortable corset, still fighting to breathe and now ducking through flying clematis petals as she panted her way to some dappled shade.

'That's great!' Nico unhooked the camera strap from his neck and framed the shot. 'The light is perfect on those butterfly wing things.'

'Ruff, Nico.'

'Yeah, you do look a bit rough, but it's OK, I can Photoshop it.'

Legs rolled her eyes and then pouted and posed for a few minutes beneath the apple tree, battling light-headedness and crouching uncomfortably to hide her feet beneath the huge hooped skirt that billowed like a sail. She would never have cut it as an actress in costume dramas, she decided, despite the obvious appeal of being very famous and maybe getting to kiss Orlando Bloom. The corsetry would kill her, as would all the crouching required to appear shorter than her leading men. She was too tall to be a movie star, and liked her breakfast muffins too much. And she was also a lousy actress. To her great regret, Legs shared none of her sister's musical talent, nor was she gifted with a creative or literary streak, despite a passionate appreciation of the arts. In her dreams, she might once have imagined herself heralded the new Tracey Emin, Zadie Smith or Emily Watson, but in reality, it was her ability to organise, charm and multi-task that earned her wage.

Life as an overworked assistant to a literary agent was perhaps not as glamorous as the stage and screen, although an office two doors away from a Starbucks proved some compensation. And as far as her nephew was concerned, she had access to the Holy Grail by working for Fellows Howlett alongside Conrad Knight, the only man to have ever knowingly met writer Gordon Lapis in person.

'Is the new Ptolemy Finch book being printed yet?' Nico asked now.

'Nearly,' she assured him.

Nico was crazy about Gordon's white-haired little hero, with his magical powers and witty irreverence. Ptolemy was wise and brave and sassy. He was also the ultimate outsider; understood by children and adults alike. Through six bestselling adventures, his thick black hair, prematurely streaked with grey, had turned pure white. Yet he never seemed to age.

Such was his success these days, when Gordon delivered a manuscript, it was a high security operation involving bank vaults and confidentiality contracts. It was the one communication that could not be conducted electronically because of the risk of hacking. His agent Conrad Knight would fetch the disk himself and never let it out of his sight until it was delivered. One hard copy would be printed and kept in the agency safe along with the master disk. Then a copy on disk was passed to the publisher. However much Nico begged, Legs would never dream of opening the safe. Just one photocopied page in circulation before the book was published would not only cost her job, but she'd probably be litter picking on community service for weeks to come. Even she was not allowed to read the book until its release into the shops at midnight on publication day, and she was Conrad Knight's lover.

But she had promised her nephew a signed copy on the stroke of that next long-awaited midnight release, and he asked about it daily. Legs now regretted boasting that she could get it signed. It hadn't occurred to her at the time that Lapis's obsession with protecting his identity meant acquiring a signed copy on launch day was close to impossible. Conrad had muttered something vague about seeing what he could do. With a ten-year-old super-fan's huge, excited eyes on her, Legs felt the weight of expectation heavy on her shoulders.

'Do you really exchange emails with Gordon Lapis?'

'I really do.'

'That must be so amazing. You know, he doesn't ever answer his fans personally any more. He has a load of secretaries that do it. But he emails *you*. That's so cool.'

Legs thought it was very arrogant that Gordon no longer replied to letters himself, but had no desire to shatter the idol worship. 'Well he does have a *lot* of fans.' She knew that, on average, Gordon Lapis received two hundred emails and letters each day.

'What are his messages like?'

'Clever.' Often obstreperous, occasionally flirtatious, she added to herself, fishing in her sleeve to read his most recent message:

Some questions for research: Speaking as a rumpled and feisty west Londoner, do you drink real coffee or instant? What radio station do you listen to? What is your morning routine? GL

A new email had already queued up behind it:

I have now been waiting three hours for a response. Julie hasn't even got to work yet, and, despite sitting at my desk, neither have I. GL

'Can I read some of them?' Nico reeled off a few more shots on his camera.

'I don't think you'd be very interested.' She hedged, imagining star-struck Nico poring over Gordon's abstruse missives. For a man who wrote such all-consuming, action-packed fiction, he was a very abstract email correspondent, leaving her hanging for days and then expecting a dozen snappy answers on the trot.

Already growing bored of his Mario Testino task, Nico wandered off to snap the family cat, Wenger, who was chasing a bumblebee between chairs on the decking.

Legs perched on a bench and hastily composed a reply.

I am so sorry! I've been modelling for a photo shoot (that should inspire him; Julie should be glamorous). *Lots of shop coffee. Radio 2. Always running late.*

Pulling at her corset again, she half watched as Nico pursued Wenger and the bumblebee back into the house, snapping away. She started composing a text to Conrad, then paused when Gordon immediately fired back more questions:

Is Julie vengeful? Does she harbour grudges? Would you be able to work alongside a man who had once been your lover?

What has Conrad told you? she tapped back in a panic before hastily resuming her text to the man himself, now paranoid that he had told Gordon Lapis that he was going to dump her. Misspelling in her haste, she demanded to know whether they were getting together that weekend or not.

As soon as she sent it off, she stared at the phone face in alarm, already uncertain whether she'd sent the right messages to writer and lover or got them muddled up as she kept doing. Yesterday she'd sent a text intended for her friend Daisy to her sister and vice versa, only realising when Ros asked what LABATYD meant. (She had quickly improvised 'love all babies and trust your dog' for 'life's a bitch and then you die'.)

Thankfully Gordon was quick to respond with reassuring directness. *Why should Conrad say anything?*

He doesn't know Conrad's my lover, she realised with relief. Be professional, she reminded herself. *My mistake. Saturday brain not in gear. Probably couldn't work alongside my ex, no. Especially not if he'd become grizzled and hard-drinking.*

Young, edgy, haunted by the past, he expanded; *lives on a house boat, plays the fiddle and has a tame badger. Intense, witty, intelligent.*

Not sure about the badger, but I could definitely work with Jimmy so far.

He's also a gambler, Gordon went on; *mildly epileptic, undergoing anger management and unable to commit to any relationship.*

I can feel sexual chemistry already.

That will do for now. Thank you for your input. GL

She tucked the phone back into her sleeve with satisfaction, envisaging him cracking his rickety knuckles over a battered PC keyboard ready to commence upon five thousand words of action-packed crime thriller. Somehow she always imagined Gordon working in a dusty, book-lined office akin to an academic's, although she really had no idea. Conrad never gave anything away about his most reclusive and successful client. For all she knew, Lapis could be their wet-lipped, bald-headed neighbour here in Ealing, working on the other side of the garden wall in the pastel blue summer-house that Ros had complained to the local conservation officer about. She could see its cedar shingles through the wind-buffeted buddleia, and imagined Gordon inside typing a description of Julie at the start of another baffling case for her and Jimmy. She hastily dismissed the notion in favour of the old wizard in an ivory tower.

The garden was full of windblown insect life that had lost grip from flowers and leaves; butterflies whizzed left while ladybirds swirled to the right.

Legs straightened up and batted away a wind-tunnelling wasp with one huge puff sleeve, making her phone fly out from its hiding place and hit her on the nose before dropping into a prickly Japanese Barberry, from which it predictably started to ring.

'Ow . . . ow . . . ow!' She managed to extract it just in time to field the call, heart beating hard because she could see it was Conrad.

'We're on!'

'We are?'

'Pick you up at eleven forty-five. Wear a dress. It's smart.' He rang off, leaving her reeling.

She was thrilled. As phone conversations went, that was long for Conrad. And she was getting to see him on a Saturday, such a rarity these days. She'd given him a hard time only this week about the fact he was neglecting her; he'd obviously listened for once.

When they'd first got together, he'd thought nothing of whisking her away every weekend, wrapped up in the first throes of passion, but now his children took precedence. While Legs didn't object – she knew how important Nico's fortnightly visits with his father were to them both, after all – she missed Conrad's company, and longed for the time when she would get introduced as 'Daddy's friend'. But as far as the four Knight teenagers were concerned, she still didn't exist.

The gossip about Conrad Knight and his comely assistant Allegra 'Legs' North was already well worn in publishing circles, but the story was always told wrongly. It was said that Conrad's rock solid marriage had ended when he took up with young Legs, whereas he'd been separated several months and already living alone before anything had ever happened between them. In fact it had been Legs' long-term relationship which had collapsed, her engagement to childhood sweetheart Francis smashed against the rocks of the affair.

Thinking about Francis yet again she felt a pinch on her heart, those familiar fingers of regret and guilt squeezing together.

Betraying her first, and greatest, love, had been the most painful thing she'd done in her life. Since those heady teenage days together, she'd always believed they would marry and raise a family

22

of blond-haired, blue-eyed children; falling in love with another man had come as a complete shock.

Across the garden, the back door banged in the wind, and Legs glanced down at the time on her mobile, realising that she must start the long pampering and perfecting ritual if she was to look her best for her lunch date, especially given Conrad was clearly taking her somewhere grand.

Picking up her skirts, she swept across the lawns and decking to the house, eager to remove the agonising corset. But the back door had slammed shut on the latch and was locked. She knocked on it, calling for Nico to let her in.

There was no answer; he was probably back in his room, already uploading gruesome close-ups of her legs. Stepping back, she looked up at his window, which was part open. Just as she cupped her hands to shout again, she remembered that Nico was meant to be setting out with a friend to be at choir by ten-thirty. It was already ten to eleven.

Trying not to panic that she was locked out of the house wearing a wedding dress, Legs phoned her sister's mobile, but it went straight through to voicemail. She left a message and started prowling around the house checking for open windows. Apart from Nico's bedroom high above her head, there were none, not even in her own little basement flat, where all the sash windows were protected with ornamental grills. Ros was pathological about security.

She stomped along the side return and let herself out through the garden gate, wedging it open with a stone so that it wouldn't lock behind her as she headed out to the front of the house without much hope of inspiration. But there, just above her head on the raised ground floor, was the answer to her prayers. One of the drawing room's balcony doors had been left slightly ajar. All she had to do was climb across from the front steps and she could get back in.

Legs liked to think she was reasonably fit and agile in her late twenties; she ran most days, swam weekly and managed the occasional pilates class with her girlfriends, but none of these activities took place while trussed in a corset and farthingale, and trailing fifteen kilos of fabric and embroidery.

By the time she'd clambered onto the outside of the little balcony that fronted her sister's elegant Victorian villa and was clinging to the neat wrought-iron railing, several passersby had gathered on the pavement beyond the front garden. Then, just as she was trying to cram her hooped skirt onto the balcony itself and edge her way to the open door, a police car drew up. Legs span around in horror to see two uniformed officers striding up the drive, demanding to know what was going on.

'I can explain – I live – aghhh!'

Any protests she was about to make were abruptly curtailed as one of her flip-flops caught against the railing and unbalanced her, the heavy weight of the dress dragging her off-centre and away from the wall. Scrabbling madly for something to break her fall, she managed to grab a branch of the monkey puzzle tree in the front garden. It couldn't hope to hold her weight, but it slowed her descent so that she landed back in the front garden with a rather graceful billow of satin and silk. It was impossible to tell whether the collective gasp from the small crowd now gathered on the pavement was as a result of her nifty manoeuvre or because they'd just been afforded a full eyeful of her meaty legs and M&S tanga as she floated down.

As she gabbled her story to the police and apologised that no, she didn't have any ID with her and no, her sister wasn't answering her phone, she realised with mounting horror that they didn't entirely believe her.

'I think you'd better pop along to the abbey and fetch her back here to let you in, madam, don't you? Been a lot of thefts and deceptions in this area recently.'

She glanced at her watch again. Conrad would be here in less than an hour. She had to get inside to change. Something about the policemen's cloddish calm lit a fuse in her.

'You can clearly see that window is open,' she fretted, knowing it was at least ten minutes' run to the abbey and the same back. 'If I go to fetch my sister, anybody could get in.' She was aware that she sounded petulant and snappish, mutating from damsel in a wedding dress to Elizabeth I addressing her court. 'Think about your public duty!'

'In that case, let me assist,' said the younger officer, hopping neatly up onto the balcony.

Legs let out a happy cry of relief, thinking that he was going to nip through and let her in by the front door, but the sound died in her throat as she saw him pull the door closed. 'There, that's now secure until you've fetched your sister and she can let you back in.'

For a brief moment, she was reminded of her anti-fascism marching days as a student, that sense of inflamed political self-righteousness which had made her lie down in front of police horses and spit at riot shields. But today was not a day to cause a breach of the peace, she reminded herself firmly. She had a 'dress smart' date with Conrad, meaning it was best to avoid a dressing down at the local nick, or equally staying dressed in bridal regalia.

'Thanks for nothing!' She turned tail and started sprinting towards the abbey, soon forced to slow down to little more than a jog when she realised the corset stays didn't allow her to breathe enough to run. As she shuffled and panted across Haven Green onto Castlebar Road, she attracted stares and laughs from passersby, but she didn't care.

It seemed to take for ever to jog the length of Blakesley Avenue, her face getting redder, lungs bursting.

'Make it to the church on time, darling!' cried a wag builder from some scaffolding.

Legs pounded on, still wearing just one flip-flop, skirts in her arms and farthingale bobbing. Conrad would never understand if he saw her like this; he was the king of cool, his suits cut perfectly, his shirts professionally laundered, not a hair out of place.

At last, the abbey loomed into sight with its familiar fairytale face, butterscotch-yellow stone and huge sweep of steps, which Legs started to scale, not noticing the photographer lurking beside one of the decoratively topped columns.

Just as she reached the top steps, lungs bursting and farthingale drooping, the black doors ahead of her opened and out walked a bride and groom, amidst triumphant organ music. It was too late for Legs to go into retreat. They looked incredibly surprised to find her standing there, red-faced in a too-short wedding dress from which her white bra was now displaying all its wares propped on an embroidered shelf.

She was now too out of breath to speak, but with a gasp of guilt she suddenly remembered the reason Nico was needed in church, and why her sister had been in such a tizz about the flowers: there was a wedding. And she'd just crashed it.

'Who is this woman?' The bride turned to her new husband in horror, clearly thinking Legs was a deranged ex-girlfriend determined to steal the show.

'Virgin Queen!' Legs managed a breathless croak. 'Traditionally *very* lucky at weddings. Have a great marriage.'

Smiling with what she hoped was great Elizabethan benevolence, she dived past them and ricocheted through amused guests to the choir pews at the rear of the church. But Nico and the rest of the choir had disbanded into an anteroom.

A quick frisk through the choristers cassocks confirmed that her nephew had already clocked out, she pictured his long robes gratefully substituted for an Arsenal strip.

'Nico's mum said something about going to the supermarket?' one of the remaining choirboys offered helpfully as she looked around in vain. 'She usually parks her car around the back of St Benedict's.'

'Thanks!' Legs darted out through the back to avoid the bridal party.

'Just missed them,' another choir mum told her when she finally located the car park just seconds after Ros and her Golf had pulled out.

'Oh no, no, no!' She closed her eyes, knowing her sister would be heading to the huge Lidls in Hanwell, where she shopped as a part of her endless economy drive, claiming Will had left her 'too poor to be organic'. It was too far to follow on foot, and now she'd somehow mislaid her phone, so couldn't try calling again, or even call Conrad to cancel lunch. It was half past eleven already. She wanted to cry.

'I'd drop you back home,' the mum offered, 'but I'm not sure I can fit you in the car.' She eyed the huge hooped skirts doubtfully.

'We'll find a way.' Legs beamed with relief, already climbing in.

Oh, the shame of travelling through west London's leafy avenues with a skirt pressed to her face and farthingale poking from the sunroof of a Citroën Picasso while her knickers were on full display to twin choirboys. But at least she got back with five minutes' grace.

The garden gate was still wedged open with a stone. Legs dashed through it, fully determined to climb up to Nico's window if it killed her. Then, to her utter relief, she spotted a full quota of clothes drying on the rotary airer at the far end of the decking.

There was no time to spare. It didn't matter that the clothes were all her sister's; they were better than the hideous farthingale.

The dress was hell to get off, but once she started pulling more carefully at the strings and laces, she found it divided into two parts so at least she could divest herself of the skirts and drag on a pair of calf-length flowered trousers that had seen better days, but had a pretty lace trim and hid her legs well. The corset was stuck put. In desperation, she raided the garden shed and found a pair of secateurs to cut through the stays. Oxygen pouring back into her lungs, she selected a red T-shirt from the washing line and dragged it over her head just in time to hear a car horn beep from the front of the house.

Hiding the dress in the shed with the secateurs, Legs dashed back out through the gate, neatly retrieving her missing flip-flop and phone from the front garden as she bounded towards Conrad's black Jaguar.

His handsome face was a mask behind expensive dark glasses, but she distinctly heard a sharp intake of breath when he saw her.

She looked down and saw that in her haste, she'd matched a pair of Ros's pyjama bottoms that had a broken elastic waist with one of her nephew's T-shirts which was not only far too small, but also bore the slogan 'Gunners Forever' across its back. Her hair was still pulled up by the jewelled scrunchy that her sister had put on her earlier and she realised her face must be puce. But such was the force of her smile – and Conrad's need of a favour – he opened his passenger door with a gentlemanly flourish and kissed her cheek as she leaped in.

'So where are you taking me?'

Before he could answer, her phone let out a message alert. *Is Julie Ocean romantically involved with her Super?* Gordon quizzed.

Insuperably, she replied before switching off her phone.

Chapter 2

Driving east, Conrad quickly slid the two Premier Admission tickets to Ascot's King George Day from the dashboard and stashed them in the glove compartment.

'Change of plan,' he said smoothly, resetting the sat nav, the cricket commentary turned down discreetly on the stereo. 'We're having a picnic in Hyde Park.'

'Heaven!' Legs settled back contentedly and listened as he made a quick call on the hands-free to Betty Blythe's to have a luxury picnic for two put on standby. His voice always thrilled her; that clipped authoritative tone with its under-note of the South African

Cape. She still vividly remembered the electric current of pleasure that had run through her when he'd said in the same husky bark 'the job is yours', liberating her from three years as a lowly small press editorial assistant to a plum role as PA to a literary agency legend. From the start, Conrad's charisma had glowed so brightly in her new world that, despite the engagement ring burning on her finger and the wedding band still branded on his, she'd allowed herself a few clichéd office fantasies about her boss pinning her up against the water cooler and thoroughly kissing her.

Legs had been working at literary agency Fellows Howlett just a few weeks when the rumours reached her that her lovely new boss's marriage was in crisis, unhitching one of London's most long-standing literary power couples. For a fortnight, it was an open secret that Conrad slept in his office, shocked and unshaven yet still taking calls and running his authors' lives like clockwork. He was a man who inspired devotion, and his work ethic never faltered. Without hesitation, his loyal team of colleagues closed ranks to protect him. As the newest agency recruit, Allegra was not a part of this inner circle, yet her heart had gone out to him, so driven and focused and damaged. To her shame, the water-cooler fantasies multiplied.

Legs heard that his wife had issued divorce papers straight away, citing unreasonable behaviour, although Legs had never met anyone more truthful and fair-minded. Apparently Conrad's children wouldn't even talk to him at first. It must have taken him great strength and dignity, Legs thought, to pull through those first weeks with minimum rancour.

Too proud to take the many offers of houseroom from friends and colleagues, he asked Legs to book him into a hotel. When he discovered that she'd reserved the suite that the agency traditionally only used for their grandest clients, he stormed out of his office to her desk, green eyes blazing. 'I don't need a Vi-spring mattress and plasma television in the bathroom.'

'I thought you deserved pampering. You look so sad.'

That was the first time he seemed to notice her, his handsome face curiously motionless, as though he was fighting back tears.

'Book a Travelodge. It's all I deserve.'

A week later he sheepishly asked her to upgrade him to a Radisson and book him a chiropractor.

Legs had worked for him tirelessly, often staying late, never complaining when he loaded her with extra duties, knowing that little by little she was becoming indispensible, showing her intelligence and initiative, and earning his trust. She soon even managed to make him laugh, a reward equalling those rare, vivid moments of praise from the man of few words and many million-pound manuscripts. But his laughter was always hard won, and she paid the price for trying too hard.

Eight weeks after she started at Fellows Howlett, Legs scored a triumph by rearranging a long-planned trip to Frankfurt in a way that gave Conrad an unprecedented afternoon off, an upgraded flight and a first-steal meeting with an American publisher eager to snap up new British talent. He was highly impressed. 'You should go far, Allegra.'

'Are you flattering me, or suggesting I remove myself to a greater distance?'

'Stick around.'

'I'll be as sticky as you want me to be,' she promised naughtily.

He had flashed that rare smile, as succinct as his speaking manner, but his green eyes remained serious. 'Flirtation is small arms fire in business; I suggest you drop it from your CV if you want to break through the glass ceiling.'

After that lecture, she stopped the wisecracks. Yet she had often caught him looking at her through the smoked-glass wall that divided their work spaces, his expression impossible to read. Breaking through ceilings and walls became a recurring theme in her dreams, where she would shatter her way through hothouses, halls of mirrors and observatories to get to his side.

As the weeks passed, her crush on Conrad had grown in direct proportion to her increasing dissatisfaction at home. Her fiancé Francis had a far better job, fast-tracking a route through the editorial department of a blue-chip publishing group, but he despised it. He was tiring of London, he said. He talked obsessively about returning to his family home, Farcombe, and the festival his father had started up. He talked about the wedding as though it was a baptism to a new life. She suddenly saw parallels with Ros abandoning all her musical ambitions, and it frightened her.

She kept these fears from friends and work colleagues. 'How's the wedding shaping up?' Conrad would ask.

Eager to cheer him up, Legs embellished plans for fire jugglers and jazz quartets, clifftop pyrotechnics and hosts of performance artists. Despite his warning, she started to made her boss laugh again, continually in fact, and loved the sound, like the surf crashing on Devon shingle. Conrad's laughter became a new favourite song she wanted to hear again and again.

Three months after his separation, he made her feel as though she was beginning to penetrate the inner circle when he took her along to an important lunch with a client, a blustery old academic whose strange fictional tomes set in the Sassanid Empire had proven surprisingly commercial, largely because they contained rather a lot of graphic sex. The academic was a terrible old letch and immediately locked onto Legs as bait, making her suspect that Conrad had invited her along purely to sweeten his client's palate. Polite and professional, Legs had tolerated his attentions, although the temptation to spear him in the groin with her fork every time his hands wandered over her thighs beneath the table was almost overwhelming. Instead, she'd drunk too much champagne, laughed along gamely to risqué jokes and sought distraction during the academic's long, boring monologues about himself by focusing her thoughts upon Francis and the wedding. But by then, these subjects were both starting to worry her intensely, as the fairytale compared increasingly unfavourably to the quality, grown-up fiction and fact she encountered daily at Fellows Howlett.

When the old letch had been put on the Oxford train, blowing Legs kisses from his first class seat, she'd shared a taxi back to the office with her unusually quiet boss.

By then, she was wound too tight and felt too worked up to keep a lid on her anger.

'I really enjoy working for you, Conrad,' she'd blurted. 'But I didn't deserve that.'

He said nothing, staring out of the window at the plane trees as they crawled along Holland Park Avenue.

'You were the one who told me to drop flirtation from my CV!' she raged.

A long silence followed. Just as Legs had convinced herself that she'd just blown her career chances, he said quietly, 'I miss you flirting.'

Conrad had also consumed a great deal of champagne over that lunch. The sleeping policemen which lined back roads to their Green Park offices had continually thrown them together, finally dislodging the scales from his eyes. For many weeks his male colleagues had all been lamenting the fact that lovely young Legs was engaged; such a sweet, sexy thing. Conrad had barely spared her a thought. Yet that day, observing her under attack at lunch, his attraction towards her was so sudden and overwhelming that his libido soared like a phoenix rising from the ashes.

He'd fixed her with his sexy, heart-battered green gaze. 'I think you're having serious second thoughts about getting married, Allegra.'

That Conrad had the guts to say it out loud, as well as the perception to see it when all her family and friends seemingly remained blind to it, won her runaway heart yet more. It might have been a lucky guess, but it had hit target with total accuracy.

'I am,' Legs had said in a small voice, hardly daring to believe she was admitting it.

'Stay behind later and let's talk about it.'

But Conrad was not a believer in talking. He might love the

passion of written words, but he was a man of physical action. That evening, after all their colleagues had left the office, he wasted no time in kissing Allegra by the water cooler, the heat between them so scorching that it threatened to boil its contents clean away, blister the partition walls and melt the office block's atrium roof.

'What about the glass ceiling?' she'd asked helplessly, knowing that if the earth moved this much when he touched her, the roof had already begun falling in on her life.

'You're in the executive lift now,' he had assured her.

From that day on, Conrad walked taller and Legs floated on air.

A year later, Conrad now rented a huge townhouse just off Wandsworth Common with rooms for each of his children that they used regularly, and he'd even taken a holiday with his entire family including his estranged wife. On the surface all was civilised calm. The divorce petition had been dropped when Mrs Knight realised how much money they both stood to lose by formalising the arrangement, and she now even wanted them to attend marriage therapy together, which Conrad wouldn't countenance. The children were reportedly struggling to cope with their parents' separation and believed, as their mother did, that the marriage could still be saved. Only Conrad maintained that it was the end of the line, which was ironic given that he hadn't been the one to pull the plug in the first place. But he certainly kept quiet about the fact that he had a girlfriend fifteen years his junior, and remained reluctant to introduce Legs into his family life, or to spare more than one Saturday in four, which was why today was so special.

★

They parked on West Carriage Drive and found a quiet spot beneath a chestnut tree overlooking the Long Water. Unfurling a checked blanket with a matador's skill, Conrad stepped back as Legs stretched out luxuriously upon it as eagerly as a sunbathing cat. His dark glasses slipped along his nose as he gazed down at her, so that two roguish green eyes glittered above the wire rims.

Even after a year, he remained the most stomach-tighteningly sexy man she had ever encountered. That rare mix of old-fashioned machismo with a poet's soul got her every time. To be adored by a man as powerful as Conrad Knight was utterly hypnotising.

Glowing in the glory of his company, backed up by the sunshine and a hamper full of iced cakes, she lay back on the checked blanket and gazed adoringly across at him as he mixed freshly squeezed orange juice with Prosecco. Her father, the drinks snob, would disapprove enormously, having always claimed buck's fizz no better than an alcopop, but right now she could think of nothing she'd like to drink more. Dorian North disapproved of everything about Conrad – his age, his pushiness, his rough-diamond charm, and the fact that he had destroyed what Dorian believed to be his daughter's greatest chance of happiness in marrying her childhood sweetheart.

Conrad was everything Francis wasn't; an ambitious gambler with a quick temper, a steel-framed ego and a super-fast corporate brain. A self-made man, he had a fearsome reputation as a brilliant business mind in the ivory towers of literary fiction publishing, and it was said that he had single-handedly dragged renowned old agency, Fellows Howlett, into the twenty-first century. Since being head-hunted from top London publishing house, Clipstone, to take over the directorship from the last of the Fellows family, he had signed a succession of radical new literary names with commercial appeal while pensioning off the worst of the dinosaurs. Literary snobs had accused him of selling out at first, but with more Booker, Orange, Pulitzer and Nobel winners currently on his books than the Athenaeum Club membership list, Conrad had proved his worth. His were high-grossing, chart-topping authors, as well as being critically acclaimed thoroughbreds with good pedigrees and perfect fetlocks, and he saw himself as the leading London trainer. Legs had noticed that the only time he became

touchy was when it was hinted that his real success could be attrib-
uted to just one author, the legendary Gordon Lapis with his
Ptolemy Finch series, a multi-million-selling runaway success that
appealed to children and adults alike and had spawned four
smash-hit movies, huge global merchandising and a brand name
as recognisable as many fast food chains, fizzy drinks brands and
football teams.

Having discovered Gordon in the agency slush pile, Conrad
held the claim of creating a megastar, but he regularly complained
that this meant he took all the shots from Gordon's legendary short
temper. He was increasingly using Legs to draw the fire away from
his busy days.

Even now, he read a message on his BlackBerry with lowered
brows. 'Gordon is trying to contact you. Why would he think I can
help on a Saturday?'

Fumbling to turn on her own phone, Legs cleared her throat
awkwardly. 'He might think we work some weekends. He does,
after all.'

'He works every day. He has more creative energy than
Hollywood.'

Legs found a new email from Gordon waiting for her: *Would
Julie Ocean fight for justice at any cost? If so, would she favour martial arts or firearms?*

'Is it about "the Reveal"?' demanded Conrad, trying to read the
message past the sun-blinding screen glare.

'No.' She hastily typed *Tai Chi* and pressed send. 'Just research
he's doing. He always refers me back to you about that. You are his
earthly portal, after all.'

Gordon's royalties alone accounted for eighty per cent of
Fellows Howlett's not inconsiderable annual profit, but pandering
to Lapis's increasing eccentricity had started to vex Conrad, who
preferred his authors bibulous and biddable. He'd told Legs that
he thought her more cheerful, informal manner might calm the
hermetic scribe. It seemed this was not happening.

'He's being impossible about the Reveal,' he sighed now, handing her a plastic flute of Buck's Fizz before lying back on his elbows and tipping his face up to the sun.

Conrad was rightly proud of his golden literary find, and he remained crucial to its success, providing the only link between the super-famous boy hero, his enigmatic creator and the real world. But like the man with the goose that laid the golden egg, he constantly wanted to cut through the feathers and see what lay beneath.

Tai Chi is non contact, Gordon had replied to Legs. *There is no point continuing this conversation as it is no longer constructive. P.s. Tell Conrad I remain resolute.*

'He remains resolute,' she told him.

'He's infuriating!'

Legs admired the thrust of Conrad's square chin, and the Grecian profile. She'd always thought he looked more a rugby player than a literary connoisseur, which was possibly why he rampaged through the publishing world like a prop forward tackling the scrum. He adored the cut and thrust of deal-making, but delicate negotiations frustrated him, and Gordon Lapis was an author who required a great deal of sensitive handling, more now than ever. The author had recently and very reluctantly agreed that it might be time to reveal his identity at long last, not least because the tabloids that had been threatening to do it for many years now appeared closer than ever, and the media man-hunt was reaching feverish proportions. Conrad saw the release of the next Ptolemy Finch book as the perfect cue for an unveiling.

But Gordon's Reveal was not proving easy to plan. At first, he had changed his mind endlessly about the time and place, the stage management and the pomp and circumstance involved. An exclusive deal with a national newspaper had been mooted then dismissed, followed by failed discussions with Oprah's production team, Hay Book Festival and Alan Yentob. Most recently, he'd settled on a venue that was laughably unrealistic.

'He's absolutely fixed on the Farcombe Festival idea,' Conrad sighed.

On hearing the familiar word, Legs swallowed a blade of dismay and dread. The most elitist arts festival in the UK, notorious for its snobbish selection process, Farcombe would no more want Gordon on their programme than an end-of-pier Punch and Judy act. For all Conrad's Booker nominees and literary grandees, he rarely ever had a client that matched up to the Farcombe entry mark. It was widely rumoured that they'd once turned down a request from the Poet Laureate to appear at the small, cherry-picked annual September festival because the role was deemed too mainstream.

'But they've already said no, haven't they?'

'Emphatically,' he sighed. 'However, Gordon won't let it drop. I even spoke with the new festival director personally last night, some old bag called Hawkes.'

'Yolande,' Legs groaned in recognition. Yolande Hawkes had been known as Bird of Prey when working in the Square Mile because she made grown men fall to their knees and beg for mercy. She had now turned from hedge funds to high culture with the belief that a brutal pruning of all but the purest art forms was required.

'Any luck?' she ventured, although she already knew the answer.

'Turned down flat.' He looked predictably offended. 'She refuses a face-to-face meeting. She won't even put it to the committee; saying the list is closed.'

'It is mixed arts,' Legs pointed out fairly. 'They can only have what, eight or nine writers appearing each year, most of those poets. It's predominantly music and visual art.'

'No doubt Gordon's deliberately suggested it as a venue because he's convinced we'll never get him a slot,' Conrad said, draining his glass and straightening up to fix her with that intense, green-eyed stare that always had such a seductive effect on her, her bra practically undid itself. 'But we have a secret weapon, of course. You know Farcombe very well indeed.'

She nodded carefully. 'Hector and Poppy Protheroe are old friends of the family.'

'Think you can swing it?'

Legs stared at him wide-eyed. 'Hector is Francis's father.'

'Exactly! You two were together for years. You must be practically like a daughter to the Protheroes. You speak their language. Talk to them, Legs. Make them see what a huge benefit this could be for them. The event will be a sell out; the television coverage alone will be priceless.'

Legs thought about Hector, six foot four of white-haired patronage and idiosyncrasy. He would love crowds flocking to his beautiful coastal retreat; he'd play his bassoon to the long queues of Ptolemy Finch fans like a busker and chat up all the prettier women. Hector was unbothered by the festival's content apart from the music, which he selected himself. But his wife Poppy was different. Legs doubted she would allow Gordon across the threshold unless he'd paid for his own ticket.

Then Legs thought about Francis, remembered his handsome, fallen-angel face just before he'd turned to leave their shared flat a year ago, the hurt and betrayal that pinched every muscle tight and drained his normally golden skin of colour. It had been the first time she had seen him cry since he was fourteen. And she had wept too; she sometimes still did. The sense of guilt never left, and it could still render her breathless with regret when caught unawares.

Returning Conrad's challenging look, Legs shook her head. 'I won't do it. It's not worth trying.'

'C'mon, where's the fighting spirit I love?' he goaded.

'I'm done with fighting,' she said wearily, thinking of all the rows, the tears and recriminations of the previous summer. 'And I wouldn't be welcome. Francis is living at Farcombe again now; he manages the farming side.' She looked away, alarmed that her eyes were already itchy with impending tears. Despite his academic bent, Francis had always loved the stock-rearing and land management of Farcombe, largely because it was an element in which Hector and Poppy had no interest whatsoever and didn't interfere; it also suited his solitary nature to spend swathes of time alone on the land there, quoting Eliot and Joyce at the flock. He liked to joke that he put the culture into agriculture, which was quite witty for Francis, she remembered fondly.

'At least call him,' Conrad urged.

'He won't want to speak to me.' The familiar Francis had long gone in her mind, replaced with one part ogre whipped up by self-justification, two parts lost soul conjured by her guilt and one part dashing blond playboy as depicted by the media who had latched onto the heir to the Protheroe fortunes in recent months, branding this son of famous, maverick businessman Hector an 'eligible bachelor'.

'Go down there for the weekend,' Conrad was suggesting.

'Are you *kidding*?'

'Your family still have their holiday cottage, don't they? Take a long break next weekend and see how the land lies.'

The thought of Spywood Cottage brought a pang of familiar yearning, the desire to revisit it never far from the surface. But Legs knew that to go there again would cause ten times the pain stored in the photograph albums that she kept hidden in the ottoman at the foot of her bed, and which contained more than half a lifetime of shared memories sealed in their plastic pages.

'My mother's there; she spends all summer painting.'

'All the more reason to visit.'

'We're not that sort of family – she likes to . . .' She drew back her lips in a pensive smile. 'It's complicated.'

It was never going to be easy to casually mention the fact her mother, for all her apparent middle-class, middle-aged conservatism, liked to be naked. Lucy North wasn't a conventional naturist and shunned shared nudity; a group ping-pong game in a seaside camp was her idea of hell. Yet she adored her solitary painting holidays in Devon, liberated from the constraints of clothes in the tiny hideaway cottage and its secluded clifftop garden. At one time, the Norths would have all gathered at Spywood for August, but since Legs' break-up with Francis, Ros had used her and Nico's church commitments and Dorian his shop as the excuses that freed Lucy to enjoy her unfettered water-colour breaks. These days, the family felt increasingly awkward about intruding.

'I'll never understand the English,' Conrad laughed, always at his most South African when he was Brit-bashing. 'You have these little bolt-holes just a couple of hours away, and you never use them.'

'Farcombe is Francis's family home.'

'We're not living in a feudal society any more!'

'Actually, Farcombe still basically is. The estate owns most of the village.'

Tucking her knees beneath her chin, Legs crammed a scone into her mouth and then found her eyes watering as she struggled to eat it whole, cheeks bulging and crumbs flying.

This conversation was starting to really annoy her. Aside from the fact that he'd procured cucumber sandwiches on a sun-drenched blanket, Conrad was being about as romantic as he would be on a Monday morning desk briefing over a Starbucks skinny latte, and just as ruthless.

'I want you to get Gordon onto the Farcombe Festival bill, whatever it takes.'

It took a great deal of effort to swallow the scone as she coughed and spluttered, 'Are you seriously asking me to try to build bridges with my ex for Gordon's sake?'

'Why not? Look at Madeleine and me. We're professional about our friendship now. We've moved on.'

'You might have moved on. She still wants you back as the head of the family.'

'Rubbish.' He rolled over onto his back. 'We're co-parents, and have business interests in common. We have to be adult about things.'

'Francis and I have no children or business interests in common.' She could cringe when she remembered their youthful dreams of setting up in publishing together, of raising a huge, clever family at Farcombe.

'*This* is business, Legs. You hold the key to releasing Gordon in a controlled environment, and keeping Ptolemy Finch as a national treasure. And you have Gordon's trust now, which gives you a very rare power indeed; don't abuse it.'

There was a long pause while Legs angrily demolished the rest of the truffle chocolate brownies, still barely able to believe that he would ask her to do this. Gordon Lapis was an exasperating sod, she reflected; he controlled them all with his big money wizardry. Having his trust felt more like a curse than a gift as it increasingly impinged upon her personal space. Yet his books were so magical, he was already engraved into her imaginative world. She only wished she shared Ptolemy Finch's ability to see into the future.

'What if Francis still has feelings?' she asked quietly.

Conrad selected a miniature pink-iced cupcake with strawberries arranged prettily on the top. 'And you?'

'I'm with *you*.' It was all too easy to say. They shared the present tense for all its occasional tension; Legs lived for the moment; Conrad, with his immediacy and drive, made every moment count. Although her feelings for Francis remained painfully complicated, she survived by keeping the two entirely separate.

Now Conrad was smiling wolfishly into her eyes, reminding her how sexy and carefree his road was through the deep dark woods.

'Good girl.' He held out the cake. 'As long as that's understood, we can trust one another. Now eat this up. I'm taking you shopping. You need a weekend wardrobe. Send Gordon an email telling him we're trying a new approach.'

Quashing visions of Julie Ocean going deep undercover at the behest of her love-interest Superintendent, she did as she was told, sending the message as instructed and adding, *Conrad attends the same Tai Chi class as myself in Hyde Park, hence we were able to discuss this today*, in a vague attempt at protecting her personal life.

He replied as they were packing up the last of their picnic: *Golden cock stands on one leg; white stork spreads wings. Draw bow to shoot tiger. GL*

'What's that all about?' Conrad read it over her shoulder in alarm.

'I think they're Tai Chi moves.'

He laughed, drawing her close and looking into her face in that way that once again made her bra feel set to ping open spontaneously. 'Good girl. He likes you. He needs his daily Leg-Up.'

'His PA keeps telling me off for distracting him.'

'Kelly.' His eyes sparkled. 'Protects Gordon's interests with admirable ferocity, don't you find? We need a forthright character like that on the team.'

Professional and personal jealousy prickled at her temples. 'Must be a saint to put up with a boss like him,' she said begrudgingly, having admired Kelly's clucky pragmatism, but still feeling that an attention-seeking, solitary genius like Gordon would thrive with more understanding, like Ptolemy, who had evolved from quarrelsome introvert to brave boy warrior through five books with the support of his amazing, intuitive sidekick Purple.

Conrad started to kiss cake crumbs from her lips. 'And you should know all about putting up with a bastard of a boss.' He still had the ability to melt her pelvis to softest putty and tie her intestines in knots.

The breeze had dropped, making the heat of the sun glow on her skin along with the sexual charge that now coursed through her, and she felt as though she was wearing a bodysuit spun from caressing fingers and electric kisses.

Soon Legs no longer cared about the impish, white-haired sorcerer and his reclusive creator. By the time Conrad found the biscuit fragments lodged by her collarbone, she had vanquished thoughts of Ptolemy Finch, Gordon Lapis and even Francis from her mind.

Sneaking into the basement flat past Ros with several bulging Browns bags wasn't easy, especially as her sister had spotted that the wedding dress was missing and clearly suspected it was in the bags, possibly in several sections, like a dismembered corpse.

'There've been three bids on it on eBay already,' she reported from the balcony. 'Is it still in your flat?'

'Yes! I'll bring it up later.'

'Coming for supper?'

'Sure! Just got to – er – check emails and stuff first. Make some calls. Have a bath.' *Fetch your wedding dress out of the garden shed*, she added with silent trepidation.

Safely locked behind her front door, she hurried to turn on her laptop, and groaned as she saw that bidding for the dress had already reached several hundred pounds. Did people have no taste?

Gordon had left yet more research queries in her inbox about Julie Ocean's character: *Do you add salt to food? What do you watch on television? What are your secret vices? How would you react to being held hostage?*

Legs sent cursory replies: *No salt, reality rubbish, buying wedding dresses on eBay, I'd crack bad jokes for a week and then crack up.* Then she turned her focus to rescuing the Ditchley dress.

There was no door directly linking the basement flat to the garden because its level was so much lower. Like an SAS commando, Legs unlocked the security grille and silently rolled it back before wriggling out through her bathroom window into the rosebed and shuffling around the garden out of sight until she reached the shed. Just a few feet away, Ros's kitchen windows were wide open, wafts of frying onions and garlic accompanied by the soothing sound of vespers on Radio 3.

The dress already smelled of weedkiller and compost. Even in the dim light of the shed window, Legs could see that the hem was grubby and tattered from her run around Ealing, and the bodice lace ripped, with several pearl-encrusted embroidery flowers now missing. The secateurs had left the stays cut to tufty shreds. She swallowed guiltily and carefully bore it back across the garden like an army medic carrying a wounded soldier back from a battlefield.

It was tricky conveying a farthingale, hooped petticoats and several acres of silk back to her basement undetected, especially when the dress kept catching on the rose bushes or trailing through the beds.

At last she fed it all through the window and clambered in with it.

On close inspection, the damage was fairly superficial, but there was no doubt that it wasn't as described in the advert.

Hurriedly, Legs created a new Gmail account and eBay identity under a false name and bid on the dress herself, putting in far more than she thought it was worth to be safe. She was immediately outbid.

'You *what*?'

She added another hundred pounds. Still it came back with the red cross. Another hundred, another red cross.

'You are *mad*,' she hissed to her rival bidders, and upped her stake by several hundred. At last a green tick. She slumped back in her chair and gazed at the dress spread across the sofa with its hoops in the air like a whale's skeleton on a beach. She doubted she could do much to repair it with just a stick of Pritt and her small collection of sewing kits pilfered from hotels.

Gordon's name was striped bold at the top of her email inbox again. *Why do you buy wedding dresses on eBay?*

You're not the only one with an altar ego, she replied.

She began Googling dress-menders in west London, but soon found herself distracted and clicking her way onto the Farcombe Festival site, unable to resist a snoop. Guest speakers for the literary side of the arts festival had been confirmed, and Legs had heard of less than half of them, so guessed they must be very worthy and learned. A poet called Kizzy de la Mere seemed to be the feature act, and there were lots of photographs of a flame-haired wraith with big lips sitting on a rock looking moody. Legs looked at her thin, high-browed face and decided she'd suit the Ditchley dress perfectly.

The website made no direct mention of Francis, who remained as quietly behind the scenes as his father remained centre stage; there were endless photographs of Hector looking dashing with young Brit Art stars, experimental musicians and dancers, usually accompanied by wife Poppy in her customary smock and turban, a style she had first adopted almost a quarter of a century earlier in the belief that it made her seem more creative but, given her tanned and wizened slenderness, now made her look like a Moroccan Berber.

Legs forced herself to stop surfing and made a big mug of tea before composing an email to Francis, telling him in the simplest terms that she was planning to spend a few days in the cottage and thought it best to let him know. She hadn't been to Farcombe since they'd split up. This was the first time she'd communicated since the day eleven months earlier that she'd crept out at dawn to post a hand-written six page letter baring her soul. She'd never received any reply. If that tearstained letter the previous year had elicited no response, Legs reasoned sadly, this brief missive was hardly likely to bear any more fruit.

She still had a first draft of that letter in her chest of keepsakes and photographs, a creased, ring-marked testament to her regret, full of misquoted Donne, but she hadn't been able to bring herself to look at it since copying out its more poignant paragraphs between weeping fits and breaks to consult the *Oxford Book of English Verse*. Even now, as she briefly thought about taking it out of its Pandora's box to revisit the moment and try to see it through Francis's eyes, the idea made her shudder in horror, ashamed of her own outpouring.

Yet after she'd had her bath, she was amazed to find that he'd already sent an email in return.

I am very relieved. Call me when you get here. We must meet up ASAP. F.

Legs let out a little cry of shock and, she knew it, glee. She only just stopped herself dancing around the flat. This had to mean that she was going to be forgiven, surely?

To Legs' relief, Ros swallowed her sister's breezy line that she'd decided the dress was safest left in her flat. She was also surprisingly enthusiastic when she heard of the planned weekend in Devon: 'It's about time you started going to the cottage again, we all know how much you love it there. And you can drop Nicholas off on the way. It's Will's turn to have him. Save him coming here. He always complains so much.' Her face was bursting with relief.

It had been a long-running point of contention since the divorce that Ros flatly refused to take her son even a part of the way to Somerset for his weekends and holiday visits with his father, not even as far as the M25, meaning that Will was forced to make the six-hour round trip twice each visiting weekend, unless Legs or one of the grandparents stepped in to help. It was Ros and Legs' mother Lucy who most often lightened his load by transporting her grandson en route to or from the family's holiday cottage when she escaped to paint and frolic naked in her garden, but this summer, her watercolour sabbatical at Spywood had already stretched from late May to high summer without interruption.

'Mum can't stay there much longer,' Ros said disapprovingly. 'She said something about finishing those watercolours of Eascombe Harbour last time I spoke to her, but the reception was awful. You know what it's like there. Best to text that you're coming so she makes space.' She carefully avoided mentioning the likelihood of finding Lucy naked among the shrubbery, although both sisters knew that was a distinct possibility, 'Dad's run out of freezer food, so she must be coming home any day. Can you pick Nicholas up on your way back as well?'

'I don't see why not; I love the drive to Inkpot, it's so pretty.'

Ros let out a long-suffering sigh.

Just as Lucy's unconventional nudity was never mentioned, the sisters kept schtum about another awkward truth. They both knew that Legs was still close to her old friend Daisy, currently six months pregnant with Will's third child, but sisterly loyalty stopped the emotive subject being raised. As far as Ros was concerned, Daisy (or 'that woman') was never mentioned in conversation, and she and Will's children did not exist in Ros and Legs' day-to-day consciousness in Ealing. It was simpler that way.

No such silent diplomacy applied to Legs' personal life; Ros fixed her with a beady look as they sat down to eat. 'Do you think you'll see Francis at all when you're at Farcombe?'

She nodded. 'He wants to meet up.'

Ros picked up her fork and stared at the prongs. 'He'll never take you back, you know.'

'That's not what this is about.' She tried not to think again about that long letter she'd sent soon after the split, saying it had all been a horrible mistake, begging him to take her back. The fact that he had never even acknowledged it still ploughed stitches of humiliated pain between her ribs whenever she thought about it. For a long time she'd convinced herself that she'd forgotten to add a stamp.

'We'll see.' Ros flashed that smug smile which had irritated Legs since childhood.

As she opened her mouth to protest more vociferously, Nico burst into the room at last and dived into his chair, breathless with excitement. 'The bidding on your dress is already at over a thousand pounds, Mum! How cool is that?'

'Very cool.' Ros lay down her fork. 'Now please don't run in the house again, or be late to table. You may say grace – *how* much?'

Legs closed her eyes. It had already gone above her top bid again. As soon as she'd finished eating, she'd have to dash downstairs and pledge the rest of her savings on the tattered wedding dress.

Chapter 3

Throughout the week that followed, now linked by instant messaging as well as emails on her whizzy phone, Legs was surprised how much she looked forward to Gordon's random, eclectic messages which came like machine-gun fire when he was seeking inspiration then stopped when he hit a productive vein. His questions were a welcome distraction as she grew increasingly nervous at the prospect of seeing Francis again.

Allegra,
How long could you personally hang off high scaffolding if gripping with only your bare hands?
GL

I have not tested my scaffolding-hanging abilities recently, but I can conduct an experiment in Piccadilly at lunchtime should you wish. A

There is no need to test scaffolding. Julie has climbed off and is now trapped in a lift with Jimmy Jimee. Warehouse is on fire around them. They could be forced to take off their clothes to create an escape rope. I may need you to research the scene. GL

As you know, I take my role as research assistant very seriously, but I should point out that our office lifts are glass. A

As well as bombarding her with hypothetical questions, Gordon forwarded a manuscript originally sent to him by a fan, *The Girl Who Checked Out* by Delia Meare. *Do look beyond her abhorrent spelling and grammatical lapses. You will find out why when you read it. Of course, you are far better qualified than I am to judge if this is what you have been dreaming of or the stuff of nightmares. And before you ask, Delia is not my new pen name.*

Touched that he valued her opinion, she printed it out ready to take with her to Devon.

As the weekend approached, Legs tried not to think about Francis, or the fact that securing a coup at Farcombe could make or break her heart as well as her career. Conrad was careful not to mention her ex by name, keeping her focus on Gordon and the agency's duty to orchestrate his Reveal perfectly. Under increasing pressure from the slavering press and Gordon's anxious publisher, he couldn't be more delighted by the burgeoning friendship between his most lucrative and tricky client and his flirty assistant. 'Keep him sweet' was becoming his catchphrase. He didn't even kick up a fuss when she accidentally blind-copied him into a message she sent to Gordon mentioning Julie and Jimmy. Julie Ocean could have been a codename for a rival agent for all he cared, as long as Gordon remained willing to reveal his true identity to the media and public that summer.

While seducing Legs in his Wandsworth house on the eve of her departure to the West Country, Conrad insisted she kept her phone on standby in case Gordon made contact. Having gone to considerable lengths to make her feel special by treating her to a night at the Proms followed by supper in The Ivy, he ruined it by handing her the iPhone halfway through a candlelit massage as her message alert chimed. 'It's bound to be him. You know how he hates being kept waiting.'

But it wasn't Gordon; it was Francis: *Please tell me you're coming tomorrow?*

She quickly replied *I'm coming*, and then cast the phone aside, turning jumpily to Conrad who had rolled off the bed to fetch more oil. The knots in her stomach suddenly seemed tied to her vocal cords and she could only nod when he asked her if all was well.

He was a consummate lover. Tonight, however, she found her body barely responding to those firm hands and expert moves that usually drove her wild with delight. In her head, she could hear her own voice repeating 'I'm coming, I'm coming', but she knew she wasn't talking to Conrad.

Legs hesitated telling Gordon she was going to Farcombe on his behalf until the last minute. Despite their short and largely abstract acquaintance, she knew he would disapprove.

So Fellows Howlett is sending an unarmed sergeant to do the Chief Super's job? he fumed through the ether.

I will wear short sleeves, she cracked back nervously, *that way I have the right to bare arms. Julie Ocean has Tai Chi on her side. White stork spreads wings. Grasp bird's tail.*

Don't fly too close to the sun.

'The sun or the son?' she wondered aloud, thinking about Francis. There was something about Gordon's reaction that unnerved her, playing to her fear. As soon as she sent the reply 'pluck off', she regretted it, knowing it was far too irreverent and coarse. If she could have leapt into cyberspace to halt the message as it crackled through the ether to his desk, she would. But it was too late.

Gordon immediately began communicating via his PA again: *G will be unavailable until further notice. He requests that you update me regularly. Regards, Kelly. (P.s. You are one plucky bird.)*

Chapter 4

It had become known as the Summer of Storms, to the ongoing excitement of the Met Office and the great British public, who were now never short of small-talk about the weather. Legs' morning drive to Somerset was like journeying from day to night and beyond as she encountered a black-skied, thundery landscape beyond the Avonmouth Bridge and drove through a hammering downpour before emerging into bright sunshine again as they climbed into the Blackdown Hills, its wet lanes hissing like snakes against the tyres of her battered old Honda.

When the red car puttered and bounced along the pot-holed driveway to Inkpot Farm, Daisy appeared briefly at the front door, rotund and hassled with a milk jug in hand, making frantic signals for Legs to park around the back and stay hidden.

Puzzled, she executed some very dodgy rally driving manoeuvres as she performed tail-snakes and wheel-spins through the rain-slicked mud to the rear yard, where she parked behind a pole barn housing a huge stack of last year's mouldering hay.

With his head lowered over a Shell garage shop bag Nico had been complaining of travel sickness since they left the A303, and now he groaned afresh. Normally, he would've jumped out and dashed off in search of his father, but this time nausea kept him in situ.

'They've got a house viewing,' Legs said, checking the messages from Daisy on her phone. 'Daddy's taken the girls out to a farm park, apparently. We were supposed to meet him there an hour ago. Oops.'

'Shall we go now?' Nico asked with only faint enthusiasm, the prospect of more motion making him look even greener.

Legs checked her watch, realising they'd missed their slot. 'Let's lie low here and the coast will be clear soon enough.'

Letting Nico sag back in his seat with his eyes closed, she

watched a bantam hen as it strutted up to check out the Honda, head tilting this way and that contemplating the front bumper with a few trial pecks. Soon it was joined by several friends who began circling around the car like prospective buyers clucking and wheel-kicking critically.

Buzzing down her window to shoo them away, Legs breathed in the sweet scent of hay, manure and silage making. It wasn't quite the brackish sea air for Farcombe that she craved so badly right now, but it was still a heady mix, and reminded her how far she had just come from Ealing to this forgotten corner of Somerset.

Ahead of her, over a low hedge, the Blackdown Hills stretched out in the heat haze like glittering green mosaic. Not as famous as their Somerset companions the Quantocks and Mendips, the Blackdowns were no less stunning, occupying an unspoilt stretch between historic Taunton and the Jurassic coast filled with deep secret valleys and breathtaking hilltops, its undulations scattered with villages of thatched ham stone cottages and smallholdings, its dense green meadows criss-crossed with rabbit run mazes of tiny, high-banked lanes with grass growing down the middle and precious few passing places.

Several miles along one such lane, so narrow and overgrown that it resembled a green bobsleigh tunnel in parts, lay Inkpot Farm, a higgledy-piggledy tawny stone farmhouse spanned by a sagging, mossy roof. It so perfectly resembled a set from a children's film that one expected to walk around the back only to find it made of cardboard and propped up with wooden supports.

Will and Daisy had fallen for its charms two years earlier on a sunny autumn afternoon, without a thought for practicality. They'd told Legs how they'd walked the sixteen acres of thigh-high meadow pasture and fruit-heavy apple orchards with dreams of baby-making and self-sufficiency, visualising chicken runs, sheep and a house cow in the paddocks, a pig pen, vegetable plots, soft fruit garden and artisan office studios in the outbuildings. Ultimately, both now claimed, they'd bought it on the strength of its name alone. What more perfect address for two writers?

But even though Inkpot Farm was the escape-from-it-all idyll that the couple had dreamed of for so long, they'd done nothing but try to escape again since arriving. It had now been on the market several months, and although it was attracting plenty of couples with roses-around-the-door-tinted spectacles, none had made an offer yet.

On the dashboard, Legs' new iPhone vibrated, making her jump.

'That's a cool mobile.' Nico managed to lift his head a fraction in acknowledgement. 'What network are you on?'

'The net that's closing in on me,' she sighed.

It was a message from Kelly.

I now gather from Gordon that you are liaising with the Farcombe Literary Committee shortly. He advises me that you are extremely confident of success. In light of this, please note the list of Gordon's requirements below:

No cameras apart from pre-approved accredited photojournalists

No questions apart from those pre-approved by Gordon's management

No public signings

No hand-held microphones

Pet-friendly accommodation to be provided with bath, not shower. Bed-head must face east, room windows west. At least three living plants in room. Large bowl of fresh fruit (Fairtrade only).

Car and driver must be available for Gordon's sole use at all times. This will be front- or four-wheel drive and have air conditioning. Must not be red.

No nuts to be served to Gordon or near Gordon.

Legs read it with eyebrows raised and quickly typed back.

I will do what I can with this list, although cannot guarantee nuts will not be served as they should be allowed to purchase a drink when they have travelled to North Devon to see their favourite author. Regrettably I cannot offer myself as chauffeur because I drive a red car. Is the bath for the pet? It might make all the difference. Fur or feather?

Knowing that she'd be fired on the spot if Conrad got wind of her impertinence – the 'pluck off' was bad enough – she moved her thumb to the 'Cancel' button. While Gordon shared her irreverent humour, she had to box clever with Kelly, who was far more hardcore protective, lightning-fast to slam down the portcullis if she sensed a threat to the extraordinary Lapis creativity. Legs guessed that Kelly was a key player behind the genius author, and was consequently very wary of her, as well as being increasingly envious of her job. The gratification and intensity of working alongside Gordon's lively mind seemed in direct contrast to her daily grind making up for Conrad's long absences and doing his dirty work for him.

Message Sent, the phone reported cheerfully.

'What?' she howled.

'Benny has an iPhone and it does that all the time,' Nico sympathised nauseously as she started shouting at her phone and threatening to jettison it out the window.

It buzzed again.

Nuts may be served outside, it read.

Legs let out a breath of relief. She liked Kelly, she decided. She could almost forgive her for being the kind of woman to make Conrad look positively skittish; he'd recently described her as having 'the balls of a man'.

Beyond the farmhouse a car engine started up then faded away along the lane.

'Sorry about that!' Daisy burst out of the back door moments later. 'That's the second time they've come and I wanted to leave them with a mental image of perfection.'

'You can't risk putting buyers off with the blight of a caffeine-deprived best friend and carsick stepson,' Legs laughed, pocketing her phone and climbing out of the car to hug her.

Pregnant, top-heavy, small and curvy, Daisy was the opposite of Legs, a full-blossoming myrtle alongside a pear-shaped baobab tree. She was dressed in a deep pink smock over black leggings, her cheeks glowing and her dark fringe as always a little too long, making her tilt her head back to look beneath it as though wearing a peaked baseball cap.

'Not at all – you look as gorgeous as ever, so you'd add value to any property.' Daisy gave her a squeeze before leaning past her to look into the car. 'Are you feeling sick, Nico, poor darling?'

'Legs drives much faster than Dad,' he groaned.

'Oh, I know – she nearly killed us both loads of times as students,' Daisy sympathised, hoofing around to the passenger side to help him out and give him a bolstering hug. 'Let's walk and have some fresh air. Daddy will be back any minute – I've just called him to say the coast is clear. Is that the new away strip?'

She hooked her arm easily around Nico and steered him towards the orchard, letting him chatter happily about the Gunners and forget his nausea. Legs followed them, allowing the sun to warm her face as she admired how natural Daisy was with her stepson. It was a far cry from Poppy Protheroe's relationship with the young Francis, she remembered. Legs still recalled the cool cruelty, her deliberate exclusion of her husband's son from family gatherings and outings, her determination that he would be packed away to boarding school, out of sight and mind.

She was dying to talk to Daisy about her trip to Farcombe, but certain rituals had to be respected first, such as the tour around the farm which looked just as idyllically run down as she remembered, the rusting vintage tractor still covered in ivy, the 'office studios' still derelict old stone barns with no roofs, the vegetable patch bursting with spring cabbages long gone to seed and soft fruit beds which remained overgrown nettle patches.

'Doesn't it look gorgeous at this time of year?' Daisy sighed as they leaned against a wooden fence.

Legs steadied herself as the rail swayed on its rotten uprights. 'So why are you selling up?'

'We can't afford to stay,' Daisy said without self pity, watching indulgently as Nico plunged through the long grass like a hound puppy, heading off to examine his beloved camp by the stream, a wobbly construction of nail-spiked planks and tarpaulin which would give Ros a heart attack if she ever saw it. 'I managed to keep working when I was pregnant with Ava, but we had mum living here then. We'll never juggle three.'

'This baby's due early September?'

Daisy nodded. 'Will's determined to get his novel finished in time, but I can't see it happening if we find ourselves in the middle of moving house.' She turned to her friend with a rueful smile.

They had been moving every year or two for as long as they'd been together, batting back and forth between practical London and their impractical West Country dream, unable to settle to either. Each move had cost them dearly, and far from climbing the property ladder, they'd now firmly landed at the bottom with no equity left.

'Are you coming back to London this time?'

'We'll go back to Spycove.' Daisy grimaced at the irony. When first together they'd holed up in the Foulkeses' family holiday cottage in Farcombe. 'Full circle. We should never have left, really. None of my family uses the place any more, and it's big enough for us all to live. The Spies are so magical. We all love it there.' The Foulkeses' holiday house was just along the track from the Norths' cottage Spywood, the two dwellings separated only by a clifftop coppice.

'I love it too.' Legs looked at her excitedly, unable to hold back a moment longer as she pressed her hands together, fingertips to her nose, bursting with anticipation. 'I'm en route to Farcombe now. Francis wants to meet up.'

'Ah.' Daisy checked that Nico was happily occupied preparing his den for renewed occupation and laced her arm through Legs', steering her towards the house.

'Is that it?' Legs snorted in disbelief. 'Just "ah"?'

Daisy shrugged, squinting up at the farm's pretty thatched dormers and then tutting as she spotted the peeling paintwork. 'I guessed it was only a matter of time.'

'Before what?' She longed for the answer to be 'before you two made friends again', but Daisy was infuriatingly pragmatic, as always.

'Before you paid the cottage a visit; Spywood is your comfort blanket.'

Legs huffed and followed her inside. She was gasping for some of the freshly brewed coffee she could smell, but Daisy pointed out that it was just a teaspoon full of grinds in the percolator acting as an air freshener for the buyers.

'Will thought it up – quite brilliant for atmosphere, but totally undrinkable, and we're down to just a few beans now. We only have herb tea, I'm afraid, although I might have some decaff my sister-in-law left here somewhere.'

'It's OK, I'll pass.' Legs tried not to foam at the mouth as she inhaled the smell of the buyer-baiting pretend coffee, 'there'll be plenty at Spywood; Mum always leaves the cupboards fully loaded for guests.'

Daisy was observing her beadily now, clever brown eyes blinking through her overlong fringe like a wise collie watching a stray sheep and weighing up whether to stay lying low or start rounding her up. 'Isn't your mother staying in Farcombe all summer?'

Legs shrugged, helping herself to an apple from a bowl. 'I've tried to call, but you know what reception's like there; anyway, Ros thinks she's back in London this week.'

Daisy's eyebrows disappeared up beyond her fringe.

'What's that look for?' Legs laughed nervously.

'You don't want Lucy knowing you're going to meet up with Francis, do you?'

'Nonsense. We just don't chat that often – we're not like you and your mum.'

Daisy and her mother spoke almost daily, whereas in the past year Legs had drifted ever further apart from her parents, who had adored Francis completely and found the broken engagement difficult to reconcile. The normally sanguine Lucy in particular had reacted to the split with near hysteria – fervid agitation followed by the cold shoulder of disapproval which distanced mother and daughter to this day.

Daisy was still watching her face closely, those clever eyes infused with affection. 'You should talk to her, Legs. Find out why she's holed herself up in Spywood all summer painting.'

'We both know she likes to kick off her shoes – and everything else – when she paints.' Legs looked away awkwardly. 'Why, has your mum said something?'

'They've hardly seen each other this year as far as I know. Mum's not been to Spycove for months. It still feels like it's a part of Dad somehow. There's so much history there for all of us. You must feel that. It's a part of us.'

The North and Foulkes families had been close for over three decades, ever since Lucy North and Babs Foulkes, both heavily pregnant, had met dog-walking on Richmond Common on a sweltering June day and had shared a breather on a bench together.

The two pregnant wives instantly struck it off. While their mutually irreverent sense of humour brought shared delight, for the husbands it was also bromance at first sight, Dorian North's charm and humour providing the perfect foil for Nigel Foulkes's ambition and drive. The two became the closest of allies; Dorian the charming Kew antiques dealer whose reupholstered Georgian chairs graced the most fashionable west London drawing rooms, and Nigel, an art dealer known as the 'City Canvasser' because of his reputation for selling outlandishly expensive paintings to bankers with deep wallets and no taste. The new fathers shared a love of sport and late-night philosophising over one too many cognacs; they adored good food, travel and adventure. Their circles of friends fused together perfectly.

Before first-borns Rosalind and Freddie were a year old, the dinner parties in Kew and Richmond had already become legendary. By the time second children Daisy and then Allegra came along, the families were taking summer holidays together to remote corners of the West Country, amongst which was an amazing clifftop estate belonging to a client of Nigel's.

Legs, who had been just four at the time, remembered little of their first trip to Farcombe, although it had been the holiday on which she and Daisy became true summer best friends, bonding over a sandcastle on Fargoe Beach that they decorated with pebbles and shells, photographs of which still rested on both the Spycove and Spywood mantels, shown off by its two little architects in swimming costumes holding buckets and spades. In those days, the families had stayed in a pair of pretty, ivy-clad cottages close to the main hall. Their enigmatic host, Hector Protheroe, hadn't been in residence, so the girls had enjoyed free range around the amazing Farcombe estate, running through the courtyards, swimming in the pool, pretending they were princesses in a fairytale castle. They imagined Hector must be a king.

Much later, Legs realised that this first summer holiday at Farcombe must have been the year that Hector's wife Ella died. The Protheroes had been living in America to enable Ella to have the best of cutting-edge treatment in an attempt to turn the tide on the huge tumour growing in her heart. After he was widowed, Hector continued to live between New York and London, and the king of Farcombe eluded his princesses.

The annual holidays at Farcombe continued for the Norths and Foulkes as the go-getting eighties were replaced by the caring nineties and the main Hall fell into increasing disrepair. Allegra and Daisy played in their magical kingdom each summer, their friendship deepening. At six, the two girls had made a friends-for-life pact in the woods above Eascombe Bay, burying their favourite Barbies side by side beneath a beech tree as a symbolic gesture of for ever friendship. As far as Legs knew they were still there, faded little plastic effigies with pert breasts and slim ankles nestling in the deep Devon loam. They knew every nook and cranny around Farcombe, every hiding spot. One summer, they even discovered a way of getting into the big house along the sea passage from

Eascombe Cove that tunnelled up through the cellars, marvelling at the tapestries and panelling, the huge oil paintings and furniture all covered with dust sheets. It became their secret play castle.

Then the king came back, and that was shattered. Hector had sold his company, Smile Media, to return to Farcombe and renovate the house in honour of his late wife. He would start up a jazz festival in his magical corner of North Devon; Farcombe Festival was going to be pure pleasure, a sabbatical project to enable him to take a much-needed rest from big business and spend time with his only son, Francis, who had been brought up and educated thus far in America.

The North and Foulkes children were told there would be no more holidays at Farcombe. The cottages where the families had stayed each summer for half a decade were earmarked for staff accommodation. Legs and Daisy mourned their lost North Devon palace.

Legs wrote a heartfelt letter to Hector, princess to king, begging him to reconsider his plans. It ran to three pages of lined A5, complete with pencil illustrations and a lucky four leaf clover that she'd found one year at Farcombe and kept pressed in her diary ever since. She Sellotaped it beside her signature – a swirly confection that she'd been perfecting all term, which made 'Allegra' indecipherable.

Thus Hector Protheroe's reply came addressed to Miss Alligator North. In flamboyant, spiky handwriting on beautifully embossed, headed paper, he apologised profusely for interfering with her summer holidays and offered a solution. There was a small farm-holding on the edge of the Farcombe estate for which he had no use, and which he was happy to sell to the two families.

Abandoned for over a decade to seagulls and rats, the small, ugly farmhouse known as Spycove and its neighbouring thatched cob cottage Spywood, were little more than tatty implement sheds perched on a cliff above Eascombe Cove, made from the same bleak grey stone as the distant hall, on the outskirts of the high woods with gardens that literally dropped away into the sea. In the years that followed, Nigel Foulkes had lavished money and attention on Spycove until it resembled a Miami beach house. Spywood Cottage, by contrast, had changed little in the seventeen summers the North family had owned it, still possessing two interlinking bedrooms beneath the eaves upstairs, and one large kitchen/living room downstairs, with a chilly lean-to bathroom jutting out amid the trees behind.

The close friendship between the families had endured for almost thirty years now, although Nigel's death four years earlier had changed the way they all thought of 'the Spies' as he'd always called them.

Daisy still clammed up on the subject of losing her father, more so than ever since her mother had remarried, settling down with quiet gallery owner Gerald, whom Daisy thought of as a very poor replacement for larger-than-life Nigel. It was a sore point, and Daisy had a lot of sore points these days, her touchiness having increased tenfold since having her own children. Unlike Legs, who wore her heart on her sleeve as she fought her way through life via the scenic route, cutting to the chase even if it meant drawing her own blood, Daisy had always been more circumspect. Her ability to see everybody's point of view had made her a terrific diplomat in her youth, and was the secret to her ability to write raucous scripts for comedy ensembles, but nowadays she saw as much bad as good in people. This newfound cynicism could be refreshingly honest, but that didn't always make her easy company.

Today was no different. Of all Daisy's sore points, the topic of Francis was always destined to hurt most.

'*Why* does he want to see you?' she asked ungraciously.

Legs tried to stop her heart racing madly. 'Perhaps it's time to forgive?'

'Hmph,' came the cynical raspberry. 'You know he's got a new girlfriend?'

'Don't talk rubbish.'

Daisy eyed her through her fringe. 'You mean you haven't heard about Kizzy?'

'Kizzy de la Mere the poet?' She remembered the self-publicising redhead on the festival website.

'I hear they're practically engaged.'

'We've only been apart a year!'

'And you and Conrad have been together how long?'

Legs brooded silently, casting aside her half-eaten apple. 'We're hardly "practically engaged".'

'Well he *would* have to get divorced first,' Daisy mused. 'But, assuming one is unattached like Fran, it doesn't take long to go from thinking one can never live without a lover to finding a future spouse. Look at my mother. Dad's hardly been dead long.'

Legs winced. Four years seemed a respectable amount of time to her, but she had no first-hand knowledge to compare. If her father died and her mother remarried afterwards, perhaps she would be just as angry? The thought of Francis getting measured up for a morning suit was certainly making her blood boil.

'He can't possibly marry somebody called Kizzy,' she groaned. 'It'll play havoc with his lisp.'

Daisy was spared answering by the loud, rattling arrival of Will in the rickety MPV, returning from the farm park with two sleeping daughters and a panting pair of lurchers.

'Gorgeous, gorgeous Legs – you look fabulous!' He immediately scooped her up into a huge hug, earning a jealous scowl from Daisy.

Neither tall nor handsome, Will nevertheless possessed a fawn-eyed kindness and ebullient energy that made him instantly disarming, the boyish looks now acquiring wise crow's feet and wolfish grey streaks to the hair as he aged. He was an incorrigible flirt, which more than made up for his moderate looks. When married to Ros, he'd become a background character, as comfortable as a reassuring armchair, easy to like and talk to, but rather flat and drab and in need of his cushions plumping. With Daisy at his side, he had been reupholstered with confidence and everybody wanted to perch on his arm.

But there was only one true love rival in Daisy's relationship with Will, and he burst in through the back door now, grass stains on his knees and twigs in his hair. 'Dad!'

Nico hurled himself at Will, as hazel-eyed and bouncy as his father. Daisy turned to Legs. 'Let's get the girls in from the car. They'll be thrilled to see you.'

Waking grumpily and hungrily to find an unfamiliar face lowered over her grappling with the car seat straps, Eva was not at her cheeriest to greet 'Aunt Legs'. Beside her, Grace was equally wary, clutching a fluffy dog fearfully to her face. Both started to mewl.

'How are you getting on with Conrad's kids?' Daisy asked pointedly as Legs hastily handed over wailing Eva.

'We're taking it slowly.' She pulled comedy faces at Grace who looked horrified and hid behind her mother's legs.

'You never take anything slowly,' Daisy laughed.

The tension between them bubbled again. Legs guessed this wasn't about Conrad at all. 'If this has to do with Francis, say so,' she rounded, preferring to get it out in the open.

'Just be careful,' Daisy warned. 'Try to read the situation before you rewrite any rules. Things have changed a lot down there.'

'I wouldn't know,' she sighed.

'Well you did rather cut yourself adrift, chucking him out without so much as a kiss goodbye.'

'I wrote to him to apologise.' She turned to Daisy indignantly.

'What good manners.' Daisy watched Grace chasing a chicken around the driveway.

Legs gazed down at her feet, her Nike Lunars looking stupidly urban alongside Daisy's dusty clogs. It was the first time she had confided about her letter to anyone: 'Actually, I told him it had all been a huge mistake.'

Daisy turned to her sharply. 'When was this?'

She dug holes in the gravel drive with her toes, 'About a month after we split up.'

'What did he say?'

'He never replied.'

Eyebrows shooting up behind the collie fringe again, Daisy blew out a puff of surprise.

'He must have hated my guts back then.' Legs carried on staring at her feet. The truth of it still hurt like glass shards through her nerve endings. She'd wept such bitter tears over that letter, writing and rewriting it, pouring her heart out. Looking back, she knew she should have been brave enough to talk face to face instead of hiding behind purple prose and clinging to Conrad for security. 'And now you say he's engaged.'

'Practically engaged.'

'It hardly smacks of a broken heart, does it?' She suddenly felt feverishly angry. Nor did it smack of one of Britain's Most Eligible Bachelors as recent press had branded him. Increasingly neglected by Conrad out of work hours, Legs didn't like to admit to the amount of time and effort she'd spent tracking down and reading the many articles that had featured Francis in recent months, but she'd been on the *Daily Mail* website so often that it now ranked high on her Explorer drop down list, and the corner newsagent had suggested she might like to take out a subscription to *Tatler* because she bought it so often. Its glossy pages regularly featured photographs of him ranked highly in Most Invited, Most Wanted and Sexiest charts, praising this good-looking heir to Farcombe, with his literary bent, healthy outdoor lifestyle, boyish sex appeal and an untarnished reputation, all of which made for a great catch. His long relationship and engagement to Legs was clearly deemed too trivial to mention, making her feel that their thirteen years together had been struck off his romantic CV entirely.

She had friends who were ex-obsessed, Googling previous boyfriends on a regular basis, and she hated the thought that she was similarly afflicted. (Surely with just the one ex to her name, an active interest was not unjustified?) But, talking to Daisy today and confessing to sending the letter that could have changed the way the past year had panned out entirely, she already suspected that her personal motivation for returning to Farcombe was less about work and more about finally making peace.

Daisy was still looking up at her through her fringe, lips pressed to the top of Eva's downy head. 'Men react to rejection in different ways. Some go straight on the rebound. Look at Conrad.' Then, before Legs had a chance to snap back that the two situations could not be compared, she added, 'What does *he* think about your long weekend in Farcombe?'

'It was his idea.'

Daisy almost dropped Eva in shock. 'Please don't tell me he's joining you at the cottage?'

'What d'you take me for?' As they headed back inside to prepare lunch, Legs explained that she was going to Farcombe on festival business.

Looking ever more disapproving, Daisy buckled Eva into a high chair before fetching salad ingredients from the fridge. 'So that's what this is all about? Nothing to do with trying to get back together with Francis?'

'Well, fate is playing a bit of a card, don't you think?'

'No! I don't think that.' A cucumber was being waved about like a conductor's baton now. Grace and Eva were entranced. 'I think that you have a horribly guilty conscience, and want to do anything in your power to lance the penitent boil.'

'Nicely put.'

Daisy glanced out of the garden window to check that Nico and Will were suitably distracted and out of earshot, kicking a ball about. Then she turned back to Legs, voice hushed, cucumber lowered. 'I think you believe you'll never forgive yourself for what you did to Francis unless you create some sort of emotional Tardis, where you try to go back in time and recreate the moment you left him, *Groundhog Day*-style, and take the other path to see where it leads.'

'You have no idea how I feel!' Legs protested hotly.

'I so do!' The cucumber struck a worksurface with a splat. 'I know, Legs, because I feel exactly the same way a lot of the time.'

'About what?'

'About stealing your sister's husband.'

Legs gasped in surprise. 'You mean you want to go back in time and hand him back?'

'Of course not!' Daisy glanced at Grace and Eva in their highchairs, lowering her voice. 'Will's the best thing that ever happened to me. But it doesn't make the guilt go away, the need to repent and the wish that it could have happened differently, with more dignity and less pain. I think you'd like to take it one stage further, and that a part of you wishes you and Francis were still together.'

'That's not what this trip is about! I'm with Conrad now. And you said it yourself, Francis is "practically" engaged.' She winced as the words physically hurt to say out loud each time. 'This is just business and, hopefully, friendship.'

Daisy gave her that age-old wise look before turning to chop up the cucumber. 'Friendship *is* important, Legs. Friendship and family; you mustn't abuse them.'

'They're everything to me.'

'Good.' She looked over her shoulder, and they shared an appeasing smile, although both knew that there was a lot being left unsaid.

Their deep bond of friendship had lasted well into adulthood despite the severest of tests. It sat comfortably beneath them, a cushion on which they both relied, which still worked better out of London, particularly away from Ros and the reminders of Legs' divided loyalty. It also worked better away from Francis. It always had. For the first few years of their friendship, the girls had known nothing about the only son of the man they thought of as their king. They hadn't even known his name.

Then the king had returned to his castle, and his heir made

himself apparent. The princesses' friendship had been tested ever since.

Throughout lunch, the knot of anxiety in Legs' stomach at the prospect of seeing Francis again tightened, seeming to pull all her entrails around it like a tight ball of wool. Speaking with Daisy had just opened up a Pandora's box of emotions that she'd been blissfully unaware of, and which now writhed like snakes around that knotted ball. Soon indigestion was raging.

'Not another faddy diet?' Will observed her picking her bread roll into small chunks without eating them. He gave her a gappy-toothed smile across the table as Nico speared up the ham on his aunt's plate.

She shook her head, suddenly fighting an urge to head back to London instead of continuing her journey west. She must have put on half a stone since she last saw Francis, and now it felt as though every ounce was in that churning lump in her belly.

'Aunt Legs is buff,' Nico offered sportingly, matching his father's smile.

Daisy almost choked on her mouthful. 'Since when did you start using phrases like "buff"?'

'Since Legs taught me to say it.'

'Nico!' She threw a little dough ball at him. 'I did no such thing!'

'So have you got a girlfriend at the moment, Nico?' Daisy asked, making him blush to his roots and stutter about not liking girls.

Still distracted, Legs held in her stomach and looked down to see how pot-bellied it was. While nothing on Daisy's pregnant bulge, it was definitely not very flat. She made a mental note to change into Magic Pants as soon as she got to Spywood Cottage.

Her iPhone was buzzing in her pocket. She pulled it out and peered at it discreetly beneath the table rim.

Gordon says he is not prepared to compromise on a bath or pet friendly accommodation, and definitely not on red car.

She looked up, wondering whether to share the joke, but

suspected the confidentiality agreement she'd signed precluded it. Will had a journalist's nose after all and, for all his assertions that he'd turned his back on the newsroom for literary pursuits, he needed the cash.

All around her, the chattering, giggling, joyful family tableau felt at total odds with the life she now had, careering through London, living alone in her basement beneath Ros's super-organised life, which revolved around Nico and church, just as her own revolved around Conrad and work.

She could see how relaxed Nico was here. He loved the easy-going routine at Inkpot, the laughter, lack of pressure and the free-range existence. She felt the same.

It made her think about Farcombe again, the memories so acute that she could almost smell and taste them. Family holidays there had been such fun. It was where she had first learned about love. She craved it again.

Fingers moving beneath the table, she typed: *Cannot guarantee anything, regrettably. Will try my best, but this could be very tricky to steer.*

Again, the reply was almost immediate. *Gordon says that is because you drive a red car. Suggests you trade in for safer colour.*

She jumped as Will waved a hand in front of her face. 'Hello? Legs?' I said what's hot off the shelves right now? Still Grit Lit and Cruci Fiction?' He'd loved drilling her about the publishing market ever since he began toiling on the great debut novel that he would let nobody read until it was finished, and which he'd only thus far described as being 'vaguely brilliant'.

'Parent Thrillers.'

'Kitchen-sink violence, you mean?'

She shook her head. 'Think *Sophie's Choice* set amid Cath Kidston accessories, Ocado deliveries and the school run. Picture a lovely but stressed professional family: by the end of chapter one, one child (preferably under the age of five) will be held hostage in a nursery-school siege, or abducted by someone planning to keep them in a cellar for twenty years, or be found to be the only match-ing donor that can save the life of their estranged, imprisoned rapist father, or be brutally disfigured and blinded in a house fire while holding the secret to the arsonist. Mother and father then face great personal sacrifice, a race against time, an impossible decision or all of the above.'

'Oh, I love books like that,' Daisy sighed. 'I cry as soon as I read the blurb.'

'The "blub" then.' Will looked sceptical. 'And they're hot in lit-erary London?'

'Conrad sold one by a complete unknown just last month; six figures for two books; film rights have already gone, it's been chosen as *Book at Bedtime* and is tipped for a certain famous couple's book club.'

'In that case I'll kill a child,' he said firmly, earning a nervous look from Nico.

'Just make sure the family have at least one spare sibling as com-pensation,' she warned him.

'You two are *so* cynical,' Daisy scoffed. 'We all know you prefer a huge body count somewhere scenic, Legs. She had a five-a-week Agatha Christie habit at your age,' she told Nico.

'You can't beat a classic formula,' she sighed.

'Perhaps you should persuade Gordon Lapis to feature an idyl-lic village with a mass murderer on the loose in the next Ptolemy Finch?' Will teased. 'A career in criminal profiling awaits our young, winged soothsayer,' he predicted in a movie trailer voice.

'Already on the case,' she beamed. 'I'm doing some research for him in Farcombe for *Ptolemy Finch and the Seagull Strangler.*'

'As long as you're not researching *Ptolemy Finch and the Sentimental Shag,*' Daisy muttered darkly.

'A shag is a type of bird,' Will told Nico, who nodded, having followed the conversation with bright-eyed interest. 'Very like a cormorant.'

'Legs has promised to get me a personally signed copy of

Ptolemy Finch and the Raven's Curse when it comes out,' he told them. 'She and Gordon are like that now.' He pinched his fingers together closely. 'I think he probably wants to give her a shag.' He smiled sweetly. 'Or perhaps a cormorant?'

On cue, Legs' phone flashed with a message from Gordon: *Julie Ocean investigating a crime that took place more than twenty years ago; she uncovers corruption at the heart of a highly respected institution. They will close ranks on her. How does she feel? What does she do?*

At least he seemed to be talking to her again, she realised with relief, replying: *Alone. Calls Jimmy for back-up.*

Too deep undercover; fears he's corrupt too.

Tempted to type 'take annual leave?', she wrote, *Goes direct to Chief Super.*

Trust nobody. He signed off without further explanation.

Chapter 5

Every familiar twist and turn on the journey to Farcombe made Legs' heart race faster and her spirits lift. She was going through the back of the holiday wardrobe of memories. Clouds scudded over the sun, flashing intermittent blinding light onto her bug-flecked windscreen as she weaved the curling miles towards the Hartland Peninsula. When the Farcombe turn came into view, her car indicator ticked in time with her thudding heart as she turned between the two wind-bent white-beam trees that stood sentinel on its high Devonshire banks.

The sunken lane climbed over the ridge that hid the sea from the main road and Legs blinked to adjust to the emerald dark as the familiar high-banked wooded tunnel enveloped her, still revealing nothing of the dramatic coastline ahead. She tucked the Honda into passing places as cars approached, tourists with sunburned noses who had spent the day in Farcombe, meandering along the steep, cobbled lanes of the fishing village, poddling along the harbour, visiting the craft shops and cafes, walking the cliff path to the beach at Fargoe Bay.

To the left were the tall stone gate pillars of Farcombe Hall, topped with their rearing unicorns which the family had nicknamed Balios and Xanthus after the horses who drew Achilles' chariot, guarding the high, wrought-iron gates. Despite its grandeur, this was not the main entrance to the estate, which was on the main coast road, with matching gatehouses shouldering a grand archway with a pinnacle in the shape of a huge-winged griffin.

Legs couldn't resist slowing as she passed, peering along the driveway, which curled away out of sight, its tall rhododendron hedges hiding all that lay beyond. The last time she'd been here, over a year ago, the fallen red and blue petals that carpeted the driveway had been turning mulchy brown, like boiled sweets caramelising in a pan; this year they were already just faint black liquorish strings running through the cobbles, pulped and rotted by the recent storms. The little sunken brook that ran in front of the gateposts was fierce as she'd ever known it. As small children, Daisy and Legs had floated folded paper message boats on it and sent them downstream, before hurtling along the lane on racing, chubby legs, pushing and shoving as they marked their crafts to see whose joined the river stream first before launching out to sea.

Legs turned down the volume on the radio and opened the window, able to hear the stream bubble and smell the sappy tang of the wooded cliffs, cut through with sea salt. It was delicious.

She put the car back in gear and hurried along the lane, passing the public car park on the right. Here the lane narrowed dramatically, with its peeling 'Private Road' sign declaring that it was the Farcombe Hall Estate, with no public access to the harbour or beach.

Dropping through the trees to the river fork, Legs felt her

stomach go weightless as though whizzing downward on a Ferris wheel. Then she took the familiar left bend, past more 'Private – Farcombe Estate' signs, and began to climb again, the sea glinting through the trees on her right. To her left, the woodland thinned again and the estate's parkland stretched up, still coyly hiding its jewel.

Another fork known as Gull Cross marked the point where the road threaded down through coastal heath and craggy stone outcrops to the private cove at Eascombe, a tunnel from which led directly to the main house. Steering away from the sea instead, Legs drove uphill on a bumpy unmade track, and into more woods, her own precious forest where every gnarled trunk was familiar, where she'd once played Little Red Riding Hood and Goldilocks with Daisy, hosting teddy bears' picnics and making dens, and later conducted midnight ghost walks and camped in hammocks between the trees. Somewhere the two Barbie dolls were buried beneath one of the old rowans, along with a time capsule created by the Foulkes and North children as instructed by the *Blue Peter* team, containing various coins, newspaper cuttings, postcards, toy cars and a retaining brace that Legs had sneaked in and then claimed to have lost.

Here in her enchanted wood, there were many trees with her initials carved in them – AN – some sharing hearts with FP, others proclaimed rather shamefully that she and DF 'woz here'. There was one tree in particular that held a special secret, which meant she loved it more than any other, and couldn't wait to lie in the deep hollow where its trunk divided into two outstretched arms.

But first she raced on to Spywood Cottage, hidden deep within the darkness, along its own small pitted track that had wrecked many an axle of the Norths' family cars. Once a gamekeeper's cottage, the thatched cob dwelling was pretty enough to reduce first-time guests to tears with one glimpse at its higgledly-piggledy perfection over the five-barred gate, nestled in its own fairy glade clearing of bottle green grass, ferns, wild strawberries and wood anemones, with a cluster of oaks and rowans at the end of the garden, beyond which was a sheer drop to the North Devon coast. The sound of the waves crashing against the stony outcrops could be so loud in the cottage at times that they would have to raise their voices to be heard. When the children were little, Lucy had been terrified that they would fall to their deaths, but although a few games of truth or dare had led to some terrifying cliffhanger moments over the years, and many a ball had been accidentally kicked over the lip to spin fifty feet down onto the sharp rocks below, Spywood had proved a safe haven to all who stayed there, and they felt as though they had a secret fairytale cottage in a cloud.

Legs parked on the main woodland track and let herself in through the boundary gate, knowing that her old Honda's suspension would never take the cottage's driveway. The ruts here were even deeper than she remembered, now filled with storm water, and it had clearly been used quite recently, although not by her mother's little runabout. These deep gouges came from a big off-roader with tyres like boulders.

Hurrying between the ruts because she wanted to get into the cottage to use the loo, Legs slowed in surprise as she noticed a bicycle propped up against one oak post of the porch. Again, the memories hit her as sharply as the sea air and cool breeze.

Francis has always propped his bike there, day after day as he paid court to her each school holiday. The kick of déjà vu to her chest was breathtaking. This was a rusting sit-up-and-beg antique, not the garish yellow and purple mountain bike of which he had been so proud, but it made her stifle a nostalgic hiccup nonetheless. Then, as she ducked beneath the curtain of clematis overhanging the porch, she let out a gasp of surprise.

There was a note on the door.

I LOVE YOU.

The latch was off, the door unlocked.

Inside, all was as she remembered – the scrubbed pine table

with its mismatched chairs, the threadbare sofas and rugs, the collected paraphernalia of tens of family holidays on the sills and shelves, driftwood and shells, bric-a-brac and bottles.

There was a vase of sweetpeas on the table, along with two champagne glasses.

Legs caught her breath, heart hammering. Still hesitating in the doorway, she saw another note pinned to the narrow stairs door. It was an arrow pointing upwards.

Hardly able to breathe for excitement, she followed its point. As she creaked hurriedly up the old elm treads, she heard strains of music coming from the main bedroom. It was the bassoon solo from Stravinsky's *Rite of Spring*.

Now on the top step, Legs froze with alarm as a cold splash of self-awareness drenched her senses. She was here to talk quietly to Francis about Gordon Lapis. She was with Conrad now. Any rapprochement should be calmly handled, with dignity on both sides. This was all wrong, surely?

Yet her honest heart continued to race with hope, and her overheating body bubbled with anticipation. She no longer cared that she was sweaty and unwashed after her journey, and hadn't had time to sport Magic Pants, fine perfume and make-up.

She crossed through the landing room and burst into the furthest bedroom. The windows were all wide open, the long muslin curtains billowing in the wind, the scent of the sea as fresh as a wave's spray.

'Arghhh!'

Hector Protheroe, a man she had once believed to be a king, and later thought of as her future father-in-law, was sitting naked on the bed playing his bassoon.

With classic sangfroid, Hector didn't play a dud note as he finished the refrain with a flourish, stretched back and reached for a towel to first dab his lips and then cover his long torso. For a man of over sixty, he had a great body, like a veteran tennis pro, all six foot four of it, lean, sinewy and tanned. Apart from a slight paunch in the middle and a soft dusting of white hairs on his chest, he could pass for Conrad's age.

'Good afternoon Allegra.' His deep bass voice let out a bark of surprise. 'We weren't expecting you, were we?'

Legs hid behind the door.

'What are you doing here?' she gasped.

She heard a creaking of floorboards as he stood up. 'Waiting for Lucy. She popped to Bude for champagne.'

Legs was dumbfounded, trying to make sense of her mother playing hostess to a naked Hector Protheroe in the cottage. Was he a closet naturist, too?

'Are you celebrating something?'

'Every day is a celebration at the moment.' Now wrapped in a jaunty, orchid-strewn silk kimono that was far too short, Hector and his bassoon joined her in the landing room, ducking beneath the low beams, his voice hushed with concern. 'My dear, you do know, don't you?'

'Know what?'

His faded blue eyes softened amid their tanned creases, and he studied her shocked face thoughtfully before steering her downstairs where it was less cramped and he could straighten up to his full six foot four and make an announcement that left Legs' jaw hanging yet lower.

'I've left Poppy.'

Legs reeled back. So that was it. Her mother was providing sanctuary for Hector, who had finally left his troubled marriage of twenty years. There had been many occasions in the past when he'd threatened to do so, and his flirtations and affairs had been legend, but he'd never actually done the deed.

Her first thought was for Francis. As a young boy with a step-mother he loathed, this was news he could only have dreamed of. Now, in adulthood, he might feel differently. How was he taking it?

Only after she'd pondered this for a moment did a second thought strike her. Why was Hector naked, and why had he written

I LOVE YOU on the door? He must have a mistress and be using Spywood to conduct his trysts. He was an incorrigible flirt, well known as a roué and a terror to barmaids at the Book Inn in Farcombe.

'Lucy has been amazing,' Hector was saying.

Legs gasped in ever-dawning shock. With typical naivety and kindness, her mother was obviously providing a refuge for the lovers, and even catering for them. No wonder Lucy had been away so long watercolouring. She'd always had a soft spot for Hector and run errands for him, forever at his beck and call, the swine.

'That's such an abuse of friendship!' Legs squeaked.

Hector shook his head. '*Au contraire*, my dear Allegra, *recevoir sans donner fait tourner l'amitié.*' He smiled benignly at her baffled face. 'Receiving without giving turns the friendship.'

'That's as might be, but there was still no need to bring my mother into all this!'

'She rather came of her own free will.'

They were standing in the kitchen now, Hector's bassoon still aloft, like a fertility symbol. Legs felt she should cast around for a phallic symbol of her own to even things up – the ornamental bedpan that hung from the wall, maybe, or one of the sausage-dog draft excluders? She could use a weapon if things got heated; Hector was hardly a threat in his flowery kimono, but his acid charm was such high grade uranium that he could flatten an ego with one barbed comment.

She'd never enjoyed an easy relationship with the man who lived up to his name by being something of a hectoring bully and vociferous critic. A controversial, anti-establishment figure and notorious gambler with a knack for making money, friends and headlines easily, Hector Protheroe had famously launched the *Commentator* magazine in the seventies when he was fresh out of Cambridge, later selling it for a fat profit which enabled him to open the Fitzroy Club in the eighties, one of the first of the swathe of private members' clubs that cashed in on London's glitterati clique. But the main source of Hector's considerable income came from Smile Media, a company at the cutting edge of mobile telecommunications, of cable and satellite and later digital broadcasting and publishing. 'Spread the Smile' had been one of the biggest advertising campaigns of the nineties, a catchphrase familiar to every Brit. Smile phones were, for a time, the ultimate in cool, along with Smile palmtops, laptops and Smile internet.

The man behind renegade publishing, trendy nightclubs and multimedia communications might maintain that he was an 'inspirer', and he certainly had plenty of hippy attributes that made him appear laidback and easy-going, but Legs knew enough to appreciate that the retired entrepreneur, reformed gambler and passionate music lover could be a tyrant, albeit one with a positive spin. He'd certainly pushed his only son incredibly hard over the years, expecting nothing less than perfection. At times, the pressure on Francis had been almost unbearable, and Legs had often stood up to his father on her lover's behalf, but that was where the famous Protheroe charm came in. Hector's seductive charisma made him a difficult man to challenge. He could turn any conversation in his favour, twisting the argument to serve his purpose so that ultimately one was left not only feeling rather silly, but also hopelessly in his awe and debt. It was why he was so lethal in business, inspired such loyalty amongst friends, and was so totally irresistible to all who met him.

Yet he was supremely selfish in his personal relationships, particularly with women. His third wife Poppy could be awkward and eccentric, but for two decades she had coped admirably with his rages, infidelity and self-absorption, and was his match intellectually. Hector self-confessedly relied upon his wife's steely stoicism to keep him in check, crediting her with bringing his long-term gambling addiction under control, stemming his drinking and redirecting his energies into supporting the many altruistic causes that had earned him such an exemplary public reputation today.

She'd also turned a blind eye to his many flirtations, which some in their inner circle put down to her incredibly short sight. Cast adrift from the marriage, he could cause havoc, and sideswipe poor, kind-hearted Lucy in his slipstream. Legs felt highly protective.

'So where are you living?'

'Here.'

'You have plenty of houses. Isn't it a bit selfish to squeeze in here?'

He barked with laughter.

Legs wanted to snap at him that he'd have to move out now that she was here (as she rather hoped her mother would, too, to clear the way for long chats with Francis), but her bladder was fit to burst now and so she was forced to retreat to the bathroom and regroup.

There were definite signs of male occupation here – an extra toothbrush, aftershave, a beard trimmer and some enormous slippers which appeared to have been stepped out of as a bath was stepped into and then abandoned beneath the antique towel rail.

For the first time, Legs began to wonder what her father made of all this.

Just then she heard a car engine coming along on the wood track. With relief, she washed her hands, splashing cool water on her face and then unbolting the door, determined to sort out this nonsense.

The bassoon was back in its stand by the chaise longue, and the front door was wide open, meaning Hector was braving the elements in his kimono in welcome. Legs dashed in his wake.

Hector had made it almost as far as the car, from which Lucy was only just emerging. His frantic hand gestures and facial expressions were not enough to alert her to danger.

'Hector, my lionheart!' She threw out her arms in embrace, imagining that he was rushing to greet her with amorous impatience. 'I have bought oysters for passion, and ice cream that we can eat from one another's most intimate love cups.'

At that moment, Lucy North caught sight of her younger daughter gaping at her over the swinging gate.

'Ah.' Lucy's smile turned from joyous to mortified, but all teeth remained on show in a brave attempt at a bluff.

Legs barely recognised her own mother. That wild peppery hair had been bobbed and bleached a flattering ash blonde, the jolly, freckled face disguised with lots of smoky eyeliner and red lipstick, and she was wearing a wraparound dress that revealed her waist for the first time in over a decade and showed a lot of leg. She looked sensational, but to Legs it was like staring at a stranger.

Her phone started to ring. She wanted to ignore it, but it was playing 'Teenage Kicks', the song she'd assigned to Francis, added to which Hector was suddenly all over her like a rash.

'What network are you on?' he demanded as she delved into her pocket to retrieve it. 'There's never a signal here.'

'Virgin,' she admitted, making him reel back in shock as she mentioned Smile Media's business arch-nemesis.

She answered the call, stepping behind a tree in a hopeless quest for privacy.

The signal was in fact so poor that the line was barely holding together. Francis sounded like he was speaking from a tin on a three-mile string.

'How much do you know about this?' she demanded furiously.

'I knew . . . should ha . . . warned you.' Despite the interference, hearing his voice was like a warm breath in her ear, his bass tone was softer and lighter than his father's, still tinged with American top notes, but the timbre strikingly similar. 'You've just caught . . . together?'

'Not exactly in flagrante, but flagrant enough.'

'We must talk. I'll meet you . . . the Lookout . . . ten min . . .' The line went dead.

Face flaming, she swept past her still-smiling mother and headed for her car. 'I'll book into the pub.'

'Aren't you coming back?' Lucy called, voice shaking.

'I'll come and see you tomorrow when we've all calmed down enough to talk. Enjoy your oysters.' *I hope they choke Hector*, she added with unspoken venom.

It was only once she was behind the wheel and emerging from woods to sunlight that she started to sob, overwhelmed by what she'd just witnessed. She drove back to the Gull Cross fork and swerved blindly down the lane towards the bay. At the point where the track started to snake down through the coastal heath, she braked hard and then cut the engine. The Honda was left parked at a jaunty angle with the bonnet crammed in a gorse bush.

The sea wind whipped away her tears as soon as she got out, and the panic subsided. Francis would make sense of it all. He always did.

Chapter 6

The path up to the Lookout was massively overgrown these days, sometimes barely passable. Legs kept losing it completely and having to retrace her steps. Mostly she navigated from instinct. Beyond the trees, almost cut into the cliff side, was a narrow stone ledge that ran deep within the gorse and heather, virtually a gully at times, uneven and precarious.

At its end, the Lookout perched on the narrowest of platforms, resembling little more than a neglected birdwatchers' hide dressed with wooden shipboard. It concealed a large cave, complete with table and chairs, a bunk and even a constant supply of freshwater that trickled along a trough of stone on one corner. Legend had it that a hermit had once lived there, before moving to the relative comfort of Spycove.

As teenagers, the Norths and Foulkes and Francis had double-dared one another to go there, convinced that it was haunted, or worse still occupied by a runaway mass murder from HMP Dartmoor. Eventually, overcoming their nerves, they'd claimed it as their own and styled it in different guises over the years – from fluffy pink to gothic black, bookish retreat to party pad. Now what minimalist signs of habitation remained were neglected, the cave showing evidence of a recent invasion of birds, bats and other visiting creatures.

Legs didn't suit high drama, and suited heights even less. She had no idea why Francis had suggested meeting here, and had been far too overwrought to think about it until now. She supposed it fitted the moment. He had always been the ultimate stage manager.

After ten minutes, just as she was starting to wonder whether the stage manager had missed his cue, a wiry little terrier wearing a checked neckerchief shot into the Lookout and barked in surprise, clearly as shocked to find her waiting there as she was to encounter a dog.

Francis followed in his wake, his high cheeks pink from running and his mop of blond hair windswept into great peaks.

Legs' heart crashed against her ribs in sympathy with the waves on the rocks below.

Of course she hadn't forgotten how good-looking he was – nobody could – but to see it afresh after a year's total separation was a shock. In the past, she'd grown so accustomed to the perfection of his profile that she'd taken his beauty for granted, along with the length and breadth of his athletic six foot two frame. She'd always jealously noted the way that new acquaintances, especially women, stole glances at him over and over again to check that he really was as gorgeous as he'd first appeared. And he was, just as he was gentlemanly and erudite and kind and almost childlike in his wonder and enthusiasm for life.

In their last few weeks as a couple, perhaps to justify her growing attraction to Conrad, she'd decided Francis's looks were far too

Fauntleroy, reflecting the fact she found him so maddeningly childlike, spoilt and petulant by then. His stubbornness had always frustrated her, along with his intellectual snobbery. And he was secretly very vain.

But now that the fallen angel had flown into the Lookout every bit as handsome as she could ever remember him, she was too breathless with the impact of seeing him again to think straight.

'I can't stay long,' he apologised. 'Kizzy has no idea I'm here, but she already suspects something because I offered to walk Byron.'

Legs tried not to feel scalded by the immediate mention of Kizzy, nor succumb to the temptation to volley Conrad's name straight back. Instead she regarded the diminutive terrier with a nervous laugh. 'That's Byron?'

'He has a limp,' he muttered by way of explanation, rushing on. 'Poppy knows I'm here so she'll cover for me. Kizzy has no idea this place exists.'

Legs said nothing, although her mind was reeling. Since when had Poppy and Francis been collaborators? And why keep secrets from Kizzy with whom he was 'practically engaged'.

He sat on one of the rusting metal chairs and pulled another alongside it for her.

Being together for the first time since the split made them both so jumpy with nerves they couldn't look one another in the eye.

She perched awkwardly beside him, 'Do you know how long this love affair between your father and my mother has been going on?' she checked, her voice unnaturally high.

'Over a decade, on and off.'

She gasped. 'That means they were at it almost the whole time we were together!'

Colour rose in his cheeks: 'Dad insists it wasn't a physical relationship until this summer, apart from the odd kiss that is.'

The image of Hector kissing her mother over the years, oddly or not, wasn't one on which Legs wished to dwell.

'So they've always fancied one another?' She winced at the term, which sounded so wrong when applied to her mother and Hector.

He winced too before nodding. 'They both recognised a growing attraction, but they resisted acting upon it because you and I were so deeply in love, it would cause such damage. From what I can gather, the affair largely amounted to secret lunches, phone calls and letters before . . .' he paused '. . . we called off our engagement.'

Legs stared at her hands. It was a typically reserved Francis-way of phrasing it. He meant 'since you ran off with your boss and broke my heart', but he would never say that.

'My father says they agreed long ago that nothing more could ever come of what they felt about one another while we were together,' he went on.

'And now that we're not they can do whatever they like,' she groaned as reality dawned with eye-watering clarity. 'Mum hasn't said a thing. No one has a clue, not even Dad as far as I'm aware. He thinks she's still painting watercolours here.'

His voice was soft with empathy: 'I'm not sure any of us believe it's real yet, not even them. They're like a pair of naughty teenagers having a holiday romance, locked away in that cottage together.'

'Do you think it might just be a summer romance then?' she asked hopefully.

'Dad claims otherwise, but he's been building up to something like this ever since his name was left off the Birthday Honours list. He was convinced he was getting his gong this year, and now he's behaving as badly as possible.'

'Are you telling me he's only wrecking his own and my parents' marriage because he's peeved about not getting a knighthood?'

'Well there's a bit more to it than that obviously.' He looked shifty. 'I'm just suggesting it might blow over, even if they say otherwise.'

'I wish you'd told me about it sooner.'

'I though you knew; I thought that's why you came.'

'What? Oh – no, that was about the festival. It's not important.'
She gazed out across the sea ahead of them, watching waves break in the distance into frothing grey ruffs of surf.

'You want this nonsense between them to stop, don't you Legs?' Francis's voice was low and reassuring, reminding her of the first love she'd adored so resolutely, the boy-turned-man who was her bedrock, who made her feel safe and cared for. He'd long since lost the preppy American accent that he'd possessed when his father first brought him to Farcombe, but Legs still always heard it in his voice, remembering their giggling delight as they had compared vowel sounds that first summer.

She continued staring out to sea, uncertain what to say. Of course she wanted the affair between Lucy and Hector to stop. It was all wrong. The thought of her mother betraying her father hurt beyond measure. The lies that must have been told over the years, the pretence at happy families when a secret desire was burning – it was almost unthinkable, undermining everything she held dear. But she also knew that it was largely beyond her control. Nothing could take back what had already happened. Hector and her mother had free will; some would say they were more wilful than most. It would be pointless trying to fight that.

Now Francis turned in his chair and fixed her with a gaze that made her skin prickle, even though her eyes still couldn't quite meet his.

'There's only one thing for it. We have to get back together, Legs.'

She snorted with laughter, a nervous reflex. He made it sound so simple and logical, like changing a flat tyre together.

There was a long pause.

'Why is that so funny?' he asked stiffly.

'It's not.' She swallowed, raising her eyes to his at last and almost rocking straight back over in her chair as a result. His eyes were as vividly blue and calm as the sea ahead was grey and stormy. She longed to dive in.

'I thought you just said their affair might burn itself out?'

'All the more reason to fight fire with fire.' He was looking so deeply into her eyes now, and she felt completely overwhelmed by emotion, so choked that she was winded by it, tears mounting in the back of her throat.

By contrast, Francis was utterly composed, only a faint quilt of the muscles on both high cheeks betraying the maelstrom of feelings swirling behind the calm facade. 'I think it's our only option. This is a frightful muddle.'

'*Muddle?*' She snorted again, laughter and tears combining to make her sound maniacal. 'It's a total car crash, Francis! When Ros finds out she'll—'

'Ros will *not* find out,' he interjected smoothly. 'It must be kept between ourselves. Please don't cry, darling Legs. We have no time for that. We can sort this mess out, you and I. We're the brave ones, remember? "Only those who risk going too far can possibly find out how far one can go." It had been their favourite Eliot quote as literature-mad teenagers, so often recited to one another here in the Lookout, when staring at the horizon had seemed like looking into a future of infinite possibilities. 'I know my father,' he went on earnestly. 'He plays the hippy well, but he has a very reactionary flipside, particularly when it comes to his children. He will stop this affair at once if we resume our engagement.' He sounded like the hero in a Restoration comedy. 'And Dorian will be spared the necessity of driving to Farcombe with duelling swords.'

'Dad would never do that. He's the real deal when it comes to hippy thinking. He'll just suffer in silence.'

'Then we must spare him that pain, Legs. If we remember why we are doing this, then nobody need get hurt.'

He seemed so strong and male, she realised in shock. She wanted to rage and throw herself to the ground in a tantrum, wailing that it was all so un*faaaaiiir*, and he was taking it like a grown-up. This was the wrong way around; she'd always been the mature one. Not that either of them had been particularly good at embracing the responsibilities of adulthood, preferring make-believe, holidays and daydreams to reality.

She mopped away the eking tears with her shirt cuffs and then fished around for something more ladylike to blow her nose.

'Here.' Francis handed her a silk handkerchief which smelled of washing powder mixed with expensive cologne. It reminded her of his pillow in their shared flat. For a moment she closed her eyes and buried her face in it.

Then Legs blew her hooter noisily and forced herself to get a grip on her sentiment overload. 'Are you going to marry Kizzy?'

'We are lovers,' he stated with an affected emphasis on the word, 'and you're still with Con-man.'

She looked away guiltily. 'Conrad.'

At Francis's feet, Byron the terrier let out a whining yawn and stared longingly towards the cliff path.

'So how can we possibly get back together?' It seemed such a wild and abstract concept to Legs, like changing that flat tyre on the Space Shuttle as their lives revolved on different orbits. And yet it already made her feel weightless with anticipation and giddy with excitement.

There was another long pause as he looked at her sideways, seemingly weighing her up, assessing the changes, searching for the perfect quote to voice his hidden feelings. She was reminded of moments of high drama in their long relationship when there would be a race to fill a silence, Francis with a quote and her with a joke. But today, while she couldn't find anything remotely funny about the situation, he turned the tables.

Suddenly his handsome face split into a laugh of charming deference, that familiar apologetic amusement that took her back to their golden years. 'Oh God, you don't think I mean get back together for real? Hell no. Sorry, Legs! You must be horrified. I didn't explain properly. This will be just an act, don't you see?'

'An act?'

'If we tell my father and Lucy that we've made up our differences and are going to get engaged again, they'll have to split up.'

The duplicity appalled her. It was totally unlike him to suggest anything as underhand as this. 'For how long?'

'However long it takes to ensure they put an end to this ridiculous farce.'

She gaped at him, astonished at the cheerful sangfroid. 'And is what you're suggesting any less "ridiculous"?'

He reached across to take her hand in his and squeezed it. 'It really is the only way. "And to make an end is to make a beginning",' he started quoting Eliot again. '"The end is where we start from."'

He came from that stiff-upper-lip school of tortured souls that could only hint at the great depths of passion and torment bubbling within his heart and soul. That was why he used quotes as emotional signposts. Whereas it was easy for Legs to speak from the heart – or indeed pen a six page letter of tearful regret – Francis had no such open vein. Brought up without the close bond of a mother's love, he needed an art form to articulate his feelings. And just as his father had always found his greatest expression through music, so Francis used poetry. He hid as much behind it as much as he emoted through it.

She could feel the solid pads of his fingers warm and firm around her palm, the short square nails brushing against the soft undersides of her wrists. She'd been the one to finally help him stop biting them, she remembered, rewarding every nibble-free week with more and more outlandish treats, largely based around carnal pleasures. The night he had finally been able to run a smooth set of nails along her naked spine from coccyx to nape had been a great victory. Her hand pressed involuntarily against his as the memory lingered, and in turn his grip tightened.

Would it really be such an act? She wondered. Perhaps it was what they both wanted?

'There's no beginning, there'll be no end,' she breathed aloud.

'That's not Eliot.'

'Wet Wet Wet.' She shook her head, laughing softly as she stared out to sea again, heart hammering. 'Do you remember when we first came up here?'

'With bottles of liqueur stolen from your parents' drinks cabinets. It's a wonder we even got back alive.'

'No, before that; my father brought us all here bird watching that first summer you came to Farcombe. Ros got vertigo and refused to come back out. You were really kind and comforted her. I remember thinking how nice you were for a boy.'

'I've always been nice for a boy.'

'What you're suggesting isn't a very nice thing to do to Kizzy.'

He removed his hand from hers and stared at his nails, she could see the habitual urge to bite was still there, then he began tapping them against his lower lip. 'Kizzy needs careful handling, but she'll want what's best for the family and for Farcombe. That's her great strength. I'm not so sure about Con-man.'

'Conrad.' She rubbed her face fretfully.

'Things a bit fragile between you two?' he asked; did she detect hope in his voice?

'We trust each other,' she said smoothly, not trusting anything right now. 'He doesn't care what I do down here as long as you and I get Gordon Lapis on the Farcombe Festival programme.'

There was a long pause. Byron whined again, edging towards the entrance.

'Gordon Lapis as in Ptolemy Finch?'

Legs nodded. 'Let's not talk about it now.'

'*Au contraire*; I want to talk about Gordon Lapis very much.'

Legs was fighting the urge to cry once more. Thinking about bloody Gordon and his stop-start messages and illogical demands was guaranteed to tip her over the edge. At least here on the cliffs she had no mobile reception at last and so was safe from his missives. But not safe from Francis and such a deep pang of déjà vu, she could taste, smell, feel, see and hear it. She'd always teased him about the phrase 'au contraire' which he'd borrowed from Hector as a teenager and never managed to shake.

As she reluctantly explained the Gordon situation, she studied his hands again, so different from Conrad's broad, tanned ones that could crush a palm in a handshake and yet excite her body like nothing else with their touch. Francis's fingers were long and slender. As so often they were tapping nervously like a pianist dreaming of a Rachmaninov solo, drumming on his frayed jeans knee which itself was bobbing up and down. He'd never been able to sit still for more than a few minutes at a time unless he was absorbed in a book.

And as soon as he heard what she had been sent to Farcombe to propose, he looked as though he was about to take off and fly out around the cove.

'This is absolutely wonderful!' he laughed. 'It's just what the festival needs. Think of the income!'

Legs turned to him in surprise. It wasn't the reaction she had expected, but nothing at Farcombe was turning out to be as she'd expected. 'The selection committee turned us down flat,' she reminded him.

'I'll just have to convince Poppy to overrule them. Kizzy will back her up.'

'She's on the committee?' No wonder she was a headline act.

'Her mother is Yolande Hawkes,' he admitted sheepishly. Poppy Protheroe's long-time best friend and arts-festival crony Yolande 'Bird of Prey' Hawkes was another turban-wearing harridan who championed obscure artists and was now the festival's director. 'Poppy's her godmother.'

'Good to know nepotism still rules round here,' she muttered, eyeing him with mounting mistrust. If it was unlike the Francis she knew to suggest faking a romance to restore family order, it was even less like him to make such a political match, no doubt orchestrated by his stepmother herself.

He was soon confirming her suspicions: 'Poppy believes Kizzy embodies the spirit of Farcombe. She was the one to encourage Kizzy to take her poetry more seriously; then Poppy put her on the committee last year, and she embraced the festival psyche totally.'

Including embracing the heir to the estate, Legs thought murderously, appalled by how painfully jealous she felt. Biting her tongue was impossible, although she redirected her anger onto Poppy.

'Talk about Cupid and Psyche,' she fumed. 'Your stepmother's so bloody manipulative!'

Hearing his old ally give a familiar war cry, Francis let his guard slip for a moment: 'Godchildren rank higher than stepchildren around here,' he agreed bitterly.

'It's so bloody corrupt, I hate it,' she huffed in support.

Francis was quick to recover. 'Actually, Kizzy does know her stuff; she has a double first from Goldsmiths, and worked at Tate Modern for two years, plus jobs in picture research and publishing.'

'Easily bored, is she?' Legs sniped.

'She's a clever girl,' he said carefully. 'She's made some positive changes.'

'By putting her own work centre stage?'

'It's very good. The *Observer* called her "a Stevie Smith for the Ecstasy generation".'

'Not raving, but drowning,' Legs sneered, which he pointedly ignored, conciliatory face back in place. She wanted to rage some more, but forced herself to stay practical. 'What makes you think Kizzy is going to recommend Gordon's big stunt to the Farcombe committee when you're proposing you and I stage a romantic reconciliation right under her nose?'

'Trust me, she'll be on side.'

She shook her head in confusion, standing up abruptly and wandering towards the clifftop arch, hugging herself. 'She must love you very much if she'd be prepared to do that.'

He followed her, 'But are you prepared to do it?' The question was so heavily loaded she stepped back, almost tripping. He caught her arm, searching her face for an answer.

She found she couldn't speak, the lump in her throat stealing away her voice.

'Please agree, Legs,' he said quietly. 'I'm only asking you to make believe, not make love.'

'And will we all live happily ever after?'

A nervous smile touched his mouth. 'Either that or we'll wake up and realise it's just been a terrible dream.'

Looking at his handsome, earnest face, Legs knew with absolute certainty that there was something he wasn't telling her.

But before she could reply, they heard a high-pitched doggy yelp from the cliffs outside and Francis let out a wail of consternation, 'Byron's gone over! Hell! Kizzy will never forgive me if I lose him,' he wailed, belting out onto the precipice.

'Unforgivable to let the dog run off, but she'll forgive you pretending to get back together with the ex,' Legs muttered before going in pursuit.

The lame little terrier must have been stalking seagulls and lost his footing, as he was now scrabbling to keep a grip on the lip of the cliff, eyes boggling. Francis scrambled after him, sending down a shower of small rocks and scree.

'Be careful!' Legs gasped, realising how close to falling he was.

'Come here, you little rat,' he growled, edging along a rocky outcrop. But before he could reach the terrier, Byron let out an alarmed yap and disappeared over the cliff completely.

'No!' Legs wailed as Francis launched after him, now dangling over the edge so that all she could see were his legs and the soles of his desert boots. 'Have you caught him?'

'He's fallen onto a ledge,' he called back, voice straining with effort. 'I can't . . . quite . . . reach him.' The legs disappeared even more, the toes of his desert boots providing the only security clamping him to the cliff.

Legs jumped forward to grab his ankles, which were hairy and sinewy. He had odd socks on, she noticed, amazed to feel a great groundswell of tenderness bursting out of her. She wanted to lay her cheek against those strong calves and kiss their dusting of blond hairs. But now was not the time, as bigger stones fell and more of the cliff edge crumbled away beneath Francis's stretching torso. She could see the foam leaping like greedy tongues as the waves lashed the rocks far below.

Byron had stopped barking and was whimpering now, genuinely terrified.

'Come here!' Francis demanded in frustration.

'Have you tried calling him rather than shouting at him?' Legs suggested.

'Don't be ridiculous! Come here you little bastard!'

He sounded just like his father. Legs took her right hand from his ankle.

'What are you doing?' he squawked.

'Searching for chocolate.' Legs rifled her pockets for a trusty corner of Green & Black's, softened in the heat beneath its foil.

'Now is not the time for a snack, Legs,' he snapped.

Ignoring him, she crept forwards and stretched her arm alongside his, which meant practically lying on top of him as they dangled off the cliff together. 'Let's try bribing him with this. And before you say anything, I know chocolate is bad for dogs, but I'm fresh out of Bonios.'

She could just make out the tip of Byron's nose as he cowered in a small hollow beneath their rocky platform.

'Here, little fellow – you'll be OK,' she soothed. 'Come on, little Ron. Come and have some choc.'

The nose twitched, sniffed and craned forwards.

In a flash, Francis's long fingers hooked their way beneath his neckerchief, took a handful of neck scruff and hauled him to safety. The chocolate tumbled into the sea below as dog and rescuers rolled away from the edge to safety, laughing and barking with overjoyed relief.

'Thank goodness for that,' Francis exclaimed, looking at Legs over his shoulder with an expression that almost made her fall off the cliff herself. His glittering blue eyes matched the bright patches of sky behind him. He was her teenage crush once more. 'What a tragedy to die before I could tell you how great it is to see you.'

Legs felt her breath catch.

There was something giddily familiar about lying side by side on the heathery grass staring up at the sky and listening to the waves behind them. As if by habit, both Francis and Legs turned their faces to one another, so close that their noses were almost touching.

Even though he was still clutching an overexcited dog, Francis stretched forwards and kissed her, long lashes lowered over his blue eyes.

It was just the briefest of gestures, as modest as a Disney prince leaning down into the casket to touch his lips against Sleeping Beauty's rosebud mouth, but Legs felt as though the cliff had crumbled and given way after all as her body spun around on its axis and her head lightened to thin air.

'Wow.' Francis pulled away. 'This is going to be very, very complicated, isn't it?'

Gazing up at him, realising that his eyes were in fact more pure cobalt than the sky, Legs knew she had come home.

In simpatico, Francis cupped a hand on her cheek. 'Where are you staying?'

She couldn't answer, not really caring while she was lying beneath him like this. Staying here in the heather six inches from the precipice sounded good to her right now.

His thumb traced the bone of her jaw. 'You can't possibly stay at Spywood. Come to the hall.'

At last, Legs felt the reassuring blade of guilt against her throat as she twisted her face away from his fingers. 'Will Kizzy be there?'

'Of course she will; she lives there.'

His no-nonsense answer made her roll deftly away from beneath him and kneel up, straightening her clothes and rubbing her flushed face, horrified at what she'd just let happen and how Conrad would react if he knew. 'I have other plans. We can talk again later. I have to be somewhere.' She made a show of looking at her watch, realising too late that she had left it on the edge of the sink in the Ealing basement flat, along with her favourite earrings. She stared blankly at the blue veins running from palm to inner arm for a moment, amazed to find that she could actually see the pulse beating there, a little pressure pad jittering up and down horribly fast.

Francis laughed affectionately. 'You always forget to wear your watch.' He reached out for her wrist, but she snatched it away.

'I live for the moment, remember? You always said that was the ultimate example of bad timekeeping. Let's text. You always said that was the ultimate example of . . .'

He took the cue, 'Bad haiku.'

Nodding, she scrambled upright and fled, realising that being one year removed from the thirteen years they'd been a couple was barely enough to stop the love and regret inside melting and boiling to reach flashpoint.

Francis was right; this was going to be very complicated.

Chapter 7

Making progress? Two identical messages awaited Legs on the iPhone, one from Conrad, the other from Gordon's PA Kelly.

The urge to type 'First Base' with hyperbolic honesty was hard to resist. To give herself time to think, she called through to the Book Inn, but the voice at the other end of the line – not one of the regular team of staff she recognised – informed her that it was fully occupied all weekend.

'Tell Guy it's Legs North.' She knew he and Nonny would fit her in, even if it meant bunking up in one of the attics.

'He's in the kitchens,' informed the voice fearfully. 'Can you call back?'

Wearily, Legs rang off. She had no intention of staying in the hall with Francis, and even less desire to stay at Spywood with the aged, naked adulterers. If she went for a walk along the Eascombe under-cliff to the harbour she could clear her head and pop in on Guy and Nonny at the Book Inn for a drink; they would find her a bed for the night.

As she walked she called Conrad, who was with his kids and clearly didn't want to speak for long. 'Easier to text when they're here for weekends,' he muttered as teenage voices moaned in the background that he was always on the phone and that they had pressed 'live pause'. 'How are you getting on?'

'Well, Francis definitely wants Gordon on the festival bill . . .' she decided to start off positively.

'That's great – tell me the details later.'

'But it's not that straightfor—' She realised he'd already rung off.

Furious, she stomped down the cliff path and started along the shingle beach, wobbly on her feet until she reached the under-cliff and perched on the ledge, punching a thumb at her little screen to address Gordon's PA.

Progress fine.

A reply flew back before she'd pocketed the phone. *Please elaborate so I can report more fully to Gordon.*

It's rather complicated.

He will require a full debrief.

She huffed, thinking that it was none of Kelly's business, let alone Gordon's. As long as she got him on the programme, surely the details were irrelevant?

She called Daisy, desperate to confide in someone, but the phone rang on unanswered.

All will be fine, she typed to Kelly. *Trying to get Gordon star billing at Farcombe, and looks v hopeful. Will update anon.*

The large A-sign outside the Book Inn announced that it was closed for a private function that night.

Holidaymakers were out in force along the seafront wearing the curious uniform of the British coastal visitor: pastel-coloured anoraks, patterned wellies and crumpled cotton shorts.

Legs sat on one of the benches overlooking the harbour and thought about Francis, uncertain whether he'd changed or whether she just saw him differently after a year apart. He seemed more mature and self-assured and distinctly sexier. Her innards squeezed deliciously as another aftershock from their kiss fizzed through her. She quashed the sensation and focused hard on a seagull dive-bombing an abandoned wrapper.

Her phone was chiming with yet another email, this time from Gordon himself.

With whom are you negotiating? Are you still unarmed and driving a red car? I hope this is being handled discreetly. GL.

Legs glared at the seagull, irritated that he wanted such forensic detail, although the joke made her smile, despite herself. She could never entirely tell whether Gordon's offbeat humour was quirky wit or just madness, but she loved its rare appearances.

I have a close personal contact within the Protheroe family, she assured him.

I abhor nepotism. He popped up on live messaging now, no longer making her smile.

She sighed even more irritably, wondering whether he really wanted to appear at the festival at all. But much as she longed to call his bluff, she knew it wasn't worth the risk.

If you would prefer to make contact yourself, it can be arranged.

That will not be necessary yet. I have heard the family can be extremely difficult to approach; I simply want assurance that this is being handled with the utmost caution and tact.

Tact! She fumed. *Tact!* The benevolent Hector Protheroe is currently shacked up with my mother in a clifftop love nest, and I'm about to upset the family applecart yet further by inventing a romance with his son to break up this sorry union, which may also result in breaking my own heart, but will almost certainly get you top billing at the festival.

However, all she angrily typed was: *The Protheroe family has always tempted fate and they can make dangerous bedfellows. Rest assured, I am taking every precaution possible, including parking the red car in gear with the handbrake on. I am also nothing if not actful.* Too late she realised that she had omitted the first 't' in 'tact'. It seemed fitting, given that she was asking to act the performance of her life. What the hell. *And armless*, she added.

Do you take nothing seriously? Gordon stormed back.

Biting her lip, Legs tapped at her screen as persistently as the seagull in front of her pecking its beak at the wrapper until she'd written more supplicating apologies and promises of utter professionalism than every politician ever accused of sleaze or expenses fiddling, footballer accused of match fixing and newspaper editor accused of phone-tapping combined. Satisfied, she pressed send. That should appease the irascible bugger.

He seemed slightly placated, replying a few moments later: *I don't doubt your professionalism, Allegra, although Conrad's is another matter. Is your close personal contact Francis Protheroe?*

He was a clever bugger as well as a capricious one, she realised, typing: *Yes.*

And he is the ex you said you could never work alongside? His memory was far too good, as were his quick-fire Googling skills. *Good looking guy.*

He clearly already had a picture of Francis in front of him, no doubt one of the many dashing shots that had accompanied gushing pieces in the *Mail* and *Telegraph*; she'd done the internet searches herself enough times to know how easy they were to find. And if one looked hard enough – as Gordon no doubt had – it was even possible to link her name with Francis's. Thus Gordon had rumbled Conrad's shabby tactics already.

Francis is highly professional, and already right behind you coming here, she assured him, eager to set his mind at rest. But he'd already signed out of their chat, no doubt to blast out a furious email to Conrad berating him for sending his silly, wisecracking assistant to do the job of a professional negotiator and agent.

The seagull had tired of the wrapper and flown off, a silhouette crossing the golden glow of the lowering sun. In the harbour, the masts clanked and jingled, and beyond the sea wall, waves on the shingle hissed and frothed like writhing serpents.

Walking into the glare of the sun with her head lowered, Legs trailed back up the cliff path to the jinxed red car and sat behind the wheel, willing herself to drive to Bude where there might be a B&B with vacancies even in high summer.

Yet she couldn't face driving away from her clifftop, such a familiar corner of her childhood. It was as though she and the Honda were held tightly there by magnets.

It took almost an hour of wrestling with her conscience before she called her father, still not knowing whether she could bring herself to tell him what was going on, yet desperate to check that he was all right. But as soon as she told Dorian that she was in Farcombe he pre-empted any clumsy attempt to declare the affair and claimed in his charming, vague manner to be well aware of the situation, thank you, and dealing with it in his own way. Hot-headed and highly emotional, Legs had never been able to penetrate Dorian's quiet, formal starchiness for all their unconditional love. He was a man who might weep through *Madame Butterfly* on Radio 3, and yet clammed up totally if asked about his feelings.

'Your mother will come back in her own good time' was all he would say.

No matter how much she huffed, puffed, barracked and demanded that he come to North Devon in person, he refused to engage. The only moment in which she heard his voice sharpen from its customary soft, gentlemanly clip was when she mentioned her sister.

'No need to involve Ros,' he snapped. 'She simply will not understand all this.'

'And I do, I suppose?'

'You're the guilty one, Allegra'

'I'm what?' she bleated.

'You always feel guilty about things and get personally involved, but you are equally quick to forgive; Ros is very moral and black and white, as you know. This would hurt her very deeply. She takes after your mother on that front. They're both martyrs to their cause.'

'Mata Hari in Mum's case,' she grumbled.

Only after the call ended did it occur to Legs that her father had let something slip, given her a rare personal insight. It seemed strange that he aligned Ros and Lucy so closely; Legs had always been the Mummy's girl, after all. She felt curiously orphaned by the drama, her entire halcyon childhood cast in doubt. She longed more than anything to speak with Daisy, but there was still no answer, nor did Conrad reply to texts. The only persistent contact on her phone was Gordon, blithering on in a long email about red cars and stalkers. He obviously had writer's block again, hadn't managed to contact Conrad and seemed to have been on the laudanum.

Conrad has no right to ask you to do this, he raged. *As if the scheming Protheroes were not enough to contend with, he knows that Ptolemy Finch fans are extremely clever, especially the cranky ones. My real identity might remain one of the literary world's greatest kept secrets – for now – but an obsessive few have long made it their business to know all about Gordon Lapis's editor, publicist and marketing team at the publishers, and even my literary agent and assistant. They have names, photographs, phone numbers, home addresses. Access to Google and a clever mind makes for easy detective work. You are highly conspicuous, Allegra, especially in a red car.*

She ignored him, deciding to be out of signal or battery as far as he was concerned. His paranoia was too much for her right now.

Even poor Kelly had dropped another line 'strictly off the record' to explain that Gordon was behaving very strangely and so it would help to know the exact situation between Legs and the Protheroe family.

Her stomach let out a loud rumble. She hadn't eaten since lunchtime and it was now after nine, the last streaks of light being pulled from the sky. Yet suddenly she was too weary to face driving for food or even a bed. She was still magnetically glued to the clifftop in the car, and feeling increasingly like a kittiwake sitting on a clutch of eggs. Parked amid the gorse bushes on the headland, she was far from any public road, and tucked safely away from sight of Gull Cross and the Spywood and Spycove track. The woods and cliffs around her held no fear; she'd camped out here often enough as a girl. She clambered into the back of the Honda and curled up into a tight ball, using her weekend bag as a pillow, momentarily surprised that her duffel bag felt smaller than expected, but too tired to really care. The sound of the sea lulled her to sleep almost immediately, cocooned in her familiar old red car.

Chapter 8

Waking to a spectacular dawn stabbing blades of sunlight through the spiked arms of gorse, Legs unfolded her stiff, cramped body and groped her way out onto the dewy grass. She was ravenously hungry. The clock on her phone told her it was five-thirty. Francis had texted at midnight: *Kizzy onside, as promised. Come for lunch. F*

She groaned, hunger still gnawing at her stomach lining, but her belly was now so acid with apprehension that she knew indigestion would chase every mouthful of breakfast. She went for a run instead, pulling on her trainers from the boot of the car and pounding the heartbeat from her ears with her feet, racing her churning thoughts along Farcombe estate's private roads, making sure she kept out of sight of the main house. Cooling off afterwards, she waded through the shingle of Eascombe Cove at high tide, not caring that her trainers got soaked. Seaweed tied itself around her ankles before slithering away as she let out high kicks which sent up salty showers that splashed refreshingly against equally salty sweat on her skin.

She should take a shower before going to the big house for lunch, she realised. Then again, staying dirty might be no bad thing. She had decided she must put Francis off. The more repulsive he found her, the more vindicated he would feel and the less tempted to enact this bizarre farce and risk damaging either his new love, or her old, battered heart. She owed it to him and Kizzy to be in a bedraggled, salt-crusted state. It was only fair. She would, however, line up the mother of all hot baths afterwards.

Back at the car, she picked up her phone to ring Guy at the Book Inn, but it wasn't yet seven. The sun was resting its chin on the top of the woods now, burning away the sea mist and dew. A fallow deer from the small Farcombe herd wandered out from the bracken and eyed her warily, tail flicking.

A chirrup from her phone sent it straight back into the undergrowth. It was Francis: *Did you get my message about lunch? Will you be there? We must discuss the plan. F*

She felt the drying sweat turn icy cold against her skin, yet a hot little flame leapt in her heart and groin. Her fingers shook as she read other messages.

Kelly had emailed again late the previous night, begging her to respond: *Gordon is in a complete state. I'm so sorry to put pressure on, but I could really use your help. He is pretty paranoid (please never tell him I said that – he tells me an overactive imagination is a part of the job spec). He seems to think there's an unfair compromise taking place.*

Conrad had sent a very dry *Sleep well?*

Daisy, alerted to the missed calls, apologised by text for juggling wailing babies and work until too late to respond in voice and asked: *Whassup? Don't tell me I poisoned you at lunch yesterday? Only saw the sell by date on the Brie afterwards. Sorry! You have Nico's bag, BTW; take care of Beekey. Seen Francis yet? Xx*

Yelping, Legs looked at the small duffel bag she had thus far believed to contain her Browns weekend wardrobe, artfully rolled to avoid creases, along with her make-up, wash-things and phone charger. Instead, it was topped by a much-washed fluffy parrot, beneath which languished several pairs of very small Y-fronts and socks, a pair of *Dr Who* pyjamas and lots of practical separates suited to a ten-year-old boy, all neatly starched and folded by Ros, some items of which Legs recognised from the garden washing line that she had already pilfered once.

With a wail, she kicked the car door to vent her anger, making it swing backwards like a starting gate before it dropped down on its rusty hinges with an ominous clank. When Legs pushed it closed again, it hung down like a broken wing and she found it would no longer shut or lock, however much she lifted and heaved. Perhaps Gordon was right; her car was hexed. She sensed fate was trying to tell her something.

'Behave like a child, dress like a child?' she suggested out loud.

Determined to stay in control, she sat on the bonnet to pull off her wet trainers and socks, then composed her very grown up and responsible replies, firstly to Francis: *Yes to lunch. Am on a sardine, citrus and boiled pulse diet. Gives one terribly bad breath, but the movements are worth it. Need to talk; not sure plan such a good idea. Pax. x*

Off it flew, followed by her response to Kelly: *Gordon is lucky to have you. Please don't worry. I will not compromise him in any way. Compromising myself goes with the territory, but you'll know all about that. He will get what he wants and is assured of my total discretion. You are an utter pro. We both are.*

Then she addressed Conrad: *I slept in the car, which is red. According to Gordon that's a bad thing. But frankly it's better than sleeping under the same roof as my mother and her secret lover of more than ten years, or my ex-fiancé and his nest of red-headed festival vipers. If you want your star to appear here, then I must get into bed with them all. This is hell. Please rescue me. L xxx*

That should get his attention, she thought murderously, dashing a final reply to Daisy, unable to hold back from total honesty with the one whose opinion she trusted most: *Don't know what to think or do. Still feel in love, like the past year hasn't happened. Am I mad? Is it guilt? Mum and Hector shacked up together hardly registers compared to this, but know it's all wrong. Help! I blame the Brie and Beekey.*

Satisfied, she lay back on the bonnet and soaked in the sun, feeling the salt crystallise on her skin.

It was only when replies started coming back that she began to panic.

Daisy, no doubt texting as she spooned breakfast into toddlers, apologised for the poisoned lunch, and said she was unaware of the sardine diet: *sounds delicious, but I have strange cravings. Are you sure you're not pregnant? Call me any time x*

Legs chewed a nail anxiously, realising that she must have sent the message intended for Francis to her friend by mistake; she hoped it was just an isolated error but then Conrad replied applauding her professionalism: *Utter pros, unutterable prose: we can read between the lines. Keep up the good work. ILY.* He had clearly been sent the message she thought she'd sent to Kelly.

Eyebrows and heartbeat shooting up, she read Francis's text: *Darling Legs, your honesty is deeply touching. Not sure we have Brie, but fatted calf and amnesty await. F. (P.s. What is Beekey?)*

Just as an email from Kelly pinged through and she read the first line, *Gordon will know about this. You must not prostitute yourself for—*, her phone battery ran out of charge.

She let out a wail. She must have sent every message to the wrong recipient.

Breathless with worry, Legs pulled everything out of the car, but the charger wasn't there. It was in the weekend bag that Nico now had at Inkpot Farm; a poor substitute for Beekey. She slumped down in defeat, realising she couldn't even double-check exactly which message had gone to whom. But it was pretty obvious she'd screwed up big time.

For that moment, she didn't care what was going on between her parents. She needed her mother, and caffeine – not necessarily in that order.

The front door to Spywood Cottage was unlocked and bassoon music hooted from the main bedroom, where its inhabitants were clearly still tucked up together in the long summer morning sleep-in.

Legs fell gratefully upon the kettle and made herself a sweet, milky coffee as strong as methadone.

There were fresh croissants in the breadbin, but she still felt too sick to eat. Instead, abandoning any noble intentions to stay off-puttingly filthy, she nipped into the downstairs bathroom and sat in the bath, cranking up the ancient hand-held shower mixer to a lukewarm splutter – its maximum output as she knew from long experience – and washed away the layers of cold sweat, sea salt and shame.

Lucy and Hector were both in the kitchen when she reappeared. Neither betrayed any surprise to find her there. Both were respectably dressed in faded summer linens, sitting at opposite ends of the table, sharing breakfast like two old friends after an early dog walk.

But while Lucy couldn't meet her younger daughter's eyes, Hector's gaze was challenging – as bright blue as his only son's, and with ten times the confidence.

'Your mother and I are very much in love.'

Legs choked on her coffee, dragging wet tendrils of hair from her watering eyes as she blinked at him. Honest anger was always her first defence. 'Don't you think it might have been wise to talk to your children about this before moving in together?'

'Perhaps,' he nodded, 'but I believe in spontaneity in all things, from music to love.' He reached across and took Lucy's hand in his, a giant lobster claw enfolding a soft anemone.

'You had secret lunches for over a decade,' Legs flashed. 'That's hardly spontaneous!'

'I would never have stood in the way of Francis's happiness,' he retaliated with characteristic sharpness, hippy turned harpy, 'but then you blew it. Life is too short for second chances, and a decade is a long time to wait for true love. That's why he is now with pretty young Kizzy, and your mother and I can declare our feelings openly at last.' He stretched across and kissed mute, blushing Lucy full on the lips.

Legs burst into tears, an uncomfortable night's sleep and too much exercise mixing toxically with coffee and the display of tenderness.

Still her mother wouldn't look at her.

'Hector, would you give us ten minutes alone?' Lucy managed to mutter.

Stepping out into the woods with his bassoon, Hector was hardly an inconspicuous presence as he paced around the cottage perimeter playing Telemann.

'Dad is devastated,' Legs cried, anger rising alongside the bassoon arpeggios.

'You've spoken with him?' Lucy gasped, unprepared for such directness after her long sabbatical in the woods, as naked truths and naked hideaways clashed.

Legs backed down a little, not wanting to shout her way out of the opportunity to talk. 'You know Dad. He won't say anything, but he's obviously in pieces.'

Lucy looked surprised. 'I was rather under the impression that he relished the time out.'

At this moment Hector appeared at the window, tooted his way through a couple of arpeggios as he checked mother and daughter were faring OK, then wandered out of sight again.

'Do you really love Hector?' Legs inclined her head towards the music in the woods.

'I've always thought him the most amazing man I have ever met.' Lucy clasped her shaking hands together in front of her and raised her eyes, making Legs blanch as they blazed with tormented honesty. 'It's been the longest of longings, so getting what's been desired for so long is quite overwhelming. We are both terribly infatuated.'

Legs remembered feeling like that about Francis once, but now her passion was muddled up with remorse and nostalgia. It felt all wrong to make believe not make love, she realised. However much she hated what was going on within her family, it was no excuse to inflict more hurt. She was determined to tell him that staging a comeback was simply not an option.

Beyond its formal griffin and unicorn entrance gates and high stone walls, tucked behind veils of oak woods, sculptured yew and rhododendron hedges, kitchen gardens, rose borders, geometric parterres and a lopsided topiary maze, Farcombe Hall was a bullish slab of pewter-grey Elizabethan stone honed into a castellated mansion by an eighteenth-century makeover. The flinty walls beneath crenellated towers and roofs were softened by festoons of red Virginia creeper on its southern and western sides, and its arched windows wore the pretty brown eyeliner of dressed stonework, but there was no denying its tough, rebellious face, especially the north elevation which gazed out to sea with battered, bare-cheeked gall, a mighty ship-head to the Farcombe Peninsula that had defied brutal North Devon storms for four centuries.

This was the face that watched Legs as she climbed up from the wooded cliffs, through the sheep-grazed parkland towards the formal gardens beyond the ha-ha.

She was waging a moral war with her conscience, which had told her she should make no effort whatsoever, and her vanity which had forced her to redeem her tear-puffed eyes with a lick of mascara and to tease out the blonde hair that had dried into a horrible rat-tails helmet while she was having her heart to heart with her mother. But she'd deliberately and forcibly dressed down in blue cotton crops that bagged unflatteringly around her bum, deck shoes and a creased white shirt, which was all she could salvage from her combined car cast-offs and her nephew's weekend bag.

Legs had been quite tempted to walk up the tunnel from the cove and burst into Farcombe Hall via the cellars, but she doubted Francis would see the joke, and it might just finish off neurotic Poppy, who was convinced a ghost of a drowned child haunted the sea passage. Now she was grateful for the sun on her skin as she cut left through the parkland to meet up with the rear wall of the churchyard, trailing her left hand along the black cast-iron spikes embedded there, which she and Daisy as macabre children had convinced themselves had once been dotted with the heads of smugglers, highwaymen and traitors.

Francis was waiting in the cloistered rear courtyard, dressed in navy chinos, deck shoes and a white shirt. They looked ridiculously cloned, right down to the zipped fleeces tied around their shoulders in case the wind picked up.

Legs hastily removed hers and tied it around her waist, which made her bum look even bigger.

'Thank you for coming.' He stooped to kiss her on the cheek, and all the delicious fizzy, squeezing sensations coursed back through her unscrupulous body.

'You smell lovely.' Francis breathed in deeply at her throat, making her skin almost melt. 'Is that a new scent?'

Legs bit her tongue to stop herself pointing out that it was his father's Douro Eau de Portugal which she'd nicked from the Spywood bathroom earlier.

He stepped back reluctantly. 'The others are waiting in the palm house.'

'Let's go.' Taking a firm grip on herself, Legs marched inside with rather more gusto than she'd intended so that she strode along the cloisters and in through the door like an eager tour guide.

This part of the house, forming the rear half of the east wing, had been fashioned like a Moorish palace and was heavy with Moroccan arches, mosaic work, gold relief and vast, intricately carved marble fireplaces. At one time, Hector had covered the huge expanse of blue and white tiled floors with exotic cushions and rugs – Legs seemed to recall a buffalo hide in one corner, a zebra in another – creating an opulent chill-out zone for house guests to gather during the festival, when the hall was inevitably filled with bohemians and academics who thronged into the ancient stone-columned rooms like endangered species gathering around a watering hole.

Now, the rugs had all gone and Poppy's sculptures dotted the floor, distorted fibreglass, stone and bronze blobs that were one part Henry Moore to five parts giant amoeba. She had produced so many over the years – and sold so few – that they were crammed all over the house and garden, even in the guest bathrooms and downstairs loos.

There were no fewer than eight in the conservatory – including one the size of a small hatchback – but thankfully the room (which the Protheroes always grandly referred to as the 'palm house') was the size of a car showroom and could accommodate dozens of Poppy originals without appearing crowded.

Not so easy to accommodate was the original Poppy herself, who might have been barely five feet tall and as skinny as a tightly rolled umbrella, but could make an empty Royal Albert Hall feel claustrophobic from across the gods. She swept out from behind a vast fern like a brightly coloured bird putting on a display, thin arms flung wide, screeching with delight. For all her pretty plumage, she had a hug like eagle talons landing on prey.

'My darling, beautiful girl – how *wonderful* to see you again!'

Poppy gushed at everybody – it was her default position. Big, doeful brown eyes lapping everyone up, she would ask endless questions, lavish endless praise, stroke cheeks, link arms, laugh at jokes and then assassinate one's very being the moment one left the room. She was so duplicitous, it was almost admirable.

Poppy genuinely liked very few people, although she pretended to love everyone and many loved her as a consequence. Incredibly short-sighted, she refused to wear glasses or contact lenses, which meant that she lived in a blurred world where anybody more than six feet away looked the same, and so she had developed a grand, theatrical way of addressing rooms at large, matched with intimate tête-à-têtes with those who came within her focal range. Needy and neurotic yet fabulously funny and welcoming, Poppy had struggled with increasing agoraphobia for over a decade and now rarely ever left the house, relying upon a small army of visiting friends and house guests to entertain her lively mind. She loved to meet new people, she claimed, but one so rarely met the right sort these days. Obsessed with class, weight and intelligence, Poppy's entry criteria for friendship was strict. A lack of education was unforgivable, anybody with an ounce of flesh on them was highly suspect, the obese were an absolute disgrace to themselves and should be locked away behind bars until thin enough to slip through them. Equally, an appreciation of mass culture was a gross moral weakness akin to paedophilia.

And yet, if introduced to a twenty-stone soap star who had left school at sixteen, she would be charm personified and seem unendingly fascinated by their life, their achievement and their talent.

Which was why, Legs guessed, right now she had a vice-like arm around Legs' waist (assessing the muffin top, no doubt) and was asking all about her career, London life, her sister and her 'gorgeous' nephew. Her dark eyes glowed with affection and interest.

'I gather you are Gordon Lapis's *confidante*.' She emphasised the word with such luscious cadence that it suggested inamorata or concubine might be just as appropriate.

'He's a client,' she said carefully.

'I can't believe he wants to come here to our little backwater,' she cooed. 'So thrilling. I have never read any of his work, but I gather he is very well liked.' Again, the insinuation was clear: 'popular trash'. 'I've even heard his oeuvre described as "magical realism", which I'm sure is kinder than "fantasy", and one does feel that genre authors still get very marginalised. I gather he's compared to Pullman and even Tolkien by many. The harnessing of suspended adolescence in literature has always been a terribly clever trick, and from what I gather Ptolemy Finch has quite extraordinary charm . . .' She proceeded to give a brief lecture that revealed a great deal of knowledge about Gordon's work for one who had purportedly never read any of his books.

Then she suddenly stopped, as though realising this, and hastily redirected herself: 'Yolande should have consulted with me when she heard that this was no ordinary request from an agent for his client. Of course Mr Lapis is not Farcombe's usual fayre, but Francis assures me that if we host this personal appearance, it will make us all wonderfully rich and bring Hector back home to me.'

Legs shot Francis a wary look. She could never have anticipated Poppy accepting the Gordon proposal this easily, and still had an unpleasant feeling she was missing something. 'He'll certainly generate a great deal of public interest,' she said cautiously.

At the mention of the great unwashed, Poppy shuddered slightly. Her bony fingers dug deeper into Legs' waist and she dropped her voice so only she could hear. 'Francis says we must all make sacrifices until order is restored, you two more than most. I know he is *so* grateful that you are prepared to help us save Farcombe.'

'I'm not sure that I—'

'Your dedication to your job is admirable, Allegra. I'm sure your boss is terribly proud of you.' The barbed comment hung in the air briefly before the turbaned one raked her nails affectionately across Legs' small spare tyre and asked her who she thought would win the Booker Prize this year.

Legs was well aware that Poppy had never liked her very much, having once nicknamed her 'the Guinea Pig', a sobriquet dating back to the squeaking laugh she'd possessed as a small girl. When Legs and Francis's childhood romance had blossomed into adult cohabitation, his stepmother had confided to family friends that she thought the girl rather plain, very lazy and highly profiteering, and that she was lucky to have him. She predicted Legs would run to fat, like her ghastly sister.

It was therefore with great caution and carefully measured charm that Legs now replied to a barrage of questions about the London literary scene as she was steered between potted ferns and giant stone amoebas.

Behind them, Francis cleared his throat. 'This is Kizzy, Allegra.'

Positively vibrating with emotion, Kizzy stepped from behind the beautifully laid table, sea-green eyes soaking in Legs' face. She was absolutely stunning, dressed in a silver-grey chiffon dress that hugged wispily to her narrow body, matched with glass beads at her neck in shades of fox, bracken and moss, her flame-red hair snaking over her shoulders almost to the elbow. She looked like Klimt's *Danaë*. Legs' heart sank.

But then Kizzy lunged forward and shook her hand, bestowing eager kisses on both her cheeks. 'I am sooo excited to meet you!' she gushed. 'I can't tell you how much I've been looking forward to it. I just know we'll be friends. We even went for the same job once, can you believe it? Is that shirt Stella McCartney? It's beautiful.'

Legs reeled back in surprise. The bony fingers that gripped hers were ice cold, the fire in her eyes a direct contrast. Kizzy looked genuinely thrilled. Legs felt her own face flame under such scrutiny, although she was switched on enough to do a quick check of the ring finger to reassure herself it was empty.

'You are *just* as I remember,' Kizzy said in a curiously lisping, girlish voice, the accent softest Scottish. This confused Legs on two counts; firstly because she had no recollection of ever meeting

Kizzy, and secondly because she recalled Yolande as a raven-haired import from NW3 complete with flat vowels, married to Howard, a boffish Canadian academic. Their daughter's Scottish accent seemed totally out of context.

'Let's eat lunch!' Poppy demanded theatrically, and then proceeded to eat practically nothing of the delicious spread of freshly baked bread rolls, smoked fish and salads prepared by Filipina housekeeper, Imee.

Equally, Kizzy pushed a few lettuce leaves around her plate, her eyes barely leaving Legs' face.

Having not eaten anything for twenty-four hours, Legs was ravenous and tucked in with gusto. Across the table Francis matched her, cheeks bulging.

Their eyes kept catching, like searchlights set in diametric corners of a top security prison wing, crossing one another to create a white-out. And even though felons were gambolling about shooting off high grade gun-power between them, they still beamed blindly.

Poppy did almost all the talking, the first half-hour of which was dedicated to deriding her husband, then Legs' mother, as though their children were not sitting directly in front of her: '*How* that dreadful little pudding of a woman could catch the eye of Hector I have no idea, although he's practically blind these days as well as deaf, which explains something of it, up until the moment he pressed flesh.'

'Enough, Poppy!' Francis flashed at last, watching Legs' ever-reddening face.

'Hector must be made to see sense,' Poppy carried on acidly. 'Once he learns that Francis has forsaken darling Kizzy for Allegra once more, he'll come straight home.'

Legs stole a glance at Kizzy, but that pretty face remained fixed on Poppy's, the expression trusting and adoring.

For once Legs was reticent, not exploding in defence of one she loved and heard bad-mouthed. Poppy naturally assumed this was because she thought the relationship between her mother and Hector as distasteful and shallow as the rest of them did, but in fact Legs' silence was due to far less noble factors: she had her mouth full of both food and her own heart, knowing Francis was so close. The presence of Kizzy also made her hopelessly tongue-tied. It was all she could do to try to follow the conversation; the heartbeat pounding in her ears meant she was constantly fighting to catch up with what was being said. She found her gaze drawn again and again to Francis, who had no half-smiles, just a look of fear and need, the big blue eyes imploring.

For her part, Kizzy said little, but those soft Scottish bon mots came at precisely at the right time for their ranting hostess and the two exchanged many half-smiles of complete understanding. They obviously adored one another.

The only time she showed any strong reaction was when Poppy mentioned her younger stepchild.

'You must have a tête-à-tête with Édith when she arrives,' she told Legs. 'Hector's behaviour is making her more cynical than ever. She'll be so relieved you're here to sort it all out. It's such a shame you dropped her when you dropped Francis. She cherished you.'

'You and Édith were close?' Kizzy's green eyes bored into Legs' face.

'She and Jax came to lunch quite often when . . .' She cleared her throat, not looking at Francis, 'when we had the flat in Notting Hill.' Legs had been instrumental in building bridges between Francis and his half-sister.

Édith – pronounced 'eedit' – was Hector's pretty, dark-eyed daughter from a brief second marriage to tempestuous French model and animal rights activist, Inès. Brought up between her mother's wildlife sanctuary in Corsica and the English boarding school paid for by her father, Édith was a rebellious mix of Mediterranean heat and British cool. After many Masters degrees and much travelling, she had now commandeered the Protheroe family's London house, where she devoted herself to running Hector's charitable trusts between therapy, theatre and holidays. She and Francis had loathed one another until Legs intervened. Their relationship remained difficult, with both sparring for their father's attention, but these days they were allies more often than rivals. Édith was also a close ally of Poppy, who had supported her earnestly when she came out several years ago and revealed her long-term lover to be a motorcycle courier called Jax (redeemed from the working classes in Poppy's mind by a whip-thin physique, an appreciation of Allyson Mitchell and a terrific ability to keep quiet and look charismatically blank in company).

'So Édith is coming down this weekend?' Legs feigned enthusiasm.

'Jax can't resist a ringside seat at any Farcombe drama,' Kizzy muttered with a flash of anger.

'They are amongst those in the know,' Poppy said smoothly, 'and this crisis calls for many a good nose.' She laughed at her pun as she tapped her tiny button snout. Among her eccentricities was a love of word play quite at odds with her hatred of all things populist. 'I spoke with Édith on the telephone this morning and told her that you were back, Allegra. She guessed straight away that you're after Francis, so we already have our first witness lined up for the "showmance".' Her deep voice made the word sound almost paranormal.

'Édith knows everything?' Legs was wary of Édith's habit of playing people off against one another. She had been amongst the first to guess at Legs' love affair with Conrad a year earlier, and had urged her to leave Francis for him. Yet it was Édith who had dropped their friendship like a stone the moment the engagement was broken. 'I thought Francis said the fewer who knew the better?'

'Édith doesn't know!' Kizzy's voice shook, making Legs start back. 'She thinks Francis is mad about me!'

Francis placed a reassuring hand on Kizzy's fine-boned

shoulder. 'What Poppy is saying is that if Édith sees Legs deliberately stealing me back from you, she will believe it to be true.'

'Only we four know that this is fake.' Poppy flashed her warm smile across the table at Legs. 'You are in the Farcombe camarilla again, Allegra. Well done.'

Legs swallowed uncomfortably. An untouched fresh fruit salad was sitting in front of her. She half expected a serpent to sidle out of it and offer her a slice of apple. Her eyes sought out Francis again, but at that moment Poppy clapped her hands together and they both turned to her like musicians to a conductor.

'Let us embrace the task at hand!' She harnessed the two ex-lovers in her dark and potent gaze. 'We all know it's going to be tough for you two to pretend to be back together, and terribly hard on darling Kizzy here.' She stretched out a jewelled, bony claw to squeeze the girl's arm. 'But it is quite essential for the future of the estate to break this union between Hector and Mrs North as quickly as possible.' She sounded like an old dowager queen discussing the succession.

At last, Legs felt her tongue let loose from its stays. Unfortunate that she had just put a large spoon of fruit salad into her mouth and spat passion fruit pips everywhere.

'I can't do it!' she cried, earning horrified looks all round.

There was an awkward pause. Poppy carefully picked off the passion fruit seeds that had landed on her smock. Across the table, Francis's blue eyes were as wide as two Delft changers. Byron helpfully filled the silence by snuffling up the grapes that had just fallen from his mistress's spoon, then spitting them out and making doggy 'bleuch' noises at ankle height.

Poppy was first to regain her composure, readjusting her turban smoothly. 'You must do what is required to save Farcombe.'

'I can't "showmance",' Legs said in a panic, stealing another glance at Francis and instantly regretting it. He looked as though he was about to cry. She tore her eyes away and levelled her gaze at Poppy, who had always frightened her like the Ice Queen in Narnia, and did so now more than ever.

She was looking irritated. 'Why ever not?'

'I can't "pretend" to love Francis again,' she said firmly. Her eyes involuntarily sought his across the table, then raced away. 'I can't possibly fake something that has never st—'

'Stop!' Poppy screeched, covering her ears. 'This is no time for sentiment. I've spent all morning planning this. It's all arranged. You and Francis will get back together tomorrow evening. I've invited the Keiller-Myleses to kitchen sups, along with Kizzy's parents. Darling Édith and Jax will be here, of course. There's even a charming beard lined up for you, Allegra. We must have an objective outsider after all.'

'As witness to the crime?' Legs stuttered, watching her with mounting alarm.

'If you like.' The dowager queen beamed back, her stage set. 'I prefer to think of Jay Goburn as Everyman.' She looked rather skittish. 'Superb prose style; reminiscent of Fitzgerald at his best. He's researching a book set in the peninsula, and we've been exchanging emails for some months now. Turns out he's in the area this weekend and would like to visit the house and gardens, so I invited him to tea and on to supper.'

Lined him up for yourself more like, thought Legs, observing Poppy on a mission. She had a penchant for last minute entertaining, which Hector rather cruelly called her 'asks'; or 'agoraphobic spontaneity kicks'. Poppy, who had always found long-term commitments like the festival terrifying, loved nothing more than rustling together dinner for twelve or a cocktail party for fifty with just a few days' notice. Few who were invited ever dared to refuse an invitation, even if it meant cancelling other commitments and hastily arranging babysitters. There was something about Poppy that defied conformity, and her parties were famously lavish, generous and entertaining. She was always utterly in control, and held court throughout, with great force and compelling charm.

Despite their eleventh hour conception, they were never casual; 'Kitchen Sups' was a well worn euphemism for 'Formal Dining'.

The minstrels' gallery players found themselves demoted from courtly dance to farce as Poppy now gave notes like an amateur theatre director at the first cast read-through: 'The American will be your blind date, Legs, but of course you are still in love with Francis,' she ordered so forcefully that Legs and Francis locked eyes again, and again got stuck there, grey clouds and blue sky converging. 'Tomorrow evening, you two will be unable to resist your mutual attraction,' she breathed in her deep alto, 'you will be publicly reconciled, and Hector will be told. After that, he and that fat—' She flashed her guilty-sweet smile as she corrected herself. 'Hector and your mother will see the error of their ways. You *must* cooperate, Legs.'

She looked at them all in wonder, certain this was a conspiracy to humiliate her. Francis was studying his fingernails fixedly, as though hoping they'd sprout Edward Scissorhands blades to claw himself out of this situation. Beside him, the reddest head in the room was tilted to heaven as though in prayer.

'And you're OK with all this?' Legs appealed directly to Kizzy.

Two glittering green eyes fixed upon her, as bright as a rainbow trout's scales. 'I'm cool if Poppy is,' she purred in her best Kirsty Young tones.

Poppy was staring straight at Legs, Ice Queen to subject.

'I won't do it.' She tried one last protest.

Francis swallowed with a loud gulp.

'In that case,' Poppy said flatly, 'the festival must be cancelled.'

Kizzy and Francis briefly united with a cry of 'no!'

'What's that got to do with it?' Legs laughed in surprise.

But Poppy's dark eyes glittered, knowing that she had played a trump card. 'Without Hector, there is no festival.'

Legs stared at the passion fruit seeds scattered around her plate, already staining the white tablecloth with little blood-red pinpricks. 'You can't do that.'

'I certainly can. I'm the Chair and majority shareholder.'

Legs looked at Francis for confirmation and he nodded almost imperceptibly.

'Gordon Lapis won't get his moment in the sun,' Poppy said breezily, enjoying the obvious panic in Legs' face. 'His desire to appear here is rather extraordinary, but this whole summer has been far from ordinary. I was rather warming to the idea of an enigma in our midst but now I have quite gone off the prospect of the festival entirely. We cannot possibly host a public event amid such family anarchy. It will be a great relief to cancel it this year.'

Looking at Francis again, Legs could see his blue gaze eating into hers, begging her not to let him down. She quickly closed her eyes, only to find Conrad in her head, along with Gordon Lapis whom she had never even met, yet his presence burned brightest of all in her mind, like young Ptolemy Finch with his white hair and wings. How she longed for the little hero's nerve right now.

'Can I have some time to think about this, please?' She gulped.

'You have until tomorrow evening,' Poppy said darkly.

Chapter 9

As Francis walked Legs through the walled gardens, along the high yew avenue and into the churchyard beyond the family's private gate, he explained the financial situation.

'Dad looks like he's still worth a fortune on paper, but the truth is he's pretty cash poor these days – has been for years. He borrowed heavily against all his properties when he was building Smile Media and then didn't repay all the loans when he sold up. The recession wiped out his investments, and he was still gambling heavily then. He'd think nothing of betting fifty thousand in a race or spending the value of a small house in a casino. He only stopped all that when he married Poppy, but by then the damage was done. It was Poppy who paid off the money outstanding on this place when she inherited from Goblin Granny, hence she's majority shareholder of the estate and its interests, including the festival. The running costs of this house, its farms and all the tenanted property are beyond belief; half the villagers pay peppercorn rents, and nothing has been properly renovated since the eighties.

'The festival is one of the few profitable income streams. The family has precious little involvement in the practical running of it these days, as you know. It's all handled by the team on site, but Poppy has ultimate autonomy. The financial side doesn't interest her; she loves such clever people coming into her orbit for a few days annually, although she gets into a panic about the event itself, worse and worse each year. With Dad staging his ridiculous rebellion this year, I think he might have truly pushed her over the edge.'

'But she loves the festival. She wouldn't want to cancel it.'

'It was always Dad's baby, remember? Sure, she took it over just like she took over the house, cramming it full of sculpture, performance poetry and installations. It used to be just music and literature at one time, Dad's real loves, but Poppy saw an opportunity to showcase her own work and naturally got her way, putting all her cronies onto the board.' There was great bitterness in his voice. 'Now that she has been proven the worst sculptress in the stratosphere, she keeps looking for an excuse to ditch the Arts in favour of an international celebration of food.'

'But she hates food!'

'Don't assume that just because she doesn't eat it, she doesn't crave it. Rather like surrounding herself by art she admires even though she can't create it.'

They had reached the first of the gravestones in the outer reaches of the churchyard, tucked behind yet more yews that shielded the plot traditionally allocated to the estate from that of the rest of the dearly departed congregation. To the left of the yews in a prettily railed enclosure stood the grandest stones and a small mausoleum belonging to the Waite family who had owned Farcombe Hall for several hundred years until they were forced out when death duties practically bankrupted them in the seventies. The estate had then passed through several developers who made unsuccessful attempts to fashion it into a luxury hotel and golf resort, before being bought by Hector at the height of his success as a private holiday home for his family.

Francis rested his hip against a tombstone's lichen crust, blond hair flopping as he bowed his head, still the self-conscious epic hero he'd fashioned himself into as a student. 'We can't let her do this, Legs; not if Gordon Lapis wants to come here. There's too much riding on it, and Poppy certainly won't get Dad back by cancelling the one thing that could save Farcombe.' He steepled his fingers to his nose for a long time before admitting, 'We have a rather large financial shortfall on our hands this year. Dad's been trying to play it down, of course, and now he's run away and buried his head in the sand completely. Poppy has no idea how serious it is, nor the limited number of options we face if the festival doesn't go ahead.'

'What are the options?'

'We'll have no option but to asset-strip – land, art, possibly even the house itself.' He eyed her face closely for a reaction. 'There's already one offer on the table.'

'You can't sell Farcombe!'

He stared down at the tombstone. 'Vin Keiller-Myles has been trying to get his hands on this place for years.'

'Isn't he the dodgy impresario? Always arguing with your father about which performers to invite?'

Back in the Fitzroy Club days, Vin Keiller-Myles had always been one of last men standing – and musicians playing – who would join club owner Hector in sinking bottles of bourbon late into the night, alternately jamming, imbibing, brokering deals and above all gambling. Both men had been high-stakes players when it came to laying bets and doing business. Hector had been one of the earliest investors in Vin's mail-order music company, VKM, at a time when few believed it would work. Not many years later, Vin repaid his due and fulfilled a lifetime's ambition by buying the Fitzroy Club for himself. Since Farcombe Festival's inception, Vin had been one of its foremost patrons.

Vin liked to collect modern sculpture to fill his echoing and bright mock-Deco holiday house perched on the cliffs just across the Cornish border, rivalling nearby GCHQ Bude for its vast, weird whiteness. He was to date the largest – and only genuine – collector of Poppy's work. In return, Poppy booked many of his avant-garde musical friends to perform during festival week, his taste these days being no less eclectic than in his rock and roll youth, often involving ageing white-haired men in black suits and dark glasses playing one note repeatedly on vast stacks of electronic instruments connected to computers. He and Hector maintained a joshing public friendship and private rivalry that verged on extreme enmity.

'Vin wants to buy out the festival as well as the estate,' Francis looked up at her through his lashes, 'but Dad's always told him he'll only get it an artwork at a time, starting with Poppy's blobs. He'd rather torch the place than see Vin playing lord of the manor here.'

'I thought they were old business allies?'

He shook his head. 'Old gamblers are never friends, not when they've lost so much to each other over the years. There's a well-known rumour that Vin won the Fitzroy Club in a bet. The same rumour says that Dad seduced his girlfriend by way of revenge, then fell in love and married her.'

'Your *mother*?'

He nodded. 'She was Vin's childhood sweetheart, and Dad stole her off him. It's all supposedly forgiven and forgotten now, but you never get over something like that, do you?' His blue eyes seared into hers, making her look away.

She'd never heard him mention the fact before, although he could have buried it in a quote.

They walked past the yews to the mausoleum.

'I often wish my mother had been buried here.' Francis stopped by the rails and gazed at the pretty building, a neoclassical mini-temple cast in local stone, inset with carved marble plaques featuring doves and angels. 'Then I'd be able to visit her grave whenever I like.'

Legs' heart gave a lurch of pity as it always did when she thought about beautiful Ella Protheroe losing her life so young and leaving her son without a mother, her heartbroken husband with an empty castle and no queen.

According to Francis, whose concept of beauty had changed over the years, Ella had looked variously like Raquel Welch, Elizabeth Siddal, Nicole Kidman and an Egon Schiele's model Valerie Neuzil. Almost all photographs of his mother had been destroyed by Hector's jealous second wife, Inés. But Ella had undoubtedly been a great beauty, and she had loved Farcombe, although illness had made her a rare visitor and she had spent the final years of her short life in New York. The Big Apple had also been the setting for Hector's ill-fated rebound marriage, an unhappy union which Francis sometimes ruefully pointed out lasted half as long as his mother's illness, but brought no less pain or respite. It was only when Hector had returned to Farcombe that he'd found reprieve and eventually love . . . or so Legs had always believed, however much Francis had tried to cast Poppy as the evil stepmother when he was a boy.

'Do you really want Poppy and your father back together?' she asked him now, almost without thinking.

'Of course. They are husband and wife.' He held onto the rails of the Waite plot, fingers drumming on the black cast iron.

'That's so reactionary!'

'Farcombe Hall is the backbone of the local community; we are all its custodians. We have a duty.'

Legs had never heard him speak like this. 'Not so long ago, you wanted her gone with all your heart.'

'I've grown up a lot in the past year,' he said, turning away.

She felt the barb dig into her skin.

'Of course; you've moved on, met Kizzy,' she said, nodding. He must be grateful to Poppy for bringing them together, at least.

'Ah yes, Kizzy.' He let out a deep, thoughtful sigh which Legs frantically sought to interpret. Was it a loving exhalation or exasperation?

'She's stunning.'

'Isn't she?' he said through tight lips.

'And very "dutiful" I'm sure,' she sniped and then regretted it as he fell silent.

As they wandered around gravestones, Legs felt torn between guilt, jealousy and fury. Reaching the far wall that bordered the village lane, they lent against an ornate stone memorial shaped like an eagle spreading its wings over a vast book.

Francis cleared his throat. 'You won't tell anyone what I've just said about the financial situation here will you?'

'Of course not.' Legs shook her head. By 'anyone', she felt sure he meant Conrad. Then, unable to stop herself, she asked: 'Does Kizzy know?'

'No,' he said tersely. 'She already holds enough Protheroe secrets, believe me.'

'You make her sound like keeper of the family closet.'

'We all have confidences we choose not to share. She has hers and I have mine.'

'I guess that's what's meant by a balanced relationship,' she said carefully.

He turned to face her, blue eyes softening. 'She still doesn't know we've kissed for a start.'

'We were once engaged, Francis, I think she'll have taken it as read that we—'

'I meant yesterday.' He stepped closer, the warm whisper of his breath joining the sun on her face.

Legs had to turn her head away to stop thinking about kissing him, reminding herself that Conrad trusted her, even if she didn't quite trust herself at the moment. 'I hadn't met Kizzy yesterday.'

He snorted irritably.

'What are you not telling me?' she demanded.

The lichen was now being scraped at a furious rate. 'I guess it's more what about what *you're* not saying, Legs.'

'Meaning?'

'I thought Farcombe meant something to you, that you cared about my family, our history, even if you've moved on from loving me.'

'Of course I care! What's happening between our parents is devastating.'

'Which is why we must unite forces.' He nodded earnestly, sounding like a world leader discussing a Middle Eastern crisis.

'We can't pretend to be something we're not.'

His voice deepened as he moved closer again: 'You heard Poppy's threat.'

'So? Let her cancel the festival. This is about our families, not Farcombe's cashflow or my career. Gordon can stay a recluse for ever for all I care. Frankly, I think he'd be happier that way. He's too volatile for fame; it's living a lie.'

'And he's not living one already? We all do that, Legs.' Two blue eyes danced between hers. 'If we said what we really thought, we'd never survive.'

'Try it, Francis,' she breathed, their lips ridiculously close now. 'Just this once, tell me what you really feel?' She searched his handsome face for clues, willing him to admit that there was nothing staged or make-believe about the way they were both feeling right now. As teenagers they'd played Truth or Dare; as adults they no longer dared to tell the truth. That conspiracy of silence had given the lie to their relationship a year ago.

He ran his tongue across his teeth, blue eyes gazing up at the statue's broken-beaked face.

'Say it,' she urged. 'What do you want most of all right now, this minute?' She tried not to pucker up as her lips tingled with anticipation.

His hand found hers and gripped it tight, fingers shaking with emotion: 'I want Gordon Lapis at Farcombe Festival!'

Legs froze. 'What?'

He looked petulant. 'Well, you did ask.'

She carefully unthreaded her fingers. 'And if I stop that happening?'

Keeping hold of her ring finger, he lifted it to his lips and kissed its bare skin '". . . if thou wilt needs marry, marry a fool; for wise men know well enough what monsters you make of them".' As so often in the past, Francis could not personalise his feelings; his words belonged to other people, loaded with emotions he couldn't express any other way.

With a polite nod, he turned and walked away, leaving Legs feeling utterly demoralised.

She looked up at the stone eagle, noticing that somebody had graffitied *To Kill a Mockingbird* on its stone book. She had a nervous feeling it might have been her and Daisy, high on alcopops on Millennium New Year's Eve.

Chapter 10

A call to Conrad from the village telephone box hardly lifted her spirits. He'd stayed up late the previous night composing a press release, he announced happily, and was poised to notify the eager media and millions of ardent Lapis fans that the author would reveal his identity at Farcombe Festival. Now sitting in the stands at Lords watching the England India test match with his kids, he was as brief and to the point as always.

'As soon as this goes live, Farcombe will be a sell out. No time to lose. Don't let me down, Legs.'

'Don't send it yet!' she insisted. 'It's very far from confirmed.'

The call left her riddled with self-doubt; her heart and head at odds. Her feelings for Francis, boxed up for so long, were now bouncing around all over the place on rusty springs, whereas Conrad remained neatly filed under 'macho' in a locked cabinet in London. What's more, she was feeling increasingly uneasy about Gordon Lapis's decision to make Farcombe his main stage. Even assuming Poppy didn't pull the plug on the festival out of sheer spite, and that the committee could be convinced of the financial benefits, Gordon himself was such an unknown quantity, he could easily change his mind. If he did, that would completely ruin Farcombe, and it would be all her fault.

She trailed down past the harbour to Fargoe beach and splashed through the sea, freezing her ankles and wondering how she might cope with losing her job, lover and family security in one weekend.

She couldn't be totally sure as she struggled to see through the maelstrom of memory and melancholy, but she was starting to suspect that she had never stopped loving Francis. She was frightened of the told-you-so clichés that were pulling and pushing her right now, trying to trip her up like the waves underfoot. In the past year, distance had made her heart grow fonder in direct proportion to familiarity breeding contempt with Conrad. Now she was back in Farcombe, nostalgia was flooding her head as fast as the incoming tide.

Children with buckets and spades, inflatables and boogie boards raced in and out of the waves around her as she trudged all the way to the rocky outcrop at Hartcombe Point and looked back across the sand to the village. The sea was racing in, forcing the holiday-makers back in its wake, sandcastles toppling, windbreaks and towels being whipped up, creams teas and ice creams sought out. She remembered the ritual so well, along with the long summers of *Swallows and Amazons* freedom that had lent her familiarity with everything around her.

Except nothing felt familiar any more, not even her own heart.

Given this opportunity to reclaim Francis and appease the guilt, surely she should grasp it? She was vacillating madly between the unexpected force of her attraction to him and the dreadful messiness of the situation. She longed for her childhood again, for those carefree holidays where the most important things in the world were winning at rounders, building secret camps and creeping out for midnight ghost hunts in the woods after the adults had gone to bed.

Now the adults were all in the wrong beds, and she had inadvertently led the way.

She needed somewhere to stay, and knowing that a second night in the Honda would leave her walking like Quasimodo, she headed back towards the harbour to stop off at the Book Inn.

The 'Private Function' sign had been turned around to offer 'Food All Day, Cream Teas and Award-Winning Accommodation'. The girl on the desk – an unfamiliar face, but with a familiar nervous voice from the previous day's phone call – told her that it was fully booked, flashing a jaunty tongue stud as she spoke, which gave her a lisp. Legs went into the bar where Guy was serving, looking very grey beneath his blond-tipped hair.

'Allegra North! You are Alka Seltzer to my hangover!' He kissed her delightedly, bloodshot grey eyes disappearing into weathered laughter creases. 'We were beginning to think we'd never see you in Farcombe again. My, but you look good – I've missed this beautiful face.' He cupped her cheeks fondly.

Built like a stocky prop forward with a jutting jaw and a permanent frown born from too many sunny days sea-angling and long nights cooking in the kitchen, Guy cut an intimidating figure, but he possessed the gentlest of souls.

'You should have come in yesterday,' he wailed when she explained that she'd arrived the day before and U-turned at the A-sign. 'We had a big party for Nonny's fortieth. You'd have been a wonderful birthday surprise.'

Nonny and Guy were the classic Beauty and Beast couple, her balletic grace and charm counterpoised by his craggy, workaholic passion. Originally from west London, they'd run a small chain of foodie wine bars in the profitable W-postcodes from Kensington to Notting Hill, Marylebone to Little Venice, many of them frequented by Legs, Francis and their gang. It was Legs who had told them about Farcombe, and the then Harbour Inn, which was hideously run down at the time and about to be flogged by a failing brewery. Seeing an opportunity at a time when they were ripe for change, they had bought it sight unseen and moved their entire family to the coast. They were followed by many of their London friends and clients, who visited on such a regular basis that some had even bought second homes in the area. The couple had made a huge difference to the village's year-round popularity. Having once worked as a music promoter, Nonny was incredibly well connected which, matched with Guy's legendary cooking skills, guaranteed the Book Inn a high level of occupancy. Always busy, it was positively heaving in high summer and guaranteed to be booked out six months in advance for festival week. At this time of year, it rarely ever had a room free at the weekends.

'I wish you'd called earlier. There was a cancellation for tonight – one of the sea view four-posters,' Guy admitted, then shook his head as Legs' face brightened, 'it was snapped up straight away – had a call first thing. We'll put you up in Skit. It's not so cold in summer, although the upstairs neighbours can be a bit noisy. You can stay as long as you like.'

Skit was the old skittle alley which ran the full length of the restaurant at first floor level and which was the subject of a long-running battle with the local planning authority because the couple had earmarked it for further accommodation, but the presence of a rare colony of greater horseshoe bats who used the roof-space as its summer roost precluded any alteration, so it was currently only used for storage and as an occasional staff bedsit. From May to September, the bats lived in a huge maternity colony overhead, rearing their young and chattering noisily all night. It wasn't ideal, but it was definitely preferable to a car seat.

'Just a night or two will be great.' Legs smiled gratefully, then remembered the Honda abandoned at Gull Point with a broken driver's door. 'Is it all right to park my car in the unloading yard if I bring it down the back way?' The Book Inn only had a tiny court-yard, and parking on the harbour was strictly frowned upon.

Guy pulled an apologetic face. 'Not tonight; we've got live music in the bar later – a seriously well-connected performer, you wait – and they need the space to unload. We might even persuade you to sing for your supper again, hey Legs?' He ruffled her hair before turning to serve a customer.

Buoyed up by the thought of Book Inn food that night, and per-haps a couple of drinks on the house over a jolly catch up and a sing-song, she headed back up the private cliff path to Gull Point to fetch the Honda and move it to the public car park at the top of the village where she could keep an eye on it. Driving along the top lane, she almost slammed straight into a taxi coming far too fast in the opposite direction. Only just swerving to avoid it, she scraped her car's wing along a rocky bank as a result. The driver lowered his window as they inched past each other.

'You want to kill someone, my love?' He told her off in a thick Devonshire accent.

Having expected to share cheery 'could-have-been-worse' apologies, Legs was instantly defensive. 'It was your fault!'

'Silly cow.' He started to wind up his window again.

'Bully!' she yelled, but he was already driving away.

In the back seat, two mournful, apologetic eyes gazed out at her through the darkened glass as the car slid past, and Legs smiled gratefully back, raising her hand to acknowledge the passenger. It was only as the car moved away that she glanced in her rear-view mirror and realised she had been waving at a basset hound.

When Legs assessed the damage, her car was even more crum-pled than ever, the front wing freshly scraped. She parked it close up against a wall to hide the fact the driver's door was ajar and then climbed out the passenger's side. Her handbag had tipped off the back seat, spilling its contents everywhere, which added to her irritation. Scraping around the seats and footwells, she could only find enough loose change for one day's parking. Carrying her nephew's small duffel-bag, the pile of crime thriller manuscripts she had brought with her to look through for work and all the loose clothes and shoes she could gather from the car, she set out along the narrow, cobbled lane to the harbour, eager to get settled then go for a run to shake off her road rage before cocktail hour.

Back at the Book Inn, Guy was nowhere to be seen, and the nervous-looking girl with the pierced tongue was trying to cover both the bar and the reception desk, where a dark-haired figure was drumming his fingers impatiently beside the guest register.

'It's B-Y-R-N-E,' he spelled out to her in a rich Irish accent as she frantically pressed keys on the computer to try to find his reservation. 'I am expected.'

'There's nothing here.'

'Jesus, what sort of a place is this?'

'I'll get the boss!' she bleated, retreating through a Staff Only door while customers called out for service in the bar.

'I think she's new,' Legs said kindly.

The man didn't turn around, and so she casually sidled along the desk to try to get a better look, remembering what Guy had said about great live music from an amazing connection. Wasn't Gabriel Byrne's son Jack in a band with Harrison Ford's boy? Now that was just the sort of act Guy and Nonny were notorious for booking, having a genius streak for promotion and an address book to die for.

Her sidling got her as far as a large display of lilies in a square vase, which liberally dusted her white shirt in bright saffron stains as she craned sideways to see his face.

He was probably too old to be Jack Byrne, she decided, although he definitely had a look of Gabriel about the curled raven wing brows, black peat eyes and glowering face. A cousin maybe?

Still ignoring her, the man reached out and moved the lily vase further along the desk, away from her shirt.

Pierced Tongue returned from consulting with Guy in the kitchen, jabbering apologies as she handed him a key.

'You're in Octodecimo, Mr Byrne,' she lisped. 'Up the stairs and then right.' All the rooms at the Book Inn were named after publishing formats from Folio through to Sexagesimo-quarto, which always played havoc with drunken guests asking for their keys. Legs imagined Pierced Tongue and her lisp didn't fare much better.

Nodding, he stooped to pick up a battered Gladstone bag and stalked upstairs.

Pierced Tongue caught Legs' eye and sucked her barbell nervously, 'I'm sorry I didn't realise who you were. You're a local legend.'

She smiled kindly. 'I'm just an old local called Legs, at a loose end.'

'Weren't you engaged to Francis Protheroe once?'

Legs stepped back, deciding that Guy should really train his front of house staff to be more discreet. 'That's right.'

'My friend says you two were the Brangelina of Farcombe.'

Legs snorted with laughter. 'Tell your friend I'm very flattered, although I've always thought Jennifer Aniston would have made Brad happier in the long-term, and that way he could have saved on tattoos.' She could feel the little ink stars on her ankle itching guiltily.

Pierced Tongue beamed, flashing her barbell. 'She'll love that!'

Taking the keys to Skit, Legs rushed up to change into her running shoes, which had been drying on the roof of the car all day and were stiff with dried saltwater, before pounding out along the harbour walls to the under-cliff and then up through the tracks to the woods. As she ran along the public coastal path, a figure pounded towards her. It was black-haired B-Y-R-N-E, still glowering menacingly, iPod earphones blotting out the world around him, and an ear-swinging basset hound blundering along behind, clearly struggling to keep up.

'Hi there!' she shouted cheerfully, raising a hand in polite recognition, but he once again blanked her, running past as though she wasn't there, his dog almost forcing her off the track as it veered across her path to cock its leg against a gorse bush. Not breaking stride, Byrne let out a deafening whistle and beckoned it forward.

'Unfriendly bastard!' she muttered breathlessly as she shambled on, wishing she'd chosen a route with less steep inclines. Running more than once in a day was always a giveaway that she had a troubled heart and mind. When she'd been breaking up with Francis, she had run her way through a new pair of trainers in a fortnight.

She returned red-faced and sweaty. Even a long shower in Skit's unconventional en suite, which had once been the pub's main gents' loo, failed to stop her cheeks glowing with sunburnt, wind-swept vigour. Nor could she get a comb through her wild, wet hair and had to settle for pulling it up into a bedraggled top-knot which revealed how milk white her neck was compared to her beetroot face. Matched with her depleted wardrobe of ten-year-old-boy-sized separates, the overall look was not an ego-boosting one. Which made her doubly annoyed to find herself walking downstairs directly in front of grumpy Byrne, his impatient breath on her hot neck.

She was about to divert to the bar for a much needed stiff drink, but Guy's blonde glamourpuss wife Nonny was front of house in the restaurant and fell on her in delight, a welcoming embrace of highly toned glamour and finely tailored chic, as delicately scented as a freesia.

'Guy said you were here! You look . . . amazing.' The word stood ironically between pauses before Nonny rushed on. 'That androgynous look is so on-trend. Eat now because we'll be absolutely heaving later and I still have one table free.' She checked her clipboard. 'Ah – that is, I did, but Gabs pencilled somebody in. Can't read the name.'

'Byrne,' said a deep Irish voice behind Legs. 'It's Byrne.'

'Mr Byrne.' Nonny held out her hand, slipping into professional hostess mode as smoothly as she might slip into one of her many killer little black dresses. 'Rhiannon Taylor. Welcome to the Book Inn; I trust Octodecimo is to your satisfaction?'

'It's satisfactory,' he acquiesced.

Legs started to back away, mouthing. 'I'll eat later.' She was quite happy with the prospect of a liquid supper – the Book Inn served dreamy cocktails, accompanied by gorgeous bar-top tapas.

But Nonny was tapping her pen against her clipboard in a way that Legs knew marked danger, eyes signalling her to wait. 'The table is laid for two . . .' she told Byrne leadingly. 'Would you like us to clear the other setting or perhaps . . .?'

'I'm dining alone, yes.' He nodded curtly.

Legs was backing away fast, smiling fixedly and shaking her head as she tugged down her tight, shiny top, which had ridden up to reveal a lot of bare-skinned midriff. The T-shirt matched with her baggy-bottomed navy cut-offs was hardly restaurant dress code, and she had no desire to small-talk with a big sulk.

Nonny's delicate, red-nailed hand grabbed her just before she could scarper through to the oblivion of cocktails and live music, 'I'll bring you something through to the bar, Allegra darling. The sea bass is fantastic. Fresh from Ilfracombe this morning.'

'Sounds delicious!' she agreed, eager to get away. 'I love bass. Hate bassoons, love bass.'

To Legs surprise, Byrne let out a sharp, sweet laugh and turned to look at her intently, raven's brows taking off.

'Allegra?'

'That's me.'

'I can't possibly let you eat in the bar. It's five-deep in there. Would you care to join me?'

Legs had thought the bass joke particularly weak, and was tempted to add something about being a 'dumbass' at this point, but she was struck so mute by surprise at his niceness, she said nothing, nodding mutely.

133

Having gobbled up so much food at lunch, she didn't really want to eat another big meal when cocktails were so much lighter and lovelier. The first Book Inn speciality that she longed to revisit was a wonderful rum-fuelled concoction called a 'Dark and Stormy Night', which she could quickly follow by a brandy-laced 'Once Upon a Time' and an absinthe-heavy 'Alas dear Readers'.

But Nonny had already summoned the head waiter to pull back chairs and was soon steering her into the restaurant behind Byrne, muttering sotto voice in her ear. 'Help! We think he must be Michelin; Guy has a hangover and is cooking like shit. Get Michelin Man drunk and flirt your arse off. *Don't* let him eat the chilli-baked crab whatever he says; the marinade is totally buggered. Anton is on side. Thank goodness you're here.' She planted the briefest kiss near Legs' ear.

With that, she was deposited at a small table by the indoor fountain and left in the capable hands of Anton their waiter, along with unsociable table companion Byrne.

While she hastily ordered a Dark and Stormy Night to galvanise her nerve, he spent a lifetime studying the menu. Legs, who was under instruction to have the sea bass, took the opportunity to assess the jogging malcontent while she swigged her drink.

He was not very tall – a good five inches shorter than Francis at a guess – and in possession of a face as sharp with clashing angles as Francis's angelic profile was soft with symmetrical harmony. He had the most amazing fiercely focused coal-black eyes, highly intelligent and faintly familiar, although not belonging to anybody Legs trusted, of that she was certain. On close inspection, they were very dark brown and flecked with fox-pelt red, like the ancient oak beams overhead that flickered in the candle's glow.

The brown eyes snapped up as Anton strode back, pad aloft, then turned their focus on her face, candlelit flecks turning to flame-throwers.

'Starter?' Byrne demanded.

He sounded like Jeremy Paxman, Legs thought suddenly,

fighting giggles. With the hastily consumed Dark and Stormy Night making her face glow all the brighter, she was grateful to have an excuse to bury herself in the menu for a moment.

'Asparagus.' She chose the first thing she saw.

'And for me,' Byrne's hypnotically *Late Late Show* voice echoed. 'Then my companion will have the sea bass and I'll have the Devon crab.'

'Absolutely not!' Legs squawked, grabbing back the menu from Anton. 'I've changed my mind. I want the Paella Valenciana.' Guy had always boasted that he could make his signature dish in his sleep.

'That is for two people,' Anton pointed out, 'but it's a very good dish. I can check with Chef if you like.' He glanced over his shoulder at the kitchens, sharing Legs' horror at the crab choice, but appearing to be equally unsure about her choice of the paella.

'No need!' Legs looked across at Byrne imploringly, convinced that a long-winded risotto would suit Guy and buy her time to charm their Michelin Man. 'The paella here is the best in Devon.'

Reluctantly, Byrne regarded the menu again. 'I'm not keen on rabbit, or snails.'

Legs started in recognition. Guy insisted on making his paella to an old, traditional recipe that contained no seafood and positively exploded with garlic and artichokes. She'd only ever tried it once, and she'd been very drunk at the time, largely because it took so long to prepare that she'd consumed most of a bottle of wine waiting. It had been Daisy's birthday, she recalled. A large group of friends and family had gathered, including all the parents. Many toasts had been raised to Daisy, and several to her late father Nigel. Dorian had recited Tennyson's 'Crossing the Bar' in his honour and Hector had played his bassoon, partly simultaneously, which had all got rather competitive. With emotions and alcohol running high, Daisy had later rowed with her mother about the presence of her future stepfather, Gerald, whom she hadn't wanted to be invited. Legs and Francis, down from London on a flying visit, had put on a united front, but she had already fallen madly for Conrad by then.

Thinking back, Legs realised it was the last time she'd eaten in the pub, not long before she and Francis had gone their separate ways. Her eyes filled with tears.

'It means a lot to me,' she managed to croak.

Looking alarmed, Byrne changed their order to the paella. 'And a bottle of the Rioja,' he added before Anton melted away. Moments later, the waiter returned with a complimentary glass of champagne each and a small tray of amuse-bouche.

Legs raised her flute gamely, 'Thank you for letting me join you.'

'Your name is Allegra?'

She nodded, practically draining her glass in one.

'Unusual.'

'Allegra Maria.' She rolled her eyes. 'I appeared nine months after my parents took their first holiday in Italy. My sister is Rosalind Celia, so one can only assume they enjoyed a good production of *As You Like It* before conception.'

His mouth flickered in a smile.

She hoovered up a thimble of cauliflower and mustard foam, 'When we were at prep school, we had a project to look up the meanings of our names. I was so jealous that my sister's translated as 'little white horse from heaven', and mine as 'gay virgin' that I changed my name to Heavenly Pony.'

'Even more unusual.'

'It didn't catch on, however hard I tried.'

'I think everyone should change their name at least once in life.'

'I've always just been Legs.' She managed to stop herself short from rattling on about the inappropriateness of her nickname and slugged back some more champagne. He had hardly touched his. She must work harder at loosening him up.

'So what brings you to Farcombe?' She picked up a ceramic

spoon of salmon mousse flecked with orange zest and licked it off greedily.

He fingered the stem of his full champagne flute. 'Family affairs.'

'Me too!' She drained her glass and picked up a tiny parmesan tuile containing minted pea sorbet, fighting not to expand upon the 'affairs' element, vaguely aware that she was already getting tight. Indiscretion had always been among her key weaknesses, along with her short temper, and alcohol inevitably unlocked both incredibly swiftly. 'So you have family living in the village?'

He gave a non-committal shrug and finally lifted his glass to his lips.

Legs had always been hopeless at drawing people out. Ros liked to claim it was because her little sister was completely self-obsessed and talked about herself too much, but kinder family members and friends would say that Legs tried to entertain and cheer glum company rather than counsel it.

Thus she found herself telling Byrne about Spywood and her family's connection with Farcombe. 'It's our safe haven and bolt-hole; we all love it here.'

'So you've all been coming here since before the festival?'

'Long before.' She nodded, smiling gratefully as Byrne signalled Anton to refill her champagne glass. 'Before the Protheroes really used the house much – Hector's first wife died of a tumour when she was barely thirty. He and Francis stayed in New York for ages afterwards.'

'But Hector's married to a local now, I gather?'

She snorted with amusement, swallowing down a black cherry tomato stuffed with a deliciously creamy, herby concoction. 'Don't let Poppy hear you call her a "local" – she is far too free a spirit. I think her family are from the area now you come to mention it. Goblin Granny certainly lived nearby.'

The raven's-wing brows shot up again at the curious name, and she laughed. 'Poppy's mother. The stepchildren called her Goblin

Granny because she lived in a gothic pile near Bideford with carvings everywhere and gargoyles peering from all the eaves; it makes Farcombe Hall look minimalist. I remember going there with Francis years ago – I think his father must have only just married Poppy. It frightened me witless. I was convinced it was a witches' coven.'

'Goblin Granny's no longer living there?'

'She died and it was sold,' she explained, realising as she said it that this must have been the legacy that Poppy sunk into Farcombe to make her majority shareholder. 'I think the family was terribly grand at one time; Poppy certainly talks about her parents hosting hunt balls and entertaining cabinet ministers on shooting weekends, but Goblin Granny was the last of that breed.'

'So her daughter doesn't host hunt balls at Farcombe?'

Halfway down her second glass of champagne, Legs was becoming increasingly careless with family gossip. 'Her first husband probably put her off horses for life.'

'How so?'

'She married a local jockey when she was very young, much to the Goblin's disapproval, as she thought him far beneath Poppy socially. I gather it was all rather – rushed.'

'A shotgun marriage?'

'There was a child,' she nodded, 'who stayed with the father when Poppy ran off. She never talks about it. I don't know a lot more, to be honest. I was too young when it all happened, although I do remember Poppy and Hector eloping. We were holidaying here at the time. Now that *was* high drama.'

Anton swept in to remove the amuse-bouche, which Legs had devoured and Byrne hadn't touched. Then he placed two rows of glossy asparagus in front of them, gleaming green fifty-calibre bandoliers of tastebud seduction.

Legs selected a spear and sucked butter from the tip.

Byrne was looking at her with the most amazingly sexy, direct expression and for a moment she egotistically wondered if she was turning him on. He was fabulously intense. Then, wiping a small oil slick from her chin, she realised that he was waiting patiently for her to carry on talking about the high drama of that summer when Poppy and Hector had eloped.

'She was one of the festival team in the early days, when it was predominantly jazz,' she told him between mouthfuls of asparagus. 'There were lots of pretty women involved back then, fragrant envelope stuffers all with their hearts set on Hector; Francis called them the Vamps after the jazz term. I remember Poppy because she was so beautiful and had hair dyed the most incredible shade of pomegranate-red, and her voice was as deep as a man's. We all thought she was amazing. We heard she had a terrible home life, but I never knew the details, just that Hector had practically saved her from destitution by giving her a job.'

'And they had an affair?'

She nodded. 'Nobody knew a thing about it until it all blew open. Hector went away on business one weekend, a last minute thing. Francis stayed with us in the cottage, which wasn't unusual because we were all friends. My sister Ros and I had a terrible fight because we both wanted to share a room with him, and I won, even though he was more her friend than mine in those days – they're the same age, you see. I remember lying awake looking at his sleeping arm dangling over the side of the bunk above my head, watching the luminous hands move on his watch, longing to touch his fingers.'

'How old were you?'

'Ten. I know it was terribly trollopy of me, but holding hands was about as hot as my fantasies got.' She fell gratefully upon the Rioja he had just poured out. 'He just seemed so sad. Then his father reappeared with Poppy at his side on Monday announcing they were going to get married, and Francis refused to move back in with them. He stayed with us the rest of the summer, and I kept the lower bunk, so I was overjoyed. And I even got to hold his hand a few times.' She blushed. 'But just as friends. He needed a friend, especially when he discovered that his father was sending him away to boarding school the following term.'

'His new stepmother's idea, I take it?'

'He hated her,' she grimaced, 'we all did, really. She banned us from the big house. Just before he left for his new school, Francis plucked up the courage to tell his father how alienated he felt by Poppy and Hector went absolutely berserk, saying he deserved happiness after all the misery he'd endured. Francis felt like he was being totally rejected. We used to write to each other during term time. He was so brave about it all, but he went through absolute hell.'

'What happened to Poppy's child? The one she left when she ran away with Hector?'

'Left the area with the father, I think. No idea where they went.' She helped herself to more wine. 'Poor thing can't have been any happier than Francis.' She felt stupidly tearful remembering his utter despair. 'The first holiday from boarding school, he brought Poppy a Christmas present he'd made, a wooden dove to hang on the tree; the ultimate peace offering. I loved him so much for his equanimity.'

'Sounds quite a guy.' He turned his butter knife on its point before spinning it around in his fingers.

'He is,' she sighed.

'And you've stayed friends all these years?' Byrne's voice was so moreish in its mellifluence, the ultimate confessor.

Legs mopped up the last of the asparagus butter with bread, pushing the rejected woody stumps around her plate to form a green mosaic smile. 'On and off and now off. I've rather buggered up the friendship in the past year, but I'm hoping to make amends.' She looked up with an embarrassed smile, and found those strange flame and coal eyes burning into her face.

Swigging more wine, she decided she had nothing to lose. Who better to offload on than a total stranger who would take his Michelin judging off to another town tomorrow and never cross her path again? She badly needed to talk.

So out it spilled, the terrible guilt about what she had done to first love Francis, about falling for her charismatic older boss Conrad and rejecting the boy-turned-man whom she had loved so long and whose family she had become a part of. The long letter she had sent which had never been acknowledged. And now, the opportunity to make amends that she had rejected.

Byrne was a very good listener. A second bottle of Rioja was discreetly ordered as the asparagus plates were removed.

'The awful thing is,' – she was wet-eyed with sentiment – 'I am so tempted to do it, to play lovers again and see what happens, but I know it would be like cartwheeling across a minefield, and I have to try to learn from my mistakes some time.'

'What mistakes are those?'

'Running off with somebody else,' she admitted, lifting her glass with shaking hands and draining a great glug, then scrubbing at her top lip as she realised it must have left her with a red moustache.

'So it was the manner of your leaving that bothers you?'

'No! Yes! Maybe I chose the wrong one of those fifty ways.' She sighed sadly. 'Or maybe I should have stayed and tried to work things out. It's behind us. He's found someone new now, too. That's what makes it all such a mess. We can't ask Conrad and Kizzy to stand aside while we play this out. Pretending to get back together is so hurtful.'

'Because he just wants to pretend, and you want it to be real?'

She was caught out by his insight. The tears swelling in her eyes started to spill. 'It's just not like him to want to mislead anybody. I think perhaps he only suggested we make it an act to protect himself in case I said no?'

'Unlikely if he's found somebody else. Men are very straightforward. We work in straight lines on a "want it, get it" basis. Why d'you think I invited you to join me this evening?'

About to protest that she had no idea, she suddenly replayed the 'want it' element of his theory in her mind and flushed deepest

141

crimson. But then he ruined it by adding, 'Truth is, I thought "I want to make that woman cry", and I just have.'

She let out a nervous laugh of shock.

He was totally deadpan.

For a moment she flashed with anger, but the amount of alcohol she'd swilled had turned her into emotional blotting paper and she let out another sniffy, gulping laugh instead. 'I know I'm a total cry-baby.' She blew her nose again. 'Francis hates me crying.'

'It's been proven scientifically that women's tears contain a chemical that represses male desire,' he said in that deep hypnotic voice. 'I think it's also been proven that watching the *Twilight* series has the exact same effect.'

She hastily mopped her tears with her napkin, too squiffy to notice that she picked up a corner of the tablecloth from her lap at the same time. Byrne showed lightning reflexes, rescuing the wine while the condiments shot towards him.

'I think I might still be in love with Francis,' she sobbed before she could stop herself.

Byrne was holding a wine glass in each hand, a pepper grinder in his lap and his male desire no doubt very repressed, but his face remained attentive and his dark eyebrows lifted inquiringly. 'That's quite a statement.' He leaned forwards and set down the wine glasses. 'Do you think he feels the same way?'

'I don't know.' She blew her nose loudly on the napkin. 'There's something so strange about the way he's behaving, like he's being held to ransom somehow. It's not like him to suggest anything deceitful, even given our parents' exploits. And I don't get the whole Kizzy thing at all – she and Poppy seem more besotted by one another than she and Francis are. I half suspect he's only lined her up to make me so jealous that I want him back.' She reached for her glass.

'Well if he has, it's certainly worked.'

She ignored him, slurping more wine before blustering on, 'There's no spark between them whatsoever, not like the one that's obviously been burning away between my mother and Hector for all these years. As far as I can tell, they have the most genuine relationship of the lot of us, but it must end.'

'Why so?'

'Because it's all so wrong!'

'Because *you* disapprove,' he corrected.

'Do you blame me? Think what this is doing to my poor Dad.'

'Let your parents sort themselves out.' That deep voice was so calm and assured, yet the fierce eyes burned across the table at her with such intense heat her face reddened further. 'It never does to interfere and play God, Allegra, not unless you want to risk everybody getting hurt in the fall out. Some deeds might deserve that sort of justice, but falling in love rarely does, certainly not when two people feel the same way about each other. You can't force people in and out of love like you can coerce anger or tears or shame.'

It was more than he had said all evening and made Legs reel back, wine stormy in her glass as she realised with a jolt all the secrets that she'd just poured out to him.

And when he spoke again, she realised his voice was not as smooth or urbane as she'd first thought. It had a crackle of burning Kilkenny peat to it. 'Take my word for it, Heavenly Pony; at best, your man Francis has moved on and found himself a nice girl to love; at worst (and this is my guess) he's after some sort of revenge. Either way, you won't come out of it happy if you try to get him back. Life's too precious. Find a new lover.'

'I have a lover!' she protested too loudly, thinking guiltily of Conrad.

There was a brief hush around them in the busy restaurant, broken only by a nearby diner dropping a fork with a loud clatter.

He raised a dark eyebrow, penetrating gaze not moving from her face.

If she blushed any more, the tablecloth would scorch, she realised. Her hypocrisy was tattooed across her hot face. 'Conrad. The man I left Francis for. We're still together. He's very good for me.'

'I don't think you'd be here pouring your heart out about still loving your ex to me if that was true.'

At that moment, the paella arrived and was set down between them, swimming with saffron, garlic, snails and rabbit. Legs had to swallow hard to stop herself gagging. She'd drunk far too much wine and gorged on amuse-bouche, bread and asparagus while developing verbal diarrhoea. Her appetite for food and conversation was dwindling fast.

And now she was paranoid about the ambiguity of Byrne's last comment. As she helped herself to a tiny ladleful of paella, she regarded him worriedly through the steam. Did he think she she was some nutty Ancient Mariner? Or did he think she was just a silly flirt, keeping her London lover amused during the week and returning to stir things up with her ex at weekends? Did he perhaps even think the fact she was sharing a table with him tonight meant she was after *him*? She deeply regretted sucking drunkenly on the asparagus spears now. He was really very annoying company, making her spill all her truths across the table like the contents of her handbag, revealing her untidy mind and intimate secrets.

He's a food judge, she reminded herself. Aren't they all horrible misogynists? She'd rarely managed to get through an entire A. A. Gill column without the desire to hurl china, particularly on the occasion he'd reduced Guy to tears of frustration by describing the Book Inn as a gimmicky gastropub with slush-pile credentials and pulp-fiction food. She owed it to her host tonight to up her game.

Byrne was staring moodily into the paella pot. It smelled delicious for all its witch's brew ingredients. Worthy of several Michelin stars, Legs decided proudly. Didn't Heston Blumenthal make snail porridge after all?

She drew breath and smiled winningly, determined to get back on course, softening him up for Guy and Nonny while making it clear that she was a committed girlfriend to Conrad.

'I can assure you I am doing all this with my lover's blessing,' she said in a measured voice which she hoped sounded mature and level-headed, but to her ear was unpleasantly Theresa May.

'You two work together in a literary agency, you say?'

He had a very sharp memory, she realised as she vaguely recalled blithering on about Conrad's genius while waving a spear of asparagus about earlier. 'Yes, I'm his assistant.'

'Then the man's no better than a pimp in my opinion.'

'How dare you talk about Conrad like that!' she huffed.

'Married men who sleep with their PAs are all slimeballs. Does he get you to buy his wife's Christmas presents?'

'He's separated!'

Several fellow diners were starting to look around at them again. Legs checked herself hard by cramming in a mouthful of paella. 'Mmm – absolutely delicious. Better than any I've had in Spain, don't you agree?' She beamed across at him.

He politely tried a mouthful, nodding thoughtfully. 'If I'd tasted the same paellas in Spain as you I might be qualified to judge.'

'He really is terribly, terribly good,' she gushed, conscious that Theresa May was morphing to Thatcher now. 'I've never had better.'

'Your lover?' he was deliberately trying to wind her up.

'No, Guy the chef.' She licked her spoon, forgetting herself as food hedonism returned. It was absolutely delicious. She had another mouthful. If one forgot about the snail thing, it was ambrosia. 'Guy's brought so many visitors to the area, mostly to try his food. He's been tipped as the next Rick Stein. Exceptional velvety depth.' She smiled again, noticing that he was staring at her mouth. Thinking he was spellbound by her cupid lips, she pursed them winningly, only to find that she had several rice grains wedged between her teeth.

He was glowering at her again. 'And he doesn't mind you being in love with your ex?'

'Guy doesn't mind what anyone does as long as they eat, drink and be merry here.' She picked up her glass, smiling encouragingly as he ate the delectable paella.

He laid down his fork to focus the full kiln-mouth heat of his angry eyes upon her once more. 'Does Conrad know you're still in love with Francis Protheroe?'

Her smile wavered. 'I didn't say I was still in love with him, I said I might be. Can we not talk about Conrad any more? I want to talk about food and Farcombe and you – your interests, like your family here. Are they Irish too?'

He shook his head. 'I don't want to discuss them. Besides, I asked *you* a question.'

Legs went to protest again, but didn't quite know how to address him, so stopped short. It was only just dawning on her that she didn't even know his first name. Having told him such intimate truths, even confessing about Heavenly Pony, it somehow seemed too late to try to find out, rather like asking a one-night stand what they were called the morning after.

She ate some more paella, grateful to feel it soak up some of the Rioja she'd swilled. He probably had no family nearby, she decided. That was just a well-worn line. He was a lonely Michelin man accustomed to getting single dining companions drunk and raiding their secrets. A lonely life on the road.

She now couldn't remember what he had asked her, so bided her time masticating, devouring every complex corner of the flavour, increasingly convinced it was star-worthy.

'Tell me about your boss and lover,' he asked in that confidential, moreish voice.

'He's lovely.'

'Goes with the territory – love, lover, lovely.' He played with the assonance, exposing her banality.

'He's sexy, manly.'

'Clever?'

'Oh, yes. Hugely. He discovered Gordon Lapis.'

'That a fact?'

'He's a genius.'

'Lapis?'

'Conrad. Well, both really, but Conrad's easier socially. I doubt Gordon gets out much.'

'You know Gordon Lapis well?'

She shook her head. 'I love his books. They just lift up life when you're reading them. But I share that intimacy with millions. And of course we all think we know him, but it's Ptolemy we fall in love with, not Gordon.'

'This would be Ptolemy Finch with the silent P?'

She nodded. 'He's such a perfect hero.'

'Surely creation and creator are never that far apart?'

'I'm not in a position to judge. I've never met Gordon. Nobody at the agency has apart from Conrad.'

'Lucky old Conrad.' He drained his wine glass and topped it up.

Legs covered her still-full glass as the wine bottle passed over. 'Isn't he just? I'd love to meet Gordon in person one day. Maybe he'll come here,' she mused idly, looking around at the dark beams and guttering candles. 'Everybody loves it here.'

He laid down his fork, dark brows lifting.

She glanced over each shoulder and craned forwards, whispering. 'Gordon might be speaking at the Farcombe festival this year.'

'In disguise, I assume?'

She shook her head, eyes widening as she delighted in sharing a much more interesting secret than her ragged love-life. 'He's going to show his face at last.'

'Wow.' He reached for his wine glass and eyed her over it as he sank an inch of deep crimson Rioja, the embers igniting in the black coals of his eyes.

'Wow indeed.' Legs nodded eagerly, grateful they were on song at last.

'And you like his stuff?' he pulled a face, although whether this was a comment on the wine or the world's bestselling author was unclear.

'Love it.' She smiled widely, eyes sparkling as she felt herself on safe ground at last. 'Ptolemy Finch is such a glorious character. My nephew Nico is obsessed, and rightly so. He's every kid in a way. He's me and my mate Daisy at that age, and he's *totally* Francis as a boy.' Her eyes filled with tears as the safe ground fell away from beneath her feet. Damn that wine. She stuffed in some more paella hoping he hadn't noticed as she rushed on: 'I can't wait for the next one. Conrad says it's shit hot.'

'Shit,' he agreed, whirling the ladle in the delicious witches brew before helping them both to more of its steaming contents. 'Hot.'

'You don't like the books?'

'I think they're formulaic,' he said flatly.

'As are Hollywood movies, soaps, magazines, newspapers. We devour formulas. This recipe is a formula.' She waved a forkful of paella around. 'It's still divine. What makes it unique is the execution, not the formula. Ptolemy Finch is divine!'

'And deserving of a fine execution.' He refilled his wine glass.

Legs had managed to keep hers half full and again held her hand over the rim to resist more. 'So what do you like to read?'

'Faces.' He stared unashamedly into hers.

Boy, was he unsettling. His expression was so critical, yet those dark eyes blazed with a lighthouse glow, steering her to safe harbour. She felt seasick.

'Read any good ones lately?'

'Just the usual trash.' He drank more wine, turning the tables on their already head-spinning dinner.

Legs ran her tongue around her teeth, refusing to rise. She was almost past the finishing line. The paella dish was all but empty. He had to give the Book Inn the thumbs-up if she just stayed calm and engaged him in light, flirtatious conversation.

She tried to think up a charming, generous way to open him up and loosen his tongue. Then she remembered something that Conrad had asked her during her first job interview which had made her laugh. She'd relaxed then, in a way that he later told her got her the job, making it hers no matter what her answer had been. 'So tell me, er,' she fudged past his missing Christian name, 'if you were a biscuit, which one would it be?'

As soon as she asked it, she realised how silly it sounded. It was hard to believe she'd been so bowled over by Conrad posing it in the first place, although she supposed coming out of the mouth of a literary maverick lent it psychological gravitas and deep absurdity, whereas from her lips it was just inane.

He looked blank. 'That's a non sequitur.'

'Is that a type of Italian cantucci?' Trying to salvage the situation with a cheery joke just made it ten times worse.

He drained his glass and refilled it, clearly trying to anaesthetise himself against her one-liners with Rioja.

She reddened, mortification crawling all over her as she changed conversational tack with mounting desperation. 'I saw you running earlier. I love a man who keeps fit. Do you do other sports?'

'Free climbing.'

'How thrilling. That must be so dangerous. Have you ever fallen?'

'Never.'

'How about in love?'

He looked at her levelly, not dignifying it with an answer.

'With someone you shouldn't have fallen in love with?' she was almost singing now, Buzzcocks in her head.

'Not lately.'

God, he was hard work.

The restaurant was crammed to the rafters. Despite being called from all sides, Nonny enveloped their table in fragranced exclusivity as she asked after the meal, patting Legs on the back before covertly signalling her with her eyes to hurry up. This was all far too subtle for squiffy Legs who raved a lot about the fantastic paella and was happy to acquiesce as Byrne asked for the pudding menu and requested more wine.

As Nonny wiggled seductively away, Legs noticed Byrne admiring her pert, tailored bottom.

'Is there a Mrs Byrne?' she asked, eager to charter a new course.

'There are many, my grandmother among them.' He drained his glass, tapping the edge of its base impatiently on the table as the full force of his eyes struck hers once more. 'I think a marriage of true minds takes too much artificial intelligence for me.' He fell gratefully on the arriving wine bottle and topped up his glass to the brim.

'Maybe you're waiting for a sublime cook?' she suggested kindly, covering her own glass once more as he swung the bottle across to fill it.

'I can cook for myself,' he assured her.

'Don't you get lonely?'

'I have plenty of company.'

'Must be very forgiving company if you only cook for yourself,' she mused. 'Or do you have lots of friends on a diet?'

He shot her a withering look, then glanced up as Anton began to clear. 'That was delicious. Chef is a talented man.'

'I will pass on your compliments, sir.'

The empty paella dish and plates were spirited away by the deadpan head waiter, whose only betrayal of glee was joyfully clicking heels and sashaying his pert buttocks, which Legs admired all the way to the swinging kitchen doors, not caring that Byrne was watching her critically. Two could play at bottom-ogling, she decided. She knew that she was behaving atrociously tonight, infantile and indiscreet and self-indulgent in equal measure. He made for completely disorienting company, so full of insight and disapproval, as though he could see straight into her soul and found it wholly lacking.

When Anton swaggered back, she lowered the standard to crotch-watching, simply because she knew Byrne was on her case. He tactfully said nothing.

The pudding list read so seductively it reignited her food lust, but she was damned if she'd show it.

'I'll pass.' She handed it back to Anton when he returned, feeling the bittersweet pinch of abstinence.

Ignoring her, Byrne ordered the dessert tasting menu for two. Legs was about to protest, but remembered that she was supposed to be helping the restaurant get a Michelin star and shut up. She'd already done enough damage.

'I have a sweet tooth.' He flashed his first smile in over an hour. 'You?'

'Just a sharp tongue.'

'To match the acid wit, I take it?' His gaze held hers.

'I was under the impression that you find my brand of humour very silly?'

The smile widened with laughter. 'Silliness is an underrated virtue. I take life far too seriously, Heavenly Pony, don't you think?'

'Maybe you've been reading too many miserable faces lately?'

'I like the one I'm reading now.' His eyes didn't leave hers.

'Not the usual trash then?' She suddenly didn't know what to do with her face.

'I thought it was fairly predictable at first, but it keeps taking me by surprise, and now I just can't figure out what happens next.'

Still under excitingly close scrutiny, Legs was struggling not to twitch and go cross-eyed as all her facial muscles developed hitherto unknown ticks. 'Probably got a lot of nasty plot twists and a sting in its tale,' she blustered. 'But then everyone lives happily ever after. Not really your thing, I should imagine.'

Those big, smouldering coal eyes glowed into hers. 'So you don't think I like happy endings, Heavenly Pony?'

He was the one getting a bit drunk now, she realised.

While she hadn't exactly sobered up, she had enough alarm bells ringing in her head to keep her senses on amber alert and advise extreme caution.

'I don't know you well enough to judge.'

Still his eyes stayed locked on hers. He said nothing, and Legs suddenly found it quite impossible to look away.

'I never judge a book by its cover,' she went on nervously, 'especially in a restaurant with so many covers.'

The candle between them was guttering. Dropping eye contact at last, Byrne ran a finger across the flickering yellow flame.

Legs was in nervous gabble mode now, 'I always used to wonder as a kid why they called it a naked flame when there were never any dressed flames. I suppose all their clothes would burn off.'

'Are old flames best naked or dressed, I wonder?' he asked quietly.

She swallowed uncomfortably.

Up came the eyes again, gaze trapping hers, 'Aren't you grown up enough to know not to play with fire, Allegra?'

Legs wasn't certain whether he was talking about the Francis situation, or something much closer to home that was threatening to ignite the table between them right now. She heard the alarm bells in her head again, this time joined by the screech of a smoke detector. She needed Conrad to come marching into the restaurant dressed as a firefighter, hose unrolled ready to douse the man who was now playing with her emotions as carelessly as a kid with matches shooting out sparks.

Even from their brief acquaintance, Legs saw that Byrne was arrogant, circuitous, and dangerously sexy. He had one-night-stand eyes and he had the better room. He'd be gone in the morning and she would never have to see him again.

I must be drunk to be this tempted, she realised giddily. Alcohol always fuelled her flirtatious streak.

A soft touch against her bare arm almost sent her into orbit as she leapt away, pulses thrumming.

But it was only Anton the waiter leaning past her to place the taster menu on the table, the serviette on his arm brushing her skin.

'It's just desserts, Allegra.' Byrne smiled across at her, those coal and fire eyes dancing like the flame of the guttering candle.

'Just desserts,' she repeated, looking at them, grateful to have more food as a distraction.

Greed overcame her once more as she regarded the tempting little ceramic miniatures and thimble-sized glasses, like doll's-house food. Her spoon clashed with Byrne's as they dived in, hooking it clean out of his hand. An entire pot of honeycomb sorbet was upended and spilled across the table. Without thinking, she dabbed her finger into the sweet, foamy spatter on the tablecloth directly in front of her and sucked it appreciatively.

She sensed Byrne's intent gaze resting on her.

'Sorry – that was really sluttish.' She reached for her napkin. 'I'm not normally this badly behaved.'

'That's a shame.' His voice was so quiet she could barely hear it.

The guttering candle let out a long, low hiss like a hot breath, then crackled as the fat end of the wick spluttered before bursting gaily into a brighter, death-throe flame. A lifelong flirt like Legs struggled not to cup her hands and breathe on the flames to fan them, however dangerous she knew that to be.

Then, looking up, she suddenly realised that the fire was out of control already.

His eyes trapped hers, and in that instant the spark between them combusted horribly and inappropriately, at least it did on Legs' side of the table. The water cooler office fantasy was nothing on this level of total, wipe-out attraction. Adrenalin and pheromones fuelled the blaze, as she felt lust grip her in a fire-fighter's lift. She wanted to climb across the table and seduce him there and then. With a monumental effort, she fought the wine and sugar rush that was warping her brain, reminding herself she had never had a one-night stand, and this was not the weekend to start.

It had been an over-emotional twenty-four hours, she told herself. Her craving for escapism had got out of control; being away from Conrad had made her weak-willed and fantasist. She needed to go to bed with a good book, not a stranger.

Byrne was still watching her face: 'Why do I have a feeling I've just reached a row of dots?'

Legs looked at him in confusion. 'I – um – I think I should – that is—'

A drumbeat started up in the main pub, making them both jump. *Boom, boom, boom.*

It broke the tension, like a gun blowing out a lock. Legs knew she had just seconds to make her escape or her sugar rush lust would take over again.

'You finish pudding; I'll order our coffees at the bar!' A triple espresso was just the chastity belt she needed. She fled with relieved glee, his eyes burning holes through her back.

Abandoning him to his rosewater and vanilla crème brûlée as she weaved away through the crowded tables, she distinctly heard him let out a long sigh, crack his spoon through the crisp caramel top and say, 'That's what I meant . . .'

Chapter 11

Mannequin cool now melting in the face of an overbooked restaurant and mutinously hungover chef, Nonny intercepted Legs en route to the bar. 'Guy is in pieces. Whatever were you *thinking* of ordering the paella?'

'You said to avoid the crab. Byrne loved it.'

'He'd better give us a Michelin star,' Nonny fretted. 'I've had to turn away our eight o'clock couple twice, and now I've lost them.'

Glancing up at the clock, Legs realised it was well past nine.

She still felt horribly squiffy as she weaved through to the bar to order coffee as the live act struck up, a jolly bluegrass band.

'What did Guy mean they were well connected?' She asked Tongue Piercing, who was looking rattled as she manned the optics.

'Check out the guitarist,' she lisped back, nodding at a chunky, bearded figure in dark glasses, hunched over a steel-stringed Gibson.

'Is that who I think it is?' she asked, but TP was gone.

Nursing two espressos and a most probably ill-advised Dark and Stormy Night-cap offered on the house, Legs backed into a dark corner, hoping Byrne didn't follow her and equally praying he did.

He did, looking sexy as hell, despite carrying a mock crock handbag.

'Yours I believe.' He handed it over and claimed a coffee, wincing at the volume of the band.

'Check out the guitarist,' she muttered in his ear, then wished she hadn't because he smelled intoxicatingly good.

'Am I supposed to know him?'

'Biggest hit of the decade. Married to a Hollywood superstar and yoga-juicing advocate. Has an organic farm in the Cotswolds. Voted world's sexiest man at least twice . . .'

But Byrne wasn't looking at the stage. He was looking into her face again and threatening to combust the room around them. Legs was certain the sparks coming off them would ignite her own clothing any minute, particularly as so much of it was artificial fibre.

Grasping around for something to say to douse the rising heat, she remembered her promise to her landlord. 'Guy wants me to sing with the band later,' she spluttered, sounding like an *X Factor* wannabe, but at least it dampened the flames, particularly as she had to repeat it three times before Byrne could hear over the music.

'You sing?' he shouted back.

'After a fashion; my parents had me classically trained as a child, but I've never had my sister's musical talent. I used to perform here with friends sometimes. The A&R men stayed away.' Her voice was going hoarse trying to be heard.

He steered her further into a dark recess. 'So you wanted to be a famous rock star?' He spoke into her ear, audible at last. She jumped away because her ear was scorching hornily, only to find the inferno was still blazing away in his eyes.

'For about five minutes,' she laughed nervously, glancing at the legend on stage. 'I could never cope with his life. If he sneezes, somebody sells the snot on eBay. Count the camera phones.'

Now they looked there were at least twenty, and Pierced Tongue was brazenly waving an HD camcorder over the bar.

'This will be all over YouTube by midnight.'

'So why is he here?'

'Because this is the closest to the old days he's ever going to get. Nobody's mobbing him, the paparazzi haven't heard he's here and it's too far to drive even if they did. Guy and Nonny know everybody who's anybody and tell nobody. That's a rare thing. I am the opposite.' She blushed as she realised she was leaning right up against him and had no idea how she'd got there. She jumped hastily away. 'I'm a hopeless blabbermouth, and would make a lousy celebrity,' she finished hurriedly.

'Hard to keep secrets if you're famous.' He watched her closely, his eyes like flame-throwers lighting up her libido.

'All one's bad habits would be exposed like a flash,' she agreed, backing quickly out of the recess so the music got too loud to speak and the clammy heat of the room soothed her lust-scorched skin.

Bad, bad habits like flirtatious, fickle all-out desire for a complete stranger, she told herself in a panic. She was practically sober again now, high grade espresso flushing her veins. She reminded herself that she was still in a relationship with Conrad and possibly still in love with Francis too, and life was much too complicated already.

Yet something kept her close to Byrne's orbit as he leaned against the back wall, finishing his coffee.

The lead singer was shouting out a catchy song about sowing seeds. Needing to dance to discharge, Legs bounced along enthusiastically and whooped at rhythmic intervals, showing off like mad but only succeeding in making Byrne back further away as her flailing arms threatened to upend his cup.

'You're right,' she called across to him. 'You do take life too seriously.' She let out a whoop, feet tapping, indicating for him to come and dance.

He shook his head with a tight smile then nodded towards the door and mouthed: 'Bed.'

Legs panted up to him. 'Spoilsport. I haven't even sung yet – not that I'm sure I'm up to singing in public right now.'

'So make your excuses and leave,' he suggested, his face giving nothing away.

It sounded like an invitation, Legs realised excitedly. Perhaps he wanted her to grant him a private audience. Terrified by the heat this idea sent coursing through her, she shook her head violently. 'I can't let Guy down.'

'Do you sing like you dance?' he asked, eyeing the stage with concern.

Legs suddenly realised that he might not be trying to drag her to bed after all, at least not his bed; he was simply eager to avoid the embarrassment of witnessing her making a fool of herself in front of a mic.

Anger chased disappointment straight to her outspoken mouth. 'I sing like I make love, with all my heart and never in public places unless I'm drunk. In fact, I need another drink. Mine's a Dark and Stormy Night.'

He didn't take the hint. Cheeks hollowing, he gave the band a last glance, all the time melting away from her. He was leaving, she realised. Suddenly she couldn't bear the idea. He was almost out of the room now. She had no idea what she wanted to say, except that she didn't want him to go. She marked him to the door.

'I love to sing, I love to drink Scotch.' She put on her best George Burns accent, resorting to Francis's old tactic of quoting for the want of emoting. 'Most people would rather hear me drink Scotch.'

He lent against the doorframe and turned back to her, almost flooring her with the intensity of his eyes. 'We all drink to forget.'

She was still doing George: 'Actually it takes just one drink to get me loaded – trouble is I can't remember whether it's the thirteenth or the fourteenth.'

'Stop it,' he snapped. 'This isn't you, Allegra.'

'No, it's your namesake, Byrne baby – Burn. He also said: sincerity is everything; if you can fake that, you've got it made.'

'Shut up.' He almost shouted it at her.

She fell silent, just as the band struck up with a cover of one of her favourite Alison Krauss tracks 'New Favourite'. Oh the gentle, sultry truth in the words, sung with such soft sentiment, telling of betrayal and lost love. To her shame, tears started welling in her eyes.

In front of her, Byrne didn't move.

A few members of the pub audience were dancing around them, knocking them closer together. Suddenly Byrne took her shoulder and wrist, none too softly, and manoeuvred her in a jolting, disunited dance back towards their quiet corner.

'I think you should leave tonight,' he told her in an urgent undertone.

'Don't be ridiculous. I'm far too drunk to drive.'

'I'll call you a taxi.'

She peered at him through the gloom in astonishment. Well, it certainly wasn't an invitation to his room. His chiselled, intense face was grave, the big dark eyes burning with embers of high emotion.

'Where would I go?'

'Back to London.' His hand tightened on her wrist.

'That's crazy. I can't leave the situation here like this.'

'That's precisely what you should do. Don't try to backtrack in life. It never works. You can't change fate. Believe me, I know better than anybody.'

The ballad came to an end to more enthusiastic applause. Legs had to raise her voice to be heard: 'How come?'

'Because, dear Allegra, I too have tried to play God and failed.' His eyes didn't leave hers, his words clearly audible now the band had stopped playing and the volume in the room dropped to hushed chatter. 'And now I am about to lose my life as a consequence.'

Legs had swilled an awful lot of cocktail, wine and caffeine that night, and wasn't entirely sure she'd heard him right, but there was something about his fierce expression that told her asking him to repeat himself would not be wise.

I am about to lose my life as a consequence. It echoed in her ears. *I am about to lose my life.*

With sudden clarity, she realised why he took life too seriously. He hadn't much of it left to live.

She felt faint with shock. Her tearful eyes went almost blind, a tsunami of hot, salty compassion flooding them. As his grip loosened at last on her wrist, she felt her hand slide instinctively into his palm and her fingers thread through his.

At that moment there was a shriek of feedback. Behind them, Guy had stepped on stage, looking grey and hungover in his chef's whites as he muttered a malevolent request to the bearded singer. He started talking to the audience, something about an old friend who was always getting into trouble, making his loyal regulars and happy holidaymakers laugh.

Unable to take her eyes from Byrne's, Legs didn't hear a word, the blood rushing through her veins almost deafening her.

'You're not a Michelin judge at all, are you?' she asked.

Byrne looked at her curiously.

'Nonny thinks you are. She'd do anything to get Guy a star.'

He let go of her hand as though given an electric shock. 'That's why you joined me tonight?'

Seeing his angry indignity, she shook her head: 'You invited me. I'm absolutely hopeless at the schmoozing anybody, as you saw. And you—'

'They're calling your name,' he interrupted.

'Allegra North!' Guy was demanding into the mic, to a round

of whistles and applause. 'Step forward and sing for your supper, baby.'

She let out a bleat of panic, gazing at Byrne, whose big blazing eyes blinked once, twice, and then he looked down so that all she could see was his lashes, no longer fanning the forest fire that was still torching her.

'I want to stay and talk to you,' she said.

'Allegra!' Guy was repeating. They'd start slow hand clapping in a minute.

'Sing.' Byrne stepped away.

She glanced fearfully at the stage, heart racing.

'Sing for your supper, girl!' Guy was beckoning her to the microphone with frantic hand gestures as the band struck up 'Coat of Many Colours'.

She looked back to Byrne, but he had disappeared into the darkness at the back of the room.

Coffee catching in her throat, Legs shot a look of apology and fear at her heroic paella-cooking host and stepped forwards, accepting a steel-stringed Gibson from the bearded singer and slotting its strap around her neck. She ran her fingers along the strings to check that it was in tune. Then she sang:

> *Back through the years*
> *I go wanderin' once again*
> *Back to the seasons of my youth . . .*

She winced as the first lines came out, knowing that she had launched into the wrong key. She was flat as a bad karaoke crooner.

The crowded bar was already shifting awkwardly, a few catcalls and titters of laughter ringing out.

She abruptly shut up, face flaming.

The band behind her ground to an unsettled halt.

She couldn't see Byrne anywhere. Guy in his chefs whites was now knocking back a Bloody Mary at the bar, looking vengeful.

'Wrong song,' she apologised brightly to her embarrassed audience, retuning the bass string and muttering over her shoulder, 'Key of D. You'll pick it up as I go along.' She turned back to the mic, trying to stop her voice from shaking. 'I want to dedicate this song to a friend, to say I'm sorry. I hope he'll understand.

'You can't judge an apple by looking in the tree.' Her voice rang out through the crowded bar as true, bright and smoky sweet as a flare over the cliffs.

The steel strings danced and hummed as she plucked and strummed the catchy old Bo Diddley number 'You Can't Judge a Book by its Cover'.

When she sang true, Legs could take the breath from a room. On she sang, through sweet verses that she had first learned with the Lookout gang over a decade earlier, jamming out to sea on an ancient Spanish guitar, maracas and a tambourine.

'Can't you see, oh you misjudge me.' She repeated the chorus and then faltered as she heard a voice join hers onstage. Her fingers froze on the guitar strings, suddenly glued into stiff bunches.

'Oh I look like a farmer, but I'm a lover,' belted a bass harmony behind her.

Recognising the new band-member, a number of villagers in the audience began to whoop.

'You can't judge a book by . . .' Legs turned to look at Francis, and the words died in her throat. His blond hair was wet with sea spray and there was sand on his boots. He looked tired and drawn, but those blue eyes that smiled into hers were filled with affection. They hadn't shared this stage for over three years, not since a stupid row when they'd performed a lock-in rendition of 'Diamonds and Rust' and she'd accused him of playing harmonica all over her lyrics. Musical like his father, able to play many instruments from piano to fiddle and pick up a tune by ear, Francis had always taken to the stage with easy-going confidence before that. Coming back tonight marked a sea change.

Behind them, the band was making an effort to keep going, but they'd lost the rhythm as the main guitar melody and both singers fell silent.

With sterling effort, Legs strummed out one final refrain, trying not to wince as she and her ex duetted like Sonny and Cher. The locals clearly loved it. What would Byrne think?

Her eyes scoured the bar, but he was nowhere to be seen. A flash of tossed red hair, however, made her heart plummet in trepidation as she saw Kizzy, predictably stunning in a midnight-blue silk tunic which fell off one shoulder to reveal the slender curve of her freckled collarbone, and spray-on white skinny jeans that showed off her fantastic legs. Aware of her own great tree trunks planted on top of feet of clay, Legs shuffled away from the mic and took a hasty bow, acknowledging first the band and then Francis with a clumsy sweep of the arm that inadvertently meant she clouted him across the head.

The room erupted into applause and cheers and whoops.

Recovering from his head blow, Francis stepped forwards to bestow another kiss on his ex-fiancées cheek, to yet more whoops. Talk of tonight's performance would be all over the village tomorrow, possibly even outstripping the bearded organic farmer rock-star's secret gig for Farcombe headline news.

Looking at Kizzy again, Legs was just in time to catch her wink at Francis before making a very theatrical flouncing exit, equally guaranteed to get tongues wagging.

Francis hastily steered Legs to the far end of the bar, which was dark and quiet. All the time her eyes raked the room for Byrne, but part of her knew that he had long gone.

'I think that went rather well, don't you?' Francis looked very pleased with himself.

She turned to him furiously, adrenalin still chasing Rioja and coffee through her veins, 'I can't believe you pulled a stunt like that without warning me.'

'Pure happenstance.' He was high on adrenalin, tanned cheeks streaked with damson. 'Thought I'd pop in for a drink with Kizz, and there you were. Perfect opportunity.'

She eyed him with disbelief. 'I wish I knew what gives between you two.'

'Total understanding,' he said breezily. 'I must say, I'd forgotten we used to sing all that old Bo Diddly stuff. That was a blast.' His eyes glittered into hers, that strange newfound affection, along with a nervous energy she remembered from his finals.

Pierced Tongue appeared with two Happy Ever Afters: 'Compliments of the boss. He's had to get back to the kitchens, but he says to tell you that song would have easily paid for your supper if the tab hadn't already been settled. Biggest tip of the year, too.'

'Settled by whom?' Legs asked.

But PT was already answering a shout at the opposite end of the bar.

Francis picked up the glass and drained a third of the velvety but lethal Baileys, Kahlua and Amaretto concoction. 'Wow, they know how to mix them. Why haven't you replied to my texts, Legs?' His blue gaze traced every angle on her face.

Aware that far more eyes in the Book Inn were on them than the band that had now regrouped to sing 'I Will Always Love You', she pushed her glass away and shifted awkwardly.

'My phone's dead. I haven't got a charger with me. I'll ask Nonny if she has one later.'

'Are you coming to supper tomorrow?' His hand covered hers, that beautiful young lion's paw with its scuffed claws, playfully predatory yet capable of drawing real blood.

'I haven't decided.' She pulled her hand away, but he gripped her fingers.

'Everyone's watching,' she hissed, edging away.

'I don't care.'

'That's just because you want us to be seen together so that your father hears about it.'

'It's because I don't bloody care. Just as I don't care who sees this.' He planted a kiss straight on her lips, a sweet, angry breath of such longing that Legs' automatic spring mechanism lifted her on her toes and she felt the stitching give way on her boys' age-ten T-shirt. As the kiss stretched from intense to intimate to mating ritual, the band belted out their chorus, '*Ieeeieeeiiiii will always love youuuuueeeooooeooooo.*'

The stage manager had executed the perfect cue.

Legs pulled away first, faint with shame and desire.

'Like the man just said . . . I will – always . . .' He went quiet, taking a long breath before looking up at her, eyes as determined, blue and horny as a pillaging Viking's. 'Shall we go to bed?' Even Francis the Viking was gentlemanly enough to ask, ever the most courteous of seducers.

Self-preservation was a rare visitor to Legs' life, but tonight it clamped her in a strait-jacket embrace of exhaustion and sexual confusion. She was far too muddled and angst-ridden. And she had the perfect haven in which to recover.

'I'm in Skit,' she told him.

If there was one thing Francis was more terrified of than talking about his feelings, it was bats. Not that he betrayed his fear for a moment, as he nodded, breathed 'tomorrow' in her ear and then lent forward to land another kiss on her lips, this one an exquisitely light farewell that lingered just long enough for Legs' untrustworthy reflex action to cause her lips to part and momentarily wish she hadn't brought bats to his mind.

With his trademark polite nod, he turned and walked out.

Legs' lips were on fire. The kiss might have been perfectly timed by a consummate pro, but there was no denying the passion. Nobody could kiss like that just for show, surely?

She abandoned her Happy Ever After untouched and headed up to Skit on legs like jelly. There, she sagged back on her dusty bed, singing hollowly to the ceiling: '*Can't you see, whoa you've misjudged me.*'

Bloody Byrne hadn't misjudged her at all, she writhed guiltily.

He had seen into her shabby soul, so fickle it transferred affection faster than a stray dog passing on fleas, desperate to be loved but ultimately destined to be cast aside for a super-loyal pedigree bred for the job.

Overhead the horseshoe bats flapped about mumsily, feeding their young broods and guarding the best pitches in the vast roof void.

She let out a low groan as a sharp sword of pain was drawn from the soft scabbard of her belly. Her period which was due on Monday had decided to stage an early appearance. No wonder she'd been behaving like a demented, angry, tearful sex maniac all night.

Remembering that her tampons were in her weekend bag with Nico at Inkpot Farm, Legs wearily trailed down to the bar and found Nonny waving off the last customers, still looking as immaculate as she had at the start of her six hour shift.

She took Legs' black-screened phone, 'I'll charge this for you, but you'll have to plunder the Ladies for tampons. I haven't had a period since my last coil was fitted. Guy says I've been switched to digital. Tell me,' she collared Legs before she could escape, 'are you and Fran really staging a comeback?'

'Oh, we're just – hmm – making friends again,' she bluffed badly, wishing that she knew Nonny well enough for a heart to heart, but she was far too jumpy and tired right now, her head already thundering with an approaching hangover of industrial proportions.

'Good for you.' Nonny creased her pretty eyes, still perfectly made up. 'Mind you, I think I can speak for everybody in saying we'll be over the moon if you two *do* get back together. Kizzy's a very odd fish. Hector calls her the Maenad Machiavelli; he thinks she's quite mad; you should have heard him ranting down here when they were first together. Half the village thinks she's Poppy's love child, you know.'

Legs took a moment to register this. 'Love child! With whom?'

'Neptune? You know what Farcombe's like for rumours. The other half think she's a mermaid washed up to avenge Farcombe Hall of sinful Protheroes. Do you think our Michelin man enjoyed his meal, by the way?' She suddenly changed topic, making Legs' tired head spin again, filled with images of Francis and Kizzy as two amoebas cast in stone.

'He loved the food,' she said eventually, appalled to find her eyes filling with tears as she thought about what Byrne had told her about losing his life, after all her ogling, confiding and bad dancing. She should have 'Trollop 28' written across her back instead of 'Walcott 14'. No wonder he'd even offered to pay for her cab back to London, poor man. Her hormones were in utter havoc tonight. She'd probably put him off women for life – whatever life he had left.

Nonny, who only cared about Guy's Michelin star, patted her arm gratefully. 'Thank you for this evening, Legs. We've missed you. Now get some sleep. And I know you'll hate me for this right now, but,' – she stood on tiptoes to breathe in Legs' ear – 'rethink the shiny tight T-shirt look, honey.'

Having plundered the machine in the Ladies, using all her pound coins, Legs trailed stiffly up to bed, stomach cramping, all the time alternating between spasms of shame about her dinner with Byrne, and obsessing about Francis and the fishy, flame-haired poet.

In the early hours, she suddenly sat up, remembering something Byrne had said: 'Shotgun wedding. Poppy's first marriage was a shotgun wedding. Bloody hell. Kizzy *must* be Poppy's daughter!'

Still mildy squiffy and riddled with stomach cramps, she got up and paced around her room beneath the restless bats, trying to ease her discomfort and make sense of the situation.

This had to be the secret Francis wasn't telling her; he was being held to ransom by Poppy and Kizzy in some way. Byrne was wrong; this wasn't about Francis wanting revenge, this was about him needing to be rescued. She had to get to the truth and then try to help him.

Chapter 12

Legs woke up far too hungover to face the Book Inn's award-winning cooked breakfast in the restaurant, which at least spared her any risk of bumping into Byrne. He had haunted her dreams all night, telling her his dying wishes as they swayed together in a smoky dance hall while Francis sang Bing Crosby numbers into an old fifties RCA microphone on stage, dressed in a tuxedo. She now couldn't remember what those wishes had been, but she had a feeling they had involved her mending her immoral ways.

Signing the Pledge would be a good start, she decided as she crawled to the bathroom and crouched over the sink with the cold tap directed at her face and mouth until the pounding in her head abated from hydraulic kanga to hand-held sledgehammer. Then she took a run to punish herself for her excess, wearing her dark glasses and her nephew's *Clone Wars* baseball cap pulled low over her nose. To her relief, she didn't bump into Byrne on the cliff paths. She hoped he had already checked out.

But when she panted into the Book Inn's back lobby, feeling as though she was sweating Rioja from every pore, she was greeted by Guy looking far brighter than he had the night before, his big hammer jaw widened by a smile that made his eyes disappear in delighted creases.

'How the tables turn,' he laughed. 'You look like you need a Bloody Mary Shelley. It's my secret recipe – lots of beetroot juice and horseradish vodka.'

'Oh, please no.' She waved her arms on front of her, catching her breath.

'Your performance last night is already the talk of the village.'

She pulled off her cap and raked back her sweaty hair, unable to resist a little puffed-out probing: 'Surely they're far more interested in Poppy Protheroe's sea-nymph love child?'

'Who?'

'Kizzy de la Mere.'

'You've obviously been talking to Nonny,' he tutted. 'She loves those mermaid rumours. Everyone round here figures Kizzy's not the Hawkeses' real daughter, but nobody knows the truth.' He leaned forwards and whispered. 'I've heard that her real mother was The Black Widow of Bideford, a gold-digging siren who married very old men for their money.'

'Well, that's reassuring.' She crammed her hat back on, glancing up nervously as she heard feet bounding downstairs, but it was just a young couple heading for breakfast with cheery 'good mornings'.

'Is Mr Byrne still here?' she asked Guy after they'd gone through.

His big, battered face lit up. 'Very dark horse, our Michelin judge. Ordered Frosties in bed for breakfast, and grilled kidneys for his dog, then booked for three more nights. And this is for you.' He handed her a Book Inn postcard with a message scrawled on the back: *Heavenly Pony, You were inspiring company last night. I was wrong; you can change hearts and minds, certainly about Paella Valenciana. With thanks. J*

'You – we – were a hit, baby.' Guy grinned, having read the card. 'He *loved* the paella!'

She reread it, wondering what J stood for. Please don't let it be Jeremy.

'And the band loved *you* too,' Guy was saying. 'You can have a meal on the house tonight.'

'I'm eating at the hall tonight,' she said vaguely, turning to go back upstairs, unaware that she had just unleashed another piece of Farcombe village gossip to be served out at the bar all day along with cocktails and tapas.

Inspiring company . . . change heart? Legs reread the note as she carried it up to Skit. And why was he staying longer? Could she have haunted his dreams too?

She already deeply regretted telling him so much about her current situation and her muddled feelings for Francis, which seemed to change with the tides. Last night she'd felt herself shipwrecked with a case of Rioja and a passing stranger to confide in. Now she couldn't shake Byrne and his fierce eyes from her consciousness. His insight and sex appeal alarmed her. He'd seemed to look straight into her heart and find it false, blasting all her claims of divided loyalty against the rocks as she'd shamelessly moved on from protesting love for both lover and ex to making eyes at the sexy stranger himself.

Then she sat down in her doorway and felt icy cold as she remembered him saying, 'I am about to lose my life.'

Spywood Cottage was deserted and locked when Legs arrived, her teeth chattering despite the fact she was wearing two jumpers. They were Nico's, and were so tight they rose up her midriff and arms like Peter Rabbit's clothes crammed on Hartley Hare. Although the sun was climbing the sky without a cloud crossing its path, she still felt bitterly cold.

Her mother's car was parked on the track so she couldn't be far away. Sitting on the wood-wormed bench by the porch, she wondered vaguely whether Francis had tried to make contact since last night's public kiss. Her mobile phone was still plugged into Nonny's charger at the Book Inn.

Experiencing another shudder of cold embarrassment, she headed down to the cove.

Sure enough, Lucy was close to the rocks directly beneath the steep path, where she had set up her easel overlooking the harbour. Although Eascombe cove was private, she was at least wearing clothes as a concession to passing dog walkers. Dressed in an old sleeveless denim dress, her soft shoulders tanned to the colour of speckled hen's eggs, she looked up from beneath her floppy straw hat as Legs clambered down.

'Be careful, it's crumbling more than ever,' she called up, stepping back as a shower of scree from Legs' slipping feet landed close by. 'Someone will fall to their death here one day.'

'You've been saying that for twenty years,' Legs reminded her, perching on the rocks behind her to admire the watercolour.

'I've been saying I'll capture this to my satisfaction for twenty years, too,' Lucy sighed, pointing at the distant harbour which was glittering with light and jostling with boat masts that poked up from behind its high walls like an army's pikes, 'and I haven't managed it yet. One or the other of them will finish me off, that's for sure.'

'It's looking good.' Legs admired the preparatory sketches.

'All it needs is an attractive girl sunbathing in the foreground,' Lucy hinted.

'Far too cold to sunbathe.' She shuddered, unscrewing the top of her mother's Thermos to sniff its contents, her skipped breakfast having left her with serious caffeine deprivation.

'Bovril.' Lucy laughed at her expression.

'Since when did you start drinking Bovril?' Legs hurriedly screwed the top back on.

'Hector likes it.'

'He's not here is he?' She looked around anxiously.

'He was going to come down and play his bassoon for the seagulls, but he's been summoned to an emergency meeting of the festival committee this morning.'

'That figures.'

'He looked terribly stern when he set out.'

'Poppy wants to call off the whole event.'

'She threatens the same thing every year.'

'This year is rather different.' Legs selected a paintbrush from the roll lying on her mother's little folding table and flicked its dry bristles across the tip of her nose.

'I know this must feel like hell to you.' Lucy stepped away from the easel and perched alongside her, covering her hand with a warm grip. She was still wearing her wedding ring, Legs noticed with relief.

She nodded mutely, paintbrush up one nostril, shamefully

aware that her hangover was eclipsing the most hellish of her feelings quite satisfactorily, both her fury at her mother's behaviour and her shame at her own. But her bad mood still niggled beneath the sense-dulling headache.

Her mother's face, once so pretty with its full lips and upturned nose, had been gently sinking south for many years now with ever-darkening bags beneath her kind blue eyes and a puffy little double chin that she hated. This summer's deep tan and the highlighted hair gave an impression of youthfulness, but today, make-up free, she looked terribly tired.

Too much sex, Legs thought sourly. 'I'm sure Poppy's throwing every threat at Hector right now to try to talk him back into her bed.' She narrowed her eyes, watching for a reaction.

The hand on hers was carefully removed. 'Throwing things rarely leads to romantic reconciliation in my experience.'

'I'll bear that in mind.'

'You've seen Francis again, I take it?'

Legs tried not to think about last night's kiss in the bar. 'We're just throwing curveballs.'

'But you two are talking again?'

'Three guesses what the main topic of conversation has been.'

Lucy looked out to sea, her voice controlled and calm. 'You said you came to Farcombe on festival business.'

'Yes, we're in discussion about a new guest speaker,' she said self-importantly. 'If the committee manages to persuade Poppy to let the festival go ahead, they'll be voting on it today. Then the printers will be notified of a change to the programme: "scratch 'Stevie Smith for the Ecstasy Generation', pencil in Gordon Lapis".'

'Gordon Lapis?' Lucy almost fell off the rock. 'Here at Farcombe Festival?'

She nodded. 'So his agent hopes.'

'Surely Poppy will never agree to it?'

'It seems she's not averse, but then again she's hardly been herself lately.' She shot Lucy a meaningful look.

'Francis must be over the moon. Gordon Lapis. What a coup!'

'Why throw things when you can drop names?' Legs shifted awkwardly. 'Although I doubt the committee will share his enthusiasm, even with Poppy on side. Ptolemy Finch stands for everything they detest. And I can't see the Titian poet surrendering top billing very graciously.'

'Oh Kizzy will love the notoriety,' Lucy said sharply.

Legs turned to her mother in surprise. Her guilt about Francis was seeping through the sides as it always did, and she couldn't resist asking, 'What do you know about her?'

'Not a lot. Just that she started working for the festival last year and then set her sights on Francis.'

'History repeating itself then.'

'She's very clever, I gather, and *very* ambitious.' Lucy watched her daughter's reaction closely, noting the pinched tightness around her red eyes as they blinked repeatedly. 'It's natural to be jealous, darling.'

'I am not jealous. Francis had every right to find a new lover, as will Dad now,' she huffed, lowering the paintbrush and using the end of its handle to dig into the gritty depths of a sea-lashed groove running through the rock she was sitting on.

Lucy refused to rise, looking out to the harbour again.

'I heard that Kizzy might be Poppy's daughter,' Legs confided. 'If so, rumour has it she's only seducing Francis to get her hands on her birthright.'

But her mother just laughed. 'That's ridiculous. Aren't these things forbidden by law?'

'They're not related. Anyway, Francis might not know her true parentage.'

'Now you really are getting absurd, Legs darling. I know you love all those exaggerated crime thrillers you read non-stop, but you must learn to temper your imagination. These things just don't happen.'

'And there was me thinking that you and Hector have been

madly in love with each other for years without telling another soul, but of course that's way too far fetched . . .'

'Don't be facetious,' Lucy snapped. 'Besides, I have always confided in one or two close friends. Babs Foulkes has known all along.'

'Babs?' Legs gasped, wondering how much Daisy knew. Mother and daughter shared every secret.

But Lucy was eager to get off the subject, 'I think you must be wrong about Kizzy, darling. For a start, I'm sure Poppy's child was a boy . . .'

'How old was he when she ran off?'

'Oh, I don't know; he must be about the same age as you, so he'd have been about ten maybe?'

'So he could have had a sex change in adulthood?' She counted through the years. 'Kizzy could be a twenty-seven-year-old transsexual, don't you think?'

Lucy chuckled, and patted her daughter's knee. 'As I said, it's natural to be jealous.'

But Legs refused to be entirely dissuaded: 'With that boyish physique, gender reassignment is a real possibility. If Kizzy's father was a jockey, then they're all tiny and fine-boned, hence no giveaway clues like being six foot with an Adam's apple. It all makes perfect sense; now he/she's returned to exact revenge for being abandoned by Poppy. Being abandoned by a mother is life-shattering,' she muttered, adding darkly, 'especially when she runs away with Hector Protheroe.'

'Now you're just winding me up.' Lucy returned to her easel, comparing the lines on the paper with those of the harbour and letting out a dissatisfied sigh, no longer happy with her composition.

'There's definitely something Francis isn't telling me,' Legs persisted.

'I should think there's a lot he isn't telling you, given what you did to him.' She picked up her pencil and changed the outline of the headland. 'You're just transferring guilt, Legs.'

'He's frightened of her.'

'He's frightened of any woman that doesn't mother him,' Lucy sighed, getting into her Freudian swing now. She'd been a home-spun counsellor ever since discovering *A Road Less Travelled* at a second-hand book fair.

'I never mothered him!'

'You mothered him from the age of eleven, darling. From what Hector says, Kizzy is a very different kettle of fish; more sea siren than earth mother. He dislikes her intensely.' She rubbed out the line she'd just drawn and tried again, 'But she is Poppy's vassal of course.'

'And possible long-lost transsexual son,' Legs muttered.

Lucy pretended not to hear. 'Given you are now Conrad's play-thing, one can hardly blame Francis for going on the rebound so wholeheartedly. And Kizzy is very pretty.'

'How *dare* you say that!' She threw the paintbrush back on the table where it rolled onto the shingle below.

Lucy stooped to pick it up. 'Well, maybe not as pretty as you, although I'm not sure that tight jumper look suits you, frankly.'

'Not that, the thing about being Conrad's plaything.'

She turned around and crossed her arms. 'Who sent you here this weekend, Legs?'

'He didn't "send" me!'

'It's obvious he did. He treats you appallingly, refusing to let you share anything much of his life beyond work, not wanting to meet your family and friends, abandoning you at weekends, then expect-ing you to be available throughout the week to cross London at all hours. Now this! You don't have to stay with him just to prove that you made the right decision, Legs, to validate what you did to Francis.'

'I've had this lecture.' She looked away sulkily.

'Then you have been getting some wise advice. You should heed it. If you still love Francis, tell him.'

'I love Conrad.' Even as she said it, she felt uncertainty prickle her scalp.

'Don't be ridiculous! It's just an infatuation. That ghastly man has taken advantage of your kindness long enough.'

'Pot kettle black!' Legs fumed, then eyed her mother suspiciously. 'What would you and Hector do if Francis and I got back together? Because a double wedding's out of the question.'

'If you two are still in love and determined to marry, we wouldn't be able to carry on.' She mixed a dash of French ultramarine into the wash to capture the growing intensity of the sky.

Mind whirring, Legs pulled down her cuffs and shivered, hugging herself for warmth. 'This is a double bluff, isn't it?'

'Darling, you've lost me. I never understand bluffs and double bluffs. You're the one who loves reading crime thrillers.'

'Promise me that you and Hector aren't staging this affair to try and get Francis and me back together?'

The sky in Lucy's painting was getting ever more purple. 'Hector and I understand one another very deeply.'

'Oh shit.' Legs closed her eyes. 'You are.'

'That's your opinion.' Lucy rinsed her brush in her water pot and started to mix up a wash of ultramarine, gunmetal and cedar green into a very unlikely-coloured sea, humming the tune to 'She'.

'Dad called you a martyr to the cause,' Legs remembered with a gasp. 'Is he in on it too?'

The humming stopped abruptly. The rattle of brush against water pot grew faster.

'I don't want to talk about your father.' From the tone of her voice, Legs knew that if pressed, Lucy would just clam up, an evasion tactic she'd passed on to Ros, who held the family record for not speaking a word: eight days.

Instead she pulled a loose thread of rubber from her plimsolls and admitted: 'Poppy's invited me to supper at the hall this evening. There'll be her usual cronies, with Francis and Kizzy in full mating plumage no doubt. It's obvious she's expecting me to make a big scene.' She shuddered anxiously, imagining herself pointing at Kizzy across the drawing room and shouting 'I know you're a man!'

Lucy splatted more wash onto her drawing before it was fully blended so the pigment in the brush clotted on the paper. 'So what are you going to do?'

'I don't know. I have to sort out the Gordon Lapis situation. It's too important; I can't let it cross over to what's happening with Francis. It's not just my career, it's Conrad's, the agency's reputation and our biggest star's welfare at stake. If I let my personal life intrude, I risk all that.'

'Life *is* muddled up, darling, especially if you sleep with your boss.' A great splash of Paynes Grey hit the paper now, carving out watery rocks. 'You can't separate it out.'

'I've already had that career lecture this week too, thanks.' Legs rested her chin on her knees, squinting up at the sun. Remembering the previous evening made a blush of heat creep up her neck to her face.

Suddenly very hot, she tried to pull off her jumper, but it was too tight to wriggle out of without a serious amount of contortion, so she pulled it back down and shuffled into the shade. 'I was also told in no uncertain terms that you can't force people in and out of love.'

'Wise words.' Lucy had mixed a wash of sepia and umber for the foreshore which she applied with angry brushstrokes. 'But remember you broke Francis's heart in the first place. That was immensely cruel, deliberate or not.'

Legs looked at the painting that was forming on the paper. Already it was wrong, all the potential of the delicate pencil drawing undermined by such clumsy splashes of paint. However carefully she sketched out her life, one impetuous brushstroke could ruin it, she realised. In London, her rash decisions coloured every day, but life was too fast paced to stop and examine the detail. Here in Farcombe, surrounded by the dreams she and Francis had laid down over so many summers, she was acutely aware of her path of destruction, like vivid red ink spilled across their clean white canvas.

Stepping back to assess the work in progress, Lucy tutted under her breath, seeing its failings too.

Legs hugged her knees even more tightly and turned her face away to hide the tears. 'Did I really break his heart so badly?'

'You shattered it, darling.' Lucy laid down her brush and looked at her over one shoulder, her face incredibly sad. 'That pretty red-head might have picked up all the pieces but she's making a big mess gluing them back in the wrong order. He's changed so much, and not for the better.'

'Oh, poor Francis.' Turning her head, Legs watched her mother pick up her paintbrush again and begin speckling ochre and umber shingle onto her painting.

'I believe Kizzy's no more right for him than Conrad is for you, but you both have to learn that the hard way, it seems.' Lucy splattered and splodged the paper. 'Just tread very carefully.'

'I'm always cautious around vengeful transsexuals.' Legs shuddered, wondering if she should take Byrne's advice and head straight back to London. But if Francis was under threat, she owed it to him to stay put and go through with this. She had to make amends. 'Have you ever heard of the Black Widow of Bideford?'

'I don't think I've ever been there,' Lucy said vaguely. 'Is it in the Good Pub Guide?'

'Very popular for wakes, I'm told.' Legs propped her chin on her knees.

Her mother was watching her closely again. '*Do* you want Francis back?'

Legs gazed at the painting, now a sludgy mess of browns and greys all bleeding into one another. It had looked so crisp and full of potential when she first saw it. 'I miss what we once had more than anything,' she said with feeling.

'The two of you shared something very rare and so special,'

Lucy agreed. 'It's such a waste not to try to recapture it. You owe Francis that much.' Her words echoed Legs' thoughts.

For a moment mother and daughter exchanged a look of understanding as the wind lifted their hair with invisible fingers and the waves sighed contentedly on the shingle. Then Legs ruined the moment completely by asking, 'And you'll go back to Dad soon?'

Lucy looked hugely irritated, turning back to her work.

'That's my business,' she snapped, ripping her wet watercolour from the easel and casting it aside before starting to mask up another sheet. 'I might take new lovers; I might wear purple and a hat that doesn't suit me; I might even have a sex change and enact terrible revenge on all who have wronged me. It's *my* life, Legs, and right now I am enjoying living it.'

Legs had a sudden vision of herself after thirty years' marriage to Francis, looking much as her mother did now and behaving much as her mother was now, although of course she'd already done that. 'Live for the moment, live with the consequences,' she breathed.

'Yes!' Lucy agreed triumphantly. After many decades of leading the younger generation by example, which quite plainly does not work, I'm finally taking a leaf out of your book and trying not to think beyond tomorrow.'

'I'm so not like that!'

Lucy said nothing. It was clearly the beginning of one of her long silent stand-offs, Legs realised. There was absolutely no point staying to shout at the waves when she had a mystery to solve. She had a duty to find out what was going on at Farcombe Hall; she owed it to Francis, as well as to Gordon. Her detective's nose scented intrigue and danger as surely as laying her Starbucks coffee beside a pile of new crime manuscripts. This was a task for Julie Ocean, despite being unarmed and unconvincing dressed in her undercover disguise as a young Arsenal fan.

She tried to think what Julie would do if faced with a dinner invitation like Poppy's, hosted by a highly manipulative agoraphobic whose guests included Julie's embittered ex-lover, now shacked up with a vengeful transsexual, whose super-ambitious parents would also be in attendance, along with a mysterious American academic and Vin Keiller-Myles, a man intent on acquiring Farcombe at any cost. Not to mention sharp-tongued Édith, Francis's half-sister, who had once been expelled from a top boarding school for planting a bomb beneath the head-master's car.

What would Julie's first instinct be?

'I'm going shopping.' She scrambled back up the perilous path.

'I rest my case,' Lucy muttered, just loudly enough to be heard. As Legs turned she saw her mother start to draw the harbour afresh.

Chapter 13

Headache now screaming in her ears and stabbing her temples, Legs hurried back to Farcombe, quite forgetting the need to buy another parking ticket for the Honda in her haste to get to the fishing village's one and only overpriced boutique before it closed for lunch.

She Sells Seashells – known to all as 'Shh' – was run by ageing temptress Cici, who had bought the little shop with her divorce settlement five years earlier. Shh contained an eccentric mix of beachwear, old ladies' twinsets and just occasionally a hidden fashion gem. The front window was its owner's post-divorce tour de force, a dramatic installation of driftwood, chains, organza, ribbon, chicken wire and crystals. Scattered throughout were photographs of Cici as a young glamourpuss, many of them accompanied by a man whose face she had carefully cut out. Several were wedding photographs. Into this packed mix she occasionally squeezed an item of stock, so that the overall effect was of a beach where a suicidal woman had examined her life in photographs before stripping off all her clothes and swimming out to sea.

Today, a few twisted looking rags were draped over the rocks, weighed down with beads and pebbles. A handmade card beside them read 'New Catwalk Collection'.

As soon as she heard the bell ping, Cici appeared with a dramatic sweep through the velvet curtain that divided her storeroom from the shop. With silvery blonde hairpieces piled up on her head like a nest of sleeping chinchillas, she was dressed in a T-shirt covered in leaping gold leopards, very shiny leggings and beaded flip-flops from which her gnarled toes poked like the knuckles of tree roots, the nail of each painted a different colour. Her eyelashes were so thick with mascara that she looked as though she had two spiders glued to her face.

Realising that she had a client who was under fifty and not plus-size, she fell ecstatically on Legs. 'Beautiful girl! You want a pretty dress for a party, no?' The Italian accent was as heavily embellished as her T-shirt. Cici in fact hailed from Plymouth.

'Nothing too fancy,' she insisted as Cici began to flick through the rails, hauling out sequin and taffeta horrors. 'It's just kitchen supper.' With optional thumbscrews by the Smeg and stocks by the Aga, she thought worriedly.

'We dressa uppa for supper!' The red talons raked some more hangers and burrowed for chiffon and silk. 'You leave it all to Cici. I weel style you from head to toe.'

Having forgotten the pushiness of the village's only fashionista shopkeeper, Legs was tempted to abandon retail therapy and raid her ten-year-old-boy capsule weekend wardrobe again instead. But she knew it had nothing to offer her fragile ego. She couldn't hope to borrow anything from diminutive Nonny, who was at least a dress size smaller, so she was at Cici's mercy.

She gazed longingly out of the window at the tourists milling past, a few of them looking in at the headless photographs, driftwood and chain window display trying to work out what the shop actually sold. Her eye was caught by an attractive man standing on the opposite side of the road, looking lost. He was gazing up at the building numbers and then down at a piece of paper. At his ankles was a very noble-looking basset hound.

Then he turned towards the shop window and she realised it was Byrne.

'Wow, he ees 'andsome, no?' Cici followed her gaze briefly before holding up something fuchsia pink and ruffled under Legs' chin.

'I'm not keen on pink.' She rejected it politely, still watching curiously as Byrne located a door further along the lane and rang a bell before disappearing from sight.

'Peacock blue!' Cici thrust out a shiny miniskirt and matching bustier trimmed with ostrich feathers that made Legs sneeze.

She shook her head apologetically. 'I was thinking more along the maxidress line?'

'Ah ha!' Cici raided another rail.

Glancing out of the window once more, a flash of Titian-red caught her eye and she spotted Kizzy wafting past in an absurdly pretty lime green tea-dress, matched with strappy espadrilles and a meshy copper shrug. She stopped by the 'New Catwalk Collection' window.

Oh God, she's coming in, Legs realised, diving behind a shelf of cashmere twinsets.

But Kizzy merely inclined her pretty head at the twisted rags and then set off again, crossing the cobbled lane to the same door which had admitted Byrne.

Before Legs could follow her progress, a huge curtain of bold print purple and orange fabric blocked her line of vision as Cici held up a maxi dress made of such cheap nylon that it was letting off static like a plasma globe.

Having realised the tea-dress was just daywear to Kizzy, Legs was now doubly determined to find something ravishing to wow them all that evening. She had nothing smarter than easy-wash football shorts and a range of branded baseball caps. Shh had to have something better that wouldn't make her look like a Moulin Rouge chorus girl.

She turned to the rails behind her and started searching while Cici tried to persuade her to try on a custard-yellow catsuit with a cut-out back that looked like a banana with a bite taken out of it.

At last Legs let out an excited gasp as she winkled out the perfect dress hidden deep within the rock-pools of glittering voile and satin. Hand crocheted in duck egg blue lace lined with nude silk, it fell to her ankles on the bias, guaranteed to hug her waist, emphasising her toned shoulders and golden skin, while hiding the pale embarrassment of her chunky legs. As soon as she tried it on she knew it was perfect.

'I think that colour is a little drab,' Cici sniffed, noticing that the price tag boasted fifty per cent off, which meant it was old stock that she was selling at little more than trade price.

'It's the perfect dress-up, dress-down day to evening wear,' Legs insisted, making Cici sniff even more as her client suddenly sounded like Mary Portas on a mission. Legs circled in front of the mirror, seeing a girl from more carefree days. It reminded her of a dress she'd worn to Francis's college's May Ball, a long, clingy swathe of silver net that had rendered him speechless with lust. The fall of the fabric and the cut were identical. The only drawback was that this one was far too long.

Sensing some profit, Cici insisted she had just the right footwear, scattering boxes everywhere in her search for a pair of sky-high strappy cream mules that were at least a size too small and cost three times more than the dress. She also decided that the outfit needed accessorising with bright colours, and was soon winding beaded necklaces around Legs' throat and wrists and draping silk and cashmere shawls over her shoulders until she resembled a Masai wife about to perform a ceremonial dance.

To Legs' horror, Cici then appeared with something which looked like an electrocuted macaw held aloft like a sacrificial offering before plonking it down on her head.

'A fascinator!' she announced, cramming in kirby grips that almost took Legs' scalp off.

Cici's black spider eyelashes did several high kicks as she stood back and admired her creation, still an early work in progress as far as she was concerned. She wiggled to the door to turn the sign to 'closed'.

'First we try lingerie, then I advice on hair and make-up, yes?' She rubbed her hands together. 'Cici haff exclusive time for pretty young client.'

'Actually I have to be somewhere in ten minutes.' Feet already throbbing to match her head, Legs bought everything she was wearing and escaped, furtively shooting across the cobbles from Shh to examine the door that she'd seen Byrne and his basset enter earlier. There was a discreet brass plaque outside engraved Marshall and Callow, Family Solicitors. The vertical blinds in the street level window were closed, a dusty fake orchid on the sill the only thing visible in the building.

Byrne would have to be a very important client to get a solicitors' appointment on a Saturday, Legs realised, pressing her nose to the window.

Suddenly the vertical blind swished open and a hand reached over the sill to hawk up the sash a few inches. Legs pulled back just in time to stop her nose flying up with it. For a brief moment, she could see a desk through the slats, with a basset hound lying on the floor beside it who now raised his head and started barking at her. Then the blinds swished closed again.

Everyone in the room, meanwhile, had been afforded full sight of her gazing in. The basset hound was still barking his head off.

Quite forgetting that the Honda was still languishing in the main car park with an expired ticket, she headed hurriedly back to the Book Inn to spend the afternoon pampering. It wasn't until she passed a wall mirror on her way upstairs to Skit that she realised she still had the mad macaw fascinator pegged on her head.

Chapter 14

Trying the crocheted dress on again in the privacy of her room, Legs realised that it had another major drawback apart from its great length. Her white underwear showed horribly. No matter how many Masai scarves she draped strategically over hips and shoulders, the bra and knickers glowed through like snowy mountain peaks. She guessed she should have stayed for Cici's exclusive lingerie after all. Knowing that Poppy kept Farcombe Hall's lighting as bright as a floodlit stadium day or night to enhance her weak eyesight, she would have to risk going without. She felt increasingly nervous.

The longer she spent tarting up, the more her confidence slipped, and she had allocated far too much time. By four o'clock her body was exfoliated, depilated and buffed, her hair was washed and finger-dried to bed head loveliness, and her make-up laid out ready to apply. If she slapped it on now, it would be sliding away by seven-thirty.

Julie Ocean had left the building; she was a glamorous go-getting action woman, not a vain literary agency assistant torn between real life and show-mance.

There was another storm brewing, the muggy air making her skin felt sticky and her throat dry.

Remembering her phone was still with Nonny, she realised gratefully that she could slip downstairs to fetch it and grab a cup of tea and a sugar fix. But Nonny, delighted at the excuse to take a break from deskwork, was eager to loosen up over a cocktail.

'You must join me,' she insisted, 'Guy tells me off if I drink during the day, but I'm allowed to join favourite guests.'

'My hangover's only just lifted,' protested Legs, who longed for a chocolate hit.

'Nonsense.' Nonny ordered two refreshing Once Upon a Times from Pierced Tongue as they propped themselves up on bar stools. 'Guy says you're eating at the hall tonight, so they'll all be out to take a piece out of you. You need inoculating.'

'What do you mean?' Legs said nervously.

'Hair of the dogs that bit you,' Nonny laughed, ordering chips and aioli which made Legs realise how hungry she was from skipping meals again. 'What are you going to wear? Please don't say the Arsenal strip.'

Legs told her about the great find in Shh, and confessed to her underwear crisis.

Remembering the request the previous night for tampons, Nonny nodded sympathetically and then held up her hand. 'I've got just the thing. Don't go away!' Two minutes later she returned with what looked like a ravel of sausage skin.

'Different type of arse strip,' she giggled. 'Transparent g-string. It's never been worn, I promise. They were all the rage in my heyday. Feels like wearing a clingfilm catapult, but you get used to it and men have no idea it's there unless you let them get a *very* close look.'

The bar was quiet. There was just one family having a cream tea and a dog-walker behind a newspaper in one corner.

Nonny was dying for the latest gossip, hanging on to the modesty pouch and Legs' iPhone like a bribe while she quizzed her. 'Is it true you and Francis are back together?'

'Who said that?'

'It's all over the village. Kizzy must be *livid*. She's only just got her foot through the hall's door.'

At that moment, Julie Ocean stepped back into the Book Inn and started speaking to Legs via hidden wire in urgent tones.

'So she's not lived there long?' Legs relayed the voice in her head.

Nonny shook her head. 'She only moved in a fortnight ago, didn't you know? She rented a room with Justin and Jon before that, the couple in the converted chapel. They say she's very odd. She eats raw fish at least three times a week.'

185

'Nothing odd about that. I love sushi. It was my sister's wedding diet,' said Legs, as Julie Ocean then demanded: 'C'mon, Nonny, nobody round here seriously believes she's a mermaid.'

Nonny fixed her with a wise look. 'This is Farcombe; there are people in this village who still leave bowls of milk out for the pixies.'

Pierced Tongue was taking a long time to wipe the bar-top nearby. Nonny shooed her away to check on the chips order before whispering: 'She's been seen swimming naked on the full moon spring tide, and she sits on the shelf rock at Fargoe headland singing some nights.'

'Sea shanties?'

'No, Kate Bush hits.'

'Does she ever sing in here?' Legs asked jealously, suddenly wondering if she duetted with Francis. 'Don't Give Up' perhaps?

But Nonny was shaking her head and laughing. 'She's got a voice like a foghorn. Quite handy for keeping boats off the rocks, I imagine.'

'Does she have a deep singing voice?' Legs asked 'Manly, would you say?'

'Not particularly.' Nonny gave her a curious look. 'Although that Scottish accent is definitely phoney. The regulars call her "the furrener" and think her poetry is the Devil's work, although it's actually quite good. You know she's been called a Stevie Smith for the—'

'Ecstasy generation. Yes, I had heard. Why do the locals mistrust her so much?'

'They like to have someone to blame for storms, shipwrecks and poor broadband coverage. It used to be Poppy Protheroe, but she hasn't been out of the house for years which doesn't give them much to gossip about. Kizzy's her natural successor.'

'But Poppy's only child was a son.'

'There's blood between them, trust me,' Nonny said darkly. 'They can smell it round here.'

'Ealing's much the same,' Legs joked to hide her mounting concern. 'I blame knife crime.'

'Kizzy was very sweet when she first arrived, all scruffy plaits and bicycle clips like Pippi Longstocking, but as soon as she got into that festival mindset, she affected this avant-garde persona, dressing like a man and trying to set up a "literary salon" in the bar here with Édith.'

'And she dressed like a man, you say?' Legs jumped on the clue, Julie Ocean still breathing down the wire at her.

'Briefly, but I think it was a fashion thing. Édith who was working the androgynous look at the time and Kizzy followed suit – literally – like a schoolgirl copying the cool sixth-formers. Then she had a huge row with her parents – that's when she moved out of their house and into the chapel and started with the moonlit swimming and singing.'

'Do you know what the row was about?'

'No idea, but that's when the Black Widow of Bideford rumours started up. Then, before we knew it, she was dressing in short skirts and flirting with Francis.'

Legs narrowed her eyes.

'Funny thing is, nobody really saw the Kizzy and Francis thing coming,' Nonny went on. 'He was always in here drowning his sorrows. So was his father. But they used to avoid the poetry nights like mad. Kizzy had her own little clique like Jacinta and Ingrid from the festival office, Carl from the bookshop, and of course Édith and Jax when they were here.'

'There was no instant spark?'

She shook her head. 'None. Their paths must have crossed dozens of times in here, but I never saw them speak. Francis just sat at the bar staring into a wine glass, talking about you. He's not a flirt like his father; he falls in love for life, like a swan.'

Legs' guilty heart squeezed on cue, despite Julie Ocean tutting sardonically down the wire that real men lamented lost love over vodka at the very least, rare malt at best, and certainly not house white.

She kept remembering Francis saying of Kizzy, *we all have confidences we choose not to share. She has hers and I have mine.*

'The villagers are very protective of Francis,' Nonny was saying. 'He can be a pompous git at times, but we all trust his integrity. Nobody around here believes Kizzy will make him happy. Some even think she'll spell the end of the Protheroe family.'

'How do you mean?' Legs gulped, already imagining grisly predictions of bloodbaths at the hall.

But Nonny giggled naughtily. '*Nobody* would call those hips childbearing. Guy says she'll need a "gestational carrier" to mix the Black Widow's genes with Protheroe blood.'

'Sounds like one of his cocktail recipes,' Legs smiled weakly.

A bowl of chips was plonked beside her. The aioli fumes were so garlicky they almost blew her off her barstool.

Nonny glanced at her watch and stood up. 'I must get back.'

'No!' Legs protested, barely started on witness cross-examination. She had to know more about the circumstances of Francis and Kizzy getting together.

But Nonny was already kissing her farewell. 'Good luck tonight. Have another cocktail on the house, and rest assured everyone here will be really happy when you and Francis are together again. We are *so* relieved to have you back. You're saving his life.' She handed over the phone and blew more kisses before heading back to her office.

'No pressure then,' Legs breathed to herself, noticing that Tongue Piercing had already lined up a fresh Once Upon a Time alongside the chips. She felt ungrateful asking for tea and biscuits now, so thanked her and took a sip before coughing so much her eyes streamed. It was almost neat brandy. At least it counteracted the taste of garlic.

She switched on her phone and checked her messages.

There were tens of texts from friends not realising that she was out of London, wondering what she was up to over the weekend. Francis had texted no less than a dozen times, clearly panicking that she wouldn't be there that evening.

Scrolling down the screen, she saw voicemail notifications from him, Ros, Daisy and Conrad.

Then she spotted an email from Gordon sent late the previous night, marked with a red exclamation mark, with the simple subject line 'You & me'. The first line leaped out at her: *As one who has sold their soul, dear Allegra, I urge you to lock up your red car and walk away from it and from this situation . . .*

She opened it and baulked as she realised it was several screens long.

Do not underestimate the past. It fashions our lives, and we wear what parts of it that still suit us, forgetting the way we really looked and that so much recollection is the Emperor's New Clothes. To reveal the truth is to undress in public.

Legs had been thinking a lot that evening about the dress she had worn to that May Ball. Now she reread the paragraph, anxious that the message between the lines was that she no longer suited crochet and would look stupidly naked.

But Gordon could see far beyond glad rags;

Some of us even take the devils we know as bedfellows so we can shrug off our memories with the lights out. You wear your devil-may-care attitude like a mask, dear Allegra. Please don't cover your pretty face.

Her eyes ran back and forwards along the lines, wondering at his insight . . . *we take the devils we know as bedfellows* . . . The poignancy of his words astounded her, and their personalised kindness. How she'd misjudged Gordon Lapis, the clever and neurotic recluse. Of course anybody capable of creating Ptolemy Finch had to have a caring side. She felt suddenly unworthy of the Curmudgeonly One's time and care.

Leaving the email half read because it was making her cry, Legs quickly scrolled back to her sent folder and confirmed her worst suspicions: before her phone battery had conked out on the night she'd slept in her car, she had sent the message she'd intended for Conrad to his client instead, or rather to Gordon's PA, who had clearly forwarded it straight on. She'd never trust Kelly again. Her own words mortified her: *If you want your star to appear here, then I must get into bed with them all. This is hell. Please rescue me. xxx*

Taking a huge slug of Once Upon a Time followed by several garlicky chips to take the taste away, she dared herself to return to his reply once more.

My cloak of anonymity is that of a coward not a superhero, Allegra, his message continued, *I have never wished to reveal my true face. It is of no great merit, and it is haunted by the past; its biography of lines carry no punches, each one a tributary to self indulgence. But you have given me laughter lines of late, and for that I am unspeakably grateful as I prepare to smile for the cameras.*

At that moment, the dog walker in the corner stood up and passed behind her, placing the newspaper on the pile lying beside her on the bar top. Folded back out of order, it flopped open across the phone in her palm.

Ptolemy Finch Creator to be Unveiled! shouted a headline, alongside a still from one of the movies starring the now super-famous child actor Con O'Mara who played the title role.

She snatched up her phone again and pressed the speed dial.

'Taking the kids back,' Conrad answered stiffly on the car's Bluetooth. 'Keep it short.'

'You bastard!'

There was a tittering from the back seat at the other end. Conrad barked for silence. 'What?'

'It's all over the Sundays that Gordon will be at Farcombe Festival in person.'

'Couldn't ask for better publicity, huh? We were too late for the first editions, but everybody's running it now, and it's been on every news bulletin today.'

'But it hasn't been formally confirmed by the committee yet!'

'They'd look bloody fools to back out now.'

'What does Gordon think about it being leaked to the press?'

'It was his idea.'

Legs took a few moments to absorb this, head spinning. He must have told Conrad what to do straight after sending his email to her, an email she'd failed to respond to or acknowledge. She had let him down so badly. Barracking Conrad would achieve nothing; this was as much her fault as it was his.

Then she stiffened as she realised she could hear a woman's voice on the line too, demanding: 'Is that *her*?'

There was a lot of muffling and clunking, then Conrad said 'must go' and cut the call.

Fuming, Legs read the rest of Gordon's message, feeling ashamed: *There is a sting in my tale, trust me*, he carried on. *Far better to choose my own stage on which to uncloak than to find myself taken by surprise and forcibly stripped of my anonymity. I am grateful for your help thus far, but I insist that I take it from here; Julie Ocean is off the case. Take your leave of Farcombe, Allegra. There is no need to get in bed with anybody. Sleep tight. Your friend, GL.*

Oh poor Gordon. This was torture for him. A tear ran down her nose and splashed on the screen.

In a daze, she drained her Happy Ever After and comfort-ate the rest of the chips before burping so toxically she could almost see the rum and garlic fumes lingering around her. At least it backed off Pierced Tongue, who was doing her bar-wiping thing again.

Retreating to a quiet corner, she rang Francis. The joy in his voice when he took her call was in such direct contrast to Conrad that she felt another wave of loving nostalgia.

'We're all waiting around for this Jay Goburn chap. I hope he's the big philanthropist Poppy promises. I also secretly hope he's gay. They've been exchanging adoring emails for months, and the last thing we need is another love affair starting up among the oldies. Please tell me you're coming to supper?'

'I'm not sure.'

'You must, Legs!' He took a deep, measured breath that told her he was about to recite something.

'OK, I'll come,' she quickly intervened, more determined than ever to cut through the verse to the plain truth. It was time to find out what they really meant to each other. Julie Ocean might be off the case, but Allegra North was still on a mission.

'You darling girl.'

She folded the edges of the newspaper in front of her, surprised by the punch of guilt that now hit her for ignoring Gordon's advice. 'How did the committee meeting go?'

'We scraped through by one vote. The old guard were up in arms about Lapis, as you can imagine, especially given today's headlines. There was lots of chuntering about selling out. Then bloody Édith rolled up at the last minute and abstained, telling Kizzy to abstain too. I could have killed them both, but Poppy was marvellous, kept her cool and convinced Kizzy to change her vote.'

'I thought Kizzy was behind Gordon coming?' Legs baulked, realising now how much this must be hurting her. She wondered whether to tell Francis that she'd spotted her outside the solicitors' offices in Farcombe, but decided against it, knowing it sounded paranoid.

'She's behaving very erratically today. It didn't help that Édith had a shouting match with my father across the committee table as soon as she arrived, saying that she would kill anyone who treated her like he's treating Poppy. Then Dad started barracking her about Jax, who it turned out was just outside the door. It all got rather personal. In the end, Poppy threw a glass of water over them both to shut them up, but missed and it went over Kizzy. You know how short-sighted she is.'

'So Poppy and Hector seem no closer to a rapprochement?'

'Not remotely. Poppy's still threatening to cancel the festival if my father doesn't come home; I think she's waiting on tonight to make her final decision. She wants order seen to be restored.'

Legs closed her eyes and breathed slowly, almost asphyxiating herself with garlic, before she ventured, 'I am not going to fake anything, Francis.'

There was a long pause. She felt the brandy drumming in her veins, holding up emotional flashcards that she didn't dare read out loud. I'm not sure I love Conrad; was it ever more than lust? I so loved what we had, Francis, but was it ever more than teenage dreams?

'No faking. This is do or die,' Francis agreed in a voice of such immediacy and intimacy that she hugged the phone to her ear, remembering the hours they had racked up on mobile bills as students, endlessly pushing their top-up cards into cashpoints to buy enough credit time to say goodbye.

Yet now she rang off as fast as a bankrupt with a cheery 'I'll see you later!', unsettled by the way nostalgia kept warping her thoughts. She was also worried by his 'do or die' line, which didn't sound like Francis at all. She tried to remember what it came from and was almost sure it was Robert Burns, part of a bloodthirsty, patriotic anthem about slaying tyrants and usurpers. Francis, who had never been beyond Edinburgh, was no Scottish Nationalist. The only Scot she knew of in Farcombe right now was Kizzy. Images of Kizzy the man flashed before her eyes, a diminutive, sinewy kilted redhead in blue face-paint waving a skean dhu about.

It made her shudder. She needed Julie Ocean onside, with Jimmy as backup. Instead she now just had a crocheted dress, transparent underwear and a promise to Francis to keep. Do or die.

She picked up the newspaper again and checked her horoscope, which was lousy, predicting conflicts, bad decisions and even disaster.

Legs trailed upstairs to Skit.

Instead of boosting her confidence, the Once upon a Times had made her feel sluggish and drained. She lay down on her bed for a moment to gather her thoughts, trying to distract herself with a manuscript she had brought in from the car. It was the crime thriller Gordon Lapis had forwarded onto her, written by his fan, Delia Meare.

The prose style was all over the place, with no punctuation to speak of. There were two spelling errors and a split infinitive in the first paragraph, followed by two grisly murders in less than a page. Usually this would lead to Legs casting it aside without another thought. Her rule of thumb was that if there were more than three grammatical errors before the first murder, Conrad wouldn't look at it twice. But there was something absolutely compelling about the way this one was written, however ludicrous, that she read on.

Both victims were redheads, both disembowelled, their bodies left in shopping trolleys on piers. Legs wondered vaguely how one got a stiff in a trolley up a pier undetected.

It was, she decided, a very promising start. There was an idiosyncratic wit to it she couldn't help liking. She let out a garlic burp and turned to page two, on which yet another redhead died, this time left in a DIY store trolley on a harbour wall. The writer's style was absolutely gripping.

She was in danger of becoming seriously hooked when she flipped over page three and howled with frustration as she realised the author had committed the heinous sin of sending non-consecutive chapters. Action had suddenly skipped ahead ten chapters, and she found herself reading through a spine-chillingly grisly scene set in a meat fridge, with even less punctuation. No longer able to concentrate, she gathered together the pages, now feeling quite sick, although whether that was from too much brandy or murder overkill was hard to tell. Her eyelids were leaden and the muggy air weighed down on her chest like hot, wet towels.

She put the manuscript on her bedside table. Seconds later she was asleep.

She awoke to the sound of her phone ringing 'Teenage Kicks'. She checked the time and realised, to her horror, that it was just a few minutes before she was due at the hall.

'Please tell me you're coming,' Francis whispered breathlessly. 'All hell's broken loose here. I need you.'

'I'm coming,' she reassured him. Scattering *The Girl Who Checked Out* far and wide, she scrambled from the bed, heart bursting with pride and gratitude that he could still trust her.

Chapter 15

With no time left to get ready, the crocheted dress went unaccessorised, and Legs barely graced her face with more than a dab of lipstick and mascara. In truth she looked a great deal better than she would have after yet more hours of pampering, she realised as she gave herself a quick glance in the mirror. Her hair was truly bedhead-ruffled and her cheeks pink, skin radiant now that it had calmed down from the previous evening, leaving a healthy sun-kissed glow. She belted out of the Book Inn barefoot during its busy Happy Ever After Hour, carrying her killer heels.

'Was that Kate Winslet?' one male guest asked Guy as he cleared empties from the outside tables.

The Book Inn landlord watched Legs hopping over the harbour cobbles towards the back lane to the hall. She looked ravishing. She had a breathless, unselfconscious air about her which had made heads turn as she dashed out. The overall effect was bombshell-seductive, but Guy knew she was far too flustered to think herself any more alluring than when she was dressed in her too-tight Arsenal strips.

'Yes. Stays here all the time,' he told the guest, picking up the cocktail list. 'Can I tempt you to another? Make Believe, with vodka and fresh lime, or Tragic Pathos with whisky and bitters?'

★

Legs paused to regroup by Farcombe Hall's gateposts, overlooked by the unicorns as she washed her feet in the fierce little brook before pulling on her new shoes. They were so unstable that she tripped along Farcombe Hall's cobbled side drive like a comedy turn who'd had half a dozen Once Upon a Times.

Seeing a flash of red hair beneath the cloisters, her heart sank as she registered Kizzy smoking a roll-up, observing her teetering approach with a frozen expression.

There was another figure alongside her, hidden in the shadow of an arch. On the grass beyond the rhododendron walk, glowing in golden evening sunlight, Byron the lame terrier was playing with a basset hound.

Legs wobbled to a halt, also cast in golden rays, unaware that the see-through g-string was doing just as Nonny had promised and the evening light angling through the crochet dress made it look as though she was wearing no underwear.

Stepping out of the shadows, Byrne regarded her warily. Ahead of him, Kizzy's demeanour was completely different than the previous day. She was clearly seething, red lips curled around her bared white teeth in an aggressive smile. Dressed immaculately in a high-necked emerald shift dress, her red hair pulled into a Hepburn chignon, she was every inch the immaculate Farcombe hostess-in-waiting, making Legs feel impossibly blousy in plunging crochet, and acutely aware that she and Francis had been locked in a clinch right under her nose last night. Her green eyes smouldered with such venom, Legs half expected a forked tongue to dart out from that fixed smile. Yet she was utterly courteous.

'Allegra. Good you could make it. Poppy apologises, but she's had a bit of a shock, and is taking a quick lie down. Mummy's with her. The Keiller-Myleses aren't here yet. Let me introduce you to Jago Byrne.'

He held out his hand to her. 'We've met.'

'We're both staying at the Book Inn,' Legs explained, seeing Kizzy's green eyes narrow. Byrne's handshake was firm and formal. His face gave nothing away; they could have shared no more than a nod at reception.

'What a coincidence.' Kizzy flicked her cigarette butt into an urn.

'Where's Francis?' Legs bleated, desperate for an ally.

Her green eyes now widened like an offended owl. 'With Édith in the kitchen. They mustn't be disturbed,' she flashed an acid splash smile, modulated Scottish voice still smooth and deep as a loch. 'If you'll excuse me, I must check that Jax and Daddy are OK.'

As Legs watched her go, she looked out for signs that she had once been a man, but apart from that whip-thin boyishness and a certain determined jut of the chin as she turned to go indoors, there was nothing obvious.

There was an uncomfortable pause, during which Byrne's furnace gaze drifted downwards followed by his brows shooting upwards, and Legs realised that in her haste she'd put her new shoes on the wrong feet, which at least explained her total inability to walk straight. Her face flamed. He must think her a complete dipsomaniac.

'Kizzy's not my biggest fan,' Legs explained, blushing even deeper because he was the last person she'd expected to encounter tonight.

'That was just bad timing. She's angry with you because you interrupted my marching orders.'

'Are you a gatecrasher then?'

'In a manner of speaking.' He let out a gruff laugh then looked up, almost knocking her off her mixed-up shoes with the intensity of his eyes. 'Perhaps I should have mentioned last night that I'd been invited here.'

'We had other things to talk about,' she said carefully, knowing that if she'd been less drunkenly attention seeking, he might have got a word in edgeways about himself. He was one of the most infuriatingly oblique men she'd ever met. Knowing that she'd confessed so much about her feelings for Francis to him made her very jumpy indeed.

'You have your shoes on the wrong feet,' he pointed out kindly.

'I know.' She perched on the base of a cloister column to refit them, regarding him warily. 'Jay Goburn. I heard you were an American academic?'

'I never said that I was anything.' He gave a guarded smile. 'Poppy is as eager to fill in backgrounds as a child with new crayons, it seems. Perhaps I should have enlightened her too. I wouldn't be in this mess.'

'What mess?' She stood up, high rise shoes now on the right feet, her eyes level with his.

He stepped closer, voice lowered discreetly, making all the hairs on the back of her neck stand up. 'It may not have escaped your notice that the atmosphere here is rather – odd. Our hostess has taken to bed and your fiancé is—'

'Ex-fiancé,' she interrupted.

'*Ex*-fiancé is conducting emergency family talks in the kitchens while his pretty girlfriend is sent outside to try to persuade me to wait at the Book Inn.'

'And why is that?'

He lifted his chin, fixing her face with those intent, dark eyes. 'Poppy Protheroe is my mother.'

Legs gasped. 'You're the . . . ?'

'The son of a shotgun marriage, yes.'

'The Prodigal Son,' she gulped, trying to take it in.

He nodded, casting his gaze to the sea, which this evening was reflecting the sun's misty-faced yellow hue so it seemed the colour of milky tea, its rocky outcrops dunked into the high tide to the far left.

'How long is it since you saw her?' Legs asked cautiously.

'Nearly twenty years; the day she left my father to run away with Hector. I thought it was about time we caught up.'

She hugged herself tightly, realising goosebumps had popped

up all over her arms; she wished she'd bought one of the many Masai shawls Cici had flogged her now. Two thoughts kept hammering through her head, the first was that Kizzy probably wasn't a transsexual avenger after all – which was something of a relief – and the second was that last night, not long after she had confided that she was still in love with Francis, Byrne had confided in her that he was about to lose his life. It made for tricky small-talk.

'So Poppy didn't realise it was you coming today?' she asked falteringly.

He shook his head. 'Jago Byrne probably means nothing to my mother. I was christened James, and she knows me as Jamie; Dad's always called me Jago.'

'And Byrne?'

'Our family name is Kelly; Byrne is my grandmother's name from her second marriage. When Dad and I returned to Ireland, he insisted we took it. He was terrified Poppy would follow and claim me back. But of course she never even tried.' He let out a cheerless laugh.

She gazed at him in amazement, remembering his comment the previous evening that everyone should change their name at least once in life. She could see the likeness now. His eyes were incredibly like Poppy's, so huge, clever and soulful, and he had her high cheeks and enviable olive skin. No wonder he was such a character assassin; it was in the genes.

The basset hound was looking up at her with even more mournful eyes than his master, longing to be stroked.

'This is Fink,' Byrne introduced her.

Legs stooped down to make a fuss of him, nerves and tension playing to her reflex action silly humour: 'And what do you Fink about all this, boy?'

To her relief, Byrne let out a gruff laugh above her head, 'Poor old Fink's as deaf as a post and as thick as a plank. Can't hear himself Fink even if he knew how.'

Legs gave the dog a sympathetic look, covering his huge ears and kissing his nose. 'Fink positive.'

Yet her own head was reeling with the looped memory of Byrne saying 'I am about to lose my life' playing over and over, like one of the maddening modern video art installations Poppy regularly commissioned for the festival.

She straightened up and smiled anxiously at him. 'Please take no notice of what I said about Poppy last night. I was always on Francis's side, remember, and theirs was never an easy relationship. She's such an amazing person. She went through a lot, and it can't have been easy coming here.'

'Easier than staying with her husband and child, though, clearly,' he muttered in an undertone before glancing across at the house as Francis came storming out from the Moroccan lobby, adding sardonically: 'Ah, a happy stepsibling.'

Blond hair on end, blue eyes blazing, fallen-angel face high with colour, Francis looked absurdly dashing in a long-cuffed shirt and faded jeans, although his expression was thunder.

'I can't believe you knew all about this!' he raged at Legs.

'I didn't!' she squeaked.

Behind Francis, his half-sister Édith Protheroe wandered onto the step and lent prettily against the doorframe, a willowy, raven-haired blade of beauty and ill-will, glass of wine in hand. It didn't look like it was her first. 'Hi Legs. Fabulous dress. We might have guessed you'd be involved in today's surprise.'

'I knew nothing!'

'You two had a very cosy tête-à-tête over supper in the pub last night before I arrived, I gather,' Francis snarled, having clearly just been debriefed, probably by Kizzy.

'We had to share the last free table in the restaurant.' Legs immediately became defensive. 'I had no idea he was Poppy's son, did I, Byrne?'

His face was deadpan. 'It was like eating in a busy Prêt. Didn't even know I'm called Jago. Spent all evening trying to avoid addressing me by my first name, so she did.'

'You noticed?' she gasped, mortified.

'Well, *Jago* here has certainly made tonight's meal one to remember,' Francis snapped, grasping Legs' elbow and steering her towards the house, calling back to Byrne. 'You can stay there. Talk to him, Édith.'

'Isn't that a bit unfriendly?' Legs muttered as he marched her through the Moroccan arches, footsteps echoing and her high heels buckling under her. 'He's family now, after all.'

'Not my bloody family,' Francis hissed, whisking her behind an amoebic statue and taking her by surprise with a long, hungry kiss. There was no courteous request tonight.

'Christ, I needed that,' he laughed with relief as they surfaced for air.

She looked at his face, so handsome and indomitable, longing to cut him down to size for manhandling her mind and body so much in the past forty-eight hours than both were dizzy, yet too fearful of hurting him again to cross him.

'What about Kizzy?'

'She's going off the rails faster than a faulty coathanger this evening. You're so right, Legs. There's no point in faking. Say the word and it's over.'

Even though she now she knew that he'd only been cohabiting with the fish-eating Babooshka-singer for a fortnight, it sounded terribly cruel. 'What word?'

By way of an answer, he settled another kiss on her lips, this one longer and gentler, but no less possessive.

Oh hell, Legs thought in a panic, casting her eyes nervously over her shoulder in case Kizzy was nearby. But there was no denying the frantic heartbeat rattling right through her, from pulse to pulse via every erogenous zone.

'Have you been eating garlic?' he asked when they surfaced again.

She had no time to answer as there was a commotion from the

staircase in the main hall and Francis dropped her like a hot brick as Poppy's deep voice boomed into earshot. 'I am going to spend time with my son, who has returned to me!' she was announcing theatrically.

'Are you sure that's wise?' Her friend Yolande was right on her heels, sixteen stone of breathless panic in a kaftan, harem pants and clicking flip-flops.

Puce in the face, her lip-gloss kissed off, Legs mustered a winning smile. As the duo swept past, she and Francis were standing a respectable three feet apart like butler and housekeeper. Poppy didn't bat an eye in their direction. Yolande, however, reserved a venomous look for her daughter's rival. Unlike her friend, whose low, jewelled turbans lent her wizened Middle Eastern ethnicity, Yolande favoured an exotic millinery modelled on well-upholstered Nigerian friends from London. Thus Legs received a furious glare from beneath a foot of orange satin, silk and feather folds of such weight and plumage that Cici's fascinator would look like a small slaughtered budgie by comparison.

As soon as they were out of earshot, Francis let out a sigh of relief.

'I need a stiff drink.' He led the way towards the service door, as though the kiss hadn't happened, adding over his shoulder. 'What's he like, Jago Byrne?'

'Pretty combustible.'

'Then we'll sit him close to a candle.'

'I think I'll just pop to the loo.' Legs dived through the door to the cloakroom, slamming it gratefully behind her and sliding the lock.

Her detective head was trying to add up facts, but there were so many new developments she was running out of fingers on which to count.

She fished a fresh tampon from her bag with shaking hands, wishing she hadn't come. A pale crocheted dress with just a transparent g-string for protection was making her paranoid, despite all the adverts for sanitary protection starring women leaping across streams and stepping stones in tight white jeans with no knicker line during their periods. But really, it was the cross-currents that were causing her heart to hammer as though taking a shower with Norman Bates holding her soap just beyond the curtain. Francis was as abrupt and snappy as she could remember. And while angry Byrne might have plenty to distract him from her silly flirtation, Kizzy looked absolutely murderous tonight. She could almost hear the knives sharpening beyond the door.

Pulling herself together, Legs washed her hands and stepped out into the hallway, turning towards the green baize service door. An angry voice just the other side made her stall.

'How could you bring her along tonight? That is so cruel.'

She stepped back, throat clutched with shame. It was Kizzy, her voice hacked through with tears.

'You lied to me! You said her love affair was just the excuse you needed to be free, and now you bring her here and rub my nose in it. You still love her, don't you? You just used me to try to get information. But you don't know the half of it. I could bring this family to its knees. You're all rotten to the core apart from Poppy. You'll get your just desserts. I am not going to be humiliated like this!' Footsteps hammered away along the back lobby.

Legs retreated hastily across the chequered marble floor to the base of the staircase, debating whether it was better to make a run for it past Byrne in the cloisters or down the dramatic sweep of entrance steps.

Before she had made up her mind, she heard the baize door swing and a click of heels as Édith appeared carrying her topped-up wine glass, along with a heavy crystal glass in which ice cubes rattled like bones beneath deep amber liquid.

She jumped when she saw Legs. 'What are you doing skulking about out here? Francis is looking for you. Do you think the Prodigal will notice this is Amaretto not Irish malt? He asked for scotch, but there's none in the house. '

'I think he might.'

'Oh well, I guess it will be a test of good manners.' She smiled wickedly and swept off through the Moroccan wing, ice clanking.

Stealing herself, Legs summoned the last traces of Julie Ocean grit and headed to the kitchen, knowing that running away would just make the situation with Francis worse; equally aware that she couldn't drag herself away from Byrne and his extraordinary revelations.

The vast Farcombe kitchen was as big and deep as a squash court, and little modernised since its Victorian heyday, apart from the replacement of the original cast-iron range with a custompainted turquoise four-door Aga and the addition of several fifties-styled fridges and quite a lot of Poppy statues.

To Legs' embarrassment, she had to edge past Kizzy who was standing directly in the doorway, stiff-jawed and wild-eyed as she spoke with Édith's girlfriend Jax. Both appeared viciously angry as they turned to let her past.

At the opposite end of the room, Francis was prowling around by the French windows looking trapped.

'There you are!' He had already poured Legs a glass of Gavi, which he quickly handed to her, blue eyes desperate to convey a message. Apart from an obvious topnote of fear and irritation, she couldn't read any more detail.

'Francis!' Kizzy called him to her side and he melted reluctantly away.

Legs watched the gathering storm clouds through the windows, wondering anxiously how Kizzy could bring the family to its knees. Perhaps she was planning to become a vicar, she thought hopefully.

Having originally planned to stick to mineral water after last night's excess and the sleep-inducing Happy Ever Afters, she sipped the Gavi unenthusiastically but discovered it was so delicious that she couldn't resist snorkelling up some more. She then crossed the room to greet Jax, who was now alone, pressed up against the Aga despite her leather jacket and the heat of the evening, her hackles raised. She had a nervous smile like a terrier. Legs had always found Jax good company and refreshingly down to earth once one penetrated the edgy coolness.

'Knew you'd be back,' Jax said in an undertone as she approached.

'So good to see you.' She kissed her cool, porcelain-pale cheeks. She smelled deliciously of Antaeus. 'I don't think I'm very welcome.'

'You and me both,' Jax snarled, then flashed another defensive smile. 'Édith always reckoned you and Fran is the real deal,' her gruff little Dublin-meets-Cockney voice made Legs suddenly homesick for city hustle and bustle.

'You're a part of the family,' she insisted, unable to comprehend why Jax would cast herself in the same turncoat mould as herself.

'They like new blood, the Protheroes,' Jax said darkly. 'Like vampires.' She stalked over to a fridge to fetch another beer, glaring at Kizzy as she passed by.

Legs sagged against the Aga, barely feeling its heat scalding her through the crochet dress. The high drama and crashing contradictory waves of Farcombe were making her seasick.

Even now, Francis was once again at Kizzy's side, putting up a united front as they discussed in sotto voices what to do with the Keiller-Myleses, who Kizzy's father Howard was right now welcoming in the main entrance hall. As Farcombe Festival's biggest sponsor and long-term supporter, Vin Keiller-Myles was always treated by the Protheroes like a visiting dignitary, even though nobody in the family liked him very much.

'At least they used the main drive so didn't encounter the touching reunion on the terrace,' Francis said tetchily, 'but somebody will have to explain to them what the hell's going on.'

'My father can show them into the library,' Kizzy suggested, brittle and distracted. Her eyes were bloodshot, Legs noticed, and her pale neck was leaping with sinews and veins.

Francis pulled at his long cuffs, nodding. 'You and Legs can keep them entertained for a bit, Kizz. Fill them in with the bare details. Legs is good at these things.' He turned to her.

'Me?' Legs gulped.

'We'll be a double act.' Kizzy looked slightly more cheerful, managing a weak conspiratorial smile at Legs. 'Partners in crime.'

'You keep him talking and I'll lift his wallet?' Legs joked.

Kizzy grabbed a jug of Pimms and raised it shakily, sounding like Miss Jean Brodie. 'If we fail to anaesthetise him with girlish good manners, Jax can go in man-to-man.'

Not apparently listening, Francis kept on nodding. 'Indeed – Jax must back you both up. Vin Keiller-Myles loves to be surrounded by pretty faces, and Imee wants us out of here, don't you Ims?' The Filipina housekeeper nodded with relief, having been battling to fight her way past Legs to the Aga with a tray of puff pastry circles loaded with caramelised onion, pears and Gorgonzola. The last thing anybody was ever expected to do at a Farcombe kitchen sups was gather in the kitchen.

Stashing a spare bottle of Budvar in her pocket, Jax shot Legs a martyred look as they trailed through to the library. 'Fran's turning into his father don'cha think?'

Legs looked at her in surprise. 'They couldn't be more different.'

'Look around you, girl. The writing's on the wall.' She bared her tiny teeth, gazing around the library which always made their jaws drop no matter how many times they'd been inside it.

The library at Farcombe Hall was a show-stopper. It was one of the few family rooms in the house that was used during the festival, a textbook setting for intimate readings and small audience discussions, creating the perfect atmosphere with the high walls lined with books and the oversized windows that looked straight out to sea. Located in one of the hall's turrets, it was almost as high as the house with four tiered galleries, accessed by glorious mechanical ladders. Engineered in Victorian times during one of the hall's gothic makeovers, these magnificent wooden climbing frames could be rotated to access the thousands of books overhead.

As teenagers, Francis and his friends had swung around on them like monkeys. As young lovers, he and Legs had dared to copulate on each narrow gallery in turn, excitement mounting with every tier. Coming in here still gave her a wistful tingle.

Despite first appearances, the room's contents contained little to excite most book-lovers. Hector was not a snob about a volume's appearance, believing that what was inside was far more important than its condition outside, so the library wasn't lined with beautifully leather-bound first editions, but instead by battered, foxed and well-thumbed volumes with fraying spines and loose pages. Visitors would struggle to find much in the way of easy bedtime reading here. Many, especially at ground level, were deeply obscure texts on subjects only of interest to Hector: unintelligible tomes on the history of jazz and bassoon, dreadful impenetrable poetry, long technical manuals detailing the geography and geology of obscure corners of the world, thousand-page theological polemics or deeply self-indulgent self-published art critiques, most often penned by his friends. Despite Poppy haranguing him for years to hire a professional librarian and indexer to create some sort of order, he relied upon his own eccentric system and brilliant memory to locate any given volume. As a result few family members could ever find a thing of interest to read there, but the incredible views from the windows, straight out to the Celtic Sea, were among the best afforded from the ground floor of the house, and tonight they were entrancing Poppy's supper guests over aperitifs and appetisers.

Vin Keiller-Myles was a barking bulldog of self-made, self-tanned self worth, with what was left of his thinning grey hair pulled back into a ponytail, his mottled jowls bulging over the stiff white collars of his shirt like pie crusts. A former music journalist and sometime progressive rocker, Vin had made his fortune in discount mail-order music sales, forming his own label to press cheap compilation CDs, then getting out just before the internet boom killed his company with download mania. His third wife, American trust-fund babe Gayle, was a younger version of his two previous wives: strawberry blonde, pseudo-intellectual and high maintenance. They alternated between vast, minimalist houses in Hampstead and North Devon, never needing to pack because they maintained duplicate wardrobes at each end, Vin's being filled with identikit pinstripe suits, white shirts and just a few very loud shirts for casual days, and Gayle's being entirely populated by white, which was the only colour she ever wore, like a blank canvas.

'I love this gaff!' Vin was pronouncing to Kizzy's disapproving parents Howard and Yolande. 'It's a man's house, isn't it?'

'I think you'll find it was a nunnery for most of the nineteenth century,' Howard droned back with flat Canadian disinterest. 'Haunted to buggery.'

'Hallelujah!' he cackled. 'Give me a few see-though novices running around the corridors over en suites any day.'

Vin had never made any secret of his desire to own Farcombe Hall, which was why he couldn't be more delighted by this summer's turn of events. The hush-hush rumours about the Protheroe marriage combined with yet another Farcombe cash crisis had stoked his interest once more. It was clear that he now finally saw an opportunity to gain ascendency over Hector. Vin had already ensured that he was more or less a part of the family firm, and his inclusion in tonight's intimate gathering made him ever more assured of his place as indispensible friend and festival mentor. The chip on his shoulder after three decades of professional jealousy and personal affront against Hector was about to splinter away. His swaggering demeanour tonight indicated that he firmly believed that it was only a matter of time before he began to run the whole shooting match, and the totty would be reward in itself.

Leering alternately at Legs and Kizzy, he sprayed them both with crumbs from the breadsticks he was stuffing back as he described his most recent purchase of a crucifixion wall hanging fashioned entirely in empty contraceptive pill foils.

'It's called the Immaculate Misconception and was the most controversial piece in Black Hole Gallery's "Blasphemy" exhibition,' he bragged. 'I've already had hate mail from all over the world for buying it.'

Vin had turned collecting bad taste art into a hobby. Although in a recent interview he claimed to enjoy spectating at a cage fight just as much as attending an exhibition, he was far from the ignorant plebeian Hector accused him of being. He might dress like a gangster with the ultimate moll as accessory, but he had a mind as sharp as his suits.

'Hear there's been some talk of calling off the festival this year? Not very clever with the Gordon Lapis news breaking.'

'It's a calculated risk,' Kizzy said smoothly, sucking up to Vin who had once listed 'dirty deals, clean sweeps and massurrealism' amongst his interests in *Who's Who*.

'Is that why you didn't want him voted in by the committee?' Legs asked her.

'It's only a small abstain on my character.' She looked cornered. 'I just don't see what all the fuss is about. He's a very mediocre writer who struck lucky.'

'He's mine and Gayle's favourite novelist.' Vin's eyes glittered. He had that rare privilege of being rich enough to be unafraid of mixing the mainstream with elitism, and cocky enough to find Poppy and her cronies' snobbery on such matters amusing.

'Good for you.' Legs beamed at him, holding out a bowl of almond-stuffed olives.

Vin smiled back, suddenly clocking the fact that she wasn't wearing a bra. Having given Gayle eight thousand dollars' worth of LA boob job as a wedding present only to find she now wore a bra 24/7 like scaffolding round a precious public artwork, he was entranced.

'You like the Ptolemy Finch books?' he asked, moving forwards to claim a few finest green Manzanilla.

'Love them.' Legs kept the smile plastered to her face while he leered down the front of her dress. She huffed out some garlic fumes to keep him at bay.

Over his bald pate, she could see Kizzy's attention being distracted by action across the room where Gayle was making stilted progress with Jax. Deprived of her warm Aga, the little motorbike-loving urchin had zipped up her leather jacket to cover her chin, sliding her tiny hands into opposite sleeves like a Geisha girl, and was perched in a window seat beside the tall shelves of books, where she could catch the last angled rays of sun as it came through the deep-set windows of the tower turret before slipping behind the woods and out to sea.

'Do you like the Ptolemy Finch books, Jacqueline?' Gayle asked in her over-sincere California accent as she kept one eye and one ear to her husband, not trusting him among such pretty young women, especially the clever-eyed, tousled blonde with the pale blue crocheted dress and beddable body.

'I prefer vampires.' Jax flashed her pointed little teeth. In their contrasting black and white, raven-haired and blonde, they looked like two allegories. 'And call me Jax, love. I ain't never been Jacqueline.'

'So what is Jax short for?'

'Ajax.' She sneered her terrier smile. 'Appropriate as I'm good with scrubbers.' She glared into the centre of the room, where Kizzy was now sniping about Jago.

'He has Poppy by the heartstrings tonight, poor darling, but he's just an opportunist. One gets so many in a family like this.' Kizzy looked up sharply as Édith floated in from the terrace, alighting beside her like a butterfly blown onto a greenhouse.

She had what must have been her fifth glass of wine on the go, eyes beginning to glaze, and she was happy to take the bitchy baton. 'Of course he's *bound* to be after the family money. Why else wait all this time to turn up? His father's family are probably as poor as church mice. He still lives with them at his grandparents' farm in Ireland, we understand. Of course Poppy's still far too overwhelmed to do the sums. They're on the terrace exchanging witticisms like Noel Coward characters. Poppy keeps crying.'

'Ah, but is she being genuine?' asked Kizzy with a brittle laugh.

In detective mode once more, Legs registered a connection between them and felt a chill draught in her veins, sensing conspiracies at work. Kizzy seemed to light up now that Édith was here, her nervous energy almost incandescent.

Édith laughed too, her tone warm and infectious. 'With Poppy, who can tell? The tears looked real enough, but then again wouldn't we all cry if this happened? Buggers up tonight's seating plan totally for a start.' She helped herself to one of the almond-stuffed olives Legs was still touting about to try to shake off lecherous Vin.

'Very fashionable to have a love child right now.' He cackled. 'Got a mate in PR who hires fake ones in from kiddy drama schools to boost his clients' profiles.'

'I believe Poppy and his father were married when he was conceived,' Édith corrected.

'My mistake. Not a love child at all! Far too late for that,' he cackled louder.

He was lapping up all the talk of the prodigal's return, knowing this development would infuriate Hector all the more. He longed to hear every detail, but Kizzy's mother Yolande had just arrived in the room and, having signalled husband Howard, the two were soon steering him out of earshot in a seamless scissor movement, well practised through many festivals of scooping overeager speakers away from their public in order to keep the timetable moving to schedule.

'Of course Poppy's secretly horrified,' Édith was saying in a more confidential voice now, although she was being far from discreet. 'After all, who wants a middle-aged man rolling up announcing he's your son? It must make her feel so *old*.'

211

Legs was outraged. 'Byrne is hardly middle-aged!' she fumed. 'And what mother wouldn't be overwhelmed with emotion to see her child again after so long apart?'

'Why did he leave it so long and why shock her with a surprise like this?' Kizzy queried. 'It *has* to be about the money. Or he's trying to give her a heart attack.'

'He's probably rolled up to bump her off.' Édith widened her eyes dramatically. 'I can feel death in the air, can't you Kizzy?'

'With this many character assassins gathered for dinner,' Kizzy's voice shook, 'I'd say there's every chance.'

Legs' detective ears were on high alert, goosebumps popping on her skin. Surely nobody could think Byrne meant any harm? A huge lump had appeared in her throat at the thought of what he had confided to her last night about losing his own life

'I'm sure he has a very heartfelt reason for making contact now,' she insisted.

But Kizzy and Édith were like a pair of Gothic writers on a roll.

'He might have already done her in,' Édith mused.

'He'll be taking his time, waiting for the storm,' breathed the redhead.

'Is that what you'd do, Kizzy darling?'

There was an awkward pause. Kizzy's green eyes flashed as she hissed, 'I'd never have come here in the first place. Farcombe's murder with or without a cadaver.'

Again, Legs was vaguely aware of a subtext, but she was too busy defending Byrne to pay it any heed. 'It must have taken him huge guts to come here.'

Claiming another olive, Édith gave her elbow a playful budge, 'Can't you see this summer is just so fantastically exciting for a boring family like ours?' she said plummily as the olive moved around her mouth. 'First Daddy staging a John and Yoko walkout with your mother, then you turning up like Rebecca waltzing back into Manderley, now this. It's thrilling.'

'I'm nothing like Rebecca,' she bleated. 'She was dead.'

'Oh yes, didn't Maxim de Winter bump her off?' Édith remembered with a giggle. 'We can't lose you again, Legs; you're such bliss to have back. We must keep close tabs on Francis. No boat trips and no guns.'

Legs glanced at Kizzy, and blanched as she received a look of such intensity in return that she stepped back. Despite the pretty smile and winning tilt of the head, Kizzy's green eyes were blazing. Yet they seemed almost as fearful as they did angry, as though trying to communicate some unspoken message or warning. This must be beyond horrible for her, Legs realised wretchedly, thinking again about the conversation she had overheard behind the baize earlier.

Even now, stalking into the room with his blond hair flopping, Francis headed towards Legs first, then seemed to remember himself and veered towards Kizzy to mutter something in her ear. Kizzy shook her head with a contemptuous laugh, but he repeated his words through gritted teeth with eyes like daggers, and she slipped from the room.

He cleared his throat and addressed the assembled guests, 'Poppy will be coming in shortly to introduce us all formally to Jamie, I mean Jago, I mean – whatever.' He looked close to explosion, but mustered his charming smile. 'First, champagne is to be circulated for a toast.'

'God, Poppy's pulling out all the stops,' Édith drawled, having joined Jax and Gayle at the window. 'If it's the 95 Krug we know somebody will be murdered by bedtime. Did you know Kizzy has a pack of tarots and pulled out Death three times earlier this evening?'

Legs felt her goosebumps spring up again. She couldn't shake the image of redheaded corpses in the shopping trolleys from her mind. Suddenly it seemed very important to get away before Byrne reappeared.

Francis moved in beside her, muttering 'You OK?'

'I'm not feeling too well,' she whispered, eyes darting to the door. 'I think it might be better if I leave.'

'No!' Francis moved in front of her, voice low and urgent, big shoulders blocking out the light as he spoke quietly into her ear. 'We agreed. You just have to say the word.'

'I can't.' She started to panic.

He straightened up, blue eyes on hers, suddenly looking terribly sad. 'I thought you felt the same way as I do.'

She looked away, her throat so full of ashes she couldn't speak at first. Then she lamely muttered something about it not being fair on Kizzy.

'Oh, Kizzy has her own agenda,' he said bitterly.

Remembering that just an hour earlier she'd believed Kizzy was a different gender as well, Legs fought an urge to laugh hysterically. Her determination to rescue Francis seemed ludicrous now, as did any plans for a romantic reconciliation amid the family drama.

'I should never have come,' she muttered to herself.

He ran a hand through his unruly blond mop, voice hardening. 'Well for God's sake don't go anywhere until we're through this fatted-calf farce. Then you can pretend you don't feel well and make your excuses.' Impossibly tense, he stalked out of the room, only to appear moments later clutching two magnums of vintage Moët followed by Kizzy carrying a tray of crystal flutes that were rattling so much from her shaking hands, they sounded like a maddened celesta player.

Édith slid in alongside Legs again, voice low and confiding. 'Isn't Kizzy a darling? *So* devoted to love and to duty – or should that be torn apart by it?'

She swallowed miserably, fighting an urge to run out to the terrace and away over the parkland straight away. 'I'll leave Farcombe as soon as I can.'

'Oh, please don't.'

'I can't possibly steal Francis back from her.'

'You must. She's quite wasted on him.'

Legs turned to face her, bewildered, but Édith was glaring over her shoulder at Jax still perched on her windowsill watching the sunset. Then she looked back at Legs, dark blue eyes wide and restless. 'My big brother is *so* deadly dull he can asphyxiate without touching his victim's throat. I never knew how you put up with him, darling, but I have to say I'm terribly glad you do. Everybody is.'

Legs looked across at Francis in alarm, but his blue eyes were fixed on the door through which a thoroughly overexcited Poppy was leading Byrne.

'Everybody, I'd like to introduce my son, Jamie!'

Byrne looked like a starving tiger that had prowled carefully and strategically into new jungle territory over many weeks, finally arriving in its new hunting ground only to find itself tranqued and transported from deep forest to city, then posted into a cage in front of an eager bunch of day trippers. He stared at them all in bewilderment.

'Good to meet you,' he said eventually in that deep, peaty burr.

'Oh my, he's handsome,' Gayle whispered to Jax, who admired his bone structure coolly.

'Great physique,' she conceded. 'But his face is too symmetrical. He looks like a character from a Vettriano painting.'

There was a hiatus as nobody seemed to know quite what to do with this newcomer, who Poppy was holding lovingly at arm's length, the prized white tiger that she'd adored as a cub, who had now been returned to her fully grown and capable of killing a man for fun.

Legs grabbed a bowl of pistachios to go with her olives and waded in.

'Hi. Welcome! I'm Allegra, as you know. Have a traditional peace offering with apologies that the branch is missing.'

Looking somewhat perplexed, he took a green olive and smiled faintly, but those dark eyes blazed in a way she was certain spoke volumes.

'Legs is Francis's loveliest friend, Jamie dear,' intoned Poppy, unaware that the two were already acquainted. 'She is like family. We all adore her, and she's been terribly clever in engineering Gordon Lapis a prime slot here at the festival next month. You know, Ptolomy Finch's creator? Dreadful tosh, but very *commercial*.' She spoke the word like a sacred oath.

'I've heard of him.' Byrne seemed to be having great difficulty swallowing his olive. 'Do you know him well?' He asked Legs in a choked voice, looking around for somewhere to spit out the little fruit.

She shook her head, but Poppy had already decided to share a sworn family secret in her loud baritone.

'Legs is Gordon's confidante. He's apparently *very* difficult and moody, more so now that ever, but Legs has a way with him. Did you know the publishers hated the name Ptolemy Finch at first? It was felt nobody would know how to pronounce it, and Finch was far too insignificant a bird. They wanted to call the character Tyler Falcon, but Gordon refused point blank and threatened to return their advance if they changed it – this is long before he became a star; the advance was paltry.'

Legs could have happily throttled her, but was too fascinated by Byrne spitting out his olive to dwell on it.

'Pistachio?' she offered brightly.

But Byrne was looking boggle-eyed, making her step back. He looked furious.

'They're organic.' She waggled the bowl temptingly.

Byrne shot her an even more disgusted look and shook his head, moving hurriedly away. Trying not to feel hurt, Leg gave a shelled pistachio to Fink who had just waddled up soulfully. Meanwhile, Poppy dashed after her son, turban bobbing. 'You must meet lovely Vincent.'

Within moments, Byrne was being circulated amongst the Keiller-Myleses and the Hawkes like an exotic souvenir brought back from a grand tour.

'And what do you do for a living?' asked Yolande, regarding

him down her long nose as though he was a particularly unpleasant smell.

'Jamie is an assistant trainer in his father's point-to-point yard,' Poppy said proudly, having already decided that the safest way to introduce her long lost son into her life was to speak for him. 'Brooke was one of the best jump jockeys of his generation before the accident. Everybody said he had a magic eye for a horse.'

'Just not a fence,' Byrne muttered drily, and Legs suddenly noticed that his knuckles were tight white and his face quilted with tension.

'Such a dreadful accident.' Poppy shuddered, closing her huge, tortured eyes as though trying to blot out the memory.

'It was no accident,' Byrne breathed, but his words were drowned as Imee rang the huge Farcombe dinner gong with a deafening stroke, making Legs jump so much that the last of the olives went flying like marbles.

Chapter 16

Aware that most popular knowledge about her first marriage was made up of myths of her own creation, that had perhaps demonised her ex-husband Brooke too much in order to cast her in a positive light, Poppy was eager to swiftly rewrite history before too many contradictions showed themselves. As soon as they sat down for supper in the exquisitely lit palm house, with Poppy softly highlighted in the rose-tinted rays of a sunset at the head of the long table, and Byrne cast in palm-striped shadows at its foot, she took up her story with customary dramatic force:

'I was very young when I married Brooke,' she told her assembled guests, 'but he was so dashing and talented, and Jamie was

217

such a beautiful child – our perfect gift to the world – that we tried to make a happy life. I had terrible post-natal depression, and Brooke was always away riding out and racing through winter, which was bitterly cold in a draughty old cottage with no heating. We lived in the middle of nowhere in a god-awful rented dump that Brooke got cheap because it was falling down around our ears, but had a small yard that he could use to train point-to-pointers, which was his real passion.

'Then he took that terrible fall at Wincanton and life changed for ever. He was in hospital almost five months. When the specialists told him he would never walk again, he refused to believe them. There was so little help in those days; my parents were from the class that thought one should just "jolly well get on with it" and said we were "marvellous" every time they visited, but still expected a full Sunday lunch and a walk through the woods with the dogs afterwards; Brooke's family were all in Ireland. I had to look after both my invalid husband and our darling boy who was still in nappies when the fall happened.'

Legs didn't dare look at Byrne, imagining the mortification of listening to it all, yet the equal fascination of knowing the other side of the story at last.

Seated between leery Vin and ultra-dry Howard, she was having a tricky time following Poppy's story in detail because Vin ate with his mouth open, grunting loudly and appreciably as he masticated his way through the blue cheese and pear tart on its watercress and walnut salad; and Howard – infuriatingly disinterested in the story at hand – had been trying to engage her in a quiet conversation about her career at Fellows Howlett throughout the starter. It was quite obvious he was angling for a way to bring his academic tomes to a greater audience. He'd certainly done his homework about the agency.

'I gather Conrad is a commercial maverick within the firm,' he droned on in her ear, 'but Dennis Nobbs sounds a good man to approach.'

'If you can take the BO,' Legs said, desperately trying to listen to Poppy talking.

'There was talk of moving away from Nevermore Cottage and the farmstead to a specially adapted bungalow,' she was saying, 'but Brooke couldn't bear to leave his horses and we had terrible rows about it because I had to look after them as well as do everything else; I used to carry Brooke up and down stairs myself, heave him in and out of the bath, dress him and help him change his catheter. He wasn't a big man, but I was even more of a swallow then and it wrecked my back, so I was always pill popping, and we both drank too much. We started to resent one another, he for being utterly reliant upon me and me for being a full-time carer. We both got terribly depressed. I felt I'd lost the man I loved and ended up with a lifetime of punishment.'

She cast a distraught, short-sighted look down the length of the table towards her son, but a huge modern arrangement of alliums and globe thistles at its centre blocked her sightline completely, so she hurried on.

'Money became ridiculously tight. Brooke was such a proud man he refused to claim the benefits we were entitled to, as though it was an admission of failure. He kept talking about getting back into training, but it never happened. Old racing friends stopped by a lot at first, but gradually they all faded away, frozen out by our fake-believe that all would be all right. The Injured Jockey's Fund helped us out, and I did dribs and drabs of work after Jamie started school, but mostly we lived from hand-outs from my parents.

'Jamie was so little when the accident happened, he probably hardly remembers his father without a wheelchair, but I remember just how tall Brooke walked for a small man; he was a brilliant talent and a total charmer. It's impossible to sum up how deeply and passionately I loved him. I was utterly enthralled by him. I turned away from my family, my class and my friends to be with him.'

'Then you turned away from him to be with Hector,' Byrne said matter-of-factly, his starter still untouched.

There was a collective gasp along the table. Few ever dared to interrupt one of Poppy's monologues.

But beyond the alliums, huge eyes swimming, she simply dipped her head with infinite regret and lowered her fork, taking it as a cue for more soul-searching.

'I still think of it as a moment of madness, especially in the light of—' she stopped herself, knowing she must focus the story around young Byrne and not herself. 'Hector made it clear from the start that Jamie could never be a part of any future we might have together; Brooke made it equally clear that if I ever took his son away from him he would kill himself.'

Byrne looked away, his face high with colour.

Again, Legs shared his mortification, knowing that Poppy was simplifying things appallingly and that it must be hell for him to listen to, yet he had been waiting so long to hear it he wasn't going to interrupt. He was the ultimate good listener after all, with the patience to know that questions could come later. She admired his guts.

'I had to escape to stop myself going mad, but leaving my boys crucified me, it still does.' Poppy's voice broke, and she took a moment to compose herself – perfectly timed to allow Imee to discreetly clear the starter. Sitting on Poppy's right, Vin patted a big paw on his hostess's narrow, silk-smocked shoulder.

She inclined her head gratefully, thinking he was offering sympathy, but then he said 'Great cheese tart, Pops,' which rather ruined the moment.

Beyond the alliums, Édith was now well into her second bottle and eager to stir. 'Lucky Hector was still alive to run away with, the way he treated my mother. Inès cannot tolerate false-heartedness. I've inherited that. We'd *kill* rather than compromise.'

There was a loud clatter further along the table as Kizzy dropped her fork.

Édith pushed her plate away for Imee to take, food barely touched. 'I think if one must leave a relationship then it's important to do it as soon as one decides, don't you?' When nobody immediately answered, she looked across at Jax. 'You agree, don't you darling?'

Jax flashed her cool smile before turning to ask Gayle Keiller-Myles whether she'd seen the latest Chapman Brothers exhibition.

Poppy was eager to rally her audience again. 'You are so right, Édith darling. It's a trait that has always marked me out as a rebel like my paternal grandmother, Clarissa, who refused to live without love and wrote the most amazingly erotic Sapphic poetry. She became a family legend – she had five husbands and countless love affairs with men and women, royalty amongst them, and was eventually murdered in Florence by a spurned lover. Daddy used to say that he got his romantic streak from her, but I think it just gave him an excuse to be a terrible philanderer.'

Desperate to hear more, Legs was still under attack from boring Howard and his questions about publishing. Showing no regard for etiquette, he refused to relinquish her to Vin on her other side as the next course arrived. But at least facing down the table afforded her a good view of Byrne, with Kizzy to his right and Francis beyond that, all three of them barely speaking, eyes forward like statues. Kizzy looked like she was having teeth pulled, Legs noted. She had hardly said a word since the toast to Byrne, the translucent pearl skin on her face pale as marble.

By contrast, Byrne was increasingly red-faced and agitated, his hand raking his hair one moment and scratching his chin the next. His mother's story was clearly getting to him, Legs realised with compassion.

Over a main course of mouth-watering sweet butterfly leg of lamb drenched in Indonesian satay sauce, Poppy regained her equilibrium enough to continue, her turban yanked back to give her an impromptu facelift, which made those huge dark eyes all the more mesmerising.

'When Hector gave me a job here, I was at an all time low. I weighed less than six stone, was crippled with pain and slept less than four hours a night. Jamie was having terrible nightmares, and bed-wetting persistently, but I couldn't get close to him emotionally. He was terribly obsessive and independent, forever disappearing; he would only talk to his father's horses. I feared autism, but what mother wants to admit their only child exists behind a glass wall? I was too much of a coward to seek help.'

Legs lay down her fork, food sticking in her throat as she realised what Poppy was doing. This was machine gun fire self-defence. But Byrne, despite his reddened face, said nothing.

'I fell in love with Hector out of survival instinct, knowing he had the intellect, wealth and strength of character to rebuild me. It was that or almost certain death.'

She left a dramatic pause. To her right, Vin continued devouring his lamb with audible appreciation, now sounding like a bloodhound with a mutton bone.

Legs was watching Byrne worriedly. Again, he had pushed his plate away without touching his food, and his red face was starting to swell. He really looked quite ill. Whatever was killing him could be staging an untimely coup, she thought in fear. Surely he should say something?

But at that moment his puffy eyes met hers and he gave her daggers, warning her off.

'Hector begged me to leave Brooke and I resisted every time,' Poppy continued, 'but I was so frail he eventually forced the situation, taking me away for a weekend and proposing. We returned to break the news to his family first – at his insistence. But then I went back to the farmhouse and found Brooke and Jamie gone, with just a note left, saying I would never find them.'

She had to break off once more to mop her eyes. Imee discreetly filled wine glasses during the pause.

Looking at Byrne, Legs saw his face was like a huge red Edam cheese, his eyes barely visible. Again they managed to seek her out and warn her off. But this time, she had to mouth 'Are you ill?'

He shook his big red head firmly and waved her away.

Her eyes reluctantly jumped to Francis, still poker-backed and facing forwards like a stone statue, although he had made good headway into the lamb, she noted. Sensing her gaze, he returned it with such bright blue, police-light intensity that she lost her breath.

'I love you,' he mouthed, damson streaks touching his cheeks, blue eyes deepening to ripe sloes. 'I love you, Legs.'

Legs glanced instantly and guiltily to Kizzy. But her chair was empty.

She must have slipped out of the room unnoticed. As she'd been sitting beside Byrne, Legs could only hope that she was fetching much-needed medical supplies. He looked close to passing out.

Poppy's bass deep, emotion-infused voice broke across the table again, 'I tried everything to find my baby, my boy.' Her eyes filled with tears and she pressed her bony fingers over her ears, which was presumably why she couldn't hear her baby gasping for breath beyond the flower arrangement at the far end of the table. 'But he seemed to have gone for ever, along with his father. I thought I'd never see them again. And now, like a miracle, here he is.' She tilted her head and gestured dramatically to the alliums, turban shooting forwards to reverse the facelift effect, instantly rendering Poppy's face like a Shar Pei dog, creases pressing down over her luminous eyes.

Unable to see much at all now, Poppy was totally unaware of her son's deteriorating state, and everybody else was too intimidated by her high emotion to point it out.

As Imee whisked in, clearing plates and shyly promising guests that the praline, yam and pecan cheesecake would be with them in just a few minutes, Legs could clearly hear Byrne fighting for breath.

She pushed back her chair in horror, amazed at the polite calm around her as Poppy's guests listened to her describing how her sculptures had always been 'a repressed cry for help'.

'Sit down, Legs,' Francis muttered across the table.

She ignored him. 'Can't you see he's ill?'

'Hector has never appreciated the pain behind my art!' Poppy was proclaiming.

It was a long time since Legs had passed her First Aid course, but she remembered the basic ABC – Airway, Breathing and Circulation.

Byrne was clutching at his chest.

'I channel my inner child through my art!' Poppy asserted behind the alliums.

Legs tried to pull him out of his chair in order to settle him in the recovery position on the cool slate floor beside one of Poppy's amoeba sculptures, but he gripped tightly onto the arms with swollen fingers, wheezing 'shot'.

'You've been shot?' she gasped.

At the head of the table, hidden from view behind the alliums, Poppy suddenly launched into an outburst against Hector of such volume and passion, her guests sat mute and fearful, torn between the action at either end. Only Vin continued to chomp noisily on a third helping of lamb.

Under Legs' ministrations, Byrne let out an angry groan, still grasping at his chest, swollen hand clutching at his jacket. As she pressed her ear to his mouth, at the same time feeling his wrist for a pulse, she heard him gasp out a few words.

'What?' She pressed her ear closer.

'Adrenaline shot,' he croaked. 'In my inside pocket. Looks like a pen.'

Anaphylactic shock, Legs recognised with sudden clarity, feeling urgently inside his jacket for the medication.

'Where do I do this?' she asked in a panic as she uncapped it.

Unable to immediately answer, Byrne slumped forwards, struggling ever more to breathe.

Legs yanked his shirt out from the back of his trousers and found an expanse of smooth, tanned skin at the base of his back, revealing the tops of heavenly spheres of paler buttock cheek rising from his jeans' belt.

Muttering a quiet apology for causing any pain, she plunged the little hypodermic pen into the first sphere.

'I feeel paiiiin!' came a wail, and it was a moment before Legs realised that it was Poppy who had let out the cry, not Byrne. And she was in fact completely oblivious to her son's discomfort, her focus remaining on her own angst, 'When I carve stone, I sometimes feel like I am cutting at my own flesh to reveal the bloodied truth beneath!'

The effect of the adrenalin was almost instant. Byrne was already trying to sit up, looking red-faced and groggy.

'Thank you,' he muttered breathlessly. 'I should be OK now.'

She slipped into Kizzy's vacant chair and stared at him in shock. The swelling was already dissipating and the redness fading, but he still looked dreadful, his eyes half closed and his breath shallow.

'Shouldn't we call an ambulance?' she checked anxiously.

'I'll be fine. Just give me time.'

'If you're sure?'

'You'd better get back to your place.' He looked past her to Francis, who was listening intently to his stepmother and ignoring the medical crisis completely, although the damson streaks in his cheeks had deepened, the muscles there quilted as tightly as a fisherman's knots.

She handed him back his adrenaline pen. As he took it, she felt his fingers hold hers for a moment.

'Thank you, Heavenly Pony,' he breathed in an undertone.

'Any time,' she said, then felt stupid because it sounded so banal.

Returning to her place, she found a great slab of cheesecake waiting there, and Howard still eager to talk about his future literary career. 'Do you think I should write under a pen name?' He asked, now extremely tight and falling over his words.

'Well Howard Hawkes might get confused with the filmmaker,' she said distractedly, still watching Byrne who looked agitated but was recovering fast.

'I was thinking of Jean Pool?' he suggested breathlessly. 'It's what I call myself when I dress as a woman.'

Legs reached nervously for her wine and checked on Byrne again.

The rest of the dinner guests seemed perfectly happy to carry on as though nothing untoward had happened. Apart from a few 'Feeling better Jamie?' enquiries, the incident was politely ignored. At Farcombe Hall, even kitchen sups were decorous enough to mean that ill health at the table was not acknowledged unless one was bleeding so profusely it threatened the napiery.

Poppy was far too short-sighted and had been far too busy talking to notice her prodigal son's allergic dice with death beyond the alliums, and was now holding forth about the festival and how hellish Hector was being: 'He's gone quite mad. We had an emergency committee meeting today, and when I threatened to cancel the whole event, he just laughed. He couldn't give a stuff about the Ptolemy Finch thing, as long as he can play his bassoon as usual. I'm thinking of getting him certified. That or dipping his reeds in cyanide.'

'Told you there'd be a death soon,' muttered Édith, licking cheesecake from her spoon before admiring her reflection in it. 'Imee really does make the most delicious puds.'

'The only thing getting killed around here is our family's reputation,' Francis snapped, now under direct assault from Poppy.

'It's your fault all this happened,' she boomed. 'Hector was fine until you lost control of Legs!'

'I'm getting confused,' Gayle was whispering to Jax. 'I thought it was her first husband who lost the use of his legs?'

Leaning sideways to get full sight of her stepson, turban over one ear, Poppy rampaged on at Francis through the alliums: 'Well you can tell your father he has burned his boats as far as I am concerned!' she was shouting, hands slamming down on the table as she addressed everyone. 'You can all tell Hector not to come back – I have a new man in my life!' She staggered to her feet and raised her glass above the alliums to Byrne, who managed a vague nod in return. 'Are you all right?' She squinted. 'You look very red.'

'I'm fine,' he insisted. 'This evening has been most enlightening.'

Édith lent behind a half-asleep Howard Hawkes to whisper to Legs over his chair back: 'Someone's obviously tried to poison Jamie already, and Kizzy is still missing, have you noticed? There'll be none of us left by petits fours.' Her eyes glowed luminously.

Legs felt her skin chill. She was rapidly losing enthusiasm for detective work in the wake of tonight's cross-currents and high drama.

Then Imee stepped between them to discreetly hand a note to Édith.

Legs' skin felt as though it had iced over as she watched the expression on her fine-boned face change from amusement to horror. 'What is it?'

Édith folded the note with shaking hands. 'It's from Kizzy.'

'What does she say?'

'I need to speak with Francis.' Her voice was tight with emotion as she pushed back her chair and rushed around the table to take Kizzy's empty space and whisper urgently with her brother.

To Legs' surprise, he started laughing. Édith looked as though she might hit him and when he demanded to read the note, she ripped it to shreds, voice rising so that Legs distinctly heard the words 'ruin us!'. Francis stopped laughing and went very pale.

But she had no time to study them further as Howard woke up from his doze with a start and put his arm around her. 'Would you like to meet Jean Pool, my dear? She loves entertaining pretty girls and sharing make-up tips.'

Rescue came from Poppy, peering myopically over the alliums again as she announced loudly that they would all take coffee in the green drawing room.

While Francis and Édith trailed behind the others deep in a hushed, intense conversation, Legs shook off Howard and tried to hang back to listen in, but Byrne foiled her with a firm hand on her back, propelling her towards the cloisters. 'Join me for a cigarette.'

'I don't smoke.'

'Neither do I, but Fink likes a quick drag.'

'Don't tell that to Howard Hawkes,' she muttered as she was marched at speed through the Moroccan corridors, shadowed by a loyal basset.

The storm was drawing ever-closer, the wind rustling madly through the rhododendrons, thunder engaged in cannon battle beyond the Fargoe headland.

Hair lifting off his forehead, Byrne was back to his old self, disapproving and furnace eyed, his cheeks showing just a hint of puffiness, like Russell Crowe between movies. 'I thought you were going to leave Farcombe?'

'*You* told me to leave.'

'It was good advice.'

Despite the fact she wanted to leave quite badly right now, she resented being bullied. 'A very good friend of mine says that red cars are unlucky, and my car is red, so I think it best not to travel.'

He gave her a withering smile, but his eyes remained restless. 'It's a lot more dangerous sticking around here.'

'Christ, don't tell me you think there'll be a murder too?'

His dark brows shot up. 'Why would I think that?'

She gave a nervous little hum by way of an answer, already feeling silly. The approaching storm and all this talk of danger, death and disappearance was making her hopelessly on edge, added to which being alone with Byrne was causing her heart to beat so hard that she was convinced it would soon start propelling her around the cloisters like a washing machine with an uneven load.

When a cough behind them made them both jump, Legs added a shriek of such heart-lurching overreaction that Fink, who was cocking his leg against the base of a column, let out a gruff bark of alarm and fell over.

Francis stepped through the arches, clipped voice reverting to Ivy League preppy as it always did when he was annoyed. 'There you are, darling. Your coffee's going cold.'

Behind him, Édith was looking more ravishingly willowy and predatory than ever as she carried out two crystal brandy balloons and a bottle of Armagnac. 'Jamie, let's have a little chat, you and I.' Her voice was a seductive purr.

Even though she knew that Byrne still just wanted to get rid of her by any means of transport available and that Édith was gay, Legs glanced over her shoulder fearfully as Francis spirited her away, washing machine heart moving from fast spin to door lock.

Still deathly pale, Francis was incredibly keyed-up. She anticipated a lecture from him for sloping off to the terrace with Poppy's son – and possibly even a telling off for breaking protocol as the cheesecake was served to administer emergency injections at the dinner table – but instead she got an eager, possessive hand on her bottom, circumnavigating her buttocks as they strode side by side. 'I adore it when you wear no knickers. Come here.' He tried to pull her behind a big fibreglass blob.

'No!' she squeaked. 'Tell me what's happened to Kizzy?'

But they were both side-tracked by Gayle Keiller-Myles gliding back from the washroom like a creamy white Andrex puppy, greeting them both with her sunny California tones: 'Such a great evening, guys. Vincent is loving it. He just adores this old place.' She fell into step with them as they meandered towards the drawing room. 'These old statelies used to give me the heebies, but I figure Farcombe is something special. It always feels so safe and cosy, doesn't it? Like nothing bad has ever happened here.'

'*Au contraire,*' Francis told her, irritated to find his clinch interrupted. 'According to the history books, there have been at least

229

seven murders at the hall during its four hundred year tenure, and I'm convinced there will be more to come.'

While Gayle giggled, certain that he was joshing, Legs swallowed nervously and glanced over her shoulder again, wishing she'd taken flight while she had the opportunity.

'What's that noise?' she gasped as they passed a small, arched window facing out to the coast, its casement frame rattling. Through it, an unearthly wailing was clearly audible.

'Sounds like a sea shanty.' Gayle cocked her head.

'It's just the wind.' Francis leaned out to pull it shut. As he did so, Legs was certain she could make out strains of 'Running Up that Hill' which were abruptly muffled as the window slammed closed and the catch clicked into place.

Chapter 17

Poppy's guests were taking coffee and digestifs in the green drawing room, surrounded by the Protheroes' personal collection of modern art, as varied and eclectic as its investors, including a large nude of Poppy herself constructed entirely from antique pin-mounted butterflies.

'Never understand why you keep the best painting in the house upstairs.' Vin was standing alongside his hostess, peering around her most treasured canvases. 'Used to hang in Hector's office at the Fitzroy.'

'The Freud?' Francis moved in smoothly.

'Cracking little picture. Always envied him it. Great little investment too; its value must have rocketed since the artist's death. Now's the time to sell.'

'In that case, we must talk.'

'Don't be ridiculous, Francis,' snapped Poppy, 'your father

would never part with that painting,' – dark eyes narrowing, her lips pursed into a smile – 'although whether I ever let him see it again is another matter.' She reclaimed Vin with a winning smile. 'I have several new works for sale if you're looking to acquire erotica.' Drawing him aside, she dismissed her stepson with a flick of her hand, seemingly no longer interested in a romantic reuinion between him and Allegra that evening, fake or otherwise.

Legs fell gratefully upon a small and potent cup of coffee, eager to clear her head, but the caffeine made her even more jittery as Francis steered her to a tall window, tightly sealed against the howling wind and sea shanty wailing.

'I think she's forgotten that he's what this evening's all about,' he muttered, and Legs jumped as he breathed in her ear, 'but we haven't forgotten, have we?'

Then, like a seagull cawing, Poppy confirmed why she no longer cared to bait the trap she had laid to bring her wayward husband home. 'Jamie, darling! *There* you are. Isn't Édith divine? I knew you two would hit it off.'

'No blows have yet been exchanged,' Édith said lightly, hooking her arm firmly through Byrne's and towing him towards the coffee.

He caught Legs' eye as he passed. She couldn't read his expression, but sensed it was far from approving. Still cornered with Francis, she found his edgy lasciviousness unnerving.

'What did Kizzy's note say?' she asked him in an undertone.

'I have no idea,' he said unhelpfully, fingers rattling on his coffee cup. 'Édith ripped it up, remember?'

'She must have told you what was in it?'

'Nothing you need to worry about. God, but you look sexy in that dress, the way your nipples poke through the knitting.'

'It's crochet, actually, and it's fully lined.' She crossed her arms in front of her chest like a scuba diver about to tip backwards off a boat.

Kizzy's parents seemed unconcerned that she was missing; Howard had nodded off on an orange velvet sofa; Yolande was taking a tour around the room with Vin, Gayle and Jax as Poppy showed off her latest acquisitions.

'This is the Stan McGillivray we hung last autumn.' She pointed to an amazing painting of a stag fashioned on a huge canvas with just half a dozen strokes of thickest black and sienna paint. Its power and simplicity was glorious, Legs thought. 'We had to go to his studio on Exmoor and practically beg at the door; he so rarely sells anything these days. We've tried to get him to the festival every year since the start, but he's a total recluse. Isn't it stunning?'

'I prefer nudes to wildlife.' Vin angled his head. 'But that ain't bad for venison.'

'Dad bought it for her birthday,' Francis whispered to Legs, 'She hated it at first – she wanted one of McGillivray's early Prosthetic Limb paintings that became part of Brit Art iconography. But absolutely everyone who sees it loves it, so she's started to come round – especially if she gets to keep it in a divorce settlement. It must be worth fifty thou. Then again, the Freud's worth ten times that. Probably why she wants to keep tabs on it.'

'Do you really think they'll divorce?'

'Might come to it.'

'But you could lose Farcombe.'

'We'll find a way round that.' His voice was caressing. But then his brows suddenly lowered menacingly over those angry true-blue eyes. 'Let's just hope that the boy wonder over there can't get his hands on the place before we figure out how.'

They both looked across to the brightly striped chaise, upon which Byrne was undergoing a rigorous cross-examination from Édith which made no allowances for his recent dice with death. 'Why not warn Poppy you were coming?' she demanded.

'It was a last-minute decision.' His voice was low and sincere.

Legs thought about his confession the previous evening. *I am about to lose my life.* If he was terminally ill, it stood to reason that he would want to seek reconciliation with his mother. She couldn't help wondering what he could be suffering from – some dreadful

232

rare blood disorder, or a tumour like the one that had stolen away Francis's beautiful mother at such an early age? It seemed desperately unfair.

She tried to edge closer to listen in, but Francis had her trapped up against a huge abstract sculpture, a complicated fabrication of rusted metal twists and spikes which looked like an instrument of torture. 'Recognise this?'

'Wasn't it outside?'

'That's right. It's a Richard Deacon. Dad's taste again. It used to live out on the terrace, but the sea air was destroying it so he insisted it be re-sited in here last winter. You remember what he used to call it?'

She shook her head.

'"Legs' parking place". It always reminds him of your old death-trap of a car; more rust and holes than motor.'

'Hondas are very reliable,' she huffed.

'You should have traded up years ago.' When they'd been together he'd tried endlessly to persuade her to upgrade the beloved Honda she'd had since her student days for one with more gadgets and curb appeal. While Francis was unashamed to drive around London in a mud-caked Land Rover, he preferred his girlfriend to be seen in a racy little hatch; he was the same about clothes, happy to look understated in classic old threads, but favouring Legs in a pretty dress to comfortable slouch gear.

'What does Kizzy drive?' She was determined to get to the truth, guiltily wondering if she was speeding along the A39 blind with tears right now – or parked up in a nearby gateway waiting to drive over Legs the moment she left the hall.

But Francis remained oblique, 'People around the bend mostly.' He was looking at the sculpture, handsome brows furled now. 'Always makes me think of a piece of torture chamber apparatus.'

Legs shuddered, her detective credentials fading yet further in the wake of mounting cowardice and desire to bolt back to the Book Inn. She could see Byrne looking at her over the back of the striped chaise, longing to escape too as Édith posed awkward questions. She smiled, but his face remained guarded.

Poppy had reached the butterfly picture. 'One really has to stand at the back of the room to get the full impact of this. It's why we hung it here so it's the first thing one sees coming through the doors from the main hall. Hector loves to shock.'

'Oh, those poor, pretty insects!' Gayle lamented, standing so close that she couldn't see the overall picture, only its delicate media.

'They would have been trapped at least fifty years ago,' Poppy insisted coolly.

'Shame the artist didn't capture Poppy in the nuddy then, too,' Francis muttered to Legs. 'Everybody comes in here with their eyes closed to avoid seeing it, except Poppy herself who is so short-sighted she can't see her ancient carcass pinned to the wall, just the seductive blur of its outline.'

'She is still a beautiful woman,' Legs pointed out, amazed to find herself defending Poppy, but equally appalled by Francis's venom. Had she forgotten how much he loathed his stepmother, she wondered, or had that enmity deepened during her absence? 'If you hate her so much, why do you want her to get back together with your father?'

'Status quid pro quo.' He turned to her. 'And there's a lot of quid at stake.'

'So it's really all just about money?'

'I want you back, Legs.' His fingers traced the underside of her arm, making it burn with fear and longing. 'We both know that's more important than anything.'

She stepped away, pressed up against the sculpture's steel ribs now. 'Not until you deal with the Kizzy situation.'

'Already done.' He tapped a finger impatiently on the rusted metal bars beside her. 'She's gone, or haven't you noticed?'

'She's really left Farcombe?' she baulked, realising that the note must have been a tearful farewell. 'In the middle of supper?'

He nodded, tapping gaining velocity.

'But where? Why so suddenly?'

'Funnily enough, we didn't ask for details or a forwarding address.'

That unexpected cruelty again; it shocked her. Just as much of a shock was the attraction she still felt hardwired through her. His hand was on her arm again. This time the heat scorched through her body, and Legs knew she couldn't trust herself at all. It was as though a chemical reaction was taking place inside her, converting all the guilt and regret and nostalgia into lust, rekindling that old spark. She'd laid off the wine all night, yet the room was spinning.

Deep in her fickle heart a voice was singing victoriously, knowing that Kizzy was no longer a threat. Her suspicions seemed entirely justified. Why, then, did she also feel like she was in a speedboat travelling far too fast into the gathering storm, with no life jackets and one man already overboard?

'Are you going to say the word?' he breathed in her ear.

She was faintly aware of Byrne still watching her at a distance, and of Poppy far closer at hand telling her guests about the Richard Deacon sculpture. 'You'll all recognise this. We bought it long before the artist was as sought after as he is now. Alas, it got rather bent when some drunkard at Hector's sixtieth climbed on it to shout at the sea.'

'That would be Hector himself.' Francis's fingers traced their way across Legs' back and beneath her hair to the nape of her neck as he whispered in her ear again. 'Stay here tonight.'

They both jumped as Yolande Hawkes struck the rusty stretch of steel on which they were leaning so that it hummed and reverberated.

'Marvellous piece this, Poppy!' She had a voice like Brian Blessed. 'One of Kizzy's favourites. The sculptor won the Turner Prize the year that she was born.'

Legs frantically did her maths. That would make Kizzy no more than twenty-four, she realised. Poor kid. Life with the Protheroes must have aged her despite the raw fish diet. It was telling that since arriving back at Farcombe, almost everybody who had known Legs here had told her how much younger she looked. Instead of keeping portraits in the attic, Francis and his father kept women ageing wearily alongside them, she thought. She didn't want to find herself immortalised on a wall in dead butterflies one day.

Suddenly the room stopped spinning. She had to get out, she realised with mounting panic. If she stayed, she'd never escape. She needed more time to think.

Looking frantically around the room to assess her best escape route, she found her gaze drawn to Byrne, who was still watching her, his dark eyes fierce, his face now almost returned to its usual chiselled proportions and drawn with desolation. Despite welcoming her son's surprise return with dramatic and open arms, Poppy had talked over him all evening, Legs reflected. They hadn't shared more than a scrap of time together and she was still largely ignoring him. He must be bitterly disappointed. He could have just weeks left to live, perhaps less.

'Stay with me.' Francis was breathing in her ear again, one hand slipping beneath her arm and caressing the edge of her breast. 'This dress is exciting the hell out of me. I know you wore it for me; I am a lucky man.'

She guessed she should feel victorious, but her panic just mounted. She'd wanted to recreate the love they'd felt at that May Ball, but all she'd recaptured was his desire to bed her. It was all happening too fast.

'I really don't feel very well,' she said in a frozen voice, ashamed at the lie.

Francis's handsome face was suddenly all contrite concern. 'Darling, why didn't you say?'

'I think I should just make my way to the Book Inn if that's OK.'

But Francis had no intention of letting her go now that Kizzy had cleared their path. 'If you're unwell, you must lie down upstairs, darling.' He hooked her arm caringly in his.

Poppy, standing behind them, was determined to get the party going. 'It's still early. I thought we'd have a little recital. Such a shame Legs is feeling ill – she sings rather sweetly – but the rest of us can still enjoy the power of the voice. And don't tell me you can't hold a tune, Jamie; you had a glorious descant as a boy.'

Shooting a panic-stricken look at Byrne over her shoulder, Legs reluctantly allowed herself to be spirited through to the main hall and up the dramatic sweep of stairs lined with vast pop art canvasses, to the landing decked with early examples of the Glasgow School where Francis steered her into the Lavender Room, a seductive dusky mauve guest suite that took up the entire West tower and looked out to sea. Despite the whimsical name, it was no innocently flower-scented bed chamber, and was crammed with the most graphic of the Protheroes' nudes, swathes of canvas depicting pink genitalia in every medium and texture, parted legs, lips, and labia, erect nipples and cocks, rounded buttocks and wanton copulation. As teenagers, she and Francis had stolen in here at every opportunity, their sex manual painted across the walls, guiding them through their carnal education as they recreated every pose with stifled giggles and mounting self awareness.

Now, averting her gaze from the walls like a WI stalwart faced with a copy of *Big'uns*, Legs stared fixedly out of the tall mullioned windows, where the last cross hatches of a red sunset were fading in the night sky, and a quarter of moon rose like a tattered ensign flying over the embers of a burning battleground.

'Why did Kizzy go so suddenly, Francis?' she demanded as he closed the door behind them. But he was intent on one thing, his hands already exploring her body and reclaiming lost ground.

'Let's not worry about that now.' His cheeks were even higher with colour, his blue gaze eating her up. His lips met her left ear and the excited breath filling its tiny hollow almost made her melt with déjà vu desire despite her squirming shame.

237

'Yes, let's worry!' she bleated, backing away. 'What if she's done something silly?' Legs the detective was still trying to put in a noble fight for answers, even if she was clueless what the questions should be.

Reluctantly, he stepped away. Sitting down on the vast carved oak bed, he patted the counterpane beside him.

Legs chose a deep window-seat instead, eyeing him warily.

His fingers tapped out a tattoo on the raw silk as he let out an impatient sigh. 'The only silly thing Kizzy did was to assume that I would choose her above you. As soon as she realised that was patently absurd, she took her leave.'

Suddenly it all made horrible sense. 'She thinks she's letting you free?'

'I told Kizzy I wanted an open relationship, which suited her just fine. Only now you're back, it's closed.'

He sounded frighteningly like his father, Legs realised with a shudder.

'What do you think she'll do now?'

'Hard to tell. She's pretty unstable,' he admitted.

'So she *might* do something silly?'

'You still read too many bad thrillers.' He looked up at the nudes on the walls. 'Kizzy's harmless, and terribly eager and sweet under all those shiny emotional scales; I really did want to make it work with her. I thought it might take away some of the pain of losing you.'

'Oh God, Francis, I'm sorry.'

'Don't be.' He stood up and crossed the room, eyes blazing. 'I have more than my fair share of consolation at hand. Christ, Legs, I've missed you. I'll wipe out anyone that stands between us.' He took her face in his hands and bent his head down to kiss her.

Legs' lips longed to soften and yield, but her mind buzzed madly, her head full of images of heartbroken Kizzy and trepidation at what she might have triggered. Falling back into his arms would be easy comfort, but it felt rushed and deceitful. She was certain she was only getting half the story, the romantic subplot within a far more political family drama.

'No!' she bleated, turned her face away from him and encountering a cold window pane. 'I mean – hell, Fran, I do feel really quite ill. It's my period, you see – awful cramps. Yuck.' That had always been guaranteed to back him off, along with bats, Marmite and power ballads.

'Poor you.' He predictably dropped her like a stone.

'Do you mind if I lie down just for a bit?'

'Go ahead,' he sighed, retracing his steps towards the door. 'I'll be back in half an hour to see how you're doing. Listen for three knocks. Don't let in anybody else. Trust nobody here tonight, Legs.' And he disappeared out into the landing.

At first just desperately relieved to be alone, Legs slumped on the window seat and took a few deep breaths. Then she started to feel anxious, Francis's warning ringing in her head: trust nobody. She certainly didn't, least of all herself. If she shared Francis's bed tonight, there'd be no going back. She wanted to escape as soon as possible.

She hurried to the door, intent on leaving the hall by the quickest exit.

But however much she rattled and tugged at the handle, it wouldn't turn. The door was locked. Peering through the keyhole to find a pawn of golden light, Legs realised that Francis must have taken the key with him, so there wasn't even a chance of pushing it through to extract from beneath the door with a wire coat-hanger as she'd read in her beloved crime thrillers. She was captive.

Whimpering, she scuttled to the window and threw open the ancient casements. She could hear the sea crashing against the rocks close by. The storm was brewing ever faster, electric crackling in the sky a few miles off the coast, distant thunder rolling towards land, stampeding rainclouds blotting out the moon's crescent.

Looking down, Legs sited the terrace at least twenty foot

beneath her, with no helpful Virginia creeper or decorative fret-work forming footholds on the bare stone walls this side of the house. There was no escape this way.

She ran to the bathroom and splashed cold water on her face, determined to calm herself down. But her heart raced on, that shameful longing for Francis combining with remorse and fear.

She curled up on the bed's coarse silk counterpane and chewed at several nails, trying not to look at all the heavenly bodies depicted on the walls around her, unashamed and carnal. So many breasts and phalluses, legs and fingers. She could so easily remember Francis's fingers first exploring between her legs, marking her sexual awakening, almost before her own fingers had ever crept there. They'd both been so tentative at first, then increasingly expert and daring. His glorious young erection had been examined from every angle, squeezed, prodded, tasted and even flicked with a teasing fingernail before it found its way inside her. She had been so familiar with its shape and feel by the time they'd lost their virginities together – under canvas on a night just as stormy as this – it was as though a long lost part of her was coming home, yet at the same time so alien and interesting and exciting that no amount of repetition ever seemed to take away the novelty.

The newly chartered romance of it all had underpinned those first explorations, lending them a magic quality she'd thought totally unique to her and Francis. She'd written long, impassioned poems describing the shards of her heart breaking with each coupling, revealing an unhealable wound of love and desire which they only needed to breathe on to make sting and sparkle. Tonight, she felt that romantic teenager inside her hurting again, the wound once more as bright and salt-seared as the shingle outside, a tide of pleasure and pain dragging her memories across the shore.

Half an hour must have passed by as she remained trapped in the room. The storm had plenty of time to brew while she waited. Francis hadn't yet come back to check on her. Thunder rumbled and crackled ever-closer. Her eyes were continually drawn to one of the smallest nudes, oil applied so thickly on its diminutive canvas that it was cast in high relief, depicting its subject with brutal yet sensual skill, a dark, uneven triangle of pubic hair, wide thighs dimpled with cellulite, a distant face cast behind the high relief soft belly, dark eyes limpid and lusting. This was the painting Vin Keiller-Myles coveted so much; Hector liked to boast that it had been given to him in his early Fitzroy Club days by Lucian Freud himself, although Legs had always doubted its provenance, and it certainly wasn't signed. She'd once hated its thickly layered coarseness. Yet now it was the picture she would take home, she realised in surprise. As a teenager, it would have been the huge and naughty Erin Home over the bed. A year ago, it might have been the powerful and thrusting Jake Ince by the dressing table, with its rugby-wide muscle men primed for action. Now she was mesmerised by a horny hairy Mary. Conrad would hate it, she decided with satisfaction. But perhaps that was a part of the attraction. Conrad featured less and less in her fantasies these days. Her desire for him, so overwhelming at first, had already faded. By contrast, her feelings for Francis were so deep rooted she couldn't hope to eradicate them, but they were all muddled up, switching between desire, guilt and affection in rapid-fire succession. Tonight, she also felt an uneasy fear of Farcombe.

It's dangerous sticking around here, Burn's words repeated in her head. Yet who was she to trust a near-stranger over a man she had known more than half her life?

Not long after the first streak of forked lightning split the sky outside, the lights in the house went off.

They'll come on in a few seconds, Legs told herself firmly.

They didn't.

She determinedly didn't scream. Instead, she slid off the bed and started to familiarise herself with the boundaries of blackness around her, again remembering that in her favourite detective thrillers the savvy girls who thought ahead usually lived, whereas the pretty ones with the big breasts died amid lots of blood and gore just before a chapter break. She had to summon Julie Ocean again, she realised. Julie wouldn't let herself become a victim; she had mounting sexual tension with Jimmy Jimee after all, and sequels to star in.

For minutes on end, she paced the ink-dark room, mapping out walls, furniture and blunt objects, alternatively whimpering and hyperventilating, but mostly remembering to keep very quiet.

Then she heard a step outside her door and somebody tried the handle.

Half suffocated by terror, fighting not to scream, Legs raced on tip-toes to hide behind the bed.

A moment later, she knew somebody else was in the room with her.

The scream inside her was building, however much she kept quashing it.

In the half light she could just make out a huge, dark silhouette between her and the door. Desperate not to be discovered, she made a strange croak as she swallowed down the blood curdling wail waiting there. Even to her pulse-pounded ears, the noise she made sounded like a startled macaw.

'Allegra?' The voice was unmistakeable in its peaty Irish soft-ness.

The scream turned into a sob.

'Oh, Byrne. Thank goodness. Francis locked me in, and then all the lights went out.'

'The door wasn't locked just now,' he pointed out.

'Well it was when I tried,' she said, suddenly feeling rather silly. Now that she thought about it, she hadn't really put her weight behind trying to open it, and the ancient doors at Farcombe were notoriously sticky. Very few of the upstairs locks worked, including the bathrooms, much to the consternation of house guests.

'Are you feeling any better?' he asked in that husky, melodic voice. 'You must be terrified up here alone in the dark.'

242

'You came upstairs just to find me?'

'No, I've been pocketing a few jewels,' he said idly, 'like the tinker rogue I am.'

Suddenly, she felt fear clutch at her throat once again. She was standing in a blackened room with a man who was dark-souled and volatile. He had already admitted to her that he had nothing to lose. He had deliberately navigated his way around an unfamiliar house in a power cut to track her down. Could he be planning to bump her off for knowing too much? She couldn't remember him confessing any incriminating secrets during their meal together last night, but then again she had been pretty blootered for much of it.

'I'm fine, thanks,' she muttered anxiously. 'Where's Francis?'

'In the cellar, looking at the fuse cupboard and swearing a lot.'

Which placed him too far away to hear her scream, Legs registered with panic. 'And the others?'

'Laying into the port when I left; Poppy is singing Billie Holiday hits a capella.'

'Oh, she does that quite often, although in the past Hector would be accompanying her on the bassoon,' Legs chattered nervously. She had started to edge around the room, planning to make a dash through the door when she got close enough. 'They used to like to fantasise they're like Johnny Dankworth and Cleo Laine.'

She heard a low sigh across the dark room, 'I'm not sure whether to be grateful or sad that I don't share her exhibitionist genes.'

Legs couldn't see his face, so it was impossible to tell his mood.

'So what do you make of your mother?' she asked, still edging around the room.

'I think we both have a nasty streak.'

Legs froze. 'How do you mean?'

'We like to settle scores, and we can wait a very long time to eat a dish cold.'

'Poppy doesn't eat anything much.' She laughed uneasily. Then

243

she gasped, realising that if Poppy had mothered her son until he was ten, she would know all about his nut allergy. Had she deliberately tried to poison him tonight? Would there have been time to change the menu?

At that moment the lights came on, and blinking through the sudden glare, she saw Byrne leaning against the doorframe. His hair was on end and he had a red mark on one cheek, but his face was back to its normal size and colour and she thought how handsome it was, those dark eyes so meltingly intense. Eyes now adjusting to the brightness, she was also acutely aware of all the nude paintings surrounding them.

Byrne didn't appear to have noticed them at all. He looked at her for a long time, those dark eyes so incredibly focused that she was sure he could see right through her skin to the ventricles of her heart pumping harder and faster.

From somewhere deep within the lowest bowels of the house, there was a bloodcurdling scream.

Byrne turned back to the open door. 'Jesus what was that?'

'We'd better get downstairs.' She rushed past him and out onto the landing, so grateful that gutsy Julie Ocean was once again taking over, she was tempted to throw in a couple of SAS rolls along the landing.

In the kitchen, they found Francis emerging from the cellars in a terrible state, cobwebs in his hair and a face as white as a sheet. His hands shook. 'I just found . . . down there . . . it's horrible . . .'

'Ohmygod, there *has* been a murder!' Legs screamed.

'Stay with him.' Leaving Francis holding onto the Aga rail for support, Byrne headed down the cellar steps.

They could hear Poppy singing 'Strange Fruit' in a reedy alto in the distance. Nobody else in the house seemed to have taken the slightest notice of the scream.

'What's down there, Francis?' demanded Legs.

But he shook his head, too upset to speak. He was close to tears.

To her surprise, Byrne looked quite cheerful when he bounded back up the steps a few moments later. 'I think you need to look at this, Allegra.'

'I really can't stand the sight of blood,' she protested. 'Surely we should just call the police? Trampling over a crime scene contaminates evidence.'

But he grabbed her hand and pulled her behind him. 'As crimes of passion go, this is extremely inventive.'

Heart thudding sickeningly, Legs followed him down to the cavernous vaulted Farcombe cellars. The first cellar looked just as she remembered it, clammy cold and smelling of the sea, the grilled door to the cove passage padlocked in one corner. To the left lay the wine cellars and a maze of old storage rooms. To the right, where Byrne led her now, was the old boiler room, then on past the fuse boxes and into the wide expanse of lower ground floor that faced onto the parkland, which Poppy now used as her studios because of the high north-facing windows and big doors which allowed easy access to one of the courtyards.

In here, it appeared Poppy had been working on her latest creation for several weeks, carving into a huge slab of limestone. But this was no amoeba. This was a human figure. Nobody could mistake that long, languid body, the sprouting beard and thick head of hair. And the bassoon was a giveaway.

Three times larger than life, Hector was depicted with such unflattering, caricatured exaggeration that he was rendered monstrous, one eye bulging, the other squinting, the nose pocked and bulbous, a dribble escaping from chapped lips as they puckered towards the reed. His body, creped as old netting, sagged and bulged and creased grotesquely. The detail was incredible, right down to the gnarled angles of his fingers on the bassoon key holes, the ragged edges of his nails, and thick cuticles. She had even etched in varicose veins on his legs, along with a scattering of moles and a few tattoos.

Most unflattering of all was what lay between his legs.

Legs whistled. 'Oh Christ, it makes Michelangelo's David look well hung.'

In the sculpture, Hector was undoubtedly in a state of high arousal, but while the rest of his carved stone body was three times its normal size, this feature was on a far smaller scale. It looked like a hyacinth peeping out between huge tree roots, waiting for the frost to pass.

'He'll go hopping mad.' She stared at the tiny stone protuberance, perfect in every detail apart from proportion. 'Hector's hung like a donkey. And he doesn't have tattoos on his buttocks.'

When Byrne said nothing, it occurred to her that her observations might be open to interpretation.

'She must be planning to exhibit is at this year's festival,' she rushed on. 'No wonder Fran's upset. The family pride will take quite a knocking.'

Byrne let out a low laugh. 'You know, I think I could get to respect my mother after all. She has an incredible talent. It's one of the most remarkable pieces I've ever seen.'

'I never knew she could actually, really sculpt,' Legs had to give grudging respect. She stepped forward to remove a dust sheet that had been abandoned by one of Hector's stone feet. Then she let out a yelp.

Wrapped around Hector's bulky ankle was a tiny bent-backed creature, part reptile, part monkey, part human, a slathering servile Gollum clinging onto the great man. Its face was Francis's.

'Jesus,' Byrne gasped in awe.

'I wonder where she's put Édith?' Legs whispered.

'Up his arsehole?'

There was a step behind them and they turned to see Francis looking pale but composed, his chin held high. The family likeness captured in the sculpture was so clear when the two were juxtaposed, it showed just how brilliant Poppy was.

'It will *never* go on show,' he announced darkly.

Neither Legs or Byrne knew where to look.

Francis cleared his throat. 'The other guests are leaving. I'm sure you want to say farewell.'

For a moment the two men stared each other down, but then Byrne conceded, turning to Legs. 'Would you like me to walk you back to the hotel?'

'She's staying here tonight!' Francis snapped.

Caught between Byrne's glowering disapproval and Francis's high emotion, she knew her loyalty should keep her here, but she craved her bed in Skit and time to think.

'I think perhaps I should go.'

To her surprise, Francis put up no more resistance. 'You're right. It's been a rather overwhelming evening, and it's not over yet. I must speak with Poppy about this – monstrosity – straight away.' He couldn't bear to look at it.

As Byrne went on ahead and Francis hastily threw the sheet back over the ankle-biter, Legs lingered behind.

'Francis, I—'

'Leave it!' he hissed, stalking past her towards the stairs. 'Some things are best left.'

In the main hallway, the party was taking forever to disband, largely because Poppy was raring to keep going until the early hours.

As soon as she saw her glowering stepson thunder out of the cellars to issue formal handshakes, Poppy registered that he was itching to have a fight, but was too well mannered to do so in front of dinner guests, and so she tried to string things out as long as she could.

'You must, must stay, Jamie,' she crooned at Byrne in her deep voice. 'We have so much to share, so much to talk about. My long lost son!' Her bony ringed fingers reached up to his cheek.

'Another time.' He smiled guardedly. 'Thank you for tonight. I apologise that I sprang such a surprise on you earlier. My plans changed at the last minute.'

'Oh, I love surprises.' She creased her huge eyes playfully, squeezing his cheek so that his mouth formed into an involuntary half-smile.

'I'll remember that.' He removed her hand gently and dropped a brusque kiss on it, which Legs considered very courteous considering Poppy had spent so much of the evening summarising his childhood so ungraciously.

By contrast, Francis kissed Legs farewell on both cheeks with lips like branding irons, then clamped her to his chest in a vice-like hug. He was so angry with Poppy, his hands were still shaking. 'We'll meet up tomorrow.'

'I leave for London straight after breakfast. I'm collecting Nico.'

'Then we'll have breakfast. We must talk.'

She nodded, not looking at Byrne. Fink the basset was already eagerly pushing his way outside, desperate to escape the madhouse and new sworn enemy Byron, with whom he'd come to blows over leftovers.

'Kizzy's left Byron behind!' Legs realised as the lame little terrier growled on the doorstep, but there was nobody to hear; Poppy was already going into rapid retreat back to her petits four and Billie Holiday, jewelled Moroccan slippers tapping lightly on the stone floors, pursued by Francis's long stomping strides. Byrne had slipped out into the darkness.

Chapter 18

Legs and Byrne walked away from the hall in silence. The storm had passed now, the rose petals underfoot a slippery river of bruised colour that ran into the veins of black lava of the rhododendron flowers lit by the carriage lamps along the rear drive. Beyond the rearing unicorns on the gate pillars the sky was clear again, stars back on show, the crescent moon now looking out to sea.

The gates were padlocked as usual. While Byrne stood in front of them wearily, assuming their way was blocked, Legs opened what appeared to be a panel in the left gate pillar itself and stepped inside, pushing another panel that led out onto the village road.

'This is amazing,' Byrne followed her.

'Hector had it put in to enable a quick dash to the pub. It only works going out, though. You can't get back this way. He has to come home through the churchyard, which he hates. That's always his excuse for staying until last orders.'

'He sounds quite a character.' His voice was unusually flat.

'Of course, you haven't met him. He's a one-off.'

'I think I might recognise him now.'

She tried not to think about the hideous stone caricature; 'When I was a little girl, I idolised him. I thought he was a king.'

'When I was a little boy, I thought he was the Devil,' Byrne said quietly.

Legs wrapped her arms tightly around herself, trying not to shiver. 'It is strange to see your mother again after so long?' The question sounded horribly nosey and awkward spoken out loud as she struggled with her intimacy switch; last night's confessions and tonight's life-saving had conspired to make her feel skin-to-skin, yet he kept three feet apart from her like a prisoner walking alongside a lawyer, divided by steel mesh and guards.

His voice, at least, remained mellifluous in its peaty warmth. 'I rather like her, which is a pleasant surprise. We have a lot in common; she has a monstrous ego and a neat line in revenge. That said, I can't say I share her taste in food.'

Legs laughed nervously, a horrible seagull caw even to her own ears. Her teeth were chattering, goosebumps like bubble-wrap now. If she hugged herself any tighter, she'd start popping like space dust.

She had so many things that she longed to ask about his childhood, and why he had come back, but she felt suddenly so shy of him she had no idea where to start. There was something so noble and tragic about him. She kept feeling she should apologise for her weak character and loose morals.

She jumped as Byrne slipped his jacket over her shoulders. It smelled of sea walks and wet dog, such a contrast to Francis's expensive cologne.

'Thank you.' She trudged on for a few paces before realising that he was no longer alongside. Turning back, she saw him rooted to the spot, staring up at the moon as it was crossed by a cloud, just its top half poking up like a luminous shark's fin.

'It wasn't an accident,' he said quietly.

'What wasn't an accident?' She walked back towards him.

He narrowed his eyes as the smoky cloud thinned around the shark's fin, transforming it into a sickle. 'You're the detective, Heavenly Pony.'

Legs wavered, mind whirring. Was he talking about the food that had almost killed him? Or Kizzy leaving so suddenly? Or even, she thought wildly, their discovery of the Hector sculpture?

But before she could hazard a guess, he stepped forwards, his silhouette blotting out the moon's sharp blade. 'You leave for London tomorrow?'

She nodded.

'You're right to get away from this place. Don't look back.' He made it sound as though staying behind spelled doom.

'I have to be at work.' They fell into step again, heading towards the dim lights of the village.

'Ah yes, with your "lover". He must be very proud of you.'

She put on a burst of speed, not wanting to think about Conrad.

'You got Gordon Lapis on the bill,' Byrne went on, matching her stride.

'Gordon did that himself, really,' she said breathlessly, almost running now as she thought about her secretive, reclusive author and his big stage show. 'He dived in ahead of me.' Her mind was replaying Gordon's incredible message: *we take the devils we know as bedfellows . . . to reveal the truth is to undress in public . . . far better to choose my own stage on which to uncloak*. 'I was just a catalyst between the Devil and the deep blue sea.'

'Is he a devil?'

'Not Gordon!' She jogged unsteadily along the cobbles as they started the steep descent along the village's narrow main lane. 'Don't tell anybody, but I think Gordon's a bit of an innocent. I love him to bits. He needs protecting.'

'And you can do that?'

'Fellows Howlett will.' She eased up the pace to stop her ankles turning on the uneven footing. 'There'll be a lot to organise, promoting the brand and protecting his interests at the festival.'

'Assuming it goes ahead,' Byrne dropped back to walk too. 'Poppy might not be prepared to step beyond her threshold without the great Hector at her side, even carved in stone. And I suspect your ex-fiancé is taking a sledgehammer to that statue as we speak, if not its creator.'

'It'd only take a small chisel to get rid of the bits Francis finds most offensive,' she pointed out.

He laughed his gruff laugh. 'He doesn't love you.'

She turned to him, offended. 'He says he does.'

'We can all say that; it's one of life's most clichéd scripts,' he muttered, then turned towards her and caught her arm, pulling her around to face him. They were standing beneath one of the village's old street lamps. His furnace eyes gleamed beneath their dark brows. 'I fell in love with you at precisely seven thirty-six last night, Allegra.' Legs could hear her heart crashing louder than the waves on the harbour walls. She felt faint, barely able to breathe for excitement. It suddenly made sense. Yesterday afternoon, for all her vacillation, she would undoubtedly have been back in Francis's bed like a shot had it not been for Kizzy. Just thirty-six hours later, her heart had staged another rebellion. Was that because she had fallen head over heels for somebody else overnight?

She stared into his face in the lamplight, his hands warm on her arms, his jacket cloaking her shoulders, and felt as though she'd been wrapped in happiness from head to toe.

'At half past eight tonight you saved my life,' he whispered, 'and I know for certain that I will love you for ever. You have my heart.'

Then Byrne abruptly let her go, turned away and started walking again, 'See? Anyone can say it. It means nothing to say it. Knowing it is another thing.'

Still reeling around in the street light, she felt like her heart had been mugged.

He halted, waiting for her to catch up.

'Francis is honest,' she defended breathlessly, her pride deeply hurt. 'He means what he says.'

'He's a shit,' he hissed.

'Francis and I were together for years and years. I trust him. He'd never hurt me.'

He laughed disbelievingly. 'You thought he'd imprisoned you in a bedroom earlier.'

'That was a silly mistake,' she fumed, ashamed at herself for having been so jumpy. 'All Édith's talk of murder, and then Kizzy disappearing like that made me overreact.'

They were now walking along the narrow, cobbled street which housed Shh, along with the family solicitors she'd seen him enter earlier.

'Did you just say Kizzy has disappeared?'

Remembering that she'd caught sight of Kizzy outside the office moments after Byrne, she was suddenly on her guard. 'She and Francis had a row. She said she wasn't going to stick around to be humiliated.'

'So he got rid of her between courses?'

She shrugged, not liking it put like that.

'If he can do that to her, just imagine what he can do to you.'

'What do you mean?'

'Maybe your friend is right telling you not to drive that old car of yours. Just make sure you check your brakes before you set out tomorrow. Better still, catch a train back to London.'

'Don't be ridiculous,' Legs scoffed. 'Francis would never do anything like that.' Now that she thought about it, he had made some very odd comments about her car tonight, but she hastily dismissed such ideas from her head. 'He might have every right to want to push me off a cliff given what I did to him, but he's shown me nothing but love and affection since I returned.'

'Beware of guilt and pity, Allegra. They are the worst possible foundations for any relationship. I've seen the way you behave with him.'

'You don't understand what he's been through.'

'I think I do.'

'His mother can never come back; Francis used to say that Ella left him with nothing but the memory of her beauty because she died young.' Tears filled her eyes. Then, realising what she had just said to a man who was self-confessedly about to lose his life, she let out a horrified gasp.

But Byrne was too agitated to pick up on it. 'At least she died before she could let him down.' He paused outside one of the little tea shops near the harbour where a poster in the window boasted two for one on angel cakes.

'Poppy running away must have been terrible to come to terms with,' she ventured cautiously. 'I can't imagine how differently my life might have turned out if my mother had left us all like that.'

'You think I've turned into some sort of screwed up misogynist as a result, don't you?'

'No!' she protested, adding, 'I'm sure you hate men just as much.'

But the joke misfired as he glared at her humourlessly, 'It's what love makes men and women do to each other I can't bear.'

253

'So what's it made *you* do, apart from mistrust absolutely everybody?' she demanded angrily.

'You just said it,' he replied matter-of-factly. 'My last girlfriend was still saying she loved me the day before she ran off with my best friend. How can that be?'

Horrified, Legs stared at the angel cake poster. 'How long ago was this?'

'Two years.'

'Did you love her very much?'

'I certainly thought so at the time, but I guess I didn't really know her. The woman I'd been in love with wasn't capable of doing that to me. Nor would the old friend I'd have trusted with my life.'

Legs thought about Francis again, and that terrible day she'd told him she wanted to be with Conrad. How long had it been since she'd said 'I love you' to him? A week? A fortnight? She'd grown accustomed to using it in place of a full stop at the end of phone calls and pillow talk.

'Did *you* want revenge?' she asked in a small voice.

He nodded, face deadpan. 'I killed them both.'

Legs' jaw dropped in horror and she felt her skin chill over. Then she saw a glitter in his eyes and laughed as she realised with a punch of relief that he was just joking, returning fire on her own wisecracks.

They turned towards the harbour again and started along the final steep, cobbled descent, the sea wind sharp against their faces. 'They moved to Cork last year to start up an IT business,' he explained. 'I heard they got married and are expecting their first child in November.'

'Can you forgive them?'

'Why would I want to do that?' He looked across at her sharply, and this time there was no glitter of amusement.

'It might help you move on,' she suggested. 'Perhaps you'll even find new love waiting at seven thirty-six one evening?'

He shook his head. 'You can't take love where I'm going.'

Legs' skin chilled again, this time to sub-zero as she thought about him losing his life.

They were in front of the Book Inn already, the sea still troubled by the storm and lashing hard against the harbour walls.

On the hotel steps, Byrne took her hand in his and shook it, which felt so formal after their two extraordinary nights' acquaintance. 'Thank you for what you did for me tonight.'

'Anytime,' she dismissed, handing his jacket back: 'There are better ways to—' She was about to say 'die', but managed to stop herself just in time and blither, 'There's more than one way to crack a nut.' In the circumstances, she wasn't sure that was a much better way of putting it.

He held open the door for her. As she was about to step through it, Legs turned back to peck him on the cheek. In her hurry, she planted her lips far closer to his mouth than she intended, almost biting his chin.

For a moment she could feel him freeze in horror and then, to her astonishment, his hand reached up to the back of her head and his mouth moved to hers.

The kiss probably only lasted a couple of seconds, but afterwards she knew for certain that she had never been kissed like that in her life. The pit of her belly sizzled like a cymbal, her head was as light as a helium balloon and she seemed to have forgotten how to breathe.

Byrne let her go and looked away, clearing his throat. 'I shouldn't have done that. Go back to your lover in London, Heavenly Pony,' he told her softly. 'There's only stormy water here, not deep blue sea.'

He turned to climb the stairs to his room, leaving her banging a palm against her head, her heart thudding against her ribs, as she tried to stop the walls spinning around her, feeling as though her morals were round her ankles.

Back in Skit, she peeled off the crocheted dress and positively danced around the urinals bathroom cleaning her teeth before falling ecstatically into bed, then picking up her iPhone to set the alarm, although she doubted she would sleep a wink knowing Byrne was lying in bed under the same roof.

One look at the long list of new messages made her want to hurl it from the room. She hadn't even replied to the old ones yet. She'd leave them all until morning, she decided, feeling bad about it. But in one corner of its glowing screen, she could see that Gordin Lapis had just sent her a live message.

Beware the Devil in disguise, was his cryptic opening.

Legs longed to press the 'offline' option, knowing the last thing she needed was an exchange with the eccentric author. But she thought guiltily about his long, heartfelt email to which she hadn't yet responded. And then she thought about Conrad, to whom she had shown no loyalty whatsoever. She'd hardly thought about him all day, she realised with a jolt, except one painful moment surrounded by nude art when she realised she no longer fancied him the way she once had. Her dedication to lover and career was feeble. She had to be professional and show Gordon that she cared tonight.

All gone v well this end. She messaged him back.

Look like an angel. Gordon's reply came almost immediately.

Know you will be a total star here during festival week.

Walk like an angel.

Conrad will confirm details next week.

Talk like an angel.

Now he had truly gone off the rails, poor man. She'd email Kelly in the morning to check what was going on, just as soon as she had escaped Farcombe and its lunacy.

Are you listening to Elvis? she asked carefully.

Title ideas for Julie Ocean and Jimmy Jimmee, he replied. *I fear sexual tension may be getting out of control. Am thinking of sending Jimmy deep undercover to a Carthusian closed order.*

She laughed. That sounded more like the old Gordon.

She started to type, *Thank you so much for the message you sent to me earlier* – but it looked so clichéd that she couldn't bring herself to finish the sentence. Instead she rolled back to the start cursor and wrote: *Sleep tight.*

Don't go! he messaged faster than she could dream of typing herself.

She waited.

Still there? he enquired eventually.

She impatiently miss-typed *Yss.*

There was another endless pause.

At last his dialogue line was refreshed, *Sleep tight.*

And he was declared offline.

Legs cast the phone aside and lay in darkness, still wide awake, listening to the pregnant bat colony budging up overhead. There seemed to be so many devils in disguise around her, she had no idea where to start looking for an angel. She certainly didn't feel like one right now.

Chapter 19

The bats in the roof above Skit woke Legs just before dawn. They were having a busy night, all the new mums dashing back into the maternity colony after foraging for their offspring, the roost overhead chattering, chirping and scolding. It was like trying to sleep beneath a school assembly.

Unable to get back to sleep, she turned on her light and picked up the manuscript of the crime thriller Gordon had recommended, but within two pages her heart was pounding and her mind jumping backwards and forwards trying to tie the clues together. *The Girl Who Checked Out* was too high grade for relaxation. She no longer had an appetite for well-crafted murders, especially those involving redheaded corpses in shopping trolleys.

Last night's antics at the hall had left her perplexed and strangely depressed. She felt silly to have been so frightened, yet she'd had a very real sense of foreboding, and Kizzy's sudden disappearance still alarmed her, as did Francis's attitude. He seemed so cruel and detached.

Casting the script aside, she switched off the reading light and padded to the window to watch the dawn steal over the village roofs. The last of the bats were flying in, soft brown missiles hurtling past on their black umbrella wings. The silver light seemed to transform the higgledy-piggledy roof tiles into pewter and pearl scales. Curling away from her up the steep hill along its two cobbled lanes, the village looked so trapped-in-time, picture-postcard medieval that she half expected to catch sight of a flapping black cloak as Francis or Édith swept back up to the hall after a night blood-sucking.

Sleep had brought her no heart-ease.

Francis had hardened and cooled, his broken heart reconditioned all wrong just as Lucy had said. Legs felt the responsibility for that new cruelty resting on her shoulders. Glimpses of the old Francis still showed through, tempting her to surrender herself back to the safe haven of nostalgia and mutual comfort, but something kept stopping her from responding to his calls to 'say the word'.

It occurred to her that in their heyday he would never have seen her off with a peck on the cheek as he had last night, however angry he was with Poppy. The Francis she remembered would have pursued her to the Book Inn and been outside her window by midnight, ready to scale the ivy and make love feverishly before talking until dawn. Admittedly the bats nesting overhead might have put him off his stroke, but he would have braved them, just as he would have braved wearing his heart on his sleeve with a few well-chosen quotes and long, heart-pulling, groin-buzzing kisses.

She found it alienating the way Francis seemed to control his passion and curb his emotions these days. She'd always been the more outspoken, impulsive one of the two, shooting her mouth off and daring to be different. Francis had traditionally chauffeured life forwards like a pro while she rode shotgun. He'd kept his foot on the accelerator throughout their relationship, turning fantasy into reality as he prepared the ground for their publishing dynasty, their wedding, their family life together. She sensed he was still in the driving seat, but now he was going round in circles, not slowing down long enough to pick up passengers or listen to directions.

She heard a door slam and looked down to see a figure setting out up the steep cobbled lane, dark hair gleaming in the first rays of sun that were now stealing over the woods at the village brow which screened off the estate walls, car park and the inland hills. It was Byrne, Fink the basset hound waddling behind.

Legs' feet itched to pull on trainers and run after him. But she forced herself to stay and watch as he strode off, his hands in pockets and head bowed, so deep in thought that he almost walked straight into the very same lamp-post beneath which he had demonstrated the meaninglessness of saying 'I love you' the night before. Now he stopped and looked up at it briefly while Fink lifted his leg at its base before both carried on with their dawn dog walk. He had his own demons, Legs told herself, and he'd made it clear he didn't want her complicating his life, whatever little of it he had left. He had kissed her just once, and even though it had felt like a whole new world to her, it had been a kiss goodbye.

Stamping into the shower, she remembered his parting words last night. 'Go back to your lover in London.'

The cool, high-pressure water rained down on her head, rattling her unspoken thoughts to the surface.

She didn't want to go back to Conrad. Nor was she yet certain she wanted to stay for Francis. Meeting Byrne had made her want something else entirely and as always, the thing she wanted most of all was the one thing she couldn't have. He'd told her that he was about to lose his life, repeatedly insisting she must leave, said 'I love you' without meaning it just to prove a point, yet she felt as though the past forty-eight hours had opened up that part of her heart which had been cauterised for years.

She distractedly washed her hair with body scrub and rubbed volume-enhancing conditioner into her armpits.

If she hadn't met Byrne that weekend, she realised, she would almost certainly have hot-headededly rushed straight back Francis's arms. She was frightened by the damage she'd already done. As her mother said, she owed it to Francis to try to recapture what they'd once had. But how could they hope to recapture it when just a year apart had pushed such estrangement between them?

And now she had to go back to London and to Conrad. She'd done what he asked. Gordon Lapis was on the Farcombe bill. She should feel delighted by the result, but she felt as though she'd traded her heart like a counterfeit note.

She stepped out of the shower and wrapped her oddly gritty hair in a towel before crossing the main room to check her phone.

Francis had texted her very late last night. *Say the word. ILY.*

Was he making a romantic statement or dictating 'the word', Legs wondered. She found she couldn't reply, still raw from Byrne's lecture about how easy it was to say 'I Love You'. The only three-letter acronym in her head right now was SOS. A well brought up man like Francis would interpret it as 'Save Our Souls', but Legs was a texting veteran whose many quick exchanges with friends like Daisy included the phrase SOS or 'Same Old Shit'. And she was definitely up to her neck in it this time.

Running away from Francis and back to Conrad again made the rock and the hard place seem indistinguishable. For now, she reached for her battered Nikes and decided to simply run.

Setting off for a final breezy jog along the cliff-path before the drive to Somerset and on to London, Legs' heart seemed to set down markers with every footfall as she breathed in the familiar sea air, hating the thought of leaving, wishing more than anything that she could stay and sort things out with Francis. She couldn't hope to say everything she needed to over breakfast. In her head, she had an image of herself weeping penitently over a bowl of muesli, crying 'sorry, sorry, sorry!' over again.

The thought of trying to make her mother and Hector see sense was another vast thorn in her side that gave her a stitch as she ran.

When she then swallowed two flies and crashed through a cow pat, Legs realised she craved Ealing Common with its neat, flat paths and poop scoop vigilantes. Before embracing that, she was equally eager to talk to Daisy, to spill beans and seek magic advice.

Running back into Farcombe from the top lane, she detoured via the Visitors' Centre public car park at the top of the village to fetch the Honda, knowing that she would have a hefty fine to pay for abandoning it there most of the weekend.

But the little red rust-bucket was missing altogether. Its broken door must have made it easy pickings for a car thief, she realised with a wail of dismay, imagining her longtime driving companion now discarded and torched on a beach somewhere.

Furious, Legs stomped back to the Book Inn, where Nonny was manning the reception desk computer, updating the guests' bills with last night's dinner and bar tabs. 'Everything OK?'

'Somebody's stolen my car!'

'No, it's cool. The man from the garage just dropped it off.' Nonny reached behind her for a padded envelope which she handed over. 'Better get it moved before the good bergers of Farcombe march on us. You know how officious the Parish Council are about illegal parking on the quayside.'

Inside the envelope were a set of Honda keys. Although these looked almost identical to her own, they were far less scuffed and dog-eared, and were attached to a large luggage tag which read: 'take outside and point at the sea.'

Intrigued, she did as instructed, pressing the 'unlock' button.

There was a chirrup immediately beside her, making Legs

jump. A shiny silver car was parked beneath the Book Inn's swinging hanging baskets, already covered in brightly jewelled petals. It was the same size and shape as hers, but far less battered.

She peered through the windows and let out a shriek, because inside was all the clutter and detritus from her own runabout, neatly stacked up on the rear seat. When she opened the door to investigate further, breathing in leather upholstery and newly valeted carpets, the log and an insurance certificate were on the passenger's seat, both in her name.

She rushed back inside the pub to corner Nonny. 'What do you know about that car?'

'Just that it was delivered here while you were out running. Isn't it yours?'

Legs raked urgently through all the paperwork and the contents of the padded envelope, but there was no explanation whatsoever.

She checked through her phone messages: Ros entreating her not to be late bringing Nico home; Daisy telling her to arrive after midday because they'd been up half the night and wanted a lie-in; Conrad asking her to ring him urgently; Francis saying that he'd just called into the Book Inn for breakfast with a surprise for her, and where was she?

She dashed down to the restaurant and then into the bar, but he was no longer there.

Running back out past the still unlocked car, its passenger door wide open and an eager seagull pecking at the trim, she panted her way up the cliff path and through the parkland to the hall, her heart on fire.

That's why he'd conducted that strange conversation about her car last night, she realised. He must have been planning this surprise all along. Byrne was totally wrong about Francis. This was a gesture of love, not revenge. He was the same man she'd loved for all those years. Francis had never been one for jewels or flowers; it was typical of him to be so pragmatic, and she found it wildly romantic. He *did* still love her. This was better than a moonlit serenade outside her window any day.

She belted through the parterre, hurdling the box hedges and scratching her ankles on the rose bushes, sending pea gravel flying as she raced around the side of the house and bombed along the raised terrace.

Francis was sitting in the kitchen with a pile of newspapers, blond hair flopping over his forehead as he flipped through them. There was more coverage of the Gordon Lapis story in almost every national that morning, along with lots of mentions of the Farcombe Festival. Speculation was rife about the true identity of the Ptolemy Finch creator.

He looked up and smiled when she panted up to the open French doors from the courtyard, as though he'd been expecting her at just that moment. 'There you are. Come in. There's fresh coffee and Imee's amazing pains au chocolat.'

Stepping in through the doors, Legs was too puffed out to be able to speak properly. 'My car!' was all she managed to wheeze.

'Is there something wrong with it?'

'No – it's lovely! Just lovely! It's the loveliest thing imaginable.'

'Well that's all lovely then,' he smiled humouringly then returned to the *Mail*, which had dedicated two pages to the Gordon Lapis true identity story and a list of suspects. 'Christ, they've even got odds here on Lapis being Jeffrey Archer.'

Legs had a brief and unpleasant vision of live-messaging 'sleep tight' wishes to Jeffrey Archer the previous night.

Francis had already poured her a coffee and placed it in front of the chair beside him.

She hesitated and then gave into temptation. It was so strange settling back into her old place at the Farcombe table as though the past year hadn't happened. She couldn't stop thinking about the car; such a romantic thing to do after he'd told her how worried he was about her safety in her red rust bucket last night. She felt a brief pang of loyalty to her old banger, but it was instantly eclipsed by happiness again, just as all thoughts of Conrad were shrouded in sea mist, increasingly reluctant to be blown inland. She and Francis could get back to their glory days, she was certain. They'd prove Byrne wrong, with his secrets and manipulative ways. Kissing Byrne had been a huge mistake. He had been right about that one fact, at least.

She desperately wanted to talk to Francis about where they stood, but Édith chose that moment to reel into the room wearing a long silk dressing gown, her face putty grey behind huge dark glasses.

'Legs, darling, back so soon – did you sleep on the doorstep?' She headed for the fridge. 'Christ I'm hungover. We really shouldn't have started on the cognacs after Poppy went to bed. Jax says she's paralysed, but I think she's just still paralytic.'

'Was there a terrible argument about the thing in the cellar then?' Legs asked.

'What "thing" in the cellar?' Édith asked, pulling out a carton of tomato juice.

Francis shot Legs a murderous look. 'Just the dodgy fusebox, Dits; I'll get someone in.'

'There *was* a furious row last night,' Édith said, alighting on a chair at the far end of the kitchen with a waft of flying silk like a heron. 'But it was about your chum Jamie-go and Kizzy.' She looked up, one eyebrow angled.

Legs felt a chill run through her. 'So they *do* know each other?'

'Of course not,' Francis snapped.

'Jax thinks they're rival bounty hunters,' Édith sipped her tomato juice and pulled a face, closing her eyes and breathing to herself 'think vodka,' before shuddering and carrying on. 'Both are after Poppy's dough with their doe eyes and doggy bags.'

'I don't think Byrne's after her money,' Legs insisted, earning another dark look from Francis.

'And Kizzy says she just wants her "lurve",' Édith sniped, casting her red juice aside, 'but she's a bright enough girl to know that's

264

impossible; Poppy's no more capable of showing real love than she is of leaving this house. Her heart's as agoraphobic as she is. She should never have played matchmaker between you two. Kizzy only went along with it to please her.'

'Kizzy is devoted to me,' Francis said stiffly, glancing at Legs.

'Spare me!' Édith laughed bitterly. 'My guess is she's always been part of Poppy's masterplan; she's been educated specifically for the job as Farcombe chatelaine. I'll bet Yolande and Poppy have been plotting it for years.'

'At least they have the estate's best interests at heart. Farcombe needs its successors in place. Poppy made it clear that she'd never let Dad sell the estate while Kizzy and I were together to run it. She even spoke once or twice about changing her will in Kizzy's favour, but of course Jamie-go turning up will have put paid to that.'

'She wanted to trap Kizzy here like one of those butterflies in her portrait,' Édith's voice shook, 'but now the Monarch's returned, the Painted Lady is liberated.'

'Farcombe must be protected,' said Francis. As he reached for his coffee, Legs noticed his hands were far from steady.

She furrowed her brows, remembering him telling her two days ago that Farcombe was all that mattered. If his entire relationship with Kizzy had been based on keeping the estate in the Protheroe name, he must feel really exposed right now. The enormity of what he'd sacrificed for her struck her afresh.

'Where is she now?' Legs asked anxiously.

'With her parents, I imagine,' said Francis.

'Doubtful,' Édith was flicking a fingernail tetchily against the rim of her glass. 'They've only just started talking again. There was a big fall out between them all about six months ago,' she told Legs. 'Kizzy moved out of the Hawkes' holiday house to a room in the village.'

Legs now remembered Nonny talking about it, along with the strange fish diet and Kate Bush shanties. She had also said that

Kizzy was close to Édith and Jax before getting together with Francis.

'I told you it was foolhardy to let her go before we got to the truth,' Édith was sniping at him.

'What truth?' she asked anxiously.

'If we knew that, we wouldn't need to find out,' Édith snapped.

'We know Kizzy isn't Yolande and Howard's daughter by birth,' Francis said flatly.

'It was a private adoption, but it's always been fearfully hush-hush,' Édith went on, seeming to know more. 'Even Kizzy was never told the full story.'

'Poppy was involved, but none of us can get to the bottom of it.' Francis's fingers were drumming on a headline about a royal scandal.

'Kizzy's slavish attitude to Poppy all dates back to that,' Édith hissed angrily.

There was a curious sibling rivalry going on as brother and sister lobbed each line of Kizzy's story out like a tennis player returning the ball faster and faster, but their delivery was secondary to the picture it created of the redheaded orphan turned femme fatale and her desperation to be a part of the Farcombe hierarchy.

'She's devoted to this house and the festival,' Francis intoned.

'She always wanted to work in London,' Édith countered. 'It's Poppy she's devoted to.'

Legs' brain went into overdrive, her original suspicions reigniting. Even if Kizzy wasn't a transsexual avenger, there was a secret history which surely placed her at the centre of Poppy's life. Why else would she consider making Kizzy her successor at Farcombe?

'Are you saying they might be related?'

'That's what we're trying to find out,' Francis closed the newspaper in front of him with an angry swish.

'We think Kizzy uncovered the truth earlier this year,' said Édith. 'It's what she argued with Yolande and Howard about.'

'Dits became a confidante and encouraged her to snoop, then blew it by picking a catfight.' Francis shot his sister a withering look. 'They stopped talking for weeks.'

'We fell out about something entirely unrelated,' Édith cleared her throat awkwardly. 'Afterwards, Kizzy would only ever say that what she'd heard could ruin this family.'

'That bad?'

'Seems so,' Francis drummed his fingers on the sugar bowl. 'But those in the know, like our father, Poppy, the Hawkes and your mother, aren't telling.'

'Mum?' She nearly choked on her coffee.

'We gather Lucy was the one who introduced Poppy and Yolande in the first place,' Édith ran a delicate fingertip along her lower lip to remove a drop of vampirish tomato juice resting there. 'She must know more.' She sucked her fingertips coyly, eyebrows raised.

She and Francis were both looking at her intently, and Legs realised what was being asked. 'Wouldn't Hector be able to tell you much more?'

'That bastard!' Édith exploded, knocking over her juice so it spilled gorily across the table. 'Maman should have pushed him off the balcony in Manhattan when she had the chance.'

Accustomed to his sister's fiery outbursts, Francis blotted the stain with the *Mail*. 'Dad's never hidden his mistrust of Kizzy, but if he knows anything, he's not saying.' He took Legs' hand. 'All we want to know is how Poppy fitted in with the Hawkes' adoption.'

'Mum and I aren't exactly on friendly terms right now.'

'You're on much friendlier terms than we are with Poppy after last night's row,' Édith pointed out. 'Not that she gives a stuff about us two now that the prodigal son is back.'

'Is he here right now?' Legs felt her heartbeat turn staccato at the thought that Byrne might be in the house and she hastily removed her hand from Francis's grip.

'Thank God not yet,' Francis rolled his eyes. 'You know Poppy – she rarely gets out of bed before midday. But no doubt he'll call by later with his Irish eyes sparkling, ready to plant his little crock at the end of the rainbow.' He hammed up a cheeky leprechaun accent.

'You don't like him very much, do you?'

'Do you blame us?' Édith snapped. 'Springing a trick like that. Christ knows what he'll do next – wheel in his father, probably; make it a proper family reunion. That's why it's vital we know more about Kizzy's birthright. We need to work out exactly who *is* a part of this bloody family and where their loyalties lie. And that includes you, Legs.' She gave her a long, hard look. With her cold, military-blue eyes, she was a great deal scarier than her brother.

Francis walked Legs as far as the ha-ha.

'You mustn't mind Dits. She's very protective these days, and she's fond of Kizzy. They were firm friends before—' He looked out towards the cliffs uncomfortably, 'before she and I . . .'

'Of course,' Legs turned into the coast wind too, grateful for its cool, embarrassed that he felt the need to behave so apologetically when Conrad was still in the picture, his fingerprints all over the frame they now found themselves in.

The sea ahead was tufted with foaming eddies and swells, the wind yet to settle upon a direction. A lone runner was pounding along the cliff path on the horizon, a dog at his heels. Legs' heart hammered as she squinted to see whether it was Byrne, but Francis put a strong arm around her and pulled her to his chest before she could identify him.

'Call me as soon as you get to London, and let me know what you've found out.' He placed a kiss on top of her head, which made her acutely aware that she hadn't yet washed her hair. Yet his embrace was brotherly and comforting rather than passionate, for which she felt grateful relief.

She stared at one of his shirt buttons, 'Where do we stand, Francis?'

'You must do what you feel is right.' His voice was stiff with formality.

She nodded, inadvertently socking him in the mouth a few times with her skull. She could feel his heart beating against her collarbone through layers of cotton. Her own guilty heart was so hopelessly overworked from its weekend of being bashed about, she now felt as though she had permanent indigestion. He had to be talking about Conrad. Was this a case of 'I've dumped mine, now you dump yours?' she wondered, an extension of the dare games they'd played as teenagers.

'Francis, do you think you can ever really forgive me?' she asked urgently.

Francis was looking over her head, presumably at the runner.

'"Your honesty should admit no discourse to your beauty",' he started quoting Shakespeare.

Legs tuned out, blood rushing in her ears as she realised that she was expected to supply the answer to her own question from the clues given. It was classic Francis, back on familiar ground, his feelings set between quotation marks.

'Did you mean it last night when you said you loved me?' she tested again.

'"I did love you once",' he breathed obediently. '*Hamlet* again, as you know.'

She supposed she should be grateful that he wasn't quoting Kizzy de la Mere at her, although the urge to scream 'yes, but what *exactly* are you *feeling*, Francis?' was almost overpowering.

'You just have to say the word, Legs,' he urged.

She remembered Byrne's cruel lesson beneath the lamp-post again and said nothing. She'd filled in far too many missing words for Francis during their time together. She used to believe that she could read meaning into his every gesture and silence, his cryptic poetry recitals, but now she just saw confusing gaps and

269

misunderstandings in the way he expressed himself. Was it really that she had once understood him so well, or perhaps it was that she'd simply always read far too much into his brooding silences and endless quotations? She found herself longing for straightforward, shoot-from-the-hip honesty, even if it hurt her to listen to the truth of it. It was one of the things she liked most about Byrne, she realised.

But Francis was as chivalrous as ever; her wounded fairytale prince who spoke through noble gestures and recitation at times of high emotion, not plain English. He'd given her a car and quoted *Hamlet* at her. In his mind, she was supposed to know exactly what to do and not spoil the moment by checking each detail.

'Take as much time as you need,' he told her now, holding her very tightly to his chest so that she could smell that familiar cologne and a great waft of fabric conditioner. 'Think about us. You promise?'

'I promise.' Her voice was muffled by crisp Oxford shirt collar and Lenor fumes. She couldn't believe how gallant and self-controlled he was being, or how ungrateful she must be for secretly wanting him to simply shout very loudly that she'd been a bloody fool, yes, but she was now forgiven and the clocks would go back five years with immediate effect.

She pulled back at last, looking up at him. 'That car means *so* much to me, you know.'

'So you keep saying.' He flashed a wary smile. Then he looked at her for a long time, eyes bluer than the sky as always. 'If you feel the same way I do, you'll do the world a favour and drive it over Conrad. Which reminds me – I have that surprise I promised you.' He felt in his pockets. Pulling out a small padded box, he dropped it in her hand and closed her fingers over it before kissing their tips and walking away.

Legs pulled open the little case. Inside was her old engagement ring.

Chapter 20

Legs walked through the woods from the hall, her head still jumbled with nostalgia as she passed the Tree of Secrets and the locations of old campsites and dens where she and Francis had first worked out what love was all about and why they were so lucky to have found it with one another.

In Spywood Cottage's little clifftop garden, Lucy and Hector were sitting in deck chairs drinking green tea. They were listening to *Porgy and Bess* blasting out through the open windows from the stereo in the sitting room. Both were naked.

Not hearing Legs arrive, they carried on talking animatedly about the Trevor Nunn production of the opera that they had both seen in London.

She hastily retreated behind the cottage wall and clattered around loudly, calling 'anybody home?' She then waited patiently behind a water butt for them to throw on a kaftan and the undersized kimono respectively and give her the all clear.

Having now had sight of Poppy's oversized stone depiction of Hector, Legs could hardly bring herself to look at him, although she braved a quick peek at his exposed chest and legs and realised that the tattoos, at least, had been a fiction, if not the varicose veins.

While he was inside the cottage making coffee, Legs quizzed her mother:

'Tell me about Yolande and Poppy's friendship.'

'Has Francis put you up to this?'

'Yes.'

After a pause for reflection, Lucy looked pleased. If her daughter was playing detective for Francis then she clearly took it to mean they were partners in crime once again, although whether those were pretty fraud or crimes of passion went uninvestigated. She'd still not forgiven Legs' outbursts during their most recent

271

conversation in the cove, and was reluctant to break her stand-off silence as she underwent a grilling that was all-too-familiar from years sharing a home with her quizzical, excitable youngest child, yet she was being asked about a time she recalled only too well and involved people that she had cared deeply about.

'It was Nigel Foulkes who introduced Yolande to the Protheroes, not me,' she finally relented a little after a barrage of questions.

'How did Daisy's father know the Hawkes?' Legs demanded.

'Yolande was something big in the City at the time, and bought a lot of art from him. Dreadful old bag.'

'Do you remember her coming here for the first time?'

She looked increasingly shifty. 'Nigel invited the Hawkes down to Spycove for a weekend one summer. We were all here.'

'And that's when Yolande met Poppy?'

The cold front slipped a little more as Lucy giggled, remembering: 'Yolande was the one who encouraged Poppy to sculpt, and even got hands on for the first few works of art. I remember them looking like two little girls with a snowman. It can't have been long after Poppy and Hector married.'

'But Kizzy would have already been three or four by then. Did the Hawkes bring her along too?'

Lucy thought back. 'They had no children.'

'Are you sure?'

'Absolutely.'

'What else do you remember?'

Lucy looked away, watching the trees being buffeted by the strange sea winds. 'They were having an affair.'

'Who?'

'Nigel and Yolande.'

'That's so awful!' Legs gasped, struggling to ever imagine Daisy's lovely, urbane father enamoured of big-boned, raven-haired Yolande with her forceful opinions and booming voice.

'Darling, *everybody* was at it in those days. I remember thinking that there should be another stage of life named 'adulteryhood' which came somewhere between early parenthood and mid-life crisis. Babs had a lover too; Howard Hawkes was clearly at it with half his tutorial group; most of our married friends in London were having affairs; your father was—'

'No!' She covered her ears. 'Don't self justify. You and Hector were obviously at it like rabbits.'

Lucy waited patiently for her to uncover her ears.

'We were the only ones *not* at it.'

'And now we're making up for lost time!' boomed a voice from the door, as Hector broke up the mother-daughter confessional with a steaming espresso pot and an open kimono.

'You've come untied, Hec,' Lucy pointed out gently.

'Oh yes.'

Legs averted her gaze. Poppy had definitely got her ratios very wrong.

Outside the Book Inn, the seagull and several of its friends had christened the new car with white good luck blobs. An anonymous note tucked under the driver's wiper warned her that parking in the quay was strictly forbidden. Somebody – possibly the note-writer – had thoughtfully closed the passenger door.

She decided to call the car Tolly after Ptolemy Finch because it was quick, young and silver-topped. She knew Francis disapproved of giving cars names – the red Honda had once been christened Wayne Rooney in an era when it had seemed ironic as opposed to just plain sad – but this time, she felt certain she was on safe ground with a literary legend.

She showered and packed hurriedly, aware that she was already running impossibly late. Yet her feet dragged as she criss-crossed Skit gathering the last of her belongings, feeling the wrench of abandoning Farcombe with so much unresolved. Ironic that Francis had given her the means of departing so swiftly.

'I'll be back,' she told the sleeping bats and their babies overhead.

As soon as she came downstairs, Nonny thrust a huge cappuccino at her and, eager to accept the stay of execution, Legs settled at the bar while the little blonde drilled her about Gordon Lapis.

'We're getting calls every five minutes from people desperate for accommodation during festival week. Our waiting list is so long we've already had to close it. All the local campsites are booked out, plus every B&B within a ten-mile radius. Is somebody arranging crowd control for this thing?'

Knowing the chaos involved in policing the midnight book launches, Legs suddenly baulked again at the scale involved in organising the first public appearance of Ptolemy Finch's genius creator.

'It's all in hand,' she said smoothly, knowing she had a lot of work ahead of her that week. The sooner she got back to London the better. Yet the emotional pull of Farcombe meant she lingered over her coffee, staring out at the tilting boat masts in the harbour, half-hoping Byrne would stride in smelling of surf-splattered walks to tell her off for being a hopeless romantic. She knew she was really only hanging about in the hope that she'd see him again.

'What's Gordon Lapis like?' asked Nonny.

'Infuriating,' she said indiscreetly. 'I have no idea how he'll react to public scrutiny.'

'He's probably hideous looking with a stutter,' Nonny giggled.

'I think he is quite old,' Legs recalled his description of his face being of no great merit and haunted by the past. 'You have to feel sorry for him; he never wanted this media mania, after all.'

'What's he worth these days? Twenty, thirty million?'

'At least double that.'

'Forgive me if I don't weep for him. Where's the great man staying?'

Realising her drastic oversight, Legs swallowed uncomfortably. 'Did you say you'd closed the waiting list here?'

Nonny went very still, her face pale. 'You *are* kidding?'

She shook her head. 'I think he'll love this place, but I warn you he's a bit of a fusspot.'

'Hey, I worked in record promotion. I know all about celebrity riders. He can have Grey Goose vodka, whores on tap and a box full of kittens. It's cool.'

When Legs listed Lapis's demands for a pet-friendly bath and pot plants, Nonny laughed in amazement. 'Is that all? What an old poppet. He can have Octodecimo,' she said excitedly, towing her towards the reception computer. 'It's already infused with the smell of sea-soaked basset hound, after all, and the bath is huge. I'll juggle the bookings and make it work.'

Unable to resist, Legs casually asked after Byrne, to learn that he'd come in from a run two hours ago, eaten a bowl of Frosties in his room with devilled kidneys for his dog, demanded to know where he could hire a horse locally and then stormed out like whirlwind with a laptop tucked under one arm. Nonny snorted with amusement, 'Who takes a computer horse riding?'

'Maybe he's hacking?' Legs suggested.

'He's one strange individual,' Nonny shook her head with a smile, folding Legs' printed receipt and handing it over. 'But seriously sexy with it. I can't believe we thought he was Michelin. Is it true he's Poppy Protheroe's son?'

Gossip travelled faster than the sea breeze in Farcombe.

'If I leave him a note, will you make sure he gets it?' She scribbled her mobile number on a Book Inn postcard, along with a squiggle that could be interpreted as a kiss or a little artistic fish depending on one's outlook.

Legs paid her bill and thanked Nonny profusely. To her surprise, Guy came out of the kitchen to see her off with the full Book Inn VIP treatment, giving her a tight bear hug and a pat on the back.

'Come back soon,' he instructed fondly. 'We can't wait to have Farcombe's answer to Will and Kate back in action.'

She went outside to put her bag in the new car. Then she doubled back and reclaimed the postcard she had written to Byrne which she screwed up and threw away.

Sitting on Tolly's very clean-smelling upholstery, protected by the high tech armour of roll bars, airbags, ABRS and traction control that Francis had given her, she took the ring-box from her pocket and flipped it open. The last time she'd looked at it properly, through puffy, weeping eyes, she had just wrenched it from her finger ready to hand back to him.

It had been his mother's ring, bestowed before Hector had made his real fortune yet showing his generosity and thoughtfulness as he'd had it specially designed in Hatton Gardens, a pretty marquise sapphire like a blue iris, surrounded by clusters of diamonds three deep and set in white gold so that it resembled an eye. It had always reminded her of the Greek good luck charms that she and Francis had brought back from holidays in Crete and Athens, and which had decorated their flat, protecting them from evil.

Carefully, she flipped the ring box shut again, an eyelid closing over a big blue eye like a knowing wink.

Chapter 21

Legs drove to Somerset in Tolly, stereo blaring, loving its nippy, shiny newness. She had plenty of opportunities to admire it from the outside when she stopped at garages for a wee, a side effect of having drunk so much coffee before setting out.

She needn't have worried about running late; Daisy and Will were still in bed, along with all their children, the family Herbert turning the superking wooden sleigh bed into a big duvet-strewn family raft on which they bobbed contentedly through the morning while napping, scrapping, snacking, reading and listening to Radio 1.

Not recognising the strange car pull up outside, they all lay low and pretended to be out. Legs had to throw pebbles at the window.

'Will and I were celebrating until the early hours.' Daisy waddled out to greet her after a long delay, wearing voluminous pyjamas covered with big red lips. 'We've accepted an offer on the house.'

'Congratulations!' Legs hugged her and the bump.

'It's a lot less than we paid for it,' she admitted, leading the way into the kitchen which was already a bombsite compared to its coffee-scented perfection two days earlier. 'We've been agonising all weekend, but now the decision's made, we couldn't be happier and realise we could have saved ourselves two sleepless nights. We're going to Farcombe!' She put on the kettle, 'I got Will to buy freshly ground coffee especially for you. Now tell me all about my gorgeous Spycove.'

Smelling coffee, Legs already needed the loo again. 'Well, you might be in for a bit of a shock when you meet the loved-up neighbours.'

'Don't tell me your parents have rented their cottage to Harry and Chelsy to try to rekindle the flame?'

Shaking her head miserably, Legs told her about her mother and Hector Protheroe.

'Man alive.' Daisy sat down heavily on a kitchen chair, and one look at her shocked face left Legs in no doubt that it was the first she knew about it. 'Are you OK with that? That must be a mind-wrecker. I thought my mum and Gerald was bad enough.'

'It's still sinking in.'

'And they've felt like this about each other for *years*, you say? Your dad must be going demented.'

'He clearly thinks it'll all blow over and that Mum should have her fun in the sun before coming home to roost. But Poppy is *livid*.'

'I can imagine. They're far too old for bed-hopping these days.'

'You mean to say they really were all bed-hopping when they were younger?' Legs baulked, trying not to think about the 'adulteryhood' years her mother had described.

'I heard rumours that the eighties were pretty wild; keys on the table type thing,' Daisy mused, then seeing Legs' horrified face, quickly added. 'I don't think your mother was anything to do with that scene.'

'Well she's certainly making up for it now,' she huffed, 'and I can't see Hector getting his longed-for knighthood if he carries on with the naked love-in much longer.'

'God, this would make such a fabulous screenplay. Is Poppy hell bent on revenge?'

'Oh, you know Poppy – she's finding solace through her art,' Legs said carefully, not liking the idea of her parents' private lives being immortalised in one of Daisy's scripts.

'Creating huge depictions of Hector as a blob, no doubt,' Daisy was never far off the pulse.

Legs accepted a cup of strong coffee and crossed her legs.

'Well she has got a bit of a distraction,' unable to resist raising the topic, she told Daisy about Byrne turning up out of the blue. 'He's her doppelganger in some ways, but a totally unique individual in others, and incredibly complex.'

Daisy was unimpressed. 'He sounds deeply dodgy.' She clearly agreed with the Protheroe children that he wanted to see what his mother was worth. 'Never trust a man with more than one name; always smacks of fraud and extortion.'

'I think it's about far more than money,' she insisted. A curious loyalty stopped her betraying Byrne's confidence about losing his life, but she suddenly wanted Daisy to like him very much. 'He has this way about him, a sort of aloofness and watchfulness, but you can see a tortured soul ablaze underneath.'

'Crikey, Legs,' Daisy snorted with laughter. 'Be still your beating heart, oh fickle friend. Isn't juggling Conrad and Francis enough for you without factoring in the tortured son of a batty agoraphobic?'

'When do you move?' Legs demanded irritably.

'They're cash buyers, so they want us out as soon as possible. We could even be in Spycove in time for the festival. I'm dying to see Gordon Lapis in person. What a story. Will is mad at you about that, by the way; you could have tipped him the wink about the man himself appearing at Farcombe.'

She bit her lip guiltily. 'It was a delicate negotiation. I wasn't sure the Protheroe family would exactly welcome the idea, or me brokering it.'

'But, don't tell me, they've looked at the projected ticket sales and now they *love* it.' Daisy gave a sardonic laugh.

'They're onside, yes.'

'I bet that Francis welcomed you back with open arms.' There was an edge to her voice as she heaved frying pans onto Aga plates.

'He was a little more circumspect.'

'And the Francis situation is what?'

Legs started to explain that her head and heart were at ever more confusing odds, but Daisy was so overrun gathering her brood, making a big champagne brunch, packing Nico's things and chasing away the flock of angry bantams that had invaded the kitchen complaining that they'd had no breakfast, she hardly seemed to be listening and kept laughing or sympathising in all the wrong places. In the end, Legs gave only edited highlights.

Sometimes the two women's long friendship was a comfort and therapy to both, but the confessional side worked better via email and long-planned phone calls these days. In person, Daisy was such a chaotic, cheerful, overextended multi-tasker that it was impossible to get her to concentrate.

'I have three episodes of *Slap Dash* to script by the end of this week,' she lamented. 'Mum was supposed to be coming here to help with childcare, but bloody Gerald's just sprung a surprise trip to France. I'm sure it's deliberate. He's furious that we're planning to move back to Spycove. I bet he wants Mum to flog it, eradicating a few more memories of a happy family life with Dad.'

Again, Legs kept quiet about what her own mother had said just that morning about the Adulteryhood years and Nigel's affair with Yolande. But she did tell Daisy about Kizzy de la Mere's mysterious parentage, her clifftop Kate Bush shanties and her sudden disappearance halfway through supper. 'I keep imagining her swimming out to sea and dissolving into the waves, like the Little Mermaid, you know?'

Cramming cherry tomatoes and fat field mushrooms in between split-skinned sausages frying in a big skillet, Daisy sucked her hot fingers; 'How fantastically fishy, although frankly Poppy is hardly about to croak so I shouldn't think the matter of inheritance is particularly important right now, unless they bump her off.'

'Don't joke. It feels like walking into *Evil Under the Sun* down there, everybody has so many grudges and secrets.'

'It always feels like that,' Daisy sighed happily. 'God, I can't wait to get back!'

Today, with an offer accepted, she was busy turning all life's punches into punchlines and seeing only the positives in life.

'This Gordon Lapis connection is such a career coup for you, Legs, you must use it to your advantage,' she insisted as she plated up brunch from the old brown Aga. 'He obviously feels an affinity with you.'

'He's madder than the tea party Hatter,' Legs sighed, reluctant to admit how many times she'd reread his heartfelt message about the Emperor's New Clothes, certain she had let him down somehow.

'And you're his Alice.'

Seeing it from that perspective, Legs felt strangely buoyed up, her resentful affection for Gordon bubbling gaily once more. She had yet to email Kelly to make tactful enquiries about his sanity, she remembered guiltily. She'd do it as soon as she got back to London.

'Maybe Gordon Lapis is the raven at the writing desk?' Will joined them. 'Oh boy, this is looking good. I can smell my cholesterol count rising already.'

He was in just as ebullient mood as Daisy, making the family brunch infectiously jolly. As the only one drinking the champagne they'd brought out to celebrate their news, he got increasingly raucous and indiscreet over lunch. Keeping the children in stitches, he pulled faces, tickled, told stories and play-fought with all of them, baby Eva on his knee, as flirty and happy as Legs could remember him.

'Why are you driving a hire car?' he asked her as they all wolfed back scrambled egg, bacon, hash browns and a mountain of fried toast.

'It's not hired.' She felt her heart drum-roll. 'It's called Tolly; Francis gave it to me.'

'Bloody hell!' Daisy spat out a mushroom in shock. 'You didn't tell me that.'

'Bloody hell!' Grace parroted delightedly from her high chair, cramming scrambled egg up her nose with a plastic spoon.

'Francis *has* changed,' Daisy was too amazed by the car news to notice. 'He was always such a tightwad.'

'He was *not*,' Legs defended.

Her confused heart rolled over a few more times in her chest, full of nervous butterflies, like tickets in a tombola with dwindling prizes on offer. She wished they could have talked more. They hadn't spoken about the break-up at all, nor had he mentioned the letter she'd sent him pouring out her heart so soon afterwards. And the Kizzy situation still mystified her.

'My mother always maintains that Francis's meanness is a reaction to Hector's gambling,' Daisy was saying. 'Children of addicts either replicate the addiction or have an almost unnatural aversion to it, as in Francis's case. He's the same with infidelity.' She gave Legs a penetrating look.

Legs side-stepped the deliberate dig. 'Hector will probably start gambling again now Poppy's not there to stop him.' She had a sudden and alarming image of her mother pawning the Spywood furniture to settle his Ladbrokes account.

'Why so?' asked Daisy. 'Poppy had nothing to do with him giving it up.'

'He always says she did.'

She shook her head. 'He stopped at least a year before they met. I remember because Dad used to talk about it; he said Hector's betting habit got seriously out of hand after he sold Smile and came back to live in England full-time. Then there was that massive clampdown on race fixing, with trainers being banned and jockeys suspended all over the place. The media loved it; rumours were rife about the big gamblers involved from the business world. It was all fantastically Dick Francis stuff. Hector's name came up more than once. Nothing ever stuck, but Hector never went to a racecourse again.'

Clearing up together after the massive fried feast that Legs would be running off all week, Daisy looked across at her friend slyly. 'Looking forward to seeing Conrad?'

'Of course.' Legs tried and failed to hold a self-assured smile.

'You know,' Daisy pondered idly as she rinsed plates, 'perhaps it would be good if you and Francis got back together.'

'I'm sorry?' Legs could hardly believe she was hearing this after Daisy had been so against it two days earlier. *Et tu, Brute*, she thought weakly.

'He can hardly care much for the redheaded poet if he lets her swan off halfway through a dinner party without a by your leave.'

They watched through the windows as Will and Nico built a bonfire outside; the girls were having a nap upstairs, the baby monitor propped on the sill between two aloes in need of repotting.

'Mind you, have you read her stuff?' Daisy went on. 'I Googled her, and it's like those dreadful poems you used to write as a teenager, Legs – "our love is a wound razed from the shards of our hearts that splinter with the impact of every quaking orgasm" . . .'

'Did I show you that?' She was mortified.

'Duh!' Daisy stretched her eyes. 'It was on the wall above your bed. Francis never struck me as the quaking sort.'

'We quaked in our day.'

'And now?'

'He's changed a lot,' Legs admitted, relieved to be able to talk about it. 'He seems so much colder, tougher too.'

'He's always been pretty impenetrable,' Daisy sighed as she thought back. 'It was one of the things we all found wildly attractive about him.'

'I can't remember him ever being this calculating. He even suggested putting on an act to break up our parents' affair at first, and he made it pretty clear that he was happy to act out the bed-scenes as well as the ensemble pieces.'

'You can hardly expect him to behave like a saint after what you did to him a year ago,' she muttered, irritation mounting. 'He's bound to try to protect himself.'

'But now he says he still loves me.'

'Well that's progress.' Daisy was deep in the dishwasher, cramming plates in any old how amid a lot of angry clanks. 'Did he mention the letter you sent?'

'Not once. My mother has a theory that his broken heart has been put back together in all the wrong order. Somebody else suggested he might be after revenge?' Legs thought back to her dinner with Byrne, when she'd banged on drunkenly about her feelings for Francis. It seemed like a lifetime ago now.

But Daisy clearly couldn't imagine honourable, conservative Francis to be capable of such a thing. She straightened up with a plate still in one hand. 'C'mon, Legs. Francis says he wants you back even if it's just make-believe for a little bit, he can't keep his hands off you and he kicks his new girlfriend out. Anybody can see he's still mad about you. Just don't break his heart a second time, because it could be fatal. You're playing with fire here, remember? Ex-lovers can be very flammable; that's why they're called old flames, especially one that was kept alight as long as Francis. I don't want you to get burned.'

'Oh, I've already got burned, trust me.' Legs felt weak, thinking about her flirtation with a near-stranger, the devastating free-fall lust of that brief kiss with Byrne compared to the bittersweet nostalgia of reuniting with Francis.

'But you two *are* getting back together, yes?' Daisy asked. To Legs' alarm, she looked as eager as she would asking Agnetha whether Abba really were going to stage that final arena tour.

'I've promised him I'll think about it.' She swallowed a lump of panic.

Daisy still wasn't tuned into her wavelength at all: 'If you two get together again that will mean you're in Farcombe lots so we'll get to see each other. It could be like the old days; we children raising our broods by the cove where our parents left off.'

Again, Legs thought uncomfortably about the Adulteryhood years.

'I have Conrad to think about too,' she said firmly, although saying it felt like secretly proving her own point. The Adulteryhood years were already upon her generation, and as usual she had been a rebellious pioneer, along with Daisy herself.

'Nico says Conrad's impossibly pompous and that he'll never marry you.'

'Since when did you listen to the opinion of a ten-year-old over your oldest friend?' she said hotly.

'I happen to think Nico has a very good take on life. And he loves you to bits. He's worried about you. We all are.'

'Well I am perfectly capable of making my own romantic decisions, thank you.' She shelved any intentions to confess all her darkest secrets to Daisy; that kiss with Byrne, which had felt like a last farewell, still haunted her lips.

But Daisy already knew one dark secret. 'Is that why you've

bought your sister's wedding dress on eBay? You always said it was hideous.'

Legs almost dropped the glass she was washing.

Daisy smiled wickedly, 'Nothing gets past a ten-year-old conspiracy theorist.'

'I should have taken him to Farcombe as my detective sidekick,' she sighed. 'He might have helped unravel the riddles there.'

Chapter 22

Driving Nico back to London was just the distraction Legs needed; he didn't pause for breath long enough for her to dwell upon the maelstrom she was leaving behind or the challenges that lay ahead.

After just forty-eight hours at Inkpot Farm, Nico was a totally different boy, his yells louder, body looser, attitude cockier and laughter endless. And he was very opinionated. Whereas Ros encouraged educational talk about subjects like history and wildlife, all carefully modulated and slotted in between church and after school activities, conversations at Inkpot revolved around people they knew, gossip, emotions and intrigue.

'Daisy says we'll all be able to have holidays together at Farcombe soon,' he told his aunt excitedly. 'Dad wants the Spycove tower room overlooking the sea as his writing study, but Daisy reckons he'll kill himself on the spiral stairs if he's drunk, which he often is, so I might get it as my bedroom, which would be so cool. Daisy says she wants a desk near a loo because she has a weak bladder and writes "loo-ney and loo-ed comedy". She's so funny. I think Daddy is a bit jealous that her stuff gets put on telly and he only ever gets things published in boring newspapers that nobody reads, but I told him his novel might make him as famous as Gordon Lapis one day, and that would mean movies and everything.'

He didn't stop chattering the entire way to Ealing, almost all sentences starting with 'Dad says' this and 'Daisy says' the other, along with many an opinionated 'I think' the complete opposite. In Ealing, he was encouraged to learn, in Somerset to debate. He benefitted from both, although the transition could be tricky at times, especially given Ros's protectiveness.

The hug between mother and son on the doorstep was all tears and delight, as cuddly as two bears reunited after a treacherous winter. But it all went rapidly downhill.

Furious that they had got back an hour later than promised, Ros was in a picky mood, her lovingly prepared supper burned beyond repair. At first she blamed her sister, 'you never look at your watch, Legs'; and then Will, 'I can't believe he let you stay in bed until lunchtime, Nicholas; it will completely ruin your sleep pattern'; and finally Daisy, although her name wasn't mentioned, as usual, 'I suppose *somebody* gave you all the wrong things to eat and encouraged you to stay up too late. *Why* aren't you eating?' She hovered over him as he picked his way through hastily defrosted and undercooked wholemeal crust pizza, as chewy and crumbly as brown polystyrene.

It was a tricky course for Nico to steer. Increasingly subdued, he agreed that he did have a bit of a funny tummy now he came to think about it.

Ros then started unpacking his bag in the kitchen, complaining that half his clothes were missing and the rest filthily covered with sand. 'Your father knows I need everything back here clean and organised. I bet he let *somebody else* pack this.'

Seeing Nico's miserable face, Daisy hurriedly tried to explain, 'Actually *I* packed it because I took it to Devon by mista—'

But Ros was on a roll. 'Will has no *idea* what it's like to scrimp and save for clothes.'

'He does!' Nico defended. 'Daddy has holes in all his clothes because he can't afford new ones.'

'Rubbish. That's because he's scruffy. He was always getting holes in his clothes when we were married, but unlike *some* people, I used to take the time to mend them for him like any good wife would.'

Nico stormed up to his room and slammed the door.

'Oh hell,' Ros rubbed her face but made no move to follow, adopting her martyred expression as she continued sorting clothes to wash. Legs hovered nearby, uncertain whether to put the kettle on and offer sympathy, tell her sister off, or scarper. As usual, the kitchen floor was spotless, but she saw emotional eggshells everywhere as she crossed it to Ros's side.

'Have you spoken to Dad at all?' she asked carefully.

'No,' Ros had that clamp-faced look which said she was close to tears. She always missed Nico dreadfully during his weekends away, counted the hours until he came home, but these days the reunion was increasingly tense and embittered by her resentment at Nico's growing independence.

'Mum's still in Farcombe . . .' she ventured.

But Ros was focused entirely on the family microcosm in W5. 'I think I'll get Mum to drop Nicholas off and collect him next time that Will can't do the run,' she said tersely. 'She never stays for more than a cup of tea. It isn't good for him to have these long lunches with you there. It gives him a false sense of perspective.'

'About what?'

'Family life.'

'But Will, Daisy and the girls are his family too.'

Ros said nothing, angrily unpairing two little socks and throwing them into the laundry skip.

'Those ones are still clean,' Legs pointed out kindly. 'I didn't wear the socks and pants.'

Ros carefully folded a pair of small Y-fronts featuring Darth Vader on the front. 'How is Francis?'

'Fine. He sends his love,' she lied, knowing it would cheer up her sister.

Ros managed a tight smile. 'Have you two made up your differences?' She made it sound like two school friends reconciled after a playground brawl.

'It's a bit more complicated than that.'

'Yesterday, I said a prayer that you two would get back together,' she sighed. 'I even lit a candle. Silly of me.'

Legs thought about the ring, still locked in the glovebox of the lovely new car parked proudly outside. In her head, she could still hear Daisy enthusing about them all raising their children in Farcombe, could see herself sitting back at the big, paper-strewn breakfast table in the hall, and she was suddenly shot through with sentimental overload. 'Not so silly at all.'

'I knew it!' The Darth Vader pants were raised like a victory flag. 'You must *fight* for him, Legs,' Ros announced zealously, as though preaching from the pulpit. 'Do whatever it takes to seek his forgiveness. Francis is everything you could ask for in a husband – financially secure, family oriented, faithful and honest. He has values that belong to our parents' generation, and that's so rare in men these days.' She whisked away a tear with the Y-fronts.

Now was certainly not the time to break the news about their mother and Hector, Legs realised. But she knew she had to tell Ros about the offer on Inkpot Farm before she left. Will clearly hadn't mentioned it when calling earlier to say that they were on their way, and her sister would be apoplectic if she heard it from Nico, being of the belief that the parents should discuss all 'grown-up' matters before children were informed.

To Legs' alarm, her sister's tears started to spill as soon as she learned Will and Daisy were taking their family to live in Spycove.

'How *dare* they live there?' Ros was distraught. 'That means I can never go to Farcombe again, never show Nico all the places I used to play as a child.'

'Of course you can,' Legs soothed. 'They lived there a few years ago, after all.'

'But that was just temporary. Before . . .' She couldn't bring herself to elaborate on Will's other children being conceived and born. 'Farcombe should be neutral territory – a refuge for us all.'

Legs privately thought that if her sister had witnessed what she had this past weekend she'd never want to go to Spywood again, but she kept quiet. Instead, she determinedly stayed positive: 'Don't you see that this could really work out for you and Nico? You two can stay at the cottage for holidays, perhaps with Mum and Dad, and me too, and he'll have his whole family around him.'

'That,' Ros glared at her, 'is one of the most hurtful things you've ever suggested.'

Realising she'd misjudged the situation totally as usual, Legs apologised and retreated to her basement flat. She could hear Ros's feet pounding upstairs before she had even closed the door.

Wearily, she unpacked her own case – Nico hadn't taken advantage of any of her Browns weekend wardrobe, she noticed – and switched on her laptop to tackle her messages. Lots of neglected friends were queued in her inbox, complaining as always that she had no time for them since Conrad had sent her careering away from her social life. She knew she must appease them soon.

First she emailed Gordon: *Back in London. Have new (non-red) car thanks to lovely ex. Know you'll approve! How's Jimmy bearing up in the Carthusian order?*

An automated out-of-office reply flew straight back saying that Gordon was no longer taking personal emails and all correspondence should be directed at his PA.

Reading it in alarm, conscience pricking, she emailed Kelly, carefully shrouding her mounting concerns about her boss's overall wellbeing and his attitude to appearing at Farcombe with a cloak of assurances that she was dedicated to assisting with this first public appearance, and so it would help to have an indication of how he was currently feeling about it and any worries he might have. She had no idea if Kelly was party to his long emails and live chats with her, but didn't want to risk further indiscretion: *I'm sure you agree we all want to make this as stress-free a process as possible.* She fought an urge to add 'ha ha' in brackets before pressing send.

Then she called Conrad. Alone in his big Wandsworth house once again, he was far more forthcoming than in recent days, if no less concise.

'So good to have you back,' he growled. 'Want to debrief my Legs in private. Come round tonight.'

'I – um – not right now. I said I'd go round and see my father tonight,' she lied. 'But I can't wait to see you tomorrow.' She winced at her platitudes, and her Pavlovian eagerness to please, ever the teacher's pet when it came to Conrad.

He accepted her excuse with unflattering complacency. 'Sure. Wear something sexy tomorrow. Dinner after work. You stay here. We have a big week ahead.' He rang off.

Stifling yawns, Legs repacked her washbag and a change of clothes into her weekend case. She had been suggesting to Conrad for months that she should leave a few spares at his place, but he always resisted, worried that his kids might find them and kick up a fuss. Now she found she dreaded the thought of going there again, like an enchanted cave that might entrap her. She wanted to turn tail and drive back to Farcombe instead.

Francis had sent a text. *Hope you got back safe.*

It wasn't exactly *Hamlet* this time, but she felt a hot glow of happiness nonetheless, replying. *Home safe. The car is truly lovely. Makes me think of you. X*

Not sure how to take that, he replied while she was changing into her running gear. *Want to talk?*

He would want to know about her conversation with her mother, she realised, the thought of Adulteryhood hanging on her conscience. Being back in London and speaking with Conrad made her guilty head spin more than ever.

Later maybe. Need time to think. x

She pocketed the phone, pulled on her running gear and headed outside to pound her way towards the common. She hadn't run this much in months. It was a sure sign of a troubled mind, she reminded herself. If her love-life didn't sort itself out soon, she'd be joining Eddie Izzard on marathons, cracking jokes about blisters and SheWees.

Chapter 23

The storm that had blown in across the Devon coast last night was buffeting west London now, its power reduced to a few electric crackles in the sky and a dark rain-cloud rumbling on the horizon somewhere near Hayes, but it was enough to make the park nearly deserted. Legs joined the hardy runners and late afternoon dog walkers lapping the windswept perimeter as she tried to sort out the muddle in her head. But all she could think about was Byrne saying 'I am about to lose my life' and that kiss which had turned hers upside-down.

Her brunch was still sitting like lead in her belly, giving her a stitch.

She stopped to rest by a bench, not caring that huge raindrops were starting to splash down on her.

Her phone was beeping with another message in her pocket. *Hope you're thinking about me . . . or are you unblocking a sink?*

Looking at it, she realised that she hadn't locked the screen properly when setting off and it had rung through to Francis's mobile as the last number she'd contacted. He must have picked up to be greeted by the sound of her panting non-stop.

Just running! She hurriedly replied.

You've been running through my mind all day; fitting that you

*should be running through my phone too. Hope you're thinking hard
about me – or should that be thinking about me hard?*

Legs wiped a raindrop from her nose, face flaming in the
knowledge that she hadn't been thinking about him at all. Now he
was text flirting. Badly. On balance, she preferred *Hamlet*. Cringing
with shame, she sat on the bench in the rain, trying to think up a
witty reply.

Only when she was soaked through did she abandon the notion
and run home. She was struggling to find her Francis quandary
funny. It just made her want to cry.

The glow of the television through the tall first floor windows
told her that Ros and Nico had made up and were snuggling in
front of a movie, no doubt indulging in a fresh batch of organic
pizza, homemade lemonade and baby talk.

Legs took a long shower before raiding her fridge, which was
looking decidedly barren, but managed to yield an unopened tub
of pesto which she was soon tipping into a huge bowl of fusilli,
cooked al dente because she was so hungry.

She wolfed it all so fast that she felt sick immediately afterwards,
all pleasure in satiation stolen from her. She guessed it was like
kissing Francis on the cliffs that first day back at Farcombe, a
greedy pleasure she hadn't earned, which had merely left her feeling spoiled and over-indulged. A fresh wave of guilt mixed toxically
with her indigestion, giving her cramp.

Another text came through. *Any chance you could start thinking
aloud? Just say the word . . .* He was getting impatient.

Lying on the floor with her legs up on her coffee table to ease
her bloated stomach, she rang him. But if she'd been worried that
he was going to come on too amorously, he quickly dispelled her
fears by demanding: 'What did your mother have to say about the
Hawkes adopting Kizzy?'

'I don't think she knows any more than we do,' she told him,
relieved he wasn't talking about her running through his mind. For
a man who could quote Shakespeare sonnets from memory, he

had an alarmingly limited repertoire of chat up lines. 'Have you found out where she went last night?'

'No idea, but wherever it is I wish Jamie-go would bugger off there too. He tramped in here to see Poppy at teatime, smelling distinctly of horse, and they've been holed up in the green drawing room ever since. Édith suggested we puff ground almonds through the keyhole to flush him out.'

Legs chewed her lip, revolving thoughts of Byrne already so hardwired into her subconscious that her eyes seemed to project his face onto the ceiling.

'They have a lot of talking to do.' She carefully modulated her voice.

'And sight-seeing, I gather. When Imee took cakes in there she overheard him trying to persuade Poppy to go somewhere with him tomorrow, but as we all know, she won't budge from this house. Not that I blame her. There are press all over the place today, and a few diehard Ptolemy Finch fans have already started to turn up. I had to turf one lot off the parkland where they were erecting a tent. One of the press boys I was talking to said we could get as many as a hundred thousand here for Gordon Lapis's first appearance. Surely that can't be right?

'His work is loved by millions worldwide.'

'Good grief. I might let them camp here after all and charge twenty quid a night. I could buy you a Ferrari with the proceeds.'

'No need. I *love* my car. I can't tell you how much I love it.'

He laughed nervously. 'I'm starting to worry that you've developed mechanophilia.'

'What?'

'Car fetishism.'

'Is that what it's called? I always thought it should be auto erotica.'

His voice softened affectionately. 'Do you remember making out in my old Beetle that time you sat on the handbrake and we almost rolled off the cliffs at Gull Point?'

'It happened more than once,' she recalled, the memories suddenly so vivid that she could almost smell the car's upholstery infused with the combined scents of Calvin Klein One, Marlboro Light and Juicy Fruit. 'We called them our handbrake turns.'

'You had a lot of funny turns in those days.'

'Still do.' She adjusted her indigestion-cramped stomach again, easing her fingers beneath her waistband to lift it away from the drum-skin tension beneath.

'I'd like to see them some time.'

She had fallen into the trap, she realised suddenly. They were flirting.

Francis's voice was laced with seduction. 'I never understood why you always got so turned on by sex on the back seat when we had a thousand acres of estate to play on, but now I'm starting to see the light . . .'

'I am definitely not a mechanophile,' she protested. 'As I recall, we used the car a lot to begin with because it was freezing outside, and I was technically still underage, so we were terrified one of the family would catch us at it anywhere else.'

'What I wouldn't give to be in a car with you now – even a Honda,' he said in a low voice. He fell silent and there was a long pause before he breathed; 'I want you to come back here.'

'We need to talk properly, Francis.'

'Not like this.'

'Face to face.'

She closed her eyes gratefully. He saw the need to talk too.

'I want to make love to you.'

She opened her eyes again. Perhaps not. Panic rose once more.

'I need this week. My career's at stake. The Gordon Lapis thing is a huge deal.'

'What about Con-man?'

She felt sick again. 'Him too.'

'You have until Friday to say the word.' He rang off.

He sounded like Conrad issuing an ultimatum, she realised in alarm. Her rock and her hard place were slamming together on her like walls closing in. Her bloated stomach let out a whine of indigestion.

She was still lying on her back with her legs up on the coffee table. Yawning tiredly, shifting her pot belly to alleviate her heartburn, she heard the beeps on the radio she'd left on in the bathroom. The news bulletins were still talking about Gordon Lapis's identity; the media couldn't get enough of the story. It was already nine o'clock; it was too late to go to see her father, she realised, twisting another guilty knife into her self-reproach.

She rang him instead, but the answerphone picked up in the Kew house. Her mother's soft voice greeted her, apologising breathlessly that Dorian and Lucy could not take the call, then asking in muffled tones how one stopped this thing. The beep went abruptly. Legs found her voice choked with emotion, heatburn raging more than ever. The only way she could speak was in falsetto bursts of forced jollity.

'Dad! Me! Hope all OK! Lots to say! Speak soon!'

She hung up and scrunched her eyes closed.

Hearing her mother's voice made the fractures in her life feel wider than ever. While Lucy's warm tones welcomed messages in the family home, she was enjoying naked tea-parties listening to Gershwin in Devon. And Legs' father was no doubt taking comfort wherever he could found it; she just prayed it didn't involve car keys in an antique bowl on the coffee table in leafy Kew. For the Norths, perhaps the Adulteryhood years had never stopped.

She snapped her eyes open again, picked up her phone and went to her saved folder to find Gordon Lapis's email, rereading every line.

Do not underestimate the past. It fashions our lives, and we wear what parts of it still suit us, forgetting the way we really looked and that so much recollection is the Emperor's New Clothes.

Looking back at her parents' marriage with the rose tint

increasingly bleached away, Legs could see that she had dressed them both in Emperor's New Clothes almost all her life.

As she reread the end of Gordon's long, clever email, she felt an overwhelming urge to talk to him. She flipped online and eyed his icon – easy to spot because he was the only person she had ever chatted to – but he was offline. She hoped he was OK in his richly layered world of make-believe and white-haired young soothsayers.

Sleep tight, she emailed instead.

Later, in bed, Legs started to reread the first book in the Lapis series, *Ptolemy Finch and the Topaz Eagle*. At three in the morning, she was still reading, as totally engrossed as she had been the first time. Legs was like a bee to honey for the sting in Gordon's tale.

Chapter 24

Having overslept, Legs ran to the bus stop only to double back in dismay as she noticed that Tolly the shiny silver car was clamped and ticketed. Her Ealing resident's parking permit was still attached to the window of the long-cherished red rust bucket, she realised with dismay.

Frantic calls made on the bus to work got her nowhere. The local council insisted she must pay the fine to have the car released, and present the original permit at the council offices that day to get it changed, bringing a mountain of documents with her as proof of her ownership, residency and ability to drive. Failing to do so would result in hefty fines, they warned. The car would be towed if the clamping fee was not paid in twenty-four hours.

'I have a permit! I am a resident!' she railed and wailed to no avail, only serving to annoy those around her on the bus. Bureaucracy gave emotional outbursts short shrift, quoting rules and regulations straight back at her like Francis quoting classics.

She called him now. He was somewhere very windswept with bad reception, meaning she had to shout to be heard, irritating her fellow passengers even more.

'Darling Legs! I knew you would ring to say the word!' he yelled down the phone to her, unable to hear more than broken fragments.

'I *said* I need the *parking permit* from my old *car* . . .' she shouted back.

'Barking hermit for your bra?'

She repeated herself at lung-bursting volume, causing her fellow bus passengers to cower away.

Francis finally understood. 'Why call *me*?'

'Can you get it for me?'

'Obviously not. I'm in Devon.'

'Well, where is it?'

'How the hell should I know? You're the mechanophile.'

They were cut off.

In near tears of frustration by now, Legs called the council hub again and finally got through to human lifeform with a soul in the form of a jolly Nigerian named Clancy who explained that lost or stolen permits could be replaced and transferred to new vehicles, but Legs would definitely have to come to the council offices in person, bringing even more documents. The offices closed at five.

Already stressed out and ragged, she got off the bus at Green Park over an hour late for work. She travelled up through the atrium in the space-pod glass lift to Fellows Howlett's floor and slipped behind her desk keeping her head low. Beyond his smoked glass office wall, Conrad shot her a furious look, but he was trapped with the finance director so could do no more than point at his watch and raise his eyebrows questioningly.

Trying to convey the horror of her morning just with her eyes, Legs inadvertently treated him to a few Bela Lugosi expressions. He looked hurriedly away. Legs busied herself with the post, knowing that his mood was hardly likely to improve when she explained that she would need to leave work early to dash back to Ealing and rescue the car her ex-fiancé had given her yesterday.

Peering at him through the glassy divide, she fought to weigh up her feelings towards him, but it was like balancing a see-saw between past and future, and she couldn't yet decide which side he was perched on. Here was her career, her present and her day-to-day normal. He'd seduced her with full-throttle testosterone charm and brio, and it had proved the ride of her life, at least at first. Seeing him now twisted her heart so tightly she got a stitch. His cheese plant needed watering again, she realised tearfully, spotting drooping leaves silhouetted against his windows. Who would look after it if she left? She'd tended it lovingly for eighteen months now, watching it grow from two-foot weakling to four-foot triffid, rather like Conrad's ego.

To add to her chagrin, Conrad was surprisingly understanding about her unpunctuality when he was finally released from his meeting. His rugby hero face almost softening as she blustered on about car compounds; 'You go back home and release your car. We'll reschedule. Besides, I've just looked in my diary and it's the *Hansel and Gretel Diet* launch tonight,' he placated. 'I should look in.' The diet's author was one of the agency's most lucrative non-fiction clients, who specialised in the sort of extreme regimens beloved of newspaper supplements. This one was being serialised in a national, and getting lots of press thanks to a celebrity wife who had lost five dress sizes and gained column inches on it. 'We'll do it later in the week. I do want to debrief you at lunchtime, however. Arrange that, if you will. Usual room.'

Not waiting for an answer, he turned back to his office to take a conference call about the Ptolemy Finch.

Thus Legs found herself taking her lunch break one block away from the agency's offices, in the hotel where they had first got together, and which had long excited them both as they reinacted the white heat of those early unions in their favourite fifth floor room.

Leaving Devon, Legs had been determined to be morally unimpeachable and as celibate as a nun until she'd sorted out her priorities, laid her cards on the table with Conrad, spoken at greater length with Francis and considered her future. Now, overwhelmed by her need to feel protected, desired and wanted by a man as powerful as Conrad, her resolve crumbled.

'This is very becoming.' He pulled her electric blue dress over her head. 'Is it new?'

It was one of the outfits he'd bought her from Browns less than a fortnight ago. Had he forgotten already?

'It's my blue period,' she said without thinking, channelling dodgy subliminal thoughts as always because she was panicking that the curse was in its last throes and her hasty office douche might not suffice.

But Conrad didn't appear to be listening as he pushed her down on the bed and lifted her legs so that her ankles rested on his shoulders as he plunged in.

'How I love to part my Legs!'

She gasped at the thrill as always, turning towards the fake suede headboard and closing her eyes ecstatically, letting out little cries with Conrad's regular thrusts. Then she opened her eyes again and squinted at the headboard. There were unpleasant greasy indents where guests had propped their heads, possibly staying up too late reading *Ptolemy Finch*.

'Does that feel good, baby?' Conrad growled, took a surreptitious glance as his watch and thrust faster, aware that he had a late lunch appointment in Chelsea to get to.

'Ohhh sooo good,' she said, looking quickly away from the headboard and smiling up at him, licking her lips.

Afterwards, back in the office, Legs felt too ashamed of herself to look up from her computer. Firstly she was ashamed for deceiving Conrad into thinking she'd enjoyed their lovemaking more – she hadn't exactly faked an orgasm, but she had made a lot of squealing, panting noises to encourage him to hurry up, knowing he'd be in a sour mood if he was late for his lunch. And she was ashamed that she really hadn't enjoyed it more. She'd hoped it would be diverting and sexy to feel desired by her confident, clever man, but she'd wanted it to be over almost as soon as it began. She didn't dare think about Francis. She couldn't help but think about Byrne, whose face now seemed to be tattooed on her inner eyelids, pillow and computer screen. Her guilt complex was escalating out of control.

She tried to concentrate on work, starting to write up a report recommending Conrad look at the dead redhead manuscript, then breaking off to check her emails. Still no word from Kelly.

She emailed the redhead murderer's author, Delia Meare: *Please could you send consecutive chapters, preferably the entire manuscript? It has an excellent beginning but to enable us to judge whether it has the narrative to grip readers, we need to read it as a whole. Many thanks.*

Within minutes, she had the entire manuscript in her computer's temporary directory, apparently sent three times, followed by twenty chasing emails to check that she had received it.

Scrolling it on screen, Legs read two or three more pages continuing from where she'd left off. They were so good that the back of her neck felt like it was plugged into the National Grid via every individual hair.

Knowing that Gordon had recommended the author in the first place, she seized upon the excuse to make something approaching normal contact, although Gordon's out-of-office status meant she had to direct these through Kelly: *Delia Meare?*

Talented writer, but will flood your inbox if left unloved. Get IT to block her email. Kelly

Done it. Thanks. How is Gordon?

Right here. He sends his best. Keep up the good work. K

It was the most conventional exchange they'd all had in days, and Conrad would no doubt be delighted to find his PA communicating with his top client with such coffee-morning politeness, but it left Legs feeling uneasy and dissatisfied. She sensed Gordon was in retreat. He hadn't asked about Farcombe or the Protheroes at all. Kelly's final reply read like a brush off, although with Gordon breathing down her neck, his PA could hardly report back on his mental state.

She started to print out Delia Meare's manuscript, but, unable to concentrate as she watched the pages shunting out, she found herself wondering what Gordon Lapis thought about the Emperor's New Clothes when it came to stripping them off seductively in front of her boss and his agent. She sensed he would disapprove enormously. For all Ptolemy and Purple's flirtation and Gordon's talk of erotic tension between Julie Ocean and Jimmy Jimee, there was a piety that allowed Gordon his dark, sexy wit and clever tropes without ever being accused of salaciousness.

Ptolemy Finch, despite being immortal, was far too young to get jiggy, and had thus far spent five books building a deep, fierce friendship with coquettish sidekick Purple without so much as a kiss. It wasn't even entirely clear whether Purple was female or male, but this whirlwind of wit and flirtation could hack any computer and hot-wire any vehicle, metamorphosise into a meerkat, speak any language and channel spirits, occasionally all at the same time. Purple also upheld the 'Ten Rules to Live By' that every child was taught at soothsayer school with almost religious fervour. Gordon clearly had high, if eccentric standards, in sidekicks as well as pet-friendly hotel rooms.

Perhaps Gordon was a priest, she wondered suddenly, imagining the media furore to find the great author standing before them in a dog-collar.

Conrad had left her with a mountain of prep work to do for the Farcombe appearance, liaising with half a dozen contacts from Gordon's publishing house, informally dubbed 'Team GL'.

Conrad's press release had unleashed a tidal wave of interest, just as he had predicted. Every broadsheet, tabloid, glossy celebrity magazine and television chat show was clamouring for interviews, big name producers wanted to commission documentaries about Gordon stepping from the shadows of anonymity, there was even talk of Hollywood film rights being sold to the story of the man behind Ptolemy Finch. Everybody involved had an opinion over how it – and Gordon – should be handled from now until the big event to maximise the hype.

What about after *the event?* Legs asked her Team GL colleagues amid the hyperbole. *How can we help him prepare for the exposure and intrusion after so long behind the veil?*

Don't jump ahead, Gordon's dictatorial editor Wendy Savage snapped back, cc-ing her email to even more people on the ever-growing Team GL list.

After two hours of circular emails, attachments and clashing opinions, Legs was close to meltdown. As well as disregarding Gordon's mental state totally, the team had no understanding of the way Farcombe worked, and how much resistance they would get if they carried on planning as they were. She struggled to get her point across, but it was a losing battle; she badly needed some backup.

Legs, who had now read Gordon's 'sting in the tale' email so many times she knew it by heart, wasn't so sure he was in a good place right now, but she felt she couldn't betray his confidence, not even to Conrad.

She composed another email: *Your message about the Emperor's New Clothes has made me think, cry, laugh and worry about you too many times to count. I can't tell you how much difference it's made to my personal life. I want to thank you from the bottom of my heart, and reassure you that I'm your emissary, ally, research assistant and trainee Julie Ocean whenever you need me.*

Farcombe is a good place and a safe place. I have taken my clothes off there many times and may well do so again. If one is going to strip bare, it's a great spot. You will be brilliant. You are brilliant. I will be there for you. A.

P.s. Just look out for the gorse bushes.

Unable to send it direct, she went for broke and directed it to Kelly with an urgent tag. As soon as it went, she regretted the p.s.

He made no reply. Nor, by four, was there any direct word from Kelly. Conrad still wasn't back from his lunch. But Legs couldn't wait any longer to hurl herself across London to fetch enough evidence to liberate the shiny silver Honda.

At seven o'clock that evening, Tolly was free and legally permitted to stay in the Ealing street on which it was parked. The Farcombe seagull droppings still tattooed on its roof had now been joined by a Jackson Pollock abstract of pigeon poo gunshot. It was a hot, airless evening that smelled of dust and exhaust fumes, thunder rumbling in the far distance. The stormy heat wave looked set to stay all week.

Legs let herself into her flat. All was silent overhead. It was choir practice night; Ros and Nico were at the cathedral.

Francis had sent an ominous text: *Say the word. ILY. P.s. Please do not mention your love of your car again before our Friday deadline. I may be forced to rethink.*

Was he going to take Tolly back again? She wondered. If so, what had he done with her old red banger of which he denied all knowledge?

Her throat was aching and her head pounding. She couldn't face running that evening.

Instead, she looked through several new manuscripts picked up from her desk today that had been marked up by the agency's readers as worth Conrad's attention. In the first, the corpse of a High Court judge was found floating in the Thames with a key crammed up each nostril; in the second, three schoolgirls kept prisoner in a cellar were drained of blood, and the third was the most gruesome of all, detailing the slow mental deterioration of a ripper

303

who kept all his conquests piled up and rotting in a remote lock up. None had anything unique or compelling about the prose style, although they were better written than most submissions. All three left her with an aching back and a fear of humankind. How could anybody trust anybody else these days? She wondered, marking the third for Conrad's attention, knowing he would love the potential of a television tie-in; drama producers couldn't get enough mass murder and mental breakdown these days. Reading them all had served to remind her how exceptional the Delia Meare script was. She wished she'd brought it back with her tonight instead of plonking it in the middle of Conrad's desk like a guilty love token.

She took a long candlelit bath in her little tub. Her involuntary thoughts drifted to Byrne as she pushed her toes up the taps, unable to stop herself wondering how he was getting on. She hoped he and Poppy could get closer. Both were such difficult buggers, hiding behind defence shields as high as cirrocumulus, yet desperate to be understood. If he had only a little time left, he deserved to break through her grand monologues to the real truth.

'Coat of Many Colours' started playing on the radio, crackling like mad because the batteries needed changing. She sank beneath the bubbles for a moment as she remembered singing it off key the night she'd told Byrne so many of her secrets.

Before she knew it, she was having an imaginary conversation with him, asking about his childhood and his illness, offering friendship and support. By the time the bubbles had all popped and the bathwater had gone lukewarm, they were firm allies.

She certainly needed allies right now, even imaginary ones.

Her iPhone started ringing with 'I'm a Believer', Conrad's designated tone.

Dripping water everywhere, she located it on the bed.

'Have you read your emails?' He demanded, launch party still raging in the background.

'Not for an hour or two.' She found herself wondering what

finger food and drink they served at the *Hansel and Gretel Diet* book launch. Chicken bones and water?

'Read it. Deal with it. We'll have a breakfast meeting at my desk at eight tomorrow. Don't be late.'

Not bothering to wait for her laptop to boot, she looked at her emails on the iPhone. Team GL had spent a busy evening forwarding attachments and cc-ing them to even more people. Gordon himself had replied to nothing, but Kelly had sent a collective message.

Dear all,

Gordon asks that Allegra North no longer works on his behalf and ceases all involvement with his forthcoming appearance at Farcombe Festival without further notice.

Kind regards,

Kelly

Legs felt the bathwater dripping down her body turn to ice as she sat down heavily on the bed.

Hands shaking, she started composing a reply and then remembered he had blocked all incoming mail. She went on to direct messaging instead. Gordon was online.

May I ask why you want me removed from the project? She addressed him as stiffly as if she was writing a formal letter. *Was it my email this afternoon? If I have been impertinent then I can only apologise wholeheartedly and beg your forgiveness. I would really appreciate your time in letting me know why this has happened. With kind regards and concern, Allegra.*

Gordon Lapis went immediately offline.

He sent an email in the early hours. She was still awake, lying in bed with the covers kicked off because it was so hot and close. Reading the last chapters of *Ptolemy Finch and the Topaz Eagle*, she'd just reached such an exciting cliffhanger that her phone's message alert beep made her scream out loud.

My dear Allegra,

You may be the only one of the lot of them who seems to understand me, but right now I do not require understanding; I require action. You do not act very well.

Your friend,

GL.

P.s. Be careful in what you say to Delia Meare; she has once again flooded my inbox; I have reinforced my firewall and changed my email. I advise caution for all her writing brilliance.

She heaved a deep, infuriated sigh, deciding she didn't like the Mad Hatter very much at all when he was in this mood. She wasn't going to waste her bedtime wishes on him tonight. When she closed her eyes to try to sleep, however, a face was waiting beneath her lids, a curious composite made up of Francis, Conrad, her imaginary Ptolemy Finch, and even Byrne, those furnace eyes full of disapproval. It wasn't a face to be ignored.

She clicked on the light and groped for her phone to reply.

Sleep tight.

Sleep tight, was returned in a less than a breath.

Chapter 25

The breakfast crisis meeting with Conrad was stickier than the melting Danish pastries that went untouched on the plate in front of them. He was wholly unimpressed by Legs' explanation that Gordon thought she acted too badly to stay on Team GL.

'This isn't an amateur production of Pygmalion,' he stormed. 'It hardly matters that you're insincere if you get the job done.'

'I am *not* insincere!' She was highly affronted.

Conrad waved her protests away. 'Gordon calls the shots and that means he can call you any name he likes. He's just being bellicose. He needs you. Let's find a solution.'

'I can hardly beg him to change his mind,' she rationalised.

He wiped his sweating forehead with a handkerchief that had 'World's Best Dad' written on it. 'This means I am going to have to take on the entire mantle of protecting his interests,' he said furiously, far more worried about his time commitments than Gordon's wellbeing.

They both knew Conrad needed her as much as Gordon. He'd shifted so much of the Lapis workload across to her in recent months that he'd lost interest as well as control. Gordon's eccentricity and lack of ambition irritated him. Looking after the Ptolemy Finch brand was a full-time job in itself, especially right now with the launch of a new book imminent, then Farcombe Festival's key event and the surrounding media furore following straight on. Conrad was a risk-taker who liked breaking new names and making new deals, not mollycoddling demanding authors. In the same way that he'd presented Legs like a treat to his most lecherous client that first lunch he'd taken her on, he had handed her to his bestselling client as a pacifier. Now that Gordon had spat out the dummy and was throwing his toys out of the pram, Conrad was at a loss.

Looking at him now, Legs felt a wave of regret that all her fantasies of sharing power coupledom with one of publishing's most fêted mavericks had come to so little. She was, after all, still just a lover he assigned to weekday nights and lunchtimes in hotel rooms, a corporate freebie he used to best advantage. But she wanted to help Gordon, her loyalty guaranteed for evenings, weekends and sleepless nights. Gordon inspired devotion, even among the newly fired.

'I'll work in the background,' she suggested, fanning herself with her notepad because she was so hot. Not thinking, she pulled forward her dress neckline and blew down into it to try to cool her sweat-slicked chest. Then she saw Conrad's eyes harden in that hypnotic, sexual way which told her he was no longer thinking about Gordon.

'No melting into the background in that outfit,' he growled, admiring another of her Browns dresses, this one asymmetric sun-flower yellow jersey, clinging softly to all the right places.

'Just melting.' She fanned herself faster. It was a sweltering day. The air conditioning in the office was on the blink. She wished she hadn't worn the dress, which was having an effect on Conrad that she found she no longer desired.

'My splash pool is wonderfully cool,' he promised, then called the meeting to a halt by asking her to book their usual table at Chez Bruce that evening, after which he promised a very long, very thorough seduction.

Legs smiled weakly, the feeling of dread mounting.

'Meanwhile, I want you to go through the *Cuthbert the Cat* contract queries with Olga and Eric,' he smiled wickedly. 'That should leave you plenty of time to be on hand to help me get up to speed with the Gordon projects.'

Legs groaned. Olga Jones, creator of the world-famous Cuthbert books, was a lovely German illustrator and cat-enthusiast married to retired accountant Eric, who'd now made it his full-time hobby to manage his wife's business affairs from home. As the most pedantic man in England, he was monstrously time-consuming to deal with. In recent years, he'd at least embraced email which had cut down on the three-hour phone conversations, but he was no less nit-picking. Olga, who trusted him implicitly, would not do a thing without his say-so and the new contract, which should have been signed months ago, was still being amended almost daily. This week, Eric had read a book on intellectual copyright. The result was a barrage of messages.

While Legs worked her way through the first of Eric's most recent twenty emails, Conrad began tackling Gordon and the agency's interests leading up to next week's launch of *Ptolemy Finch and the Raven's Curse* followed by the Farcombe appearance.

A new Gordon launch was always huge, involving so much global communication and massive secrecy that it was exhausting to orchestrate. Protecting copyright was paramount. No printed copies could be allowed out of the warehouses until the last moment, and all those were guarded by hired-in security teams. The midnight bookshop launches, synchronised to GMT and held simultaneously across the globe, were a military offensive. The ebook would be released a week later.

But artwork for the exclusive collector's edition had been rushed back to the illustrator when it was spotted that Ptolemy looked like he had a hard-on from certain angles. Meanwhile Gordon was laying down more codicils about Farcombe, mostly about increasing security and limiting the media, the detail of which curiously seemed to revolve around protecting the Protheroe family.

'That's so generous of him.' Legs was moved by his forethought as the tiny, family-run festival faced a tidal wave of his fans, most sane but a few certifiable.

'It's bloody inconvenient of him!' Conrad raged. 'I've got far too much on my plate already!'

He consequently spent all morning thrusting his head out of his office door and bellowing 'Legs!' as he demanded that she both brief him and run errands, Frau Whiplash meets whipping boy with no coffee or loo breaks. The more hectic the task, the more apoplectic he grew, taking it out on her first and others second. By the time he set off for a client lunch, he'd argued with almost everyone on Team GL, including Gordon.

'The man is maddening!' he raged. 'He's refusing all interviews, and insists his first appearance can't be televised, which buggers up the Farcombe sponsorship with EuroArts TV. He's just called me a "media pimp".'

'He's Gordon Lapis,' Legs said soothingly. 'He calls the shots and the names, remember.'

Conrad and his BlackBerry stormed off to hail a taxi on Piccadilly.

Legs returned to her Eric Jones emails. In the time it had taken her to reply to his first ten, he'd sent fifteen more. She wished she could get IT to block his emails like they'd done with Delia Meare.

Feeling guilty about Delia, who she now saw as Gordon's protégée, she wrote her an old-fashioned letter, a very rare event in Fellows Howlett's offices these days. In it she explained that she was personally very excited by her writing, which was boundary-breaking in this ultra-cynical era when so many readers were impervious to shock. She went on to say that Delia's enthusiastic submission approach was to her credit; tenacious and original material could help make an agent live and feel the book. But she then gently advised that the same follow-up might not work for Conrad. Satisfied that she'd got her point across and spread some cheer, she threw it in the pile for the afternoon post and sagged back at her desk, wiped out by the humidity.

Throughout the afternoon, she got hotter and hotter. Her head was pounding again. By five-thirty, she was pouring with sweat, the yellow dress now glued to her skin.

Conrad kept forwarding Team GL messages from his BlackBerry for her to deal with, telling her to pretend to be him. He wasn't returning to the office after lunch, he explained; he'd see her later at the restaurant for a 'debrief'.

Working through the messages, Legs wasn't sure she could face being debriefed by Conrad twice in one week. She was trying not to resent the fact that he was probably at his club or the gym right now, avoiding the Gordon issue while indulging in what he would call 'networking' and she would call 'skiving'.

Legs needed to go home and shower before heading across the river with her overnight bag. The thought of a huge meal and a sexual marathon with Conrad exhausted her. She knew she had to address her doubts, and even though she felt too drained to know where to start, she was determined to tackle the situation with maturity and in privacy before another day dawned.

But when Legs got back to Ealing, Ros was out of the upper entrance like a shot. 'There's someone been waiting here to see you since five,' she hissed. 'You really must explain to your friends that

I can't abide dogs in the house.' For a strange, illogical moment Legs imagined Byrne and Fink the basset calling by. But Ros quickly shattered the illusion. 'She's in the garden looking suicidal. You must get rid of her soon; I have my embroidery ladies coming at six-thirty.'

Thinking longingly of her shower, Legs headed through the side gate.

Sitting on Nico's old swing was what she first took to be a teenage girl. Dressed in baggy shorts, her hair scraped back beneath a green cotton bandana and thin freckled legs dangling down to scuffed trainers, she cut a pathetically frail figure.

Then Legs spotted a terrier in a matching bandana cocking a wonky leg on her sister's begonias and realised its owner was Kizzy de la Mere.

As soon as Kizzy saw Legs, she burst into tears.

'I'm so sorry to come unannounced, but I have to talk to you!' she sobbed.

Legs could see her sister glaring at them through the kitchen windows.

Feeling like a large sweaty banana in her yellow dress, she led the waif-like Kizzy to the bench behind the apple tree, out of sight of the house. It was a relief to know she was alive, at least, and hadn't swum out to sea the night she disappeared, or been bumped off in a dastardly Protheroe conspiracy. She tried not to look at her watch too obviously.

'I've been going demented with worry,' Kizzy wailed. 'Francis won't s-speak to me or tell me what's g-going on.'

'How did you find me?'

'My friend Gabs w-works at the Book Inn. She looked up your address on the computer.'

Tongue Piercing was a spy, Legs realised. No wonder she'd been shuffling around with a dishcloth every time Nonny or Guy asked Legs about Francis.

As they sat down side by side on a wall, Legs could guess that

Kizzy was here as a part of a campaign to try to win Francis back. She'd heard the word 'ambitious' in connection with Kizzy too often to trust her motives. Yet she felt curiously calm. Sitting in her sister's back garden after a day from hell at work, Francis and their lost love seemed worlds apart, an abstract shape she had yet to fit back into the geometry of her life.

Kizzy did seem genuinely upset. 'I came up to London yesterday.' She gulped the words out. 'I'm staying in my parents' flat. I j-just need to know if you and Francis are b-back t-together?'

'Not really. Not at all, in fact.'

Cue more sobs, no doubt relief joining high grade self pity. Legs braced herself for an onslaught of tearful begging and pleading as Kizzy demanded that Legs step aside so that she could have Francis back.

But to her surprise, the redhead sobbed, snorted and spluttered: 'Francis will only ever love you!'

Legs wasn't sure she'd heard her right, but Kizzy was making too much noise to interrupt. She was a very pretty girl, but not an attractive crier. Within seconds, snot was trailing from her nostrils like stalactites and her face as puffy as Byrne sucking on a peanut.

'He would d-do anything to have you back.' She looked up at Legs, green eyes like wet frogs' backs. 'He thinks I'm Poppy's pawn, and now that Jamie's turned up, and you're back, I'll never see the Protheroes again!' She started to howl.

'Of course that's not true,' Legs said reassuringly.

'But it is!' Kizzy howled. 'I knew from the start that Francis would never love me. How can I hope to compete with you? You are Isolde to his Tristan.'

'Not the happiest long-term relationship,' Legs pointed out in an undertone before looking at her levelly. 'Do *you* love *him*?'

'I love them all!' she wailed. 'Poppy has been like a guardian angel to me, and she was s-so enthusiastic when Francis took a romantic interest, encouraging us to spend time together, and then inviting me to live in the house.'

'That wasn't Francis's idea?'

'No! We had separate rooms. I adore the way he's so old-fashioned. He just wanted to talk about poetry and farming. He's very simple to please, isn't he?'

Legs smiled weakly.

Kizzy hung her head miserably. 'It was obvious that if you returned, there'd be no future for us, and I accepted that. I just wanted to be a part of the family, to be close to them all. But now it's over, I realise I've sacrificed my greatest love . . .' She dissolved into sobs again.

Legs dug wearily through her bag for a tissue. There was no mistaking how heartfelt her tears were. But when Kizzy snorted and dribbled out the story of her short love affair with Francis, it wasn't quite as she'd expected.

'We only really had a few dinner dates before Poppy latched onto it and made a big fuss. You are his first and only love, Legs. He's been so wounded by what happened between you. He has this sort of twisted defence shield around him, like a suit of armour that had caved in and stabbed him in the heart, you know?'

Fitting that she looked like Guinevere, Legs thought sadly, trying not to steal another glance at her watch. This was a conversation she really didn't want to have.

'He used to joke that Poppy must have created me in her studio at Farcombe, I was so perfect for him.'

'But you must have met him before, surely?'

'A few times – I met you, too.'

Legs looked at her disbelievingly.

'I was just a geeky kid; thick glasses, plaits, teeth in braces. You two were so glamorous – the Brad and Angelina of my world.'

Legs smiled nervously, grateful at least that she'd moved on from Tristan and Isolde whose forever lust had been so tragically thwarted by other lovers.

'I idolised you both, but I'm not surprised you didn't even register me. Nobody did. I was away at school most of the time, with camps and self-improvement courses in the holidays. Yolande is very hot on education. It was the same at university.'

'Doesn't sound much of a childhood.' Legs batted away midges.

'Oh, I'm incredibly lucky.' She smiled a wobbly smile that turned into more tears, 'It could have been so different if Poppy hadn't saved me. She desperately wanted me to marry Francis and I've let her down.' She howled and hiccupped again.

'You can't force people in and out of love,' Legs breathed, hearing Byrne's voice in her head. She jumped as a police siren wailed through the Ealing streets nearby.

'I've missed that noise,' Kizzy sighed tearfully. 'I adore London's sounds, don't you? They're my lullaby.'

Legs looked across at her in surprise. 'I thought you loved Farcombe?'

'I know it's a magical place, and I've enjoyed living there.' She looked up at a droning jumbo jet climbing away from Heathrow, 'but I've always felt at home in London. I'm happier in a big city. I envy your life here – this lovely family house, your friends, your amazing job.'

'My job's pretty crap right now,' Legs thought about Gordon firing her and Conrad's stress.

'I interviewed for it too.'

Legs almost fell off the wall. 'You applied to be Conrad Knight's assistant?'

Kizzy nodded, mopping her damp green eyes on her sleeves. 'I wanted it more than anything; I read profiles of every Fellows Howlett author, researched the deals, found out everything I could about the agency. Conrad told me it was in the bag, then you were next in the room after me and blew him away.'

'I did not blow him to get my job!'

'I was talking metaphorically.'

'Oh.' She rubbed her sweaty forehead.

'That was when Poppy offered me part-time work at the festival. It was like a lovely holiday, getting to know the Protheroes, hanging out with Édith and Jax and the Book Inn crowd. It was supposed to just be temporary, but then Francis came back from London heartbroken, and my part-time work somehow became full-time, and then Hector started misbehaving and . . .' She was gripped by sobbing again.

Legs fished for another tissue and handed it over before putting a comforting arm around the redhead's shoulders, eager for the tears to end. 'Do you mind terribly if I make a quick call? I'm supposed to be somewhere.'

If she hoped Kizzy would take the hint and leave, she was mistaken. In the throes of the sort of lovelorn agony that's entirely blinkered to the everyday lives of others, Kizzy wandered around the garden smoking a roll-up while Legs lurked by the shed and made a whispered call to Conrad. The midges were starting to bite with a vengeance now. She swatted great clouds of them away as she spoke to him.

'Can't you reschedule her?' he asked, as though Kizzy was an inconvenient appointment that had run late.

'She's in floods of tears. I'm sure the restaurant will put the booking back. Just give me another half hour or so.'

He rung off irritably saying he'd see what he could do.

Legs jumped to find Kizzy leaning against the shed door just around the corner finishing her cigarette, Byron panting at her feet.

At least the frantic sobbing seemed to have abated.

'Would you mind if I used your loo?' she asked.

Reluctantly, Legs took her down to the flat, pulling an apologetic face as they passed the kitchen window where Ros was mouthing 'No dogs! No smoking!'

Byron settled straight on the striped settee while his mistress spent an inordinate amount of time in the bathroom. Just as Legs was starting to panic that Kizzy might have slit her wrists in there, she re-emerged looking puffy-eyed but calm.

'You have such lovely things here. It's a gorgeous flat.'

'It's my sister's place.'

315

'But these are the possessions you had when you lived with Francis?' she asked, looking at the shelves cluttered with souvenirs from their travels together.

'Some.'

She picked up a little carved wooden box from Nepal. 'You were together *such* a long time.'

'Yes. Ages. Kizzy, I'm afraid I have a dinner da—'

'Do you possibly think I could let Byron have a drink of water in a bowl or something?'

'Of course. Sorry. It's so hot, he must be dehydrated.' Legs shot hurriedly into the kitchen, Kizzy let out a little dry cough then another.

Legs felt a needle prick at her conscience. 'Would you like some water too? I can stretch to a glass instead of a bowl. Or something stronger? Wine, maybe?' She closed her eyes as soon as she said it, already certain she was making a big mistake.

'Oh yes please!' Kizzy settled down on the sofa, staring around her, eager to memorise everything. Something about her reminded Legs of a beautiful sea anemone bedded firmly into a sandy bed, with a deadly sting at the ready.

'I thought you left the dog at Farcombe?' She regarded Byron warily as he limped around the flat inspecting everything with his nose.

'Édith brought him back to London.' Her blotchy face coloured. 'We had a terrible argument.' The tears were threatening again. 'It's the reason I'm here. I have to make things better. I shouldn't have run away like that. I should have stayed and let Francis do it his way.'

'Do what precisely?' She headed to the sink to fill a bowl of water for panting Byron.

'All that stuff about pretending to get back together with you to split up your parents was just a smoke screen. It was obvious Francis was still mad about you. But he didn't want to frighten you off or alarm Poppy, who is incredibly fragile right now, what with Hector behaving so badly and the festival coming up.'

'How considerate of him,' Legs muttered, putting the brimming bowl down on the kitchen floor. 'It would have helped to let me know what he was planning. In fact, what *was* he planning?'

'Actually it was my idea. Francis told me that you'd feel impossibly guilty if he dropped me like a stone the moment you came back.'

Legs closed her eyes. He knew her far too well.

'So we were going to have an argument over supper and I'd tell him it was over,' Kizzy went on, 'but of course Poppy's son turned up and stole all the limelight.'

'I was under the impression Poppy kept that firmly on herself,' Legs muttered, eyeing her curiously. 'Were you really prepared to do that for Francis?'

'Oh yes, I was looking forward to it.' Her damp eyes glittered. 'I was spoiling for a fight that night.'

'So why run away?'

'I didn't like the company at supper. One too many guests.' She looked at her hands, not offering any more detail.

She must be referring to Byrne. Legs realised uneasily. If Kizzy knew a secret that could bring down the family, then it could well involve Byrne. Detective nose twitching, she was avid to get to the truth, but knew better than to give away how much she already knew.

She went in search of wine. Then she span back round, remembering: 'You *did* have an argument, though. Before supper, in the back lobby; I heard it. You told Francis that you refused to be humiliated.'

The blotchy colour on Kizzy's cheeks deepened from salami to bresaola. 'I wasn't talking to Francis.'

'Then who was it?'

'I'd rather not say, but I promise it wasn't him.'

Legs looked at her red face, suspicions now on high alert as she added together more clues. She'd spotted Kizzy outside the family solicitors in Farcombe that day just minutes after Byrne, then there had been the angry confrontation she'd interrupted between them when first arriving at supper. Could the hushed, unseen conversation she'd heard taking place behind the green baize door have been Kizzy talking to Poppy's long-lost son? The thought made her feel sick.

Eager to change the subject, Kizzy had picked up the copy of *Ptolemy Finch and the Topaz Eagle* which Legs had abandoned on the coffee table. 'D'you know Poppy has read all the Ptolemy books at least twice?'

Legs gaped at her. '*Poppy* is a Gordon Lapis fan?'

'She wraps old Faber and Faber dust jackets around them so nobody knows. It's so sweet, and so typical of her – like wrapping Francis and me up in Farcombe Hall and thinking it makes us a power couple. It really is true,' Kizzy intoned in her strange Scottish lisp, giggling at Legs' astonished face. 'It's her guilty secret. She's read them all several times, each one tucked up in *Mrs Dalloway*'s dust jacket like a stolen baby in a shawl.'

Chapter 26

Half an hour later, Legs phoned Conrad from the privacy of the bathroom, leaving a tap running to avoid being overheard. 'I don't think I'll make it.'

'I've given them hell changing that booking.'

'I can still come to the house later, maybe?' she offered.

'Don't bother,' he hung up.

Still no pillow talk to counter all the office chat, Legs thought sadly as she splashed her face before turning off the tap. But a part of her was very relieved to be let off the sexual hook again. Her body felt drained and aching, and her headache wouldn't budge despite painkillers. She was also guiltily eager to know more about the connection between Kizzy de la Mere and Farcombe, most especially Poppy. The detective in her was back on the case; Julie Ocean had clocked onto the night shift, grateful to be back in her familiar west London patch.

The wine bottle was already half empty. Kizzy, who had no head for alcohol, was looking increasingly glazed, but she certainly loved to talk, giving a five-minute monologue on the wonders of Poppy that could have been scripted by the be-turbanned one herself: 'She is so supportive and nurturing, so full of love and empathy and just the most energising and maternal person to be around, don't you find?'

Try telling that to Byrne, Legs wanted to say, but she could feel Julie Ocean at her side now, reminding her that the truth had to be teased out: 'She must be an amazing godmother.'

'She is very special.' There followed another long homily on Poppy's magnificent talents, kindness and general saintliness. 'Although I'm not strictly speaking her god-daughter at all,' Kizzy reached for her wine glass. 'Legally I'm her ward, I suppose, or at least I was before I went to live with Howard and Yolande.'

'How old were you when they adopted you?'

'They're actually my foster parents. Private adoptions aren't legal in this country, but my mother didn't want me taken into care. I was three when they took me.'

Lying contentedly between the two women on the sofa, Byron was quietly working through the trimming on one of Ros's Laura Ashley brocade cushions.

Legs was far too fascinated by the story at hand to notice. 'And before that you lived with your mother?'

'On and off. She was never a very capable parent, I'm afraid. She has lots of – difficulties. Poppy looked after me sometimes, but her life was hardly easy.'

'How did they know each other?'

Kizzy looked at her for a long time, weighing up her trustworthiness. 'It's a long story.'

Legs said nothing, even though her curiosity was now completely ignited. She kept finding her mind returning to Byrne, convinced that there had to be a link between them both.

'My birth mother is called Liz Delamere,' Kizzy told her, watching her face for reaction.

Legs knew the family name. The Delameres were big North Devon movers and shakers. But she had never heard of Liz.

'She used to help Poppy out at Nevermore Cottage, caring for Brooke and Jamie when Poppy was out working,' Kizzy explained.

Legs' eyes widened. 'So you've known Byrne, I mean Jamie, since childhood?'

She shook her head, 'I don't really remember him at all. I was too young.'

Byron had now tired of chewing the piping off the cushion and started a thorough ablution of his private parts, snorting vociferously.

'Do you still see Liz?'

Kizzy's face grew even warier. 'She moved around a lot; we lost contact until quite recently.'

'And now?'

'We did meet up again once, not long ago. She lives in a sheltered community near Torquay now. It's very tranquil. Her great passion is writing.'

'Perhaps that's where you got your talent from?'

'My spelling's better.'

'And your father?'

'What's this, an SAS interrogation?' Kizzy giggled nervously, eyes crossing as she reached for her wine glass and missed.

'Sorry – I'm incurably nosy,' Legs blushed, realising she'd been hammering out the questions like Julie Ocean putting together a criminal profile. 'Your life has been so unusual, and you're so clever and pretty, it's just fascinating to get to know you better,' she enthused, wincing at her sycophancy.

But Kizzy lapped up the compliments. She was thoroughly enjoying all the focus being on her.

'And you are *sho* much nicer than everyone shays,' she slurred as she managed to grasp her wine glass and raise it to Legs before carrying on with her life story. 'Dad was a Highland laird. I spent holidays with him, but he drank and womanised away his fortune and died when I was fourteen.'

'Really?' Legs was staggered, but it made sense of the incongruous Scottish accent.

'No!' Kizzy shrieked with laughter. 'I can't believe that story still works. I made it up when I was at school – I was sent to this awful hell-hole in the Borders. I hated it there. It was hugely academic with breakthough teaching techniques based on the Chinese system; one of Howard's friends was the headmaster, and it was thought I'd be better off there than London because Mum was working twenty-four seven. Ironic given the school worked its pupils pretty much twenty-four seven too.' The laughter wobbled towards tears once more. 'I survived by making up stories about my real dad and his amazing adventures around the Ballachnaughty Estate.'

She looked at her hands. 'The truth is I have no idea who my birth father is, some village stud from the Hartland Peninsula, I think. Mum was very young and a bit capricious.' She smiled ruefully, tears still wet on her freckled cheeks. 'They'd probably call it ADHD now, but in those days it was just seen as waywardness, and a family like the Delameres could still brush such things under the Axminster – or keep it in the nursery wing. Liz is incredibly bright, over-bright really, but she didn't finish her education; she had no social skills by the time she reached adulthood, and was hopelessly naive, just living at home in their big country pile like a neglected pet, which is probably why she loves animals and lame ducks more than anything. Poppy's family and the Delameres were close friends, and it was Goblin Granny who suggested Liz become a mother's help at Nevermore to give her something to do.

'Liz was probably nineteen or twenty by then, but acted like a little girl playing house. She clucked around Poppy's brood like a little mother hen, living in her own fantasy world, which is what she does a lot of the time. She loved caring for all the horses, and it meant Poppy could get out of the house. Brooke used to get Liz to wheel him to the local pubs – his alcoholism was legend – and it gave her her first taste of a social life. She was terribly pretty back then and men found her charming, even though she was wild as celandine with no grasp of social mores whatsoever. She was also far too kind-hearted to say no.

'But then she got pregnant. She was so innocent it's easy to see how some local letch took advantage. She was almost six months gone by the time anybody found out. She wouldn't say who the father was, but a few discreet enquiries made it pretty obvious that by then she was thought of as little more than the village bicycle. The Delameres disowned her, and so it was left to Poppy and Goblin Granny to pick up the pieces.'

'And you were the pieces?'

She nodded again, big green eyes cheerless. 'Poppy got Liz on the local council house list and she was already in a little flat by the time I was born, but her benefits didn't go far and she had no real understanding of the world. She can behave inappropriately, obsessively sometimes; it's hard to explain. People took advantage of her, difficult situations frightened her. She started having panic attacks. The Delamere family had played down her differences so much as she grew up that there had never been formal help or any diagnosis of a mental health issue, so she got no extra money or assistance. She just had Poppy.'

Legs suspected there had to be more to the connection between the two women than an old family friendship, but she wasn't about to interrupt with awkward questions.

'Poppy had just started to work for the Farcombe Festival at the time,' Kizzy went on, 'Liz still did a few part-time hours for her, bringing me along with her, but she became unreliable, not turning up on time or not turning up at all. I think Brooke had to go into respite care for a bit; Jamie kept running away. Poppy was really struggling and terribly unhappy.

'Then Liz made a suicide attempt – not her first by any means, but her most determined by a mile – and that got social services on high alert, given I was still under two. They were soon talking about taking me into care. That's when Liz asked Poppy if she could sign over my custody to her.'

'Isn't that a bit extreme?'

Kizzy stretched out a thin freckled hand and stroked Byron's soft undercarriage. Now lying belly up between them, lame leg twitching in sleep, he was snoring contentedly.

'Liz is incredibly loving, but she isn't at all maternal. It's hard to explain. She'd abandon me on the pavement as a toddler to cross the road and pet a dog. She'd stay up all night reading a book or writing stories of her own and then sleep all the next day, forgetting my needs totally. Goblin Granny used to call it a goldfish memory, but she's just hard-wired differently.'

Legs watched her small, pretty face, amazed at how rational and sane she was about it all. She looked terribly pale, the puffiness from crying having subsided to reveal big grey smudges under her eyes.

'Could I possibly scrounge a biscuit or some bread and butter?' Kizzy asked faintly.

'Of course! When did you last eat?'

'Imee's walnut starter thing.'

'Kerist! Hang on in there.' She headed to the kitchen. 'I'm afraid I don't have any raw fish.'

'Francis stopped me eating raw fish,' Kizzy sighed. 'It's full of B vitamins, but he said it was weird and made me spotty.'

'He used a similar argument with me about chocolate,' Legs sympathised.

Having not yet shopped for food, she knew her fridge was on its last offerings, but she managed to scrape the mould off a slab of cheddar and grate enough to cover a slice of pitta bread that she hacked from its icy tomb in the freezer compartment. Toasted under the grill, it delighted Kizzy, who fell on it like a famished refugee, sharing it with the suddenly alert Byron while Legs made herself a cup of tea.

Kizzy was still plundering the wine, raising her glass in a wonky salute now. 'You are so kind, Legs. I can see why Francis says you're the sweetest person he ever knew.'

'He said that?' She spluttered hot tea in shock.

Kizzy looked into her glass as she remembered. 'He used to shout it really, when he wanted to get at me.'

'I'm sorry.'

'Don't be. We both went into the relationship with such huge agendas, we needed a secretary to take minutes. This is delicious.' Kizzy was already noshing the last corner of pitta bread. 'Is there any more?'

Legs shook her head apologetically. 'There's some elderly Stilton I haven't explored yet, and I might have some biscuits . . .'

'Please!' She gazed at the photos framed on the walls and shelves while Legs raided cupboards in search of digestives. 'You have lots and lots of friends, don't you?'

'Very neglected ones,' Legs pulled a regretful face as she lifted bags of spilling rice and pasta looking for biscuits. 'They keep hitching and hatching while I'm – well, busy,' she fudged around the Conrad issue. It had all been so much easier with Francis at her side. Granted, her school and university friends hadn't always taken to him at first, her long distance, bright yet aloof boyfriend with his quasi-American accent who had been presented as a fait accompli and had always prevented her sowing her wild oats alongside her old London pals and peers. But that was a long time ago. They'd all eventually grown to love him as a part of her. Over the years many had become close to Francis's school and university friends, knitting together the social circles, and in time this embroidered alliance had been joined by other colourful new threads, acquaintances from jobs and pastimes. It had made for a muddling tapestry to unpick when they'd split up. In the wake of the broken engagement that nobody had seen coming, a few had sided pointedly with Francis, the wronged party, banished to Devon. Many had stuck with Legs, the friendly socialite, who had stayed conveniently in London. Quite a few had dropped out of contact totally.

'When a couple split up, the address book quickly changes from current affairs to history in the making,' she admitted to Kizzy now.

Between them, they demolished all the digestives and aged Stilton, which was actually sublime, even though Legs knew it dated back to the previous Christmas; the only thing that had been in her fridge longer was the Fridge Fresh Egg that Ros had given her as a moving in present. Legs found her appetite as sticky as the weather, but Kizzy was comfort-eating like a Tasmanian Devil on a binge.

'Francis and I had no friends in common apart from Édith,' she admitted in a small voice as she chased biscuit crumbs from creases in her shorts.

'And Jax,' Legs added automatically.

Kizzy started crying noisily again. She was really very drunk now, Legs realised. She wondered whether it would be terribly rude and uncaring to call her a taxi. As Kizzy threw herself against Legs' side and sobbed into her yellow dress, she decided it would. Besides which, she felt certain she was close to uncovering the big secret.

'It was Édith who persuaded me to try to find my mother again,' said Kizzy. 'Liz had been a live-in c-carer for a long time and moved all over the c-country. She'd m-married one man she looked after and had a bit of a breakdown w-when he died and his family tried to take her to court over money. Then she went on the rebound and married somebody else, another old m-man who treated her horribly before he died too. Her life was a mess.'

The Black Widow of Bideford, Legs remembered with a shiver.

'She's always frightened me,' Kizzy admitted. 'She'd write to me from time to time, long, rambling letters full of potty conspiracy theories. I threw them away and never wrote back. It was Édith who said I should face my fear, but I kept flunking it. I refused to talk about her; it was like my memory had blotted her out. It drove Édith mad. Then we had a horrible argument and I went to see Liz to prove I had the nerve as much as anything.'

'And what did you find out?'

'That I was right to be frightened.' Her voice shook and she picked repeatedly at the frays on the chewed cushion, unable to look up.

'Have you talked to anyone about this?'

'Not properly.' She shook her head. 'Édith had stopped speaking to me. I t-tried to have a quiet word with Francis, but he thought I was propositioning him. That's how we ended up on a first date.' She looked up apologetically, pale skin starting to colour. 'And I'd never tell Poppy, just as I've never dared tell her the t-truth about my real f-feelings,' she hiccupped, tears welling afresh. 'I'd do anything for her, and I couldn't let her down. Without her, my life would have been utterly different. I thought Francis was s-so lovely and safe, that he w-would look after me. Poppy wanted me to be an official part of the Farcombe dynasty, not just a cuckoo chick she was forced to g-give away.'

It was starting to dawn on Legs that Kizzy had not just been abandoned once as a young child, but twice over. It was enough to make anybody unstable. 'You say your mother made Poppy your custodian?'

'That was the legal term, yes,' she nodded tearfully. 'When Liz's life reached crisis point, Poppy was in a very unhappy place too. Brooke was hell to live with; Jamie was such a wild child, obsessed with his horses, fearless of danger and lost in his own world. He'd stopped talking to her. Nevermore Farm is something to behold; it hasn't changed much, even now. Back then, it was an angry, male dominated house with practically no home comforts. Poppy saw

326

me as compensation, the pretty little girl who danced for her and giggled at her jokes, the daughter she never had maybe. She didn't take a lot of persuading to become custodian.

'But I wasn't so pretty and entertaining to live with twenty-four seven. I woke ten, fifteen times a night screaming, I had tantrums and was impossibly clingy.'

'You must have been so traumatised.' Legs hugged Kizzy's shoulders tightly.

But the green eyes facing her glittered with a little of the old Kizzy that she remembered from Farcombe. 'I was attention seeking even then, and I think I must have sensed my biggest rival close at hand.'

'Byrne?' Legs whispered, finally getting to the secret she longed to hear most.

But Kizzy shook her head woozily. 'Hector,' she corrected. 'He was already circling overhead like a big eagle when I came into the nest.'

'And you got cast overboard when he landed?'

Settling back amongst the cushions on the sofa, Kizzy played with the soft little flaps of Byron's ears. 'Poppy had never mentioned my existence to Hector. Their flirtation was already in evidence when she took on my custody, but they were in their own little bubble. She says theirs was a courtship based on cerebral and carnal compatibility; their home lives were of little interest, although he knew her marriage was a living hell, and she knew he was desperately lonely and wounded by grief. When the love affair took off, they were blown out of the water by its intensity. Everything around them disappeared, or was made to disappear.'

'Loving Hector clearly has that effect on women.' Legs thought about her own mother whose real life no longer seemed to exist to her.

'Poppy is so full of regret now.' Kizzy hugged Byron closer. 'But at the time, it was a case of out of sight, out of mind. Brooke took Jamie to Ireland, of course; Francis was sent away to school. And

I went to Goblin Granny, where I was placed in a spooky attic with a hired nanny and told to keep quiet.'

Legs could barely conceive of the trauma that would cause such a little girl with an already blighted life.

But Kizzy remained calm as she recited events: 'Then Poppy met my parents. Yolande had spent so long battling the sexes in the City that she hadn't found a window in her diary for conception until long after the recommended deadline for childbirth had passed. Years of IVF had brought no joy. She was desperate to adopt a child, but Howard has a criminal record – don't ask; we always say it's political – and the British system kept spitting them out. The media was full of stories about Romanian orphans, and they had started a long application process, but then Poppy spoke to them about me, and Yolande knew it was kismet.'

'Is that where you got your name?'

'Sorry?'

'Isn't Kizzy short for Kismet?'

'No, my real name's Clarissa. It's a family name. I've always hated it.'

'Oh,' Legs smiled, 'everybody should change their name at least once in life.'

'Yolande and Howard never pushed me to call myself Hawkes or refer to them as "Mum" and "Dad". They're not the most conventional parents. I sometimes wonder if Yolande thinks I'm an asset she's best investing offshore to accrue the highest interest, and Howard sees me as a living repository for all his knowledge, but they have given me every opportunity, with such heart and thought. I shall always be grateful to them for that; they will be so disappointed that it hasn't worked out with Francis; Yolande shared Poppy's vision of our taking on the mantle of Farcombe together.' Her eyes filled with tears again. 'They even cooked up the idea of getting me a job at the festival so I'd be perfectly positioned to attract Francis's attention.'

'Ah, Francis.' Legs pressed her knuckles to her nose, the familiar twin sword hilts of guilt and jealousy trapped in her hands. Her fingers smelled of Stilton. She eyed Kizzy over them. She couldn't help but like her, this curious landlocked mermaid who loved her city sirens despite dipping her tail in the sea. Her childhood had been horribly disjointed, and yet her loyalty to Poppy was extraordinary.

But something wasn't quite adding up. She distinctly remembered Édith mentioning a big argument with her parents which had left them barely on speaking terms, with Kizzy forfeiting the Hawkes' coastal retreat for a room in the village.

'When I got to Farcombe, I found it really hard to settle. I missed my London life desperately. I went to see a fortune teller who told me my soulmate was lost at sea, but I could call them home. And she told me all about the guardian angels and spirit guides helping me. It was so cool. I really felt I could let down my hair and trust in fate. I made lots of amazing new friends.'

Legs eyed her warily. 'You don't really believe in all that clairvoyant stuff do you?'

'You sound like Howard and Yolande,' she sighed. 'They totally disapproved of my "rebellion" as they called it. We fell out big time.'

'Until you called Francis home from sea.' Legs looked away, surprised how much it still hurt.

'If you can call it that,' Kizzy muttered. 'I think he was already in a dry dock. I was naive to think that I'd love Francis just because we'd both lost our hearts elsewhere and might find comfort with one another. I knew when I moved in that I couldn't ever love him. Then Hector left and the pressure became unbearable. When Poppy agreed that the best way to get him to come home was for you and Francis to get back together, I saw a way out. I'd begun to feel so trapped, it was a liberation.

'Liz says we both take after her grandmother – my namesake,' she went on. 'Clarissa had our red hair and writing passion, and she couldn't live without love.'

'"I am two fools I know, for loving and for saying so",' Legs sighed.

'How perfectly put,' Kizzy smiled wanly. 'Is that Byron?'

'Donne. Francis wrote a thesis on him at university.'

Kizzy groaned and closed her eyes, relaxing into a strange laugh of relief. 'Oh God, I should have known that. I feel like one of those hapless girls one sees photographed on Hugh Grant's arm at parties, knowing full well that nobody will ever suit him as well as Elizabeth Hurley and vice versa. You two are just destined to be soulmates for ever.'

Legs closed her eyes for a moment, hardly able to believe that she could add Kizzy to the list of people telling her that she and Francis were the perfect couple. She rubbed her aching forehead. The smell of Stilton was making her feel queasy. 'Friendship is love without his wings,' she sighed.

'Now that *is* Byron,' Kizzy was instantly tearful once more. 'Francis is in love with you, Legs. And his wingspan is wider than the Farcombe Hall roof.'

Legs unfurled her fingers to cover her cheeks, but not quickly enough to stop Kizzy seeing the red blush that was racing up her face. She had a sudden, ludicrous image of Francis soaring over Eascombe cove like a sea eagle while she perched nervously in the rocks uncertain if she could take off or not. They'd both been sea eagles once, but now she was more of a fledgling guillemot.

Kizzy's green eyes were crossing a great deal now. 'You two *must* get back together, Legs. Francis is lost without you. Édith is right; I should never have come between you, like Conrad Knight should never have got in the way in the first place. That's my fault, too. If I'd got the job, you and Francis would still be together.'

'You can't think like that,' Legs gaped at her in shock.

'It's true! I want to make things better. You have to see that there really was nothing more between me and Francis than two friends comforting one another because they couldn't have the people they really love.'

'You're in love with someone else?'

'Mine is a lost cause.' Kizzy nodded miserably. 'In secret we met, in silence I grieve.' Quoting Byron, she hiccupped and excused herself to go to the loo again.

Byron the namesake terrier was still snoring loudly on the sofa, emitting contented puttering noises from his dewlaps one end and occasional gentle parping Stilton farts from the other.

Yawning, Legs thought how much simpler it would be to share her life with a dog. She and Francis had talked often of their dream puppy, a blue-eyed Husky. They had even thought up pretentious literary names: Virginia Woolf if it was a girl, von Goethe for a boy. The nursery slope to raising a family together; childish make-believe befitting of their childhood romance, now lost in growing up and growing apart.

There's had been a Peter Pan love, she reflected wretchedly. She'd once imagined it would never change, never grow old, but the truth was that it remained trapped in childhood. Then Wendy had run away with Captain Hook, which had been a terrible mistake. And now Tinkerbell was locked in her bathroom here.

Heading through to her little kitchen to put on the kettle, she picked up her phone from the surface and scrolled messages, more friends checking her whereabouts and wellbeing.

Francis 21.54.

There was his name. She felt cold and sweaty with remorse just at the sight of it, glancing towards the bathroom door to check Kizzy was still inside. Then she touched his name on the screen with a shaking thumb.

Bloody Jamie-go causing mutiny. Can you call him off? He likes you. If not, I will feed him nuts. Need you back so badly. Please say the word. ILY xxx

As she reread it, three things leaped out at her. But it wasn't the kisses, nor the ILY. It was those three words 'He likes you'. Byrne liked her. She felt as though wings had sprouted to lift her three feet off the floor. Oh, what a mess.

'That's such a cool phone.'

She jumped in shock, dropping it back on the counter as Kizzy came out of the bathroom, yawning widely. She looked so pretty and young, a long red plait trailing from her bandana and snaking over one shoulder. She'd make a wonderful classic heroine, Legs decided, perhaps in a Thomas Hardy or a George Eliot.

'Would you mind terribly if I slept on your sofa?' Kizzy asked sheepishly. 'I can't face the night bus back to Docklands, and I promise I'll be gone first thing.'

'Sure,' Legs looked at Byron warily. 'Shouldn't we take him out to a lamp-post?'

'Oh, he'll be fine,' Kizzy was already snuggling into the cushions, pulling a fake fur throw over herself. 'He has the bladder of a camel.'

Legs was too distracted by Francis's text message to argue, bolting into her bedroom and cranking the window up as far as it would go in the wake of Ros's many security locks so that she could gulp a little fresh air. It was hotter and closer than ever.

Picking up her bedside reading to fan herself, she remembered Byrne saying the Ptolemy Finch books were formulaic.

He likes you.

She fanned her face faster.

Having known Francis since he was a boy, she had always found it difficult to see the man. Meeting Byrne, it was equally hard for her to imagine the little boy Poppy had abandoned. He seemed so evolved and adult, layer upon layer of depth and cleverness marking out his unique character.

He likes you.

'Friendship is love without wings,' she breathed, book held aloft like a flying bird.

Gordon Lapis had an extraordinary ability to write about friendship. Ptolemy and Purple were symbiotic, fiercely loyal and the closest of allies. They had been through scrapes and escapades, survived almost certain death many times, showing incredible allegiance and trust. Sometimes they argued – Ptolemy was an opinionated sort and Purple's recklessness bordered on lunacy at times – but friendship always won through.

Suddenly Legs slammed the book shut in recognition.

She had a word to tell Francis. If her phone was to hand she would text him it right now. *Purple*.

She sat up excitedly. She had been agonising so much over her feelings for him, but the way forward was in fact incredibly simple.

Friendship. Legs and Francis had the makings of the very best of friendships. She couldn't wait to make it work. She just hoped she could keep Tolly the car.

Chapter 27

Despite setting three alarms, Legs overslept again the next day. Her head pounded more than ever as she stumbled around getting dressed, although she'd hardly touched a drop of wine last night. The empty bottle lined up on the kitchen surface was entirely down to the redheaded guest sleeping on her sofa. That guest now woke with a start as Legs trod in something wet and let out a shriek.

The dog with the bladder of a camel had, it seemed, created several wet oases of wee on the basement flat's seagrass carpeting overnight and deposited a small and very smelly poo on the doormat.

'Oh, hell.' Still bleary-eyed, Kizzy started flapping about ineffectually underfoot with a roll of kitchen towel and a bottle of Cif. In the end, Legs was forced to abandon her in the flat, telling her to let herself out. She hoped Ros didn't find her there. She also hoped Kizzy didn't snoop in the tea chest in the bedroom which contained all the photo albums of her Francis years, along with his love letters, her diaries and more personal keepsakes.

'I'll buy you lunch to say sorry!' Kizzy called after her as she made her escape, carrying the doormat, poo and all.

Depositing it stealthily in the council's dog waste container at the end of the road, Legs headed for the bus stop. She then had to wait so long for her bus that she had ample opportunity to watch two local dog walkers stop by the bin and point furiously at the Welcome mat poking out.

'Did you see anybody fly-tipping in the poop scoop bin?' one asked Legs as she sat fiddling with her phone, red-faced.

'Gosh, how dreadful,' she said brightly. 'I'm afraid I didn't see a thing.'

You'll get struck down for your lies, she thought as she reread Francis's text from the previous night. In hindsight, she was glad that she hadn't had her phone to hand during her friendship epiphany. She doubted he would have quite grasped the 'Purple!' moment as she had. He'd probably have thought she was going on about cars again.

Instead, she now lamely texted *What has Byrne done?*, and stared at the words 'he likes you' until her bus finally arrived.

Staring out of the window as sun-baked west London slid by, she tried to envisage Byrne causing mutiny. Perhaps he was stoking discontent among the estate workers? There was something heroically Tolpuddle Martyr about him. But she could hardly imagine the assorted band of Farcombe retainers rioting.

The bus brakes hissed to a halt at traffic lights just as Francis's name lit up her phone screen. Outside the window, a pneumatic drill drowned out the 'Teenage Kicks' ringtone.

'Hello?' she yelled as she took the call.

'. . . Poppy to the pub . . . Dad there . . . pissed . . . ended up . . . huge fight . . .'

This time, Legs was the one unable to hear the conversation.

She covered her free ear to blot out the hammering kanga. 'Are you saying your father and Poppy have had a fight?'

'Jamie . . . started out . . . war of words . . . got nasty . . . gun . . . threatened to shoot the little bastard.'

'Your father threatened to *kill* Byrne?' At last the bus moved on and Legs could hear him. Her fellow passengers were agog.

Francis quickly recapped a confrontation at the Book Inn involving a drunken Hector propping up the bar as Byrne tried to coax agoraphobic Poppy inside for a disastrous lunch outing. 'Jamie-go insists she can get over her agoraphobia,' he snorted with derision. 'And she'd been fine on a few walks around the grounds and so forth, but lunch in a public place was pushing it too far, particularly when she saw my father there. Poppy had a dreadful panic attack and locked herself in the loo; Guy had to break in with a crow bar to get her out. That's when there was a huge public argument between Dad and Jamie-go, each blaming the other. In the end, the prodigal son more or less threw Hector out of the pub, shouting that the only thing wrong with Poppy was her marriage.

'Dad was spitting mad. He turned up at the hall later and told Jamie-go there's no money left so he must fuck off his property and leave Poppy alone.'

'And he had a gun at this point?'

'I believe so; I was upstairs discussing the Freud painting with Vin Keiller-Myles, but I gather Jamie-go told Poppy she must choose between him and Dad, and she told the Prodigal to leave.'

'She threw Byrne out?' Legs' fellow passengers leaned closer.

'She threw them both out. I think she expected the two of them to cool off and make up their differences before apologising, but Jamie-go's disappeared like smoke, and of course Dad rushed back to your mother's comforting arms.'

'Let's not bring my mother's arms into this.'

'Poppy clearly thought Dad was going to move back to Farcombe after a proprietorial display like that, but it seems he just wanted to show Jamie-go he's still lord of the manor, even if he hasn't got the manners return to his wife. Now she's going spare. She's changed all the locks. You must tell your prodigal friend to pacify her. He'll listen to you.'

'I barely know him.' She closed her eyes, realising that was a lie. She felt as though she'd seen into his heart, however briefly; she was a confidante who knew that his life was about to end. 'I haven't got his number.'

'Then you must come back here,' his voice deepened. 'I need you to take control, Legs.' He sounded worryingly like a gimp talking to a dominatrix.

'I can't get away from work. You know Gordon needs delicate handling if he's going to reveal all.'

Francis let out an irritable sigh. 'I suppose I can get Imee to slip more valium into Poppy's cocoa. Whatever it takes to flog the Freud without her noticing. Let's speak later. Say the word. I'm waiting.'

'Hang on, did you say you're flogging the little nude?' She gasped, but he had already rung off. She smiled politely at her fellow passengers who all abruptly turned away and feigned fascination with the safety notices.

She wanted to call Francis right back and demand to know why exactly Farcombe's financial crisis had got so bad that he was selling the Lucian Freud to Vin Keiller-Myles, but self-preservation stopped her. If he thought she was going to say the word, it was kinder to stay quiet until the words queuing up in her head had fewer question marks and explanation marks punctuating them.

Besides, she reminded herself firmly, Farcombe Festival was strictly out of bounds now that Gordon had fired her. She no longer felt quite so hurt, although she still didn't understand why. Reading the first Ptolemy book had drawn her back into Gordon's incredible imaginary world, and she felt increasing sympathy for him, the clever old eccentric with his love of privacy. She was surprised how much she missed his messages, especially now that she was back in London. She hoped they were still friends.

She picked up her phone again and emailed, *How are Julie Ocean and Jimmy Jimee getting on?*

He didn't reply.

Legs closed her eyes and tried not to imagine the restraining order landing on her desk.

When she finally made it to the office, Conrad was glowering more than ever from behind his glass wall. He was trapped with the head of foreign rights for another hour, but managed to tap into his computer keyboard without looking at it, like a newsreader, during the meeting to send her an internal email that read. *Hotel lunch?*

It was his shorthand for a quickie in their usual suite.

I'm meeting a friend, she typed back with relief. Then she sighed, knowing that she had to be grown up and tackle the situation by telling some tough truths, adding. *Tonight?*

I'm committed.

Legs knew his diary was empty. She watched at him through the glass partition, but he was still utterly focused on his colleague, that clever mind thinking three lines ahead in the conversation to stay two steps in front of the competition. Conrad could run intellectual and physical rings around men half his age. He could still run intellectual and physical rings around lovely, rock solid Francis. That had been so much of the attraction in the first place.

It's over, she realised with a jolt as painful as a kosh in the ribs. I don't love him any more. It's over.

A colleague beamed at her over her monitor. 'Are you devil or angel today?'

'Sorry?'

'I'm popping to Starbucks; caramel macchiato or skinny latte?'

'You know me! Devil all the way.' She laughed dementedly and her colleague melted swiftly away. She put her head in her hands. It's over, it's over, it's over. It was as simple as that. It wasn't even very painful. As revelations went, it was effortless.

Fingers shaking, Legs picked up the phone and called her

father's Kew antique shop, inviting herself around to her childhood home that evening. 'I'll bring supper.'

'Marvellous. I want to hear all about your romantic rapprochement with young Francis.' He rolled his 'r's theatrically.

'There is no romantic rapprochement, Dad,' she muttered, eyeing Conrad through the glass, adding determinedly, 'but I am hoping for a Purple patch.'

Ringing off, she rubbed her searing temples and wearily began to wade through Eric Jones' many communications. He was now reading a book about product placement, he reported. Could Fellows Howlett amend the contract to enable Olga to mentioned favoured cat food brands in the Cuthbert books for which he could seek remuneration?

No, she replied deftly and returned to her inbox, scrolling past eight more messages from Eric. She noticed that Delia Meare the redhead-massacring author of *The Girl Who Checked Out* had managed to get past IT with a new Gmail address; she thanked Legs profusely for her letter, promising to help her and 'the esteemed' Conrad Knight 'live and feel' the book in every way she could. *I will be happy to lay you and Mr Knight a trail . . .*

Hoping this didn't mean Delia was going to flood the server with messages again, Legs read through other messages. A lot of the Team GL stuff was still filtering through. Then she spotted something amongst her cced emails that made her baulk.

She emailed Conrad immediately, forwarding the message in question. *Does Gordon know he's expected to sign copies in the warehouse before launch?*

He was as brusque as ever: *NYP.*

Too late, Legs realised she had accidentally cc-ed all the message's original recipients when forwarding it, including Gordon's PA Kelly who now replied brusquely: *Gordon asks me to remind you that you are fired.*

'Old cow,' Legs fumed.

As soon as the head of foreign rights came out of Conrad's

office, she stepped in. 'Isn't a warehouse signing a potential publicity leak? It would only take one photo sent from a mobile phone to a tabloid to ruin the festival unveiling.'

He didn't look up from typing something into his computer. 'All security staff will be vetted twice. You got my message – Not Your Problem. This is no longer your responsibility, Legs.'

It's over, it's over, it's over her head chanted.

She tried to stay focused on Gordon.

'He'd be guaranteed privacy at home. He's always turned around signed copies there before.'

Conrad finally stopped typing and looked up at her. For the first time, she realised how haggard he looked, as though he hadn't slept all week.

'It hardly matters. Gordon *isn't* at home, Legs. He's AWOL. Nobody knows where he is.'

'Since when?'

'Last week some time.'

'But we – I mean you've had contact with him since then. We've had emails.'

'Emails can be exchanged anywhere with a phone signal these days. I've not heard from him since the argument about television coverage yesterday. He was very, very jumpy. Now he's not returning calls.'

She sat down heavily on the chair opposite him. 'Do you think he's disappeared because he can't face the idea of revealing his true identity?'

'He could be pot-holing in the Lake District for all I care; the end result is the same,' Conrad rubbed his deeply furrowed forehead with his fingertips. 'Let's keep a lid on this in the hope he'll turn up. Team GL will go into a tailspin panic if they think Farcombe's in the balance. We *must* keep them focused on the new book. Christ knows, that's going to be controversial enough when it comes out.'

'In what way?' she asked vaguely, still trying to work out where Gordon might be.

'You know I can't divulge that information,' he blocked tersely. 'Let's just say we need to make sure he has maximum security around him, and that means knowing where he is.'

Legs was too distracted by Gordon's disappearance to take in what he was saying. Fellows Howlett's star author disappearing a week before launch was potentially catastrophic. He might be having a complete breakdown.

'Oh poor Gordon,' she said shakily, imagining her Mad Hatter on the run. That long, impassioned email he'd written to her should have rung alarm bells, but she'd just used it like self help.

'Don't waste your sympathy on *him*!' Conrad fumed. 'This is my neck on the line here too. I have spent all bloody week getting Piers Morgan's people ready to sign on seven zeros for an exclusive interview straight after Farcombe, and Gordon's gone fucking walkabouts.'

'What does Kelly have to say?'

Conrad looked at her curiously. 'Surely you know? Kelly *is* Gordon. She's his alter ego.'

'Gordon's Kelly?'

'One and the same.'

Her first thought was that the Mad Hatter was even more eccentric than she imagined. 'He's a cross-dresser?'

'I doubt he dresses up, although I wouldn't put anything past Gordon. But he uses the fictional PA to back people off, and to flush out the real fakes. It's a clever tactic.'

'That's awful. It's so duplicitous! I loathe duplicitousness.'

'I think you'll find that's "duplicity" not "duplicitousness".' Conrad had an annoying habit of correcting her grammar just when she was at her most passionately heated. His mental red pen was constantly poised over the contents of her conversations. He'd even done it in bed a few times. It inevitably threw her off stroke and made her feel stupid.

It's over, her aching head screamed. OVER!

'Well I'm glad Gordon fired me,' she said hotly. 'I'd had enough of his ego, and his alter ego come to that. The man is a monster. No wonder he has to have a pretend PA – no real one worth her salt would go near him. He messes with people's heads and hearts and expects way too much.'

Conrad narrowed his olive green eyes. 'Legs, *why* precisely did Gordon sack you?'

'I have no idea! I guess wasn't a very good research assistant; I didn't get in nearly enough life-threatening situations, although the sexual tension was pretty heated at times.'

'What?'

'I muddled up an email meant for you and sent it to Kelly when I was in Farcombe,' she hurried on. 'Then Gordon sent me a long email I didn't handle very well because it made me cry and I didn't know what to say to him. And I've stopped wishing him goodnight on live messenger which might have pissed him off.'

'You wish Gordon Lapis goodnight?'

'He started it!' Her face flamed. 'He's basing a character on me, Julie Ocean.'

Suddenly Conrad slammed his fists on his desk, making his laptop screen flicker.

Is he jealous? She wondered wildly, the drumrolls of 'it's over' starting to fade in her head.

But Conrad was laughing with relief.

'Legs, you must deal with this!' he demanded. 'He trusts you. You "understand" him, so he says. You can track him down, Constable Ocean.' He indicated the door, his tone adamant.

She hesitated. 'He fired me. And it's Detective Sergeant Ocean, actually.'

Conrad was already lifting his phone to make a call. 'I'm the boss, I'll fire you if you don't do as I'm asking. Pretend to be me. Email, text and hire a psychic for all I care. Get the stroppy bastard back to us.' He dismissed her from his office once more with an impatient wave, already spinning his big leather chair away and dialling out.

Legs stood her ground.

'It's over!' she said through gritted teeth, mortified that it came out as little more than a hiss of hot air.

Conrad didn't even hear. Thinking that she'd gone, he had his big back turned to her and was already talking into the receiver: 'Darling, there's a crisis on at the office. I might not make tonight. Can we reschedule?'

Legs froze. Who was 'darling'? One of the children, perhaps . . .

'Of course I'm committed to these sessions; I want our marriage to work as much as anybody, but one cancelled appointment in six months is surely not bad going?'

Legs caught her breath.

As he swung around in his chair, he saw her still standing in the room and had the grace to look abashed.

She shrank away.

Returning to her desk, feeling absolutely washed out, Legs contemplated her inbox. It was no wonder Gordon hadn't replied to her message about Julie Ocean. He probably wasn't in a compatible timezone. She envied him. What she wouldn't give to run away from life right now.

Then she suddenly remembered Kelly replying within seconds of receiving the accidental cc, reminding her that she was fired.

Feeling like Morse interfering after he's been laid off a case, she wrote one paltry line: *Where are you?*

Her fingers hovered over the keyboard before adding. *P.s. Your agent is a slimeball.*

She glanced up to see Conrad was still on the phone. He didn't look at her, but she sensed he knew that she was watching him because he backed towards his office door and shut it.

She wanted to compose an email full of fury and vitriol telling him it was over, but stupid tears kept welling up.

'*It's over,*' she began.

A skinny latte landed on her desk.

'I thought I said devil?' She looked up to see her colleague reading her screen over her shoulder.

She quickly minimised the window.

'Oops! Sorry. My mistake.' The colleague skipped off, saying 'You're just too nice to be a devil, Legs.'

Legs rubbed her forehead, knowing that nice girls didn't dump their lovers by email.

Deleting the half-composed message to Conrad, she clicked into Explorer and looked up the latest press theories on Gordon's identity. Stephen Fry was the current favourite; Russell Brand's odds had shortened dramatically since joking in a television interview that it was him. Jeffrey Archer was now a rank outsider, she was relieved to note. All the tabloids were inviting readers to fill in an online suggestions box.

Why couldn't Gordon be a woman? Legs thought indignantly. She typed 'Kizzy de la Mere' and submitted it to the tabloid.

She then Googled Clarissa Delamere, trailing through a few genealogy links before changing to Google Images. A familiar-looking little redhead glared out from a school photograph, with thick glasses and braces. She then Googled Kizzy de la Mere. The same redhead, after a 'why, Miss Jones' transformation from geek to chic, pouted in wet chiffon dresses on sea-lashed rocks alongside acres of self-indulgent poetry.

Amongst this year's new works was a series of poems in homage to Kate Bush. One stood out, a reworking of 'The Man with the Child in His Eyes', its bittersweet humour counteracting any mawkishness as it spoke of abandonment and fear of loneliness. Then she spotted a footnote:

To my secret lover; we were born into the same family but shared no childhood and have no future; our couplets have no rhyme, our verses versus. You have my heart.

Reading it, Legs remembered Kizzy saying that her love was a 'lost cause'. She now knew that it wasn't Francis, which only left Hector amongst the Protheroe family, an unlikely candidate even in her wildest imaginings. There was another possibility, but it was one that she longed to dismiss. Kizzy and Byrne had briefly shared a family home before being separated. He'd told her he had no future. Could they have been lovers?

She cancelled the screen, wiping away the pouting images and doggerel, determined to get to the truth.

An apologetic email from Conrad was waiting in her inbox, full of contrition that he was covertly seeing his estranged wife 'she's been terribly depressed . . . need to show a united front to get Finlay through GCSEs . . . takes time to unpick twenty years of marriage . . .' Legs speed-read it, amazed at her calmness and dis-passion. It was too late. She just felt hollow.

Conrad had rescheduled his meeting with PR man Piers Fox so that they could talk over a long lunch, he explained, going on to say that he very much wanted to save what they had both personally and professionally. *Cancel your friend*, he begged.

Legs sent just one word back, knowing that by doing so, she was finally sounding out the overture to the end of the affair. The relief was like headrush.

Chapter 28

Leaving Conrad marching around his office with steam practically coming from his ears as he shouted at somebody about ebooks, Legs stubbornly kept her lunch date.

Byron panted beneath his mistress's aluminium chair as they waited outside La Strada on Lansdowne Row. Even hollow-cheeked, make-up free and dressed in a very creased T-shirt and the ubiquitous baggy shorts, Kizzy was a breed apart. Sitting down on a sun-baked seat as hot as a branding iron, Legs swept aside Kizzy's apologies about the damp patches on her flat's seagrass.

'How do you think Poppy feels about having her son back in her life?' she asked with barely any preamble.

Kizzy didn't betray any surprise at her directness. 'Terrified. I gather he's kicking up quite a fuss. He keeps trying to get Poppy out of the house – seems to think her agoraphobia is Hector's fault.'

'How do you know all this?' she asked suspiciously.

'Gabs called me earlier. It's her day off. She says there was a terrible scene at the Book Inn yesterday. All the village is talking about it. Jamie accused Hector of ruining Poppy's life.'

'Why would he think that?'

'I suppose it's the gilded cage principle. Hector indulges her and yet controls her. Francis treats women just the same; father and son are like those matching griffins on the Farcombe gateposts. Their intellects are vast, layered, fascinating; but those equally large-scale egos are as unsullied and over-suckled as they were in infancy. It takes a special person to love men like them, although they attract incredibly loyalty. Poppy still loves Hector to bits, and of course you love Francis. I don't know how you both do it.' She was a great deal more cocky and upbeat today, all last night's high emotion replaced by a brittle cheerfulness. She reminded Legs of Édith. Even the way they spoke was identical, the witty, bitter tropes.

'So why did you become Francis's girlfriend if you knew you could never love him?' she asked, starting to wonder if she had run into Conrad's arms a year ago to avoid being trapped in the gilded cage with an over-suckled ego herself.

'To be a part of the family. Seeing Liz again frightened me; I don't want to turn into her, a lonely obsessive with a twisted imagination. When we met, she read her latest work aloud to me for five hours. I literally couldn't get away.'

'That's quite intense.'

'Especially when she's reading non-consecutive chapters,' Kizzy rolled her eyes. 'We have nothing in common, for all the genetics. She just wants to take over. It's like Jamie trying to force Poppy on random day trips.'

Legs heard the fury rattling in her voice.

'Do you mind that he's back in her life?'

'I just want Poppy to be happy,' she said earnestly. 'I know it would never have worked out between me and Francis, but she was so desperate to make the match from the start. She even started talking about changing her will in my favour. The Protheroe family solicitors were up in arms.'

Feeling her detective skin prickling with unease, Legs eyed her sceptically. 'Marshall and Callow?'

Kizzy looked blank. 'Who?' She turned to smile as their waiter arrived at their table and began listing today's specials.

Sagging back in her aluminium chair, Legs ordered goat's cheese salad. Kizzy took for ever to choose, changing her mind several times before settling upon the sashimi special 'to start. Then does the ribeye steak come with chips? . . . Great, then I'll have that with a side order of deep-fried zucchini, some creamed spinach, a tomato salad and a huge glass of red wine.'

Legs was amazed someone so fragile could have such a voracious appetite, especially in this heat. She was born to work in publishing, where so many movers and shakers still clung on to the two-bottle lunch. Handing her own menu up to the waiter, she asked for a jug of water.

Kizzy had let her hair loose today, and it flowed across her shoulders and back, glowing in the sunshine like a huge rippling copper curtain. Passersby caught their steps and breaths to look.

She must have some amazing genes to get bone structure like that, Legs thought suspiciously. How could Francis not love her? She was Millais' Ophelia. So what if the initial attraction had been the prospect of merging two compatible birthrights. Wasn't that how many great dynasties started? Between them, they could rule the Kingdom of Farcombe beautifully.

She fanned herself with the *Big Issue* she'd bought on the walk from the office. It was just as swelteringly close today as yesterday. Her head throbbed. Gordon was out there somewhere in possible turmoil while she was obsessing about Francis and the Protheroes.

She was on the wrong case. Julie Ocean would at the very least be down to her undies by now, cutting her wrist ties loose with her teeth while a stampede of wild horses advanced on her. Yet she couldn't resist delving for more, and her guilty heart knew it wasn't the Protheroes she was obsessing about.

'Are you sure you don't remember meeting Byrne – I mean Jamie – when you were little?'

'Not really.'

'Did Liz talk about the time she helped at Nevermore Farm?'

'She mentioned it in her letters sometimes,' Kizzy fell on her red wine as it arrived. 'It's hard to distinguish fact from fiction with Liz, though. She has such wild imaginings, seeing ghosts and murder plots everywhere: she's even been banned from her local Sainsbury's because she kept throwing scenes in the frozen food aisles claiming there were mutilated dead bodies hidden amongst the chicken nuggets.

'When she found out I was dating Francis, she wrote warning me not to get involved,' she went on. 'It's about the sanest advice she's given, although she then went on to say she thought he was an alien.'

'So she still writes to you?'

The expression on Kizzy's face changed, and Legs suddenly knew that she'd found the lock that she needed to pick to get at the truth. 'She reads the Farcombe Festival blog obsessively. She even attended a talk Francis gave on coastal conservation so she could get a closer look; that's when she came up with her alien theory.'

'I can't imagine he was impressed.'

'He doesn't know. I've never talked about her.'

'Why not?'

'If Poppy found out it would hurt her terribly. She's tried so hard to protect me. Liz might live in an imaginary world, but it's been grown from grains of truth.'

'So Francis *might* be an alien?'

She smiled warily. 'It's in the genes, according to Liz. Hector's got two faces and acid for blood, after all.'

'Nothing Hector is capable of doing will ever surprise me.'

Kizzy raised a red eyebrow. 'She says Hector had Brooke crippled so that he could woo Poppy.'

'She thinks that?' Legs laughed disbelievingly.

Kizzy nodded. 'Actually, it's one of her few theories that I think might have some substance,' those vivid eyes were earnest. 'She's convinced that Hector was involved in Brooke's accident. She has pages of cuttings as evidence. She sent them to me after we met.'

Legs abruptly stopped laughing, pennies dropping faster than a slot machine paying out. Julie Ocean was equally dumbfounded. This was it. This was the secret.

Now that she'd found somebody to confide in, Kizzy perceptibly relaxed. Gone was last night's stuttering fear, replaced by an overwhelming eagerness to offload the dark truth she'd been carrying around so long.

'Brooke fell in a fixed race.' She swished her hair theatrically. 'Big gamblers had teams they'd pay to put on cash bets in bookies all over the country, five thousand here, ten there. The cumulative pay-off for a fixed race could be a half a million or more, but it cost horses' lives and jockeys' careers. Nowadays punters can bet on a horse to lose a race, so it's possible to fix it by paying a jockey to deliberately ride slow, but back then gamblers bet on a horse to win, so to guarantee a pay-out they had to ensure the opposition got nobbled, which was hugely dangerous. It was a very dark phase in racing.'

'Hector's name came up in the press scandal, but it was never proven,' Legs remembered Daisy talking about it.

'Brooke was riding the odds-on favourite in a minor little weekday hurdle. It was bread-and-butter stuff and should have been of no great consequence, but the betting pool was huge, which is a classic sign of a gambling ring at work – especially in those days. Brooke was deliberately boxed in coming into the strait, held up to scupper the win. Most jockeys would have decided it was too risky to try to fight their way out and left it to the stewards to sort out. But Brooke rode every race to win it and made a break. One of the bent jockeys pulled his horse right into his path at the last fence. Brooke never walked again.'

'And Hector was behind that?' Legs was struggling to take it all in.

'After the accident, Brooke used to rant and rage, and kept scrapbooks full of those newspaper cuttings Liz sent me, about all the dirty deals going on. The name Protheroe comes up more than once. I guess he needed to blame someone. So when Poppy began her affair with Hector, he finally had a villain.'

Legs sucked her lips uneasily. If true, it was a terrible travesty and tragedy, certainly, but it really didn't tally with the Hector she knew. His addiction had always been driven by the desire for good luck, to beat the odds and feel the sugar rush of kismet. She could never imagine him wanting to gamble on a fixed outcome. Nor equally would he want to remove the opponent in sport, business or love. 'Surely, even if Hector was involved, it had nothing to do with stealing Brooke's wife? He would never have wanted a man injured for life like that. And he hadn't even *met* Poppy then, had he?'

'That's where Liz's theories become a little fantastical,' Kizzy sighed, 'or Brooke's; it's hard to tell. I think they egged each other on in the Nevermore days, concocting ever-wilder conspiracy theories, him drinking to self-pitying excess and her – well, Liz is just like that.' She adopted a stoic expression. 'But there's truth in there somewhere.'

'Truth enough to convince a ten-year-old boy,' Legs breathed, suddenly realising the implications of what she'd just learned. Had Byrne grown up believing that Hector Protheroe had crippled his father and stolen away his mother? She suddenly heard his words as clearly as he had spoken them to her the night of Poppy's ill-fated supper 'it was no accident' . . .

'Who could blame him for thinking love is valueless when entire lives can be gambled for profit?' she breathed aloud, not noticing that Kizzy was licking her lips and looking excitedly over her shoulder.

Legs almost jumped out of her hot skin as her iPhone was dropped onto her place setting.

'"Profit or prophet?",' a deep voice rolled over them. 'Both are music to my ears, along with "let me introduce you to my pretty friend" and "Gordon Lapis on line one".'

She looked up to see Conrad's silhouette eclipsing the sun, broad-shouldered and masculine. It was the sexiest shadow she knew, but now she felt chilled to the bone as it blocked out the sunlight.

'You left this in the office, Legs. It seems Gordon has found his bat phone. Read on.'

She fumbled through the screens to read his response to the message she'd sent earlier asking where he was.

Am in a huis clos, *or should that be a cliché? Second thoughts are never as original as first ones. GL*

P.s. Agree about slimeball. Would you like me to fire him too?

She chewed her lip, where a small smile was forming. She was so relieved that he was OK. And sometimes she just loved his obstreperousness.

'You must keep him talking,' Conrad ordered.

'You make it sound like a hostage situation.'

'Tell him we'll send a car for him wherever he is, or a helicopter. A private jet if he wants one. And who is this "slimeball"?'

'Just a shared Ptolemy Finch joke,' she fudged.

'Good girl. He loves you. Keep it up.' Conrad was over-effusive because he was trying to make it up to her. The overheard phonecall to his ex-wife made him artificially smiley, along with the Lily Cole lookalike at the table who was pouting up at him like jail-bait.

'Remember me?' Kizzy stared up at Conrad, big green eyes

sparkling like cloned Gachala emeralds as she batted her long lashes.

She was certainly quick to drop the little girl act when needed, Legs noticed.

'Of course!' He beamed back at her reassuringly, just a nudge of the eye towards Legs indicating doubt.

'Sorry, I should have reintroduced you two—' she started, but Conrad was already moving away.

'Later. I have an urgent meeting with Piers Fox. I want Gordon mollified by the time I return.' He looked over his shoulder at Kizzy, 'Come back for a tour of the office!' Then he waved his phone at Legs. 'Text me.'

A guided tour of Fellows Howlett in a crisis? Legs watched his departing back, broad shoulders swinging, butt cheeks taut. He was clearly either trying to avoid being left alone with her or up to something even more calculating. With Conrad, everything was deliberate.

It's over, she breathed out with silent relief, reaching for her water glass. Across the table, Kizzy was surreptitiously checking her reflection in her knife and smirking. Not so pathetic at all, Legs realised. She had a sudden and unpleasant feeling that she was being used. Yet strangely, it hardly bothered her. Such was the maelstrom of emotions coursing through her, she was immune to further pain. And she couldn't help feeling a begrudging admiration for Kizzy in spite of all her twisting and turning. She was terribly like Poppy – over-bright, over-critical, attention seeking and gushy, but internally in shreds of self-doubt. By comparison, Poppy's rival heir apparent Byrne was like an avenging angel.

Her phone vibrated with a text from Conrad. *Who is the redhead?*

Feeling slightly mollified, Legs replied: *Kizzy de la Mere. You interviewed her for my job. I was better.* Conrad rarely forgot a name, and certainly not one as distinctive as that.

To her consternation, he didn't reply.

Kizzy's sashimi had arrived and she was making a big fuss about needing low salt soy and extra wasabi. The waiter fell over himself to help her. When she finally fell on her raw fish like a hungry seal, Legs surreptitiously emailed Gordon, deliberately playing dumb to elicit a response. *Are you in France?*

Looking up, she realised Kizzy had donned a very fifties pair of dark glasses and was talking about her childhood again. 'I always knew I'd make something of myself. When you're born with a birthright like mine, you have to chose between self-doubt and self-fulfilling prophecy.'

'Or self-obsession,' Legs muttered, deciding she could only take Kizzy in small doses.

'Exactly! It would be so easy to fall into that trap, but I'll never let it happen. You are going to be such a good friend, Legs, I know it.' Her positive outlook today was as unrelenting as the sun burning overhead.

Talking seemed to have liberated her, whereas Legs found that unpicking the lock to Kizzy's secrets now caged her in worry. Had Byrne returned to North Devon for revenge, she wondered. He was already picking fights with Hector. How much further was he willing to go to punish the man he'd always thought of as the Devil?

'You and Francis are such a team,' Kizzy was saying. 'He needs someone who truly loves and understands him, and who finds him interesting.'

'He *is* interesting,' Legs snapped, watching unenthusiastically as her goat's cheese salad was delivered. It was far too hot to eat anything.

'I find him limiting,' Kizzy said unapologetically then started to wolf back her rib-eye, carrying on between mouthfuls, 'he thinks Eliot's lyricism can't be bettered.'

'Better than thinking *Cats* lyrics can't be bettered.'

'He's has inherited his father's blinkers. At least Édith was spared that; Poppy *adores* Édith.'

'Bully for Édith,' Legs said distractedly, picking up her phone to email Gordon again, simply asking: *Can I come back on Team GL?*

Byron was noisily scratching beneath her chair, his collar spinning round and round with a tinkle of identity tag.

'Francis could learn a lot from Édith,' Kizzy droned on between mouthfuls of steak. 'He lacks her sangfroid. He's always seen Poppy as a direct threat to his mother, Ella, but who in life can really threaten a perfect memory?'

'Memory,' Legs sang quietly, 'all alone in the moonlight.' She thought about Byrne as a boy coping with his father's rages and the tales of corruption behind his injuries, and suddenly found her chest full of hot ashes, tears dangerously close to erupting.

Her phone chimed.

You're still fired, Gordon replied, *Will only hire you again if you can find me, click your heels and say . . . ?*

Legs stared at the message for a long time, certain she recognised the phrase. But her head was full of Byrne, Lloyd Webber, and Kizzy's incessant yakking: 'Francis and his father, both live predominantly in the past.'

'I remember the time I knew what happiness was.'

'What?' Kizzy looked at her quizzically.

'Nothing – sorry.' She stopped singing and started to compose a reply to Gordon, soon distractedly humming 'has the moon lost her memory . . .'

What's the difference between a raven and a writing desk? she typed. That should fox him.

'Francis never let me text when we were eating together,' Kizzy speared an inch of pink meat as Legs threw her phone down on the table. 'He says it's bad manners.'

'Mine are mostly just bad spelling,' Legs apologised. 'Now you have my full attention.'

Kizzy's green gaze was challenging, 'You know, I never understood why you could leave someone like Francis for an old man like Conrad—'

'He's only forty seven,'

'—but seeing him again, he is *so* inspiring.'

'Do you think so?' She was just finding him maddening right now. It's over, it's over, her heart intoned.

'Absolutely.' She laid down her knife and levelled her green gaze like shotgun barrels aimed between Legs eyes. 'I can so see why the thought of life in Farcombe suffocated you. I think my future lies here in London too. It's my home town.' The trigger was pulled. 'And I w-w-and t-to c-come h-home!' Teardrop shots started to spout.

Not at her most sensitive, Legs let out a sudden shriek of recognition. 'There's no place like home!'

'Exactly,' Kizzy's eyes gleamed like wet jade, tears still spilling.

But Legs wasn't listening as she reached for her phone, laughing. 'Gordon, you old wizard, you!'

She wrote *There's no place like home!* and sent it to Gordon three times. When she looked up, she found Kizzy staring at her, wide-eyed and tearful.

'The rest of my life starts right here right now,' Kizzy breathed in a dramatic vibrato.

'Good for you,' Legs humoured distractedly, throwing her phone in her bag and wondering where exactly Gordon was if he wasn't at home. 'I have to get back to the office.'

'I'm coming too!'

As Conrad Knight had offered her a personal tour, Legs could hardly say no.

'I'll just pop to the loo first.' Kizzy picked up her chunky duffel bag and fled inside so fast that her chair upended and liberated Byron who'd been tethered beneath it, his lead attached to an aluminium leg.

Another inordinate wait ensued. Kizzy spent longer in the loo than your average drug dealer, Legs thought tetchily, knowing she'd run well over her lunch hour. She'd have to work seriously late. She hoped she had enough paracetamol in her desk; her head and throat were battling it out for pain threshold bashing. At least she had the excuse of supper with her father to flee to and avoid any more confrontations with Conrad. She didn't want to get stuck alone in the office with him. They owed it to one another to part more nobly than with a slanging match over the water cooler, where it had all begun. Conrad, she knew, would try to win himself back into her favour with power games and seduction first. He hated to lose at anything. And she needed her anger to simmer down before she could turn the 'it's over' mantra into anything other than a hysterical rant.

Hoovering up some dropped chips en route, Byron limped disconsolately up to Legs and cocked his lame leg on her handbag which didn't improve her temper.

A total vamp was undulating towards her table dressed in a wisp of translucent tunic made up from the lightest layers of green silk, long red hair falling in a single seductive twist over one shoulder, slender legs propped up on five-inch orange heels.

From below, Byron let out a welcoming whine.

Legs' jaw fell. 'You look . . . amazing.'

'I want to be as glamorous as you, Legs. I just love your life!'

Legs picked up her handbag and shook the dog pee off it. 'You know what, Kizzy? Right now, you're welcome to it. Walk this way.'

Chapter 29

Kizzy spent all afternoon at Fellows Howlett, enchanting everyone and passing on valuable Farcombe Festival lowdown to Team GL while the dog with the bladder of a camel nosed around the office waste paper baskets and lifted his leg repeatedly against a three foot cardboard cut-out of Cuthbert the Cat.

When Conrad returned from a very successful meeting with

Piers Fox much later that afternoon, he was even more artificially smiley than before, sitting on the edge of Legs' desk, muscular thighs bulging through his expensive linen suit trousers. Although his stress level had been numbed by several glasses of Prosecco, his forehead remained veined like a Derby runner's neck.

'What progress with our missing star?'

He was asserting sexual power as she'd known he would, believing that if he puffed his feathers out wide enough, she wouldn't notice his head buried in the sand. A slight delay in his pupils focusing betrayed a long, liquid crisis meeting with his favourite publicity guru. Piers Fox was an old-fashioned, private-club-loving PR man who Conrad had long had in his sights to handle his biggest star. Legs was certain Gordon would hate him.

'He says I'm still fired, and that there's no place like home.'

'You darling! I knew he'd trust you enough to tell you where he is,' Conrad disappeared into his office to make a call, but quickly reappeared, brows lowered. 'You're wrong. He's not at home. Keep on the case.' His eyes were already trailing towards Kizzy again, unconscious male response to a belisha beacon in his peripheral vision, as though the office plasma screen which normally showed cricket had been tuned to hardcore porn, or a Christmas tree had just been brought into the office in the midsummer heatwave.

Bracing herself, Legs observed Conrad's focus run the length of the redhead's long, slender legs and very high heels.

It's oh-vah, she reminded herself, noticing critically that those moss green eyes were really very close together and his forehead far too low.

Pulling her chair forward to hide her own tree-trunk legs, she hammered away on her computer keyboard, pretending to be busy.

'Helps if you enter your password first,' Conrad said smugly, wandering away to chat up Kizzy. 'So you went on to work for Farcombe Festival once you slipped through our fingers?'

'Actually I'm looking for a new job right now . . .' Kizzy said in her coyest Scottish burr, eyeing him through her lashes.

Legs glared at her screen which was now covered in error messages telling her to log on.

When she did, she found Delia Meare had sent another email from her Gmail account, this one distinctly more bonkers than the last: *I am in the midst of preparing a live happening to enhance* The Girl Who Checked Out. *Terror must be felt to be understood. You will feel it.*

Legs had no idea what a 'live happening' was, but she was certain Conrad wouldn't appreciate it. For a moment she was quite tempted to reply 'go right ahead and scare the bastard,' but she managed to temper herself and suggest that Delia ran any details past her first.

She sent this and then started cross checking locations that might be construed as 'home' in the Ptolemy Finch books, but given that most of the action was set in another universe and time continuum, there wasn't much to go on.

'I always think Ptolemy will be sex on legs when he grows up,' a voice giggled behind her.

Legs stiffened as a curtain of red hair cut off all the light to her right and Kizzy stretched across to pluck up one of the framed photographs from her desk. 'And this one is mighty preddy too.'

'My nephew.' She snatched back the shot of Nico at his tenth birthday party striking a Ptolemy pose complete with the beautiful silver wings that Ros had spent weeks making. 'An ardent Finch fan, and a hater of girls. I thought Lapis was far too mainstream for your tastes?'

'I find him rather prosaic, but I've persevered for Poppy's sake. She's beyond excited that he's coming to Farcombe.'

'Don't tell me she'll be taking Gordon's canon out of *Mrs Dalloway*'s dust jacket for the occasion?'

'Gordon isn't afraid of Virginia Woolf!' boomed a voice.

Kizzy honked and peeled with laughter, hooking her burnished curtain of hair behind her tiny ear to reveal that Conrad was standing at her shoulder, looking delighted.

Legs didn't find it particularly funny, but plastered a smile to her face for professional damage limitation.

'Why exactly *has* Gordon chosen Farcombe?' asked Kizzy. 'It does seem a very odd choice given the festival's reputation.

'The chair of the selection committee *is* a huge fan of Ptolemy,' Legs reminded her.

'Yes, but Gordon can't have known that Poppy Protheroe devours his work in secret, can he?' Kizzy queried.

'Gordon is a very odd man,' Conrad huffed, 'and very, very difficult to handle.'

'He's a genius,' Legs flared.

'Poppy would agree with that,' said Kizzy. 'She claims his books have an Oedipal subtext and contain carnivalesque satire which is a moral map of modern society.'

'Bloody good reads, too,' Legs muttered.

'I like "carnivalesque satire".' Conrad pursed his lips, one eye closed as he committed the phrase to memory.

Legs replayed her own subtext, past, present and future. 'It's over; it's over.'

When Kizzy finally left Fellows Howlett, she gave Legs a tight hug farewell. 'You're so lovely. Please marry Francis and have lots of babies so I can have your job.'

'Don't say you heard it from me,' Legs whispered, 'but I have it on good authority there'll be a vacancy here very soon,'

Letting out a little shriek of excitement Kizzy rushed back into the office to press her new contact details into Conrad's palm, cheek-pecking him ostentatiously and with so many gushing thanks for his time that Legs was half convinced she was going to drop to her knees and unbuckle his flies.

Afterwards, Conrad retreated to his tinted glass lair to make some calls. Legs could see testosterone smoking off him like petrol fumes on a start grid.

Please don't call me through, she prayed silently, knowing that if he did she'd be tempted to wrench up the water cooler by its base and cart it into her office to hurl at him. She quickly called up Google on screen to trawl all online history of Brooke Kelly, race-fixing and Hector Protheroe's involvement.

He called her through.

As soon as she entered, Conrad pulled her behind the big potted cheese plant and started necking her, lips sucking on her skin with clumsy urgency. Still drunk from lunch and no doubt randily excited by Kizzy, he obviously thought this was the best way to appease her.

'No!' She pulled away. 'Anyone in the office could see.'

'I've wanted you all day.'

'Not here.'

It's over, it's over, it's over, her head screamed.

'The boardroom then. Ten minutes. Be tender.' He raised an eyebrow. It was Conrad shorthand for a blow-job.

She returned to her desk for her ten-minute stay of execution, barely concentrating as she flicked up and down the Ptolemy Finch references, 'it's over' screaming in her head. Then a word caught her eye, bringing the blessed silence of focus.

Never Moor.

It was the place Ptolemy had been born, a miserable hellhole the boy had only just escaped with his life. She had heard it said several times in recent days in quite a different context, but it hadn't registered until now. She'd even been talking about it with Kizzy over lunch. The farm where Byrne had grown up with Brooke and Poppy had the same name.

She Googled 'Never Moor Cottage'. Nothing. She changed it to 'Nevermore Farm'.

Bingo! There it was, just a few miles from Farcombe, buried deep in the hinterland of uncultivated inland valleys.

Legs felt her palms start to sweat as the mouse raced, clicked and zoomed.

Streetview flew her down to the nearest lane, from which she spied sagging roofs, broken chimneys and derelict outhouses that made Inkpot Farm look like a new-build.

She emailed Gordon, heart racing. *Nevermore Cottage.*

She waited for a reply, fingernails hooked over her lower teeth. She hadn't looked up from the screen in a quarter of an hour now. Conrad would already be waiting in the board room, she realised. It's so over.

One line winged back. *Don't come here. GL*

Gordon Lapis. She stared at his name in the Sender box for a long time. Gordon Lapis.

She'd always assumed he was old because he was so wise and opinionated, but so was Byrne, and he was her own generation. That dry wit was so distinctive, the sense of fair play and the brusque charm unique to them both for one reason; they were the same person. Jago Byrne was Gordon Lapis.

Grabbing a pen, she wrote out the letters G-O-R-D-O-N-L-A-P-I-S in a big circle and then started rearranging them.

Prodigal Son.

None of those clever, obsessive Ptolemy Finch fans had ever spotted it, she realised with a gasp.

No wonder Gordon had been so insistent that he had to make his first public appearance at Farcombe. He was going to show Poppy what a success her son had made of his life. Would he bask in the schadenfreude of the moment?

But even as she thought it, Legs knew it didn't ring true of Byrne, who was so intense and private, and had only agreed to the Reveal at all under the greatest duress. She knew she should have protected him, instead she'd paved his way to hell. She closed her eyes and groaned as she remembered drunkenly boasting about Gordon's forthcoming apparence that first night she and Byrne shared a table in the Book Inn. He'd been so rude about the books, calling them formulaic – and she had flirted so shamelessly. Then her eyes snapped open as she remembered him telling her, 'I am about to lose my life.'

He'd grown up believing that Hector had crippled his father. Now he was back, was he planning to get even? She heard his words in her head again, that deep Irish burr: 'When I was a little boy, I thought he was the Devil'.

She felt clammy with fear despite the cloying heat of the day. How far was he prepared to go to take revenge for Brooke's accident, she wondered. She had to stop him.

I know who you are, she emailed again with shaking fingers. *And I know why you are about to lose your life, Byrne. I am so sorry. It's all my fault. I'll make it better.*

Two words came back. *Stay away.*

Queuing up behind it, Conrad had sent a curt message from his BlackBerry. *Your ten minutes are up and my ten inches are up for tender.*

With a sob, she ran towards the boardroom knowing that the only thing she was going to tender was her resignation, from both her job and her love affair.

Another storm was breaking outside. Rain was lashing the glass roof as she crossed the gallery around the big office block's atrium. Somebody had left a wet golfing umbrella puffed out to dry on the rails. It was printed with Gordon Lapis's first four covers. She grabbed it like Ptolemy plucking up his faithful sword, Lenore.

It didn't help that Conrad was already ready for action, leaning back on the chair at the far end of the board table, flies lowered to release his expectant hard on.

'Have you been singing in the rain?' He took in the umbrella with surprise.

'I'm having a Mary Poppins moment.' She lifted her chin.

'How thrilling.' He was tapping his gold fountain pen on the sleek, polished beech of the board table. 'Now slip under here. I have something to pop in you.'

Realising he wanted her to approach him on hands and knees beneath the table, Legs let out a soft laugh and instead, she climbed on board it.

Conrad looked both alarmed and highly excited as she clanked towards him, scattering notepads and corporate goodies that had been laid out for a big foreign publisher the agency were hosting later.

She stopped a metre short of him and looked up. The false ceiling was made up of opaque illuminated panels. She tried one with the sharp end of her brolly and it shattered beautifully.

'What are you doing?' Conrad yelped, leaping up from his chair.

'Breaking through the glass ceiling,' she laughed, shattering some more panels.

He made a dash for the door.

'You might want to do up your flies first,' she called after him.

Chapter 30

'You were lucky not to get arrested,' Ros said disapprovingly later. 'They'll probably have you for breach of contract. And how are you going to pay your rent?'

'You were lucky not to get arrested,' Daisy said when she called Legs not long afterwards, having heard the story from Will, who had heard it from Nico. Legend now had it that she had scaled the Fellows Howlett atrium roof and smashed her way through that too.

'You were lucky not to get arrested,' said her father when she dropped in to see him at the Kew house that evening. 'And it doesn't do to be unemployed at your age. You can come and work with me at the shop if you like.'

'What are the wages like?'

'Don't talk nonsense. I can only offer Saturdays to start with, but there are digestives at tea break. I *can* purchase groceries myself you know,' he chided gently as he watched her stacking his fridge with Waitrose ready meals, half-moon spectacles propped in his thinning grey hair, one side of his collar up, and kind grey eyes amused.

'Yes, but you forget, Dad. You're already looking too thin.'

'You sound like your mother.'

Legs cast him a long, watchful look, waiting for more.

He stared her down. 'I'm *not* going to talk about it.'

'*You* sound like Mum.' Emotion caught in her throat.

He looked stubbornly away.

She wondered briefly whether his glamorous lady shop assistants were rallying around to help; Vegan Megan was probably lovingly baking him lentil loaf each day, while Scented Rose tended his garden and Clever Heather lured him out to the theatre to take his mind off things.

Holding up her hands in despair, she turned away to fetch the last of the Waitrose bags to the fridge.

'Have you got flu? You look unwell.' He observed her clumsy movements and the pallor of her face.

'Just a summer cold.' She made light of it. Her headache still wouldn't budge despite dosing herself up with painkillers all day, and she was increasingly short of breath, but she didn't want her father to go in search of the home medical journal to start diagnosing life-threatening ailments, one of his favourite occupations. 'I'm fine. Tired and jobless, that's all.'

'So are you going to start work with me on Saturday?' he persisted.

'I'm going straight back to Devon.' When she turned back towards him, his face had brightened with delight.

'Have you got a message for Mum?' she asked hopefully.

'No. But you can tell Francis I'm looking forward to visiting the British Museum together again soon.'

'Dad, I'm not with Francis any more.'

'Oh.' He looked incredibly sad. For years, he'd assumed his role as father-in-law was a fait accompli. 'Please think about this very carefully, Legs. Didn't you say that he's just given you a car?'

'You gave me a car when I was eighteen. Does that mean I have to work in the shop for ever?'

He screwed up one eye. 'Your logic is not entirely linear, although I do get the thrust of your point.'

Legs laughed, ignoring the razorblades of pain in her throat. She loved his erudite predictability, the sayings and phrases he had repeated so often through her life that they were now familiar motifs. Friends had often teased her that in Francis she'd chosen a man just like her father.

She had intended to drill him about her mother again that evening, to probe into his feelings, demand a reaction other than this gentle, resigned apathy. She'd even dared herself to ask him about his own infidelities. But she felt too wiped out, and had already lost heart. He seemed so fragile for all his customary clever bravura. It would be like interrogating an old teddy bear with Guantanamo Bay torture techniques. Instead, she bunged a Waitrose meal for two in the oven, made a pot of tea and settled beside him in one of the sagging conservatory sofas.

'Do you have a copy of "The Raven" you could read to me?'

'Since when have you been interested in Edgar Allen Poe?'

'Just a passing fancy,' she reassured him.

He chuckled, heaving himself up to search the bookcase in the hall, calling back over his shoulder. 'It's rather long.'

'I've got all night.' She curled into the sofa arm, fighting tiredness, her chest on fire. She really did feel ill now she came to think about it. 'Can I sleep in my old bedroom?'

'You'll have to make up the bed.' Reading glasses on the end of his nose now, releasing the unkempt grey coronet of hair to spring up like wild grass around his pink pond of a bald patch, Dorian brought in a battered volume of poetry from the hall.

Then he settled back to recite the Poe classic in which a raven traps the soul of a heartbroken man beneath his shadow with the incessant cry of 'nevermore' in answer to every question about his lost love Lenore. To her shame, Legs drifted in and out of sleep.

'I think on balance I'm more of a T. S. Eliot fan,' she admitted sleepily afterwards.

'Me too,' he chuckled, closing the book and kissing her on the forehead, 'You're very hot, Legs.'

'It's the weather,' she assured him. 'And a guilty conscience.'

'Nonsense. You're right to get away from that Knight chap. Francis will take care of you. When do you go to Devon?'

'Tomorrow,' she said wearily, feeling too ragged to explain that she wasn't driving there to see Francis, although she knew she owed him an explanation and an unmitigated apology. She seemed to have nothing but apologies to make at the moment.

Dorian was ecstatic at the prospect of having order restored – his beloved future son-in-law back in the fold, and then surely his own wife Lucy to follow. He genuinely envied Legs her first love.

Now he was plundering the shelves for T. S. Eliot.

'This is your mother's favourite.' He settled back beside her and began to read 'The Love Song of J. Alfred Prufrock'.

She listened with her burning chest full of fireworks. It was a poem of exquisite compassion; the outpourings of an ageing, timid man whose love was as deep as any; the summary of her father.

He's so like Francis, Legs realised in renewed amazement as she listened to Dorian's beautiful voice bring the words to life. He tells the biggest emotional truths through high art and third party tricks. He never rants or rages. It was no wonder Francis had become a surrogate son to him.

Afterwards she hugged him as tightly as she ever had.

'You're very, very hot.' He held her anxiously.

'My generation take "hot" as a compliment.' She kissed him goodnight. 'I'm fine.'

'Francis is a good man,' he said with quiet purpose.

'I know.' She pressed her burning face to his neck for a moment. 'I know.'

Later that night, she lay in her old bed, staring up at the ceiling where a few luminous sticker stars still clung on for dear life. Her life was spinning on its axis. She kept going hot and cold, and her raging headache was worse than ever. Her chest was an inferno.

The phone on her bedside table lit up. Gordon Lapis was online.

Sleep tight, Heavenly Pony.

Sleep tight, Byrne.

He didn't tell her to stay away this time. That was all the cue she needed.

Chapter 31

Legs drove to the North Devon coast with what felt like a bonfire blazing in her lungs, a thunderstorm on her tail and the new car's unfamiliar sat nav on her case.

'In one hundred yards, turn right. Turn right!'

'Exit roundabout!'

It was like driving with her sister Ros map-reading. Her head screamed with pain. All the time the windscreen wipers swish-swish-swished sheets of rain in front of her. The deluge was relentless. She had to blink continually to stay focused.

'Turn sharply right!'

Doing as she was told, she almost collided with oncoming traffic several times before finding herself turning into private driveways and industrial estates because she'd misinterpreted the directions. At least the sat nav didn't complain of car sickness.

But as they diverted far from familiar roads to navigate the labyrinth of lanes deep within the Devon countryside, she was grateful for the bossy female voice. She would never have found the route to Nevermore any other way. The narrow lanes here were so overgrown that her bumpers snarled up with grass and high, banked verges flipped both her wing mirrors back like a hawk's folded wings as she dived down the steepest of hills into a hidden valley.

Black clouds overhead had brought a false dusk. Rain was coming down in sheets now, so loud on the roof she could barely hear the voice announce 'You have arrived at your destination, on right.'

Legs swung into a gateway overgrown with elder, the battered wrought-iron gate swinging off its hinges as though the last person to arrive had rammed straight through it. On closer inspection, there was thick ivy growing around the rusty hinges and the grass was several inches high beneath it, making it impossible to open further. Beyond it, the long driveway that stretched away between rain-lashed chestnut trees was so pot-holed, it was as though a meteor shower had landed there. She abandoned the car and shrugged on her raincoat, head lowered against the deluge as she splashed her way along the final hundred yards. Lightning crackled directly overhead as the storm threw its most ferocious temper tantrum yet. It felt like walking through a waterfall.

The farm was in a terrible state, the outbuildings little more than ruins, its cottage utterly desolate. Clearly unoccupied for a very long time, the windows were boarded up and half its roof slates missing. A threadbare tarpaulin whipped and cracked like a war-torn flag from one chimney where it had ripped loose from its ties. Through the gaping hole it had once covered, beyond the ribs of rotten wooden trusses, Legs could see what had once been a child's bedroom with peeling teddy bear wallpaper. It was the sort of place that would cause even the most ardent of doer-uppers to refuse to get out of the car on a first viewing. No wonder Poppy had longed to escape, she realised as she looked around in horror.

Yet even as she recoiled from the storm's whip-lashes and gun-fire, she could see that there was a curious lost beauty surrounding her. It had been Byrne's home once. Its connection with him enfolded her like a safety cage. Abandoned in its lush acres, it remained alive, its heart beating fiercely against the ravages of angry skies.

'Byrne?' she called out hopelessly, but the hammering rain drowned out her words.

Forked lightning was crackling through the black clouds overhead, angrily seeking somewhere to discharge its force. Exposed to every element in the middle of a desolate farmyard, Legs was suddenly gripped by panic as she imagined herself struck by a bolt and frying on the spot. She hadn't told anybody she was coming here. A deafening crack of thunder made her dive for cover, and she crouched in the shelter of an old stable, shaking with cold and fear, waiting for the worst of the storm to pass. Each breath felt as though it was ripping the lining from her lungs.

As she huddled against a wood-lined wall, looking out at the lightning slashing its way into the old orchard beside the farmyard like a god stabbing his trident down in search of apples, she tried to imagine what demons must have possessed Brooke Kelly to keep his young wife and son here after his accident left him wheelchair-bound. His rages against Hector Protheroe must have ripped through the crumbling farmstead like the storm surrounding her now. It was hardly surprising Byrne had run wild as a boy, disappearing from home for hours on end, living a daydream world in which his closest allies were horses. He'd grown up to create an immortal fictional hero who took on the forces of evil and avenged wrong-doings. Was that how Byrne saw himself, too?

A headcollar was still hanging on a peg, its stiff leather layered with dirt, dust and mould. She scraped her thumbnail along its blackened brass name-plaque and read Finch.

★

368

How Legs made it to the Book Inn she would never know, but the satellite navigator said 'recalculating' at least a dozen times, and 'if possible make a U-turn' at least twice. The twisting back lanes that fell sharply downhill through the estate to Farcombe harbour made her feel faint with vertigo. Almost flattening a memorial bench, she parked illegally on the sea front, scattering several seagulls.

The wind nearly took her head off when she stepped out of the car, but at least she'd finally shaken off the storm, leaving it inland. Despite the ferocious wind, sea-spray over the harbour walls and the red flag flying on the beach, there were blue patches in the sky.

Almost too bedraggled to be recognisable, she stumbled into the pub. Her face was grey beneath the wet rats' tails of hair; her clothes were plastered to her body and she was coated with dust and straw.

Pierced Tongue was lolling behind the bar reading the *Daily Star*. She took one look at Legs and disappeared like smoke through the staff only door. Legs could hear hushed voices with the words 'hippy' and 'stalker' being hissed in a lisping undertone.

Coming through from her office, Nonny rushed forwards in alarm.

'Darling Legs! What happened to you? Gabs thought it was another Ptolemy Finch crank coming in. You poor duck. Come and sit down. Have a Dark and Stormy to warm you up.'

Legs shook her head, teeth chattering, 'I've had enough of storms for one day, thanks. Is Byrne here?'

Nonny shook her head. 'He checked out on Wednesday. He's staying up at the hall, I think. Darling, you look really poorly. We're fully booked, but you can have a lie down in our quarters if you like?'

Thanking her but shaking her head, Legs reeled back outside and performed a perilous three point turn on the harbour front before rattling up to the main house, now driving so badly that she dented one wing of the silver car swinging into the gates.

Just turning off the engine felt like a major victory. She was boiling hot, her skin clammy and her muscles aching. Her hands were shaking so much she couldn't take the keys out of the ignition. She thought she might black out.

Somebody wrenched open the driver's door. She looked up, focus coming and going.

It was Francis.

'Oh thank God, Legs. Thank God you're here!'

'Has something happened?' Her voice sounded miles away in her pounding head, hoarse with pain. The wind was howling through the courtyards and into the car, making all the clutter on her dashboard take off.

Crouching down, Francis took her hands. His hair was being buffeted off his face, his blue eyes watering in the blasting wind – or were those tears, she wondered in amazement.

His voice crackled with emotion. 'Your letter arrived this morning.'

'My letter?'

He bent down to kiss her fingers resting in his. 'Welcome home, my darling. I don't need to tell you what my answer is. You wrote the word so many times and, as if I could ever doubt your sincerity, now here you are. Actions speak louder than words as you always used to tell me.'

She stared at him in bewilderment.

Frowning, he reached up to touch her forehead. 'Legs darling, you're burning hot. Are you ill?'

'Feel a bit fluey,' she managed to wheeze.

He gathered her into his arms and lifted her up, grunting with the effort.

The wind tried to knock him off his feet as he carried her into the house, accidentally banging her bottom on the door frame.

'Your letter is quite beautiful,' his voice shook with emotion as he reeled around, not knowing where to put her. She was a dead weight now.

'My letter?' she checked again, struggling to make any sense of what was going on. The room was spinning, or was it just Francis lurching in circles in search of a convenient chair?

'It's one of the most moving things I've ever read,' he panted along the hallway towards the door to the cosy oak-panelled sitting room, 'and I am extremely well read as you know: "Childhood, adulthood and old age are lost in the infinity of a love like ours."'

'God that's awful,' she groaned weakly. In the confused maelstrom of her fevered mind, Legs had a vague recollection of the phrase – horribly self-indulgent – written almost exactly a year ago, not long after she and Francis had split up, when her second thoughts had seemed to rip out her heart, and she'd poured her regret and remorse onto six pages of tear-stained paper to post to him.

'Second thoughts are never as original as first ones,' she muttered before passing out in his arms.

She awoke in the Lavender Room, surrounded by suggestive nudes, and almost blinded by sunlight streaming in through the half-open curtains. She felt so hot, she thought she must be wearing layers of clothes and tucked beneath a host of thick duvets, but when she checked she was just in her underwear beneath a cotton sheet. Her hair was soaked with sweat, her skin slick. She ached so much she could barely lift her arms or legs. Her head still throbbed.

It had to be late afternoon, she realised. The sun was still high over Eascombe Cove.

She longed to open the window to let in the sea breeze. With a supreme effort, she made it off the bed and reeled towards the sash. But she only took a couple of steps before her vision tunnelled and an ice cold sweat enveloped her. She flailed for something to hold, falling to her knees.

The door flew open and Francis crossed the room.

'What are you doing out of bed? Darling you must rest. Let's get you back in.'

She desperately wanted to ask him what was wrong with her. In her crazed, fevered mind she half believed she had been drugged. But her voice was trapped in her spinning, aching head. As soon as he lifted her into bed, she fell into a restless, sweaty sleep once more.

She dreamed that she was a young girl, and Francis was dressed up as a doctor asking her all sorts of questions. Or was he answering the questions while somebody else pretended to be a doctor? Lights flashed in her eyes, cold metal was held to her chest. Thinking it was a gun, she tried to scream out, but her throat hurt too much to do more than squeak breathlessly. She could hear a male voice talking quietly about 'rehydration' and 'analgesia', and signs of drowsiness versus delirium.

'Aren't they two of the seven dwarves?' She heard her own voice coming from some strange place in her head.

The man pretending to be a doctor – or was it Francis? – stooped over her and asked her if she knew what day it was.

'Of course I know.' Her voice now appeared to be coming from the other side of the room. 'It's the first day of the rest of my life.'

Why was she saying these things? Dreams were so weird. She tried to voice a few more random observations about how she felt like Alice in Wonderland and how much she wanted to talk to the mad hatter, but the razor blades in her throat soon stopped her.

She could hear Francis laughing gently and explaining to the pretend doctor that they had just had an emotional reunion and he would take the utmost care of her.

In her dream, she very much wanted to have the utmost care taken of her. Francis's handsome face moved closer, those eyes as blue as Neal's Yard Remedies bottles, full of soothing tincture.

'We love each other,' he said in a voice as soft as a caress.

★

The next time she woke it was dark. She could hear the sea, and a distant storm offshore. The window had been opened a fraction and the breeze shifted the heavy curtains like a Victorian nurse-maid's skirts.

Her throat was still full of razorblades and her chest seemed weighed down by molten lead. Swallowing was agony. She was desperately thirsty.

Flailing her hand blindly around her in the hope of finding a drink, she hit something soft and heard a groan.

She let out a croak of alarm in turn.

A light went on, making her flinch away.

'What is it Legs darling?'

Francis was in bed with her, although he was at least still fully clothed and lying on top on the counterpane.

'Drink!' she managed to splutter, sounding like Father Jack.

As he busied himself with a water jug and glass on the bedside table, she took in the nudes frolicking on the walls around her and remembered where she was, although she couldn't remember for the life of her how she had got there.

She looked at her wrist to see what time it was, but her watch was missing as usual.

'It's after midnight,' Francis turned back with a glass of water. 'I must have nodded off while I was sitting with you. How are you feeling?'

Fireworks were going off in her head. When she took a gulp of water, it was like trying to swallow a fireball. Her vision was tunnelling again. It took all her effort to rasp, 'Not feeling too hot.'

'*Au contraire*, you're still far too hot.' He brushed damp tendrils off her sweaty forehead. 'My poor darling. It's time for your med-icine.' He reached behind him for two packets of pills.

Seeing a look of panic cross her face, he smiled reassuringly. 'Just antibiotics and paracetamol. The doctor came again this evening. There was talk of admitting you to hospital, but I won't let them take you from me.' He helped her to some more sips of water as she swallowed back tablets that felt like boulders. 'I'm looking after you. I have a private nurse coming tomorrow to help.'

'What's wrong with me?' she managed to rasp.

'Pneumonia.'

'Thank God for that,' she sighed, sinking back into the pillows and closing her eyes. 'I thought I might be really ill.'

She woke again in the early hours, whimpering with terror. Francis was at her side within seconds. 'Darling, what is it? Is it your poor head?'

'Pneumonia is really bad! I want to go to hospital.' Her voice was so hoarse she sounded like Tom Waits.

'You'll get better care here.'

Nothing made any sense. She wasn't supposed to be here. Her head was caving in. She couldn't breathe. 'I want to talk to the Mad Hatter!'

Francis held her in his arms until the panic subsided, replaced by feverish, muted confusion.

He'd brought in a scuffed leather wing chair that she recognised from his bedroom and placed it near the window. There were blue pages of writing paper by its side, covered with her own hand-writing.

'I'm never going to let you go again,' he breathed into her hair.

Chapter 32

Legs lost all sense of time. Her fever seemed out of control. At its height, she thought she might die. Incoherent with pain, she was vaguely aware of ranting deliriously about her childhood, her

374

family, Farcombe and the Protheroes. The early hours were the worse, the suffocating claustrophobia of battling for breath, her throat and chest on fire. She begged the darkened room around her to turn into a nice clean hospital ward.

By day, a super-efficient Indian nurse called Gopi tended to her every need.

'You don't want to go hospital. Dirty places. Come back very sick.'

At all other times, Francis did everything for her. He bathed her face and hands, helped her clean her teeth, and he even brushed her hair.

Ironic, she thought in a more lucid moment, that her bedhead mop had never been silkier and sleeker than when bedbound. The feverish torpor of being an invalid appalled her, but she had no voice to argue nor the strength to do anything for herself; the shame of letting him carry her into the bathroom and lower her onto the loo before retreating discreetly behind the door broke through her delirium, making her cry.

Most of the time, she was too ill to think straight. She soon developed a cough that ripped through her hour after hour, bringing up phlegm and even blood. She'd never felt this weak in her life. Just the tiniest of efforts left her reeling with fatigue. Thankfully, she slept a lot of the time. She had no idea when or if Francis slept at all. He sat up with her night after night, moving from his chair to the bed to hold her when she started to panic. She could never remember what she raged about afterwards, but she raged a lot.

Francis allowed no visitors. Legs had no idea where her phone was. London could have been washed away in a tsunami in the past week for all she knew. He wouldn't even let her have a radio in the room.

'You need complete rest,' he insisted, and for a while she was content to surrender to the order. He was so kind and attentive, reading her poetry for hours, telling her what was happening on

375

the estate, the last of the hay being baled, the lambs being weaned onto aftermath grazing, the preparation of shearlings for the sales. She guessed he might be avoiding the topics of the festival and the family, but she was too wiped out to care. Her sense of reality flitted back and forth from their long years together to the muddled present, which she couldn't work out at all.

When it became clear that the first course of antibiotics and analgesics weren't taking effect, the doctor pumped her full of a more potent mix, but it was still two more days before she felt strong enough to sit up and tackle anything more ambitious than a sip of water. Even then, she needed Francis's steadying hand to stop the glass of juice she was holding from shaking everywhere.

As soon as she had drunk it, she threw up everywhere.

He made no complaint as he changed the bedding while she shivered and shook on the wing chair beneath the window, noticing her letter still beside it, now acting as a bookmark in a volume of twentieth century poetry.

'Why are you doing this for me?' she asked groggily.

'Because you wrote the truth about us and I love you for it,' he said. 'I'm going to look after you for the rest of your life.'

Sick as she was, Legs could feel panic join the infection in her veins, stoking the coals of her lingering fever. As she lay sweating on her crisp, clean bedding, she tried to piece together the clues through the fog of nausea and tremors. She'd sent him that letter a year ago. Surely even by the GPO's occasionally wayward standards that was a very long delivery time. It was possible she had forgotten to add a stamp after all. Or had he kept it all along and not read it until now? It felt like it had been written in a different lifetime and language. She couldn't even remember exactly what she had said in it. She longed to read it again.

That evening, while Francis recited W. H. Auden, she spent a long time plucking up the courage to risk the bathos of saying: 'Could you read my letter to me?'

He seemed amused. 'Why?'

'I want to talk about it.'

'Wait until you feel better.'

She started coughing as she struggled to sit up, 'we *must* talk about the letter, Francis.'

'Listen to you; you can hardly speak, my poor darling. Wait until you feel better.'

The more wound up she got about it, the harder she found it to express herself. Eventually, when she was left so raw from coughing she couldn't speak at all, Francis gave her a double dose of codeine linctus.

He settled down in his wing chair to recite Auden again, then stopped as he noticed she was crying.

'Please carry on,' she croaked. 'It's a beautiful poem. It was so perfect when John Hannah's character read it in the film.'

'What film?'

'*Four Weddings and a Funeral.*' Legs and Daisy had been to see it together three times, and both now kept a DVD version on standby in the cupboard in case of crisis – like chocolate, white wine or Lemsip. Francis had always refused to see it, thinking Richard Curtis far too asinine.

Now he closed the book. 'Let's revisit a text we both adore.'

That evening, the volume of twentieth-century poetry was replaced by *Ulysses*, which he read aloud as a special treat.

'I know how much you love it.'

Oh how she regretted her pretentiousness now, remembering through the foggy soup of analgesia that when he'd been set it as a text at university, she'd lovingly taken the James Joyce classic out of the library at home, immediately telling him it was her favourite book of all time and then battling to get beyond the first few pages. They'd had long, stimulating conversations about it during the Christmas holidays, largely based upon her mugging up with York Notes and agreeing with everything Francis said. He'd even taken her to Dublin on Bloomsday the following summer as a birthday treat.

Tonight, she fell asleep after five minutes.

The next day, feeling stronger, she tried to get at the letter again, but Francis was insistent that she needed more rest. It became like a mad circular poem:

'I want to see the letter.'

'When you're feeling better.'

Her mind kept telling her there was something really big at stake now, a life-changing event, a birth or a death, and a mammoth change of heart. But when she tried to concentrate on what exactly it was, all she could see were fictional characters: the Mad Hatter, Ptolemy Finch, the Wizard of Oz and even Toto the dog kept walking through her head, the latter with a strange limp. Her dreams featured endless battles and sword-fights, and the alarming repetitive theme of Hector Protheroe riding a unicorn into the Book Inn wearing nothing but a kimono. And then there was Byrne, the man with the coal-furnace eyes, playing constant tricks with her memory and trust. Was he fact or fiction? She half believed she'd dreamed him.

Asking Francis about Byrne bought the portcullis down even faster. 'Let's concentrate on getting you well again, darling.'

He read out another long tract of *Ulysses* that evening, focusing on the affair Leopold Bloom's concert-singer wife Molly has with her sleazy manager, Blazes. Legs could see exactly what he was doing. He was quoting at her instead of talking as usual, but at least his message was being spelled out as clearly as those York Notes she'd once read instead of the book itself. She was Molly to his Bloom. Discuss.

Her year-long affair with Conrad was dead in the water, she knew that much as fact, but every time she thought about Conrad she started crying, which didn't help. Hardly pausing in his narrative, Francis handed her a box of tissues.

She blew her nose loudly.

He'd skipped ahead to Penelope now, the final episode of the impenetrable book, far beyond anywhere Legs had managed to reach in her school days. Known as Molly's Monologue, it was a series of long unpunctuated sentences in which Molly's stream of consciousness is let loose.

Legs' mind, meanwhile, was stuck on the same page. With Conrad out of the picture and Kizzy given the kiss off, there was nothing to stand between her and Francis reconciling amid great family approbation, she realised, hysteria mounting. God, what *had* she written in that letter? Her own stream of consciousness had none of Joyce's timeless lyrical brilliance, but Francis had obviously taken it very seriously indeed.

She found she couldn't shake the melody from Kate Bush's 'The Sensual World' from her head. Had Kizzy sung it as part of her clifftop medley? She wondered, her thoughts jumping randomly around the page now as her mind tired and lost concentration.

I am so shallow, she thought wildly. If someone quotes Eliot at me, I think of *Cats*. If it's *Ulysses*, I think Bush. God forbid Francis starts reciting Coleridge's 'Kubla Khan' because it'll be Olivia Newton-John and sweatbands all the way.

She found laughter catching in her throat, making her cough more, tears running even faster.

On Francis droned. He'd adopted a Dublin brogue, trying to capture the essence of Molly with jaunty banks-of-the-Liffey cadences. Legs couldn't follow it at all. His Irish accent was very strange indeed, she realised. He sounded like a cross between Graham Norton and Mrs Doyle from *Father Ted*, which was fitting given that she still sounded like Father Jack. It was nothing like Byrne's lovely deep, peaty burr.

The giggles were digging in; her coughing was ferocious.

'What's the matter, darling?' Francis looked up and saw the tears on her cheeks, his face suddenly contrite, thinking she was sobbing her heart out. 'Oh, Legs my poor darling. I'm a brute. Do you want some more water?'

She shook her head, unable to speak or look at him.

Closing the book, he tucked her up in bed, kissed her wet cheek and returned to his chair to read in silence. She could hear the pages turn while she shuddered and convulsed beneath the covers, coughing between giggling spasms, imagining the camp Craggy Island voice still twittering on in his head. At last her laughter subsided and, to her dismay, she found panic and fear still lying beneath the silliness like sharp rocks beneath a high tide, just waiting to rip the heart from her hull.

Sleep was her refuge. The high emotion had already exhausted her. She couldn't believe it possible to feel this tired. Dosing fitfully, she dreamed that she was sitting on a chamber-pot on the main stage at Farcombe Festival while Francis and Kizzy duetted 'Islands in the Stream' accompanied by Hector on the bassoon.

For hours Legs' butterfly-light sleep was punctuated by the pages turning on Francis's book like wings slowly unfolding, the dreams and thoughts alternating in her mind. Her memory was scatter-gunned all over her head by the infection, and her short term memory had been shot to bits more than the rest, but gradually she was starting to piece together more fragments, although not necessarily in the right order.

Her first real breakthrough that night was that it suddenly seemed terribly important to tell Francis that she had seen Kizzy.

'She came to see me in London,' she ranted in the early hours. 'She's alive! Isn't that great?'

'Calm down, darling,' Francis leaped up, assuming she was delirious again.

'She told me how you two tried to make a go of it. She seems so perfect for you. Much better suited than me. It's so sad. So sad. It's a sad, sad situation.'

'Shh.' He hugged her. 'I don't need to hear this.'

But on and on she blustered, coughing and spluttering, desperate to get her point across, although she really only succeeded in repeating Elton John lyrics and saying how pretty and clever Kizzy was. Somewhere in the midst of her pitch – probably when she thought about Conrad lusting after the ravishing redhead, if the truth was to be told – she began to cry. Soon she was saying one word for every two nose blows, eight hiccups, ten coughs and twenty shudders, still struggling to get her point across. No longer listening, Francis gave her a slug of something in a tiny cup that tasted salty. Whatever it was knocked her out for hours.

She opened her eyes the next morning to see Gopi reading a book with a familiar-looking cover.

Her head was still so soupy with sleepiness it took her almost a full minute to register what it was.

'It's out!' She heaved herself up onto one elbow, then sank back down pathetically as it gave way beneath her.

'What is out?' Gopi looked up in alarm, casting a professional eye across her patient as though anticipating a ruptured hernia.

'*Ptolemy Finch and the Raven's Curse.*' She wriggled up the pillows, trying not to cough.

'My husband queued all night in Newton Abbot to purchase a copy,' Gopi informed her, already a third if the way through the book's six hundred pages. 'It is quite marvellous. The writer is so clever.' She set it down and went about checking her charge's vital signs, making her drink lots of fluids and take her antibiotics.

Because Gopi hardly ever spoke, Legs had assumed her English wasn't very good. Now she felt ashamed, guessing that, as patients went, she'd been far too ill and deranged to want to strike up a conversation with. She was determined to make amends. She was equally determined to get her hands on that book. Suddenly her year-old letter paled into insignificance. It was lightweight tinder compared to this incendiary device to speed her recovery.

But Gopi was far too engrossed in Ptolemy's latest adventure to be drawn on any subject for long. Yes, the book was very good thank you. The Protheroe family seemed very nice from what little she had see of them, yes; and housekeeper Imee was a lovely woman who had made her feel most welcome. Nothing major had happened in the world, no. The weather had been fine since the terrible storms a week earlier. The Royal scandal was still being talked about. Gordon Lapis's identity was still a hot topic.

'My money is on Salman Rushdie,' she said, eagerly turning a page.

Legs coughed so much at this that she thought her lungs were going to turn inside out, and Gopi gave her a draught of Galcodine, telling her she was talking too much.

Letting the nurse read on undisturbed, she sagged back and studied the book's jacket again. It was the collector's edition. Ptolemy Finch's ambiguous trouser bulge had been cleverly disguised by the illustrator adding in his sword Lenore, she noticed groggily, the linctus making her drowsy. The author's gold embossed name swam in front of her eyes – the letters that made up Gordon Lapis rearranging themselves into Prodigal Son before darkness descended.

Although Legs still felt hellish, she was no longer sleeping for great tracts of time. She napped for just a few minutes before her mind was alert and clanking again, trying to add up dates and memories. The Gordon Lapis launch had already happened. That means I must have been in bed for over a week, she realised in shock.

She started to piece together recent events in the right order at last. Kissing Francis on the clifftop. Kissing Francis in the Book Inn. Kissing Francis behind one of Poppy's sculptures. She and Francis had done a lot of kissing, she realised in alarm. No wonder she'd given him the wrong impression, letter or no letter. And – oh hell – her mother and Hector were no doubt still shacked up at Spywood Cottage, nakedly discussing their favourite opera productions and indulging in aphrodisiacs. In Kew, her father would have let all those ready meals pass their sell by date as he pretended he was fine, wasting away in denial in front of BBC Four. Was Ros looking after him at all? Legs wondered. Had she discovered the doggy pee patches on her seagrass in the basement flat yet? Was she still stressing about the rent now that her tenant was jobless?

She closed her eyes, remembering that she had attacked Conrad – or rather the ceiling above him – with an umbrella in the boardroom. There might be charges pressed.

But all the time that her head was racing with a kaleidoscope of recent memories, one face eclipsed the rest, a face she had only seen a few times in her life but which had now stamped itself and its deep, compelling voice in her consciousness so strongly that it was the one she'd been reaching out to touch and hear in her sleep all week. Byrne.

Jago Byrne was Gordon Lapis, the Prodigal Son. She had kissed him too.

Legs was suddenly maddened by the need to know where he was. Sitting up in bed like Linda Blair in *The Exorcist*, only just stopping her head from spinning, she quizzed Gopi frantically. 'There's a man staying in the house – a dark-haired man. Have you seen him? He has a long-eared dog with a sad face.'

'I know of no such man.' She eyed her warily. Francis paid her very well, and she had strict instructions to say nothing, although she felt bad that the girl was sweet, and had been very ill indeed. 'I may have seen the dog.'

'Is he OK?'

'He has a wet nose and wags his tail. I think that is an indication of health and happiness in such species. I have not seen the man.'

Easily defeated in her weakened state, Legs slumped back into bed and stared out of the window at the scudding clouds.

She heard another page turn followed by an intake of breath.

'Is it exciting?' she asked.

'It is very exciting, yes, but I do not like what he is doing with young Ptolemy.'

'Tolly's immortal,' Legs reminded her. 'He'll be fine.'

To her frustration Gopi said no more until it was time for her next dose of drugs.

'Who's it dedicated to?' she demanded after she had knocked back her pills, tinctures and the usual gallons of water.

Gopi checked, 'A woman called Ann.'

'May I see?'

Jealously, Gopi handed the book across, marking it with her dark eyes. Legs felt its weight in her hands like a newborn baby that she longed to nurture. Turning the pages made her weightless with the butterflies of anticipation.

For Ann O'Nymity

'A lover, you think?' Gopi asked, already pulling the novel back into her care.

'An old friend,' Legs watched it disappear into a big handbag as Gopi prepared to clock off her shift. 'Can you ask Imee a couple of things for me?' she asked urgently.

'Of course.'

'Can you ask her where the basset hound is sleeping? Also does she know where my iPhone is?'

That evening, when Francis produced a fat, dog-eared collection of the Romantic poets, Legs closed her eyes and feigned sleep, shamed by a desire to ask him if he had any meaty crime thrillers in the house.

'Sleep tight,' Francis kissed her forehead.

Suddenly her eyes snapped open as another memory was triggered so sharply it seemed to pinch at her skin.

'Sleep tight,' she whispered and scrunched her eyes shut again, Byrne's presence blazing so vividly in her consciousness that her head seemed floodlit inside.

★

Gopi was back the following morning, *Raven's Curse* just thirty pages from its end. As soon as she'd made sure Legs was alive and well and had tucked her in tightly to ensure she couldn't kick up a fuss, she opened its covers.

Pinned to the mattress, Legs eyed her hopefully. 'What did Imee say?'

Gopi didn't look up from the novel. 'My friend says that there was a very terrible argument with guns and the man with the long, sad dog with silly ears has left,' she reported distractedly, already reading.

'Where is he now, the man with the silly ears and sad dog? I mean the sad man and his silly . . .' She struggled to sit up. 'Where is Byrne?'

'I didn't ask.' She waved a vague hand. 'I will try to find out at lunchtime.'

But by lunchtime the normally mild-mannered nurse was far too furious to care to play detective. 'Gordon Lapis is a horrible man! *Ghar ka bhedi lanka dhaye*!' She threw the book down on the floor, where Legs eyed it like a loose rugby ball on the pitch, ripe for the taking. If only she wasn't trapped in bed by Gopi's over-tightened sheets and her own frailty.

'What does that mean?' she demanded hoarsely as Gopi picked up the capacious handbag.

'It is a Hindi saying: "A person who betrays his own can bring down Lanka". It means that an insider can bring down a great city.'

'What's Gordon done?'

'You do not want to know, Allegra. He is a cruel man. Many will hate him now, trust me.' She stooped to scoop up the book. Legs marked it eagerly with her eyes, convinced that it held essential secrets about its creator, Jago Byrne the prodigal son, and why he had chosen to unmask himself at Farcombe.

'Can I borrow it?'

'Certainly. But my husband will read it next, then my sister's nephew, two aunts and several of my cousins. They will all hate it. After that, you may borrow it.'

'Has Byrne left Farcombe?' Legs asked Francis when he popped in for lunch, bringing her freshly squeezed orange juice.

His smile was giveaway edgy. 'Legs, darling, I really couldn't care less.'

'Are he and Poppy still not speaking?'

'*Au contraire.*' He sat down on the bed. 'He's most definitely on her Christmas card list.'

'What happened during that argument with Hector?' she demanded, clear-headed now. 'Gopi said something about guns?'

'I had no idea Gopi was stoking you up like this; she and Imee are far too close. Legs, darling, you mustn't worry yourself with family gossip. You're only just turning the corner.'

But she was like a dog with a bone, fitting given she was starving hungry suddenly. 'When I was in London, you told me your father had threatened to kill him.'

'Did I? I forget.'

'What did Byrne say to him to make him so angry? Did he talk about Brooke Kelly's accident, or about race fixing? Did he threaten revenge?'

'Why would he do that?' Francis looked baffled. 'As far as I'm aware they were arguing about Poppy and the estate. I only saw the very end of it. What's all this nonsense about revenge?'

Legs fell silent, aware that she was in danger of giving too much away as her head raced, remembering Byrne's terrible childhood, the bleakness of Nevermore, his mother abandoning him with a drunken father who was convinced that his career had deliberately been ruined by the man who had stolen her away.

'It sounded like such a terrible argument, I thought there might be more trouble brewing,' she said feebly.

'Well he's left the house, so let's not worry about it,' he said conclusively. 'Now drink your juice.

Legs did as she was told, already overcome with weariness again. No sooner had she felt her fighting spirit course back through her veins than she felt it gallop off again

'I want to phone my family,' she sighed disconsolately.

'I've spoken to them all in the last two days – both your parents, and Ros.'

'You have?'

'Of course. They're all worried about you. Your father sends special love. He's delighted to hear you came back to me.'

'I'm not back,' she croaked, wondering what sort of propaganda her father was spreading. 'I've had a near-death experience.'

'Now you're just being a hypochondriac.'

She stared grumpily at the framed nudes cavorting across the opposite wall. Then her eyes narrowed as she spotted a familiar velvety crotch in their midst. Her gaze must have crossed over it every day for almost a fortnight now, but it was only now that she took in the implication of it still being here.

'You didn't sell the Freud to Vin Keiller-Myles after all?'

Francis looked edgy. 'We're in discussion.'

'I thought Farcombe badly needed a cash injection for the festival to go ahead?'

'We just have a couple of administration issues to iron out, that's all,' his voice had the monotone quality he always adopted when hiding something bad. 'Nothing for you to worry about. Gordon Lapis's appearance is bringing in plenty of new revenue.'

'You can't trust him!' she bleated, thinking about the pressure on Byrne, and the very real possibility he was set on revenge. 'It's not safe.'

'His welfare is no longer your concern,' he pointed out, leaning forwards to tuck her hair behind her ears. Then suddenly he smiled, eyes still bluer than the sky, lighting up his handsome face and reminding her how gorgeous he was. 'I can tell you're feeling better. You are getting argumentative again. It's sweet.'

Gopi didn't return to Legs' bedside that afternoon.

Legs was well enough to be put in his sole care, Francis announced when he returned from the estate office, explaining that Gopi's agency had asked her to transfer to a broken hip in Great Torrington.

'Does that mean I can get up?' she asked hopefully, although propping herself up on her elbows to look at him still felt like advanced pilates.

'Don't be silly,' Francis plumped up her pillows to support her. 'You have a long way to go yet.'

But the strength was coursing back through her. That evening she managed a bowl of clear soup without throwing up, and was proud to be able to venture to the loo unassisted at last. When she caught sight of herself in the bathroom mirror, she was shocked at the reflection gazing back, grey eyes huge in a shrunken white face, pimples rearing from her chin, and her filthy hair like a fright wig. The weight had dropped off her.

And her emotions were still wired up all wrong. Francis had brought up a CD player as a part of his concession to her need for stimulation and proceeded to play a compilation of all the most miserable Leonard Cohen and Joni Mitchell tracks they had indulged in as undergraduates. By the time they got to Leonard singing 'Hallelujah' she was howling like a baby and in need of the tissue box again.

'Haven't you got any Björk?' she asked.

He compromised with Radiohead, which wasn't much of an improvement. Humming along, still nodding off occasionally, Legs was itching for something more fun. She was starting to feel her isolation from news, friends and family. She had no means of communicating with the outside world, or at least her inner escape hatch.

'I'd love to read the new Ptolemy Finch,' she entreated.

Francis didn't look up from *The Anatomy of Melancholy* which had now replaced *Ulysses* as his own current read. 'There's one in the house somewhere.'

'Don't tell me Poppy's reading it in secret under the bedcovers with a torch?' she asked, suddenly brightening at the thought that Gordon's pages might be within her reach.

'You know about that?'

'Kizzy told me she was a fan.'

Francis looked disapproving but then let loose a chuckle: 'She's been quite unable to put it down for three days. Nobody can get a word out of her. It's absolute bliss.'

'Do you think I can read it after she finishes?'

'I don't see why not, although how one can tolerate such tosh is beyond me.'

'You can go to bed, you know,' Legs noticed him shifting uncomfortably on the wing chair. 'You said yourself I'm much better. I'm not going to die in the night.'

'I'd rather stay, thanks,' he muttered. 'You have no idea who might be out there.' He nodded towards the dark window.

'What do you mean?' She pulled the covers up to her chin anxiously.

'I'm looking after you, Legs,' he assured her, putting his feet up on the dressing table ottoman and closing his eyes.

Legs lay awake, imagining a *Day of the Triffids*-type Devonshire disaster that she had totally missed through illness, and the hall now under siege by giant man-eating vegetables.

In the early hours of the morning, an enraged scream echoed through the first floor of Farcombe Hall followed by the distinctive sound of something heavy being hurled against a wood panelled wall. Francis shot off to investigate. Legs cowered groggily and fearfully in bed.

'Just Poppy,' he reported back a few minutes later. 'She's finished *Ptolemy Finch*.'

'Did you bring the book back here?'

'I forgot to ask.' He settled back in his wing chair. 'But from Poppy's mood, I wouldn't say it was as good as the others.'

She lay awake for hours, feeling boxed in and out-manoeuvred. She didn't need escapism, she decided. She needed to escape.

She was determined to get out of the room the next day.

Chapter 33

No longer policed by Gopi, Legs had several hours to make good her escape the following morning while Francis was distracted in the estate office.

Her first obstacle was a lack of clothes. Her bag was still missing. She was even wearing a borrowed nightie which was far too short and heavily embroidered with Moroccan stitch-work and beads, so probably one of Poppy's. She could find none of her own things in the room whatsoever, forcing her to raid the huge, ornate built-in wardrobes which appeared to contain nothing but ancient hunting gear and ball gowns that reeked of mothballs.

It seemed to take hours just to pull on a dress, her hands shaking with nerves and feebleness. She was mad at her body for still being so weak. Even though the sun was blazing outside, she found her teeth chattering.

Dressed in a twenties flapper frock and pink hunting coat, she stole out through the door and along the landing beneath the Glasgow School canvasses.

She had to take a breather at the top of the stairs, already light-headed from her efforts.

She could hear voices in the hall below her; Poppy's distinctive husky tenor and a man's deep, angry bass, too low to be Francis.

For a moment her heart lifted, wondering if it was Byrne. But then she recognised Hector's booming tone:

'Poppy, this is quite ridiculous. You insist I come here and then make me wait on the doorstep for an hour. How *dare* you change the locks. It's my home!'

'You should have thought of that when you walked out to shack up with that frump. I was busy getting dressed. It's a perfectly pleasant morning to sit outside. Hector, we have a situation.'

'A situation so serious that it takes you an hour to get ready to tell me about it?'

'You know I can't function properly unless I am suitably attired. I must dress to suit my mood.'

'So do I take it the situation involves you goat herding in Kurdistan?'

'That is very cruel, Hector. I bought this kaftan from Liberty.'

On they scrapped.

Backing away, Legs tiptoed to the opposite end of the landing and slid through the old servants' door to the back staircase.

She had to clutch on tight to the banister rail as she descended to stop herself blacking out. Her legs felt crazily wobbly, but she plunged on, making it as far as the back lobby.

She could hear Imee moving around in the kitchen, from which the smell of cake baking was wafting enticingly.

Legs' belly let out an eager rumble. She crept in the opposite direction, along the narrow passageway that ran past the old butler's pantry, cellar door and storage rooms to another service door, this one leading directly into the morning room which Hector had always used as an office.

Legs knew there was a phone on there, although to her shame the only numbers she had memorised were her childhood home and her father's shop. She relied upon her mobile to know everything these days.

But just as she started to creep through the door, she let out a shriek as a wet nose was pressed to the back of her leg.

'Fink!' She gasped in delight as she recognised the basset hound.

The solemn eyes looked up to her beseechingly, long tail swishing. Legs stooped to hug him. Byrne would never abandon his dog. He was still nearby, she was certain.

'Who there?' Imee demanded from the kitchen.

Legs slipped quickly through the morning room door, Fink at her heels.

For a man who had once made a fortune in high-tech communications, Hector was profoundly old-fashioned when it came to his work space, preferring to surround himself with the gadgetry familiar with the era when his business empire was at its height. Thus his computer was a vintage Sony that belonged in a museum, as did his printers, a scanner the size of a small sunbed and a telephone system which would make anyone at Smile Media these days weep.

Legs regarded the huge old-fashioned fax phone on the baronial desk with suspicion, having never seen anything quite so archaic in her life, and that included her father's ancient mobile phone from which he refused to part. She approached it nervously, certain that it would whirr into life beeping a lot if she pressed the wrong button, and she could hear Poppy and Hector arguing in the entrance hall just beyond the door. She was starting to go hot and cold in rapid succession and was feeling horribly weak. She knew she had to hurry before a coughing fit overcame her.

As she lifted the receiver, she dislodged a transmission poking out of it, sending pages fluttering. Hastily picking them up to restack them, she caught sight of the first line of the covering page and baulked. Unable to stop herself, she read on in astonished horror. It came from the Protheroes' decrepit family insurance brokers whom Hector adored because like him they had yet to master scans or email and preferred to communicate by the slowest, most gentlemanly means possible, preferably involving lunch.

The fact this had been sent by fax showed the urgency of the missive.

The festival was in serious trouble. To satisfy new industry regulations, the insurers had this year been obliged to conduct a safety survey using an independent assessor. The resulting report highlighted no less than six 'life-threatening hazards' to the paying public, in addition to the thirty-nine 'serious dangers' and almost two hundred 'urgent recommendations'.

These had to be the 'administration issues' Francis had referred to. He'd known about it for weeks and had clearly been trying to rectify the situation; there was mention of private underwriters and guarantors, but none had been forthcoming and the situation was now so critical the insurers had withdrawn all cover just days before the big event. The fax made it clear that the words 'death' and 'trap' went hand in hand with 'Farcombe' and 'Festival', urging the family to cancel the event.

Legs looked up in alarm as footsteps approached the door. Still clutching the fax, she dived under the desk's foot well just as somebody entered the room.

'I can see you, you smelly monster!' Poppy screeched, rumbling an intruder straight away.

About to crawl back out, Legs felt anger flare in her infection-weakened chest. That was really a bit personal, even for Poppy. But, shooting a long-suffering look at her over his shoulder, it was Fink that padded out into open view to take the flack.

'Shoo! Shoo! Put him outside will you Hector? Dog hair plays havoc with my asthma.'

There followed a lot of scraping of claws on polished floors and the sound of the front door being opened and closed with Hector's muffled voice commiserating with the basset: 'know how you feel, old boy.'

Beneath the desk, Legs quaked, now shivering uncontrollably.

'Jamie's dog keeps hanging around the house.' Poppy had moved across the room, calling over her shoulder to Hector, whose shadow Legs could just see framed in the doorway. 'I don't think he's quite taken to a life under canvas.'

'Owner still keeping his distance?' Hector asked with obvious satisfaction.

Legs cocked her head with interest, then ducked it again as she saw a Liberty's kaftan flapping around just inches away from her hiding place.

'You shouldn't have got involved, Hector. You overreacted terribly as usual. Your rages are quite uncalled for.'

'Wish I'd fired a couple of shots to see him back across the Irish Sea,' Hector said unapologetically. 'He had no right to force you out of the house like that. What he did was cruel, Pops,' his voice softened slightly. 'Thank God I was there to protect you. He's unbalanced. You heard how he spoke to me.'

'How odd,' Poppy was leaning over the desk on the opposite side. 'I'm sure I heard the fax come through just now. Bother. It must be out of paper. I'll call Rex and ask him to send it again, but he made it quite clear on the phone last night that we shouldn't be going ahead under any circumstances. The festival is doomed, I tell you!' She sounded just like Private Frazer in *Dad's Army*.

Hector let out a bark of derision, mercifully masking the snort of laughter that came from Legs under the desk.

'Doomed!' Poppy repeated, sensing her point wasn't being taken on board.

But it was like the boy crying wolf. She had said it so many times over the years that nobody in the room, hidden or visible, took much notice of her.

Hector sounded bored. 'I'm sure Francis has the situation under control. He knows all about these things. That boy has a mind like an accountant.'

'He's all wrapped up with Allegra.'

'Ah yes, his lost asset; I heard she was staying here. That going well is it?'

'You'd think she'd got bubonic plague the way he's policing her.

394

'I'm sure it's just a little head-cold; she always was a hypochondriac, but Francis *loves* a gallant mission, as we know. He's been like a dog with two tails.'

'I'm surprised you don't keep putting him outside to spare your asthma,' Hector snapped tetchily.

'I've hardly seen him all week. They're bound to be at it non-stop.'

Legs sat up in horror, almost hitting ear head on the underside of the desk.

'Always knew she'd come back to him in the end,' Hector was saying.

'So why did you take up with her frump of a mother?' Poppy's voice rose hysterically.

'It will break Francis's heart if Allegra leaves him again, of course,' Hector blustered on, dodging the question. 'The boy isn't going about this the right way at all. I've told him he needs to get her straight up the aisle this time. Allegra is a sterling girl, and impulsive like her mother. He should whisk her off on a road trip across America, hire a vintage open-top Cadillac, swim naked with dolphins, marry in Vegas – or if he insists on his usual tight budget, he could do much the same in Scotland with a modest hatchback, finishing in Gretna Green. Either way, he must move fast to transform Ms North to Mrs Protheroe.'

Under the desk, Legs now found herself shaking her head so violently she went dizzy.

'Is that what you and the Frump plan to do?' Poppy squeaked in horror.

'Don't call Lucy that.' He heaved a deep sigh laden with self-pity. 'She and I have been on a road less travelled, our gratification a delayed pleasure and the boundaries of our egos ever-widening to let in others, but our journey together is nearing its end. She really is the most selfless of women. We've both agreed that I shall have to come back to you should Francis and Allegra be serious about this reconciliation.'

Legs' headshaking sped up. Her vision was tunnelling. Poppy's voice suddenly seemed to be coming from a distant clifftop: 'What makes you think I'll have you back?'

Hector's reply was even more faint and distorted, the only words Legs could pick out being 'your son', 'bloody festival', 'kills someone', 'knighthood' and 'wedding'.

She must have blacked out against the pedestal briefly because the next thing she heard were Poppy's nails drumming on the leather desktop overhead. A row was raging.

'I refuse to be bullied by bad-tempered men!' Poppy was shrieking. 'You're all the same! Jamie has a quite impossibly short fuse, just like his father. You can't dictate to me any more either, Hector.'

'Don't compare me to that poisonous little upstart!'

'Jamie's my flesh and blood.'

'Who will draw my blood to get his pound of flesh,' Hector muttered darkly. 'I won't let him hurt you, Pops, d'you hear? I'll fight to the death for the things I love. You're still my wife and this is still my house.'

Boxed in her shadowy lair, Legs blinked anxiously, trying hard to focus.

'God, I miss darling Kizzy,' Poppy lamented with a stifled sob. 'She never once told me what to do. I've asked her to come back and see me, but she tells me she's got an important new job in publishing and can't take time off. It's all my fault for pushing her too hard towards Francis.'

'The muse is not amused,' Hector barked sarcastically. 'No doubt she's much happier indulging her natural proclivities for women's-only poetry salons, knocking back mojitos with Édith and Jax at the Candy Bar to get over the shock of life here.'

'Don't be so judgemental, Hector!'

Wiping cold sweat from her forehead, Legs craned to listen above the rush of blood in her ears. Something was still stuck to her temple from resting it against the pedestal. Panicking that it was a spider, she reached up to swipe it away and realised that it was a loose segment of plastic electrician's tape. Looking up she saw that it was part of a criss-cross cat's cradle which was securing a small, leather-bound notebook to the underside of the desk.

'Dreadful harpy,' Hector was still ranting jealously about Kizzy. 'She would never have the backbone to run Farcombe. Francis and Allegra will make much better guardians once they marry.'

Legs started so abruptly that she head-butted the tape-webbed notebook and the desk almost shot across the room, but Hector and Poppy were too busy arguing to notice.

'We'll see about that!' Poppy thundered, sweeping towards the window. 'We have other interested parties now.'

He let out a sarcastic scoff, 'I suppose you're planning for the Prodigal Son and the Mermaid Muse to team up as lord and lady of the manor?'

Legs groaned aloud, partly at the thought of Byrne and Kizzy getting together and partly because quite a lot of the electrician's tape was now stuck in her hair.

'That would be *quite* out of the question, Hector,' Poppy's deep, sombre voice more than drowned out any noises from beneath the desk. 'By interested parties, I'm talking Vin Keiller-Myles.'

'I'm having nothing to do with that bastard's money!' Hector roared.

'Francis says Vin's the only one who can bail us out. He can get us out of this impasse, don't you see? We both know the festival can't go on, and what's the point of keeping Farcombe if we can't host the festival? It costs so much to run the estate these days. If we sell the whole shooting match to him, he'll take on all the liability. He can easily afford to cover the work needed.'

'I'll never sell to him!'

'He offered us twice the market value last year with that consortium he put together.'

Legs was grappling with the tape, which was now wrapped

around her wrist as well as being matted through her hair, the little book coming loose from its hiding place and flapping about like a giant moth.

'Are you really prepared to leave this house?' Hector asked Poppy in disbelief.

'If I must, and I really think this situation means we must.' She let out a throaty sob. 'As if these dreadful death threats weren't enough, now this . . .'

'What "death threats"?' thundered Hector.

Legs stopped grappling with the tape, stayed stock still and listened, her skin icy.

There was a rustling of paper as Poppy drew something from her pocket.

Heavy footsteps crossed the room. Another paper rustle and Hector let out a gasp. 'Abominable prose style. Compelling stuff, though. You say there are others?'

'This is the second. We dismissed the first as a one-off, but now . . .'

'Who else knows about them?'

'Just Francis. He now thinks we should go to the police, but we can't risk any adverse publicity, particularly now the insurance fiasco means we're looking disaster in the face. Oh Hector, can't you see? We might lose the festival for good!' She started to sob in deep, mournful cries, like a howling collie.

'There, there my little one.' There was genuine tenderness in Hector's voice. 'It won't come to that. Let me talk to Francis. I'm sure we can get the Friends of the Festival to collectively underwrite the risk. This Gordon Lapis appearance is worth a fortune to us all. If we can just get through the next few weeks, we'll be able to afford to make the changes for next year.'

Poppy gave a doubtful sniff. 'What if Gordon Lapis trips over one of the "serious dangers", breaks his writing fingers and then sues us for millions? Or, worse still, gets murdered by the mad person behind these letters?'

'I will personally follow him around like a bodyguard, my darling little one, and catch him if he falls, just as I will shoot anybody who tries to do any harm to him, to you or to our family. And I'll make it my mission to get my hands on whoever is writing these damned pieces of filth, as if I can't guess. This time the safety catch is staying off.'

He thinks it's Byrne, Legs realised in alarm.

But Poppy remained baffled. 'Who do we know who is this cruel . . . and uneducated?'

'Leave it all with me.'

'My hero,' she growled in her deep voice, then giggled teasingly. 'Actually, Gordon would do the reading public a favour if he broke his bloody writing fingers. His latest book has the most infuriating end. I still can't quite believe he's done it.'

They had started walking towards the hallway, much to Legs' relief because she still had one wrist taped to her head, was developing severe cramp in one calf and feeling increasingly faint again.

'We will get through this, Pops.' Hector's voice was weighted with such affection that there was a catch of tears at the back if his throat, cutting through his soothing bass like a split bassoon reed.

Hearing it too, Poppy was full of her old vigour. 'Why don't we have a lovely big fundraising dinner after the press launch this week to save the festival? It can mark your homecoming, Sir Hector!'

'Let's not get ahead of ourselves,' he muttered, but he sounded terribly pleased. 'I think a dinner is a fine idea. By then, we may even be celebrating the news that we'll be hosting a wedding here after all.'

'Maybe I'll invite Jamie as guest of honour so that we can all make peace.'

'One thing at a time, my darling. I'm not sure we have enough long-handled spoons as it is.'

'Don't be cruel, Hector.'

As they left the room, squabbling yet again, Legs finally pulled her wrist free, wincing as clumps of hair were ripped from her head. The notepad was still attached to the tape around her wrist, so that she was wearing it like a dance card now.

Too uncomfortable to care, she rubbed her cramping leg muscle and hoped her mother would survive the fall out if the summer romance was coming to a close. But Lucy's temporary diversion from the road less travelled was the least of her worries in the light of what she'd just heard about death threats and impending financial disaster at Farcombe.

Crawling out of her hiding place, she tugged at the bracelet of sticky tape only to find it tightening like a tourniquet.

She could hear urgent voices in the main hall. Francis had discovered her disappearance.

'She's still terribly ill and delirious at times. She's a danger to herself.'

Now Legs thought about it, she did feel distinctly ill. She was incredibly dizzy and chilled to her bones.

Footsteps were running all over the house now, voices shouting her name.

She hastily crept back through the service door, holding onto the walls for support. It took all her energy to retrace her steps through to the back lobby and up the rear stairs. The search party hadn't started looking beyond the green baize yet, but Legs was feeling so rough now that she no longer cared if she was found as long as they gave her an arm to lean on and promised to catch her if she fainted. She crawled the last flight of back stairs on her hands and knees.

Nobody was on the landing when she crossed it and returned to her room, peeling off the hunt coat and balldress with arms as weak as string before kicking them under the bed, which she clambered into just as Francis charged back into the room.

'Where have you *been*?'

'Here,' she said faintly, mustering a smile. She was drenched in icy sweat again. She was acutely aware that she still had a small, leather-bound notebook and a large amount of her own hair taped to her wrist, which she kept firmly under the covers.

'You went missing.'

'Perhaps you're getting what I've had? I hope you're not delirious and a danger to yourself.' She closed her eyes, grateful for the blanket of exhausted darkness that immediately enfolded her.

Chapter 34

After her gruelling excursion, she slept for a couple of hours. Waking to hear a tray clanking its way towards her along the landing, she managed to wrestle the electrical tape from her wrist and hide the notepad under her pillow before Francis appeared with more clear soup. She ate it hungrily, although she was secretly dying for some of Imee's cake that she'd smelled earlier. But Francis was insistent that she must follow his prescription for recovery, and she could hardly reveal that she'd been on the loose that day after all, sniffing the baking and eavesdropping on calamitous family secrets.

'I think I could manage something sweet,' she suggested.

'No need to get into bad habits,' Francis teased, having already wolfed his way through the huge steak baguette he'd brought up to keep her company. 'You've lost so much weight, after all. You look fantastic.'

He picked up her hand and examined her reddened wrist. 'Darling what have you been doing to yourself?'

It did look pretty horrific, the tight tape having left deep creases which were stained with the leather's oxblood dye. It must have run while she'd sweated her way back upstairs after her break for freedom.

'It's nothing – touch of psoriasis,' she lied. 'I must scratch it in my sleep. All that poetry has been giving me incredibly vivid dreams.'

Looking at his creased brow, she had an unpleasant feeling that he now had her on suicide watch as well as runaway watch, meaning that she wouldn't get to examine the contents of the little book beneath her pillow, let alone plan a better escape.

'I keep dreaming about letters arriving,' she fished, scratching her wrist for effect.

'Well that's hardly surprising.' He removed her hand and patted it. 'It was your love letter that brought us back together.'

'In my dream, they're death threats.'

'Death threats?' He looked alarmed.

'And the house starts falling down around me as I read them, floors collapsing, walls caving in, ceilings coming down, that sort of thing. I think Gordon Lapis is there too.'

His eyebrows shot up. 'What a disturbing reverie.'

'I'm sure it's my unconscious mind trying to connect something,' she insisted, studying his face for a reaction. 'What do you think?'

He gave her a curious look. 'I think you're right. Perhaps you have had too much poetry recently. Good job I've found something else for us to look through.'

He'd brought up a lot of old photographs with him that evening, eager to reminisce far beyond the past fortnight. Soon, they were spread all over the bed like a patchwork quilt of memories.

Every photograph that featured her, Francis and their families happy and smiling made Legs doubt the messy blond stranger she now saw captured in front of her eyes. Given his recent comments about her looking so good for losing weight, she kept wondering if Francis had always wanted her to be thinner. Perhaps she should have developed pneumonia on a regular basis?

She was certainly no oil painting as a child, with her National Health specs and puppy fat. Christ, her legs were awful. The first bikini shot Francis had taken of her was a shocker – she looked like

Alan Carr in a string two-piece – but she comforted herself with the fact that she'd been twelve with no boobs yet to speak of, and she was poking her tongue out. On closer examination, she stuck her tongue out for every photograph from the age of eight to fifteen. The sight of Francis as a teenager still flipped her heart over. He'd never suffered the greasy-skinned, spotty, bum-fluff moustache trauma of other teenage boys she knew. He had looked like something from a boy band, all floppy-haired, blue-eyed, cupid-lipped coy intensity. She'd fancied him so much. Her fingers now lifted a shot of him sitting moodily on the shelf of rock outside Lookout that could be a publicity poster for *The O.C.* She was sure she had the same picture in her ottoman at home; Ros had taken it during her arty photographer stage.

'God, I was guileless, wasn't I?' He noticed her looking at it. 'That was about the time I got stopped by a scout and asked to go into a model agency, but I couldn't think of anything worse.'

'Being stopped by a scout and asked if he can help you cross the road?' she suggested idly, thinking him rather vain to remind her of the incident when the evidence was laid out in front of them that she'd spent most of her teens looking like Ugly Betty's even uglier little sister.

It still baffled her why he had chosen her above all the others, above Ros and Daisy and assorted pretty friends who'd holidayed with them and had all harboured crushes on him. At the time, she'd probably questioned his choice less because it had just felt so exciting and right and she had loved him; they'd got on like two sparks from the start, always joking and talking, the age gap between them irrelevant because her sense of humour was so grown up and his sense of fun was so childlike. Now she looked back at printed reminders of herself, the baby of the group, so goofy and gauche and immature compared to the flicky-haired sleekness of his closer peers, she wondered why he'd looked at her twice. He'd seemed so shy and complex to her at the time, but the photographs suggested a self-confidence and charisma she'd never registered back then.

She studied shots of Francis now with his arm around her on the harbour-front, then at the beach, in this house, in the wooded garden at Spywood and on the terrace at Spycove. There they were lined up with the Foukes family when Nigel had still been alive – Daisy's brother Freddie was holding up two fingers like rabbit ears behind her head, and Daisy herself was looking furiously sulky. Daisy had been so upset when Francis fell for Legs and not her. Her crush on him had been just as fierce and phosphorous as her younger friend's after all. The two had compared their love for Francis Protheroe like a secret pact before the ultimate betrayal happened. Daisy remained jumpy on the subject even today, as well as being very protective of Francis.

'Why did you ever fancy me?' she asked now, holding up the tongue-poking Alan Carr in a bikini shot as evidence.

'You were my best friend,' he said simply. 'I woke up one day realising I wanted to sleep with my best friend more than anything else in the world.'

'But I was such a goof.'

His hand closed over hers. 'You've got more beautiful every day that I've known you, Legs.'

'I couldn't have got much worse,' she scoffed, quickly removing her hand and casting the bikini shot aside, embarrassed that she'd fished for that compliment so shamelessly and now wanted to cast it back out to sea.

Seeing their travel photographs, she couldn't help but be transported back, remembering those budget mini-breaks that she'd worked loathsome weekend jobs to fund, and which had matured their fledgling romance from kiddy summer holidays to seasoned globe-trotting, or so they'd believed as the world opened out to them like a giant multi-lingual playground.

There were many European snaps of Francis and Legs dressed in the sort of student street fashion they had thought super-cool at the time, posing artily alongside smiling Pacamac tourists as they climbed the Eiffel Tower, crossed the River Danube, pretended to push over the leaning tower of Pisa and just stared and stared up at the Gaudi cathedral in Barcelona. Given their inability to work the camera's timer and the unreliability of asking fellow sightseers to frame a shot, many had heads and ears cut off.

Legs studied them again closely. Francis looked the same in all of them, she suddenly noticed. There was that same floppy hair, always cut the same way, handsome as a pop pin-up, his wildest fashion gestures being to pull the white shirt from his jeans waistband and add a waistcoat. She'd always thought he was so trendy. She, meanwhile, appeared to have travelled to many of the most romantic capitals of Europe dressed as a bag lady with a different hair colour and hat on each occasion.

'Am I wearing a tam-o'-shanter?' She peered closely at herself posing wistfully by Oscar Wilde's grave. 'Christ, I've got a ruffle-front shirt on, too.'

'That was during your Walter Scott phase. You'd been studying "The Lady of the Lake" at school that term.'

'As Oscar said, "You can never be overdressed or over-educated" – and here is proof.' She hastily moved on. 'Oh look, here's Bali! I loved that beach. And you don't look nearly so boffin-ish here.' He was sitting on a rickety hired moped, his linen shirt unbuttoned. Around his throat he wore a leather bootlace threaded with turquoise and green beads that she'd bought him from a street market. Skin tanned the colour of coffee and hair bleached white in the sun, he was incredibly foxy.

'What do you mean "nearly so boffinish"?'

'Finnish – Nordic, you know; pale,' clearing her throat, she quickly changed the subject. 'Wow! Look at that sunset over Angkor Wat. Was it really that colour?'

The Big Trip photographs were the most evocative, making her heart lift as she remembered the heat and buzz of the dusty road trips and the shimmering beauty of island hopping, dancing at midnight on the beaches in the firelight, slicing through perfect turquoise sea in rickety long boats, snorkelling through caves to dive for shells, and making love again and again and again, insatiable in their little beach hut rooms on stilts. She'd never been as brown as that before or since, she realised. Her teeth looked pure white in the photographs, her hair as blonde as Francis's. And by that point in her life she had learned to artfully tie a sarong on one hip to detract from her vast thighs.

'You look amazing here, he lifted a shot of her sunbathing topless, laughing into the camera and coyly covering her chest with crossed arms.

'It was the happiest I can remember being in my life,' she said honestly.

They hadn't taken many photographs of their little London flat. Heading off to work for the first time was hardly like heading off to school, with indulgent parents lining up youngsters in the doorway wearing their crisp school uniforms. Nor had they taken shots of their very pretentious dinner parties, where they had served 'truffle galettes avec jus' on Woolworths plates to guests crammed around a wobbly table that was such a tight fit in their flat's kitchen that the guest at one end ate in constant peril of falling out of the window.

But there were captured moments from family Christmases and birthdays and holidays spanning their five cohabiting years, and also many of the festival as it grew from tiny, friendly jazz gathering to highbrow arts clique. Legs and Francis with a famous dissident poet; Legs and Francis with a strange Siberian sculptor who fashioned all his work from reindeer milk, horsehair and goat dung; Legs and Francis with lots of drunken jazz musicians.

There was the engagement party they'd held at the Book Inn, a raucous all-nighter with live music and Prosecco flowing endlessly, and such fun, culminating in a brave few skinny dipping off the harbour walls at high tide. They were lucky they hadn't got hauled in by the coastguards.

'Did you bring the ring back here with you?' Francis asked.

'Um, no, it's in my bedside drawer,' she lied, knowing it was still crammed in the car's glove compartment where it had been since the day he'd handed it back to her.

She felt the prickling heat of trepidation on her skin. Surely he hadn't intended that ring-giving gesture as some sort of new proposal? She had admittedly taken it without argument, but that was because he'd walked off leaving the ring box in her hands before she could do a thing about it. If he had been asking her to marry him again, then had his entreaties to 'say the word' in fact not been about telling him she loved him, as she'd thought, but simply to say 'yes'?

She *had* to get her hands on that letter and see what she had written so that she could start minimising the damage. She was also eager to know what his father had meant by saying 'once Francis and Allegra marry' like it was a done deal, but she still didn't want to give away the fact she'd been wandering around the house eavesdropping. Equally, the little leather notebook was still burning a hole beneath the pillow behind her but she couldn't hope to sneak a peek with Francis around, and he was showing no sign of budging.

Looking through the photographs had unsettled her, making her irritable and nit-picky, and badly in need of the loving comfort of her family.

'I can't believe my mother hasn't been to see me in a whole fortnight,' she grumbled. 'She's only ten minutes' walk away.'

'She's not exactly welcome here right now,' he reminded her.

'Surely Poppy could call a truce on hostilities just to enable her to visit the sick? I've been very ill.' She succumbed to a fit of coughing to prove her point.

'That's why you're better off without visitors.' Francis stood up to fetch her next dose of antibiotics which were due. 'I've kept Lucy totally up to date.'

'How is she? Please tell me the Spywood love-in is coming to an end?'

He refilled her glass with a long-suffering sigh. 'They're still behaving like children.'

Legs eyed him with suspicion, Hector's loving entreaties for Poppy to take him back still fresh in her ears, along with his spiel about his adulterous road less travelled. 'I shouldn't think Mum was very happy about him brawling in the pub, or waving a gun at his stepson. Naturism is less idyllic with a black eye and a twelve-bore.'

She chewed her lip, now increasingly worried about her mother. Whatever Francis said, she suspected that the summer of love in Spywood Cottage had developed an autumn chill which meant clothes would have to be put on before both parties faced a wintry dressings down at their respective homes. It might be the outcome Legs had wanted, yet she guessed it would be no less painful for soft-hearted Lucy after the greatest rebellion of her life. She had no idea how distraught her mother might be right now, nor did she trust Francis to impart all the facts during his telephone updates. It seemed unlikely he'd reported that her younger daughter had suffered pneumonia, coughed up blood, been delirious, unable eat for ten days and seemed to have lost all her possessions. Even in the throes of heartbreak, Lucy would have battled her way into the hall via the sea tunnel to find Legs had she known that.

Another fear was gripping her, one which she knew had little logic yet she still couldn't shake off. If Byrne had come to Farcombe to enact some sort of revenge on Hector, surely her mother was in danger while she was still living under the same roof as him. The sooner he returned to the hall the better, she felt; she'd slip him a set of new keys personally if necessary.

'Can you take me to the cottage to see her tomorrow?' she asked now.

Francis predictably flashed a patronising smile and shook his handsome head; 'You're still far too ill to leave the house. You need to rest more. You look shattered, poor darling.'

I'll just go without him, Legs decided recklessly. But even as she thought it, cold grey slabs of concrete weariness were boxing in her head.

He was right, she realised as tiredness mugged her. She was wiped out again. All this reminiscing and worrying was making her feel enervated. She increasingly resented her body for succumbing to such weakness, making her usually ox-like constitution so frail. Ten days ago she'd been able to run up the cliff path without breaking a sweat. Now she dripped with exhaustion after the slightest effort and the thought of running was laughable, even running away.

When she awoke after a doze, she saw that Francis was sitting across the room in the window seat watching her, the florescent pink and lilac sunset behind him as bright as a tacky neon sign. She couldn't read the expression on his face at all.

'I found your dressing up clothes,' he said quietly.

'My what?'

'Under the bed. Uncle Larry's hunt coat and a silky negligee.'

She could feel a blush stealing its way through her pallor, 'I got cold in bed,' she lied.

He sucked his lower lip thoughtfully. It was obvious he didn't believe her, but he was too well-mannered to say so. 'You just have to say, darling. I'll fetch you another blanket.'

She stared mulishly up at the light from the pink sunset spilling across the ceiling, her hand automatically reaching beneath the pillow behind her to check for the little notebook. It was still there, sticky with electrical tape. She tucked it further into the folds.

'Could I have a glass of juice?' she croaked.

'There's water in the jug.'

'Bit of a sugar low,' she rolled her eyes pleadingly towards him.

The moment he'd gone, she felt under the pillow and pulled out the notebook, peeling the tangle of tapes from its dark red leather covers. It was filled with that same spiky handwriting she remembered from the 'Dear Alligator' letter she'd received as a young girl, and it seemed to date from the same era. The pages were packed with columns containing tightly written words and numbers that made no sense to her. It looked like code.

Hearing Francis struggling with the stiff door handle as he returned, she thrust it under the pillow again just in time, her face turning telltale pink.

She drank the orange juice with such guilty speed and lip-smacking appreciation she could have been auditioning for a Del Monte advert.

'Better?' he asked, returning to his sentry post in the wing chair.

'Much,' she nodded, and realised it was. The concentrated sugar-rush after all that clear soup was like a dose of speed.

It had all started coming back to her clearly now, the reason why she'd driven here from London in that storm: Byrne, the man behind Gordon Lapis, blamed Hector for his father's racing accident, and now he was seeking revenge.

'How long exactly have I been ill?' she asked, turning her face to Francis.

'Almost a fortnight.'

She gaped at him in disbelief for a moment. 'I must have missed so much happening here.'

'Such as?'

She wanted to demand 'death threats?'; 'insurance crisis?'; 'Byrne going native, possibly plotting to kill Hector?', but managed a vague wave of the arms instead and said, 'There must have been repercussions from the argument you told me about for a start?'

'Nothing much.' He looked away shiftily. 'All quiet on the Western front.' He clearly wasn't going to spill any gossip.

Legs let out a frustrated sigh, reluctant to trigger a barrage of evasive Remarque quotes, possibly in original German. 'Can I make some phone calls?'

'Maybe tomorrow. You look wiped out, darling, and Poppy's hitting the landline this evening arranging one of her last minute soirées; you know what she's like. But I've spoken to everyone important on your behalf at least once this week. I even called Conrad.'

'Conrad?'

'I hadn't appreciated that you'd,' – he cleared his throat – 'handed in your resignation. I thought you might be missed at work.'

She sat up in horror as she remembered that awful day afresh. 'I walked out.'

'So I gather.' His eyes glittered with approval. 'You could hardly stay at the agency after your relationship ended. It would be like Kizzy still working here.'

Legs knew she was definitely getting better because she could now think about Conrad without wanting to cry. Instead she felt a more familiar blend of irritation and intimidation.

'Oh God, he'll probably sue me for breach of contract,' she groaned.

'I very much doubt that, given that you introduced your successor the day you left like the good PA you are.'

'What do you mean? Conrad's a shit to work for. He'll never replace me before the festival.'

'He already has.'

Legs didn't need to ask who; Francis's expression said it all; he was clearly dying to deliver the punchline. This must be the new job Poppy had mentioned earlier which was keeping Kizzy so busy.

To his surprise, she burst out laughing. 'How wonderful! It was obvious Kizzy was the perfect fit when she came into the office that day after she'd slept on my sofa. Conrad should have hired her in the first place.' Laughing had triggered a racking cough and she reached for the last of the juice.

Francis was looking horrified. 'Kizzy stayed overnight with you? Did anything happen?'

'I *told* you she stayed. She drank all my wine and Byron pooed on my doormat.'

'When you said that, I thought you were delirious.'

'I was quite annoyed actually.' She slumped back into her pillows, sweat rising and painful breaths shallow. She was feeling sick now, the orange juice burning acidly in her belly, threatening to come back up.

She waited wanly for Francis to probe her about what Kizzy might have told her, the big family secret that she'd eagerly let slip as soon as she was away from Farcombe and Hector's reach. But he said nothing, and she realised that it would never occur to him that Kizzy might confide in her. He really didn't understand the way women worked at all, she realised. In the same way, he was no doubt currently anticipating that she would explode with indignant fury that Kizzy had walked into her job, but she was secretly relieved, guessing that the redhead had the brain, guile and charm to cope admirably with Conrad.

Legs just hoped Kizzy looked after the agency's most important client, Gordon Lapis AKA Jago Byrne AKA Jamie Kelly. Her eyes filled with tears and she turned her head away so Francis couldn't see. If the insurance crisis meant the festival was really called off, she might never see Byrne again, she realised. He would get his revenge on Hector and move on. Then, sooner or later, Byrne would lose his life to Gordon Lapis in another carefully staged *coup de grâce*, and become public property protected by private security guards. Legs would never be able to get up close and personal after that. She would just have to kidnap his dog, she decided feverishly.

She was dying know where exactly Byrne was and why Fink the basset was still hanging around, but she was feeling increasingly vile and finding out from Francis would be impossible. He was still choosing the conversational subject headings, tonight's being employment.

'You have a job here now.' He perched on the bed and handed her a glass of water to ease the orange juice reflux. 'When you've got your strength back, of course; I could certainly use a good PA in the coming three weeks. Now drink your fluids. Doctors orders – boss's too.'

She stared at him in disbelief, wondering if he was winding her up. But Francis didn't *do* winding up.

'You want me to job swap with Kizzy?'

'It makes perfect sense, you must agree.'

'Is that all you want me to swap with her?'

'You know it's not.'

She drank her water, eyeing him over the rim of the glass, revisiting that feeling of not trusting him at all. She kept remembering what Byrne had said about Francis wanting to hurt her, and being out to teach her a lesson.

'Don't you feel at all sad about what happened between you and Kizzy?' she asked.

"Women were made to be loved, not to be understood',' he said in a plummy Pathé newsreel voice and he picked up the photograph of Legs sporting her tam-o'-shanter in Père Lachaise cemetery.

'Meaning?'

He rubbed his chin. 'You were the big Oscar Wilde fan as a student; you tell me.'

She gave up in frustration, sulked for a few moments and then changed tack.

'You've been so kind, looking after me. Thank you.'

The photographs of their years together were still scattered around her bed. She picked up one of them posing in a dinghy. She must have been fourteen by then, but still sticking her tongue out for any camera. It was high summer. Her skin was freckled and pink, clashing with her orange life jacket. Francis was doing his handsome pouty thing, staring into the mid-distance, although he had a proprietorial suntanned arm slung over her shoulders. Dangling at his wrist was the digital watch that had so entranced her the first night they'd ever slept together, wholly respectably, in adjacent bunks.

'That was taken the week we camped in Eascombe woods and your tent collapsed,' he reminded her.

He didn't need to say more. Legs was transported back to the night they had first slept together very unrespectably, in a too-tight sleeping bag with their underwear entwined around their ankles.

She peered more closely at the photograph, looking for signs that she had recently been deflowered, but the tongue-out, cross-eyed immaturity was there for all the world.

All the North and Foulkes children and assorted friends had set up camp in the woods that week. She and Daisy had been sharing a terrible old ex-army tent with rotten guy ropes which they'd failed to slacken off meaning that the night it rained a monsoon, they firstly got soaked and then almost suffocated as the tent came down. Daisy decamped to share with big brother Freddie and a friend who were doing their Duke of Edinburgh award that year and bossed her about a lot. Legs, who was by then almost-officially Francis's best friend too, happily accepted his offer of a place in his high tech bivvy. They had been practising their kissing techniques together for quite some time by then, neither acknowledging the racing excitement it elicited within each heart.

Alone together in the bivvy, Legs and Francis had practised kissing a lot.

Then, the day the sun finally came out and set steam rising from the tent skins, they skipped the early swim and sat up in their favourite tree together to tease, touch, giggle, gaze and tell the truth. The Tree of Secrets still bore its 'FP loves AN' scar within a chipped bark heart to this day. Francis told Legs he loved her, Legs said she loved him too. It was time to learn more than just kissing.

She was acutely aware of him sitting beside her right now, still silhouetted by the sunset. She could hear his breathing and smell his aftershave. He had his weight propped on one outstretched hand, and she noticed the soft blond hairs running along its length. His watch was a silver and expensive-looking Tag now.

She suddenly wanted to be transported back to that day in the tree so desperately, she could barely breathe.

He shifted closer, a warm hand reaching out to cup her face.

'I feel the same way,' he breathed.

When they kissed, the tears on their cheeks touched and blended at the same time as their tongues met. Legs wasn't sure if it was nostalgia or lust – or even pneumonia – that was making her chest pound so hard and her head go light, but it felt so exciting she couldn't stop.

They kissed for a long time, but she hadn't the strength for more. Her coughing soon became too obtrusive to even kiss.

Penitent, Francis tucked her in and fetched the bottle of Galcodine.

He didn't retreat to his chair that night. They slept curled up together. Plagued by nightmares in which she was suffocating, Legs clung to him in her sleep and then felt the familiar kick of guilt when she woke the next morning feeling much stronger, her head clearer than it had been in two long weeks. She was determined to take back control and get away from the hall.

Francis brought her a breakfast tray of apple juice and dried toast, with a jaunty bunch of scented sweet peas crammed in a little Delft jar. He certainly knew how to make a girl feel bad about her fickle-hearted shabbiness.

'We shouldn't have kissed last night,' she said apologetically, echoes of another voice ringing in her head.

Still holding the tray edges, he looked up at her through his dark gold lashes and said nothing, not even retreating behind a quote.

Feeling awkward, she bolted back her breakfast too fast and got indigestion. She then started to make her way shakily towards the bathroom, her legs bandy with lack of use. 'I thought I might take a shower. My hair's revolting.'

'Better leave it a couple more days,' he insisted. 'You're still having night sweats. You were wringing wet last night.'

'Was I? Ugh. Even more reason to wash.' Her voice, strained from so much coughing, had started to sound like Tom Waits again.

'Listen to you. We can't risk you getting a chill,' he lectured. 'You still look dreadful, darling.'

She now felt so repulsive she scuttled back towards the bed like a slimy toad to its familiar rock.

'In that case, perhaps I'll make a couple of calls instead,' she told him fractiously, voice croaking ever-deeper. 'Do you know where my phone ended up?'

'Probably still in your car with the rest of your stuff.'

She felt further aggrieved that for all his immaculate bedside manners, he hadn't thought to bring in her bag. It was no wonder she had to resort to pilfering clothes from the wardrobes when her own personal items were denied her. She was experiencing that unpleasant sense of being kept prisoner again. She longed to escape, but didn't want to appear ungrateful, and after yesterday's escapade she was acutely aware that she had the stamina of a gnat.

'I'll go and have a look for you.' He loped off.

She watched him leave, feeling ungrateful. Heaving herself out of bed again, she went into the bathroom to splash cold water on her face. Her reflection stared back more wraith-like than ever, her filthy hair a limp mass of greasy rats tails tipped by frizzy ringlets after all Francis's brushing.

He'd been so attentive, she thought wretchedly, and so forgiving. She should be indebted to him for nursing her through illness, not itching to run away like this. Kissing him had been blissfully nostalgic, after all. Perhaps the magic was still there. There had been moments in recent days when she'd felt genuinely adoring. They shared so much history. Now that she was getting stronger at last, she could try to work things through with him. If she felt clean and healthy again she might start to feel sexy too.

Unlike the window in the bedroom which looked out across the lawns to the sea, the bathroom window was angled, overlooking the courtyards. She could see the converted coach-house that now housed the festival offices, a hive of activity this close to the event, with figures racing around behind the windows, white vans galore parked outside and huge banners propped up against the walls ready to be raised above the marquees when they were erected.

There was her little silver Tolly car still abandoned on the cobbles where she'd parked it a fortnight ago, horribly dented from its prang with the Farcombe gatepost.

She saw Francis walk up to it, so handsome and kind. He peered inside, kicked a tyre, and walked away.

She then cleaned her teeth for a long time, wondering if kissing was fate's way of keeping your tongue tied.

To her shame, she could only think about kissing Byrne and how amazing it had felt, knowing that it had blown her away so much she was utterly spoiled for Francis now.

'Your car keys are locked inside,' he reported back a few minutes later, sitting back on the bed beside her and drinking a cup of strong Arabic coffee, the smell of which made her both crave caffeine and feel queasy. 'I can break in if you like.'

'No! I love Tolly.' She was Don LaFontaine with laryngitis now, deep voice crackling its way out. 'I'll get out the AA or something.'

He shrugged and sipped his coffee. 'What happened to your old red car by the way? I thought you loved that like no other?'

Legs stared at him wide-eyed, then rasped: 'Don't you know?'

He laughed fondly, eyebrows lifting questioningly. 'All I know is that you kept banging on about how much you loved it, then you turned up here close to death in a racy silver number. You are *so* contrary, darling Legs. Marriage will never be dull.'

She was too shocked to speak, then started coughing too much to speak.

He rubbed her back, reaching for the Galpodine bottle. 'Poor darling, you must let your body recover. I have to drive into Barnstaple this morning to meet with the insurers. There's some fuck up about public liability for the festival. Then I have to – well, there's other business to attend to.' He looked strangely shifty. 'Will you be OK while I'm gone? Do you want anything to read?'

'The letter I wrote to you,' she managed to splutter.

Laughing fondly, as though she'd just kitten-clawed him with playful ironic wit, he gave her a plate of fruit and a copy of James Joyce's *Portrait of the Artist as a Young Man*. Then he kissed her on the lips, breathing 'Stay here. No dressing up this time. Don't let me down.'

Legs' squeaky clean teeth stayed clamped together as his lips formed a seal with hers.

Her hand was under the pillow before he'd even closed the door, extracting the leather notebook. She was going to go and see her mother and Hector, and she was going to get some answers. If she happened to see a basset hound on the way, she'd follow it wherever it went.

As soon as she heard the Land Rover start up in the courtyard, Legs raided the moth-bally wardrobes again, this time pulling out a long olive green velvet dress which was outrageously Maid Marian but at least looked warm, and a man's black tailcoat with frayed piping and a few trails of party streamers still clinging from its wide shoulders. She slipped the little notebook into a pocket.

Putting them on over her nightie, she stole out of the room and along the landing to the back stairs. She still had bare feet, but had already planned ahead and, sure enough, lined up by the gun room door were several pairs of sturdy walking boots. She stepped into the warmest looking pair. Then, stealthy as a daylight raiding fox, she crept outside and stole across the gravel into the topiary maze, where she ducked and dived behind the cover of clipped green geometry to the parterre, dashing across that, through the rose garden, behind the kitchen garden walls and over the rails past the lake until she finally reached the safety of the woods, Spywood in her sights.

Chapter 35

When Legs finally trailed along the track to Spywood, ragged with exhaustion, she found her mother's little car missing and the cottage locked up.

She knelt on the doorstep and felt like weeping. It had taken every ounce of energy to get there. Her chest was roaring, and coughs ripped though her like machine gun fire. She could hardly breathe. Her legs were wrung-out rags, her head mush. And her mother wasn't here.

Worse of all, the spare door key was missing from its hiding place. Lucy was always mislaying hers and borrowing the spare, then forgetting to put it back. It drove the rest of the family mad.

On behalf of the rest of the family, Legs was now very mad indeed, and very frightened. She didn't want to go back to the hall, but she had nowhere else to turn. She could hardly ramble down to the village – even supposing she had the energy to walk another mile, which right now she didn't – and wander into the Book Inn wearing one of Poppy's old ball dresses and Hector's tailcoat asking to be saved. This was Francis's home turf, his future life. She'd make a total fool out of him and herself by making a scene. It wasn't as though he'd done anything wrong. She'd been nursed lovingly in the past few days, after all, waited on hand and foot, adored and idolised by the man the entire village wanted her to get back together with. She should have no complaints. She had to see this through like a grown up.

But Legs didn't want to be a grown-up. She wanted her mum.

She buried her face in her shaking hands for a moment, fighting to breathe. Then she remembered the old-fashioned red call box in the village. She'd phone Daisy! Of anybody, Daisy would understand and help. But what was the number? She and Will were bound to be ex-directory. And Legs had no money to even call directory enquiries to find out.

She groped in the tailcoat pockets and found a clutch of raffle tickets, an expensive petrol lighter and several bassoon reeds, along with a roll of many thousands of Italian lire, which told her just how long it had been since the coat had been in active service. There was also the little leather notebook.

She flipped through it again, waiting for her lungs to stop burning. Page after page of codes floated past, all in neat columns. There was something vaguely familiar about the numbers and abbreviations. Then it struck her. This was a betting system, a record of every horse Hector had laid, its odds and its outcome. In that distinctive spiky hand, he had made a note of the name, date, course, handicap, race odds and initials of the jockey along with his stake and outcome. The sums involved were astonishing, seldom less than five thousand, often ten times that. He bet mostly on favourites and he often saw his money returned which, given the sums involved, meant doubling or trebling the investment. Far from being a hapless gambler, he'd made a decent profit. There was a final column on the far right of each page which he'd only filled in after a win and was made up of acronyms she didn't understand, ICA, BDRS and NYO amongst them; she assumed it had to be something to do with the ground or whether the horse ran the race from the front or behind.

The record stopped abruptly with an entry that read *Thelonious Monk, 15/02, W'canton, 2mH, 10st, 10/11, BK £75K. Fell.* There were no more entries after that.

She stared at it for a long time. Byrne's father's fall had been at Wincanton. BK had to be Brooke Kelly. If so, Hector had bet on him to win; he couldn't have had anything to do with fixing the race for the opposite outcome; it was his biggest cash bet to date.

Looking back through the list of horse names, she let out a snort of recognition. His system was very simple. Not only did he bet on favourites, but they all had a musical or jazz association in their name – Bass Clef, Gershwin's City, Bebop, Scott Joplin, Trumpet Solo and so on. No wonder he'd placed such a huge lump on

Thelonious Monk, a genius of jazz improvisation and one of Hector's all-time musical heroes.

She closed the book and pressed its spine to her lips, knowing this changed everything. If Byrne had really grown up believing that Hector was a part of the gambling ring that was responsible for his father's accident, he had to want reparation. They had already had one furious row, and now Hector was once again on the rampage. If their paths crossed, it could spell disaster.

Pocketing the book once more, she pulled out the lighter and sparked it, so amazed when it burst into flame that she almost dropped it. She flicked its lid shut disconsolately, realising she would have to go back to the hall. With any luck, nobody would have noticed she'd been gone this time. It seemed imperative that she avoided alerting suspicion; she'd stolen the notebook, after all, and asking Poppy seemed the only way to find out where Byrne was. All paths led back to Farcombe Hall.

She should be grateful Francis hadn't tagged her ankle, she reflected, the feeling of being a fugitive returning. Chewing her nails in angst, not realising the lighter was still aflame in her hand, she almost burned off her nose.

She knew she had to start back again if she stood any chance of her flit going unnoticed.

But still she waited on the Spywood doorstep, hoping to hear her mother's car engine on the track. Another half an hour, maybe more, passed. She had no watch to judge the time. She'd never asked for it back. Time had stopped mattering this week.

'Go back,' she groaned to herself, raking her foul, greasy hair. 'You have to face this.'

When she stood up, her legs felt like burned-out tapers. In the depth of the woods with no sunlight on her, she couldn't stop shivering. Instead of retracing her steps, she took the lower path through the deepest old forestry of Spywood to call past on an old friend.

There it was, the gnarled old oak with a trunk as broad as a double bed, shaped like a tuning fork at its first intersection, with a perfect seat for a first kiss, then higher up on the left, a cradle of equally weighted starfish branches for the most democratic of secret friendship pact meetings; on its right, two parallel branches hidden deep within the canopy of foliage where young lovers had once traded truths.

Standing at its base, she sank the knuckle of her forefinger into the gouged outline of the heart that encircled hers and Francis's initials.

A branch snapped behind her. Something panted.

Pressed motionless against the hefty trunk, she watched as a figure moved closer, a long-eared, short-legged dog breathing hard at his heels as it snorted into the undergrowth. Byrne was pulling up fallen branches and gathering them under one arm, his ragged grey T-shirt covered in bark chips and lichen. His wide shoulders twisted down as he pulled the dry timber from the bracken and bilberry, separating the rotten, louse-pulped wood from recent fallen branches.

He moved closer, focused on his task, head bowed in concentration.

Legs stayed utterly still, heart racing as fast as a wren's. A weak sun was threading dusty amber fingers through the woodland canopy, barricading the undergrowth between them with tightly focused light-beams that she felt sure would set off a loud alarm as soon as he crossed them. But cross them he did, closer and closer, crouching and sorting.

Then, inevitably, he saw her, spotting the boots first – those borrowed clodhopping size eight crag-climbers. He studied her boots for a long time.

Thud, thud, the firewood fell from under his arm as he straightened up. Thud, thud thud-thudthudthudthud.

Up his eyes trailed, past the mothball velvet the same muted green as the bracken, the frayed tailcoat, to the pale, anxious face.

Very slowly, he tilted his head, his big dark eyes shifting right for a moment, thinking hard, muttering under his breath, 'Now I'm really bloody seeing things.'

She opened her mouth to point out that she was real, then closed it again, remembering she had two-week filthy hair, greasy skin, a face as grey as a gull's wing and a voice like Linda Blair possessed by Satan. She suddenly wondered if it might be better to stay quiet and let him think she was some sort of apparition? This way, she could hand over the notebook before floating off into the trees in a mystical, willow-the-wisp fashion. It could be straight out of the pages of a Gordon Lapis fantasy adventure.

He stepped forwards, crossing more dusty sunbeams, inching into her space.

The sea was so calm they could barely hear it, just distant sighs through the trees, the gulls cawing.

Legs regarded Byrne warily as he walked right up to her, halting just a couple of feet away, furnace eyes blazing.

'Allegra.'

'I'm a ghost,' she croaked in panic, her broken voice sinister even to her own ears.

She felt very silly as his brows creased down crossly. But then he seemed to change his mind and decided to humour her for now, a spark of bravura in those dark eyes, like hot coals jumping out: 'A ghost, you say?'

She nodded and he tilted his head the other way, more coals flaring as he regarded her face in detail. 'I must say, you do look pretty ghostly.'

She flicked a nervous smile.

'And real-life Allegra would never be this quiet.'

The smile flicked on and off again.

'Jesus, this is weird.' Byrne laughed huskily and raised a hand to his black forelock, pulling his fingers through it so that it stood up. 'This week just keeps getting crazier. I half believe you are a ghost.'

Legs felt as though she was having old-fashioned palpitations; she was far too hyped up to speak. His hair had grown, she realised. And he had a week's beard. He looked dishevelled and absurdly sexy, like a hunk in a Davidoff advert going native.

Gazing at her intently again, he pursed his lips in thought. They curled like perfect scrolls. Legs found she couldn't stop staring at his mouth.

'Are you haunting anything in particular?' he asked.

'I haunt this tree.' She sounded like an emphysemic old man, a death rattle in her chest.

'It's a good tree.'

'Isn't it?' She tried to inject a little femininity into her voice, but it was still Tom Waits after a bender at best. She watched his lips pursing in thought.

He looked away, tapping the bark of the trunk beside him. 'I take it this is you? AN?'

'AN Other lifetime,' she sighed hoarsely, then cast him a wise look. 'How's your friend Ann O'Nymity?'

'Fading fast.' He reached up a hand to one of the oak's tuning fork branches, using it to keep balance as he leaned forwards so his face was inches from hers.

At last she lifted her gaze to his eyes which glittered between amusement and concern, head tilting the other way again, watching her so closely she was certain he was counting each fleck of grey in her eyes. Suddenly her insides were hollowed out and packed with incendiary devices.

'You're not a ghost, Heavenly Pony,' he said, but there was just a thread of a question mark at the end of the statement, and she knew he still didn't quite believe what he was seeing.

She could hardly blame him. She'd just appeared from nowhere in private woodland looking deranged. The outfit was gothic; the weight-loss was dramatic; the skin was marble pale and spotty; the hair was wild and must smell of decay if not ectoplasm.

She sucked her lips nervously, noticing that he was watching her mouth now. They were taking turns. Her belly squirmed. A match was being lowered to the explosives packed in her shrunken stomach.

'Do you know how to tell a real ghost?' she found herself asking in a voice that could have been mistaken for Darth Vader threatening Obi-Wan Kenobi with total annihilation. It certainly scared her because she had no idea what she was saying until it was out there, hanging in the woodland air between them like a dare.

'How?'

'You try to touch them. If they're real, your hand goes right through.'

A smile touched his lips. 'Is that a fact?'

She nodded emphatically. Being a ghost was incredibly empowering, she realised with relief. She felt as though she could say anything she liked. She tested the theory: 'Kissing counts as touching.'

As soon as she said it, she felt faint with embarrassment and then, seeing the expression on his face, she felt equally faint with the desire to be kissed.

Now they were both looking at each other's mouths.

He tipped closer, his lips almost touching hers and, just as she almost exploded with excitement at the thought that he was going to kiss her, he whispered in her ear, 'Isn't it easier to simply admit you're real?'

'But not nearly as much fun.'

'Jesus,' he laughed, still not moving away. 'You're the flirtiest woman I've ever met.'

'Ghost. Flirtiest ghost,' Legs corrected, still watching his mouth, aware of his warm breath on her skin. He was definitely going to kiss her and test the theory, she realised giddily. But she could feel a cough welling in her chest now. As Byrne's lips touched hers, she fought her damndest stop the cough happening, only for it to crash open in her throat like a wave over a breakwater, hacking out with phlegmy heavy-smoker pensioner sound effects.

'Jesus!' Byrne was back on his heels in an instant.

Coughing even more violently, Legs watched in horror as two spools of snot flew from her nostrils like green party poppers.

'Bother.' She turned her head away, fishing in the tailcoat pockets, past raffle tickets, lighter and cash. There were no tissues there at all.

As she was about to unroll a wad of lire, Byrne held out a spotted handkerchief, the sort she imagined one knotted around sandwiches and tied to sticks when running away.

She blew her nose loudly.

Having plundered his pockets again, he now handed her a Fisherman's Friend, which she sucked up gratefully. Over a week of intense analgesia, and all it took was a high grade lozenge, she realised as the hoarseness started melting away. She was amazed.

'Any better?' he asked.

'Much, thanks,' she nodded, her voice already softened from evil baddie to butch hero.

A dark cloud moved in overhead, suddenly wiping out the sunshine birdcage bars around them. It instantly broke the spell. There was nothing very normal about the situation, but it no longer felt paranormal.

'Ghosts don't need to suck throat tablets,' Byrne said pragmatically.

'Headless ones might.' Embarrassed, she gazed down at her oversized boots. Then, realising she was giving him a face full of her filthy hair, she looked up again.

'You look different,' he studied her again, eyes intent with worry for a moment.

'I'm trying out a new look.'

'I liked the old one better.' He lifted his hand to rake his hair and looked away to glare at AN and FP in the crudely carved heart. 'What are you doing here, Allegra?'

She was tempted to blurt that she'd been held prisoner for a fortnight and had just escaped, but stopped herself. The ghost line had already over-stretched his credulity. And the truth was she could have left the hall at any time. Being ill had stopped her thinking straight.

Instead, she mumbled: 'I came to see my mother, but she's out.'

He gave her a look which made it clear that she might as well have said she was taking a basket of goodies to grandma and trying to avoid the big bad wolf.

'Do you usually dress like this to see your mum?'

'No, I usually accessorise with better shoes and a hat, preferably a fascinator.'

He was watching her face, and she felt self-conscious knowing he was taking in her pale face and sunken cheeks. The green dress did nothing for her complexion, she knew, and she must have become pretty gaunt. 'You've been ill.'

'Touch of girl flu,' she joked to fill the long silence that followed. 'Just dieting with a fever basically.' Knowing she looked deathly, she ducked behind one of the tuning fork branches, reluctant to be examined in any more detail. Then she eyed him through the greenery, remembering Poppy mentioning that he was under canvas. 'Are you living rough out here?'

'Not exactly.'

'Researching a survival book?'

When he didn't answer, she pulled a branch of thick leaves aside to peer at him. It was hard to marry eccentric Gordon whose neediness she had looked after for so long with practical, rugged Byrne doing his best Bear Grylls impersonation. He certainly looked very healthy and well.

'So you're feeling OK?'

'Perfectly.' He was leaning against the trunk of the Tree of Secrets now, looking up at its canopy as though seeking illumination. 'Has Conrad sent you deep undercover to determine this?'

She let the branch swish back, almost taking her nose off. 'No!'

On the far side of the tree, he let out a long sigh. 'Allegra, I don't know what you're really doing here, but it's not safe to hang around long. Trust me. You can report back to Conrad that I am perfectly well. I won't let him down. Now go home.'

She loomed over the tree's tuning fork V and glared at him,

crunching up the last of her Fisherman's Friend. 'I am *not* spying on you for Conrad! I no longer work for him.'

He stared at her for a long time.

'It's over between us,' she said shakily.

He nodded, face guarded.

The notebook was burning a hole in her pocket, her heart burning a hole in her chest. But there was something about his defensive expression that tied her tongue in knots. She wanted to scream I came back to find you! I am Julie Ocean! You're Byrne and Gordon and Jimmy Jimee, and I would run here from London on my bare feet for all three of you.

He sucked his top teeth uneasily. 'Go home. It's not safe here.'

'Why ever not?'

His eyes blazed more than ever. 'Trust me, you don't want to know. I'm not good for you, Allegra. You don't want to come where I'm going next. You're better off not knowing me.'

'You sound just like Ptolemy Finch.'

'Funny that.' He held up his hands and turned away, suddenly listening like a hare hearing a lurcher coursing towards him. A puttering car engine juddered along the pot-holed track on the far side of the woods. From the open driver's side window they could distinctly hear Jenni Murray talking about breastfeeding.

Legs let out a little cry of relief. It was her mother listening to Woman's Hour as she returned to Spywood. She turned to Byrne urgently. Not pausing for thought, she came out with a blithering, urgent muddle in a breathless croak: 'I know why you insisted that Farcombe has to be the place Gordon reveals his identity, I mean *your* identity, I mean you reveal yourself. No – that sounds wrong. Oh hell, Byrne. Nobody would blame you for wanting to get your own back on your mother, and I know you've just had a big argument so probably feel even more aggrieved, but I can't let this happen without saying something. You're so right that it's not safe. The house is falling down, and Poppy's in a terrible state. I heard there have been death threats. I can't just stand back and watch you or anyone else getting hurt. And I know that your father's accident happened because of the race-fixing racket that was going on at the time, which was truly awful, but if you think Hector was behind it in some way, he really wasn't I can prove it – here!' She groped in her pocket for the little papery rectangle and thrust it at him.

He stared at the spilling roll of cash she'd pressed into his hand. 'Italian lire?'

'No! Not that! Hang on . . .' She felt deeper in the pockets, scrabbling past the bassoon reeds and the lighter which clicked open as she fumbled. The next moment there was a hissing whoosh and her pocket combusted, mothballs igniting like little tinder petrol bombs. 'Agh!'

Byrne had lightning reactions. Before she could even take in what was going on, he'd dragged off the tailcoat, thrown it to the ground and was stamping on it.

As soon as the little blaze was out, he took her hand very gently in his to examine it. Apart from a red thumb and a broken nail, it was unharmed. The coat, meanwhile, was a smouldering wreck, its pocket totally burned out.

Legs looked down at it, suddenly wanting to cry. 'I found Hector's betting system. He wrote it all down in a little book, but I've just torched it, so now you have no reason to believe me when I say he had nothing to do with race fixing. He had money on your father to win on a horse called Thelonious Monk.'

'I know,' he said tersely.

Before she could question this, he held his fingers up to his lips again. Jenni Murray was interviewing a breast-is-best advocate at close range now as the little car bounced over the woodland track potholes just beyond the brash. They listened as she shared an anecdote about maternity bra clips.

'It's just my mother coming back,' Legs whispered to Byrne.

'Is Hector with her?'

'I have no idea.' She eyed him nervously, wondering what he might do to Hector if he *was* there. Was that why he was here out in the woods, about to spring his revenge? Was there a booby trap already set? She sucked her burned thumb, which was starting to throb quite badly now.

'How did you get his notebook?' Byrne was craning to catch a sight of the car.

'It was taped under his desk.'

His eyebrows shot up, but he kept his gaze trained on the track. 'Did you drive here?'

'My keys are locked inside my car. It's a long story. Nobody followed me, if that's what you're worried about. And I don't drive a red car any more,' she added brightly, eager to reassure him that she wasn't bad karma.

'I know that,' he replied drily, finally turning to look at her.

'How do you . . . Oh. My. God.'

He lifted his finger to his mouth as the penny dropped in Legs' head amid a gold rush of gratitude and repressed squealing. 'It was you, wasn't it?' she whispered in amazement. 'You gave me a car! That was so kind!'

'All the better to drive away from me in quickly.' He glanced over his shoulder as the car engine on the track fell silent, his voice dropping to an urgent undertone. 'Now you *must* go.'

'How can I go without thanking you properly, and helping you with all this? You gave me a car! I can't believe I thought it was Francis.'

'Shh!' He held up his hand, listening to angry voices drifting through the woods.

But it was just the car radio which Lucy had left on, no doubt listening to the last few minutes of the breast-is-best debate, which now featured a furious male interviewee ranting that it was a public decency offence. Moments later, Jenni was plugging the scone-baking feature on tomorrow's show and the radio was switched off.

Now they could hear nothing except the breeze in the tree-tops, the distant waves raking the shingle and the gulls crying out greedily and mournfully.

'Why do you want to get rid of me so badly?' she asked quietly.

'You're hurt.' He turned to her, voice barely more than a hiss of breath. 'Go and see your mother. You need to soak that hand.'

'Come with me.' She couldn't bear the idea of him disappearing, leaving so many unanswered questions, 'Hector's obviously not with her.'

He shook his head.

'Just come for a cup of tea,' suddenly the thought of her first cup of tea in a fortnight almost made her weep with joy, but she didn't want to let him slip away. 'You'll like Mum.'

'I *do* like her.'

She stared at him in amazement. He kept doing that to her, taking facts she told him and revealing that he already knew them. Well two could play at that game, she decided, as anger and fear coursed through her. She'd show him just how insightful Julie Ocean was and just how brave she could be when fighting to protect her loved ones.

'So you've befriended her to get closer to Hector, have you?' she challenged. 'I might have guessed. You did the same to me that first night, after all, wheedling all that information out of me to further your cause. And now you're here spying on him, desperate not to have me blow your cover. What are you planning to do? Leap out from behind a tree and cudgel him?'

'Hardly,' he said witheringly. 'He's got a gun.'

'Oh God!' Legs gasped, clutching her chest in horror. 'Has it come to that?'

He gave her a dubious look, uncertain if she was teasing him or not. 'He's been out since dawn bagging pheasants for a big dinner Poppy's hosting in a couple of days. Peace offering, I think.'

Realising her mistake, she breathed out with relief. 'It won't be very well hung.'

'How unlike Hector,' he muttered sarcastically. 'Poppy called me last night to tell me about the party and let slip that she intends to come here today and demand that your mother relinquishes Hector before aperitifs. Apparently they've recently exchanged letters; it's all very Jane Austen. That's why I'm hanging around here. I thought it best to be close by in case it's more *Pride and Prejudice* than *Sense and Sensibility*. Poppy gets very overwrought away from the house.' There was genuine concern in his voice.

'In that case, what are we waiting for?' She stooped down and gathered basset hound Fink in her arms, buckling under the weight. He was as heavy as a sack of wet sand and already enthusiastically washing her face.

'What are you doing?'

'Kidnapping your dog.' She stumbled off as fast as her weary legs would carry her, grateful that she had planned for just this eventuality.

Chapter 36

When Legs burst into Spywood Cottage carrying a tail-wagging basset hound, her mother was sitting naked at the table writing a letter on blue paper, a glass of white wine at her side despite the morning hour. Tears were streaming down her face.

'Legs! Darling!' She looked up in shock. 'I heard you were still bed-ridden. You look terrible.'

'I'm much better, thanks.' She averted her eyes from her mother's full frontal.

'What on earth are you doing with Fink?' Lucy made a hopeless attempt at false cheer, mopping her cheeks with the tablecloth, then squealed and held the cloth to her chin to preserve modesty as she spotted Byrne racing in after her daughter. 'Goodness! What drama here at Spywood. Hi, Jago. Is everything OK?'

'I could ask you the same.' He immediately took in the tear-streaked cheeks, the wine and the letter, which she was now sweeping beneath today's unread *Guardian*.

'You two *do* know each other?' Legs gasped, dropping Fink on a sofa and collapsing onto it with him for a moment, her lungs scorching again and the room spinning.

'We met on the beach when I was painting,' Lucy sniffed shakily. 'Glass of wine?'

'I'll make tea,' Legs took a few bolstering hot breaths ready to cross the room, but Jago held up his hand, already heading into the recessed kitchen to put on the kettle.

He seemed remarkably au fait with the cottage layout, Legs realised distractedly, but she was more concerned that her mother's nakedness, entirely visible from the back, was now inches from Byrne as he searched for teabags. Lucy was looking tearful again. 'It's j-just lovely to see you, darling. I've left so many unreturned messages on your mobile; I thought you'd stopped t-talking to me.'

'Of course not,' she said croakily. 'My phone's been locked in the car all week.'

'And I've been feeling too shame-faced to question it,' Lucy gasped. 'I was desperate to come and see you, but I was told I wasn't wanted.'

Without warning, a wave of empathy coursed through Legs with such force it swept her off the sofa like flotsam, and she launched herself across the room to give her mother a mammoth hug, wrapping her in the tablecloth as she went, complete with the *Guardian*, writing paper, spilled white wine and a small vase of wild musk mallows.

It was the best of all hugs – tight-armed, tearful, laughing, loving, all wrapped up in a length of old William Morris-print cotton that had seen the family through a plethora of meals and crises. Legs wanted to stay there for ever despite the white wine dripping into her crotch and the musk mallows on her head.

433

When Byrne placed tea mugs on the bare scrubbed boards of the table beside them, mother and daughter broke apart, palms cupping each other's cheeks. Legs' eyes slid gratefully towards him, but he'd already melted out of range as her mother kept her face locked forwards, eyes brimming with emotion.

'I hoped I might finally get to see you at the big house this morning, but I was rather ambushed.'

'You've been to the hall?' Legs asked, trying not to cough.

'I knew Poppy intended to come and talk to me today and I was so worried about it I didn't sleep a wink last night,' she admitted shakily. 'So I thought I'd go myself and save her the fright of trying to get out of the front door.'

'Was it awful?'

'It was strangely civilised. I think she was so relieved not to have to leave the house that she welcomed me like an old friend, even though I was there to apologise for having an affair with her husband. And you know how gushing she is with everyone, even if she hates one's guts. She's terribly lonely. We had coffee on the terrace and compared notes on Hector. He really is a *very* difficult man. Poppy says he absolutely has it in for poor Jago.'

Again Legs tried to look for Byrne to catch his eye, but her mother still had her in a loving headlock.

'It's strange to learn so much about oneself from one's most headstrong child,' Lucy smiled sadly at Legs, pulling her closer so their noses touched. 'I thought you were utterly mad leaving Francis, when I had adored his older doppelganger all those years. Now I can see how wrong I was in imagining he would be an easy man to love.'

Legs eyes' crossed as she tried to fix her mother with a meaningful look. 'Actually I have escap—'

'And you're together again!' Lucy finally let go of Legs' cheeks so she could clutch her daughter's hands in hers and kiss them jubilantly, making her burnt thumb throb. 'You are so brave. *So* brave and true. You and Francis have that spark of magic that endures and forgives errors of judgement. Like Poppy and Hector.' She sat back down with a troubled sigh.

Coughing hoarsely, Legs looked around for Byrne, but he'd vanished, leaving a large bowl of iced water on the scrubbed oak beside her. Fighting not to wail in frustration that he'd deserted her, she plunged her reddened thumb into the water where it practically sizzled before dropping its needles of pain away like a diffused magnet.

'You look so terribly pale.' Her mother was regarding her closely across the table, still wrapped in the William Morris cloth like a sarong. 'I wish I'd been allowed to see you.'

'Did Francis really say I didn't want you to come?' Eyes still scanning the room, she noticed that the front door was still open and realised Byrne must have slipped out again.

'He said no visitors,' Lucy sighed. 'I tried to get more out of him, but you know what the mobile reception is like here. At least I knew you'd be getting the best possible care. Francis seems over the moon you came back to him.'

'Francis isn't the reason I came back,' Legs laid claim to her tea, too drained and bereft to waste time going into detail. She hugged the warm mug in her free hand and breathed in its steam, wanting to spin out the pleasure, knowing Byrne had made it. He'd given her a car and made her a mug of tea. Both took on equal importance right now, her mismatched tokens of a mismatched love.

Then she heard a guttural snort and spotted Fink working his way forensically around the kitchen recess vacuuming up crumbs and she suddenly found herself beaming from ear to ear. If he'd left the dog, he had to be planning to return.

'I do love bassets,' Lucy followed her gaze. 'They remind me of your father. Fink and Jago stop to talk to me on the beach most days; I gather he's camping nearby. He came in here and fixed the trip switch once – you know how antediluvian that board is with its awful fuse wires; only your father ever understood it because he grew up with one just like it. Jago turns out to be exactly the same.

Hector is utterly impractical with such things.' Her face crumpled once more.

'Is it over between you two?'

She shrugged sadly, big bluebell eyes draped in shadowy lashes. 'Hector is terribly difficult to live with, you know. In concentration, he's far more contrary than I ever imagined, and *so* boorish. What starts out as a lively conversation inevitably becomes a lecture. He's just so hyper critical, and he is *such* a baby.'

'Sounds like Francis,' Legs sighed before succumbing to another coughing fit.

'He calls me "domestic" as an insult,' Lucy ranted on, 'but I *like* being domestic. "The practical aesthete", Dorian has always called me. I trained as a picture restorer after all. Art *is* a practical process. It requires hard work. God, I miss your father.'

'He misses you.'

Lucy said nothing, doubt etched on her face. She looked unspeakably tired, her sleepless night having ravaged her hollow cheeks and drawn the darkest of rings beneath her eyes. Legs reached her free hand across to take her mother's.

'So it's really, really over?' She tried to disguise the hope in her voice.

'Almost,' she offered uncertainly through the waves of high emotion. 'We're mature creatures; we don't "dump" each other like your generation – it's more of an osmosis. Nobody gave us a date for summer's lease running short, although we knew it would end; certainly if you and Francis reunited.'

'Was that always the plan?'

She shook her head guiltily, squeezing Legs' hand tightly in hers. 'I only wish we were so noble. That was simply the excuse.'

Legs returned the pressure.

'But you *are* back together!' Lucy laughed tearfully. 'Francis says you've even taken your engagement ring back.'

Legs' eyes widened. 'The phone signal must have been remarkably good when he called to tell you that.'

'He came to the cottage in person not long after you left for London. Francis said you had his mother's ring and that you two were still very much in love. Hector told him you'd have to return to Farcombe to prove it, and now you have.'

She shook her head violently, coughs racking her chest again, 'That's not right. I simply didn't know what to do with it for the best. When a man gives you a ring it's like taking a part of his heart, isn't it?'

If she expected her mother to pick up on the unhappiness in her cough-ridden voice, she was mistaken, as Lucy's thoughts went straight to Dorian, lifting her hand to study her own trio of rings, engagement wedding and eternity. 'Your father will be so pleased! He just adores Francis. Having him as a son-in-law will make up for all this upset.'

There was a low, welcoming woof from the sofa, and Legs looked round to see Byrne standing in the doorway. If he'd heard any of the preceding conversation, his face gave nothing away. Crossing the room, he put the tailcoat on the table, no longer smouldering but smelling strongly of charred mothballs, wool and paper.

'I found the notebook.' He placed it carefully alongside the coat like forensic evidence, the red leather cover blistered around charred pages.

Still numb from her mother's proclamation, praying that Byrne hadn't heard it, Legs managed a nervous smile. Coughs ripped through her again.

'You are the very best of research assistants.' He didn't look very pleased about it, taking her hand which she'd been waving around for emphasis while talking to her mother and putting it back in the water.

Across the table, Lucy stood up with a great scraping of chair and scattering of more mallow as she tugged the tablecloth around her. 'If you'll excuse me, I'll just pop upstairs and get dressed.' She picked up her writing paper and pen. 'Maybe I'll have a little lie down first. I have something important to think over.' She tripped her way up, trailing a vase, two candlesticks and a rapidly unfolding G2.

Leg continued staring fixedly at Byrne, one hand in a bowl of water once again.

He stared back, waiting until Lucy had closed the bedroom door audibly upstairs. Then he held up the notebook. 'Hector laid a huge bet on my father to win the day he fell.'

'So I was right! He can't have been responsible for his accident?'

'Oh, Hector was still to blame,' he said bleakly. 'Why d'you think he put so much money on the horse?'

She looked at him questioningly.

'He had an insider tip.' He remained unblinking. 'It was my father who told him to back it in the first place.'

Legs hand flew to her mouth in surprise, splashing drops everywhere.

'Hector loved the races so much, he bought a couple of point-to-pointers on a neighbour's advice to keep with a local jockey who'd started training. That was Dad. It was over twenty years ago. The neighbour was Goblin Granny. They all partied together regularly.'

'So Hector knew Poppy before the accident?'

'The first spark of attraction dates back to those early days.' He reached out and took her hand, making her heart rev excitedly, but he was just steering it back to soak in its water bath again, his face set with anger. 'Hector plays a long game. Look at your mother.'

Legs glanced anxiously towards the stairs.

'Dad gave him regular tips,' he went on. 'There's nothing underhand in a jockey tipping, provided it's one of his own rides. And with Thelonious Monk, he knew the horse couldn't lose. What he didn't realise until too late was that the race was being targeted by a gambling ring, so the horse would be hampered to hell.'

'And he'd lose his whole career,' Legs breathed.

'Hector tried to help financially after the accident,' Byrne went on, his voice bitter, 'but I think that was just an excuse to keep Poppy in his sights. Dad hated him. He convinced himself that Hector had deliberately set him up for the fall. He had a girl who came in and cared for him – another of Goblin Granny's recommendations – full of conspiracy theories that played to his paranoia; her imagination was amazing. I can't remember her name.'

'Liz.'

'That's right – Thin Lizzie.' He looked at her in surprise. 'Jesus, my research assistant strikes again.'

Legs bit her lip, realising that he had no idea that Liz Delamere was the reason she was so well informed, and that her daughter was tied up in the Protheroe dynasty too.

She opened her mouth to explain, then stopped herself because she wanted to hear more. Witnessing Byrne opening up was like watching the most extraordinary dawn breaking. She was hypnotised by the intensity of his face and his voice.

He picked charred leather from the notebook's cover: 'Dad used to play "Whisky in the Jar" to her; she had the patience to listen to him rant on for hours, which nobody else did, trying to make sense of his ramblings – if you can call it sense. Between them, they created this scenario with Hector as the personification of evil. That suited me just fine at the time.' He looked up at her, and the rage in his eyes seemed to scorch right through the room, 'I wanted to hate him too. Thin Lizzie came and went, but Dad stuck to his story religiously. He knew Hector wanted his wife for himself. When Poppy took a job working for the festival, that plot twist had already been written in his suspicious mind many times over. Dad had his bags packed long before she left him.'

'Did his storyline include you coming back to Farcombe for revenge?' she asked before she could stop herself.

He looked away, evading the question, eyes focusing on her hand resting on the table between them. He reached out for it again, and she felt an electric charge course up it as he placed it back in the bowl. She half expected to see the water inside boil with the heat sparking off their linked fingers.

'Would you want revenge?' he turned the tables.

'Quite probably,' she said honestly. 'But I don't play the long game in anything, so I'd have tried to cut Hector's brakes with a pen knife aged ten. If that didn't work, I'd have written him a very long, very angry letter. It's pretty pathetic.'

'I've done one of those already.' He let out a gruff laugh. 'All six novels of it. Who do you think Rushlore is based on?'

Legs let out a gasp of delight which turned into a predictable chesty cough as she instantly recognised Hector as Ptolemy's gargantuan, waspish enemy who breathes poisonous wind, fire, sand and ice through the many fluted tentacles that rise from his neck and shoulders, has a weakness for country music and flirts outrageously with Purple at every opportunity.

Byrne relaxed briefly, that intense face watching hers, his trust burning loyalty deeper into her heart as he sank back in his chair. 'There was a big argument last week. I shouted a lot, mostly at Hector. Now Poppy wants me to come to her grand dinner and "all make friends". I hate formal gatherings; I can't stand the pretence.'

'But you're keeping up the biggest pretence of all,' she pointed out, her voice growing hoarser. 'You're Gordon Lapis.'

Trust destroyed, he glared at her as though she'd just shouted 'the butler did it!' at curtain up for *The Mousetrap*.

'When were you planning to break it to Poppy that you're the festival's star act?' she went on, rasping now. 'Or is revenge going to be your mother and Hector learning the truth about you at the same time as an audience of millions across the world?'

'I've never wanted publicity.'

'Pretty hard to avoid it now.'

He rubbed his face uneasily. 'I always planned to come back here to find my mother,' he admitted. 'I wanted to do it as soon as I got published, to show her how well I'd done; I thought it would make her love me. But in the end I couldn't do that to Dad. He was still so bitter, and terrified of losing me. And he was going through hell around that time trying to quit drinking. His liver's so shot to pieces; the doctors kept warning him that he'd be dead in a year if he didn't stop. My kids' fantasy book didn't seem important compared to his life. The advance was tiny; I had no idea it would be such a success. I asked to stay anonymous to protect my father, and then it seemed easier to keep it like that.

'Dad knew the truth, of course, and he was incredibly proud. Not long after that, he started turning his life around. He's stayed dry five years now; he's back training full-time and his horses are winning some decent races; he's even found love again. Last year, they got married and he finally gave me his blessing to come to England to see Poppy.'

'By which point Gordon Lapis was publishing's best kept secret,' she realised, her strained voice barely more than a whisper now.

He nodded, 'I never dreamed it would be such a success story: Ptolemy Finch is a huge global franchise, but of course it's all happened remotely. I just wrote the books and banked the cheques. I like it that way.'

'Didn't you resent getting no public credit?'

'Any publicity would inevitably rake up Dad's accident; I had to protect him. What he's achieved in the past few years is far more glorious than my writing career. He couldn't have done that in the shadow of Gordon Lapis. Nowadays, he's the one who is frustrated that he can't boast that Gordon is a part of the family, but I enjoy my life just the way it is; I love my family and friends, my freedom. I've never wanted that to change, although the money is grand.'

'But you've always wanted to contact Poppy again?'

'All my adult life. When I thought about coming to England, I'd get very keyed up about needing my mother to acknowledge my success, and getting one over on Hector. I was too twisted up with anger and hurt to know how to deal with it. I kept starting letters to her and not knowing what to say or how to explain. Then, out of the blue, she emailed me – or rather she emailed Gordon.'

'Poppy sent Gordon Lapis fan mail?'

He nodded. 'She signed the message with her maiden name, but it came from the Farcombe email address so it was obvious who she was. Of course she had no idea it was me. She said reading Ptolemy Finch was her secret vice, and that she absolutely adored my books.'

'You must have felt so thrilled.'

'Not entirely. I didn't want Poppy to love Gordon; I wanted her to love me, her son. I really resented the fact she could write such gushing praise to Gordon but hadn't sent me a birthday card in fifteen years.'

Put like that, Legs could see his point. 'What did you do?'

'I telephoned her, but I was so tongue-tied that she heard my name wrong, calling me "Mr Goburn", and when I said that I was a voice from the past, she seemed to think I was a historian, so I bottled out and decided to email instead. At first, I just sent her a couple of lines apologising for the strange call. My private Gmail address doesn't have an automatic signature. She replied to 'Jay Goburn' straight away and was so charming, sending lots of details about the house and its history, that I couldn't bring myself to disillusion her.'

'So you corresponded as yet another alter ego?' Her strained, whispering voice had settled into a comfortable niche now, somewhere between inflating bagpipes and a snooker commentator.

He shrugged. 'I guess, albeit accidentally. It gave me an opportunity to get to know her again, and it was obvious how unhappy and frustrated she was. I stopped feeling quite so angry with her, although I still longed to shock her into action. She seemed to be living a half-life, using her agoraphobia as defence shield.'

'Like you use Gordon?'

'Perhaps a little,' he acknowledged. 'Maybe we both needed a way out. By that point, Conrad was really getting on my case about revealing my identity as Gordon's creator, threatening to frog-march me onto Oprah or to Hay-on-Wye, so I Googled this place for the hell of it. I read a profile of Hector in an online newspaper, full of praise for his championing of the Arts and his charitable benevolence, tipping him for a knighthood this year; it made me so angry.'

'He didn't get it,' Legs glanced at the stairs, remembering Francis saying that he'd started the affair with Lucy as a result of that snub.

'I told Conrad I'd come here to Farcombe out of bloody-mindedness; I knew enough about the festival to see the selection process would never allow any commercial writer past, let alone a monstrous mega-seller like Gordon. I didn't think it could really happen but I figured that if it did, it was fate. Then you got involved and tempted fate.'

'Is that why you turned up to try to stop me?' She eyed him hopefully.

He shook his head, turning the notebook over in his hands, not looking at her. 'You mentioned that Hector had left Poppy. I had to come.'

'Oh.'

'Besides, Gordon had grown very fond of you, and it was obvious Conrad was exploiting you. It wasn't fair.'

'You're Gordon, Byrne. *You!* And you're Mr Goburn. And even Kelly the PA!'

'I know.' He still wouldn't look at her. 'Having alter egos is the ultimate in egotism, according to my father. He says Gordon is my excuse to be cantankerous and anti-social; my OCD. I guess that makes Kelly my bossy and conscientious streak.'

'I was so mad when I found out she was you,' she remembered irritably, coughs blasting though her chest like firecrackers.

He reached for her hand again, long since escaped from its water soak. The electric current ran across her skin the moment he touched her; her burned thumb throbbed. She waited for him to lift it and drop it back in its watery harbour, but he held on tight.

'I'm sorry. You were the only one I wanted to break through the alter egos and overturn the tables. And you have.' He looked up at her face.

Legs found that once their gazes met, it was impossible to tear them apart. Her stomach seemed to burn away faster than the shredded tailcoat pocket still crumpled in front of her.

'I adore Gordon,' she said truthfully. 'His sense of humour is so wonderful. I even like his cantankerousness. It's all that angry energy that fuels his talent.'

'He was certainly pretty angry when he arrived here.' He looked away abruptly, placing her hand back into the water bowl. 'And yes, when I first planned this, perhaps I did think there'd be a great deal of satisfaction in revealing who I really was while my mother and Hector watched on, unaware. What better platform to announce what an immoral crook Hector Protheroe is than his own festival stage, after all?'

'So that's what you're planning to do?' Legs gaped at him, torn between fear and admiration.

Reaching for the leather notebook, he flipped trough to select one of the least burned pages and started reading out the list of abbreviations running down the final column, the acronyms which Legs hadn't understood, 'ICA, BDRS – they're all charities,' he explained. 'Mostly art funds. That's where all his winnings went – about two million in total in this book alone.'

'Hector gave his winnings to charity?'

Byrne closed the book angrily. 'It's pretty irresponsible to fund one's charitable donations through gambling, perhaps, but that fits the character perfectly; it was his money to lose and he mostly made a profit after all. I guess that was a part of the thrill. His philanthropy is still a matter of record. He won't be judged any differently if this fact is made public, in fact many will admire him all the more for that famous loveable roguishness. That he stole his wife from another man and fucked up my childhood in the process is neither here nor there in the world at large, particularly all these years later. It's just a romantic aside to a long, benevolent calling as a patron of the arts.' His eyes flashed angrily. 'I should thank you, Allegra. This has saved me.' He held up the book. 'If I try to publicly discredit Hector as planned, he'd have me laughed off the stage. And wouldn't he just love to see me squirm?'

'You've certainly stoked his anger,' Legs thought about the threats she'd overheard in the study.

'He knows I hate him. This makes no difference.' He turned the book in his hands. 'It wasn't just a broken back Dad suffered; what Hector did to my father's heart is just as bad.'

'So what are you going to do?'

He looked around the little cottage, scene of a summer's love-nesting. 'You tell me. You must hate him too.'

'Hector's armour-plated; trying to fight fire with fire just means getting burned.' She glared at the bassoon resting on its stand in the corner, coughing angrily. 'You have to wait for him to trundle off and find a new target.'

He turned to her again, taking in the dusty velvet dress covered with twigs, the pale skin and wild hair. 'Is that what you think I should do, Heavenly Pony? Lie low in the woods until he goes away?'

'Obviously not,' she said hotly, wondering if it would be petty to suggest they smash up the bassoon and quickly deciding it would. 'But he's had life his own way for a very long time, and now Poppy has a new hero just as he's been caught behaving very badly indeed, he's bound to be defensive. You already have the perfect comeuppance to hand. If I'd written all those amazing books and held claim over the world's most famous pseudonym, I'd stand up and shout my real name to the rooftops. That was always the idea in coming here, after all, wasn't it? Forget Hector. Let him join the congratulatory queue.'

Byrne was staring angrily at the bassoon now too. He stared at it for so long, Legs half expected it to start leaping around the room batting the crockery on the draining board into orbit and playing refrains from 'The Sorcerer's Apprentice'.

'Even if it were as straightforward as you say.' He rubbed his forehead with his fingertips. 'I'm not sure Poppy could take it. I had no idea how fragile she was until now. I can't stand back and watch her get hurt just to revel in schadenfreude.'

'So tell her the truth beforehand.'

'That won't stop the media invasion,' he pointed out. 'Exposing her to public glare could damage her very deeply.'

'But she's always courted publicity; she's the ultimate attention seeker.'

'Good publicity, yes – the sort that means she doesn't have to leave Farcombe. But this isn't about hosting a jolly lunch for Brian Sewell then giving him a tour of the sculpture garden. This is the ugly, angry, resentful public exposure and invasion of privacy that comes with mass media popularity. You know as well as anyone the sort of attention Gordon attracts, the stalkers, begging letters and hate mail. As soon as this secret gets out, Poppy will be exposed to that alongside the feature pieces and photo shoots.'

It was starting to dawn on Legs that he'd hidden behind a pen name all these years to protect his father, only to find that when he had Brooke's blessing to reveal the truth, his mother needed shielding just as much.

'Maybe that's what the threatening letters which have come to Farcombe are about.'

His eyes fixed on hers. 'Who exactly were they addressed to?'

'I'm not sure, but Poppy opened them first,' she whispered. 'There have been two, I think. I don't know what they contain, but I'm guessing it's something like the potty ones we used to get through the agency when I still handled your snail mail. Conrad got a temp in when it started arriving in sacks, so I have no idea what they write these days.'

'Still much the same: mostly that they love Ptolemy; sometimes

446

that they love me; occasionally that they want to kill me. It goes with the territory. The more imaginative ones add diagrams and illustrations of how they'd go about it.'

'What do they want to do to you?' she asked in trepidation.

'Pretty much the same as I did to Ptolemy in *Raven's Curse*, I should think.' He looked away. 'If someone's sending threats direct to Farcombe, it's my fault. I've screwed up big time.'

Legs remembered Conrad saying that the novel would be highly controversial, and that Gopi and Poppy had both despaired in the final chapters. 'Is it something to do with what happens at the end of the book?' she asked quietly.

'You mean you haven't read it?' He looked hurt, Gordon's fragile ego flashing through the customary Byrne cool.

'I haven't quite finished.'

'Where are you up to?'

'The dedication.'

'That's a crushing blow for an author's ego.'

'Ghosts don't read too fast,' she joked feebly then jumped as a gunshot cracked in the woods nearby, water splashing everywhere.

Reaching out automatically to catch the rolling water bowl and return her hand to it, Byrne turned towards the noise. 'If I hang around here together much longer, I might be able to test that theory.'

'It's just Hector shooting game,' she reminded him, clinging onto his fingers underwater. 'Poppy should really add a brace of pleasant to her sculpture for authenticity.'

His eyes watched the windows warily. Then he said, 'Inside each and every one of Poppy's abstract fibreglass sculptures are amazing caricatures like the one we saw in the cellars.'

'You're kidding?'

'She calls them "the hidden truths".' He turned to her. 'The smooth outer shell conceals the real grotesque within. It's conceptual, but even the concept is kept secret.'

'So they were really works of genius all along.' She laughed in

447

amazement, thinking of the hundreds of blobs littered around Farcombe, each containing a detailed sculpture one could only guess at.

'She says she wants their secrets to be discovered after her death because she doesn't deserve the recognition in her lifetime. She's so trapped by her own veils.'

'Like mother like son,' Legs sighed. 'I want to break them all open like Easter Eggs straight away, don't you?'

'My offers to liberate them haven't gone down too well so far.' He looked out distractedly through a clematis-veiled window towards the woods, 'Nor did sailing, horse-riding, local galleries or anything beyond Farcombe's walls. Our biggest adventure was lunch in the village, and of course Hector gatecrashed that. I can't stand her blind devotion to him. He's her jailer, but she can't see it.'

Another shot went off, much closer by, making them both jump this time. Across the room, Fink woke from a sonorous slumber and barked. Byrne pulled his hand free from the water bath, ever more alert.

'Did Hector really threaten to kill you that day?'

'He said he'd put a bullet in me if I did anything to upset Poppy again.'

No wonder he was now so jumpy around Hector's gunfire, Legs mused. Then she gasped as she remembered: 'Hector thinks you're the one behind the death threats!'

On cue, a blast went off at such close range, shot showered down on the roof. Upstairs, Lucy screamed.

'Jesus!' He glanced towards the door, reaching to pick up the charred notebook and pocket it. 'I told you I wasn't safe to be around. I must go.'

'Where will I find you again?' She realised she had no idea where he was even sleeping. He was like the Farcombe hermit, she thought wildly. She had visions of him and Fink holed up in the Lookout.

'You won't; I'm not putting you in any more danger.' He

448

reached out to lift her hand from the bowl of water, examining the wrinkled, burn-whitened skin of thumb before tracing each of her fingers with the tips of his until her hand felt newly baptised. 'There'll always be a sting in my tale, remember, however many times you try to rewrite it with a happy ending.'

'Don't go,' she was punched back by the force of her own longing.

'Goodbye, Heavenly Pony. Don't meddle any more or you'll get your fingers burned.' He dropped his lips tenderly on the tip of her scalded thumb before turning to leave. The gunshots were moving away again now.

Legs covered her mouth, slumping back down on her chair in defeat, angry tears sprouting from nowhere. 'Why couldn't you just leave Ptolemy snogging Purple at the end of *Raven's Curse* like everyone in the world wants?' she shouted after him.

He slowed in his tracks, not turning round. 'Who says I don't?'

The sobs in her throat caught a crab of laughter. 'Do you really? Is Purple a she or a he? Is it a good kiss?'

'You must read the book to find out,' he said with infuriating Gordon Lapis pedantry, stooping down to clip a lead on the sleeping Fink's collar. But then he dropped it, the sleeping basset not even stirring. Turning, Byrne marched back to the table, stepped right onto it and sat down in it directly in front of her so their faces were level, his legs to either side of her.

Reaching his hands to her cheeks, he drew her into a kiss that broke their personal best one kiss record for unforgettableness, although Legs was pretty sure she blacked out completely this time as lust dragged all the oxygen from her brain so fast that her erogenous zones were the only things thinking for themselves.

At last, Byrne pulled away, whispering breathlessly: 'It's pretty much that sort of kiss.'

Legs found it was a long time before she could speak. 'Please don't tell me Purple wakes up and it's all been a dream?'

Shaking his head, he let out his gruff, bittersweet laugh, but his face was pinched with sorrow. 'Don't skip ahead. It's a good book.' He pulled away. 'Now leave me alone to lose my life the way I see fit.'

'You can't mean that?'

His beautiful scroll of a mouth twisted into a half-smile. 'I've already lost my heart and my head. What's left hardly counts.' Kissing her cheek, he whispered something into her ear which she didn't quite understand. '*Gráim thú.*'

Dark eyes even more regretful, he blew her a kiss and slipped out through the door.

'Wait! What did you just say to me?' she called out, but the door was closed.

She slumped her hot face down on the table, chest burning. Exhaustion and emotional overload enveloped her along with a merciless coughing fit. She badly needed another Fisherman's Friend. Her lost heart thundered. It was cannoning over the clifftops.

She tried to repeat what he'd whispered in her ear again, but whichever inflexion she gave, it still sounded like 'Grime poo.'

A call came from overhead. 'Legs, are you still down there?'

She trailed upstairs.

Still wearing the tablecloth, Lucy was stretched out on the bed, an eye-mask in place, along with her iPod now to drown out the gunshots.

She lifted the mask briefly to smile before dropping it back like a letterbox flap, talking over-loudly because she had opera in both ears. 'Could you fetch me another glass of wine? I have a terrible headache!'

'Wouldn't a paracetamol be better?'

But Donizetti had taken over once more.

Tucked into the William Morris fabric were several pieces of scrunched up writing paper. She didn't have to look very hard to see that every one was addressed to *My darling Dorian,* and invariably began, *How can you ever forgive my summer madness, my darling*

man? What visions have I seen! Methought I was enamour'd of an ass.'
Feeling guilty of prying, she carefully retreated downstairs.

There was a knock on the door. Abandoning the bottle of wine on the table, Legs found Byrne leaning against the oak porch, draped in fronds of overgrown clematis and rambling rose, like a woodland god, his face in dappled shadow.

'I forgot to give you this.' He took her hand in his, placing a little parcel into her palm before enfolding it in her fingers and drawing them hurriedly up to his lips. Then he said it again: 'Grime poo.'

As Legs opened her mouth to ask what he meant, a shot rang out, the closest yet, twelve-bore lead hitting the porch roof at such velocity its whole frame shook, throwing down great veins of oak splinters and thatch from above along with pellets of shot.

Legs screamed, her hand still gripped in Byrne's as she ducked low and he shielded her with his body.

'Keep *very* quiet,' he breathed, covering her mouth to stop her screaming again.

Another shot blasted higher into the trees surrounding the cottage, splintering bark so that it showered over their heads. Hector was shouting from beyond a line of poplars at the wood's boundary with estate parkland. 'Show yourself, you little bastard!'

'Stay here and don't move,' Byrne breathed. 'I'd give you all my heart if I had a life worth living. Grime poo.'

A kiss landed on her lips with such speed and lightness it was as though her mouth was visited by a zephyr before it blew away. He was gone, crossing the garden and into the woods.

'Over here!' he shouted at Hector, who had now reloaded and blasted a shot after him.

Head buried in her hands to muffle the sound and terror, Legs sat shaking for a long time before realising that her own heartbeat was crashing far louder than any gunfire. The woodland around her had fallen silent.

She uncurled her fingers and let out a sob of disbelief as she saw a packet of Fisherman's Friends creased in her palm.

Then she noticed something else in the packet. It was a gold signet ring. The engraved crest on it featured a tower supported by two lions rampant. With shaking hands, she slid it onto her little finger, but it was too big. It fitted exactly on her ring finger and she held out her hand to admire it, cursing herself because it was still trembling so much that the lions danced like two punks in a mosh pit.

Legs found laughter and sobs tangled in her throat. She looked up to the gnarled beams overhead, and told their wise eyed knots. 'I love him. Both of him.'

'I need that wine,' came a voice from the top of the stairs as her mother reappeared dressed in an inside-out smock dress, sleep-mask round her neck like a velvet choker, one iPod earphone dangling. She started downwards then paused, cocking her head, removing the other earpiece. 'Why is Hector making all that noise? I thought he was shooting wildlife not giving it a forty-one-gun salute?'

Legs groaned as she heard familiar, barracking shouts from the far end of the garden.

Dressed incongruously in a kaftan and ancient cords, Hector had several brace of pheasant swinging from an old leather belt around his hips so that he looked like he was wearing a feathery game tutu. Matched with the cartridge bag slung jauntily over his shoulders and the hippy beads around his neck, the look was psychotic transvestite meets trapper. Far worse, he had Fink the basset pressed up against a gnarled oak at gun-point, just a few feet from the cliff's edge.

'Admit you wrote them, you little bastard, or the dog gets it!' Hector was snarling in his deep drawl.

Was he referring to the threatening letters or the bestselling novels? Legs wondered wildly as she ran towards them, watching in horror as Byrne stepped from the shadows to place himself squarely between the gun and his dog.

Crashing through the undergrowth like a wild boar, Legs panted up to Hector's side. 'Stop it!'

'Legs, poppet, what in the name of Charlie Parker are you doing outside in a party frock?' he demanded, aim not faltering.

'Get back inside,' Byrne warned. Only Fink showed grateful relief that backup had arrived. Taking advantage of the distraction, he wriggled away from his master and raced up to Legs, long ears swinging.

'Hector, please leave the poor boy alone,' Lucy said soothingly as she appeared behind her daughter. 'He's doing no harm.'

'He is doing a great deal of harm!' Hector raised the gun to Byrne's throat. 'And he's about to admit the truth.'

Byrne looked at him levelly. 'I have indeed written something I regret,' he said. 'But it wasn't a letter, I can assure you.'

'I want you to get off my bloody land!' Hector raged.

'This is the North family's land actually,' Lucy pointed out.

'It's leasehold; it belongs to me.'

'How typically feudal,' Byrne hissed. 'I suppose you think that gives you the right to claim your tenants' wives as mistresses whenever you feel inclined?'

'Take that back.' Hector fingered the trigger.

'Stop this!' Legs wailed in horror as the gun moved closer to Byrne's face.

'You certainly had no qualms about stealing Poppy from my father,' Byrne went on, hardly seeming to notice the gun's presence.

'She was trapped and dying of unhappiness.'

'She still is.'

With an enraged howl, Hector lifted the stock to his shoulder.

Byrne's reactions were breathtaking. Before anybody could take in what was happening, he'd reached out to grasp the gun-barrel and wrenched it upwards. The shot that went off cracked through the oak canopy, showering them all with twigs and acorns.

Lucy let out a high-pitched scream and grabbed Legs' arm, dragging her back towards the house as another shot went off, this time blasting into the garden shed.

'Get in before they kill us!' Lucy pushed her daughter into the cottage porch.

'The gun's empty now,' Legs pointed out, but Lucy was taking no chances as she slammed the door behind them, then chivvied her upstairs, where they peeked out nervously from one of the tiny thatched dormers overlooking the garden.

Hector and Byrne were squaring up to one another amid the trees now. Fink retreated hurriedly beneath the old wooden bench.

'Where's the gun gone?' Lucy whispered as Hector reached for his cartridge bag. But instead of opening it to draw out more ammunition, he hooked the strap off his shoulder and took a swing at Byrne with it.

'He's hand-bagging him,' Legs gasped.

Byrne caught the flying canvas sack by its straps and tugged it from Hector's grip before aiming a punch towards him. But before he could land it, he received a face full of feathers as the older man hurled a pheasant at him.

Caught by surprise, Byrne reeled back.

'Ha!' Hector laughed. 'The early bird catches the worm!'

'This is the only bird you deserve,' Byrne flicked up his middle finger.

'You bloody thug!' With an enraged bellow, Hector threw two more pheasants which Byrne ducked to avoid. As he did so, his eyes alighted on the shotgun lying in the undergrowth. The cartridge bag had landed just inches away from it.

Spotting it too, Hector lunged towards it at the same moment and the two men clashed foreheads with matching cries of pain.

Seeing an opportunity to pillage, Fink had now re-emerged from beneath the bench to lay claim to the nearest pheasant, just as his master finally landed a punch on Hector, who lurched back and inadvertently trod on the dog's tail. With an incensed howl to rival those of either human fighter, Fink sank his teeth into Hector's ankle.

'Good lad!' Byrne whooped, but then his expression of delight turned to horror as the ankle kicked out violently and Fink shrieked with alarm, flying through the air before landing in a clump of forget-me-nots.

Glaring at Hector with open venom, Byrne stooped quickly for the gun and the bag.

'No!' Legs cried in horror, starting back towards the stairs. 'I must put a stop to this.'

'It's not safe to go out there.' Her mother tried to bar her way, but she pushed past.

By the time she made it outside, Hector had let loose his remaining stockpile of pheasants like plumed cannonballs and Byrne had reloaded the gun, which he now pointed at his nemesis.

'Go on, shoot me!' Hector goaded. 'I'll see you in hell soon enough.'

'Birdshot's too good for chicken-shit like you, Hector.'

Legs panted up to them. 'Will you two stop talking like cowboys in a bad Spaghetti Western? Give me the gun, Byrne.'

'I want Hector to apologise.'

'What for?' Hector goaded. 'Falling in love with your mother? Never!'

'In that case, keep pointing the gun while he apologises to me for that one too,' Legs joked nervously, glancing up at the cottage window through which Lucy was watching, then baulking when she realised her mother had a fresh glass of wine on the go, as though watching Shakespeare in Regent's Park.

Hector stubbornly said nothing. He didn't look remotely frightened.

Clambering out of the forget-me-nots unscathed, Fink flapped his long ears and sat down briefly to scratch his neck before waddling towards the scattered pheasants once more, issuing a low, possessive growl to nobody in particular.

'Please just give me the gun, Byrne,' Legs beseeched.

'Do as the girl says,' Hector barked irritably before turning to her. 'Shouldn't you still be in bed? You've had pneumonia.'

'You've had what?' Byrne swung round in shock, not realising he was pointing the gun straight at her now. 'You said it was just a touch of flu.'

Legs held up her arms nervously. 'I'm better now,' she insisted, trying not to cough or faint, both of which she had a sudden overwhelming urge to do.

'Does Francis know you're here?' demanded Hector.

'I have a right to see my mother without his written permission.'

'Well get inside the house, for goodness' sake. Lucy will make you herb tea. Let us settle this man to man,' his eyes flicked over the gun, clearly plotting a heroic lunge to wrest it back. He seemed to be almost enjoying the drama.

But before Hector could make his move, Byrne broke open the breech and pulled out the two cartridges.

'I think we've all had enough excitement for one day. You're right, Allegra needs to rest,' he smiled at her anxiously as he handed her the gun. 'Can you look after this? It's not too heavy?'

'It's fine,' she insisted, slinging it over her shoulder like a hearty mercenary and almost falling over backwards.

'Just till I'm gone,' Byrne's brows lowered with concern as he watched her. He turned to Hector, face hardening. 'If you'd hurt my dog, I'd have shot you right here. For hurting my family, that's far too merciful.'

'Get off my bloody land or I'll have the police on you,' Hector snapped.

'You don't own the sea.' With a final glance at Legs, Byrne turned towards the cliff.

'You can't go that way!' she cried. 'There's no path down.'

But he didn't even look round, and she watched in astonishment as he disappeared into the bright sunlight between the two outermost trees and seemed to drop off the edge of the garden to the sea. Only Fink looked unsurprised as he set off purposefully in the direction of the track towards the cliff path that led safely down to the cove below, a pheasant still clutched proudly in his jaws.

'I'll take that.' Hector snatched back his gun and hurried to his abandoned cartridge bag, clearly eager to open fire over the cliff side like an overzealous Home Guard brigadier.

'No!' Legs tried to grab hold on his sleeve to stop him, but he was too fast, marching towards the trees to look over the precipice. He then let out a loud huff of frustration. 'Damn man's disappeared!'

Realising that she was shaking so much her knuckles were rattling together like a Newton's cradle, Legs rushed to the cliff's edge and looked over, but all she could see was the long, rocky drop past the gulls' nests to the sea below.

Hector's hand landed heavily on her shoulder. 'Only wanted to scare him off. Bloody troublemaker.'

She looked up at him in shock. There was something truly bizarre about a twelve-bore Browning resting on a Barry White kaftan with hand-embroidered slash neck. Looking very pleased with himself, he turned to gather up the scattered pheasants.

'He's just like any Irish tinker you meet.' He tied feathery carcasses to his belt. 'Mannerless trespassers the lot of them, but cowards underneath.'

'He's your stepson.' She tried to control her anger, aware that he was once again carrying a loaded gun, and had fresh game to slingshot too. 'And he just went over a cliff! Shouldn't we call the coastguard?' Her eyes raked the rocky face below her once more.

'Odds on he swung along the ledge like a thief along guttering and is back with the happy campers already.' Hector was entirely unconvinced of his demise. 'Probably gathering a lynch mob. Can't be too careful with all these proles pitching tents out round the place.'

He appeared alongside her again, pheasant carcasses to the fore, his long face looming over hers like an Easter Island carving out-staring a rock climber. And at that moment she remembered something that left her in no doubt Byrne was safe.

The night they had shared a table at the Book Inn, he'd told her he was an experienced free climber. He had never once fallen, he'd said.

She felt the ring on her finger positively glow as relief pumped through her, and she pressed its gold warmth to her lips. She knew that when Francis had handed her back the engagement ring which had belonged to his mother, it had felt like a curse; Byrne's felt like an enchanted power, a magical token that would guard her against evil.

Smelling menthol and eucalyptus, she realised that she was still carrying the Fisherman's Friend packet crumpled sweatily in her tightly fisted hand.

'What did you just say about camping?' she croaked at Hector, groping for one of the little lozenges.

'Nothing to worry your pretty head about. I'll take you back to the hall.' He grasped her arm. 'Francis will be going spare. He said you were staying in bed all day.'

'I must talk to Mum.' She started back towards the house, with Hector still clasping her arm so that she found herself hawking him along too like a long-legged, feathery handbag.

'You wait there,' she told him at the door, remembering the crumpled letters with a guilty start. 'I'll just pop upstairs and check she's OK.'

'I shall come too.'

'Actually perhaps we should go straight back to the hall after all. She's probably asleep.'

'I am not asleep!' came a rather slurred voice from the bath-room, followed by the sound of the cistern flushing. Lucy appeared, sleep mask on top of her head now, iPod earpieces trailing behind. She looked even more puffy-eyed, and had clearly been crying again.

'I'm taking Allegra back to the hall,' Hector announced firmly. 'Francis will look after her. She really has been very ill lately.'

'Yes, that's probably best,' Lucy shot her daughter a regretful look. 'I might just go up for another nap. This has all been very emotional.' Her face crumpled as reached up then fled towards the stairs, crashing into the bedpan as she went.

'Better wait until you're *in* bed before putting your sleep mask back on,' Hector snapped witheringly.

'Oh yes,' Lucy pulled it back up, sobbed again, and scuttled upstairs.

Legs tried to follow, but Hector still had her in his vice-like grip 'Let's get you back to bed too.'

Much as Legs longed to race upstairs and curl up alongside her mother, clinging on for dear life and taking her refuge, she knew that would do neither of them any favours. Hector still had his gun under his arm, cartridges at the ready, eyes darting from window to window in case Byrne brought his lynch mob back. He was not a man to argue with today, and she had no energy left with which to argue or ask any more questions. She was utterly wrung out in body and soul. The thought of bed, any bed, was so inviting she felt almost tearful with longing. She was sure everything would make sense again after a few hours' sleep.

'Best get you back.' He hurried her outside and on through the trees. 'Come on, the old truck's just on the cove track here.'

Legs was too wiped out to argue, tripping along half supported by him like a rag doll.

Bouncing around in the back of the Land Rover en route to the hall across the parkland – Hector never bothered using the tracks if he could cross turf at speed – she tried and failed to pull Byrne's signet ring off her fourth finger, not wanting Francis to see it. She tugged and sucked and prized and scraped, but it was stuck tight. In the end she gave up. She supposed it would at least give her a useful talking point to help open up a very difficult conversation she was about to have with him. She pressed her lips to the lions with their tower and drew strength.

Chapter 37

Francis was predictably apoplectic to learn that she had been discovered at Spywood while his father took pot shots at 'that trespassing tinker son of Poppy's'.

'Have you got a death wish?' he yelled. 'You walked there alone through the woods. If a secondary infection doesn't kill you, some crackpot will!'

She tried to explain, but her coughing had reached fever pitch and she was sent straight back to bed like a naughty child. She was too exhausted to put up a fight. She had terrible shakes again. He gave her another slug of the salty-tasting barbiturate. It knocked her out like a tranquillised cat.

She woke up hours later with him stretched out alongside her on top of the counterpane like a carving of a medieval knight lying on a plinth, his head turned towards her. Moonlight cast his beautiful, sleeping face in stone. Then he opened his eyes, bright blue sapphires set in the marble mask.

'I love you.' He tilted his head to kiss her.

'I'm too ill!' She shrank away.

He reached for her hand, the pads of his fingers, stroking her nails. 'You don't make it easy to look after you, Legs darling.'

'I don't need looking after. Francis. We must talk about—'

He lifted his hand to her mouth to silence her, her fingertips still gripped in his. 'You don't understand what's going on. You need protecting as much as the rest of us, darling one – more so, according to Conrad. I spoke to him again today. He's in a terrible state; always lacked backbone,' he added with satisfaction, sounding just like Hector.

'What's Conrad got to do with it?' She had a sudden vision of her ex-lover threatening to enact a terrible revenge on her for her maddened umbrella resignation.

But she couldn't have been further from the truth.

Francis took her hand again. 'We think Gordon Lapis has a stalker who's already hanging about here at Farcombe – not just a random crank; a fully fledged nutcase.'

'Since when?' She sat up, clutching her head as she went dizzy.

Francis propped himself up on one elbow. 'Well according to Conrad there have always been unhinged mega-fans.'

'Lots,' she agreed.

'And God knows there are enough turning up here in Farcombe each day to bear that out – but this one is a breed apart.'

'Is this to do with the letters?'

'You know about those?'

'Your father accused Byrne of writing death threats.'

'It's not him, not unless he has an accomplice. A third letter turned up just today, hand-delivered as before, at about the same time Dad had Jamie-go at gunpoint. It's obvious that whoever it is watches everything that goes on here. That includes you.'

'Me?' She remembered Byrne's very real fear for her safety, and Hector's hurry to get her back to the hall.

'You've got a couple of personal mentions in the stories.' He took her hands in his.

She felt her scalp tighten with fear. "Stories'?'

'They all start "Once Upon a Time" – Dad's trying to persuade the police to have a forensic psychologist looking at them, but they're not taking it terribly seriously to be honest, and obviously see it as a waste of resources. They've got all the notes. I met with them again today, but their hands are tied unless a crime actually committed.'

'Surely poison letters count as a criminal offence?'

'It's termed "malicious communication", but of course the fear is that something much worse will happen before they can catch whoever it is playing postman. The police say they've increased their presence, but we get one patrol car passing by a day if we're lucky, and that's only really to remind the happy campers that Big Brother is watching them.'

461

'What happy campers?'

But he wasn't listening. He had discovered the heavy ring that was stuck on her finger.

He held up her hand to examine it, lifting it up to the moonlight. 'Why are you wearing Kizzy's ring?'

She snatched her hand away. 'It can't possibly be Kizzy's.'

'She never takes it off. She's got these lions tattooed on her . . . ' He cleared his throat. 'Somewhere intimate.'

Mind whirring, Legs' first illogical reaction was to be livid that Byrne had fobbed off Kizzy's ring as a love token, and to wonder why he was in possession of it in the first place. Then she was illogically offended that Francis had once made her feel so grubby about the little stars on her ankle, and yet Kizzy clearly had a minor safari park inked somewhere private. Finally she felt paranoid that Francis would never let her leave the hall again, keeping her for ever entombed amid erotic paintings and poetry readings. Her thoughts were still so jumbled up with tiredness and barbiturates, and talk of death threats and stalkers. Somehow it seemed vitally important not to give anything away about her recent encounter with Byrne.

'I . . . found it,' she improvised hopelessly. 'In the woods.'

He tutted in disbelief. 'Don't lie to me.'

'It's not a lie.' She *had* found it – in a Fisherman's Friend bag, she told herself, staring determinedly back at him in the half darkness. His face was light and shadow dancing as clouds scudded across the moon. He looked both incredibly handsome and eerily predatory.

'You mustn't go out alone, it's not safe,' his voice was carefully modulated, both caring and censorious.

She found herself thinking about Byrne asking after the threats earlier, the man for whom they were almost certainly personally directed. He had been typically cool and level-headed, claiming to be more concerned about Hector waving a gun about than hate letters and cranky fans. If anything, he had seemed far more concerned for her safety. But if the perpetrator was really wandering around the estate by night, didn't that put him in terrible danger?

'Where is Byrne tonight?' she demanded in a panic.

Francis looked at her warily. 'He's camping.'

'Where?'

'On the Isle of Wight,' he snapped, sounding bored. 'Here, of course, on one of Home Farm's old hay fields.'

'Isn't that a bit unfriendly, not to mention frightening out there with mad stalkers running around?' She felt terrified for him, ready to raid the wardrobes for more evening wear and storm out to stand guard over his tent with Hector's shotgun.

'It was his choice.'

'But it must be lonely.'

'Legs, darling, it's a *city* out there. Didn't you notice when you were wandering around earlier?'

She shook her head. 'I went via the lake.'

'Come and look,' talking her by the hand, he led her from the room and across the wide landing into his old bedroom which had mullion windows looking over the walled kitchen gardens up to Home Farm and its pastureland.

There she saw acres of tents in the monochrome moonlight. There must have been more than a hundred, thrown scattergun fashion into the hills like little glacial boulders. A few, where the inhabitants were still awake, glowed like illuminated lanterns. Closer to the farm were campervans and motor-homes in serried lines.

'All paying handsomely for their pitches,' Francis looked very pleased with himself. 'I'll buy you that Ferrari. If they keep turning up at this rate, it'll be a 250 GT. Who knew trash fiction could be so rewarding? I can't wait to shake Gordon Lapis by the hand.'

'If he survives the death threats and mad stalker.' She stared at him in horror.

'It's all under control. We're hiring in a private security firm.

Conrad has it covered. We can't cancel now. This lot would riot, not to mention the thousands we're expecting in the next fortnight.'

'And you'd lose a fortune,' she muttered quietly.

'This place *costs* a fortune.' He turned to her suddenly, cupping her face. 'You've saved us, Legs. You've saved me.'

'I have?' She bleated.

'You brought me Gordon Lapis. You did this for Farcombe Hall and for us. You did it to beg forgiveness. I love you for it. I never stopped loving you. And my God I'm going to protect you.' He pressed his lips down on hers.

She hurriedly faked a few coughs to back him off.

'And Byrne is out there right now?' Her eyes raked the endless little pods shimmering in the moonlight.

He let out a caustic laugh. 'Old Jamie-go hates being cooped up indoors, it seems. Probably misses bunking down in a stable in Kildare. Poppy says he loves it out there with all the oddballs, although the dog isn't quite so keen on sharing his personal space with the great unwashed.'

The first light of dawn was breaking over the horizon. Legs gazed out across the steely fields, knowing Byrne was out there somewhere, sleeping among the superfans. And suddenly she knew what he was doing. He was getting to know his readers face to face, meeting them in person, breaking bread and sharing firelight while he remained behind the cloak of anonymity. He was testing the water to see whether he could cope with the full onslaught of sharing the rest of his life with them all as an active part of it.

'Nothing will stop this festival going ahead now,' Francis was saying. 'Crowds are estimated as high as a hundred thousand. We're going to close public access to the village and bring them in through the estate gates from the main road, charging anyone without a ticket a tenner each.'

Legs felt foreboding trickling the length of her body; whether the mad stalker would get to Gordon before he got to Hector was debatable; either way it was set to be a dramatic festival. And the crowds could be the most unpredictable force of all.

'Where exactly is Gordon Lapis's first public appearance being staged?'

'The current plan is the library. Given the threats to Gordon's safety, it's thought that the main marquee is too much of a security risk. Gayle Keiller-Myles has come up with the brilliant idea of taking out all our books and replacing them with thousands of Gordon Lapis ones in every edition including the hundreds of foreign language ones. It will look fantastic on the live screening.'

'Live screening? On EuroArts?' Legs knew the budget satellite arts channel which sponsored the festival had an outdoor broadcast unit consisting of one freelance journalist and a digital camera hooked up to a laptop. They didn't *do* live.

'Auntie's finest from Four are dedicating an hour to us.' He touched his nose, indicating a secret. 'It's being announced at the press launch tomorrow. EuroArts are cool as they get fifty per cent of all syndication rights, plus the chance to run endless repeats. The broadcast has already been sold around the globe. And the Beeb will show edited highlights as a part of a Gordon Lapis Omnibus special.

'We're also laying on big screens in the parkland here,' he bragged, sounding as though they did it every year whereas Legs knew Farcombe's most newsworthy festival speaker to date had been a photogenic Iranian female poet under fatwa. 'We have a company coming to place a fifty square metre LED in front of the parterre – it sits on top of a huge pantechnicon.'

'I guess that will make up for the fact that you don't have a television in the house,' she said faintly.

Legs felt weak as she took in the sheer scale of the operation and its total lack of foresight or understanding about Gordon and his readers and their long, loving relationship with Ptolemy. She'd spent enough time at Fellows Howlett dealing with the cranky post and email – just a tiny fraction of the Lapis phenomena – to know what a demanding lot they were. They would want to be close to him, she was certain, not fobbed off with a glorified webcam screening.

The one person possibly best qualified to judge right now was out in the parkland, counting down the days to the moment he revealed himself as an imposter not only to those fans all around him, but also to the mother with whom he had only just made contact. Legs adored Byrne with an intensity that frightened her, and she loved Gordon's work with an addict's passion, but now that she knew one man to be the flipside of the other, she feared for his stability. What had he got planned for Hector? Now that he knew he couldn't publicly discredit him, would he risk something even more shocking? If it involved a crowd of thousands, no public liability insurance and a live BBC screening, he could bring down Farcombe like the House of Usher.

She was suddenly very angry with all those who had let Byrne down; Conrad with his negligence and cowardice; Francis with his greed; Hector for his bullying selfishness, but mostly angry with herself for playing her part so artlessly, living for the moment as always and now faced with the possibility of truly catastrophic consequences.

'You're shivering, Legs darling.' Mistaking her shaking anger for fatigue, Francis was instantly back in condescending carer mode. 'You need to get back to bed.'

'I'm fed up of being in bed.' She shrugged away the hand on her shoulder. He'd be quoting at her next, she predicted wearily, suddenly realising she was very tired indeed.

As soon as she clambered into bed she conked out, gold signet ring pressed against the tip of her nose for comfort, only to dream that she'd been entombed in the family mausoleum in Farcombe's graveyard, the festival in full swing in the parkland beyond the walls. Then blinding lights flashed on and she realised she was facing a television crew with live action being fed to the big screens outside. Alongside her sat Byrne and Fink the basset, both wearing dark glasses. She was interviewing the duo, a producer who sounded like Conrad shouting in her ear. Beside the camera's all-seeing eye, an autocue starting to roll with questions, the first of which read ALLEGRA: 'So, Gordon Lapis, tell me, if you were a biscuit which one would it be?'

Chapter 38

Legs woke abruptly mid morning to the sound of one of Poppy's bloodcurdling screams which was clearly distinguishable above the wind, howling wilder than ever now.

She scrambled out of bed and onto the landing, reeled around, coughed a lot and looked for a weapon in case she needed to take on the assailant. Despite her years reading racy detective fiction, she made for a hopeless female lead as she crept downstairs in a short nightie, wheezing consumptively, holding aloft a stone doorstop shaped like a pineapple which was so heavy she was forced to rest it on the banisters halfway down before resuming her mission.

Now wailing in anguish, Poppy was flapping about in the hall-way, beaded jewellery rattling like castanets. She was clutching a piece of paper in her hand.

Legs hovered on the bottom step. 'Is everything OK?' she asked dumbly, because it plainly wasn't.

Barely pausing in her lament, Poppy wailed past like a siren, then wailed back again to snap: 'Put that pineapple down, Allegra. It's from Goblin Granny's roof! It's one of the last th-things we laughed about – and the only things h-a-ave to r-r-remember her by. It almost f-fell on me the d-d-day she d-died.'

467

Goblin Granny had always possessed a very dark sense of humour. She would no doubt have been highly amused by the note Poppy thrust at Legs now.

'Isn't this j-just beastly? The spelling's di-diabolical.'

The single page of standard cartridge paper was printed out in neat twelve point font: *Once Upon A Time there was a woman who culd never be trusted and used to pathetically hide behind tall walls creating misery in the name of art . . .* it started.

Legs read on in alarm as the deranged note described the brutal killing of Farcombe's headline act and most of the festival organisers by a shadowy figure who disembowelled them all before throwing their corpses over a cliff. As she scanned it, she thought she recognised the style, but couldn't think from where. It was surprisingly readable. Many of Fellows Howlett's esteemed clients would struggle to get this much action-packed plot into three hundred times the page length.

Then she caught her breath as she read: *and the blonde girl came running through the woods to rapashously meet with her evil lover wearing a long black coat and eating sweets and nobody heard her scream as her throat was cut for stealing . . .*

'What do you think?' Poppy asked fearfully.

'The punctuation is rather reminiscent of the final episode of *Ulysses,*' she joked, her first defence reflex when scared witless. At the bottom of the page, the author had finished with the line *and if I do not get what I want you will ALL die!*

'At least nobody gets to feel left out.'

'It was delivered in the early hours. I've told Francis we *must* install CCTV. Anybody can get close to the house through the graveyard, as you know.'

Legs swallowed uncomfortably, realising that it was quite possible the stalker had hand-delivered it while she and Francis were gazing out of the window at the fields of camping Ptolemy fans. Had she just glanced down, she might have seen a shadow stealing through the cloisters.

'Are you still thinking about cancelling the festival?' she asked, suddenly thinking that might be a very good idea after all.

But Poppy had entirely changed heart in the light of the enthrallingly large crowds flocking into her beautiful gardens and grounds. 'Don't be ridiculous, darling. It's far too late for that. I'm thinking of asking Gordon Lapis to unveil my latest sculpture on the live television broadcast. He can hardly refuse given the hospitality we're extending – and the peril we're putting ourselves in. I will check with Conrad Knight that it's all arranged when he dines with us later.'

Legs reeled. 'Conrad is having dinner *here*?'

'He and his colleagues are here meeting with the festival team now; Francis is kindly sitting in for me because I really have so much to do, what with the press launch and tonight's party.' She cleared her throat. The truth was that her terror had now reached such a fever pitch that she couldn't even bear to cross the court-yard to the festival offices. 'In fact, I must press on now,' she reached out to snatch the letter back. 'Shouldn't you be in bed? That nightie must be letting in a frightful chill. Isn't it one of mine?' She eyed it suspiciously.

Legs hung tightly onto the folded paper with one hand and the hem of her nightie with the other. If she kept hold of the letter, she realised, she could try to get it to Byrne. It suddenly seemed ter-ribly important that he saw it. 'Don't you think somebody should tell Gordon about this?'

'I'm sure Conrad has all that under control,' Poppy wrenched the letter from her, leaving Legs just clutching the envelope. 'His author will be escorted everywhere under heavy security, I can assure you, although I may personally finish him off. He's bru-talised Ptolemy. If he gets murdered, he probably deserves it for what he's done to that poor boy!'

Legs sucked her teeth, realising that Poppy still had no idea that her son was the fêted writer, currently living unguarded and under canvas amongst his most fanatic fans, one of whom might well be hand-delivering highly personalised death threats.

She wondered if she had the physical strength to make another run for it and race through the tent-strewn fields in search of him with a warning, but even if she had been wearing something that fell lower than her buttocks, she was terrified that by doing that she might lead any killer straight to him. She clearly recalled Gordon telling her once that the crankiest Ptolemy fans knew all about his publisher and agent and their staff. Even though she no longer worked for Fellows Howlett, she was clearly in this mad stalker's scrapbook under 'blonde girl' and had been observed in the woods yesterday with Hector's tailcoat and a Fisherman's Friend. The thought made her feel faint with fear.

Then it occurred to her that all she had to do was break into her little silver car and get her phone back so that she could message him. Delighted, she hurried past Poppy through the green baize door to the back lobby and out into the main courtyard where several big, glossy cars were now parked, including Conrad's sleek black Jag. But her little silver Tolly had gone, she realised with a cry of frustration.

The wind was wild, promising more storms. Gusts were threatening to hoist her crotch-length nightie up her torso like a flag. Still clinging onto the hem, she looked around wildly, catching sight of several faces watching her from the big glass windows of the festival offices which had once been a vast arch to the coach-houses.

A moment later, Francis had rushed out carrying a long Mackintosh.

'For Christ's sake, darling, get back inside the house!'

'Where's my car? I want to break into it.'

'We had it removed.' He propelled her back through the door to the hall's rear passageway, where Poppy was lurking behind a hat stand looking thrilled at the brewing row.

'Where did you have my car removed *to*?' Legs demanded.

'Just one of the barns.'

'Take me there.'

'Not now, darling, I'm in the middle of a meeting.'

She gaped at him, suddenly reminded of Basil Fawlty at his most laconic.

'Tell me where it is then.'

'The other side of Home Farm.' He looked unapologetic. 'We need all the space here for the festival, and the new security chaps suggested it might be a bomb threat.'

To get to Home Farm would mean crossing in front of the campsite, she realised. It was completely counter-intuitive. She'd still be the Pied Piper to their switched-on stalker, and the mention of bombs was seriously off-putting too.

'I have to get back – I can't let this meeting overrun; I've an important lunch lined up with Vin Keiller-Myles,' Francis was already retreating through the door, looking to his stepmother for help. 'Poppy will keep you company.'

But, patting her turban, Francis's stepmother announced that she was going down to the cellars to work on her sculpture again, where she must not be disturbed.

Legs felt so trapped and incensed that she was death-rattle deep-breathing again. 'I must have Tolly!'

Francis faltered. 'Who?'

'My Honda. He's called Tolly!' She lifted her chin defiantly.

Francis stepped back inside hurriedly, his tone tightly conde-scending 'I know you're bored, darling, but this really is a very tricky day for me, and "Tolly" will have to wait.' Basil Fawlty was on the verge of exploding into a rage. 'But I promise as soon as this meeting is through, I'll call a locksmith to get the bloody thing open. Then you will have everything you need to read a few crime thrillers, redo your nails and text your chums.'

'And look ravishing for tonight!' Poppy called over her shoulder as she headed for the cellar doors.

Legs started in horror. 'What's tonight got to do with me?'

'You mean you haven't told her yet, Francis?' Poppy doubled

back in consternation. 'You were the one who insisted I include her in the first place. It's been arranged for days; I've finalised the seating plan.'

Francis gave his stepmother a withering look and drew Legs aside. 'As you know, there's a rather dreary formal dinner here to follow the press launch; Poppy and Dad are putting on a united front and hosting an emergency schmooze for the great and the good to try to nail enough private backing to underwrite a small shortfall in liability cover this year,' his eyes didn't quite meet hers as he glossed over the true extent of the problem. 'The family would like us to put on a united front too.'

'Who's going to be there?' she gulped, already aware of at least one guest she preferred not to see, particularly in her current washed-out state, surrounded by Protheroe propaganda.

'Oh, everybody basically,' Francis said airily. 'I know you're still weak, so you don't need to come if you feel too ill. It'll all be too much for you, I think.' He clearly didn't trust her recent erratic behaviour.

But Legs saw freedom beckoning. She could surely make a run for it with a big, rowdy dinner going on to divert attention away from her escape. Kizzy had once managed it in similar circumstances after all. This time she'd plan ahead and have money, correctly fitting shoes and – with any luck – car keys. 'Of course I'll be there. Count me in!'

'Well that's a relief,' Poppy headed back down into the cellars again, her seating plan safe, along with Hector's secret plans to announce his son's re-engagement over a champagne toast.

Francis looked irritated. 'In that case, I'll ask Imee to prepare clear soup and plain noodles for you.'

'Great,' she smiled a little less enthusiastically. 'I'll take a shower and wash my hair.'

About to go outside again, he stopped in his tracks. 'That's really not wise. The boilers here are playing up as usual, and you can't risk a chill.' He suddenly flashed that chivalric smile, as bright as a blade of steel caught in sunlight, 'Why don't you spend the day in bed and read the new Lapis? It's in my room.'

Legs didn't need asking twice. She rushed upstairs and gathered up *Ptolemy Finch and the Raven's Curse* into her arms like an injured bird. The copy was seriously battered from being hurled against a wall by Poppy, its spine twisted and broken, but she conveyed it to the Lavender bedroom as delightedly as a Victorian slum orphan with a new toy.

She fell on its pages hungrily, speed reading in her haste. By lunchtime, she was already almost halfway through and glutted with fictional pleasure overload.

Her head soon throbbed, but whether this was from the lingering vestiges of infection or just reading too much, she couldn't tell, and was far too engrossed to break off and take a paracetemol. It was Ptolemy's greatest adventure yet, flanked by lion-hearted pragmatist Purple. The plot twisted and turned from the first page, propelling her from one chapter to the next, spiralling through time and space with the little white-haired hero and his sidekick, fighting their battles alongside them, hanging from cliffs between them, sharing their wisecracks and wielding Lenore at a cornucopia of vividly described evil foes.

As the day wore on, wracked with coughs that seemed to turn her lungs inside out, she lost all sense of time. Still she read like a demon, forgetting to take her antibiotics and analgesics. She sat in a lukewarm bath with the book, then on the loo, then back in bed. While erotic canvases flaunted their sexual chemistry with shameless guile on the walls all around her, the little Freud more than any, promising untold pleasures beyond those soft furls of skin, Legs found a relationship that was far more innocent yet no less sensual within the fast-turning pages of the book.

For the first time, she saw it in absolute black and white. Ptolemy and Purple were in love.

Chapter 39

Legs was just two chapters from the finish when Francis came in, already dressed for dinner. He was using a crutch and had one foot heavily bandaged, although she was too distracted reading to notice until he banged the crutch on a wooden bedpost and propped the injured foot up alongside her.

Even so, she remained too distracted by the Ptolemy's quest – and the very chance that he was about to enact 'that kiss' with Purple at any moment – to afford his injury a second glance, very much doubting that he'd just assailed the Farcombe stalker in a manly fashion.

'What happened?' she asked vaguely.

'I broke my toe on a stone pineapple some idiot left on the stairs,' he said, in a very black mood. 'I'm sure it was Poppy. She's incredibly annoyed about us two getting back together again. You think she'd be pleased; after all, Dad is just waiting for her signal to move back in, but that's Poppy for you. She thinks it's my fault there's a financial crisis. I've been too diverted by you to deal with it, she says.'

Legs would have taken issue with the 'getting back together again' line were it not for her desperation to get to the end of the book.

Francis heaved his foot back down, mood blackening by the second in the face of her selfishness. 'I've been in a meeting with Vin all afternoon trying to put together a rescue package.' He glanced at his watch. 'Will you put that book down? We must be on show in ten minutes. You haven't even dressed!'

'All my clothes are in my car,' she reminded him, turning a page.

Limping across the room, he pulled open the wardrobe of ball gowns. 'You've already taken full advantage of these. I'm no Saint Laurent, but I'd say they're more suited to parties than running around woods, darling. Let me choose.'

Suitably chastised, she cast around for a bookmark and picked up a crumpled envelope from the bedside table, realising guiltily that it was the one the poison pen letter had come in and therefore probably an important piece of evidence.

Francis was rattling through coathangers. 'There's bound to be something in here that fits you.'

'Won't Poppy mind?' she asked, cramming the envelope between pages.

'That didn't exactly stop you before,' he pointed out. 'She's worn nothing but smocks for twenty years. She'll never recognise anything. Here – try this.' He threw something at her that was Angelina Ballerina over Angelina Jolie any day, with more stiff net petticoats than the cast of *Swan Lake*.

'Coral really isn't my colour.'

'You'll look gorgeous,' he snapped impatiently, looking at his watch again.

'I have no shoes.'

In a flash, he'd extracted a basket of Moroccan slippers from the wardrobe – a tiny sample of Poppy's huge collection – and selected a pair that looked baggy enough to accommodate her feet. Garish purple and green, and covered with orange beads, they were still so tiny that her toes curled inside them like springs in a mouse trap.

'My hair's filthy.'

'I'll fetch you a turban.' He limped out of the room and along the corridor. Usually, Legs would have gone ballistic at the very thought, but she was so desperate to be able to read a few more pages of *Ptolemy Finch* that she barely noticed, even when he returned and plonked a pre-moulded green satin wrap on her head. She was far more irate that he wouldn't let her take the novel downstairs with her.

As he hurried out of the room, she lingered behind briefly, picking up the book to read two more lines like an addict snorting up a fix. Currently in mortal peril, Ptolemy and Purple were going to kiss any moment now, she was certain of it. Leaving them behind to face a room full of literary snobs was agony.

Francis was calling from the top of the stairs.

Surfacing reluctantly, she noticed the envelope bookmark had dropped to the floor and she stooped to pick it up.

Printed in the same font as the letter itself was *FAO Allegra North, Farcombe Hall*.

She let out a whimper. It was addressed to her.

As she ran from the Lavender Room in a blind panic, she cannoned into a tall figure hurrying in and threw herself into the dress-shirted chest, clinging to Francis's familiar broad strength in terror, desperately seeking comfort.

'My fragile little bird!' He gripped her back so tightly she thought she'd suffocate, cheek pressed heavily down on top of her turban. 'I'm never going to let you down again. Tonight is our reincarnation. My beautiful, precious Poppy!'

'Eh?' Legs wrenched out of the embrace with some difficulty. It was Hector, breathing champagne fumes all over her.

'Legs! You gave me a terrible shock. Thought you were Poppy catching me red handed.' He reeled back in alarm, hastily pressing a finger to his lips and whispering. 'You haven't seen me here, darling. Just popped up here to, er, see an old friend.' He looked around at the erotic paintings on the walls.

Legs stepped aside and nodded politely before bolting downstairs, far too terrified by the name on the envelope to care what he was doing skulking around his own house.

'That's my dress!' was the first thing Poppy said when she saw Legs belting into the main entrance hall. She and Francis were huddled together in what appeared to be an urgent confab, but now sprang apart as Poppy rushed forwards to air-kiss Legs. 'Coral really isn't your colour, but I do like the turban. How are you enjoying *Raven*? Isn't the ending *dreadful*?'

'I haven't got there yet.' She slid to a halt, looking urgently at Francis who was folding something into his pocket.

'You *are* a slow reader,' Poppy exclaimed, hooking her arm through Legs' and towing her towards the sound of guests gathering. 'I was *most* disappointed, but I won't spoil it for you. I only read it as an academic exercise, after all,' she added with a sharp smile, aware that she was about to be surrounded by the festival faithful who hadn't read a book with a print run longer than that its page count in their entire adult lives.

Legs looked around for Francis, but he had shot off through the baize door into the back rooms and she was forced to accompany Poppy to her pre-dinner drinks, cast as reluctant co-host.

'I need to talk to you about the letters,' she whispered desperately as they climbed the little-used marble staircase leading to the east wing.

'Not a word,' Poppy hissed back, hostess smile already in place. 'This is an important night for the festival. We must put on a united front. Not a *word* about the letters.'

'But they were addressed to me!' Legs was still struggling to take this in, aghast that Francis and the rest of the Protheroes had kept it from her. She no longer even worked for the agency that represented Gordon. If this was a crackpot fan, they needed to see her P45. But she couldn't stop a mounting fear that this was far more personal.

Poppy ignored her, beaming out largesse short-sightedly, even though there were very few people there yet.

The guests were being gathered for drinks in the hall's long gallery which ran the length of the first floor above the cloisters, and was by far the most formal of its reception spaces, a Victorian Gothic concoction of dark wood panelling embossed with coats of arms, flamboyantly carved stone fireplaces, ornate plaster ceiling and polished elm floor which the Protheroes had typically challenged with a riot of technicolour rugs, along with modern glass chandeliers shaped like thousands of rainbow fingers that pointed down from above. Poppy's blobby stone statues predictably outnumbered the guests. The furniture was modern, minimal and uncomfortable.

Dosed up with drugs, but still feeling weak as a marathon runner hitting 'the wall', Legs sank onto a lounger made from Perspex while Poppy eyed her critically from beneath her own particularly ornate, jewelled turban. 'I'm amazed you fit into my clothes. You have lost weight. You must be thrilled. Good rest today? All better now?' She had no sympathy for the ill.

Legs nodded wanly. With no make-up to hand, her face was a white mask. The only colour in her pallid skin was a spot sprouting between her eyebrows like a bindi. Matched with the turban, it was a very odd, cross-dressing anaemic maharajah look. She knew it as far from Merchant-Ivory flattering, although when finally Francis reappeared, discreetly slipping through the panelling door from the back stairs, he seemed happy to be cast as the devoted lover.

'Glass of water, darling.' He limped up with his crutch and bestowed it like a Holy draft. 'I brought you still up from the kitchen especially because sparkling might be too much for you.' He sat down heavily beside her, propping his walking stick against his knee.

'Thanks.' How she longed for a Dark and Stormy Night. But her mouth tasted like battery acid and her stomach felt far too delicate to risk drinking alcohol.

'Poppy's right; coral really isn't your colour.' He seemed to prefer her publicly unappetising. She half suspected he'd like her best in full burqa.

But then he surprised her totally by pulling a heavy velvet-covered box from his pocket. Inside was an exquisite five-string pearl choker. 'It was my mother's,' his voice cracked with emotion. 'I thought it would set off that frock rather well.' Before Legs could say anything, he was putting it on her. Ella Protheroe must have had a neck like a swan because when Francis did up the clasp, it almost garrotted her.

'That looks lovely.' He leant back and admired the hundreds of pearls strangling her. 'You're terribly pale, darling.'

'I've had a real fright,' she whispered, worried she'd break the necklace if she spoke any louder. 'I know Poppy says I'm not allowed to talk about the letters tonight but—'

'That's right, darling,' he snapped, patting her knee and turning to watch as Poppy issued Imee with instructions about the champagne cocktails. 'Lips *absolutely* sealed.'

Eyes narrowing, Legs wondered what else he was keeping from her for the sake of the guests. 'That was another one you were reading when I came down, wasn't it?'

'Let's not talk about it.'

'Yes, let's!' She didn't care that her voice was climbing scales. 'It was addressed to me, after all!'

'I can assure you, it wasn't.' He turned to her with a pacifying smile. 'It was in fact a very large banker's draft. I've just put it in the safe, hence I saw my mother's necklace and thought it deserved an outing. We want to keep a lid on it for now, but let's just say that Farcombe's liability shortfall is no longer an issue. Not that it was ever going to stand in the way of the festival; Poppy blew it out of all proportion when she found out.'

Legs took a moment to understand what he was saying, her head still full of death threats. Then she recalled his meeting with Vin Keiller-Myles and talk of a rescue package. He must have sold him the Freud. Hector would be livid.

'How pleasant to receive a very large draft for such a small shortfall,' she muttered, eyeing him mistrustfully. 'Just the mad stalker to worry about now.' Her mind kept drifting back to *Ptolemy Finch*, who she'd left on the brink of plunging to certain doom, his wings clipped as he and Purple dangled above the Pit of Pi, edging along balance ropes that were being nibbled by fire rats at either end.

Francis was speaking again, eager to steer her to safer conversational topics: 'The festival press launch has gone very well,' he enunciated pointedly, as though talking to a dimwit.

'Oh yes?'

'I was in too much pain to stay for Dad's speech, not that you've noticed how much agony I'm in.' He slung his injured foot onto a stool with a martyred sigh. 'It's excruciating. Your turn to look after me next week, I think.'

She was spared answering as there was a commotion at the door and Gordon Lapis's London publishing contingent entered the room noisily and glamorously.

Conrad led the way, richly upholstered in a new Boateng suit the same deep, ecclesiastical purple as Gordon's latest book jacket. Seeing him again made Legs even more nervous, remembering her glass ceiling umbrella-poking departure. It felt like a lifetime ago now, as did her love affair with Conrad himself, who tonight was just another beefy, flamboyant suit among many.

Alongside him was super-slick PR man Piers Fox in wide pin-stripes, Gordon's ultra-protective editor Wendy in even wider pinstripes, two very corporate men Legs didn't recognise in shiny three-pieces and – horrors – Kizzy playing the dutiful new PA. She was predictably ravishing in a lime green bandage dress that clashed fantastically with her hair and created unfeasible curves on her whip-thin body.

'Are you OK with this?' Legs muttered to Francis under her breath, looking from him to Conrad to Kizzy, who was trapped amongst the suits, but turned to look at her now with huge, haunted eyes as though desperately trying to convey a message.

'Of course,' he breathed smoothly, reaching out for her hand. 'I have you back, darling.' His fingers closed over the rampant lions ring still stuck there, twisting so that it pinched. 'It's all about Farcombe,' he said quietly. 'That's why I need you by my side. Think of Farcombe.'

'Yes, Farcombe,' she hissed under her breath, playing on the mispronunciation that they had delighted in hearing from tourists and repeating as children. 'Farcombe Hall. Farcombe bloody all.'

Individually marked by charming and comely members of the Farcombe Festival team, Conrad, Piers and Gordon's editor

Wendy were being fêted as though Ptolemy's great creator himself was amongst them. The two shiny suits sipped mineral water and eyed the windows.

'Bodyguards,' Francis explained to Legs in an undertone.

'Hired in for Gordon?' She felt relieved; they were butch as hell now she looked more closely.

'No, they're Conrad's personal entourage. Ladbrokes have him as three to one for the real Gordon Lapis now.' He raised his eyebrows smugly. 'I hear he's already getting fan mail, not all of it very lovely. He's scared stiff.'

'He's getting threatening letters too?' she squeaked.

'Lips sealed,' he reminded her, flashing his pacifying smile again.

At that moment a champagne cork went off with a bang and Francis betrayed his nerves by jumping out of his skin, burying his face in Legs' armpit.

He quickly withdrew it, composure recovered sufficiently to criticise. 'Do I detect a lack of depilation?'

'I didn't have a razor,' she snapped. 'You clearly think I'm far too much of a suicide threat.'

Francis was looking anxiously around the gallery. 'Where the hell is Dad? He promised we'd have a conversation about private armed response companies before we went through. He finished the press talk ages ago and went to fetch his bassoon. He should be here by now.'

'Depends where he left his bassoon,' Legs said idly, deciding not to mention the fact Hector had been wandering furtively around the bedrooms when she spotted him earlier.

Chewing at a corner of broken nail, she suddenly felt anxious for her mother; Legs didn't like to think of her alone in Spywood cottage with the author of the poison-pen letters on the loose, especially now that she knew at least one of them had been addressed to her.

Francis reached for his stick, 'I suppose I'd better start working the room. You stay here; you're still weak. Can't have you fainting over a canapé.'

Or talking about stalkers, Legs thought bleakly as he stood up with a self-conscious groan of pain, the walking cane making him look more than ever as though he'd wandered in from the wrong century. She watched more guests arriving, amazed at the way being ill for two weeks had made her feel as though she was set behind glass, separate from the world, watching it through a fish tank.

The publishing suits were being very loud in one corner, although Kizzy had predictably cleaved to Poppy's side and was hugging her tightly. Then she seemed to freeze, eyes widening as she watched someone coming up the marble stairs. Following her gaze, Legs spotted a wan-looking Édith arriving alone and immediately laying claim to the champagne table, looking unusually understated in drab black.

Then Hector appeared through the doors behind her making a far grander entrance, bassoon aloft and his pale hair on end. 'Welcome all!' he boomed. 'Where is my beautiful wife?'

Breathless and overexcited, he made a beeline for Poppy and, brushing Kizzy aside, kissed her so effusively that her jewelled turban fell off to reveal a little stocking skullcap. Stooping hurriedly to retrieve it from Byron the terrier's head, he crammed the turban back on a positively red-faced Poppy and announced. 'I am back, my darling! What a night of celebration we shall have!'

'At last.' Francis limped across the room to corner him about a hired protection team.

But Hector was clearly in no mood for talk of safety and precautions, particularly once he learned that a fat banker's draft was now stashed in the safe to amply cover any liability for Farcombe's six life-threatening dangers to the public. His press speech that afternoon had been a triumph. Raspberry-cheeked and swaying, he was still tight as a tick from chatting up arts editors for two hours with nothing but champagne for sustenance before his dash to Spywood to fetch his trusty instrument.

'Half the press are still partying down there in the library,' he boomed in his too-loud voice to his wife and son. 'I wanted to invite them through to eat with us, but Imee insists it would ruin her numbers, and woe betide her chilled almond soup gets spread too thinly. It is pure elixir. I asked for it especially.'

Legs recognised the coded message and looked quickly to Poppy. Imee's almond soup was her absolute favourite, and one of the very few dishes that actually tempted her enough to ingest food. Her huge, baleful eyes were blinking tearfully, but she still pushed Hector away when he dived in for another kiss, not ready to swallow his lines just yet, nor threaten the stability of her turban.

Unrelenting, he lifted his bassoon and started serenading her and the rest of the guests with a taster of the music by Iranian composer Mehdi Hosseini that he was featuring at the festival along with his customary jazz. To Legs' untrained ear it sounded like horror film music just before the frenzied stabbing takes place. It did nothing for her nerves.

Trying to insert a finger beneath the pearl choker to alleviate the pressure on her windpipe, she itched to make a run for it. But as she plotted her exit strategy, measuring up the dash to the door, Conrad slid in beside her on the Perspex chair. His voice bore its customary touch-line tyranny as they spoke facing forwards like two spies liaising at a public gathering.

'Legs.'

'Conrad.'

'You well?'

'Fine.

'Don't look it. Take a holiday.'

'Will do.'

'Know where Gordon is?'

'You mean you don't?' She turned to him in surprise.

He kept his eyes out front, sinews at high strain on his broad neck. 'Not heard much. You?'

'I know where he is.'

'He well?'

'Fine.'

'Is he still on for next week?'

'Last I heard.'

'He'd better be. Tell him I *must* speak with him. The book's outselling all the others, but the Americans are up in arms, demanding a new end. Piers Morgan's team are so hungry for him they'll pay double what anybody else are offering. The tabloids are baying for blood, and crackpot fans are really coming out of the woodwork now. It's not just my problem.'

'I don't work for you any more, Conrad.'

'If Gordon wants to live to tell the tale,' his voice was dark with menace, 'get him to call me. *I* know who he is, remember.'

'You've had threatening letters at the agency too, haven't you?'

He looked at her sharply. 'That's confidential. As you say, you no longer work for us. Your business mail is the agency's property now. Kizzy is dealing with it.'

'You mean those were addressed to me, too?'

Just for a second, as he glanced across at her, those green marble eyes betrayed a flicker of worry before narrowing and scanning the room once more. 'The Protheroes are looking after you now, Legs. Let's you and I keep the focus on Gordon, shall we? I need that call.'

He stood up smoothly to join Poppy, who was eager to introduce the local MP, leaving Legs wondering whether Byrne's life was in danger from a stalker or just Conrad.

She eyed the doors again, but her escape route was blocked as more and more festival high-flyers arrived to be plied with champagne and canapés.

It was a seriously corporate affair, Legs realised. The Keiller-Myleses were in evidence, plus Kizzy's boorish parents in a replay of the murder-that-never-was mystery night. Mixed in with festival stalwarts, village hierarchy, local landowners and boho Devonians, there were over twenty to supper.

'Thank God you're here,' Édith flopped down gratefully in the vacant spot beside her now, champagne flute askew. 'That turban is hilarious – you always had such a wicked sense of humour. Thankfully Poppy is taking it as a compliment. Isn't this dullsville? I can count eight suits, not all of them sartorial. We'll be sued to hell if Gordon Lapis backs out now. Nobody knows if he's actually going to be here next week, do they?'

Close to, she looked deathly pale and red-eyed.

'How are you?' she asked carefully.

'So so. Jax has left me.'

'God, I'm sorry.'

'Don't be. We've been at each other's throats for months. I'm madly in love with somebody else.'

'Well that's a blessing.'

'Isn't it? I should be grateful, really, but Jax was so practical, I'm at a bit of a loss. I had to call out a plumber yesterday to show me how to use the washing machine. Come through to the dining room.'

The Farcombe Hall dining room was among its most flamboyant creations with its gold columns, deep crimson panels, ornate plaster ceiling and vast chandelier.

Imee had been in overdrive. The huge table, as long as a cricket wicket, was laid for a banquet, glittering with finest crystal and polished silver, vases bursting with vibrant pink zinnias that clashed fantastically with the red walls, deep orange tablecloth and emerald napkins. Guest names and menus were fashioned like little bookmarks propped up in miniature Poppy Protheroe sculptures.

Édith trailed around the table looking at the place cards. 'I'm so thrilled you and Francis are back together. You're soulmates.'

Legs made a non-committal humming sound, but thankfully Édith wasn't really interested in her brother's love-life when her stepmother was misbehaving: 'I see Poppy has Kizzy back in her spell again. She's so evil with her, moving her around like a pawn.'

'I think Conrad Knight's trying for checkmate.'

'Horrible man; Kizzy will tire of him even faster than you did. And she'll never sleep with him, whatever he hopes.' She plucked up her own name card and prowled around the table deciding where to move it. Then a wicked smile crossed her face as her eyes alighted on a place setting in the shadow of a Taj Mahal of silverware. 'Have you got a pen?'

'Not even a lipstick,' Legs apologised.

'Shame. I was going to change "Howard Hawkes" to "Jean Poole",' Édith sighed, prowling on. 'Isn't tonight such a joke, and so typically Poppy? She's probably spent as much as she stands to recoup here, but that's my stepmother; completely devoid of logic. She probably won't summon the nerve to cross the gravel to the marquees next week, but an impromptu party is fine, just so long as everybody writes fat cheques and nobody mentions the insurance fuck-up. Francis says it's all under control now and Hiscox will underwrite the entire thing with a few exclusions, but Poppy never really cared about that anyway.' She plucked a few more place cards out of their holders and swapped them around. 'There! Now I've got a camp Goldwin twin to either side to keep me entertained, and you're sitting between lovely Frank Parish and Jamie-go.'

Having been about to confide that the fattest of cheques had already been written, Legs found the words dying in her throat and the blood drained from her face. 'Byrne's here?'

She'd never for a moment imagined he would accept any invitation given his dislike of socialising and excessive pomp. But she hadn't taken into account his Achilles heel, the need to understand his mother. Poppy's olive branch had been grasped, and the consequences were potentially cataclysmic. Conrad would recognise him as Gordon straight away.

'He's taking a bath,' Édith dropped her voice, glancing towards the hall. 'Francis is livid Poppy invited him; he and my father are both convinced the prodigal son's about to enact a *Kind Hearts and Coronets* family-tree felling. I suppose they could have a point. Jamie-go's got to be prime suspect for the death threats. Hector's under strict instructions to be civil to him, but you know how volatile my father can be after a couple of drinks. I thought we were lucky to get away without a murder last time, but tonight's a dead cert.' Looking at Legs' left hand, her eyes narrowed. 'Why are you wearing the Kelly coat of arms on your ring finger? Is Francis buying engagement rings at Dublin Airport these days?'

'I can't get it off.' Legs eyed the ring. 'Did you say "Kelly"?'

'A friend of mine has one just like it. Want help?'

She wasn't sure she did want to take the ring off, but Édith had already taken her hand and was at tugging the ring. It was stuck fast. Before Legs could stop her, she'd put her finger in her mouth and was sucking at it, trying to loosen it with her tongue.

'I always said you could twist anyone round your little finger,' said a voice behind them.

Seeing two figures silhouetted in the door, Legs let out a nervous laugh.

'What on *earth* are you two doing?' Francis snapped.

Standing immediately behind him, Kizzy let out a startled cry. 'I told you, Francis! I told you she wanted to punish me!' She stormed past them and fled through the panelled service door with a sob.

'Is she talking about you or me?' Legs asked Édith shakily.

'Now look what you've done!' Francis huffed, starting to limp in pursuit, then letting out a few over-dramatic gasps of pain and deciding against it. 'One of you two must go after her,' he lowered his voice to a whisper; 'she wants to talk about the *letters*.'

Raising a pair of amused, narrow eyebrows at Legs, Édith pulled off the ring with her teeth, almost swallowing it. Then, spitting it out onto her palm and wiping it dry with her opposite sleeve, she handed it back to Legs before sweeping out after Kizzy.

'What does she know about the letters?' she turned to demand of Francis.

'Shh!' Still framed in the doorway, he glanced over his shoulders at his stepmother's guests. 'I'd rather we didn't speak about them in public tonight. And please don't encourage my sister, Legs. You know full well she has a very malicious streak. 'She . . . ' He took his deep, I-am-about-to-quote breath and Legs felt herself adopt the familiar brace position: identify quote, endure quote, interpret quote.

But to her relief, before he could start, his father's booming voice called him away. 'Francis! Come and tell Lord Palumbo about your plans for the new gallery in the tithe barns'.

It wasn't a summons to be ignored. Nodding at Legs with that familiar, old-fashioned, 'duty calls' expression, he turned and limped away.

With a lump in her throat so big the tight strings of pearls around her neck threatened to shoot far and wide, Legs wondered whether that might be the last time she ever saw him. The dining room was empty. To her left, just a few paces away, was the service door in the panelling through which Kizzy had made her escape. It led to the back lobby from which she could run down onto the courtyard and out across the fields to Spywood.

But even as she pushed it open, she knew that she would be turning to climb the stairs not descend them. She had to warn Byrne that Conrad was here.

Chapter 40

Slotting Byrne's heavy gold signet ring onto her little finger and clenching her fist to keep it there, Legs hurried along the back lobby in her toe-curling Moroccan pumps, taking the service stairs two at a time and racing around the first stair-turn with such silent speed that she didn't notice the couple sitting at the top of the flight kissing until she almost landed between them.

She cannoned off bare scented shoulders, soft Wonderbras and bony collarbones, her face full of first red hair then black. Finally regaining her balance and straightening up, she clutched onto the banisters as Kizzy and Édith looked up at her in surprise, both rumpled and pink-cheeked with their lipstick worn off.

Muttering apologies, she edged hurriedly past them.

'Wait, Legs!' Kizzy called out. 'We have to talk. I need to explain—'

'No need,' Legs raced on, realising that she'd just run head-first into a romantic reconciliation. It suddenly made perfect sense. Édith was the secret lover Kizzy had spoken about. It was Édith who had encouraged Kizzy to meet her birth mother, Édith from whom she always sought approval and with whom she matched one-liners like two bookends propping up a private joke collection. They must have fallen out because Édith refused to leave Jax, forcing Kizzy to run into Francis's waiting arms, egged on by Poppy. Poor Francis had been completely out-manoeuvred. But Legs wasn't concerned about Francis right now.

She burst out onto the main landing before knocking upon and then pushing open the doors to each bathroom on the landing in turn.

In the third bathroom along, magnificent naked male shoulders greeted her, tanned the colour of toffee and curved like the back of a Louis XV settee as they enfolded the end of the roll-edged bath.

Byrne was lying back in the deep, claw-footed tub, eyes closed. Fink was spread out wearily on the bathmat chewing a loofah.

As Legs stepped backward on tiptoes, Fink let out a gruff hello bark and Byrne's eyes snapped open.

'Sorry!'

'Allegra!' He reared out of the bath like a whale's tail, dripping water everywhere as he grabbed a towel.

'I'll wait on the landing.' She turned and bolted back out.

Legs couldn't look him in the face as he stood framed in the doorway, dressed in hurriedly pulled-on jeans. Then she caught sight of his torso and found she couldn't look him in the body either. He had a six pack. Who would have thought Gordon Lapis would look like one of those 'Hunk of the Week' posters stapled in the centre of teen girls' magazines? The press would go mad for him.

'I told you to go home,' he whispered urgently, glancing towards the main stairs from which guests could be heard filtering between long gallery and dining room.

'I haven't told *anyone* who you are,' she bleated, staring fixedly at a piece of cornicing.

'What in hell are you doing here?'

Losing concentration on the cornicing, Legs found she was gaping at his chest again, marvelling at the breadth of his shoulders and the flat stomach. He had an outie belly button, she noted, and across one breastbone was a tattoo of a line of writing in an elaborate script that she couldn't make out. She hurriedly forced herself to check out the ceiling once more. 'I've been here all week.'

He let out a long sigh. 'How did I guess you hadn't just popped down from London to visit your mother yesterday?'

'I was ill. I tried to leave – twice – but then Francis gave me the new Ptolemy Finch book to read.'

He didn't appear to be listening, those flaming coal eyes wide with worry.

'You kill him at the end, don't you?' she asked, looking him in the face once more.

He nodded vaguely, eyes so intense they almost fired her back against the wall.

Legs felt a bolt of illogical, angry grief. She hadn't let herself fully believe it until now, even having left the book ten pages from the end when there seemed no other conclusion. 'If your neighbours in the park out there find out who you are, they'll lynch you.'

He shrugged. 'They're not too happy about the book, it's true.'

'How can he die if he's immortal?'

'He sacrifices his immortality to kiss Purple.'

She knew that she must have read to within a few lines of this. She'd sensed it coming. Now he'd told her, she felt a great wash of emotion pulling her ankles from under her and spinning her round. She wanted to run along the corridor and grab the book from her bed. It all made such sense. But as usual, she went for the wisecrack in self-defence.

'A lesson to us all in the dangers of open mouthed kissing,' she muttered, eyeing him again.

They stared at each other for a ridiculous length of time. Fink moved on from the loofah to a sponge. Neither of them noticed a spider lowering itself boldly between them like a jewel thief on a wire.

But the call to dinner downstairs accompanied by the gong made them both jump.

'I'd better get dressed,' he said, not moving.

She nodded, equally frozen to the spot, her eyes tracing those words along his breastbone. 'What does your tattoo say?'

'*Is geal leis an bhfiach dubh a ghearrcach féin,*' his deep voice breathed the words like a spell. 'It's Irish Gaelic: *the raven likes his own nest*. It's a family saying.'

'I have stars on one ankle,' she told him. 'It's a family shape.'

He didn't laugh.

'What does "grime poo" mean?' she asked.

His eyes softened with amusement, melting into hers. '*Gráim thú,*' he corrected. 'It means *I love you*.'

She stared at him for a long time, not trusting her own ears.

'That would make some tattoo,' she breathed.

His eyes were so intense they almost burned hers out. 'Tattoos aren't like rings; they're not a part of your heart you give away. They stay with you.'

Slowly she held up her fist, uncurling her fingers one by one until she revealed the gold ring. 'So take this away.'

Before she could react, out flew his hand, grasping hers, closing her fingers over the ring to keep it there.

Unable to stop herself, Legs launched herself forwards to kiss him.

'You.' He pulled her into the bathroom, talking urgently between kisses. 'You – I – gorgeous creature – I – love –'

'Grime poo too,' she laughed, returning his kisses, amazed at the energy coursing through her, the sheer abandon of being in love.

But suddenly he pulled away, holding her face in his hands, those burning peat eyes unblinking.

She stared back at him in disbelief, lips buzzing so much she could barely speak. 'Please don't stop.'

His thumbs traced those pins and needles lips as though trying to erase the kiss.

'What's wrong?' she begged.

'You tell me.'

'Conrad's here.'

He took a moment to take this in before his face drained of colour.

'He's a pro,' Legs assured him. 'He won't give you away. But he'll use this, Byrne.'

'It hardly matters does it? They'll all know soon enough.' He sounded like a man on death row, turning away to fetch the rest of his clothes.

She stayed in the doorway, watching him. Picking up a pair of socks, he straightened up, looked across at her, muttered 'oh hell,' before pulling her into the room and kicking closed the door to kiss her with knee-quaking thoroughness.

'Please don't tell me to go away again.' She kissed him back eagerly, curling into his arms.

'We couldn't have met at a worse time.'

'We couldn't have met at all. *That* would have been so much worse.'

Fink and his sponge dodged out of the way as they span around the room kissing now. Far from getting dressed, Byrne was making terrific headway into the coral frock, his warm hands touching the most delightful of places. 'I knew you'd catch me out, even before I met you. You flirted with Gordon for God's sake. *Nobody* flirts with Gordon.'

'I fancied Gordon from the moment he said he was going to call his new detectives Julie Ocean and Jimmy Jimee. I *knew* he couldn't be as old and curmudgeonly as he made out to use Undertones song titles.'

'You told me my skill was to build sexual tension over many months, years, books.' He started to prise the dress off her shoulders, kissing the bare skin as it was revealed an inch at a time. 'This isn't months, Heavenly Pony.'

'Sometimes.' She kissed him back urgently between words, 'sexual tension . . . is too . . . bloody huge . . . to need . . . building.'

The dress fell off one way and the hated turban flew off the other until she was sporting nothing but a pearl choker and a discreet star tattoo on one ankle.

'Do you never wear underwear?' he asked, taking a nipple in one mouth and making her stifle a squeal of pleasure.

The dinner gong was going again.

'We'll be in *such* trouble,' she giggled.

'I think we'll skip the starter.' He kissed the other nipple, manoeuvring her back against the wall.

'Oh God – it's almond soup to start tonight!' she remembered.

'Well that counts me out for a start.' He put his hand between her legs and found her molten with excitement, 'I'd rather drink from you.'

'Oh please do.' She managed to unbutton his trousers while still kissing frenziedly.

He lifted her knee to his side, running his hand from hip to ankle as he tilted his head to admire her tattoo, fingers lingering on the little inked stars. 'These are neat.'

'The family shapes,' Legs laughed between kisses. 'I always

thought I should have had "live for the moment, live with the consequences" added.'

'If it's written in skin, you must live by the word.' He moved closer still, kisses deepening, his hand enfolding hers and tightening as he felt the signet ring still encircling her little finger. 'Until then, never let this go.'

'I won't,' she promised, the ring a magic talisman now, making her fearless as she climbed his sides with her thighs, barely able to believe the excitement coursing through her veins.

There was a hammering on the door. 'You in there Jamie?'

It was Francis.

'Shit,' Byrne breathed, quickly stepping forwards and putting a hand across Legs' mouth to stop her squealing.

'Yup – just shaving.'

'We're all waiting on you. Did you see Allegra at all before you went in there?'

'Uh-huh,' he said, not committing either way, holding her tight to his naked chest.

'Well bloody hurry up.' Francis moved off, calling out her name.

Byrne wrapped his arms around her and pressed his lips to her ear, speaking in barely a breath, his voice as soft as an Irish breeze. 'We can both run away together. Tonight. You and me. Julie and Jimmy.'

She laughed breathlessly. 'Do you mean it?'

'I don't want to be Gordon Lapis, Allegra. I want to be Jago Byrne, with you, on the run.'

'I thought you wanted revenge?'

'Right now, I want you more.'

She laughed even more, feeling increasingly hysterical, and he covered her mouth again. Then, sliding his hand away, he kissed her until all the oxygen seemed to float away from her brain in little bubbles containing exclamations like 'wow!' 'zonkers!' and 'kerwizz!'

'What about the festival?'

'There's still a week before Gordon's due to appear. Run away with me tonight, just tonight.'

'Live for the moment, live with the consequences,' she said shakily.

'Your motto.' He held her tightly.

'How do we do it?'

'You have to go back down there, sit through the meal; I can't risk Conrad seeing me and it'll ring too many alarm bells with the family if we both disappear. Tell Francis quietly that I'm unwell, that you've just found me throwing up in here. I'll make sure I stagger around looking suitably putrid for half an hour in case he checks, then I'll get out and wait for you.'

'Eascombe Cove,' Legs said urgently. 'I'll take the tunnel from the cellars. We'll meet there.'

He nodded, kissing her again. 'I'll be waiting.' Then, as she reached for her clothes, he pulled something from a duffel bag on the chair by the bath and handed it to her. 'Wear these.'

'What the—?' She unfolded a pair of freshly laundered Calvin Klein boxers.

'Put them on,' he insisted, looking up at her through his lashes. 'It's windy out there.' His dark eyes sparkled. 'And besides, if I can't get in your pants right now this minute, which I sincerely wish I could, at least you can get in mine.'

He kissed her again, and it was all threatening to get completely out of hand when Fink, losing patience, crammed his wet nose and solid head between the two of them, wagging his long body for attention.

'Eascombe Cove.' Byrne planted one last, unforgettable kiss which seemed to breathe her right inside him. 'I'll wait all night if I have to.'

But no sooner had Legs pulled on the pants, along with the hated coral dress and turban, creeping out onto the landing, than Francis stepped out from the shadows of a doorway. Tie loosened and cheeks stained with colour, blond hair spilling across his face, he looked as angry as she'd ever seen him.

'Legs . . . Jamie.' He nodded to the figure silhouetted behind her in the bathroom.

'Jago's not feeling too well,' Legs lied badly.

'And he hasn't even tried the soup,' he drawled. 'The trouble is, neither has anybody else. You really are spectacularly late for dinner, darling.'

'Legs was very kindly looking after me,' Byrne was a far better actor than her, wandering out onto the landing looking very ill indeed. 'I told her not to bother, but she's got too kind a heart.'

'Very true. She's had pneumonia herself; I've been looking after her,' Francis hissed. 'She can't risk a set back. Are you OK darling?' He felt her forehead. 'Do you need a rest?'

'I think Jago's the one who needs to lie down,' Legs spluttered.

'Of course – use my room,' Francis stepped aside and beckoned him through the doorway. 'Imee's rather busy, but I'll get her to bring you up some herb tea when she gets a moment. There's poetry by the bed there if you want something to read.'

The moment Byrne was through the door, Francis slammed it shut and gripped Legs viciously under the arm, steering her back along the landing. As he did so, the signet ring slipped from her little finger. She fumbled to grab it, but it dropped out of reach, ricocheted off Francis's bandaged foot and flew back along the corridor.

Craning to watch its progress over her shoulder Legs let out a whimper as it rolled to a halt in front of the recently slammed door. Not noticing, Francis marched her downstairs at high speed.

'Be careful around that Jamie-go, darling,' he said stiffly as he limped alongside her. 'He's very underhand, and frankly I think he's unbalanced.'

'I'm fine,' she snapped, unable to think about anything but running away with Byrne.

'We both know there's a lots of ill-will against this family out there at the moment, and I'm here to look after you. I'm not letting you out of my sight again.'

'I don't need looking after!' she bleated.

They had almost reached the dining room doors, beyond which Poppy's guests were already laying into the first course.

Drawing her aside, he fished in his pockets. 'I think you should see something that came through the letterbox today.'

'Poppy's already shown me the letter.' She turned away, knowing Byrne could never have written prose like that. 'And I know it was addressed to me, although she kept quiet about that. Were they all meant for me?' She shuddered, longing to get away from Farcombe more than ever. Byrne would protect her; she trusted him with her life.

'We didn't want to alarm you, darling. Conrad is certain it's the same crank who's been targeting the agency, misguidedly using you to get to Gordon Lapis. But now this has arrived, which rather changes things.'

The piece of paper he thrust into her hand was a supermarket receipt. On one side it itemised six bottles of scrumpy, discounted chicken thighs, *Ptomemy Finch and the Raven's Curse* and a magazine called *True Life Crime*. On the back of the receipt, in jagged biro was written *ALLEGRA NORTH WILL CHECK OUT TONIGHT.*

'I'm not letting you out of my sight,' Francis repeated in an undertone, taking her arm and leading her into the dining room with his usual impeccable manners as he saw her to her chair before taking his own place, apologising politely to those around them for being so late.

'Francis and Allegra have recently rekindled their romance, so we can forgive them a little unpunctuality,' Poppy announced theatrically, reaching for her glass and peering short-sightedly along the table at her wayward husband.

'Hear hear!' Hector thrust his Chablis in the air, inadvertently emptying most of it over Gayle Keiller-Myles. 'Let's all raise a toast to rekindling!'

While the Protheroes smouldered lovingly at one another through the candles, silverware, zinnias and the blur of short sight in Poppy's case, Legs avoided Francis's watchful gaze across the table. To her right was Byrne's empty seat. She could imagine him already in his running shoes, heading out across the parkland to the cliff path. Her own feet, crammed into tight Moroccan pumps, were jumping and tapping beneath the table as they subconsciously ran alongside him.

Somehow, Legs got through the first two courses of dinner, her mind in a haze as she pushed the uneaten clear soup around her bowl and occasionally inserted a finger beneath her pearl choker to ease her breathing. All the time, she was aware of Francis's gaze on her like a jailer.

For once, Poppy wasn't holding court and regaling her guests with monologues; instead, their hostess gazed lovingly and shortsightedly the full length of the table to Hector gazing adoringly back. Conversations cross-currented around Legs like eddying waves pushing a little boat further out to sea. Mostly talk was of Gordon Lapis.

'Quite unbelievable to have him come here.'

'Literary coup of the century.'

'It'll put Farcombe on the map.'

Not caring that Gordon's publisher and agent were both present, Yolande Hawkes was taking no prisoners in her outspoken criticism of the festival's star turn. Sporting a feathered yellow turban that looked like a dayglo cycling helmet with a fluffy aerial, she was holding forth from her seat between Francis and his father: 'The real Gordon Lapis is bound to be a dreadful little weirdo; look at all the undesirables he attracts amongst his devotees. Howard once wrote a pamphlet entitled *The Pseudo-Intellectual Pseudonym* which shows that writers hiding behind pen names usually harbour inadequacies.'

'Or just have the misfortune to have been christened Phyllis Stein,' Édith muttered, exchanging a long-suffering look with Kizzy, with whom she appeared to have made forever friends again.

'I have only had one book published,' Yolande droned on. 'A slim volume about the hidden misogyny of the Suprematism Movement, but I was always incredibly proud to see my name on the cover.'

'Which is a relief given you still have twenty boxes of unsold copies at home in the garage, my darling,' said Howard, earning himself a black look from his wife which grew blacker when he lent across to Legs and whispered. 'Not a patch on Jean Poole's pamphlet.'

'I'm sure both are very good reads,' she said vaguely, glancing along the table and noticing that Conrad had laid down his spoon and was fumbling in a strange way beneath the tablecloth. Opposite him, Kizzy's chair was empty, the soup barely touched. Legs' first illogical thought was that the redhead must have dropped her napkin as an excuse to dive beneath the table where she was currently either biting her boss's ankle or performing a nefarious act. But that hardly rang true in the light of the emotional reunion she'd just witnessed. She had a chilly feeling of déjà vu.

As Conrad pushed back his chair slightly, she spotted his BlackBerry on his lap and realised he was reading a message. She knew immediately it wasn't good news; all the veins were sticking up on his neck and his thumb was scraping the little device's touchpad as urgently as a bankrupt with a scratch-card as he scrolled down. Moments later, he made a polite apology to his hostess then hurried around the table to summon Piers Fox before both men left the room.

'You would definitely enjoy *Black Circles and Menstrual Cycles*, Allegra,' Yolande was enthusing. 'I'll look you out a copy. It's a marvellous read, isn't it Poppy?'

'Mmm, yes darling,' murmured Poppy, who had been smouldering at Hector throughout the conversation, neither giving a hoot that three dinner guests were now missing. 'Riveting stuff.'

Suitably encouraged, Yolande launched into the reason why the revolutionary Russian art movement had led her to associate its geometric shapes with female oppression.

Legs stopped listening. All she wanted to do was get to Eascombe Cove to meet Byrne. She felt increasingly sick with excitement and nerves. She barely noticed that Kizzy had reappeared and was staring straight at her, white-faced. She no longer cared what was going on with Conrad and his posse. Grateful that Édith's card-swapping meant she was sitting six places down from Francis and didn't have to look him in the eye, she counted down the seconds and mouthfuls until she was safe to leave the table.

Excusing herself straight after dessert, she bolted to a downstairs loo, where she drew deep, galvanising breaths and splashed her face with cold water before creeping back out. She half expected Francis to be waiting there for her, but to her relief he was still trapped in his seat at the table, politely listening to Yolande Hawkes as she told an interminable story about authenticating an unattributed Malevich painting. She knew she'd had no time to spare to make a run for it along the sea passage, but she had to retrieve Byrne's ring first.

Gathering up her coral skirts, she dashed across the main entrance hall towards the stairs, then slid to a horrified halt.

Kizzy was barring her way. She reminded Legs of a mermaid more than ever as she curled around the huge stone newel post like a siren on a rock, red hair spilling over her shoulders, face trembling. 'Don't abandon him, Legs.'

'Abandon who?' she bluffed.

'You are Tristan and Isolde! Liz and Hugh! Sartre and de Beauvoir, Brangelina! Please stay!'

'Who says I'm going anywhere?'

'I watched you just now at dinner.' Her pretty face softened with sympathy, reminding Legs how sweet and sensitive she could be. 'I know the signs. I ran away myself, remember?'

'Then you'll understand why I have to do this,' Legs shook her head, trying to pass, but Kizzy threw out a deep sea tentacle arm, barring her way.

'You mustn't leave the house tonight.'

'Why not?'

The green eyes blinked fearfully, brimming with emotion. Her voice dropped to an urgent whisper. 'My mother's a brilliant woman, but she's a total fantasist at times. She can't tell the difference between fiction and real life. Right now, she's totally out of control.'

Legs glanced in the direction of the dining room, praying that Yolande's Malevich anecdote was still going strong. She personally didn't care whether it was a fantasy or not as long as it kept Francis distracted.

'She believes her book is a work of total genius,' Kizzy went on, still barring the way. 'She lives and breathes it; she thinks it's *real*.'

'Well it was non-fiction,' Legs said distractedly, knowing she'd tuned out most of Yolande's monologue about art. 'Please let me past, Kizzy.'

'No!' She shook her head so violently that red Medusa curls whipped Legs across the face. 'You don't understand! I thought it was just Gordon she was targeting, and he's protected by anonymity, at least for a little bit longer. I had no idea until this evening that you were a part of it.' She took Legs' hands in hers, which were shaking and clammy. 'She's here right now, and she's determined to catch your attention.'

'Well, that yellow turban is certainly a show-stopper.'

Kizzy didn't appear to be listening as she rattled on. 'It's my fault for encouraging her. The book is brilliant; she read it to me. I know it has something truly magical about it. But now you've taken an interest, it's become dangerous.'

Legs hardly thought a slim volume of feminist criticism about paintings of squares and circles worthy of the fear staring at her from Kizzy's eyes right now.

'She'll stop at nothing,' she breathed. 'She knows all about the coast here, the cliff caves and this house, where to hide and where to run. She's been here in secret many times this past year, watching me as I walk and compose and sing. I never knew. She's always one step ahead. She's like a wild animal.'

Legs was amazed at Yolande's stealth; she'd never seen her without a twenty litre handbag, a technicolour pashmina and at least one mobile phone ringing non-stop.

'She calls it a "paperchase of clues full of hidden meanings",' Kizzy went on. 'I put everything in my poems, and she's so clever that she sees straight through the metaphors. We're just the same like that. She was the only one who guessed about Édith, who's written in every line.' Her green eyes were brimming. 'But she hates Édith almost as much as she hates Francis.'

At last, Legs thought she could guess what this was about. 'I won't betray you to your parents or anybody else, Kizzy, I promise. You two have every right to keep your relationship private. I adore Édith.'

She started to cry in true Kizzy fashion, with trails of snot and red, blotchy skin. 'Édith will never forgive me if you get hurt. She loves having you in this family. She has no idea who's really behind the letters and why. That's why I have to put a stop to it, don't you see? You mustn't leave. You mustn't leave!'

'The letters?' Legs froze, not liking the amount of bloodshot whites showing around Kizzy's wet eyes right now. With a jolt like a lead bar in the back, she remembered Francis saying that Kizzy had wanted to talk about the letters.

'They got terribly out of hand,' she was wailing, 'I know how frightening they must have been. I'm so sorry. There was really no harm meant; they were just supposed to set the mood.'

'I'd call a death threat quite harmful.' Legs started backing away. 'For mood setting, I prefer scented candles and background music.'

'But you asked for it! They were written with love and attention.'

Legs gaped at her, deciding that Kizzy was a very serious threat right now. If she was behind the letters, as seemed increasingly likely, then she had to get away from her, and fast.

She took a deft side-step, almost at the first stair tread. 'Just let me get past, Kizzy, and I'll be out of your hair for good.'

'You can't leave the house tonight!' Kizzy lunged forwards, Titian tresses lashing Legs in the face and blinding her so there was no getting out of her hair, let alone up the stairs. Two small but vice-like hands gripped at her wrists. 'My clairvoyant warned me this would happen. She turned the Death card in the tarot deck three times. I *will* stop you! It's for your own good.'

Seeing nothing but red mist and red curls, Legs struck out her arms in a maddened star jump that was probably more Village People than martial arts, but succeeded in loosening Kizzy's grip long enough for the red hair sea to part and her route past the manic mermaid to present itself.

Adrenalin coursed through her. Suddenly she felt like Julie Ocean on a mission. She knew exactly what to do to get away. Reaching up to her neck, she gripped the tight pearl choker and gave it a hard yank. A split second later, with satisfying hail-like thuds, five strings of liberated pearls were raining down around them.

'Oh, your beautiful necklace!' Kizzy dropped straight to her knees to start gathering them.

Pushing her way past, Legs scaled the stairs as fast as she could in the Moroccan pumps, which were now causing such cramps in her feet that she had to almost bunny hop up sideways. Halfway up the stairs she kicked them off and let the mousetraps of her curled toes spring out to sprint up the rest. Running the length of the landing, she searched around for the signet ring, but it was no longer there.

The door to Francis's old bedroom was open in front of her. There were loose pages scattered across the bed. Stepping inside, she saw the ring sitting on top of one of the six crumpled sheets of writing paper spread out there, the top page of a long, heartfelt letter. She recognised her own handwriting straight away.

Stifling a sob, she snatched up the pages and started to read.

My darling Francis, I have made such a huge mistake, I hardly know where to begin. You are the lost part of my soul. I love you with all my heart. To quote Donne—

'No!' she shrieked. 'Not Donne!'

It was worse than she'd thought.

Tears rising faster than floodwater on already saturated ground, she skimmed in horror through the sprawled pages, complete with her crossings out and mawkish prose. There were even asterisks and footnotes. And she suddenly realised what she was looking at. This wasn't the letter that she had sent to Francis a year earlier. These were the notes she'd made, her first rough copy, ten times as sentimental, mawkish and tear-stained. And Byrne had just read it.

It had been in the trunk in her bedroom at the Ealing flat, she realised in shock, buried and forgotten beneath photos and diaries. The only person who could possibly have got access to it was Kizzy.

But that hardly mattered because Byrne had gone. He'd gone.

She could hear raised voices as footsteps rang out from the main stairs. Francis was calling out her name.

Slotting the ring back on her little finger and closing her fist tightly over it, she raced out onto the landing and through the baize door to the back stairs before anyone spotted her. She knew, however blind her hope, that she must make it to the beach at Eascombe Cove.

Chapter 41

Still dressed in the coral ballerina shock-frock and turban, Legs stole down along the back stairs and through the Farcombe Hall service passages, this time slotting her bare feet into a pair of plastic gardening clogs lying amid the piles of boots in the rear lobby. Through the glass pane of the courtyard door, she could see the contingent of smokers gathered beneath a coach-light on the cobbles just a few feet away, Kizzy amongst them, her hair gleaming in red corkscrews, like Medusa sporting corn snakes.

She turned silently to the cellars, hooking down the key to the sea passage from the little candle alcove beside the door, clutching it tightly in her palm to stop her shaking fingers from dropping it.

Tripping down the stairs in the dark, she made it across the uneven flagstones and fumbled with the padlock. The wind was whistling up through the passage like a giant's mournful blows through a longhorn.

She'd only just managed to slot in the key when she heard voices behind her that made her dive into one of the narrow wine stores, leaving the key dangling.

The lights flashed on with a buzz of tungsten.

'Come quickly, before anyone spots we're gone . . .' It was Poppy, obviously three parts cut.

'What are we doing here?' came Hector's deep drawl, infused with several large cognacs.

'Darling man, I have a very little something to show you which I think you will like. I believe it is quite my best work to date.'

Nose-to-nose with a row of dusty claret bottles, Legs held her breath in disbelief, waiting for the deafening bellow of outrage when he spotted the stone statue and its miniscule manhood.

Instead, she heard a lot of loving cooing noises, some slurping and 'my darling!'

It was just as Byrne had said, she realised. Poppy had covered the grotesque with a fibreglass blob like all her other shapeless artworks, veiling her acerbic critique in gentle soft focus.

Amazed, but no less desperate to get away from the house, she edged back toward the passageway entrance, knowing it was out of the line of sight from Poppy's studio.

But the key had gone, the padlock pushed fast shut again.

She stared at it, disbelief and terror mingling in her blood like ice and fire as she tried to tell herself that there was a perfectly logical explanation. But the only one she could come up with was that somebody else was in the cellar besides herself and the canoodling Protheroes, and she had no intention of hanging about long enough to find out who.

Poppy and Hector appeared to be enjoying a very passionate reunion in the studio beyond the boiler room.

'Oh, my *big* honey bear.'

'Oh honeybee, little honeybee. Drink my nectar.'

With the sea passage now locked, Legs had no choice but to head back up to the house. As she crept hurriedly towards the cellar stairs again, she was certain she saw a shadow crossing behind her out of the corner of her eye. She swung around, but there was nothing to see.

The slurping noises were increasing, joined by grunting now.

'Oh my darling, don't stop!'

'What about our guests?'

'Let's make them go away.'

Legs started tip-toeing quickly up the stairs, her plastic clogs making sympathetic sucking noises to match those she was leaving behind.

'How can we make them go?' Poppy was asking plaintively. 'They'll be here for hours.'

'Not if we kill the lights.'

'We can't. Francis will be straight down here.'

'No he won't. Look – the cellar door key. I've locked it from the inside.'

Legs stifled a terrified bleat as she heard him striding loftily to the fuse cupboard, size thirteen footsteps hollow on the flagstones. A moment later the lights went off.

'Oh, Poppy.'

'Oh, Hector.'

Legs started cautiously down the steps again, wringing her sweaty hands together. She heard a metallic clink and Byrne's ring fell off again, skittling away in the darkness, and she closed her eyes in dismay. It was absolutely pitch dark. He ears were on elastic. Even though her heartbeat was becoming too thunderous to hear much, she distinctly made out light footsteps crossing the room in front of her.

She was now quite certain there was somebody else in the cellars alongside herself and the ageing lovers.

The door at the top of the stairs was rattled furiously: 'What's going on? Hey! Open up.' It was Édith, her drawling voice torn between amusement and irritation. 'It's dark up here, you know.'

Legs let out a little sob of relief.

'I warn you, we have a gun out here and we'll blow out the bloody lock!' Kizzy shouted, sounding frenzied.

The sound of a barrel cocking just above her head made Legs dive forwards, groping wildly for the wall, trying to picture the cellar's layout in her mind and plot the best place to take cover. But as she did so, she suddenly she remembered that there was another way out. The big doors at the far end of the studio were simply bolted from the inside as far as she recalled. She started to sneak towards Poppy and Hector, who seemed oblivious to the gun-toting on the other side of the cellar door,

'Oh yes, darling . . .'

'My big, *big* man . . .'

Legs was now so drenched in nervous sweat that her plastic shoes squelched as she made it past the boiler room and started to edge across the huge space. Here, a faint light filtered in through the high windows. She was almost at the doors, able to make out their big square bulk, the black smudges of the bolts.

Then, as she reached out towards them, she felt a cold, claw-fingered hand on her arm and a strange Gollum voice whispered 'Ring'.

Looking round, she found her face full of familiar curls and caught a glint of white-eyed zeal. Not stopping to think how Kizzy could be both here and at the top of the stairs behind a locked door simultaneously, she let out a scream that even threatened to pierce her own eardrums. Pure reflex made her lash back with her foot, plastic gardening shoe making contact with a shin. She heard a grunt of pain behind her as she threw herself at the doors and started pulling at the bolts.

Poppy was screaming now too, Hector bellowing. Above their heads, Francis joined in the fray yelling ever-louder for attention behind the cellar door.

As Legs slid the second of three bolts, the claw-like hand made a grab for her shoulder and a voice again gasped, 'Ring!'

'This is just too much!' She jabbed an elbow back, feeling the fingers lose their grip, then pulled the final bolt and wretched the big sliding doors open just as a gun went off overhead. The wind almost knocked her back in as it hit her with a smack in the face. She ducked her head and slip-slapped her way out into it, plastic shoes making obscene raspberries as she tore away towards the cover of the rose garden, diving in and out of the thorny arms, dress ripping, towards the tall rhododendrons and the gap she knew from childhood, three trunks along. Ducking through the low arch, she reached the back driveway not far from the gatepost with the secret cut-through to the coast lane.

Already she could hear feet hammering along the tarmac behind her.

'Ring! Ring!' called a breathless voice, making her think illogically of Abba.

Head now full of seventies pop that matched the beat of her own rushing blood, she crashed her hands against the stone wildly in search of the catch before finally feeling it yield so that she could push through and out onto the village lane, slamming the hinges hastily behind her before diving out of sight beneath the church-yard wall.

A long shadow appeared in the light cast from the house security lights, falling across the lane and sweeping left then right. Nobody could mistake that silhouette of untamed Pre-Raphaelite hair.

Kizzy clearly didn't know about the gatepost trick. Feet stamped and turned, the gate rattled on its hinges and then Legs heard the footsteps retreating.

She fought for breath for a moment, her weakened lungs already flayed to shreds. An owl shrieking overhead almost finished her off.

Flinching at every squeak and hiss from her plastic shoes, she crept along the lane beneath the church wall until she was safely behind the veil of weeping willows that marked the point where the little stream gurgled under its bridge from the village side and chased its way down to the sea. The wind was far too loud to hear it bubbling, the willow's branches thrashing like Medusa's snakes.

But one noise was clearly audible above the gale as, behind her, the church gate slammed with a whipcrack.

Legs ran, heedless of the stones and twigs gathering in her clogs and bruising her soles, almost blind with fear as she navigated by instinct along the sea lane, left at the ford, over the bridge and up towards the woods. Her legs were cramped with lactic acid, her body leaden with exhaustion, but sharp spikes of adrenalin still prodded her on.

At Gull Point she forked right towards the cliff path, tripping through bracken and gorse as she lost the track in the darkness, then fighting her way back onto rough packed stone again.

She could hear a car engine in the far distance, grinding and groaning as it careered over the bumps. Still she ran on, looking frantically around for the natural rock steps that led down to Eascombe Cove, certain they would appear behind a patch of heather at any moment. But then she reached the dogleg where the public path turned into the woods and she realised that she must have overshot them by a hundred metres or more. Ahead of her, the narrow half-hidden path along the cliff's top only led to the Lookout.

Not pausing to doubt her decision, she forged straight ahead and stumbled through the heather onto the Lookout path, ducking behind the gorses, thoughts accelerated by fear. She could seek refuge in the Lookout, she realised. Nobody knew it existed apart from her closest allies.

But even as she tripped along the half-buried path, wind threatening to batter her against the rocks, she heard the bracken breaking behind her.

The route to the Lookout was one way. Beyond it was nothing but sheer rock. The sea crashed mercilessly below, the cliff path beneath her feet was becoming ever more narrow and crumbly. The only way out would be to lure her assailant over the cliff first, gun or no gun.

Then a voice cried out behind her, 'Wait! My flip-flop's broken!'

Legs stalled.

'Your what?' she howled, swinging around to face her pursuer, prey to hunter.

The long red hair danced in the wind, cast pewter by the moon darting in and out of scudding clouds, pale face grey in the half light, whites of eyes glinting. She was wearing a bold print tunic dress Legs recognised from Next, matched with broken flip-flops. It was hardly Ninja.

'I just want to give you your ring back,' a strange voice pleaded. Part Joanna Lumley, part Diana Rigg, frightfully posh and wholly unexpected. 'And talk to you about my book.'

Legs gaped at Kizzy. Only this wasn't Kizzy. There was that chipped toothed smile again. There was no tight bandage dress. She'd matched the tunic with leggings and a crocheted shrug.

'Wh-what book?' Legs bleated.

'*The Girl Who Checked Out.*'

Legs racked her brains, which wasn't easy while balancing on a gale-lashed clifftop in a coral tutu dress that was threatening to billow her up into orbit, her lacerated lungs so starved of oxygen that five Kizzy lookalikes in Next tunics were dancing in front of her now.

Delia Meare, Legs realised, her adrenalin-filled head working at speed. Byrne had warned her that the author of *The Girl Who Checked Out* was quite potty but absurdly talented. When Legs had encouraged her to smarten up her submission for Conrad, Delia had offered to stage a 'live happening'. This must be it.

She was closing in. 'So you really liked my book?'

Legs stepped back. 'Yes. There's *lots* to like. I marked it for Conrad's attention before I – ah . . .' Even this dizzy from running too fast, she realised it was important not to let on she'd lost her job. 'Before I came here.'

'Clarissa's got all her talent from me, you know,' she was saying. 'Of course, you call her Kizzy. She's very like me, I think.'

'Doppelgangers.' Legs was far too stressed for detective-fast lateral thinking, yet rag-legged and buffeted on a clifftop, she couldn't stop her mind adding facts up like a windblown Jessica Fletcher. Delia Meare was a pen name for Liz Delamere. Kizzy had tried to warn her, but Legs had misunderstood her. It all made horrible sense. This was Kizzy's birth mother, Liz.

Just as she made this connection and remembered just how extraordinary she had found the manuscript with the supermarket trolleys full of dead redheads, she realised the multiple Kizzy lookalikes were disappearing into blackness.

'I say, are you OK?' asked the Joanna Lumley voice.

'Oh fuck, I'm fainting,' she realised, pitching sideways over the cliff edge.

Chapter 42

'Ohhhhhhhhhhhh fuuuuuuuuuuuuuuuuuu . . .' The wind whipped away her words.

Staring at the black swell of angry sea lashing its tongues around below, Legs knew it could be worse. She could be in there already, smashed against the rocks. Instead she was hanging upside-down over the cliff edge, hugging onto a rock for dear life while a mad stalker woman held her ankles.

'Nice underpants,' said the Joanna Lumley/Diana Rigg voice chattily, trying to keep her spirits up, although her grip was weakening by the second.

Legs told herself that was another thing to be grateful for. She may not have got to love Byrne with her body in this tragically foreshortened life, but at least he had saved her dying quite so ignobly by covering up her ladyhood in its last moments. And he was right; it was windy out. Her face was stripped bare, the sea spray salty on her lips even a hundred feet above the waves.

'Can you really not pull me up?' she pleaded with Joanna Lumley.

'I haven't the strength right now,' she panted, sweaty hands having already slipped their grip from knee to ankle. 'Spot of sciatica, you see. Help will come soon. It's bound to. I've got a good hold here now.' She tightened her manacle grip. 'I really didn't mean to scare you,' she apologised in her lovely, reassuring voice.

'Chasing me all this way in the dark was a bit extreme,' she said faintly. '*This* is a bit extreme.' She peered down at the sea again and hurriedly closed her eyes as her head went giddy, nausea rising.

'You dropped your ring in the cellars,' Liz explained kindly, then suddenly shifted, loosening her grip as she said, 'I've got it right here in my bum bag.'

'Don't let go! Really! It can wait!'

The ring appeared briefly in her eye line before landing hard against her shin as Liz grabbed at her legs again to stop her plummeting down.

'Clarissa has one just the same.'

'I know.' Legs could feel the ring edging down between Liz's hand and her leg.

'The Kelly crest.'

512

'Yes.' It was at the tips of Liz's fingers now, and she scrabbled to try to hold onto it.

'Her father is a Kelly.'

'You don't say?'

The ring was finally released and ricocheted down off Legs' knee to her tutu before spinning away to the sea far below.

'Oh God, I dropped it!' Liz howled, grip loosening dramatically.

'Well don't drop me!' Legs howled, hugging her jutting rock tighter.

The hold on her ankles tightened. 'Clarissa's father was such a sweet man, and so grateful. Poppy was terribly cruel to him after his accident. Terribly cruel to me too. But she's always been kind to Clarissa.'

Legs opened one eye: 'Brooke Kelly is Kizzy's father?' Then she closed her eye again, deciding she didn't much care in the face on imminent death. Let Byrne and Kizzy unite in sibling grief at my funeral, she thought wildly, wind-whipped tears running down through her eyebrows.

'I'm not supposed to tell people,' Liz pointed out. 'Poppy made me swear not to say who fathered my baby, not even to Kizzy. My sister has never forgiven me for seducing her husband; I turned him from martyr too satyr in her mind.' The truth was spilling out like surreal Last Rites.

Both Legs' eye snapped open again. 'Poppy's your *sister*?'

'I'm not allowed to talk about that either,' she said kindly. 'Not that anybody's ever asked, but you must *promise* not to blab. All I can tell you is that Daddy preferred chaps, so Mummy sought solace elsewhere. Oh listen, somebody's coming.'

Legs let out a sob of relief as she heard voices on the cliff path beyond her feet, a man's shout louder than any other, calling her name. That noble, courtly voice she knew so well. Francis; her old-fashioned hero, still true and fair, however many times she broke his poor heart.

'We're here!' she shrieked. 'Here! Francis! Arghhhhhhhh!'

The grip on her ankles slipped yet further, and Joanna Lumley's voice hissed. 'Loathsome man. I watched him at a meeting once, sounding like a Tory MP lecturing the underclass, and it was all I could do not to hurl eggs. Don't let him near me!'

Legs closed her eyes. 'Please can you just let him rescue me, Liz, then you two can settle your political differences afterwards?'

But Liz was cocking her head as she listened through the wind to the urgent conversation now taking place just a few feet away.

'Call the police. Hostage situation. Psycho. Stalker. Just found out she's my ex-girlfriend's mother currently holding my fiancé over a cliff. Been sectioned more than once. That's right. Helicopters, dogs, the works. I'll try to keep her talking, but I think we're looking at minutes to go here.'

The blood that had rushed to Legs' head in the time she'd been upside-down now swirled and pounded through her brain as she visualised the moments leading up to her end caught by helicopter camera while the Sea Rescue team battled vainly to help her. It would no doubt be a huge YouTube hit. There she would be, dangling upside-down off a cliff, wearing men's underpants and a hideous coral dress with its great ballerina's tutu of nets now blowing inside out, her awful huge thighs and fat knees on full display to the world as the worse of legacies.

She spat out a mouthful of hair. At least the ghastly turban had fallen off when she fainted, no doubt swirling into the sea below. She peered down at the rocks forlornly, acquainting herself with her fate, and then blinked away the sea spray and wind in astonishment.

There was a figure moving about down there.

Up above, Francis was edging closer again. 'Liz – *Liz*,' his voice deepened with false affection. 'Let's stop all this nonsense.'

'Back off!' Liz screamed.

'Agh!' Legs felt herself slip further down, her grip slipping from the rock, hands scrabbling vainly for a hold, but she was swinging from the overhang with nothing but her net skirts within reach now. She could see the ledge below her where Byron the terrier had landed that first day she'd come back to Farcombe and he'd scrabbled after a seagull over the cliff side. The little shelf ran along the cliff·beneath the overhang, just beyond her reach, but was far too narrow to hope to land upon if Liz let go, which looked increasingly likely as Francis inched towards them waving a bright torch about.

'Liz, I can help you. We all want to help . . .'

The grip slipped further. 'Horrible, bullish, boring man,' she started muttering feverishly. 'No good for my girl. None of them are. Bloody men. Full of lies.'

Getting dizzier by the second, Legs was watching the figure on the rocks below start to free-climb the cliff face. She quite forgot all her detective story advice to keep one's captor talking. She just stared, lacy skirt nets billowing against her face, heart in her throat, head swirling.

'Liz – Liz,' Francis was trying again, now only a few feet away, yet shouting loudly into the wind. 'It's Kizzy I love, not Legs. Trust me. I just don't want to see this lovely young woman here die!'

'No. Francis,' Legs protested weakly, head swimming through layers of dizziness now. 'You've got it all wrong! Don't say that—'

'Be quiet, darling, I'm dealing with this. Now don't worry, Liz – I'm not going to make any sudden moves; I have a broken toe. Let's all be sensible about this. In the words of Kipling, "Hold on when there is nothing in you except the Will which says to them 'Hold on!'"'

Legs closed her eyes. Liz was right. He was a horrible, bullish, poetry-quoting bore and he did sound like a Tory MP.

'Now Liz, you are going to keep on holding tight to Legs' legs,' he went on. 'And I am going to come alongside you veeery slowly and take hold of Legs' legs.'

The blood rushing around her head and the adrenalin on full choke was playing tricks on her as she started to giggle. It all sounded so silly, all those legs.

'Stop that, darling,' Francis's voice was rigid with tension, making him sound like Basil Fawlty once more. 'You're not helping.'

With great effort, she stopped giggling, hysterical panic and hysterical laughter all muddled up. Her eyes raked the cliff below her for the climber, but she could see nothing. It must have been an illusion, brought about by the fitful, desperate head-rush of certain death.

'Right, Liz,' Francis had edged much closer, his voice much louder. 'I am going to—'

'Get back!' she screeched, swinging around so that Legs swayed sideways too, net skirts catching on the rocks and bringing down a shower of loose scree.

'Oh please, Lord, no,' she whimpered, and then almost passed out as a firm arm steadied her shoulders and she gazed out through layers of net to see Byrne standing on the ledge beneath the overhang, his upside-down head level with hers. He pressed his fingers to his lips.

'"If you can fill the unforgiving minute—"' Francis droned on, quoting Kipling again.

'Will you shut up!' Liz screamed at him. 'I can't think straight.'

Legs let out a moan of fear as she slipped yet lower, but this time two arms had her safely in their grip

As strong as Nureyev whirling Margot Fonteyn overhead, he lifted her away from Liz's grip and slid her down one of his broad shoulders, turning her the right way up and landing her lightly on the ledge beside him where she swayed groggily, blood rushing away from her head again. His arm reached out like a fairground safety bar, pressing her back against the rock-face beneath the overhang.

'Oh fuck,' came a shocked voice from above, 'I've just dropped her.'

Francis's wail of grief could have graced a repertory production of *Lear* as he stood on the edge of the cliff screaming at the sea. It was existential.

'It was an accident!' Liz was shrieking too, barely audible over

Francis's screams and the rush of the wind. 'It wasn't my fault! It was an accident. That poor girl.'

Francis let out another howl.

For a terrifying moment, Legs thought he was going to push Liz over and possibly even jump himself, but he seemed to gather himself together remarkably quickly and, as sirens and blue lights raced towards the clifftop, he sobbed: 'You are right, of course. I saw it all. It was an accident. A tragic accident. The police must be told straight away,' his voice tapered away as he limped off to greet the emergency services pursued by a sobbing Liz.

Legs' eyes bulged in fury. He hadn't even looked over the edge to check if she was hanging there. She knew he was pretty phobic about the sight of blood and gore – and seeing a lover's body smashed on the rocks would be a sight no man would willingly endure – but surely he could have tried? He was a total coward.

She turned her head to look at Byrne, seeing his big, dark eyes like two clifftop braziers. Again, he held a finger to his mouth and then nodded to her far side, where the ledge widened as it ran up towards the cliff's edge at the Lookout.

Swallowing in terror, she started to shuffle along sideways, gripping tightly on to his arm. Together they edged twenty yards to a point where it was possible to turn around and clamber onto the plateau of windswept scrub and heather directly beside the old hermit's cave.

Chapter 43

Legs embraced solid ground with such passionate relief that she half expected to sink into it and take root there. Eventually, she let Byrne prize her up into a sitting position, and he stooped down to pick her up, carrying her into the cave.

'Thank you thank you thank you!' she sobbed, clinging to him. 'You saved my life.'

He settled her down on one of the rickety chairs and then stepped back, raking his fingers into his hair which had been whipped wild by the sea-spray and wind.

It was sheltered from the wind inside the Lookout, and very dark, just a faint thread of moonlight stealing in between black outs of cloud cover. Byrne started pacing around, still supremely edgy.

'What is this place?' He looked at the old furniture and effects, eyes squinting into the darkness.

'An old hermitage. We used to come here as kids.'

'You and Francis?'

'All of us.' She was starting to regain her breath at last, her heartbeat gradually coming down, but her teeth rattled like castanets at a fiesta and she wasn't sure how much longer she could last without a large brandy and a warm hug. She stood up unsteadily. 'We must go out there now and tell them I'm OK.'

'Why?' he snapped.

'They think I'm dead!'

There was a pause and Byrne seemed to gather himself together, shaking his head briefly, clearing his thoughts.

'Of course.' He stepped back into the shadows. 'You must go to Francis.'

She picked her way cautiously towards the entrance then turned back to him. 'Aren't you coming?'

'Not right now.'

'You must, please, Byrne. I need you. I can't . . .' Her eyes filled with tears as she looked from him to the cliff path. 'I'm scared.'

'Hey.' He rushed forwards to wrap his arms around her. 'Hey. Shh. Poor little one, poor Heavenly Pony.'

She clung onto him gratefully. She could hear his heart pounding in his chest, impossibly fast. The warmth of his body against hers gave her strength, and she curled more tightly into it, listening to his breathing, her teeth no longer chattering as her hands reached up to his face, fingers exploring the sharp angle of his jaw and the soft hollows beneath his ears.

He trapped her hands with his, gently pulling them away and holding them together under her chin as though in prayer, his eyes blazing into hers through the darkness.

Aware of her bare fingers, she blurted. 'I dropped your ring – well Delia Meare did. I'm sorry. I'll buy you another one, I promise.'

'Delia Meare was the woman on the cliff?' His brows creased, trying to place the familiar name.

'She wrote *The Girl Who Checked Out*,' she explained, still getting to grips with it herself.

Byrne took a moment to make the connection, then looked stupefied. 'Oh God, I sent that to you,' he remembered. 'Strange correspondent; brilliant plot.'

'She's Kizzy's mother. Didn't you see the likeness?'

'Funnily enough I wasn't studying her too closely.' He looked up at her sharply from beneath his curling black brows. 'Why would Kizzy's mother want to kill you?'

'The poison pen letters have been a sort of misguided attempt to capture our attention including Gordon's – yours – and Conrad's.'

'I know it's hard to get representation these days, but surely that's a bit excessive?'

'I just hope she doesn't try the same stunt with the Booker judges.' She leaned closer into him, desperate to be hugged. She couldn't stop shaking, her teeth chattering and her body uncoordinated.

He let go and stepped away, his forehead creased with discomfort. 'I'm going back to Ireland tonight.'

'No!' She reached out for him again, but he crossed his arms defensively in front of his chest.

Then suddenly, in technicolour, high definition, 3D flashback, she remembered what she'd discovered before her imagination became so overactive that she'd started running around the cellars, lanes and clifftop in a panic, imagining a murderer on her tail. 'Oh Christ, Byrne, the letter!'

Face immediately shuttered, he looked away. 'Forget about it.'

'I wrote it over a year ago, but it was never intended to be sent. That is, I *did* send a version, probably almost as bad only with fewer spelling mistakes and no Donne, but Francis never acknowledged that one, and then this—'

'I said forget it! I should never have read it. It's your private business.'

'It's not!' she implored desperately. 'I love you! *Gráim thú*. Let's run away together like we planned. Let's live for the moment. I love *you*.'

But he was a stone wall of self protection, his head low and shaking slowly, so that all she could see was his lovely, wild black hair in thick heroic tufts on his crown.

'"I love you",' he quoted bitterly, and she remembered the moment he'd told her that he loved her under the lamp-post and she'd believed him even though he was only teaching her a lesson. 'You write it eighteen times in your letter to Francis.'

She closed her eyes as she realised he'd counted them up while she had been counting down the minutes through dinner.

'Nineteen if you count the quote from Donne's "Batter My Heart",' he added.

And suddenly Legs realised she was talking to Gordon Lapis now, just as she had been that night walking back to the Book Inn. Paranoid, infuriating, hyper-critical Gordon, her old friend and sparring partner, so clever and so contrary. The two halves of Byrne coexisted so closely under his skin. To kiss one was to taste the other, the bitter skin on the sweetest fruit.

'I know you've written things you regret,' she said hoarsely. 'I've heard you say it.'

'But I can't take them back,' he replied coldly, 'What's written, once read, is like ink in skin to me. You can't undo that, however much you long to go back and change it.'

'Well, it's not like that for me! It's never been like that for me. My love-life might be short on emotional damage compared to yours, but its annals are still layered with Tippex and eraser crumbs, and if I could spend life leaning on the backspace key I would. Unlike you, my writing isn't a matter of public record. When I want my words to be published, I'll get another tattoo, ink on skin.'

'Take my advice and stick to shapes,' he muttered, 'or hire a copy-editor first. Your spelling's atrocious.'

She knew his flippancy was born of hurt. He was more Gordon than ever. But knowing it did nothing to quell her rage. Her voice was climbing scales of panic: 'That letter you read was never meant to be *read*. I should have destroyed it a year ago.'

'Live for the moment, live with the consequences.'

'But don't ever die young wearing men's underpants,' she said shakily.

He shrugged, turning away. 'It worked for Ptolemy.'

'Why did you kill him?'

'I figured if I had to sacrifice my life for him, he could return the favour.'

'So you made up a rule saying he loses his immortality if he falls in love?'

'I just wanted him gone.'

'You must really mistrust love to want to publicly destroy it like that.'

'That's right.' He steepled his fingers over his nose, and looked across at her. 'I built an invincible boy and killed him for love. What a fucking waste.'

Legs shook her head angrily. 'He doesn't die for love, Gordon. He dies because he can't *live* with love. You won't let him. That's the fucking waste.'

He stared at her for a long time, taking this in.

'People can hurt you when you love them.'

'Like Poppy hurt you by running away?'

'This isn't about Poppy. I only came back here to teach Hector a lesson.'

'I don't believe that. This has been all about Poppy from the very start.'

'Hector screwed up my father's life!'

'And I'm sure you entertained ideas of throwing punches in retaliation, humiliating him, seeing him financially ruined and sexually undermined, all of which you've achieved in some way or another, but Poppy has always been your primary target. You wrote Ptolemy for her in the first place, Byrne. It's so plain to see, and so heartbreaking. It's the longest and saddest letter an abandoned child could write home to his mother, a story about a boy who can never grow old and can never love. This is all about her; Ptolemy is *all* about Poppy. He's you as a child, isn't he? He's your avenging angel and you brought him back to his mother after all these years, only to kill him in front of her eyes. If that isn't revenge, I don't know what is.'

His eyes blazed from his face. There was a yawning silence before he spoke.

'I can't change it,' he hissed. 'It's out there now.'

'And your fans are heartbroken. They're in outcry. They blame you for murdering their favourite hero; no matter that you created him in the first place. You just shot your career to hell days before you're due to go public. But what the hell – you upset your mother, which is all this was ever really about, so you got what you wanted. Now you can go home to Ireland and bury your head under a Bushmills.'

'I am not ashamed to stand by my work.'

'You don't regret it! That's great! You should get it tattooed on your chest in Gaelic: "I killed Ptolemy Finch and I don't regret it." Hollywood will rewrite the end, but Gordon Lapis could never compromise his artistic integrity and admit he got it wrong. What's written, once read, is like ink on skin to you, after all. Remind me to get "Allegra requires discipline to achieve

522

amelioration" tattooed on my buttocks. It was in my school report at thirteen. Once written . . .'

'You should go into psychoanalysis,' he muttered. 'And your arse is too small for that tattoo.'

'Never do a job you can't spell; the same goes for tattoos. How about "take firmly in hand"?'

'I'm sure Francis will attend to that.' He turned sharply away.

'He doesn't like tattoos.' She wanted to weep, knowing that fear had made her attack when all she longed to do was throw her arms around him and beg him to take her with him. But he was a wall of defensiveness now, ten brick courses higher than before for her onslaught.

He moved further away. There was a long pause. Then she heard a piece of paper being unfolded.

'There's a reply.'

'What?'

'To your letter. There was a reply with it. It's here. I was going to put it in a bottle and throw it out to sea, but I guess it's quicker to hand-deliver it on his behalf. You two don't want to wait another year for the post to deliver, after all.' He handed her the page. 'He writes beautifully. Better than I ever could.'

'I can't read it.' She thrust it back.

'Here – use this as a torch.' He reached through his pockets and pulled out a lighter; as it sparked, she recognised the big Zippo from the charred frock coat.

'Thanks.' She took it from him and thrust the paper over it.

'What are you *doing*?' He whipped it away from her as it caught light, damping out the flames against the wall. 'What is it with you and setting light to things?'

'I said I can't read it.' The words came through gritted teeth.

'After I've gone, then,' he snapped, pressing the lighter into her hands followed by the letter. 'Then burn it for all I care. I almost did. But you must read it first. I'm sorry I misjudged Francis. I had no idea of the strength of feeling you two share. I should have listened that first night we talked, when you said you still loved him. It's his ring you should be wearing by now. You were right to cast mine out to sea.'

'I don't! You shouldn't. That is, I – I should really talk to him, yes. He thinks I'm dead, after all. He deserves to know the truth about everything.'

He nodded, turning away.

'Don't leave tonight,' she begged again. 'Wait until I've spoken with him.'

He shook his head. 'Second thoughts are never as original as first ones.'

'Of course they are! Like second love and second chances.' Her throat was so clogged with tears, she gasped out the words as though drowning.

'You once told me sexual chemistry needs to be built slowly, and you were right. Ours simply blew up in our faces.'

'It's more than that.'

He shook his head. 'You're right about me too. My canon is pure self-defence, full of self-pitying hubris. I've turned love into a punishment. Now I'm about to start my life sentence, so I don't want visitors.'

'Can I write to you?'

'I'd rather you didn't.'

Mortified by his coldness, Legs pushed past him out onto the cliff path.

As she disappeared into the night, she passed Fink the basset hound, who had clearly endured a laborious and windy time navigating his way up the steps from the cove. His ears were blown inside-out now, as he rejoined his master with an ecstatically loud greeting, panting from his exertions between happy howls. What Legs couldn't hear over the wind was the dog letting out a frustrated whine as he was forced to retrace his steps back along the cliff path alongside his anxious master to monitor her precarious, tearful progress back to firm ground.

Ears still flapping, he did as he was told, watching mournfully as she disappeared between the gorse bushes.

Just for a moment, Leg paused in her tracks and listened.

'*Gráim thú.*' She could have sworn she heard the words on the wind. But as she looked back, she saw Byrne turning away to take the track down to the village without a backward glance.

Legs stumbled along the cliff path, wobbling around on her oversized plastic shoes on the uneven footing with faster steps until she was running, netting skirts flying up into her face, out over the bracken and heather, across the tufty grass tussocks and rock boulders, through the pointed promontories of woodland to the parkland and the caring, professional arms of the emergency services.

Then she ground to a halt. There were no flashing blue lights, no reflective silver stripes or uniformed officers, nor any red and white tape; just a big black sky, white stars, and the lion's share of a cowardly moon hiding its blushes behind the gathering storm-clouds.

She turned in a slow circle, hearing nothing but the wind and the sea.

The weather was on the turn. The wind and the sea were playing together like tussling boys now, angry waves catching elbows and skins of rocks while the foam smiles grew nastier and the howls and hisses became bullying.

Legs looked across at the hall, its lights beaming once more through those deep set, uneven windows, a landlocked frigate fighting its wars below decks. Were the occupants all lined up in the drawing room being grilled by a West Country police detective with a creamy accent and a wily smile, she wondered, knowing she should go there straight away and declare herself alive and well. Yet she had no desire to offer deliverance to Francis yet. Whatever he had written in his unfinished reply to her eighteen 'I love yous' had just stolen Byrne away from her. The letter was still in her hand along with the petrol lighter.

It was far too squally where she stood for flamelit reading. The boisterous sea was still slinging insults up at the wind, blowing raspberries as its tide turned, and getting long wolf whistles through the rocks in return.

She remembered Édith jokingly comparing her to Rebecca, whom Maxim de Winter had let die at sea with such relief. For a moment she longed to see Farcombe engulfed in flames like Manderley, but it remained stubbornly twinkly and fairytale-castle rugged, about as combustible as Battenburg cake.

Legs changed her mind abruptly about going there. In a toss-up between marzipan castles and gingerbread cottages, the latter won all the way. She needed her mother's sweet refuge.

Kicking off her shoes and picking them up, she diverted off the track onto the mossiest grass to cool her aching feet, and padded into the woods towards Spywood Cottage.

Chapter 44

There were cars parked three deep on the track in front of Spywood Cottage's gate when Legs arrived. She recognised her mother's runabout, the Farcombe Estate Land Rover and, to her surprise, her sister's sensible saloon. Lights glowed from all the downstairs windows.

She peered in through the little casement window beside the door. An emotional gathering was taking place at the scuffed table over a pot of tea and a rapidly emptying brandy bottle.

Sitting with Lucy and Ros with his back to her, Francis's big shoulders were shaking. He rarely betrayed emotion, but he was openly weeping.

She was suddenly reminded of her most self-indulgent, morbid fantasies as an angst-ridden teenager, watching her unappreciative family and friends mourning penitently at her graveside. The reality was not so satisfying.

Before she went in, she unfolded the letter to read in the spilled light.

'Oh no no.' She felt tears bubble up instantly as she took in the pure emotion and poetry. Byrne was right. This was written exquisitely. It was breathtaking. It was a letter to fall in love to, to fall back in love, to stay in love. It was a letter written by a man who understood love.

She reread the first paragraph, brows curling at the familiarity of the words.

Squinting to see, she clicked the petrol lighter alight and reread a few lines in its orange glow.

There wasn't a single phrase of Francis's own on the page. It was *all* quotations, mostly from Joyce, cut and patched together like one of the music compilation tapes he'd made in the nineties; some *Dubliners* here, *Portrait of the Artist as a Young Man* there, a splash of *Ulysses* elsewhere amid riffs of Eliot and Donne.

She sagged back against the wall and closed her eyes with a groan. Byrne had no idea what he'd just read, she realised. How could he ever compete with the beauty of Joyce in montage? Joyce was a master; he felt through his pen like others feel through mere mortal nerve endings. Francis, meanwhile, was an emotional parrot. She opened her eyes and looked at it again miserably.

A ball of flames glowed back.

'Aggh!'

The crackling inferno in her hand made her panic and throw letter and lighter up in the air. While one caught the drooping, parched clematis leaves and ignited them, the other landed heavily at her feet to start flame-throwing its wind-dried roots. Slotting her feet back into the clogs, Legs stamped out the blaze underfoot before hurriedly damping out the other against the porch wall with the doormat.

Amazingly, when she looked back in through the window, nothing had changed. Her mother and sister were still hand-wringing and eye-dabbing; Francis's shoulders were still shaking. Only the level of the brandy bottle had gone down.

When Legs pushed open the door, the universal intake of breath that greeted her seemed to suck the air from the room. The smoke surrounding her added significantly to the impact, along with her smouldering plastic shoes.

'Hi.' She smiled anxiously. 'I'm here. Really sorry if you were worried.'

Her sister and mother both screamed. Francis just sat with his mouth open, staring at her.

'I'm not dead,' Legs said brightly. 'Isn't that great?'

Ros screamed again. Lucy burst into tears.

'Is there any more tea in that pot?' Legs asked apologetically.

When nobody answered, she made her way to the kitchen to fetch a mug.

Minutes later, everybody was talking at once. Lucy, crying with delight, was arguing with Ros about whether Legs should go to hospital, and so completely muddled up in her excitement that she was trying to make fresh tea by putting bags in the sugar crock and pouring boiling water on top.

Refusing to let go of Legs' hand, Francis managed to be both defensive and contrite at the same time, expressing loud amazement that his 'extensive search' of the cliffs hadn't found her and then taking all the credit for wrestling Liz Delamere away from her hostage.

'I fell off onto a ledge,' she explained.

'Thank goodness for that.' He was too busy exonerating himself to really care for practical detail. 'The police are questioning Liz at the hall now. Kizzy's there too. They'll both go away for a bloody good stretch, I'll hazard.'

'No! We must go there to explain!'

'It can wait.' He knitted his fingers lovingly through hers, raising them to his lips to kiss. Spotting her crustily burnt thumb, he hastily diverted towards her little finger.

Legs snatched her hand away. 'But Liz really did nothing wrong, Francis. I overreacted.'

'She broke into the cellar via the sea passage.'

'I left the key in the lock.'

'Then she tripped all the lights and locked the door from the inside,' he pointed out, adding: 'Why were you down in the cellars by the way?'

'You know it wasn't Liz who locked the cellar door,' Legs cleared her throat, glancing at her mother, but Lucy was distractedly pouring boiling water into the tea caddy now. 'I'd dropped my ring; she wanted to give it back.'

'She chased you down to the cliffs!'

'Yes, and when I fainted, she caught me. She saved my life really.'

'*I* saved your life. What ring? Not my mother's I hope?'

'No. And what d'you mean, *you* saved my life? You thought I was dead just a minute ago,' her voice was rising uncontrollably. She suddenly felt hysterical, tears mingling with laughter in a giddy, helium mix.

'You really *must* go to hospital to get checked out,' Ros was insisting bossily as she waved her phone about in search of a signal. 'You're obviously still in shock and might well have been concussed. I'll call you an ambulance.'

'I'll drive her,' said Francis firmly.

'You've had at least a gill of brandy. So have I.'

'I'll take her,' Lucy was putting teabags in the milk jug.

'You polished off the rest of the bottle, Mum,' Ros snapped, holding her phone out of the window, the howling wind knocking all the pot plants from the sill.

'She needs to stay here with her mother looking after her!' Lucy bustled up to the table with a teapot brimming with boiling water but no teabags.

'I'll be looking after Legs at the hall,' Francis clutched her hand even more tightly.

'I'm honestly fine,' Legs insisted, overwhelmed by weariness. 'What I could really do with right now is a bath. And somebody really had better tell the police that I'm not dead. Are they searching the cliffs?'

'They said they were waiting until daylight,' Francis shook his head. 'The wind's just too dangerous to risk launching a boat or flying the chopper, and more storms are forecast.'

'I'll get the water running,' Ros offered, still holding her phone up in hope of a signal as she headed into the little room beneath the stairs.

Lucy bustled back into the kitchen recess and re-emerged with a pot that now contained hot water, teabags, milk, sugar and several biscuits all ready mixed. 'You can drive up to the hall to talk to the police while Legs is having a bath, can't you Francis? They can hardly arrest you for drink driving on your own private roads. Tell them Legs can't possibly speak with them until the morning. But tell Hector *I* must speak with *him* urgently.'

Francis reluctantly limped to the door, towing Legs behind him out onto the porch, where he covered her hand with both his and held it against his chest. 'I'll be back as soon as I can,' he promised. 'The police will want to talk to you about Byrne too, but I'm sure it's just a formality.'

'Why do they want to know about him?' She asked, colour mounting on her cheeks. 'It was Liz who wrote those letters.'

'The Lucian Freud nude is missing.'

'I thought you sold it to Vin Keiller-Myles?'

'I did. He was going to take it home with him tonight, but when I went upstairs to fetch it, it had disappeared. It must have been taken when the lights went out.'

Legs' laughed incredulously. 'Why blame Byrne?'

'He had access and motive. Now he's disappeared too. It all adds up'

'What "motive"?'

'Money, of course.'

'He doesn't need money!' She bit her lip, realising she mustn't betray Byrne. 'Are you sure it hasn't just fallen off the wall? It could be a Freudian slip.'

He gave her a withering look, but then his handsome blue eyes creased with amusement, 'Darling Legs, you are my light relief at the end of the tunnel. How could I survive without you? I knew my mother's ring would be safe with you.' To her horror, he stooped to kiss her. She kept her mouth tight shut and wriggled quickly away.

'I need that bath.'

'Of course you do. You must feel like hell. I will dedicate tonight to you, as I will dedicate the rest of my life. I love you. Now don't you dare go away.' Kissing her nose, forehead, each cheek and chin before blowing her a kiss from his fingers, he turned to go, then turned back. 'Why *were* you in the cellars when Liz came up through the sea passage, by the way?' he asked again.

'I was checking on progress on Poppy's sculpture,' she bluffed, emotion suddenly wiring her jaws so tight they hollowed like pricked balloons.

'Much better, isn't it?' he smiled fondly. 'No idea why she tried for that awful Scarfe caricature stuff. Abstract naive is definitely her limit.' Nodding farewell, he headed off into the gathering storm, Land Rover engine roaring louder than the approaching thunder.

Legs waved him off with relief, wondering if it might have been preferable to tumble over that cliff after all. A life without Byrne was unbearable. She slumped down on the porch step of Spywood, her little haven of comfort, and hugged the oak upright of its porch.

She had to be strong and tell Francis there was no future. But while dumping her motherless, romantic, scholarly first love once looked like misfortune, to dump him twice looked like deliberate cruelty. She raked away mounting tears with her palms.

Now the Land Rover tail-lights had disappeared down the tracks, Lucy appeared at her side on the Spywood doorstep. She was proffering a vast brandy, having raided the Christmas surplus which was stored in the trunk below the stairs. When Legs shook her head, she had a large swig herself. 'Thank God he's gone, you're alive and you're here. Oh Legs, darling.' She dropped her voice to a whisper and sat down beside her. 'Lucian Freud's nude's upstairs.'

It took Legs' overwrought mind a few moments to comprehend what her mother was saying. 'The painting's here?'

Lucy nodded, looking frantic. 'Hector took it – it was hanging up amid my watercolours in the kitchen when Ros arrived this evening. I only spotted it there because she accused me of painting disgusting filth, but I recognised it straight away, of course. It used to hang downstairs by the old butler's pantry at Farcombe, and Hector would get guests to guess whether it was genuine or not.'

'Is it?'

'I very much doubt it,' Lucy shook her head, art restorer judgement reigning supreme despite her panic. 'But Hector never let on, and I have no doubt the Protheroes think it is.'

'Francis has just sold it to Vin Keiller-Myles for a fortune,' Legs told her, the truth about Farcombe's financial shortfalls spilling out.

'Then it must be a fake. Why else would Hector smuggle it here? Vin's bound to want it authenticated. Hector knows I always liked it enormously. It was no doubt intended to be a noble parting gesture before he goes back to Poppy. But you can imagine the trouble it will cause if it's discovered here.'

'Why didn't you just tell Francis?'

'We were rather distracted by the thought that you'd just gone over a cliff.' She started to snivel as the horror of that struck her afresh. 'Now I just want it gone. It's another reminder of Hector's wild flights of fancy.'

'I'll get rid of it,' Legs reached across to hug her shoulders. 'Francis need never know. If the police really are involved, it must get returned to Farcombe as soon as possible.'

'But Hector will get in such terrible trouble.'

'It's Francis who sold it,' Legs muttered. 'He'd do anything to save Farcombe.'

'Whereas his father would still gamble it away on a whim,' Lucy sighed, patting her daughter's arm. 'He was always sending me into William Hill in Bude with a roll of fifties.'

'Do his bets still all have musical names?'

'How did you know that?'

Legs told her about discovering Hector's old system, the winnings going to charity. Then she found herself confessing that she had worked it all out in a frantic attempt to persuade Byrne his father hadn't fallen victim to Hector's cruelty, but rather his legendary and over-effusive philanthropy. 'Of course, Hector stealing Poppy away from Brooke is rather harder to forgive.'

'How he could have a son as upstanding and trustworthy as Francis still amazes me,' Lucy eyed her closely.

'Yes, Francis lays down the law while his father lays bets and wives.'

'Poor darling Legs,' Lucy gripped her daughter's hand on her shoulder. 'There was me thinking that you were so lucky to have the son all these years when I was denied the father, but the sins of both have been waged against us. You don't want to marry Francis at all, do you?'

'No.' She hung her head.

Lucy squeezed her hand, 'We all love Francis, of course, and he's family to us, but you're both young. You'll both find—'

'Don't say it. It's already happened.' Legs tipped her head against her mother's shoulder and watched lightning flashing like a distant rave party over the horizon.

'Jago,' Lucy sighed, 'the man with barbed wire round his soul.'

She nodded, breathing in her mother's familiar scent. 'I've lost my heart to somebody who thinks love is a weapon of mass destruction.'

'I guessed as much when I saw you together. Such a clever man,' Lucy sighed again. 'Do you want to talk about it?' She was trying very hard not to slur her words, but it was obvious she was struggling to keep focus.

'Not particularly,' she apologised. 'I think only a bath can take my tears right now.'

'Your father always says that you carry more guilt in your shoulders than the rest of the Norths put together, including your God-fearing sister and all the Catholics on my mother's side. He used to call you our Madonna child, do you remember?'

'That's because I sang "Like a Virgin" into my hairbrush in front of the mirror, Mum.'

'Was it?'

They stood up, arm in arm, and went inside. Ros had been putting the finishing touches to a bath brimming with Hector's muscle soak bubble bath. She'd even lit a few candles, and placed a freshly brewed mug of tea between the taps.

While Lucy reeled cheerfully back to the newly opened brandy bottle, Legs stifled a yawn and lent on the door frame as she watched her sister pulling clean towels from the laundry cupboard. 'This is such heaven. Thank you.'

'It's not every day we get you back from the dead,' Ros said chirpily, testing the temperature in the bath.

It only now occurred to Legs that her sister must have set out from London long before her clifftop drama began. 'What are you doing in Devon?'

'I came on here after dropping Nico with his father,' she said then lowered her voice to a whisper. 'I think Dad's about to stage a walkout with Vegan Megan from the antiques shop. I went in there yesterday and she was giving him . . . head . . .' a clap of thunder overhead blotted out all noise '. . . in full public view.'

Legs stepped hurriedly into the bathroom and pulled the door closed, whispering: 'Did you say "head"?'

'That's right. Indian.'

'Indian head? Is that a Kama Sutra thing?'

'*Massage*, Legs. Indian head massage,' she hissed it as though it was the Kew equivalent of soliciting on a street corner.

'Oh that's all right then,' Legs said with relief. 'Vegan Megan is totally not Dad's type. The only pulses she sets racing are mung beans.' She stared at Ros as something ground-breaking occurred to her. 'Did you just say you actually went to Inkpot Farm?'

Ros straightened her neat bob in front of the mirror over the basin. 'Of course not. We met Nico's father at Taunton Services. He was late, of course.'

'It's so great you're doing some of the driving.' She yawned tiredly, knowing Will and Daisy would be hugely gratified; they desperately needed Ros to be more practical and onside.

But Ros looked pained by the compliment. 'It's just this once. I wanted to come here and say goodbye to the old place before I lose it.' She gazed around the bathroom tearfully, at the bowing whitewashed beams, the cracked old enamel, broken tiles and rusted taps. Then her eyes alighted on her sister. 'You look terrible, Legs. Are you feeling cold? Clammy? Difficulty breathing? Let me look at your pupils.'

'I'm fine.' She pulled off the tattered coral dress, exhaustion overwhelming her.

Ros eyed her with concern. 'Why are you wearing men's underpants?'

'I'm toying with the idea of a sex change.'

'I really have never understood your sense of humour. That letter you wrote to Francis had some very odd jokes in it. I was in two minds about sending it frankly, but I'm terribly pleased I did. It's made all the difference, hasn't it?'

Legs gaped at her. 'You sent it?'

With a saintly smile, Ros turned to the door. 'I discovered it when I was cleaning your flat after that dog stayed the night. The letter was spread out on your bed, along with my wedding dress which you bought from eBay. That is just *so* sweet.'

Legs closed her eyes. She'd blamed Kizzy for falsely framing her, but it had been a team effort all along; working independently, one had dug out the misleading clues, the other had packaged them up and labelled them as evidence.

'I would have given the Ditchley dress to you had I known, Legs,' Ros went on. 'I always said you should wear it to marry Francis. The least I could do was help fate along with a first class stamp. You scrub up for his return – he'll be back any minute.' She blew her a kiss as she slipped out of the door, immensely proud of her act of big-sisterly kindness.

Legs plunged into her bath as eagerly as Ophelia seeking oblivion.

It was such heaven to wash her hair at last that for a brief moment Legs almost forgot her woes, water lifting every follicle, threading its warm fingers through the loosening tangles and caressing her scalp like Vegan Megan's Indian head massage. She lay for a long time in the bath, letting the water go cold and running more hot in, listening to the candles guttering and the storm circling around the headland. Spywood's little, flickering bathroom felt safe, this deep enamel tub she'd once shared with her sister and later shared many times with Francis, those summers that they had spent nights here alone, crammed together in the hot bubbles, legs hanging over the side of the bath, lust and laughter keeping the water hot.

She topped up again with a scalding jet from the hot tap and sank back more miserably, dreading the conversation to come.

To add to her turmoil, she could hear Francis returning now and talking loudly to Ros outside the door, obviously about to come in and see her.

'Nobody there apart from Imee,' he was complaining. 'The police have all gone home. Kizzy's taken Liz Delamere back to her wardened flat. Édith's buggered off too, and Dad's had to take Poppy to hospital – she's still quite convinced Liz wanted to kill her, and that she mistook Legs for her because she was wearing Poppy's turban and dress. She's suffering the most ghastly panic attack, although Dad seemed quite cheerful about it when we spoke on the phone, saying that at least he was getting the old girl out of the house for once. Is Legs in here?'

Splashing water everywhere, she managed to clamber out of the bath and wrap herself in a towel just as he came in.

'Darling, don't get up on my account,' he joked. 'You look much better.' He'd put on a jumper and was wearing old jeans now. He looked so incredibly handsome and cheerful, she wanted to cry.

'I just need to – um . . .' She rushed past him into the main cottage room, towel trailing and hair dripping. 'Mum, can I borrow something to wear?'

Having had another schooner of brandy, Lucy was flying high on nervous energy and alcohol. 'Of course! Anything!'

Legs started up the stars, Francis predictably on her tail.

Suddenly Lucy let out a scream, remembering that the questionable, pilfered Lucian Freud nude was lying on the bed. 'Francis! Wait! Tell me how everything is at the hall?'

He hovered politely but reluctantly. 'I've just told you that.'

'Tell me again!'

Legs dived into the bedroom and borrowed a bright blue kaftan which made her look like a floating portaloo, but was at least cool and clean. She carefully put the tiny hairy Mary oil painting in a spare pillowcase from the wardrobe and folded it up tightly before hiding it behind a beam at the top of the stairs.

'Well tonight will certainly give you some material for your wedding speech, Francis,' Ros was laughing happily at something he'd just recounted.

Halfway down the stairs, Legs swayed in horror, and then caught her mother's tormented, sympathetic eyes over Francis's head.

Already reaching for Legs' hand to help her down with customary gallantry, he smirked back over his shoulder at Ros. 'I shall be far too busy complimenting my wife's beautiful maid of honour to recount such horrors.'

'As well as thanking me for getting you two back together in the first place,' Ros simpered.

'How do you mean?' asked Francis.

'"More than kisses, letters mingle souls",' she quoted warmly. 'Let's just say I Donne right.'

Francis beamed back at his future sister-in-law. They'd always basked in mutual admiration.

Legs felt the room closing in. 'I have to get some fresh air.' She headed towards the door.

'It's about to pour down out there,' Francis pointed out, once more in control and exerting his authority, 'You've almost fallen to your death tonight, darling, best not risk catching your death now.'

Laughing at his witty turn of phrase, Ros backed him up. 'Yes Legs, don't be selfish. You have wet hair.'

'At least wear a hat,' Lucy hiccupped from the table.

Cramming a floppy straw hat on her head, which was the only one she could find, Legs dipped her feet into her mother's flower patterned wellies by the door and extracted the walking socks before stepping into their rubbery depths again. Then she turned to look at Francis over her shoulder. 'Come with me.'

'I haven't got an overcoat.'

She wrenched open the door just as thunder rolled directly overhead. A huge gust of wind blew her hat straight off, spinning it back into the house where it hit Francis on the nose. 'Neither have I.'

'Legs, this is ridiculous.' Picking up the hat, he turned up his shirt collars and hurried after her.

Chapter 45

Amazingly, the storm held off its big, wet machine gun attack. It blasted them with wind and thunder, lit up the sky with flashes rather than forks, made the sea spit and roar beyond the cliffs and the trees creak and shudder, throwing twigs everywhere. But it stayed dry, as did Legs' tears.

She marched purposefully through the swirling, eddying leaves to the Tree of Secrets where she kicked off her wellies and climbed up to settle on one of its twin arms, waiting for Francis to haul himself up into the trunk's crook in front of her. He was still carrying the straw hat, she noticed, which he settled on his lap like a shield, hands protectively on top, as though she was planning to attack his groin. In a way, she was.

Wearing just an oversized kaftan and a sad smile, she tried to soften the blow: 'You are a wonderful man, Francis. I care for you very deeply, but I don't want to marry you.'

'I haven't asked you to,' he snapped back.

'Then we're agreed?'

'Absolutely.'

Legs almost wept with relief. That had been so much easier than she imagined. Overwhelmed by a wave of sadness and affection, she reached forward to take his hands in hers. But then he started to kiss each one of her fingers and she realised she might not have got her point across yet.

'We need to take it much more slowly than that,' he went on. 'Get the festival out of the way, have a holiday, spend time together. You need to build up your strength again. I thought a safari in Africa, or if you prefer the beach maybe the Maldives . . . or Pembrokeshire?' he offered the last option with added gusto, eager to push the budget option.

'No Francis.' She prised her fingers away. 'You don't understand. I don't want us to get back together at all.'

He looked up at the branches swaying and rustling madly overhead, 'That's not what you said in the letter.'

'It was written a year ago.' She hung her head. 'I originally sent it the week we broke up, but that copy obviously got lost in the post-traumatic stress.'

What he said next almost made her fall out of the tree in shock. 'I got your first letter.'

She stared at him for a long time. 'Why didn't you reply then?'

'It was very overwritten. The original was much more real and raw. It felt as though it had been written for *me*, not for yourself.'

'Thank you for the literary criticism. Maybe you should add a foreword and footnotes?'

He glanced up again as more lightning flashed through the sky. 'You always dumb down too much, Legs.'

'I wrote that letter from my dumb heart which was bleeding. Entirely self-inflicted, I know. Only an academic would differentiate between the version I sent and the first draft.'

'Actually they're almost entirely different,' Francis started to lecture, but stopped himself when he saw her murderous expression. He flashed a nervous smile. 'Perhaps I knew it was past tense even when I read it. All those references to last year's Summer Exhibition were a giveaway (wasn't it *X Factor* in the first version?). But then the day I got it, you drove here like the clappers and collapsed in my arms and . . . here we are.'

'Here we are,' she echoed hollowly. 'I got your reply.'

'I never intended it to land in your hands!'

'Touché.'

'What did you think?'

'I've heard it all before, Francis.'

A spirit of stagnant indignation reigned, undercut with wistful regret. They sat in silence in the Tree of Secrets for many minutes, listening to the circling thunder. Legs felt swords of emotion push and pulling at her sides. Still offshore, the storm turned and began

540

retreating towards Wales, taking its heavy rain-clouds with it, saving its force for more worthy star-crossed lovers.

But then Francis let out a furious bellow, rallying to his own indignant cause.

'I can't *believe* you're doing this to me again!' he suddenly exploded, the tree shaking as he shifted upright, looming in its hollow. 'You carry my heart with you, Legs. Are you trying to set it loose or cut it out a string at a time? Either way it bloody well hurts. I wish you'd never come back here.'

She hid her face behind her arms. 'I'm *so* sorry!'

'You have no idea how painful it's been trying to fathom out what's going on in that capricious head of yours, while all the time my father has been sharing a bed with your mother.' He was waving the straw hat about like Lear in the storm ranting about his ungrateful daughters.

She pressed her forearms tighter to her head, face buried in the crooks of her elbows, hating herself. 'I know, I know. And now Hector has gone back to Poppy, so nothing we could have done would have made a jot of difference anyway.'

He let out an ironic grunt, part anger and part regret. 'That's good at least.'

'And you and Kizzy split up because of me—'

'Actually I'm *very* relieved about that.' Another conciliatory grunt. 'So is she.'

Legs couldn't reign in her dam-burst of penitence. 'Then you were so kind looking after me when I was ill, and I've been so ungrateful.'

'I rather enjoyed it,' he admitted, sounding quite surprised. 'It meant I reread some favourite works and it spared me enduring Poppy.' He sat back down in the crook of the tree, anger already spent, like a Labrador exhausted from barking on Bonfire Night. 'Although I must say you behave even more unpredictably when you're ill than well, running off to find gold rings in the woods.'

'Oh, God, what have I put you through, Francis?' She peered

out at him between her forearms. 'You thought I was dead. That must have been awful.'

'After the initial shock that bit was quite cathartic,' he confessed. 'But the publicity would have been appalling.'

She laughed hollowly. 'Woe betide my death were to cast a negative light on the festival.'

'Indeed. Gordon Lapis is really going to put us on the map this year. You did Farcombe an enormous favour there.' Francis was looking increasingly cheery. 'Even the insurance fiasco has turned out rather well thanks to our star attraction. We have no premium to pay at all. Vin Keiller-Myles is underwriting the lot, saving us thousands.'

Legs remembered the banker's draft that had gone into the safe before dinner and Francis's gloating expression. She felt as though she was swallowing dust. '*If* the Freud is recovered.'

'Of course it will be. The police are supremely confident of bringing this to a swift conclusion. And Vin's not going to see the festival called off while that's happening.'

'That's very charitable of him.'

'*Au contraire*, Vin's also taking a hefty share of any profits, and a private supper with Gordon Lapis for himself and Gayle as reward.'

They've already eaten together, Legs found herself thinking wildly. 'But Gordon's not . . . that is, he's . . .'

'Entrenched in Ireland, we know.'

'You do?' she baulked, knowing he couldn't have even caught a flight yet.

'Conrad got a text from Gordon tonight saying he's planning on staying in Ireland until the very last moment and is not to be disturbed. Apparently he's working on something big. A pop-up dinosaur story or lift-the-flap monster book, one presumes,' he sneered.

Legs swallowed hard, realising that Byrne had texted his agent while counting up the eighteen 'I love yous' in her letter to Francis, plus one from Donne. Her voice crackled with emotion: 'Are you sure he'll come here?'

Francis narrowed his eyes. 'Conrad's given Poppy his word that our star act will *not* back out of his Farcombe appearance. He's got his most trusted girl on the job, he tells us.'

'I am no longer his trusted girl or whipping boy,' she huffed indignantly.

'Not you, Legs,' he scoffed. 'Kizzy's booked flights to Dublin already; I think we can rest assured Lapis will be policed all the way here. That girl would do anything for Poppy and the festival. She'll seduce him if she needs to.'

'But they're—' about to say 'brother and sister!' Legs managed to stop herself and splutter 'lesbians!' She wasn't sure the statement had as much punch, despite an element of truth.

For a moment, Francis looked stunned, but he swiftly regained his composure. 'I shouldn't think Kizzy would let a minor detail like that put her off her career trajectory. Con-man has her under strict instructions to deliver Gordon to Farcombe at any cost; I overheard the pep-talk. One can't help admiring his bravado.'

Legs felt as though the branch beneath her was whipping around like a serpent's tail. She sat up, gripping on tightly. 'Conrad is an utter bastard!'

Francis chuckled. 'Say that again.'

'Conrad is an utter, utter bastard!'

He smiled up through the tree's branches at the clearing night sky. The clouds were rushing off as fast as socialites moving on to a better party now, allowing the half moon to stage a shy epilogue, casting a faint light on his amused face.

'Perhaps you have suffered enough,' he reflected, tilting down his face to look along his perfect nose at her. 'After all, neither of us is going to die of a broken heart, are we?'

Her battered but unbroken heart was bursting with relief. 'I'm so glad you feel like that.'

'I won't pretend I'm not hurt, but the truth is, darling, I'm not sure you were clever enough for me. You have such a *carpe diem* mind.'

Relief turned instantly to outrage. '*What*?'

He flashed his handsome, condescending smile. 'When you were ill, I was reminded of the thing that used to irritate me about you most: your inability to concentrate, to engage; to care for the written word beyond its first reading.'

'You only say that because you talk in quotes all the time!' she defended, hot tears of indignation chasing away all those of guilt. 'Even your letter was full of Joyce.'

'You weren't supposed to read it yet; I haven't finished the appendices.' He looked indignant, but then a hint of vanity crept into his voice. 'What did you think of it?'

'Flammable.'

'You mean inflammatory?'

'I mean inflammable.'

He let out a long, patronising sigh. 'Which just goes to show how much you know about literature.'

'Does that make me a lesser person?'

'Frankly, yes.'

Legs fell silent. This time she would let him take victory. She recognised his need for a deadly verbal blow, that final word she must nobly concede, especially when it was accompanied by the sort of expression Francis now bore, which in most other men she knew would relate to a hat-trick scored in injury time followed by an orgy of two-girl-on-one-hatrick-scorer bedroom action. He had won the match. And while he didn't exactly rip his shirt off and thrust his groin at the crowds for adulation, he still needed to make his victory salute.

Crouching over her now, he bestowed a kiss of such tenderness on her cheek, the heat of her tears creeping out to meet his lips seemed to melt her skin.

'Is it utterly pointless hoping for friendship?' she asked in a fractured voice.

His coldness took her by surprise. 'Utterly pointless.'

Thus, without warning, she found the scream bellowed from her like a toddler staging the mother of all hissy fits: 'I WANT my CAR back! NOW!'

He took several seconds to comprehend what she was saying. 'I'm hardly going to get it right this minute.'

'Yes you are! I'm going to Ireland.'

Francis's ancient Land Rover racketed along the tracks through the moonlight, pulling up outside a Dutch Barn located amongst the cluster of neglected piggeries and sheep holds in one of Home Farm's outer yards.

As soon as she saw her little silver dream machine stored inside, Legs threw her arms over its firm back like a small girl with her pony, visualising herself galloping away.

Francis watched her from the big double doors, silhouetted in brightening moonlight, 'You can hardly call the AA at two in the morning and expect them to be here within half an hour.' He stepped forwards.

'No need.' She scouted around, spotted an ancient rusting scythe propped up against an old corn thresher, and grasped it, holding it aloft victoriously.

With a terrified wail, Francis leaped out of sight, clearly believing the Grim Reaper had arrived.

Taking no notice of him, Legs hurled the weighted base of the handle at the driver's side window, which smashed obligingly, the car alarm shrieking straight away.

Leaning inside, she extracted the car keys and silenced the alarm with the fob button. Across the Home Farm fields, dogs barked inside tents.

'I would have knocked out the passenger's side,' Francis said helpfully, peering around the barn door again. 'Less wind in the face.'

'I can't wait to smell fresh Eire.' She shivered happily, jumping in.

As soon as she started the engine, the sat nav burst into life, still seeking its last requested destination.

'*At the next available opportunity, take a U-turn*,' came the bossy voice.

'This lady's not for turning,' Legs shouted back just as bossily, and pressed her foot on the accelerator.

She drove straight to Spywood Cottage, which was now in darkness.

Ros was dozing on the sofa, and woke with a start to find her sister hurriedly writing a note at the kitchen table.

'I've left the spare bed free for you.' Still half-asleep, yawning and rubbing her stiff neck, she sat up stiffly. 'I made it up with fresh sheets and put out my spare pyjamas.'

'I'm not staying.'

'You can't leave Francis!'

'I don't love him any more. I did when I wrote that letter you sent, but it was just aftershock, afterthoughts, after burn . . . after Byrne.' The words caught in her throat. 'The writing was on the wall; I should have had "Live for the Moment" tattooed across my brow before I came back here to bang it against Farcombe's brick walls.'

'They're stone,' Ros pointed out, regarding her suspiciously. 'You're not thinking of getting another tattoo?'

Legs could hear Byrne's voice in her head, *What's written, once read, is like ink on skin.* She hit upon a sudden idea. It would be the ultimate love letter. 'You know, I just might.'

Her sister's grey eyes marked her as she screwed up the note, 'You're running back to Conrad, I assume?'

She shook her head: 'I'm going to County Laois – louse – leesh,' she struggled with the pronunciation.

'You will find nothing but louses, leeches and letches out there, Legs,' Ros stood up and headed wearily into the kitchen. 'I'd better make you a Thermos of coffee if you're driving.'

'Is Mum asleep?' Legs craved a Lucy hug, longing to explain what she was doing to the one person she was certain would understand.

'Cognac coma,' Ros switched on the kettle then stretched out her arms between the handles of two wall cupboards crucifix-style, drooping her head at forty-five degrees. 'I can't believe you're swanning off, leaving me to pick up the pieces as usual.'

Legs ignored the martyr pose. 'Get Mum and Dad face to face ASAP. They can sort it out for themselves. Just don't let them trust to letters. You know what they're like; they only open post once a month to avoid the scary bills.'

Her sister looked up quickly, appalled. 'Is that your expert advice in marriage guidance?'

'What do you suggest then?'

Ros could only focus on the detail as usual. 'Mum told me tonight that she's had "intimate waxing".' She dropped her voice, glancing up. 'Dad can't see her until it's grown out, don't you agree?'

'He might like it.' Legs pointed out, then remembered the miniature fake Freud, whose nude model had definitely not had any intimate waxing before she was painted.

'Don't be absurd,' Ros was going redder by the second. 'He's far too old.'

Legs quickly scaled three quarters of the stairs to retrieve the folded pillowcase. 'Can you do me a massive favour?' She thrust it at her sister. 'I need you to get rid of this.'

'Is it drugs?' Ros held it by her fingertips like a bomb that might explode at any second.

'No.' She picked up the Thermos gratefully; 'Just a naked truth that needs covering up.'

Ros handed it straight back, 'I'm all for covering up nudity, but I draw the line at smuggling. Just post it into the nearest police station's letterbox.'

'I am no longer a woman of letters,' Legs sighed as she carried it out to the battered, breezy car to stash it in the boot. 'This time I'm going to say what I need to face to face, even if I have to write crib notes on my skin first.'

Chapter 46

'Legs!'

'Daisy!'

'At last! Where have you *been*?'

'Long story.'

'What's that noise?'

'I'm on a ferry.'

'Brian or Otis?'

'Ha ha. Going to Ireland. How's Inkpot?'

'Actually, I'm in Farcombe. Your tyre tracks are still smoking outside Spywood, you minx. I heard you were on the run. What have you *done* here? Even Ros stopped to tell me about it, she's so shocked.'

'What do you mean?'

The signal cut out and the line went dead.

Having plundered her dwindling current account to book a cabin for the crossing, Legs had liberated her weekend bag from the boot of the Honda at last and fell on it like an old friend, pulling out clothes that she'd personally chosen and were in fashion with the ecstatic gratitude of a released prisoner no longer obliged to wear arrows. Byrne had never even seen her in her own clothes, she realised in amazement. When they'd first met she'd been sporting an Arsenal away kit, followed later by the party frocks of an ageing society hostess. At least he'd been spared her mother's blue kaftan which resembled something

Nelson Mandela might wear on a state visit. She dragged it off now like a tarpaulin from an Aprilia, eager to put on her race farings.

But when she started to try things on, she had a confidence crisis. She had lost so much weight while being ill that nothing fitted any more. She knew she should feel elated, but all her jeans had unflatteringly baggy bums, and her boobs appeared to have shrunk drastically, leaving her bras gaping at the top like mussel shells.

She took a shower and then tried hard to have a power nap, aware that she was running almost entirely on adrenalin and coffee having not slept properly in two days. But it was impossible to settle with her heart racing so fast. No matter how many times she told herself that she was simply going to Ireland to tell Byrne that Kizzy was his half-sister, she knew she was also on a mission to hand-deliver something far more personal and life-changing for herself.

She got up and painted her face with great care, trying for the barely-there look but just ended up with a matt pancake render that she hurriedly washed off before settling for pale and interesting with bedhead hair, lashings of mascara and a lick of lip-gloss. Matched with a clingy dove-grey tunic that slipped seductively off one shoulder and sea-green pedalpushers that made her thighs look almost slender, she started to buck up. Lifting her hair up, she pouted at the mirror, turning this way and that, astonished at her newfound cheekbones. The old Allegra was back, and ready to live for the moment with all her heart.

It was almost time to write her letter. First, she needed the address.

Within half a mile of Rosslare, she got one signal point on her phone and a welcome text from her new Irish host network. She dialled straight out: 'I need to locate a family called Byrne, or possibly Kelly, in Laois or possibly Kildare. They train horses.'

'Initial?'

'No idea.'

'Oooookay, madam. I am the White Pages, and I have no intention of turning the air blue here, but have you any idea just how many people we are talking about roughly?'

'Fifty? Eighty?'

'Thousands.'

'The initial would be B, I think. Brooke. That's it! Kelly, Brooke.'

'Kelly Brook?'

'Yes. I need the address.'

'She'll be ex-directory. And she doesn't live in Ireland. Lovely girl.'

'OK, forget that. I just need the number of a tattoo parlour in Portlaoise.'

'Is this to do with Kelly Brook?' asked her operator excitedly.

Legs took the number and rang off. Bracing herself, she called Conrad.

'Where does Gordon live exactly?'

'Right here. But the bastard isn't in.' He held his hand over the phone and talked to someone at the other end, presumably Kizzy. 'I catch a flight back to London in an hour. Why d'you want his address?'

'Good luck card.'

'You've typed it on enough letters in the past,' Conrad reminded her rudely, hanging up.

Legs had a similar blank spot with addresses as she did telephone numbers if they were stored in electronic media that she could simply cut and paste or speed dial. She closed her eyes and tried really hard to concentrate, even clicking her heels together and saying 'there's no place like home' a few times for luck, much to the amused alarm of her fellow passengers, one of whom started videoing her.

Then she let out a whoop and opened her eyes, remembering: 'Coolbaragh Farm!'

'That seriously stings,' Legs winced as the needle painted its way delicately along the top of her neck.

'You want me to stop, darlin'?'

'No, I can take it. My friend likes a sting in his tale.' Legs smiled at the artist, who had worryingly cross eyes and clearly used his body as a portfolio for both his ink and his piercing needlework 'You wouldn't happen to know how to find somewhere called Coolbaragh Farm by any chance?'

'How would you be spelling that? There're a lot of "cools" round here – Coolanoma, Coolbanaghar, Cooltoran, Coolnacarrick.' He lifted his gun and reached for a sterile swab. 'This is a cool place.'

She wrote it down for him while he changed needles.

'Doesn't look familiar.' He peered at it, 'but then again I'm dyslexic.' He started the machine up again and peered at her neck, irises sliding closer together. 'Funny, I don't get asked for this phrase much any more. Can't remember the last time.'

She cleared her throat nervously. 'Why's that d'you think?'

'I guess "*tá grá agam duit*" would be more accurate.' He nodded towards the 'Buy One Get One Half Price' poster beside her head. 'It'd look grand on your lower back.'

'I'll stick with the one, thanks. I wrote too much last time I tried something like this.' Legs gritted her teeth, eyes watering, grateful she'd chosen only two words, and hoping that he wasn't writing it phonetically.

An hour later, listening to the whining grinding of a needle engraving into gold, Legs flinched as she reached up beneath her hair and pressed her tentative fingertips to the fiery new mark protected by a clear dressing there. 'You wouldn't happen to know how to find somewhere called Coolbaragh Farm by any chance?'

'Sure, that's Mr Byrne's place, a mile or two off the Kildare Road.' The whining stopped as the jeweller wetted his newly marked signet before holding it up to examine. 'He buys a lot of pretty gems for Mrs Byrne in here, and the son's been a good customer since he took to the foreign wife.'

Legs stared at him in disbelief. 'Did you say wife?'

'That's right. They've grand stables up there, I hear. Fine horses. Now who would be living there with the initial P, I wonder?' he pried.

'The P is silent,' Legs explained as she took the ring with shaking hands and turned it between her fingers, admiring the curling monogram. 'Do you suppose there's room to add "rick"?'

The jeweller gave a nervous laugh. 'We sell a very handsome titanium identity bracelet with gold accents which I can engrave at no extra cost.'

'I'll just take the ring, thanks.' She handed it back. 'It's best the corpse isn't identified until after I leave the country. Could you give me directions?'

The Byrne family lived in a white farmhouse on the outskirts of the tiny village of Coolbaragh just south west of Kildare, with a ruined stone tower squatting by its front gates like a truncated dragon leg and fields full of glossy, tail-flicking thoroughbreds. It wasn't at all as Legs had expected, although her imaginings had always veered wildly between the sort of romantic hideaway castle Gordon Lapis could afford, and a modest rural hovel adored by home-loving Jago, with chickens wandering in and out of the kitchen and peat loaded on the fire.

Instead, Coolbaragh Farm was large and immaculate, with newly painted render, freshly creosoted fencing and tarmac so uniform and glossy black it looked like polished granite. It was alarmingly WAG-mansionesque. There were smart carriage lights dotted along the drive, beautifully edged flowerbeds bursting with red valerian, and a large stone horse rearing in the centre of a fountain on the flawless green grass in front of the house. Electric gates with a discreet CCTV camera were the only hint at the security required to protect its occupants, although that could equally have applied to the ones in the stables of its adjoining stud.

It wasn't very Byrne-like. It felt wholly anti-climactic. It was also punishingly hot, the storms in England having long since left its near neighbour which was basking in a late summer heatwave. She could smell the tarmac melting.

'Who's that?' a cheerful female voice crackled through the intercom attached to the gatepost.

'Legs,' she said without thinking. Driving there from Portlaoise, she had been too busy veering between emotional extremes to formulate any sort of plan, one moment convinced that the jeweller's hearsay had to be wrong and Byrne couldn't be married; the next, wanting to kill him. Now that she had arrived, all she wanted to do was see him.

'Did you say "Legs"?' The accent wasn't Irish. It sounded deeply European.

'Yes. I'm here to see Byrne – Jago – Lapis – Gordon – Finch,' she struggled. He was everything to her. He had no need for one name.

But the cheerful voice was clearly more than satisfied that she'd passed muster. 'At *last*! My husband's been waiting on you all day. Come on in.'

To her amazement, the gate was opened with an electronic whirr.

A gorgeous blonde was already coming out of the front door, in possession of the sort of endless legs, pale blue eyes and cream complexion that only the purest gene-pool could contrive to reproduce. To prove the point, she carried a perfect Silbury Hill bump between her narrow hips and her pert bust, the advanced stages of pregnancy sported like a fashion accessory. Hopping along as she pulled on boots, she beamed across at Legs.

'Come straight to ze yard. Ve are so glad you're here.' Her accent was very thick indeed, possibly Polish or Russian, with American vowel sounds and curiously Irish intonations. 'My aul man's on phone. He'll be here shortly. He hasn't slept in forty-eight hours. No doubt you have been told of ze situation.' The blonde vision began striding ahead on those endless slim limbs, now

553

pursued by Fink the basset who cast Legs a mildly penitent look, like a serial adulterer caught out so often he no longer raised more than an eyebrow.

'Not really . . .' Having not slept for almost as many hours, Legs was struggling to keep up mentally and physically too. The blonde could cover ground like an ostrich, pregnant or not.

'My husband has been frantic for you to get here.' She was leading the way along the granite shiny tarmac to a stable yard of such gleaming perfection it looked like a little girl's toy, complete with another pretty fountain and lots of hanging baskets bursting with colour like pick-n-mix scoops. The blonde headed to a far corner, where the half door had an ominous prison cell metal grille above it. 'Ze vorst one's over here. Nobody can get near him right now, so be careful.' She slid open the bolt and ushered Legs in. 'Can you see how poofy zey are?'

Before she could answer, Legs found herself sharing a very small space with very big, angry horse that was standing on three swollen legs. He hopped one way, Legs jumped the other.

'I think there's been a mistake . . .' she bleated at the door.

'I'll make tea an get my aul man.' The blonde walked away.

Legs flattened herself back against a wall as the horse bared its teeth at her. 'Um . . . help!'

There was nobody outside to hear any more. Hay was munched, hooves stamped, and another horse whinnied. She crept to the door and reached through the bars of the grille to slide the lock, only to find the door was still stuck fast, a lower bolt on the outside holding it closed with steel force.

Legs' disconsolate new companion, eager to see what was happening on the yard, limped towards its door too, still shooting her evils out of the corner of its eye which sent her scuttling against a side wall. A moment later its very large, glossy brown bum was facing her. She had very little working knowledge of horses, but she remembered a line saying that they were equally dangerous at both ends. She edged away into a corner and fought panic.

Her mind was in overdrive. Byrne was married to the leggy blonde, she realised. They had a child on the way.

She reached automatically for the back of her neck, feeling the heat burning there, horrified by her misjudgement.

Her touch-paper ignited again, this time blazing out of control. She felt so livid and humiliated that her skin seemed to blister, and she was amazed the stable didn't combust around her. She'd been a total fool for coming here with her heart on her sleeve, for assuming such a deep connection based on their brief acquaintance. He'd told her from the start that he had nothing to give her, but she'd blindly assumed that it was because he didn't trust love, never assuming that he was already taken. She wanted to mule-kick him, which fitted nicely with her current circumstances. If her puffy-legged stable-mate would oblige, she'd very much like him to kick Byrne too, then bite him, after which they could both roll on him. She'd show him just what a Heavenly Pony was capable of if betrayed.

No wonder he hadn't wanted a relationship with her in the face of public exposure, she thought furiously. Away from the media gaze, Gordon Lapis could get away with whatever he liked, but as soon as his life became public, keeping a mistress would be impossibly messy.

She let out an angry sob.

The horse snorted back, far from sympathetically.

Legs snivelled and hiccupped.

A big brown head swung around and glared at her.

She gulped, looked at him apologetically, and started to wail.

A moment later and there was a loud rustling of wood shavings and a big hairy shoulder thudded against hers as the horse rubbed his cheek against her head with a deep sigh, slamming her against a wall as it sympathised with her woes.

Legs put her arm around his neck and wailed into his warm skin. She wailed for a long time. Nobody came back to check on her or bring her tea. Eventually, she and the horse started to clear their throats and feel embarrassed. He shuffled off to pull at a haynet. She slid down the wall and buried her face in her hands, knowing that she had to get away somehow. She'd judged it all wrong. She didn't know Byrne at all. He was a married man.

There was a voice shouting out in the yard now, deep baroque Irish, husky and whip-crack hoarse. It was a mesmerising voice, but not Byrne's.

'Where is she? Paddy Flynn definitely said his new man is a man. Why d'you not ask for ID? She could be one of O'Grady's lasses sent here to dope the few sound ones we have left. Where is she now?'

The door was thrown open and Legs found herself staring at the most mesmerising older version of Byrne, with all the same chisel-boned beauty and those huge, fierce eyes, but these were deep grey to match the grey streaks in his faded red hair.

The man was sitting in a wheelchair, so white hot with anger that the heatwave-baked tarmac around him seemed destined to melt into bubbling lava.

'Who are you?' he demanded furiously.

The horse sharing its quarters with Legs whickered cheerfully, knowing no fear of him. She quailed by comparison.

'Legs!' she bleated.

'I told you, Brooke.' The blonde raised her palms in self-justification. 'Ze leg person.'

'Now there's a thing,' Brooke had the same gruff laugh as his son, eyeing Legs with supreme scepticism, taking in the pedal-pushers, off-the-shoulder top and the reddened eyes. 'Where's your bag?'

'In the car. The thing is, I—' she started to explain, but he interrupted.

'Think this one will race again?'

'I couldn't say.'

'Half my yard is hopping around with fetlocks like footballs, so they are. My son thinks it's a virus.'

'Could be right, yes, only I'm not really—'

'Sure you have a way with big Lappy, d'you not?' he laughed as he watched the horse nuzzle her hair, now quite fond of the impostor in his stable. 'Lapis here is a brute and he'd usually eat you as soon as look at you. Zina puts all the pretty girls in with him first.'

The blonde smiled innocently, making Legs wonder if Zina had already guessed that she was an imposter with murderous intentions towards her husband. The best course of action seemed to be keeping quiet and making a swift exit.

But Brooke was clearly enjoying the show.

'Come and see the others,' he'd already started wheeling away. 'Now this little grey mare is Purple; she's not so bad as the others – Finch here has been off colour all week; this chap Necrodorn is born idle, but he's got filled legs on him too as has his neighbour Rushlore.' Legs recognised the names of two of Ptolemy's arch rivals, at least one of them based on Hector.

'They're all named after Ptolemy Finch characters,' she said, stating the obvious.

Brooke was delighted. 'Clever girl! Zina's mad crazy on those silly books about the little grey-haired fellow, so she is. I'm not a one for reading about wizards, although I liked the movies, sure enough.' He eyed her cheerfully, and Legs knew full well he was relishing the craic of talking about his son's career in front of a stranger, unaware that she knew exactly who Gordon was in real life. Except the Jago Byrne she had fallen in love with was was no more real than his alter ego. He was as illusory as Ptolemy Finch himself, a fictional creation she'd coloured in with her imagination, joining the dots to make sense of the contradictions. Not once had she thought to draw a wedding ring on his finger.

A buzzer indicated another visitor at the gates. Zina trailed away towards the driveway muttering as she went. 'I hope it's not zat creepy Conrad fellow again, always turning up out of the blue wanting Jago to run this errand or that one, and calling me 'Kelly'.

Jago's a computer programmer, not a dogsbody. Fink is ze dogsbody round here.'

Panting in the heat, Fink trailed after her.

Legs was in even greater shock. Could it be possible that Byrne's young wife had no idea he was Ptolemy Finch's creator? She felt dangerously close to tears again. Her skin had started prickle afresh with hot needles of indignation, her breath shortening and her mule-kicking legs tensing, torn between running away and planting hard until she found him and gave him hell.

Meanwhile, Brooke was looking at her askance, both suspicious and amused, well aware of his son's cachet as a romantic catch. And it was obvious that Brooke had a shrewd suspicion who *she* was, or at least what she wanted.

'You mustn't mind Zina – she's overprotective.' He narrowed his eyes speculatively as he took in Legs' dishevelled blonde appearance and obvious agitation. 'And she calls all vets "the leg man" because that's what we call Paddy, who usually cares for the beasts here. What he doesn't know about a nag's pins isn't worth knowing. But you're obviously no vet, nor any sort of horsewoman. I take it you're another one come to see my son?'

Legs' eyes met his clever grey ones. He had all of Byrne's directness with less brooding darkness. Do not cry, she told herself firmly, too choked to speak

'You are,' Brooke nodded with certainty. 'I have no idea what you girls see in a waste of space like him, dreaming his life away on computers when he has such a talent to ride a horse. I suppose you two met on the internet?'

She nodded vaguely, realising it was technically correct, alarm bells ringing ever-louder in her head. How many others had there been? No wonder his pregnant young wife was such a crosspatch, left to look after her father-in-law while Byrne was gallivanting around leading his secret double life. And no wonder, again, that he had resisted losing the anonymity that allowed such deception.

His father, clearly complicit in all this, seemed remarkably unbothered.

'You're not the first pretty caller of the day. The other girl waited all morning. I told her he'd not be back from the quarry before dark, but she insisted on waiting here in the tower.'

It must be Kizzy, Legs realised in horror. She'd been too over-wrought by the disovery that Byrne was married to give it another thought until now, but Conrad had charged the redhead with the task of bringing Gordon back to Farcombe at any cost, even if it took all-out seduction. Legs doubted a brush with incest would put Jago off given the hypocrisy she'd just uncovered, but she knew she couldn't run away and leave them to it. They had to be told the truth.

'Is she still here?' Legs looked across at the crumbling stone wreck by the entrance gates, wondering what sort of family would let anyone wait in there, although the idea of locking Kizzy away in a medieval dungeon for a bit quite appealed to her.

'Not that one,' he cackled, following her gaze. 'Jago's tower, up there,' he pointed through the archway at the rear of the stable yard to a corner of hilly woodland hidden from the road, through which a steeply raked path led up to another sun-baked limestone tower, this one intact and gloriously, totally Ptolemy Finch. 'She's gone now. Left about an hour ago, she did. I told her if she was going to the old quarry she'd need to change her shoes, but she took no notice. I'd lay you any odds she'll be limping back here any minute. His last girlfriend used to set off up there dressed up to the nines with champagne picnics – always spraining her ankle and needing first aid, she was; it drove Zina mad.'

She felt again for the hot new brand beneath her hair, knowing she'd been a total fool for coming. But she had to see it through.

'Where is the quarry?'

'Oh, you don't want to go there. It's impossible to find unless you know the local area.'

'I have a sat nav. Just give me the location details.'

'You'll never drive there. The old road in is shot to pieces. Francis took a horse.'

Stubbornly, Legs took the coordinates.

Chapter 47

'You have arrived at your destination. You have arrived at your destination.'

'How can I have?' Legs howled driving on through a haze of dust on the bumpiest, steepest and stoniest road she'd ever tried to navigate, raised high on the limestone escarpment, so narrow and precarious that it was like trying to drive along a lumpy tightrope. 'I can't see anything!'

Then she let out a scream as the car seemed to lurch sideways, tipped at an acute angle, the nearside wheels now spinning uselessly.

At boiling point, she hauled up the handbrake and clambered out to assess the situation. It could have been worse, she realised; she could have driven another three feet and plunged to her death. Instead, she'd been grounded in a deep rut inches from a precipice.

Ahead of her stretched a miniature Grand Canyon cut out of the ground like an inverted cathedral. It must have been disused for many years, and had now been reclaimed by nature, the quarry floor carpeted with wildflowers, a deep pool at its centre dancing with insects and dragonflies, the strata in the steep stone sides filled with nesting birds, and the grassland ridge was the brightest emerald green, patrolled by hundreds of blue butterflies.

Slumping against her wonky car bonnet in a haze of dust, she gazed out across the wide drop and spotted a horse tethered on the opposite side, grazing peacefully. A few yards away, she could make out a figure sitting beneath an ash tree, his back propped against the trunk, earphones blotting out all outside noise as he worked on a laptop propped on his knees.

For a moment, Legs wanted to turn and flee, mortified to have chased after him across the sea, living for the moment yet again with the consequences certain to humiliate her. But her car was beached, and she had to tell him the truth about Kizzy. At least she'd beaten the redhead here. She just had to say her piece and leave as swiftly as possible by whatever means, even if that meant racing all the way back to Laois on foot. She had her running gear in the car, after all.

She looked for something to wear to cover the back of her neck, determined that he mustn't see the heartfelt declaration she'd so foolishly had stamped there. She remembered Francis's appalled face when she'd revealed the precious little stars on her ankle, and his pious pronouncement that all tattoos became labels of regret one day. No doubt he'd derive great satisfaction from her current situation. But she was determined to keep her cool and maintain her dignity. She would even give him the ring she'd had engraved to replace the signet with the Kelly family crest that had gone over the cliff at Farcombe the night he'd rescued her. It would be her parting gesture, a reminder that he'd thought her life worth saving once, even if he could never share it.

Collecting a fluffy pink polo-necked jumper from the back seat of her car and dragging it over her head, she pulled a small box from her glove compartment and she set out around the lip of the quarry.

She was pouring with sweat by the time she reached him, the horse starting back in alarm to find another human penetrating this remote spot.

Byrne looked up and pulled out the earphones, equally surprised, dark eyes stretched wide. 'Are you going to tell me you're a ghost again?'

Legs wiped the sweat angrily from her face, 'Of course not.'

'How on earth did you get up here?'

'I drove.' She nodded across to the Tolly car, now a dusty wreck poking from a huge pothole at a jaunty angle as though abandoned there by teenage joy-riders.

'Looks like it could use a valet.' He raised his eyebrows and then closed his laptop, casting it aside on top of a copy of *Finnegan's Wake*.

Legs was overheating fast. She felt faint being so close to him again. 'I have to tell you something important. It's too personal for an email or call.'

He looked up at her, his face shaded by his hand as he squinted against the sun. 'Isn't an announcement in the *Telegraph* more standard practice?'

She stared at him dumbly, guessing he must think she was here on festival business. This was going to be tougher than she'd imagined. Just looking at him was turning her inside out, and her polo-neck was suffocating her. She was starting to sway dizzily, like a Carpenters fan listening to 'Close to You'.

'Here, sit down.' He patted the ground beside him. 'This sun's punishing today. You look dressed for the arctic.'

'I'm fine!' She perched awkwardly beside him, grateful at least that he was being quite amicable. She'd expected him to shout at her to go away. As long as she could curb her own emotions and her mood-swinging desire to both kiss and punch him, she'd be fine. She simply had to make her point in a straightforward, unemotional way:

'It's about Kizzy. She's on her way up here right now; your dad doesn't think she'll make it in her high heels, but she's very determined. She's here in Ireland with Conrad to talk you back to Farcombe; that is Kizzy thinks she's going to meet Gordon but as soon as she sees you she'll realise you're Jago Byrne, Poppy's son. And Conrad doesn't know you're Poppy's son at all, but he will as soon as Kizzy puts the two of you together. And Kizzy might even try to seduce you – in fact I'm pretty certain she will –

but you mustn't let that happen because what neither of you know is that—'

He put his finger up to her lips to silence her, making Legs' mouth so tingly then numb with longing she felt as though she'd kissed a nettle leaf. 'Breathe, Legs.'

Realising that she was starting to hyperventilate, Legs went even hotter and started to pant. Even her eyes were sweating. She could see Byrne's concerned face swimming in front of her, dark brows lowered. He probably thinks I'm ill again, she realised in horror; first pneumonia, now swamp fever. She didn't want to come across as sickly. She wanted to be cool and calm as she relayed the truth about Kizzy before departing with her dignity intact, possibly elbowing him over the quarry precipice as she went.

'Let's get that jumper off. Ridiculous thing to wear on a day like this.' He reached out to haul it up over her head.

'No!' Legs protested, but her face was already surrounded by pink mohair and it was too late as Byrne tugged it off, almost removing her ears in the process.

Even though she leapt away as fast as she could, he still caught sight of the reddened skin at the top of her spine. 'What's this? Have you hurt yourself?'

'It's nothing!' She covered it with her hair, edging further away from him.

He sighed, casting another wary look. 'So what exactly is it you've come here to tell me? You lost me somewhere after the high heels bit.'

'Kizzy's your sister, Byrne. Half-sister.'

He stared at her incredulously. 'She's Poppy's daughter?'

'No. Her birth mother is definitely Liz Delamere. Kizzy has no idea who her real father is, but Liz told me it's Brooke.'

'Ah.' He tipped his head back against the tree and looked up, closing one eye as he took in the implications of this. Then he suddenly laughed. 'Dad's longed for a bigger brood all his life and I always hated being an only child, so I guess we just got what we both wanted. Thank you for telling me.'

Legs didn't know what to say. She'd expected him to seethe with anger in classic Byrne fashion, berating his irresponsible father and mad Liz for forsaking him just as her mother had with Hector. Instead, he shook his head in bewildered delight and laughed again.

'Thin Lizzie the conspiracist. Who'd have guessed? She can't have been much more than a child back then. I wish I could remember her better. I know she made Dad laugh, which was an amazing thing. There had never been much laughter at Nevermore before that.'

'Oh, she's still quite a joker,' Legs muttered. 'We had a hilarious time on the cliff's edge. Shame you climbed up to put an end to the fun really. It was all downhill from there that night.' Tears were welling again as she thought about following him here to Ireland. Stop it, she told herself. Don't go there. You've said all you need to, and now you can give him the ring and go before you make a fool of yourself by shouting at him for deceiving you into loving him.

But she stayed glued to her rocky perch, unable to tear herself away as Byrne looked out across the quarry. 'This is where I taught myself to climb,' he told her. 'I'd come here after school as a teenager and worked my way up those walls from every approach, sometimes in the pitch dark.'

Still caught between fury and fascination, she followed his gaze across the sheer stone sides and imagined how dangerous it must have been navigating them in total darkness.

'It made me feel alive, that huge adrenalin rush; it was one of the only things that really moved me. Inevitably I fell off a few times, and one day I smashed up my leg and ribs so badly, I was laid up in bed over a month. Dad was livid, as you can imagine. I might have died here if the local hunt hadn't found me, and of course he ranted and raged about me ending up in a wheelchair like him. That's when I started writing, stuck in that bed with my leg in plaster. Then Dad bought me a laptop for my seventeenth birthday and I didn't look back. After that, I came here to put Ptolemy in dire straits.' He packed his laptop into a courier's bag.

Legs didn't trust herself to speak. Anger kept bubbling up inside her like boiling caramel then dying back just as fast, knowing that she was hearing a story that had probably never been shared. Counting back, she realised that she'd still been at university when the first Ptolemy Finch book came out, a pretentious undergraduate who recited Eliot down the phone to Francis while Jago was already a published author.

'This is Byrne land,' he was saying. 'The family used to make their money from stone until the quarry was closed in the seventies. After that, the farm had to pay its way and it was always a struggle, especially once Dad, me and the horses arrived. Nan's husband Mal is a generous man, and he never complained once, but it's amazing to be able to put something back. They've got it just how they like it now; even Nan agrees that the front lawn can't take another ornamental Greek urn, which is an anagnorisis I thought I'd never see. '

So the footballers' wives perfection and garish potted petunias weren't to his taste, she realised. His wife certainly seemed to love them though, she thought wretchedly. The caramel was boiling over again, spilling into the cooking flames in a cloud of black smoke.

'Does Zina know you're Gordon Lapis?' She struggled to keep her voice level.

To her astonishment, he didn't seem to find anything odd in the question, shaking his head: 'Just Dad. He's known from the start; I had to explain who Conrad was and why he calls me Gordon when he comes here, plus all the letters that come addressed to Mr Lapis. He covers for me when I need him to, but we both find it's easier to forget about Ptolemy Finch while we're here. Coolbaragh's about the horses, not little winged soothsayers. None of the rest of the family knows. They think I'm some sort of internet entrepreneur.'

'A paragon of virtual,' Legs hissed, eyeing up the distance between Jago and the quarry edge and wondering how hard she'd have work to drag him there after she'd hit him over the head with his laptop.

The caramel anger was pouring in hot black rivers like lava now, she thought about poor, heavily pregnant Zina, totally unaware that she was married to the man behind a mega-selling global franchise. How could she not know? It was like Picasso's wife believing his paint-stained fingers were down to a busy day mixing Dulux in B&Q.

'I must go.' She stood up quickly, realising she was going to make a huge, wailing, violent, tattooed spectacle of herself if she stayed a moment longer. Fumbling in her haste to cover the evidence, she knotted the polo neck high around her shoulders, taking care to keep her hair underneath so her neck was totally covered.

'That car doesn't look like it's going anywhere.' He stood up too.

'I'm sure I can get it out.' She fished in her pockets and pulled out the little box, thrusting it at him before she could change her mind. 'I remember you telling me rings are like a part of your heart you give away. This is for you because I lost yours, and it was never really mine to keep. I hope it works out with Kizzy and Conrad and Zina and the baby everything.' Saying it out loud hurt like a body blow.

Not giving him time to answer, she hurried back to her car, stumbling and tripping and almost pitching into the quarry in her haste to get away and to keep the tears stemmed until she was out of sight.

But Byrne was right. The car was stuck fast and no amount of furious revving could make the wheels gain traction. She simply created a dust cloud. In despair, she grabbed her phone, but she had nobody to call for help and no signal.

Eventually, he rode up through the dusty heat haze like a Wild

West pony express, despatch bag slung across his back. 'I'll give you a lift back to the farm. We'll come up with dad's truck and pull it out later.'

She clambered out of the driver's door, still clutching her phone. 'I can't ride a horse!'

'I'm not leaving you here in this heat.' He reached out a hand. 'Use the car as a mounting block and hop up in front of me here.'

'Absolutely not!'

'You'll be quite safe,' he assured her. 'You just gave me a sapphire ring. The least I can do to thank you is make a cup of tea before you head off again.'

'Did you say a sapphire?' she gulped.

'It's . . . totally unexpected, and very generous of you,' he said carefully, not wanting to offend her.

'Oh shit,' Legs wrenched open the car door again and rootled through the glove compartment.

There, still wedged between an ice scraper and several audiobooks, was the little box from the jewellers in Portlaoise containing the gold signet she'd bought that morning, engraved with an initial because they'd had no rings bearing the Kelly family crest. How she'd agonised over whether it should be JB, JL or even GL, finally asking for a P monogram in elaborate Celtic lettering. Now that she had just exercised every molecule of self-control to hand it over in her noble gesture of closure instead of hurling it at him, she found she'd presented him with her old blue-eyed engagement ring by mistake.

She straightened up and held out the monogrammed signet ring shakily, pulling an apologetic face. 'Can we swap? That sapphire belonged to Francis's mother.'

He reached into his pocket and pulled out the velvet ring box, weighing it in his hand as though contemplating whether to hurl it into the quarry. 'Rather mean of him not to fork out on a new one. When's the big day?' He lobbed it at her, forcing her to drop the signet to catch it.

'There won't be one.' She stashed it back in the glove compartment then turned back, stooping to retrieve the dropped signet. 'I could never marry Francis.'

Straightening up, Legs saw that Byrne was staring down at her open-mouthed, dark eyes like two oilwells aflame.

'I was totally right to leave him when I did,' she sighed. 'I just did it in completely the wrong way, running straight to Conrad.' She turned the dusty gold ring in her fingertips. 'I always wondered if I'd made the right decision, but it was only when I got a second chance that I finally realised I'd mistaken guilt for regret. I couldn't get engaged to Francis a second time, real or fake. I just don't love him any more.' Without realising what she was doing, she had slotted the signet onto her ring finger. Lowering her hands out of Byrne's line of vision, she tried to ease it off, but it stayed glued to her sweaty finger. She tugged harder. It stayed put. She hauled and groaned. It had stuck fast.

Byrne's horse was stamping an impatient hoof, and he played on the reins to soothe it as he watched her curiously. 'You OK?'

'Fine!' She thrust her hands behind her back and looked up to find she was almost blinded by the fire in his eyes.

Suddenly smiling, Byrne jumped off and put his hands around her waist. For a disorienting moment she thought he was going to kiss her and had no idea whether she should kiss him back or sock him one. But instead he man-handled her onto the horse's saddle as deftly as a Highlander slinging a dead stag over his pommel. Feet flailing, she scrabbled astride just in time to find him swinging back into the plate behind her and picking up the reins.

As they moved off, Legs let out a terrified squeal and clung on for dear life. 'Stop this! I want to get off!'

'Have you ridden before?'

'Only the donkeys on Fargoe beach when I was little.'

'You're doing great,' he laughed, kicking his horse into a steady canter along the escarpment. 'You're a natural.'

Despite her protests, the next two minutes were amongst the

most exciting and addictive Legs could remember as the wind threw back her hair and the sheer speed made her laugh with amazement. Held firmly in place by Byrne's arms to either side, she had no choice but to enjoy the ride.

When they slowed to a walk, she was clinging onto the horse's mane too tightly to stop him reaching up to draw her hair to one side, revealing the nape of her neck.

'*Gráim thú.*' He read the new tattoo there, visible through its clear dressing, the skin around it still red and tender.

Legs' face burned with utter mortification. She hung her head, appalled to have embarrassed him – and herself – so much. 'It means nothing,' she muttered, desperately trying to salvage some pride. 'I thought it would be cool to have something Gaelic tattooed, and it was either that or Eejit.' When he said nothing, she raced on, 'I hear *tá grá agam duit* is all the rage, but I couldn't take the pain. As love letters go, silent Ps are by far the best. Ow!' She howled as the horse stumbled and her head rocked back against the tender flesh.

He steadied her with his rein arm, his voice in her ear, soft and incredulous. 'Is this a love letter?'

She shrugged, knowing there was really no point bluffing any more. 'Hand delivering letters is always a bad idea, isn't it? I feel like Delia Meare. I should have stuck to internet messaging. At least you could block me.'

He made no reply and they rode on in silence, Legs squeezing her eyes shut and grimacing, utterly ashamed of herself.

Then he dropped a kiss on her shoulder that felt like the touch of a monarch's sword. 'It's the most beautiful thing I've ever seen in my life.'

As the horse's metal shoes rang out on tarmac and they closed down the last few hundred yards to home in a heady haze of scorching sunlight and dancing midges, Legs could say nothing more, the lump in her throat so huge that she was struggling to breathe. Anger was still raging in her belly, trying to burn away the shame and lost-cause love, but but she had no voice to express any of it.

As they rode into the Coolbaragh stable yard, Brooke came wheeling out from his office beside the feed room, squinting up at them as the sun hit his face. 'Ah, there you are, Jago! I'm glad this one found you. She was quite determined. The other one's back here again too.' He waved towards the second tower. 'Pretty little redhead with a broken shoe. I sent her straight up there while Zina is having a siesta in the house. You have such a complicated life.' He turned to wheel back into the cool shadows of his office again.

Byrne jumped off before helping Legs dismount, gripping tightly onto her hand as she landed so that he could examine the ring. 'P?'

'It's a silent P,' she croaked, blushing because her noble gesture had got crammed on her own finger. Now that they were off the horse and facing one another again, she found she couldn't look him in the eye. 'As in Purple.'

'That's not silent.'

'Sidekick, then.'

'You mean psychic?' He stepped to one side to avoid being visible from the tower, looking at her face in wonder. 'Because I sometimes think you must be just that.'

Feeling very wobbly from her ride, the lump lodged in her throat now the size of a wicked stepmother's entire apple basket, she took a few stiff steps back, still unable to look at him. 'Let me talk to Kizzy.'

'Get rid of her.' His voice had a dose of familiar ferocity in it. 'She mustn't see me.'

Legs felt thick-headed and drooping with tiredness having barely slept in forty-eight hours, her reserves now being fuelled by adrenalin alone. She wasn't sure she had the strength left to physically remove Kizzy from the farm, nor did it seem the right thing to do.

'Surely I should explain about things?' She lowered her croaky, lump-muffled voice yet further so that Brooke couldn't possibly overhear through the open office door. 'She hasn't a clue that she's at her own father's house. His identity's always been kept a secret from her.'

'Let's keep it that way a little bit longer,' he whispered back, taking her hand in his, thumb tracing the engraved P on the ring. 'I'll have to speak with Dad first, and now's not the time. Right this minute, the only person I want to talk to is you. She must go. Please.'

Snatching her hand away, she knew she should tell him to get lost, shout that she knew all about life of lies and his callous womanising, and stand up for poor Kizzy who was such an unwitting pawn in all this. But then he stepped closer, a warm hand cupping her cheek as he breathed in her ear: '*Gráim thú.*'

She leaned against him for a moment, drawing his heat, the lump in her throat inflating like an airbag. 'Give me ten minutes.'

Chapter 48

Legs raced up the path to the tower, her breath like dragon's fire in her lungs, a stitch of anxiety already tightening into her side.

The tower was accessed by a thick oak door set in a deep arch. As soon as she stepped inside, she heard Kizzy's voice above her head, obviously placating Conrad on a mobile phone. 'I promise I won't leave until I see Gordon this time. He's definitely been staying here. The computers are still switched on . . . OK, I'll look.'

Legs glanced around the semi-circular entrance hall she now found herself in, like the inside of a stone moon, the most amazing light playing on its walls and ceiling. At her feet was a huge pond, taking up most of the floor, filled with carp and under-lit so that the reflections danced all around her. The curved walls were skirted with a continuous bench seat, topped with a thick green velvet cushion, and their straight counterpart was hung with incredible art, the sort that Poppy publicly despised and privately coveted – sensual, literal, and emotive, there were huge modern canvases depicting horses, dogs and landscapes. Legs recognised several as Stan McGillivray's, the notorious recluse and Brit Art rebel turned realist, whose work was amongst the most coveted of any living artist. Nothing hanging on this wall made any ironic statement whatsoever, it was a collection intended to bring pure pleasure.

She was in the Wizard of Oz's hideout, she realised.

Above her head, Kizzy's husky little Scottish voice was reporting to Conrad: 'It's OK, it's definitely a Ptolemy Finch book, not crime. I don't know where you got that idea from . . . hang on, I'll read a bit out to you—'

Her anger ignited, Legs stomped up the spiral staircase.

'Stop it!' She burst into the room, then reeled back in shock. 'Jesus!'

She'd never seen anything quite like it. With its windows covered with heavy tapestry blinds, the room was as dark as a cave. There were huge computer screens on every wall and just one enormous leather swivel chair in the middle of the polished oak floor, in which Kizzy was currently sitting like a seductive *Mastermind* contestant prepared to tackle anything asked of her, especially passes. Her delicate frame appeared to be swathed in little more than a few wisps of butterfly-bright twisted silk which Legs vaguely recognised from the Shh window as the 'latest catwalk collection', several layers of which she had undone to reveal a lacy pink bra.

Still dressed in the dusty pedalpushers and creased tunic she'd been travelling in, new tattoo itching beneath her hair, Legs felt at a disadvantage, as though she was bursting into an artfully shot Hollywood scene looking like an extra from Albert Square market.

Kizzy cut her call, mouth forming into a little 'o' of surprise.

'Gordon would like you to leave now,' Legs said, her voice high and strained, like a school prefect on her first day.

'Legs!' Kizzy dropped her phone and went bright red as she fumbled to re-knot a few of the rags. 'This isn't what it looks like.'

'It is, Kizzy,' Legs sighed. 'You were reading out new Ptolemy Finch material. That's totally against Gordon's wishes, and Conrad knows that.'

Far from being the seductive panther of business espionage she'd first appeared, Kizzy was more like a kitten found hanging off the budgie cage now. If she could have run up and down the curtains with her tail bushed and a startled expression on her face, Legs thought she probably would have.

So flustered that she'd tied her dress up like Gandhi's *dhoti*, she scrabbled around for her dropped phone. 'What are you doing here, Legs?'

Momentarily asking herself the same question, Legs suddenly hit upon an answer. 'I'm Gordon's new PA,' she announced brightly. 'I've taken over from Kelly. And he would like you to leave now. He was most emphatic, and it doesn't do to upset Gordon, as Conrad has no doubt told you. Shall I call you a taxi?'

'No need, I have a hire car,' mustering some dignity, Kizzy started out across the room with her chin held high, limping on her broken shoe heel like Sarah Berhardt making a dramatic exit, then stopped as she realised her knots were a serious handicap. 'You can tell Gordon I'll be back in touch as soon as I've discussed the situation with Conrad,' she said as she adjusted her dress, trying very hard to maintain her professional edge. 'I take it he doesn't know about your new job?'

'Gordon didn't ask for references.'

'Please reassure him I wasn't reading new material. Even I know that's *Raven's Curse*.' She pointed at the screens around them. 'And I've only sped-read it.'

Glancing around, Legs realised she was right, but she was too busy shepherding Kizzy down the stairs and through the glittering, watery hall to dwell on it. 'I'm sure Gordon will be in touch very soon,' she said, suddenly feeling sorry for her, and guilty for throwing her out when her secret history was right in front of her here.

On the doorstep, Kizzy looked incredibly shocked to find herself on the receiving end of a warm hug.

'Gordon won't let his fans down,' Legs reassured her. 'He's an amazing person and really lovely underneath all that cruel and hurtful selfishness,' Pausing to regroup, she flashed an anxious smile, 'But of course he's so protective of his private life that he bulldozes over people emotions and . . .' She stopped herself again. 'You'll like him a lot. You have so much in common. In fact you'll think of him as family, I promise. I know he's over the moon that you're going to be a part of his life.'

Kizzy smiled in amazement, her green eyes brimming with gratitude. She lingered for a moment in the arched door. 'I haven't had a chance to apologise for what happened with my mother. She was quite mortified afterwards. She's going to write to you.'

'Tell her she really doesn't have to,' Legs said hastily, not wanting to receive another of Liz Delamere's creative letters. 'All is forgiven. Speak soon. And don't let Conrad bully you into doing anything you don't feel comfortable with.'

She waved Kizzy away, watching her pick her way back down the path and cross the stable-yard before stepping into a very shiny little red hire car and driving away. Only then did Legs feel safe to retreat back into the wizard's lair.

She wandered upstairs again, looking around at the screens. They were all lined with writing, each showing a different page of a Word document. She picked out the words Ptolemy and Purple before she heard a door slam below her and turned to watch Byrne bounding up the creaking wooden treads, battered despatch case under one arm. 'You just saved my life. Thank you.'

'Hardly on the scale of climbing up a cliff or pulling me up on a horse.'

'I'm researching damsels in distress.' He strode into the room.

'You know what they say about authors; nothing is ever wasted. You haven't been snooping, have you?'

'Of course not.' She blushed, realising that she'd been about to indulge in exactly what she'd told off Kizzy for doing.

She watched him nervously, this caddish squire with his wild black hair and determined manner, striding between his computer screens. Here was Gordon Lapis in his tower, a master of description and deception; Jago Byrne at home, a horseman and a gambler, Ptolemy Finch in his attic observatory, reading the stars before flying off to save the world. He was a mass of contradictions, yet seeing him here in context made them all add up at last.

He sat down in his chair and started unzipping his long leather riding boots. 'No matter how many times I tell you to steer clear of me, you keep turning up.' He glanced up through furrowed brows, fierce eyes sparkling. There was a smile playing on his lips.

She found she couldn't answer, anger, love and compassion fusing her vocal chords closed. He seemed so sure of himself suddenly, whereas mortification and disappointment filled her with self-doubt.

The screens flickered around them still. Unable to stop her eyes being drawn to them, Legs read a few more lines on one, recognising a scene from the closing chapters of *Raven's Curse*, not long before she'd been forced to stop reading.

Swinging a hinged table across in front of him, Byrne pressed a couple of buttons on the keyboard there and the white screens were all simultaneously wiped to be replaced by a 3D screensaver of tropical fish around a coral reef picked out in extraordinary life-like detail, so that suddenly it felt as though they were in a submarine.

'Tell me you'll stay a while?' he asked, casting his boots aside.

'You offered me a cup of tea, remember,' she muttered edgily, watching a clownfish dart from one screen to another. She couldn't look at him now, the new tattoo burning shamefully on her neck. She was damned if she was going to embarrass herself any more than she already had by throwing herself at his newly liberated feet in their bright red socks.

On cue, Fink the basset waddled breathlessly upstairs carrying a pair of slippers which he placed at his master's toes before turning back to welcome her, tail swaying, pressing his muzzle between her ankles.

Byrne looked abashed as he stepped into the soft leather mules. 'Fink's an old-fashioned hound. I'll put the kettle on to boil.' To her surprise, he then simply pressed a couple more computer keys and one of the screens flashed up with a message announcing the *kettle on* before returning to the reef once more. He really was the Wizard of Oz, Legs realised, straightening up from patting Fink.

'Don't you have a fireside one of these?' She pointed at the fishy landscape. 'We could toast crumpets.'

With a few more keystrokes they were surrounded by flaming logs.

'I was only joking.' She swallowed, circling the room, looking at each fireplace in turn.

He swung around in the chair, marking her progress. She felt like a performing pony in a big top watched by the circus ringmaster.

'You have to be in control, don't you?' she asked, getting more wound up again with every circuit, the virtual flames surrounding her finally igniting her incandescent anger.

He shrugged, saying nothing, tilting his head as he watched her.

'You're basically just a big geek, aren't you Byrne?'

'If you say so.'

'Incredibly clever, granted, but a control freak geek nonetheless. You have no idea how to handle women at all.'

'Is that a fact?'

'I think you're scared of us.' She started to walk faster.

'I'm more frightened for my monitors right now. I think you should change direction. You'll get dizzy.'

'I feel so sorry for Zina.'

'Why?' he laughed softly. 'She's happy. I don't ask her to clean in here, if that's what bothers you.'

She couldn't believe his arrogance. 'You entertain girls you meet on the internet up here all the time. That's so disgusting!'

'Whatever gave you that idea?'

'Your own father told me.'

'Dad thinks the internet is the Devil's brothel. He won't even have a computer in the house, which drives Zina mad because she's desperate to get on Mumsnet.'

Again, his arrogance took her breath away, and she panted to a halt. 'She doesn't even *know* you're Gordon Lapis, does she?'

'No woman knows but you, Allegra.'

'Why *me*?' She swung around to face him. 'Why confide in me?'

He was looking less self-assured now, dark brows furrowed low. 'I didn't confide. You guessed.'

'Come on, all the clues were there!'

'Only to you.' His voice was as soft as hers was shrill and accusing. 'Nobody here is interested. Dad's the only one who knows and he doesn't even read the books. He only cares about things with four legs, which technically includes his wife right now.'

'Zina reads the books.'

'She tries, but she only understands about one word in three; she learned all her English from watching *CSI*, so she thinks soothsayers and sorcerers are forensic detectives.'

'God you're heartless!'

He stood up smoothly and walked towards her, those furnace eyes as bright as the screensavers around them, reflecting the dancing flames. 'You are right about me, Allegra. Totally right. I am supremely selfish and I am a geek. I am Ptolemy, an immortal boy who cannot grow old, playing with my wizardry and plagued by my childish hang-ups. I am quite hopeless with women. My father brought me up to be highly suspicious of love.'

'And now your grime poo is spreading far and wide to make up for it?'

He turned away, hands in his hair, laughing bitterly. 'Perhaps you're right to call it that. It's like shitting on somebody from a great height.'

'How can you say that if you've never tried trusting a woman?' Legs exclaimed. 'Even your wife doesn't know who you really are.'

'I'm not married.'

'And you treat her—' she stopped herself mid-sentence, cocking her head, eyes darting left then right. 'What about Zina?'

'She's my stepmother.'

She gaped at him disbelievingly as he turned to look at her over his shoulder, a slow smile curling the corners of his mouth. 'You thought she was my wife?'

Legs felt her face flaming again, appalled at her misjudgement. 'But she's our age.'

He grimaced. 'Dad has a lot of hang-ups about that, so best not mention it. He wouldn't believe she loved him for a long time. She came through the agency as a live-in carer a couple of years back – one of the benefits of my income is that I could get him a decent housekeeper. My Nan and her husband have lived in a bungalow beyond the orchard for years; they prefer their independence. Dad and Zina have the house to themselves now. She's restored his faith in love.'

She felt her face redden yet more. Then, like a porthole bursting open, the relief came flooding in, whooshing around her, bubbling and swirling and lifting her towards the beamed ceiling as grateful laughter caught in her her throat and tears touched her eyes. He wasn't married. He was a single man; one who she had just called a geek, disgusting and a control freak and accused of being frightened of women, she realised uneasily. The tide of relief quickly turned into a cold sweat of contrition.

'And you?' she managed to splutter.

He deliberately misread the question. 'I eat with them often, but mostly I'm working in here or away travelling. I keep meaning to buy a place of my own, but then I get writing and get too busy. I just write, Legs. That's what I do. I'm a geek – you said it. I write day and night sometimes. It's the world I most want to live in.'

'Along with the rest of us,' she agreed tearfully. 'Your world is magic to millions.'

'Yeah.' He ran a hand through his hair again, turning away to look at the flickering fires. 'Trouble is I'm as scared of fame as I am of love. Scared of everything, me.'

'You're one of the bravest men I've ever met,' Legs protested, remembering him running into the cellars the night they thought a murder had taken place at Farcombe, drawing the gunfire to himself when Hector was taking pot-shots at Spywood and finally climbing up the cliff-face at Eascombe Cove to rescue her.

He shook his head. 'I like my world just as it is. I write, run and ride – my three Rs. I'm just a typical Oirish farm boy.' He thickened his accent. 'Sometimes I climb mountains. I have friends I trust, but they can be forgiven for not trusting me when I keep so many secrets. I love my family. Conrad's like a portal to another world. He's the real sorcerer, turning my words into more cash than I know what to do with. I hate him sometimes, but what he does for me pays for the repairs here, so he's OK.' He looked around at the fires burning on the screens and gave his soft laugh. 'I just wish I had his literary knowledge.' He walked to his despatch case and pulled out a pile of paperbacks along with his laptop. 'Can you believe I've never read Joyce until now?' He held them up. 'That's a crying shame for an Irishman to admit.'

'His work's best appreciated when one's lived and loved a little, I think,' Legs bit her lip, heart starting to roar with hope. 'Now's probably the perfect time in your life to start.'

He smiled, looking down at the covers. 'When I got to Dublin airport, I realised I hadn't got anything for Nan – she wouldn't forgive me if I came back from a trip without a gift. So I found some god-awful gift shop, and there, on a tea towel, was the first line of the letter Francis wrote you.'

'They weren't his words,' she breathed. 'They didn't come from his soul. He arranged them like a bouquet of florist's flowers to win me over, but my heart was already lost to a whole new garden I'd found growing wild all around me. I love you.'

Moving slowly up to her face, his eyes found hers, and blinked in wonder. 'Christ, I'm so fucking naive. You had to have it tattooed on your skin to spell it out to me.' He looked away, raking his hands through his hair. 'The farm boy geek who has no idea how to handle women. Can you sue the tattooist?'

She shook her head, laughter and tears catching together in her throat. 'I think you're the most incredible man I have ever met, the brightest, the bravest and definitely the sexiest.'

'You do?' He looked at her again, eyebrows curling up in genuine amazement.

'I can't believe you're for real. You're no typical Oirish farm boy. Or geek.' She bit her lip, shame-faced.

He stepped towards her almost cautiously, thrusting out his hands. 'Feel there.'

She reached out for them, amazed at their warmth.

'Those calluses are from typing, these from riding. These cuts here are from climbing up a rock a couple of days ago helping some eejit girl who was hanging off a cliff in my favourite pants; I want those back, by the way.'

Laughing, she touched the bumps and grazes with her fingertips, and fought an urge to sink her lips to those honest, hardworking hands. She wanted to kiss every finger, and then his strong sinewy forearms, his wide shoulders and strong neck and most of all his mouth, eagerly rediscovering that kiss which she already knew had spoiled her from enjoying the kiss of other men for a lifetime.

But his lips were moving too much to kiss, words tumbling from them like tennis balls fired from a rally machine, holding her back from approaching the net.

'I thought that when you read that letter, you'd go straight back to Francis,' he said, his mouth tantalisingly close to hers, 'I was so angry at myself for screwing it up for you two, banging on about revenge and love meaning nothing, dragging you down into my darkness. That was all that seemed to matter at first. Then suddenly you were all that seemed to matter, but I'd already made your life hell by then, costing you your job, putting you in danger, questioning your heart. Even Liz Delamere's mad stunt was my fault for passing on her manuscript when I knew she was half crackpot, half genius. I'd misjudged everything, so it seemed only right to make amends after being proven wrong on all counts.'

His lips were frustratingly close. Legs couldn't take her eyes from them.

'Then I saw the light on a tea towel.' His voice was a seductive whisper.

She burst into laughter, blowing the kiss away. She wanted to catch hold of it and drag it back, but he was talking again, the tennis balls rapid-firing at faster, trickier angles now.

'I might not be as well read as Francis, but I do understand what he's feeling. A year ago, I thought my heart was broken, too. I'd have plaguarised any text going to have her back – the Bible, *War and Peace* or *Bridget Jones's Diary*. Whatever it took.'

Legs was broadsided by jealousy as she recalled the girlfriend who'd told him she loved him before running off. And hadn't Brooke talked earlier about champagne picnics and twisted ankles? It conjured instant images of an Anne Hathaway beauty tripping prettily through the meadows, breaking fragile bones, crockery and hearts.

'She went off with your best friend,' she remembered, the prospect of a kiss blowing further away by the second. 'They're expecting a baby in Cork.'

'The cork's popped,' his brows curled thoughtfully. 'I got a text yesterday.'

'How do you feel?'

'Yesterday I was too wretchedly in love to care. Lost-forever love. I'd moved on to a whole new level of misery. That news barely salted the wound.'

'And today?'

The kissable mouth laughed, showing lots of tasteable red tongue and lickable white teeth; the dark eyes blazed brighter than ever. 'Still in love. Totally in love. Different love. Better love. Shout out loud in love. I just want to thank them for finding each other so that I could find this love. I want to tell Francis to hang on in there and wait for this sort of "bloody marvellous love".' He adopted an upper class drawl. Then he took her face in his hands and drew her lips to his. 'I want to tell the world I'm in love. I AM IN LOVE! The Oirish farm boy geek is in love with Allegra North.'

Faint with happiness, Legs shut her eyes tightly in giddy anticipation and puckered up. The kiss was back on course.

As his lips closed over hers, the shock of energy between them rocked them onto their heels. They pulled apart.

Byrne's eyes melted into hers. 'Wow.'

'Wow,' she whispered back.

His fingers slid along hers and gripped her hand tight, steering her towards the stairs leading upwards.

As she tripped along behind Legs was aware that this might all be part of an elaborate seduction enacted many times on internet lovers. But to her shame, she didn't much care. She'd follow him to the ends of the Earth for another kiss right now. His trust was an aphrodisiac like no other. She was knock-kneed with lust.

On the level above the cave of computer screens was a top floor that seemed to have walls entirely made of glass, looking across miles of green hills. Almost blinded by light after the darkness below, Legs' eyes watered as she tried to take it in.

'I wake up to this every day,' Byrne led her to the window. 'It's hard to beat.'

'You live in heaven,' she laughed, eyes adjusting as she realised she was looking back towards the quarry, its vast, yawning chasm just a stony scar from this distance.

'The sea at Farcombe comes a close second, but I just love this.' He turned to watch her expression as she looked out across the green miles. 'What man needs any other castle?'

Legs thought about her dingy basement squeezed in amid the packed urban cubism of London and couldn't argue, although looking around the glass walls she couldn't help wondering where the loo was.

'The raven likes his own nest,' she whispered, then wished she hadn't because saying it made her think of the tattoo on his beautiful, wide breastbone, just above that tightly muscled torso and just beneath the dusty T-shirt he was wearing right now, which was close enough for her to reach out and pull off over his head in a heartbeat.

There was a huge, low bed in the middle of the room, covered with rumpled Egyptian linen. Its presence made her acutely aware of Byrne watching her in his dusty rip-offable T-shirt, and of her knocking knees keeping time with her castanet heart. She was so charged up with nervous sexual energy that she could no longer stand still for fear of sounding like a percussion section.

So she began lapping this room as well, the big, tousled bed seeming to mark her as she circled it. 'How many women have you seduced in here?'

He watched her maddened circuits with troubled eyes. 'None.'

'Let me rephrase that. How many women seduced you in here?' 'None.'

She stopped lapping and turned to face him across a huge and very sexy claw-footed bath. 'You're no bloody virgin.'

He raised a dark eyebrow. 'This room is. I don't sleep here often, and when I do I'm too exhausted for company.'

She started circling the room again. 'Great. Glad we cleared that up.'

'Are you feeling OK?' He watched her fanning out her vest top, cheeks growing pink.

'Fine! Just have a touch of what nineteenth-century heroines called the vapours.' She realised she must be coming across about as comely and beguiling as an amorous hamster on a wheel, but she couldn't seem to stop herself. She'd overindulged in romantic anticipation, and was now experiencing an endorphin high, a sort of sexual sugar rush that made her as manic and silly as a toddler after gorging on sweets. Growing dizzy, she did an about turn and started racing in the opposite direction.

She was suddenly reminded of the riding lessons she'd begged her parents for as a child. She'd wheedled and cajoled, written petitioning letters, drawn winning pictures, slaved lovingly over domestic chores and gone down on bended knees to secure her hour on Bo in a dusty indoor arena on the outskirts of Twickenham. Tacked up, docile eyed and obliging, he'd been presented to her beside the mounting block with his stirrups pulled down and his sweet-smelling muzzle outstretched to investigate her pockets. At which point she'd burst into tears and run back to the car to sob uncontrollably on the back seat, unable to explain to her confused parents that the pleasure was simply too great to sustain, the fear of disappointment too huge to contemplate. She'd folded under the pressure of her own expectations.

Byrne stepped back towards the stairs: 'This is making you uncomfortable. Let's go down.'

'No, the virtual fireplaces are worse!'

'The ground floor—'

'Not the glittery pond! That's far too . . .'

'Too?'

'Seductive. Don't you have a kitchen? Weren't you going to make tea?'

'Ah, yes. It's beyond the seductive glittery pond. You can close your eyes and I'll lead you to it if you don't want to look at that.' She couldn't quite tell if he was joking or not.

'I'll be fine!' She belted away from the bed and the 360-degree heavenly view and hurtled downstairs, past Fink the basset puffing steadily up towards her, past the fires and on to the illuminated carp amid their stunning artwork, pushing gratefully through the first door she found.

'That's the loo,' Byrne said helpfully from a discreet distance. 'I'll put the kettle on. I'm through the next door on your left.'

Legs admired the slate-tiled wet room, heart careering around madly in her chest. For a moment, she wondered how long she could hide in here, then realised that would look weird and took a few deep breaths before locating the kitchen.

This, she realised, was safe – the other half of the tower's ground floor moon had curved, shiny black units with a red gas range at their heart, a Smeg and a pinball machine acting as outriders, a long, thin glass refectory table with benches taking up the majority of the polished stone floor, and a black leather sofa flanking far left along with a pair of double doors far right. It was bachelor pad-tastic, uber-cool and totally without warmth.

'I hate this room,' Byrne threw open the double doors. 'My Nan chose it, God bless her. She says it's very "Versace", according to her magazines.' He headed outside.

He was gone so long, Legs edged towards the doors and peeked through.

There was a huge decking balcony overlooking a steep wooded valley. The tops of the trees were level with its railings. Byrne lent on these, his hands knotted together around the back of his neck, staring into the crown of a tall pine, deep in thought.

She rolled her lips between her teeth and stepped out onto the deck, sunlight soothing her face and shoulders.

He didn't look round.

'This was ruined like the other tower up until a couple of years ago,' he told her. 'Local legend has it the land belonged to a brother and sister who fought over its legacy. Every bitter tear they wept turned to stone and eventually incarcerated them in the two towers here. They're known as the Sibling Stones. They were ruined because they kept hurling bounders at one another.'

'You made that up,' she spluttered.

'It's my job.'

There was a long pause. He continued staring at the pine, where a woodpecker was drumming furiously. Now he was the one behaving oddly.

'Are you OK?'

'I'm not sure I like this place with you in it,' he admitted.

Legs felt as though her heart had suddenly been ejected from her between her ribs at high velocity.

'This place is all about Gordon Lapis,' he explained, narrowing his eyes as he turned to look back up at the tower. 'The money I earned as him has paid for it. Ptolemy lives and dies here, and Gordon never steps beyond these walls. It's not a part of the real world. You are very real indeed, Legs. You don't belong here.'

'I'll go.'

'No! I want you to stay.'

Her heart, finding itself on bungee elastic at maximum stretch, was pulled back into her chest again at even higher speed. There was another long pause.

The woodpecker was excelling itself now, drumming so fast, Legs half expected the top of the pine tree to drop off. Then she watched a spotted, feathery figure streak past overhead, red under-tail twitching. Yet the hammering continued, and she realised it was her own fingers rattling involuntarily against the wall beside her. Pulling her hand away and folding her arms, she caught Byrne's eye.

He laughed, holding out his own hands. 'Look.' They were shaking too, the fingers dancing like a dreaming pianist's.

'Look.' Uncrossing her arms, she held out hers which accompanied his, twitching and jerking like a slumbering harpist's. Now laughing too, she blurted: 'Sexual tension!'

'Is that what this is?' He looked delighted.

'It's either that or lithium poisoning.' She was in danger of getting all-consuming giggles in a minute. 'I don't know about you, but I'm far too tense for sex.'

Nodding, he trapped his shaking hands beneath his arms. 'How do we take the edge off it?'

'Going for a run helps.'

'Good idea.' He sprang up and burst back through the doors, sweeping her up in his slipstream. They made it as far as the long glass table, where he braked hard to avoid a loose chair and she slammed into him.

Both winded, they staggered aside, eyes watering.

Breathless, Byrne turned to her and held out his arms. She hurled herself into them.

The kiss he landed on her mouth was elixir. Far from dispelling any sexual tension, it pulled her every heartstring to breaking point and tightened every nerve ending in her erogenous zones.

Unable to stop herself, she took hold of the hem of his dusty T-shirt and pulled it up over his head, feasting her eyes on his broad shoulders and muscle-quilted belly, kissing the line of intricate black text along his breastbone. It was a quote she couldn't hope to pronounce, but she hoped it would be on her lips every day for a very long time to come.

Later, Byrne looked up through his glass dining table and exclaimed. 'I love this kitchen. I so love this kitchen!'

Legs curled tighter into his warmth and hoped his change in interior design taste was a temporary spell brought about by carnal mania. She loved this kitchen too. She never wanted to leave it for all its very Versace tackiness.

He reached out a hand to her face and turned it to his to kiss it. Soon she was rolling on top of him feeling like a magnet that had attached itself so totally to its counterpart they might never pull apart.

'I love you.' He looked up at her in wonder. 'I love you here. Never leave.'

Later still, she watched the sun setting over the crests of the pines through the double doors. 'I should get my bag from the car.'

'It can wait.'

There was an echo of déjà vu. This time, she had no desire to break free and reclaim her toothbrush and knickers. She felt as though she had come home. Suddenly she understood her mother and the summer of love. She had no care for the permanence of her situation here or the thoughts of others, just so long as each minute passed this exquisitely.

They drank coffee on the decking, wrapped in one shared towel, they ate toast between kisses at the glass table, they soaped one another with slithery abandon in the wet room and ventured up to the top of the tower to look at the stars and make love on a bed at last, revelling in its bouncing comfort and support as they twisted and turned, arched and weaved together.

As they curled up ready for sleep, Byrne traced the tattoo on the back of her neck in wonder, 'This is so beautiful. *You* are so beautiful.'

'You've always been able to read me like a book.' She reached drowsily for his hand to draw his arm beneath her chin like a warm stole. 'I thought you deserved a signed copy.'

Chapter 49

Dawn arrived, then bright sunlight, then dusk, all back-lighting their love-making, naps, chatter and teasing. Byrne made love with that same extraordinary intense focus and energy with which he wrote and spoke. They talked endlessly now, opening new avenues of honesty and laughter with each pause between breath-snatching kisses and tongue-tying sex.

Another sleepless night ensued, as Legs learned more about his childhood and his amazing rapprochement with Poppy. 'I had no idea what a clever woman she could be. Such bitterness is the richest of chocolate with her, smooth to taste if you take time to acquire a palate. She is desperate to be loved, but too rare to be appreciated by many. I adore her.'

'What about your father?'

'He would be the first to admit that he loved drink more than her by the end. Sure, he's never really forgiven her for abandoning us, but that she didn't take me was her saving grace, the ultimate sacrifice. He needed me more than she did.'

'And you forgive her that?'

'Now I do. I really do. I can think of no worse fate than being raised at Farcombe like Francis.'

She flinched away, guilt spearing her.

'Look at your misplaced penitence, Heavenly Pony. I swear you're more a Catholic than any member of this household. My father will love you as a daughter. He'll buy you a new rosary for every birthday.'

She stayed very still.

'I am an old fashioned geek,' he pointed out. 'I will propose one day, be warned. Just not yet. You will have plenty of opportunity to run away beforehand. I have to get dressed and go out to buy a ring for a start. Although.' He picked up her hand and admired the P signet still firmly stuck on her fourth finger, 'you may have beaten me to that with that amazing foresight of yours, Psychic Purple.' He kissed her finger.

'I'm not great at engagements,' she pointed out in terror, not wanting to break the spell.

'I don't think it'll be a very long one. I love you, you love me. It's absolutely right.'

She chewed her lip, still not trusting herself to believe something so lovely could be happening to her. 'It wasn't so long ago you lectured me about the fact any fool can say "I love you".'

'I meant everything I said that night.'

She started back in horror, but he reached out to stop her retreating further across the mattress, dark eyes glowing with honesty. 'When I said I'd fallen in love with you at half past seven the previous evening, I was telling the truth, although I hated myself for it at the time.'

Legs gazed back at him in amazement, blown away by the intensity of his eyes. 'Seven thirty-six,' she corrected breathlessly. 'You said you fell in love with me at seven thirty-six.'

'And you?'

'I always forget to wear a watch.' She wriggled closer again, 'but I'd hazard a guess at seven thirty-sixish. I felt the same,' she laughed, snuggling up to him once more. 'I've never reacted so strongly to anyone in my life. I absolutely, totally loved you from that point.'

'As long as you keep saying that to me, I think I can finally start to believe it.' He reached out to touch his fingers lightly on the words at the top of her spine in wonder.

'I love you, I love you, I love you, I love you, I love you, I love you!' She repeated over and over again until he was forced to kiss her again to shut her up.

Making love amid the flickering computer screens in Byrne's writing room was one of the most thrilling sexual highs of Legs' life. She loved the imaginative potency of the space and its dark, gothic intimacy; it was part monastic medieval study, part sci-fi fantasy. The big leather chair was particularly stimulating as she climbed on board to straddle him and it whirled around giddily, the illuminated screens blurring in front of her eyes until she lost count of the minutes they span round, just as she'd already lost count of the number of times they'd had sex. Byrne's beautiful, athletic body was her Seventh Heaven and his clever mind her Cloud Nine, fuelling her sexual imagination as they found more and more delicious ways of slotting together, from Legs Eleven to Sixty-Nine.

Afterwards, exhausted, they took a long soak in the claw-footed bath and collapsed into bed to sleep. When Legs woke up it was the early hours and Byrne was missing beside her in the bed.

She could hear computer keys tapping in the room below and crept halfway down the stairs to watch him working in his big chair, no longer a plaything as he focused on one of the many screens, typing furiously. He was wearing just an old shirt and the inevitable Calvin Klein boxers, his hair on end, gorgeously dishevelled and much-shagged. So besotted that her libido was on permanent tick-over like a waiting getaway car to sexual oblivion, Legs felt the engine revving on her sex drive again. She tried to let out the choke, not wanting to disturb him.

Around the room, other screens were open on reference websites and emails. She could see one from Conrad written entirely in capital letters.

Legs had checked her own phone earlier that day while Byrne was asleep and had found tens of messages from her ex boss and ex-lover queued up on it demanding to know what was going on and whether she was really now Gordon's PA. Conrad was back in London now, as was Kizzy, desperately preparing for damage limitation in the event of Gordon's big reveal being cancelled. It seemed Brooke had finally sent Kizzy packing by telling her that his son had just flown to New Zealand, which was panicking Conrad totally. Peering at the screen now to look at his email to Byrne, she could make out at least ten capitalised obscenities.

Aware that he wasn't alone, Byrne stopped typing and looked up at her perched on the curving staircase.

'I wasn't snooping,' she promised, then blushed. 'Well maybe a bit. I like watching you work.'

'You'll have to get used to it.' He smiled apologetically. 'I'm something of a workaholic.'

'Oh I'm sure I can help you deal with that.' She started down the stairs. 'The secret of getting rid of a vice is to acquire another one.' She dropped the bed sheet she was wrapped in as she weaved her way towards him.

'And what did you have in mind?'

She climbed back on board the chair. 'I was thinking of sex addiction.'

'Too late.' He started kissing her as she eased the boxers off and herself on. 'I'm already totally hooked.'

Curled up on his lap later, she watched as he flipped through more emails while he printed out his night's work.

'What is it?' She watched the sheaves of A4 churning out of the laser.

'Something I was working on that day at the quarry. It's finished now. I'll show you soon. Shit!' He sat up, spilling her off his lap as he read a message, anger mounting in his face.

'What is it?' She turned to see, but he minimised the screen, making her suddenly jumpy, even though romantic fires were glowing and cracking all around them once more.

'Is it Conrad going on about the Reveal again?'

He shook his head.

'Have you decided what you're going to do?'

Still his head shook, those big intense eyes lifting to hers, rivalling the fires all around them. 'Can you live with Gordon Lapis as a public figure?'

'Of course I can. If you wrote bestselling sex confessionals as Tess Tosterone I'd be proud to be outed as your lover. I love you.'

He smiled distractedly, looking at the fires on screen, but his head shook on like a dancing bear kept chained up too long in a Russian city square.

'The message is from Poppy in total histrionics,' he admitted, although Legs sensed he was trying to change the subject away from Gordon's forthcoming public appearance rather than wanting to talk about his mother's overwrought state. 'I sent her a line saying that I now know about Kizzy being my half-sister.'

'She's angry that you know?'

'Upset,' still his head shook on. 'She thinks I'll never forgive her for keeping us apart. I suppose I was pretty cold. I thought she'd told me absolutely everything, after all, and now I find out she's still withholding secrets.'

'But you do forgive her, surely?' she asked, remembering that he'd said he adored her that very day.

'For that much, yes. I'm sure she had her reasons.'

Legs was about to point out that he similarly had reasons for keeping Gordon a secret, but something about his tension stopped her. 'So what is it you can't forgive her?'

'I told her that I'm in love with you.'

She went very still. 'What does she say?'

'That I'm a bloody fool. That you and Francis have a love that can never be extinguished. She's told Hector and he's raging to the rooftops.'

'They're wrong!' Legs took his face in her hands, forcing his head to stop shaking. 'They're wrong!'

'Poppy says that you two have always been the future of Farcombe and I've just brought that down.' His eyes were bright flares of anguish. 'It's true, you were going to go back to him and I stopped you.'

'That,' she started to kiss him with incredible tenderness – 'was the bravest act of all your heroics.' Tears of gratitude stole onto her cheeks. 'It was the thing that really saved my life.'

Sliding to the floor, they made love again in front of eight roaring fires and one long-suffering basset hound.

By the third sunrise, they were both growing faint with hunger, the trendy Versace kitchen plundered of any edible contents. They'd lived off beans on toast and tom yum noodles for three days. Only Fink had eaten well, having discovered an unopened bag of dry dog food left unguarded in one corner, which he'd broken into and been gorging happily upon ever since in between voyeuristically observing all the sex taking place in his master's tower.

'We'll go to the main house,' Byrne told Legs. 'Zina is a fantastic cook.'

He went to fetch her bag from the abandoned car at long last, leaving her snoozing on the bed, unable to believe she had stumbled upon a haven of man and place that made her feel as though she was existing in a floating bubble that she never wanted to pop. With Francis it had been a prison; here she was in the clouds – literally. She watched the highest, tuftiest streaks of cirrus float by, shaped like seahorses.

It vaguely occurred to her that she should call her parents and reply to the many messages on her phone. But Legs was floating in a guilt-free place for once, so the outside world felt unimportant.

Then Byrne came back, loaded with unfamiliar women's clothes.

'Whose are those?' Legs eyed them warily, noting a high percentage of coral.

'Zina's. Your car is no longer there.'

'My car's been *stolen*?'

'Impounded.'

'Since when did the Laois County Council put double yellows on a disused quarry?'

'That's pronounced "leesh" not "louse", and it's nothing to do with illegal parking, although they're very strict on car dumping round here. That's a popular beauty spot; I guess a local walker reported your car abandoned there, and when a check was run on the British numberplate, it came up red hot. You are wanted by the police.'

'For what?'

'Something to do with a stolen painting?'

'Shit!' She covered her mouth in anguished recognition. 'I drove off from Devon with the Protheroes' Lucian Freud in my car boot.'

'That'll explain it,' he said drily, 'not to mention the family's sapphire ring in the glove compartment. Dad knows the local Garda well, and managed to persuade them the car left all the way up there was nothing to do with the family here at Coolbaragh, but it won't take a lot for them to add you and me together. They'll be back first thing tomorrow at a guess.'

'Technically, it's Vin Keiller-Myles' Freud,' Legs breathed as she realised the full scale of the man hunt she was now unwittingly framed within, 'or rather his fake Freud, but he obviously doesn't know that yet. Hector smuggled it to Spywood to avoid the truth getting out; he gave it to my mother as a romantic gesture. He was probably too blootered to remember he did it in the first place. I meant to drop it back in the hall postbox the night I left, but I was so desperate to get away I didn't stop. I'm guilty as charged.'

'Then you have no choice.' His dark eyes glowed.

Legs nodded, terror gripping her. 'I know. I have to turn myself in and explain exactly what happened.'

'Are you crazy? Hector will frame you like that little painting if you do that. I always knew he was a crook. He didn't give it to your mother as a love token, Legs. This is an insurance fiddle.'

She gaped at him, 'He wouldn't do that to Mum.'

'He's a gambler who bets on loyalty. If he loses a wager, the innocent go down in flames.'

'But Francis sold that painting, not his father.'

'Your innocent old flame.' He wrapped his arms around her. 'Hector probably acted in a panic, I grant you, but then all the die turned up sixes for him.'

'I don't understand how you can still hate him so much.'

'Trust me, I'm through with hating him,' he sighed, resting his forehead against hers, lash-veiled eyes scanning between hers. 'There's a bigger gambler in play here, and he's raised the stakes sky high.'

'Who?'

He cupped her face in his hand, looking away. 'When you found that notebook proving that Hector couldn't have been a part of the ring that brought down my father, I knew there had to be something I'd overlooked. It just didn't add up. So many trails I followed in the past had led to Farcombe, apparently to Hector and his years as a heavy gambler. Then when I came back here, I looked again at everything I have on file and struck upon the truth. The trails didn't lead *to* Hector. They led *past* him, to Vin Keiller-Myles.'

'Vin?'

He nodded, eyes on her again. 'Vin was right at the centre of the most corrupt betting circle operating in the UK for almost a decade, but his businesses were so interwoven with Hector's money and investments at the time, their lives running so parallel, it's hard to pull the threads apart. He didn't care if the finger got pointed at Hector; that was partly the point. Vin's name was never brought into it. For all their old-poker-cronie camaraderie, they hate one another, as you know. Hector's never forgiven Vin for taking his club; likewise Vin loathes Hector for stealing the love of his life. They've always looked for ways to out-gamble one another. Vin's been badgering Hector to sell him the Freud for years, but knew Hector would never oblige because both men know it's fake. But Francis didn't know that, and he has the authority to sell estate assets. With Hector distracted, Vin finally succeeded in the hustle.'

'What's he planning to do? Have the painting authenticated and sue the Protheroes for misleading him?'

'Something to that end. He has them in a financial noose. His main goal has always been the hall.'

'Might he get it?' she gasped.

'Not if he's threatened with evidence that could reveal him as a key figure in horseracing's most corrupt years. The police would arrest him like a shot. If convicted, he'd miss at least twenty festivals.'

'What are we waiting for? We must do it!' She grabbed his arm delightedly.

He stayed put. 'You think I want to help Hector and Francis out of this tight spot?'

'No, obviously not them.' She tugged at his arm, desperate to launch into action like Julie Ocean and Jimmy, 'but what about Poppy?'

'She's better off without them.' He shook away her hand.

Legs stepped back in shock, gazing anxiously at his lowered brows, that dark expression he wore when thinking and brooding, a portcullis of concentration.

'But they want to arrest me!' she whimpered, feeling suddenly very vulnerable. 'What about *me*?'

The arms came out again, and this time he enfolded her so tightly she was in no doubt that she was the right side of the defending drawbridge. 'I'm going to look after you, never you fear.'

'So what do you suggest we do?'

'We're going on the run, Bonnie.'

'We can't!' she yelped. 'The festival is less than a week away.'

'The perfect excuse for a road trip.' He kissed her decisively.

Chapter 50

'I used to drink to forget but I'm damned if I can remember why that was now!' Brooke cackled in an accent so creamily Irish that he made the old joke sound like a million hit YouTube clip. He was a head-on collision between cliché and *joie de vivre* that made him a delightful *bon vivant*. His politics, however, were not for the faint-hearted: 'I hate the British, I hate the Germans and I especially hate the fecking French, arrogant cowards. But I love their food – that's why I sent Zina here on a cordon bleu cookery course last year.'

Before they left Coolbaragh, Byrne insisted he and Legs must share a meal with his father and Zina. He clearly didn't believe in quick getaways when it came to going on the run, and when Legs tasted Zina's food she hardly blamed him. The soft, sweet chicken bursting with tarragon was almost worth getting arrested for, and she would have willingly served time for a third helping of her chocolate and orange mousse.

Brooke wasn't at all as Legs had first thought. She'd seen a jockey-sized, angry malcontent with his son's darkness, dry wit and his own demons to boot. Instead, Byrne's father had an unending appetite for life and food. He was Henry the Eighth on wheels, forever calling for more wine, women and song, although in his case it was endless tea, Zina and his fiddle. He had strong opinions on everything and, unlike Byrne, he delighted in expressing his emotions, his accent far thicker and his spoken voice far quicker than his son's.

'Me oul wan and her fella will be mad to have missed you, Legs,' he apologised now, slotting his fiddle under his chin, 'but it's Tuesday so they're getting ossified at Shaney's.'

'Nan and Mal are out at the local pub,' Byrne translated.

Brooke fixed Legs with a beady look. 'Jago needs to settle down with a good wife. We're all muck savages apart from him. Ignore any shite he gives you about being a typical Oirish farmboy. He's the black sheep of this family.' He launched into 'Rose in the Heather', bow jigging across the strings.

And it was a big family, the shelves and mantels of the farmhouse crammed with framed photographs of uncles and aunts, cousins, nephews and nieces. Brooke had been born third of six. Byrne had over twenty first cousins alone. There were many parties held here, Brooke boasted happily, huge Christmas and Easter gatherings, visitors constantly coming and going.

All her misconceptions were quickly turned on their heads as she re-evaluated Byrne once again. There he was in the photographs, surrounded by his huge close-knit brood, joining in the laughter and merrymaking. Far from being an aloof loner, he was known as a family joker and a daredevil, an unpredictable risk-taker that they all adored, mothered by the aunts and idolised by the younger cousins, forever being set up with ravishing single women he failed to appreciate.

'Sure, we thought he was of the gay persuasion at one time,' Brooke admitted as he lay down his bow between jigs to take a swig of tea. 'All those pretty girlfriends and never a hint of a proposal.' He eyed Legs' P signet ring beadily. 'There was the dusky one who ran off with Peter, of course, which came as a relief all round because she was terrified of the horses. Not a natural like you, Allegra. I haven't seen aul Lapis looking that loving since he shared his summer pasture with a feral goat.'

'That's enough, Dad.'

With a wise look, Brooke launched into 'King of the Fairies', Zina swaying along adoringly from the sofa behind him, swollen feet propped up on a pile of race cards on an occasional table.

For all Brooke's teasing, he clearly doted on his son: 'I don't deserve one as loyal and selfless as this man here. Jago was put on this earth by God to do good. His family are everything to him.'

Seeing them together, it was even more obvious to Legs why Byrne wanted to protect them all from the public world of Gordon Lapis and the media interest his wealth and fame would bring. Exposés about his childhood and his father's bleakest years would never be welcome here amid such hard-won contentment.

And Brooke made no secret of the fact that Byrne was responsible for his survival: 'He's been my minder since he was knee high to my wheels, always looking out for me, helping me with the horses, driving the wagon as soon as he was old enough, bullying me to clean up my act. He even bribed me into giving up the drink by offering to get As in all his exams. I remember saying to him, "surely it's supposed to be the other way around, son"?'

Brooke had great charm and warmth, and Legs saw why a young Poppy would fall for him against her family's wishes, and why wild-child Liz Delamere had been seduced by his charm. Zina obviously doted on him. And while he refused to be pitied, it was impossible not to feel compassion for a man whose lifelong mission had always been to race horses, and yet who could no longer ride them.

He seemed to derive pleasure from life itself these days though, and drew delight from those closest to him, sharing in their joys and loves. He took to Legs from the off, telling her she looked like a young Sinéad Cusack, relishing in her sense of humour and even sharing her great love of crime thrillers, 'Sure I've read everything that Dick Francis ever wrote, most so many times they've fallen apart. I love a good murder.

'My beloved boy Jago has introduced me to a new girlfriend!' He raised his fiddle in salute. 'I never thought I'd see the day the love could shine out of him like this. And what a girl to love!'

Even her perceived connection with the world of international art theft seemed to enhance her appeal. 'Byrne likes to live life on the wild side. He comes from a long line of clever scoundrels and brilliant horsemen.' And he'd not forgotten the fact that bad-tempered, lame Lapis had nuzzled her like a favourite companion. 'Sure, she has a way with horses, Jago. You'll have lots of little baby jockeys, although Zina and myself will beat you to the maternity suite.'

'You're not expecting a *baby* . . . ?' Byrne feigned astonishment as though this was the first he'd heard of it, his jaw swinging open, making his father laugh so much his tyres bounced. On the sofa, Zina snoozed on oblivious, slim fingers cradling her perfect semi-sphere bump.

Brooke laughed until tears ran, his delight in being a father again clearly a running joke at Coolbaragh.

Wiping his eyes, he sighed happily, 'At least God didn't take the tune from my flute as well as the use of my legs, although whether the instrument's playing the right music remains to be seen. I'd love a little girl. I'd hoped to have a pretty brood step-dancing to my fiddle by now, not a *sean-nós.*'

Byrne cleared his throat. 'Actually, Dad, I need to talk to you about something which may have a bearing on that.'

While father and son went outside onto the terrace so that Brooke could smoke a cigar and Byrne could talk, Zina jerked awake and, blinking sleep from her eyes, drew Legs over to one side, her long face guarded.

Now that Legs had studied her closer, without the jealous demons poking at the backs of her eyes, she could see Zina was not as young as she'd first thought and not as pretty, but she had a fire in her eyes that seemed a prerequisite to being a member of the household.

'You hurt him and you will be covered with Byrnes, you understand? Legs wasn't sure whether she was using the family name or threatening her with smouldering skin torture, but it was definitely not the moment to ask.

'I'm afraid my family are rather demanding,' Byrne apologised while they waited in the hall under strict instructions from Zina who was thumping around upstairs gathering yet more clothes for Legs. Fiddle music filled the house as Brooke played 'Drowsie Maggie' from the sitting room, shouting out "Is this not bloody good?" between refrains.

'They're lovely,' she assured him happily.

'I told you I'd give you plenty of opportunities to run away before I propose. Now is one.'

'I like it here,' she insisted, knowing she'd be happy to stay indefinitely.

Byrne's dark eyes flashed. 'We're leaving tonight. It's too risky to stay.'

Nodding, she kissed him, toes and fingertips buzzing as they had been all day, as though she was now so infused with love it was trying to fire itself out of her nerve endings.

'How did your father take the news about Kizzy?' she asked quietly as Brooke launched into 'Irish Washerwoman' with such aplomb the thumping feet overhead started tapping.

'I am the *daddy* of fecking fiddle players!' came the ecstatic cry from the sitting room.

'I think that answers your question,' his lips closed over hers and that devastating kiss just got better, as it had upon each replay for three days. It also got terribly out of hand if left to its own devices, and they were far too accustomed to being alone. When Zina finally came back downstairs clutching a bulging stack of pastel separates between her bump and her chin, Byrne and Legs were knocking framed photographs of Coolbaragh racehorses past and present into jaunty angles against the pattered wallpaper as they slammed from wall to wall, bodies craving chemical synthesis. They pulled apart as Zina dropped her pile beside them.

'I know you cannot keep your clothes on for more than a few minutes at a time,' a look of wistful reflection passed through her tired eyes, but then she hugged her bump and smiled broadly, nodding at the pile. 'These are all unwanted – rip them all off. Please do.'

From the sitting room, 'Irish Washerwoman' was reaching an ecstatic conclusion.

The first thing Legs noticed about Byrne's car was its colour.

'It's *red*!'

'Burgundy.'

'Red.'

'It's burgundy, Allegra. I asked for a custom purple one, but the Bentley dealer persuaded me that might attract the wrong attention.'

Legs looked around at the tan leather and walnut of the high-class convertible. 'And this *doesn't* attract attention?'

'The locals call it "the English car"; I bought it from Belfast. Sure, they think it's a bit flash, but they covet Paddy Flynn's new Isuzu pick-up far more.'

Chapter 51

The not-quite-red English car weaved its way from Laois to the Wicklow Mountains, its hood up, luxury interior filled with constant flirtation and laughter. Asleep on the back seat, Fink snored loudly, chin propped on a leather armrest.

Legs loved being a runaway, however irresponsible. She shivered with anticipation at the thought of a five star hotel, signing in as Mr and Mrs Prodygal-Sonne or suchlike, then playing with a four-poster and a marble bathroom all night.

But as dusk fell, Byrne pulled into a campsite on the banks of a lake glowing like molten copper.

Legs turned to him in surprise. 'Do we have a tent?'

His face gave nothing away. 'Know how to work one?'

'Is this a test?'

He smiled, saying nothing.

Legs was torn between throwing the bagged tent she found in the Bentley's boot straight at him or creating a framed canvas structure to screen sexual tension that was growing to intolerable levels between them. In the end, it was no contest.

Having camped since infancy, Legs erected the two man hiking dome in less than twenty minutes while Byrne cooked up a feast on a humble gas stove.

'There's more room in the car,' she complained after laying out two ground mats and a double sleeping bag in the tiny dome. Then she sniffed the air indulgently. 'That smells like campsite nectar.'

Byrne presented her with a plate of caramel-sweet, spicy sausages, baked beans and curling bronze toasted doorsteps with the reverence of a butler lifting silver cloche from a plate of Wagy steak. He was a master of fireside food.

'If we're going to live our lives on the run on the road, this is a great start.' She speared up her bangers blissfully, caramel, pepper and smoke exploding on her taste buds.

'I'm just an Irish tinker at heart.'

'Perhaps we should scrap the Bentley and buy a camper van then?'

'Irish tinkers like their big bling motors,' he reminded her, feeding Fink a sausage.

For desserts, they took ripe pears, slabs of chocolate and instant campsite coffee to the banks of the lake, its expanse now silver and blue shot silk in the moonlight.

'Where are we running to?' Legs asked quietly, the heat of the coffee burning her lip and blowing steam up her nose, yet filling her with strength.

In the moonlight, Byrne's flame-hot eyes flickered with steely light. 'Each other.'

Legs nodded, watching a full moon climbing the oblique angle of the lake's western mountain, like a silver ball being rolled uphill by a determined child.

'That's worth wearing out our soles.' She shared her last corner of Maya Gold with him before savouring the exquisite aftertaste with that mind-blowing kiss. Still kissing, they dived hurriedly under cover to share intimacies behind canvas walls which kept them awake for many more hours.

'I love all of you,' she whispered into the crook of his arm in the early hours.

'All of me?'

'Jago Jamie Kelly Ptolemy Finch Gordon Lapis Byrne.'

'Not Gordon.'

'Why not? I knew him first.'

'I wish to God he'd never existed.'

'You wouldn't be camping with me and a Bentley Continental if he hadn't.'

He turned his back to her and pretended to sleep.

The following morning, they ran for miles through breathtaking mountainous countryside, although Legs' breath was taken far more by the kiss at the highest point than by any scenery around them. She was now so high on love that they could have jogged along the central carriageway of the M6 and she would have been just as happy.

Why was it, then, that she had an uncanny knack of saying exactly the wrong thing, always?

His phone, which had no reception in the campsite, was in his pocket and chiming with messages now, like a morning Angelus. One was from Poppy, ever more panic-stricken that her long-lost son had lost faith in her.

'What does she say?' Legs demanded, ignoring her own phone bleeping sociably from her bum bag.

'She wants to meet up.' He read the message, hollow cheeks leaping with muscles. 'She's even prepared to forsake Farcombe.'

'She's going to leave Hector?' Legs gasped.

'I sincerely doubt it.' He looked at the message again. 'By "forsake" I think we can read "cream tea with tranquillisers in the village", or "car park at a Travel Inn" at bravest.'

Acutely aware that Gordon Lapis's scheduled appearance at Farcombe Festival was now just days away, Legs couldn't stop herself pushing the point. 'If you meet up, you can tell her the truth about your writing career, surely?'

'Why? We just keep running. Sooner or later Ptolemy Finch will be forgotten.'

'You know that's not true!'

'I'm no liar!' he exploded. 'If I don't tell the truth it's because I write fiction. I killed Ptolemy. He's currently dead, as thousands of readers are finding out on a daily basis. That's not fact, granted. Based on his track record, rescue should be guaranteed; one takes it for granted. Author and reader have an unwritten agreement nestling cosily between the lines that good will eventually triumph, however slim the odds may appear at times. That's fiction. I write it, I don't live it.'

'But isn't life on the run just make-believe too?'

'If you want to get real, Allegra, you can rewrite the script.' He stood up and started pounding down the mountainside, only to double back to catch her in his arms as she stumbled blindly in his wake.

'I'm sorry, I'm sorry, I'm sorry.' He held her so securely she felt as though she was drowning in him, his lips tight to her throat. 'I love you. Please don't let's stop running yet.'

When they returned to the banks of the lake, he took both their iPhones and hurled them into the water.

'Isn't that terribly environmentally unfriendly?'

'Shit, you're right!' He stripped off his clothes and waded in to dive for them, dipping around like a dolphin.

Stripping off, Legs waded in too. Soon they were getting beyond friendly in their environment, the phones forgotten.

They drove to Dublin in the not-quite-red car, where Byrne had booked a suite in the Gresham once occupied by Taylor and Burton. There, they made love half-on, half-off the four poster bed, shared a deep bath, dressed in such a hurry that both their buttons were one out, and ran on foot to the Abbey Theatre to catch the last night of the sell-out, highly acclaimed production of *The Playboy of the Western World*, starring a Hollywood bad boy originally hailing from Ballymun.

'How did you ever get tickets?' she gasped as they claimed their balcony seats seconds before curtain up.

'Like everyone else. I booked online as soon as they were released.'

'But you can't have known we were going to be here?'

'I was going to bring Nan. She loves this guy playing Christy.'

It was an extraordinary performance, the actor proving he was far more than a brooding heartthrob with a well publicised drug problem and sex tape to his name. He could act. Legs was moved to tears by his reconciliation with his father at the end and his rejection by Pegeen, who she knew made the right choice even though almost every woman in the audience would have taken the brooding Hollywood actor then and there.

'I'm only sorry your grandmother didn't see it,' she said to Byrne as they emerged, hands still buzzing from clapping.

'I'm not.' He took her buzzing hand and held it to his lips to kiss it, making it buzz even more. 'When she learns he didn't even take his shirt off, she'll not think it was worth coming. Do you want to eat?'

She shook her head. Being with him was doing bizarre things to her appetite, ravenous one moment, no appetite for days thereafter.

They walked back arm in arm, weaving through the trees in front of Clery & Co. like bending poles and kissing beneath each one.

In front of the statue of Joyce, Legs gave the great man a salute and silently apologised for the fact that she would never understand or appreciate him as much detective fiction, adding that she dearly hoped that Francis one day found a woman who could.

Byrne waited patiently, not entirely sold on the tribute, but respectful enough to let her worship as he leaned against Joyce's walking stick.

'What did you make of *Ulysses*?' she asked Byrne as they walked the last short stretch to the hotel.

'Is this a test?' he asked.

She shrugged. 'Quicker than putting up a tent.'

'Takes a lot longer to read *Ulysses* than to put up a tent.' He took her arm in his.

'I'm still unravelling the narrative groundsheet. Do you think I'm incredibly thick?'

'Heavenly Pony, I haven't even started sorting out the tent pegs. Who am I to judge?'

To their delight, they soon discovered a whole new bedroom to their suite in which to make love, along with a balcony overlooking the still whooping, revelling streets and the city skyline, and then it was back to the deep bath to lather each other with every miniature soap product on offer.

The following morning, Legs slept very late and then luxuriated with breakfast in bed. She ordered enough for two, but Byrne, who had gone for a run, was missing for hours. In the end she shared his ration with Fink then got indigestion.

'Did you get lost?' she asked when he finally reappeared, heading straight into the shower.

'I had to make some calls and send a few emails.'

She dangled off the bed so that she could see his reflection in the long mirror opposite the bathroom door, 'Shouldn't have thrown away your phone.'

He turned on the water, stopping the conversation. Legs admired him for a bit, belly squirming with lust, but her indigestion was giving her a stitch, so she got up to dress.

It seemed like an eternity since she'd had any of her own clothes for more than a few hours. She flipped through the selection Zina had kindly lent to her, a cornucopia of pastels. So far she'd worn the same baggy pink linen trousers each day, but they were now looking decidedly grubby, and the only alternatives – a little pale yellow dress or tight white pedalpushers – had been bought by somebody with great legs they liked to show off. She plumped for the dress as the lesser of two evils, knowing that to encase her thighs in white would be about as flattering as sporting voluminous bloomers stuffed with bubblewrap.

Pulling it over her head, she went to the mirror to check how much cellulite was on show, then did a double take. Somebody with very shapely legs was staring back at her from the mirror.

They couldn't be her legs, she thought excitedly. Smoothly curved, hand-turned to perfect symmetry and creamy taut. No, they couldn't be.

Behind her, Byrne stepped out of the shower and let out a long, appreciative wolf whistle.

Legs turned an amazed circle, wondering how that had

happened. She supposed that she hadn't really looked at herself for longer than a few seconds in a full length mirror since before falling ill. She'd had plenty of opportunities to scrutinise her face, quite liking her cheekbones yet missing her rosy cheeked glow. And she could tell her stomach was a bit flatter and her waist a bit smaller – although right now she had a decidedly rounded belly from eating two breakfasts. But her thighs, which had always resisted every diet, exercise programme, expensive cream and undignified wrap in the world, were a revelation.

She struck a model pose, laughing in utter delight. She didn't care if she only had slim legs for a few short weeks; she was far too greedy to keep them, after all. The fact that she had them at all, however fleetingly, was wondrous. She wanted to dance along O'Connell Street in her bare feet and her short dress like a sixties flower child performing the odd high kick. To know what it felt like to wear a miniskirt was heaven.

To know what it felt like to stand in front of a mirror with a naked lover starting to kiss her shoulders, lift up that miniskirt and part her slim legs was even more heavenly.

Byrne's gaze met hers in the mirror and she shivered deliciously, her body absolutely rippling with desire. 'You are the loveliest creature alive. My gorgeous Allegra.'

'Your gorgeous Legs,' she corrected, deciding it was time he used the name she knew best. Then, as he slid a hand beneath her buttock to lift one thigh, she smiled deliciously. 'You're stretching your Legs.'

Over her shoulder his smile creased his eyes as he slid inside her. 'Pulling my Legs.'

Afterwards, ravenous, he ate all the food out of the minibar and the complimentary biscuits from the coffee tray.

'We could order room service,' she laughed, watching him indulgently from the bed, knowing that she would never tire of admiring his buttocks. 'Or go out and get something round here?

Look at the shops?' she hinted. She didn't want to get all *Pretty Woman* on him, and would be happy to buy herself some new clothes, but her purse was still in her impounded car.

The trouble was, Byrne liked her most naked at the moment, so had no real interest in acquiring items to cover her up. The thought wouldn't even occur to him.

He clambered on the bed beside her, shaking his head. 'We're checking out in a minute.'

'Where are we going?'

'Sea Legs.' He dropped a kiss on her bare stomach.

By lunchtime, they were on a ferry headed for Holyhead. On deck, beneath an angry grey sky, they leaned on the rails and looked out at the rumpled, creased sea.

'What's the plan?' Legs asked.

Byrne's fingers threaded between hers. 'I'm taking your advice.'

She smiled with delight, gratified that he trusted her. 'So where are we going?'

'The West Country.'

She felt immediately queasy, her two breakfasts repeating on her. 'If one's on the run, isn't it rather counter-intuitive to run directly to the place where one's wanted most?'

He looked out to sea for a long time, wind blowing the hair back off his face, revealing its intricate contours and angles, and deep furrows in his brow. 'You were quite right when you said we can't keep running.'

'I didn't mean "let's go to Devon".'

'We're not going there right now.'

'Well that's a relief,' she said. 'At least I have a few hours before getting arrested for taking possession of a picture of . . .' She glanced around, aware of the number of people close by.

'Yes, what was the picture you stole *of?*'

'A front bottom,' she whispered prudishly. 'And I didn't steal it. I mistakenly drove away with it in my car, which incidentally is the unluckiest car I've ever had. I've had a speeding penalty, three parking tickets, been clamped and almost driven into a quarry since getting it, and now it's been impounded. I loved my old red Honda.'

He put his arms around her, laughing, 'I'll buy you it back as a wedding present.'

'I'll pin up its photo in my prison cell,' she grumbled.

Still laughing, he kissed her, hands on her face, his lips so familiar against hers now that she struggled to know or care where one pair started and another ended.

'Aw, isn't that romantic. Just like *Titanic*!' a voice exclaimed in broad Irish brogue.

'We haven't hit an iceberg yet,' Byrne whispered when they came up for air.

'It's only a matter of time,' Legs muttered, watching over his shoulder as the lighthouse at the end of the Holyhead harbour wall grew ever-closer, like the last pawn on a chessboard as the endgame approached checkmate.

When Byrne stopped to refuel at a service station on the M5 – the not-quite-red Bentley Continental now attracting huge amounts of attention everywhere they went – Legs took a loo break and saw the front cover of the *Express*, stopping dead with total horror. Her face was on it.

FARCOMBE INTRIGUE LINKED TO SPURNED LOVER; DEATH THREATS AND ART THEFT. COULD PTOLEMY FINCH SAVE THE DAY?

Buying a copy along with a pair of cheap dark glasses and a baseball cap, she slunk back to the car.

Byrne was unimpressed. 'The festival team are going after maximum publicity for Gordon. They're working with Conrad and Piers Fox now, remember. Nothing will be sacred.'

The article left readers in no doubt that Ptolemy's creator would be unveiled in two days' time. Speculation about his identity had gone mad; the prime suspects were under siege. Stephen Fry was being door-stepped, and Salman Rushdie was threatening to go into hiding again. Investigative journalists and paparazzi were beside themselves trying to get to the truth first.

'Gordon can't leave it any longer to reveal his face,' Byrne said darkly. 'Any day now, they'll find him for themselves and make up their own truths.'

'Catching him on the run with an international art crook won't do a lot for his reputation as a children's author,' Legs joked flatly. 'It's OK. Drop me at the nearest moor. I'll take the tent and take my chances.'

'Let's try to enjoy tonight.' He indicated to join the Bridgewater slip road. She noticed his knuckles were white against the black leather of the steering wheel.

'Where are we staying?'

'Watchet.'

'I was only asking.'

To her surprise he laughed, the tension seeming to drop away from him. 'We're going to Watchet marina. A friend has a yacht there at our disposal.'

'Generous friend.'

'I met him travelling. He's lives in Costa Rica now, so the boat's never used. He hasn't got around to sailing it over there yet.'

Legs had sudden visions of her and Byrne hoisting mainsails and tacking between North Somerset and the Pacific Rim.

'So when you say that we must stop running,' she asked carefully, 'does that mean you want to start floating instead?'

He took a long time to answer, pulling a pair of dark glasses from the glove-box and putting them on as a low sun burst through the clouds at last. Now Legs couldn't even read his expression as he again said: 'Let's enjoy tonight.'

With the car's roof down, Fink propped his paws up on the rear door trim so that he could catch the slipstream and sniff the air, ears turned inside out. It was a very balmy afternoon to breathe, thick with the scent of harvest and autumn approaching, a bonfire tang in the air and hedgerows crammed with ripening blackberries and sloes.

Letting herself daydream idly, Legs found the idea of life aboard a sailing boat increasingly erotic, imagining herself in a bikini, deeply tanned with sun-bleached hair standing at the prow of a glossy white cruiser with Byrne, mahogany-skinned and superhero-chested at her side, surrounded by turquoise sea.

By the time they reached the marina, her fantasy had got thoroughly out of hand. As the Continental's soft-top closed back over them, she was out of her seat and kissing Byrne before he'd even pulled up the handbrake, which wasn't wise so close to the quayside, but she didn't much care right now, just as it didn't bother her that the Bentley attracted immediate attention as usual, and two faces were soon peering in at them while conducting a loud discussion as to whether it was Simon Cowell in there being molested by a blonde nympho.

'Simon likes dusky beauties,' one of the onlookers pointed out. 'I think that's a footballer. Doesn't John Terry have a GT?'

'Jesus!' Byrne laughed, pulling away from her lips. 'I'm definitely selling the car. Fink might approve of dogging, but it's not my thing.'

'Boats are much more private,' Legs couldn't wait to get aboard. 'There's only sea-life to watch us once we're in open water.'

'And Fink.'

'He'll be far too busy dog-fishing,' Legs pointed out, throwing open her door. 'Let's go straight below deck and get naked.'

'You can make a start on that while I tell the harbour master we're here.' Smiling up politely at their audience, he got out too before turning back to Legs. 'I expect you ship-shape and Bristol fashion by my return.'

'I'll be waiting, bristols flashing.' She blew him a kiss over the top of the car.

'She's the big cruising yacht called *Chastity*. She should be unlocked by now,' Byrne told her then loped off to the marina office, Fink at his heels.

Still admiring the Bentley, the two onlookers crossed their arms in front of their chests, one of them breathing: 'Did he just say *Chastity*? You know what they say about her.'

'Owned by *drug smugglers*,' the other confirmed in a nervous whisper.

'I've already seen someone go on board today. They must be planning a run.'

Chastity was not exactly the glossy-white Cannes harbour dream Legs had envisaged while making her steamy seduction plans in the car, but she had a vintage sex appeal nonetheless. She was the forty foot grande dame of the marina, bobbing at the far end of a pontoon, with peeling powder blue paint and faded woodwork. Legs raced on board.

Clanking below deck, she started to undress hurriedly, ripping off borrowed clothes, eager for the fantasy to keep distracting her from reality. She knew Byrne felt exactly the same way. Sex was the easiest, happiest place to escape to right now, along with crazy daydreams of setting sail. Down to her underwear, she shook out her hair and ran her hands up the back of her hot neck to scoop it up from her shoulders and roll the tension from her spine.

'Hello Allegra,' a figure walked through from the main berth. 'You've put on weight.' It was Poppy.

'What are you doing here?' Legs yelped in alarm, hands still on her head as though being held at gunpoint.

'I could ask you the same thing.' She squinted short-sightedly at her. 'Is that a tattoo on your neck? Who on earth is "Graham"?'

Chapter 52

'I got a taxi here,' Poppy was shaking with nerves. 'I had to wear my eye mask throughout the journey. I've had two Valium.'

She'd commandeered the only dry, upholstered bench in *Chastity*'s main deck, which she was stretched out upon like a patient on a psychiatrist's couch with a snoring Fink squeezed in alongside her.

Legs and Byrne were sharing the lid of a damp storage chest.

Byrne had been livid to find his mother on board waiting for them, but Legs had to admire her guts. Poppy hadn't left Farcombe in over five years as far as she was aware, apart from one brief recent visit to a hospital under Hector's escort.

For once she wasn't wearing her turban and smock, her deep red hair liberated in a surprisingly neat bob, her narrow frame layered in a long blue cashmere cardigan, matching polo neck and slim white jeans. She looked unexpectedly stylish and normal, but equally unstable as she fished a hipflask out of a cavernous handbag and helped herself to a large tot, watching with huge, turbulent dark eyes as Byrne paced around the confined space like Odysseus waiting for the tide to turn, clearly longing to set sail.

'You could have suggested somewhere closer to Farcombe to meet, Jamie,' she complained. 'This is decidedly Ancient Mariner.'

Chastity was a salty, seafaring vessel with few home comforts. Outside, masts were clanking, waves lapping and gulls calling.

'We weren't expecting you until tomorrow morning.' He shot Legs an apologetic look. She returned an anxious smile, biting back a repost that she hadn't been expecting Poppy at all. She only hoped he wasn't planning on taking his mother with them to Costa Rica.

'I *knew* I had to get here as soon as I received your call,' Poppy's smoky voice almost as low as her son's.

'We must talk,' he sighed. 'I guess tonight's as good as tomorrow. Let's get it over with.'

Suddenly Legs realised what Byrne had meant when he said he was taking her advice; he was going to tell his mother the truth about Gordon Lapis after all. She wanted to whoop, cheer and kiss him all over, but suspected audience participation would probably be unwelcome at this precise moment, as would any desire to kiss him repeatedly.

'I might go for a run,' she said tactfully, eager to give them some privacy.

'No, stay!' Byrne reached out for her hand.

As ever, Poppy approached any frank and open discussion with the defensive tactic of a dramatic monologue, employing her deepest and throatiest emotional tenor: 'I only found out that Brooke was Kizzy's father when Mummy died – Goblin Granny as the family knew her. I'd guessed at it, of course, but I had no proof. Mummy never told another soul, but she did write it all in her diaries, in code. I started to read them when I was clearing her house. They were easy to decipher. That's also when I learned that Liz and I have the same father.'

Byrne let out a cry of surprise. 'Liz Delamere is your sister?'

'Yes. Isn't it ghastly? Mummy was Liz's godmother, just as I am Kizzy's. How many notes we could have compared! Can you imagine being godmother to one's husband's illegitimate offspring? It's a wonder the fonts didn't boil. Of course Liz was a total force of nature from the start. It's amazing she survived to adulthood, frankly, although hardly surprising that she was promiscuous. She's very like our mutual father, so over-dramatic and impetuous, and a terrible parent like him. She had no interest in poor little Kizzy until recently.

'When those death-threats started arriving at Farcombe, I guessed it was her,' she said in a shaky tenor. 'I thought she was going to try to kill me for interfering in Kizzy's life, but it turns out she was just trying to impress you, Legs. God knows why. Nobody can have told her you'd lost your job at the literary agency; we'd have been spared a great deal of upset if they had. Darling Kizzy never tells her anything, but one can hardly blame her, and it was far too late by the time she realised what was going on. Liz is utterly wilful when she gets going, as we all bore witness that night. She's lucky she wasn't arrested, frankly. But she wrote me a very charming letter afterwards; we're going to meet for lunch. I think she has a rather fanciful idea of appearing at the festival to read from some book she's written. Trying to prove she's one of us, no doubt.'

Legs cleared her throat and glanced at Byrne, but his face was a mask.

'Didn't you ever think Kizzy had a right to know who her father was?' he asked.

Poppy looked surprised. 'I never saw what possible use he could be to her unless she wanted to learn to ride. The Hawkes have given her every love and care a child could want. Brooke can only hurt her.'

Legs watched Byrne in alarm, certain he was going to explode, but to her surprise he shook his head with a rueful smile, sitting beside Poppy and taking her hand tenderly in his. 'She deserves to get to know her father. It might even straighten her out a bit.'

'Oh she'll never be straight, darling. That really was always the greatest flaw in matching her with Francis, who quite frankly would take a beagle as a girlfriend as long as she looked at him adoringly and listened to his endless opinions. *So* like his father.' She shuddered and shot Legs a steely look before carrying on: 'Darling Kizzy's heart has been quite lost on another throughout.'

Legs let out a sigh of recognition. 'Édith.'

'How do you know that?' Poppy looked astonished.

'Nothing gets past Julie Ocean,' Byrne reached out to take her hand, his own icy cold, betraying the tension he was feeling as yet more home truths were revealed.

'I suppose Julie Ocean's one of the arty crowd that used to gather at the Book Inn,' Poppy was saying. 'Kizzy and Édith were a part of it. Last year they had a very passionate affair which ended very unhappily. I guessed at it at the time, but thought it was just a phase, like Virginia Woolf. Kizzy did try to make a go of it with Francis, poor girl,' Poppy sighed, 'and I know that she would do anything for me, but frankly it was torture to watch in the end. If anything Francis pushed her further in the direction of Sapphic love. He takes so much looking after.' She let out a deep sigh. 'I do wish you'd reconsider him, Legs. You're so good for him.'

'She will *not* reconsider,' Byrne thundered.

'Hector is terribly disenchanted by all this. He's desperate for grandchildren. He always thought Édith was going through a stage and would settle down eventually to have babies, but this latest development rather refutes that – and now you and Francis look unlikely to reconcile, Legs, he'll have to stop practising lullabies on the bassoon, poor darling.' She let out a long, soulful sigh, but if she expected to garner any sympathy on board *Chastity*, she was mistaken. 'He's hugely disapproving of Édith taking up with Kizzy,' she went on. 'He only tolerated Jax because she was so practical to have around the house and looked rather like a chap. He says decorative women like Kizzy and Édith should never take up together because it limits the high end heterosexual market, leaving only poor quality goods available. He's such a corporate reactionary in some ways – my darling caveman.' She shuddered, but this time from pleasure as a smile spread across her face. The idea of a limited heterosexual market available to Hector clearly pleased her a great deal. 'He's even threatening to boot Édith out of the London house, but I suspect that's only as an excuse to sell it. He's convinced the only way to secure a knighthood is to bung another few million to charitable causes, and we're stupidly hard up.'

'Can't he stage a few more art thefts and claim them on insurance?' muttered Byrne.

'Oh that's just Hector being silly,' Poppy dismissed, as though it was no more than a mislaid cufflink.

'He can't really believe I took that painting deliberately?' Legs asked nervously, reluctant to reveal the full truth about how Hector's love token came into her possession.

'Well he's certainly been shouting down the phone and annoying the police a lot. They even seem to be taking him seriously, which is quite amazing given Liz's death threats turned out to be harmless creative over-enthusiasm, although I suppose the fact you ended up hanging upside-down from a cliff in front of witnesses added some weight to his argument, Legs. Then of course you ran off with that painting, and focus shifted from malicious threats to art theft. It's insured for a hundred thousand, which would have come in jolly handy.'

'Oh God, he'll have me banged up,' she groaned.

'I'm sure all will be forgiven if you come back to Francis,' Poppy gave her a knowing look.

'I can't do that!' she yelped, looking at Byrne whose dark eyes glowered furiously.

Poppy folded her long fingers together in front of her nose and crossed her eyes as she regarded her large, brightly coloured glass rings before glancing across at Legs. '*Nobody* will arrest you over that dreadful geegaw, Legs. Quite honestly you did us a favour getting rid of it. Hector and I always argue about it because he once told Francis it was a Freud, showing off as usual, and now he can't bring himself to admit that he painted it himself as a young man. Now that it's been recovered, it's bound to be authenticated, and of course the truth will come out. It's actually a portrait of one of the waitresses at the Fitzroy Club. Hector told me he had an affair with her while Ella was pregnant with Francis, but I don't think it will help to tell him that right now.'

'Probably not,' Legs agreed shakily.

'The man's shameless!' Byrne exploded at his mother. 'How can you bear to take him back?'

Poppy looked at him levelly. 'For all his considerable sins, I love him a great deal,' she sighed. 'It's such bliss to have him in the house again, I feel reborn. It's been so deathly quiet without him. He's my music, my conversation and my laughter. I know he's terribly wayward, more so than ever these days, and he probably should be taught a lesson, but with the festival so close at hand, I need him to stay strong for all our sakes.'

'I'll happily teach him a fucking lesson,' Byrne raged.

'Please don't hate him, Jamie. I know you two haven't got off to the best of starts, but Hector really terribly charming once you—'

'Never!'

'Oh, what a mess,' Poppy let out a deep sigh, pressing a finger-tip between her eyes to relieve the pressure of a headache there. 'Everything surrounding the festival is very fragile this year, including the house. Thank *goodness* for Gordon Lapis. He is Farcombe's saviour.'

'You think so?' Byrne asked darkly.

Legs watched him anxiously. There was a muscle pounding in his cheek.

'I know it,' Poppy seemed greatly cheered by the thought of Gordon as she reached for her hip flask again. 'Such a talented chap. Do you know I'm probably the reason he asked to make his debut appearance at Farcombe? I wrote to him once in appreciation of his work (I'm sure the poor man hardly ever gets a letter from anybody with a decent education) and had a charming reply from his PA saying how gratified he was. I can't wait to meet him. I think we might have rather a lot in common, he and I.' She checked her reflection in the flask's silver side, its convex curves widening her cheekbones to flattering Marianne Faithfull proportions.

Byrne's brows lowered over his furnace eyes. 'The man's a selfish bastard. He'll let you down, trust me.'

'Do you know him then?'

'Intimately.'

'How thrilling! I had no idea you were bisexual.'

Byrne was looking up at the cabin's wooden roof in frustration. Then a wry smile touched his tight lips. 'Poppy, *I* am Gordon Lapis.'

Her hands flew to her face again, huge eyes gazing at him over her fingers, her voice muffled as she gasped: 'Would you mind saying that again?'

Sitting down at her side, he took her hand in his and told her about his writing alter ego as calmly and simply as he could.

Afterwards, she kissed his hand like a fervent disciple kissing the Ring of Fishermen, 'You are so clever and so brilliant and so unique and so – rich! And you are about to be so, so famous.'

'I don't want to be famous.'

She gaped at him in horror, almost more shocked by this bombshell than the news that he was Gordon. 'Why ever not?'

He stared across at Legs. 'I want to marry the woman I love and have a huge family, ride horses and write new books. I don't want that life to be in any way public. Gordon's done a fantastic thing, but now it's time for him to retire.'

'Nonsense! You have no idea what influence such notoriety has. It's power to do *so* much good. What I wouldn't have given for this opportunity. Admittedly you are very populist, but that has its plus sides. And your books are so terribly clever, I have no doubt they will outlive you by many generations. You could do so much for the arts as a patron and spokesperson. You must see this as your duty!' She was positively evangelical. 'My son! My clever, clever son.' She sprang towards him in a rare, affectionate embrace.

Crushed in her bony crab grip, he admitted mournfully. 'I have absolutely no desire to do it.'

'You have no choice. What else are you going to do? Trawl this old boat out of harbour and set sail across the oceans?' She released him from the hug.

'Something like that.' He looked to Legs for reassurance, jumping as his mother slammed her ringed finger down on the narrow galley table in front of them.

'You mustn't! Think of the millions of fans you're letting down.'

'I've already done that. I killed Ptolemy.'

'And I was very, very angry about that at first too,' Poppy admitted, 'but I've reread the book and it's obvious that you've put down markers for his resurrection, Purple's abilities in necromancy for a start, and the ghost narrative in the mid section. In fact the whole series is littered with references which could be tied together to create a quite overwhelming sequel to *Raven's Curse*.'

'You know the books better than I do,' he laughed sadly. 'But you're not going to change my mind.'

She looked terribly sad, her dreams of more Ptolemy Finch adventures shattered. 'Do you really hate writing them that much?'

He shook his head. 'I enjoy writing them. Ptolemy's world is so real to me now I can escape there simply by closing my eyes. I've even written something new in this past week.'

'You *are* writing another!' she cried, hopes reigniting as she demanded excitedly. 'Can I read it?'

'It's not a sequel. It's an apology of sorts.'

She grasped his arm determinedly. 'You will read it aloud at the festival even if I have to take you hostage tonight. This is your duty, Jamie!' She turned to Legs, 'Tell him he must do this. It's entirely selfish of you both to want to set sail, not to mention cruel to the dog.'

Legs had to admit that life on the high seas was starting to lose its appeal. Just bobbing about in the harbour was making her feel quite sick, and Fink certainly looked pretty queasy too, but she remained staunchly loyal, brimming with such love and pride that she'd set sail across oceans in a two-man barrel if he asked her to. 'I will go wherever Byrne goes.'

'Then I'll have to take you both hostage,' Poppy said in a sinister undertone, reaching into her cavernous handbag.

Seeing a glint of metal, Legs thought for a terrifying moment that Poppy was pulling out a gun, but it was just her hipflask which she unscrewed with shaking hands before taking a very long tot.

'I hardly think you are in a position to take us hostage,' Byrne pointed out gently. 'You came by taxi, for a start.'

Poppy conceded the point, staring fixedly at Legs now, eyes narrowing. She gazed so intently and for so long that Legs shifted uncomfortably, frightened by what she was going to do next.

But Poppy merely raised her hip-flask in a toast with a gallant smile. 'It seems I am destined to be your mother-in-law one way or another, Allegra. I'm very glad.'

'You are?' Legs gulped.

'You're really quite witty and it's useful having a strong soprano like yours at singsongs. You have a lot of brio, and I've always rather liked you. It was your taste in men that's always been too abhorrent to countenance. But you've obviously changed your ways completely.' Her big eyes glowed with affection. 'I do hope we'll be friends. I could use someone spirited like you on side.'

'I hope so too.' Legs beamed back, knowing that such barbed praise from Poppy meant everything; when she gushed, it was just habitual affectation but when she gave a reluctant tribute like this, it was spoken from the heart.

Now Poppy was staring at Legs even more intently as she announced with great theatricality: 'I see the solution to your dilemma, Jamie!' She didn't take her dark eyes from Legs' face. 'It's right in front of us.'

'It is?'

She nodded earnestly, turning from Legs to him and then back again. 'Gordon Lapis must have a sex change!'

Horrified, Legs and Byrne held hands, fingers tightly knitted for mutual support.

Chapter 53

The traffic crawling along the main North Devon coast road was worse than any Legs had ever known. For hours it was at a standstill, only edging forwards when the intrepid few turned off to try to forge a way along the back lanes, or simply executed a three point turn to head back the way they had come. Drivers and passengers got out and chatted, complained and shouted into their mobile phones. Only motorbikes and pedal cycles were making it through, weaving in and out of the static line.

'There must have been an accident,' Legs groaned.

'This is all festival traffic,' Poppy pointed out cheerfully from the back seat which she was sharing with Fink, watching as a motorcycle roared past. 'It's been the same all week apparently.'

The local radio station confirmed this, warning listeners to avoid the area around Farcombe at all costs, and reporting tailbacks of ten miles or more.

'They're all coming to see Gordon,' Poppy beamed through the window as the driver of a neighbouring car, stepping out for a leg stretch, peered in nosily.

The Bentley Continental was yet again attracting a great deal of attention.

'Why didn't I come in something less conspicuous like my dad's horsebox or cousin Caron's gipsy caravan?' Byrne muttered, getting increasingly tense as he pressed the button to close the roof and it flipped protectively over them like a black wing.

'I think they might be onto us,' Legs looked around anxiously as more onlookers gathered, unable to see through the darkened privacy glass. Fink barked at them sociably.

A couple of people had begun to take photographs with their mobile phones now. Word was going around the traffic jam that the great man himself might be amongst them. Someone rapped at the door and asked if they could have their book signed.

Byrne buzzed down the window fractionally. 'I have no idea what you're talking about. Can you leave us alone, please?'

'Irish!' someone called out. 'The *Mirror* said yesterday that Gordon is Irish!'

'Are you him? Are you?'

Byrne hurriedly wound up the window.

Then, to his alarm, a man on a moped cruised up with a big digital camera and high powered flash which he pressed against the windows and fired off repeatedly.

'It's the paparazzi!' Poppy declared ecstatically, whipping out her lipstick and compact.

'We've got to get out of here.' Byrne put the car into drive again, now at snapping point.

There was a turning about fifty yards ahead of them. Nosing his way out into the path of oncoming traffic, almost mowing down several bystanders, Byrne sped along the wrong side of the road and swerved into a tiny, high-banked lane, ignoring the cry from the back of the car as Poppy and her make-up were catapulted across the leather upholstery and Fink fell off the seat entirely. They'd barely driven half a mile before they realised the moped was on their tail.

'Shit!' Byrne accelerated.

'We should have stayed there calling their bluff,' Poppy grumbled, lipstick now all over her cheek. 'Now he knows we're trying to hide something.'

While Legs fiddled frantically with the sat nav, Byrne blasted through the countryside trying to shake them off their tail.

'We need to try to get back towards Bideford so we can cross under the main road again,' Legs called out, gripping hold of the dashboard. 'Otherwise we'll be in the sea any minute.'

'This is Goblin Granny's land,' Poppy recognised excitedly, looking out at the fast-moving greenery. 'I used to ride all over it on my pony as a girl.'

'Know any short cuts to Farcombe?'

'Hundreds,' Poppy was rattling around in the back. 'Such a shame we're not in a four wheel drive.'

'This *is* four wheel drive,' Byrne pointed out. 'Just point the way.'

Not content with taking his two-hundred-thousand-euro car camping, he was soon off-roading as they pelted along dusty, rutted farm tracks, through woodland drives no wider than the wing mirrors. Their moped outrider fell back and then finally gave up as they sped across stubble fields which rattled their papery tines against the low-slung car and flicked stones up from the wide wheels.

'This is thrilling!' Poppy whooped as they splashed through a ford and slithered up a rough stone track. 'Where did you learn to drive like this?'

'I just followed Legs' example. Foot down. Close your eyes. Pray.'

'I'm an atheist,' Legs protested, then wailed as they plunged down a steep escarpment, G-force pulling all her vital organs up into her chest.

'You might be about to regret that,' he said through gritted teeth as he steered against a slide to stop the car rolling over.

Eventually they came out on the headland overlooking Fargoe beach, driving through a field of sheep.

'We're very near the Pleasure Drive,' Poppy pointed out. 'Once we're on that, we can get all the way to the village and cut across to the parkland below Gull Cross.'

The Pleasure Drive was a private road that had been laid in the late nineteenth century by Farcombe Hall's great Victorian improvers the Waites to enable the family and their guests to ride, drive and walk through lush rhododendron borders and artfully planted woodland with enticing glimpses of the sea. It had been closed for many years and was practically impassable in places. The land around it was now all leased out for forestry and farming, its once carriage-smooth contours only ever navigated by tractors and pick-ups, if at all.

'Is it safe?' Legs asked uneasily as they rattled over a cattle grid and started along the narrow, crumbling hoggin.

'Bound to be,' Poppy insisted, not wanting the adventure to end.

As Byrne clicked the button to open the roof again, Legs clung onto her seatbelt, wondering at the transformation in Poppy which had taken her from a nervous wreck who needed two Valium to travel in a taxi to thrill-seeking backseat driver in less than twenty-four hours.

Poppy had been forcibly liberated, she realised, released from her self-imposed prison as surely as breaking her extraordinary sculptures from their fibreglass shells, albeit temporarily. Legs didn't doubt her agoraphobia was far from cured, and probably never would be – she was clearly desperate to get back home, insisting loudly that she had no intention of leaving Farcombe again if she could help it. But a sea change had taken place after her night in safe harbour on *Chastity*.

'I'd forgotten how much I like cars,' she was saying brightly now, admiring the plush leatherwork. 'I used to adore driving. Do you remember that old red sports car I had, Jamie?'

'How could I forget?' he said flatly.

'I just loved that car,' Poppy sighed nostalgically. 'Such a speedy little thing. We used to have such fun racketing around the lanes near Nevermore with the top down, didn't we?'

'When we weren't trapped upside-down in ditches waiting for the emergency services.'

Legs began listening in with interest as Poppy giggled and said, 'There were a few little mishaps, weren't there? Nothing serious.'

'The concussion wasn't great that day I fell out when you cornered at a flat seventy.'

'I'd forgotten about that.'

'And there was the time you killed a cow.' He looked at her in the rear view mirror.

'Well it just walked out in front of me.'

'At two miles an hour, while you were doing a hundred.'

'Oh you're exaggerating. I can't have been doing more than sixty.' She took in a deep breath of brackish air as the shade of an artfully planted lime tree avenue gave way to the bright sun of a stretch of clifftop. Poppy craned out of the side of the car to catch the first glimpses of the village appearing around the headland far below. 'Maybe I'll get myself a little banger to pootle around in on the estate? I'm sure I'll be fine as long as I keep the house in sight.'

'And have a speed limiter fitted,' Byrne watched her nervously in the mirror, but he was smiling again now, delighted at her growing confidence.

'Keep your eyes on the road,' Legs muttered as the Bentley started veering towards the sheer drop.

For Legs, the Pleasure Drive could not have been more of a misnomer for the ten minutes that ensued, swerving around rubble, inching along precipices with tyres almost tipping over the side, bouncing over potholes and scraping between trees. Poppy shrieked with delight throughout. Even Fink was propped up on the back seat, barking his head off, ears flapping. Byrne, clearly a rally driver in another lifetime, was utterly assured and still smiling broadly. When they reached a stretch of unbroken road, he reached over and took Legs' hand.

'Tell me we're doing the right thing.'

'We're doing the right thing.'

Looking across at him, Legs suddenly found herself laughing, joining in the group high. They were heading back to Farcombe. She had the man she loved at her side, with all his identities intact. Worse things happen at sea, she reminded herself firmly.

The park around the estate was now one enormous campsite, the little canvas clusters had spread across the faded green velvet of Farcombe's ample acres like thousands of fallen kites. Many hundred of rows of cars were parked in colourful jewelled string necklaces across the flattest of the farm fields. The camper vans and caravans had swelled to form a great mosaic arc around Home Farm. No hotel, B&B, holiday cottage or chalet park within a twenty-mile radius had a vacancy.

Closer to the house, the customary big festival marquees had been erected. There were cubist blue rows of Portaloos, along with the usual monolith Portakabin offices and more signage than the M25. But the police barriers were new, as was the massively expanded army of stewards and security guards, and the big television screens Francis had put in place to amuse the masses, currently showing a rolling promo shot by EuroArts TV.

'I'll call an emergency family meeting tonight,' Poppy's deep voice was authoritative and calm now as she clicked into practical mode. She reached into her handbag for a turban, slotting it over her devilish red hair and then tucking in loose strands as though adopting a disguise. 'Legs cannot stay in the house.' She held up a hand to silence the protests. 'Francis will not tolerate it. You have a tent, I gather. Better that we drop her off with that and you stick with me, Jamie.'

'I want to be with Byrne!' Legs panicked. The scale of Gordon "coming out" was finally starting to hit her, and with it the reality she was about to be thrown into the heart of a cyclone.

'And I'm staying with Allegra,' Byrne insisted.

'As you wish.'

Suddenly the air was filled with strains of 'Ain't Misbehavin'' as Poppy extracted a small, jewelled mobile phone which was ringing in her handbag, an ancient relic in technological terms, but encased in a ravishingly arty skin. 'Oh, it's Édith!'

Legs' fingers tightened in Byrne's grip and both listened with concern as Poppy spoke in an excited undertone to her step-daughter, interspersed with alternate gasps of alarm and cackles of laugher, which hardly inspired confidence.

As their surreal route gave way to the familiar, the lane climbing from the ford to the cliffs, she finally rang off. 'Édith says Hector and Francis are holding court in the pub, which is predictable if no less disappointing. Apparently some prankster broke into the room reserved for Gordon Lapis last night and took lots of photos to post on Twitter. Guy's livid because the room's unoccupied, and there are plenty of photos already on the pub's website. But Gordon's secret identity is getting the world tweeting more than any super-injunction. But so far, nobody's even close to guessing.'

'That's reassuring,' Legs gulped, playing anxious cats cradles with Byrne's fingers. 'Let's go to Spywood.'

They dropped Poppy off at Gull Cross before speeding along the Spywood track, the dusty Continental making light work of the potholes after its cross-county run.

Lucy North was naked in her wooded holiday cottage garden, sporting just her floppy straw hat – now very battered from its stormy night in the Tree of Secrets. She was painting at her easel.

'Ah there you are, darling.' She greeted Legs as though she'd just wandered out of the cottage from a siesta, reaching unhurriedly for a large silk sarong from the branch of a nearby birch to cover her modesty. 'After two decades, I've given up on that bloody harbour. My boat simply won't come in. I'm trying life drawing. What d'you think?'

Legs studied the portrait carefully. 'It looks like Dad.'

'That's because it is.'

Then she noticed a figure swinging in the hammock who now raised a glass of wine affably.

There was an awkward cough behind her.

'You remember Jago, Mum,' Legs turned to take his hand proudly, pulling him alongside her. 'And this is Fink.' She gestured to the panting basset. 'This is my family. Our family.'

Lucy turned in surprise, clutching her slipping sarong tightly with her underarms. 'Oh, I'm *so* glad she found you again.' Her face brightened. 'Dorian darling, this is Jago!' she called out across the garden. 'The one I told you about.'

The figure in the hammock raised his glass again. 'Welcome!'

'You must get Legs to introduce you to our daughter Rosalind and grandson Nico,' Lucy was saying to Byrne.

'They're in Farcombe?' Legs gasped.

In the hammock, one finger flicked up from the glass rim pointing south. 'Just through the woods there.'

'Staying at Spycove with Will and the family,' Lucy confirmed, smiling proudly.

'Is Daisy in situ too?' she spluttered.

'Go and see for yourselves.' Her mother gave her a wise look, somewhere between I-told-you-so and push off.

'We thought we might camp in the woods for a couple of days,' Legs explained before they left.

'How lovely,' Lucy beamed at them both. 'Jago must sit for me while you're staying.'

'He will *not*,' came a gruff bark from the hammock.

'I think I'm already at risk of over-exposure right now,' Byrne smiled uneasily.

As they walked away arm in arm, Legs dipped an apologetic forehead to his shoulder. 'My parents are rather self-obsessed, I'm afraid. They've never exactly been standard-issue, but this past few weeks has set new standards of non-conformity.'

'I like them.' He swung her round in the path. 'Your mother's got the sharpest, kindest wit about her. Like you.' He fired those blazing eyes straight into hers. 'Being conventional is very over-rated in my opinion.'

As Legs towed him along the track to Spycove, she chewed her lip. 'Best not mention that to my sister just yet.'

Ros was camping at the furthest end of the garden from Spycove, like a peace protestor.

'We could hardly stay with Mum and Dad,' she pointed out. 'They haven't got a stitch on most days and never eat regular meals. Everywhere else is fully booked and I promised Nico we'd come here to see Gordon Lapis.'

On cue, a wiry streak of joy in an Arsenal strip hurled himself at Legs. 'You're here! Are you camping with us? Did you bring my signed book? This summer is so cool!'

Nico was delighted to be able to flit between families, it transpired, luring his mother ever closer to his second home; she had participated in a rounders match, volleyball and a barbecue, he reported gaily.

'Somebody has to keep watch,' was Ros's excuse for the arrangement, adding with some satisfaction, 'There's no sense of safety around here. Daisy is hopeless.'

'She's a fortnight away from giving birth,' Legs excused her wryly.

At this, Ros's eyes began twitching, so her sister hastily introduced Byrne.

'You're Irish,' Ros registered the accent as soon as he said hello. 'Are you Catholic?'

'I am.'

Ros's eyes glittered as she regarded Legs with newfound respect, realising the family might yet host a wedding at Ealing Abbey with Nico singing before his voice broke. The Ditchley dress could star again.

'You always appear at the luckiest times!'

Daisy was on a celebratory high because she'd completed all her commissioned scripts while Will and a bunch of friends hurriedly packed up Inkpot Farm to make way for their cash buyers and they could now kick up their family heels: 'Before you ask, everything we own's in storage, which is why it's so tidy,' she laughed, struggling to open a bottle of cheap fizz. 'We are on a long holiday because we can't face our own mess and we all want to have a gawp at Gordon Lapis. Have you *seen* how many people are here? Mum turned down six thousand pounds for one week's holiday let in this place to let us stay. Isn't that amazing? Nico is beside himself at the thought of seeing his hero in person.'

She was clearly fascinated when Legs introduced Byrne, who smouldered in his reserved, intense way: 'So do you two want a place to stay? We have a futon.'

Byrne squeezed Legs' hand hard. 'We've got a tent. Could we claim a pitch in your wood?'

'Be our guest,' Daisy was delighted at the thought of less bed-making and bathroom-hogging. 'It's such perfect timing you're here. We're hosting a barbecue tonight for family and local friends. Tomorrow is the big day. Will's hoping to get an interview with Gordon if he can get past security, although they're even body-searching people going down to the beach. Now you're here, Legs, you can put in a request to Gordon personally, can't you?'

'I have nothing to do with the agency any more,' Legs blustered, holding Byrne's hand tighter.

'But I thought you two were email buddies. Surely you're meeting up?'

She shook her head far too emphatically. 'He has a huge entourage. I'm sure he won't want me hanging around.'

Her friend adopted a shrewd look, potent baby hormones at their most disarmingly direct as she eyed Byrne through her collie fringe. 'What did you say you do for a living again?'

'I write crime thrillers,' he said with a wry smile. 'But I haven't had any of them published yet.'

'You and my husband will have so much in common,' she said cheerfully. 'He wants to write a novel and hasn't even started it yet. I'd introduce you both, but he's been struck dumb and I don't want to break the spell just yet.' She nodded across the garden to the driveway where Will and Nico had both been gazing at the Bentley with their mouths open for over five minutes now.

Leaving the old friends together, Byrne headed off to introduce himself to Will and fetch the tent. Daisy steered Legs to the decking that boasted the best coast view on the Hartland Peninsula.

'Nice car for an unpublished author.'

'He's selling it,' Legs said casually. 'No good for dogging.'

Daisy laughed. 'Thank goodness you're not back with Francis. I knew any rapprochement between you two was doomed.'

'You said we should get back together so that I could live here and gossip with you all the time.'

'Did I? Pregnancy does terrible things,' Daisy waved a dismissive hand and then eyed her shrewdly. 'Does Francis know you're here with Poppy's son?'

'Not yet.' She shook her head. 'He'll be livid.'

'Will and I were in the pub last night. Hector was in there playing his bassoon while Francis propped up the bar looking utterly miserable. Your reputation as an international art thief is growing. Anybody would think you limbo through laser beams and cut through security glass on a nightly basis.'

'Oh for Chrissake this has to stop!' Legs huffed in exasperation, leaping up. 'I'm going running.'

'Not on the run again?' Daisy wailed. 'You've only just arrived . Stay for the party, at least.'

'I'm going *for* a run, not on it.'

'Is everything all right?' Daisy eyed her. 'You look incredibly tense.'

'Fine! Never better! Living for the moment, you know?'

'Live for the moment, live with the consequences,' Daisy remembered her friend's old self-punishing motto.

'Bugger the consequences.' She went to claim back Byrne for a quiet word.

'I'm coming with you,' Byrne insisted as soon as he heard what she planned to do, his face tight with worry.

She shook her head. 'I have to go in alone. We can't risk you being seen. Conrad's staying in the Book Inn. If he sees you, our cover's completely blown. You're best staying here.' She was aware that she sounded like Julie Ocean briefing Jimmy before a raid, but she couldn't stop herself.

'I'm not lolling about in a holiday cottage while you go down there all by yourself.' Byrne was clearly not happy playing junior officer.

'Then wait for me in the village. I'll call if I need back up.'

'You haven't got a phone,' he reminded her.

'It's a small village; I have a very loud scream.'

He sucked his teeth doubtfully. 'They'd better not try anything funny.'

Legs had a sudden image of Hector and Francis dressed up as clowns with long shoes, frog-marching her along the harbour wall at water-pistol gunpoint, or forcing her into a colourful flowery car that fell apart a wing at a time. The thought cheered her up immensely, fuelling her resolve.

'I won't let them. I really can handle this alone, trust me. I'm a big girl; I can stand on my own two legs.'

'There's only one Legs in my world,' his eyes ran admiringly down her body, making her tug down her T-shirt self-consciously and regret coupling 'big girl' with 'legs'. She'd finally been forced to sport the white pedalpushers today, which predictably made her thighs look like two roly-poly seal pups, even in their slimmed-down state.

'You do this your way, Ocean,' he conceded, putting on a throaty Ray Winston rasp. 'But I'm treating you to some new threads afterwards, no arguing. You name the shop.'

Legs laughed, although she secretly couldn't help wishing he'd offered when they were staying in Dublin. 'There's only Shh.'

His dark eyes looked quizzical. 'What?'

'Shh.'

'I am shushing. What is it we're listening for?'

She kissed him.

Chapter 54

They ran the cliff path together, parting at the ford, where he kissed her thoroughly and took the rising lane towards the church and Farcombe Hall while she picked up the private estate road to

635

the harbour, dropping down the steep incline and pounding along the cobbles to the Book Inn. The drinkers were five deep outside, spilling over all the extra tables, sitting on the harbour walls and crowding in huge, jolly groups all along the seafront. A small army of temporary staff were clearing glasses and serving food.

Legs fought her way to the bar where Nonny was serving alongside Pierced Tongue, barely able to keep up with orders.

On two barstools at the furthest end, Hector and Francis resembled two magnificent eagles on perches, larger than life and so eye-catchingly handsome that the drinkers in the crowded pub seemed to be grouped around them like tourists around totem poles. They were holding court to several female admirers, Hector accompanying his son on the bassoon while Francis recited *The Waste Land* from the battered Faber edition of the collected poems he'd owned as a student.

They rocked back on their barstools in shock when Legs marched up to put her case. 'That painting was never stolen, Hector, and you know it! Just like you've always known it's a fraud not a Freud. You know the truth.'

'You do?' Francis turned to his father.

'Do I?' Hector clutched his bassoon like a boy with a teddy bear, shifty and flustered.

Francis lowered his voice, glancing around nervously. 'You said only this morning you've always thought it was genuine.'

'I did?'

Turning back to Legs, not quite able to meet her gaze, Francis's handsome face was apologetic. 'We only heard from Sotheby's in Dublin today. I took the call. They say the painting's a fake. A seriously good one, but a fake.'

'You didn't tell me they said that, Francis.' Hector looked indignant.

'I did!' he hissed back, patience rapidly dwindling. 'You were standing next to me at the time.'

'Yes, but you didn't tell me they thought it was "seriously

636

good".' Hector looked delighted, blowing a couple of top notes before reaching for his pint.

'What does Vin Keiller-Myles make of all this?' Legs asked shakily.

At the mention of his name, Hector started to play 'Leaving on a Jet Plane'.

Legs looked searchingly at Francis, who was quite unexpectedly beaming from ear to ear, nodding his head in time. 'Gone.'

'Gone where?'

'No idea, but according to their housekeeper who's very thick with Imee, he took a long phonecall in his study two days ago, after which he got Mrs K-M to go out and buy a pile of suitcases which they packed in a hurry before setting out for Bristol airport. The next morning, an estate agent came round to value the place, so it doesn't look like they're planning to holiday here again.'

She gaped at him. Two days ago, Byrne had sloped away from their Dublin hotel room to make a series of calls. Had one of them been to Vin telling him what he knew about his past? Perhaps he had decided to be lenient to Hector and Francis after all. She felt weak with relief.

'So you're not going to have me arrested?'

'Of course not. That was never going to happen. Dad just got a bit carried away.' He shot his father a withering look. 'It's all in hand now, and I'll arrange to have your car shipped back by way of apology. I've already spoken with the police here and in Ireland.'

'The Laois police dismisseth us,' she sighed with relief.

'I love Eliot's use of everyday ditties.' Hector smiled woozily, clearly several pints up on his son. 'My memory's appalling. Tell me, is that from "The Fire Sermon"?'

Just for a moment, Legs' eyes met Francis's and they shared the joke. Then he ruined it by saying: 'I think you'll find that's Leith police, Legs, which is in fact Edinburgh.'

Hector started playing the famous opening to Dukas's 'The Sorcerer's Apprentice' and Francis's blue gaze hardened as he glanced around before leaning forwards to hiss. 'I hear you're working as Gordon Lapis's PA now?'

She nodded, reddening. 'I'm just temping.'

'He *is* going to appear on stage tomorrow, isn't he?' he whispered, real fear starting to show.

She nodded. 'He won't let Farcombe down.'

For a moment he looked as though he was going to hug her, then thought the better of it. 'This calls for a huge drink. It's the least I can offer. A Happy Ever After would be fitting, don't you think?'

'Another time.' She shook her head, glancing at the clock above the bar. 'Daisy's throwing a party at Spycove; I don't want to get blootered and fall off a cliff on the way back.'

'A party!' Hector stopped playing briefly. 'Have we been invited, Francis?'

'No.'

'Bloody cheek. Always used to get stiffies for the festival parties. Will this Gordon Laptop chap be there?'

'You never know,' she smiled, exchanging another look of amusement with Francis. 'I'd better go. I said I'd meet someone five minutes ago.' Without thinking, she reached out to give his arm an affectionate farewell squeeze.

When he seized her hand, she felt the familiar cloy of panic, worried she'd misjudged the gesture.

'I've changed my mind.' He smiled, lifting her hand to his mouth and kissing it lightly. Then he smiled widely and let it go. 'There's nothing pointless whatsoever in hoping for friendship.'

On her way out of the Book Inn, a fiery display of long corkscrews of red hair in the restaurant caught Legs' eye. Then she heard a familiar, dominant voice infused with South African undertones and she backed up towards the front of house lectern to take a better look.

Conrad was wearing his flashest handmade suit and sitting

beside Gordon's fierce super-cool editor, Wendy, in equally sharp tailored lines, along with Kizzy, looking predictably ravishing in a gauzy stretch butterfly-print dress that was barely more than a tattoo on her skin. So far so relatively normal, except that Kizzy had her hair tightly constrained in a bun. Beside her, Liz Delamere was thrashing her pre-Raphaelite curls like Medusa and loving the attention.

'Everybody in my family always assumed I was too thick to function or too mad to care,' she gushed in her lovely Joanna Lumley voice, 'but I was simply never understood. I've spent most of my life in therapy and institutions. *The Girl Who Checked Out* is my bridge to the mainstream world.'

'It's a great title,' Wendy nodded earnestly.

'Your life-story will sell it,' Conrad nodded. 'And if we can get a quote from Gordon Lapis for the front cover, we're made.'

Byrne was already waiting outside Shh with Fink sitting on the cobbles at his master's feet, leaning against him. The Catwalk Collection had been removed from the window display, which now featured Autumn Separates draped over the pebbles, chains and photographs of Cici as a glamorous young bride.

'How was it?' He leaped forwards, making Fink tip sideways.

'We can ditch the recipe for nail file sponge cake,' she told him. 'You're no longer looking at a fugitive from the law.'

He seemed delighted, but she had a feeling he knew it already.

'You spoke to Vin, didn't you?'

'I figured if you and I were going to set sail to Latin America, I should tie up a few loose ends first. Now he's the one crossing continents and we're still on dry land.'

'I'm sorry. It wasn't the justice you wanted for what happened to your father.'

'It felt good enough. Dad doesn't want to be dragged through all that again right now. He has a baby on its way, or "her" way as he insists on saying.'

She swallowed anxiously.

As sensitive as a horse, he picked up on her tension straight away. 'Is it Francis? Was he difficult?'

She shook her head. 'Francis was a gentleman as always.' She took his hands in hers. 'Kizzy's in Farcombe, Byrne.'

'Ah.'

'You must talk to her. She deserves to know the truth.'

'Can't it wait?'

She shook her head. 'We both know all hell will break loose tomorrow. Tonight's the calm before the storm.'

'Which is why I want to spend every minute of it with you.'

'Liz is here too. Don't you see it's a perfect opportunity to get it all in the open?'

'Then let's get her to tell her daughter the truth!' he snapped. 'From what I've seen of Kizzy so far, I'm not wild on a family reunion, frankly.'

'She's really very sweet when you get to know her.'

He looked at her angrily, a childhood of fury burning from his eyes. 'Her mother used to serve me undercooked fishfingers after school and shut me in the kitchen with Radio One turned up really loudly so I couldn't hear her and Dad talking in the next room.'

'That must be where Kizzy got her taste for raw fish and Kate Bush.' Reluctant to let it go, Legs looked away irritably, and found her eyes inadvertently drawn to the solicitor's office across the lane. Suddenly she realised something didn't add up: 'I saw you go in there the day after you arrived.'

'That's right. I had to collect some papers.'

'Kizzy was there too.'

He shook his head. 'Not with me. Perhaps she went next door?'

Suspicions mounting, Legs towed him across the road to study the building alongside Marshall and Callow. Its door was painted purple and bore a sign over it that she'd never noticed before.

'Merle Peters, Medium and Clairvoyant,' she read out loud then reeled back in surprise. 'She was consulting a soothsayer!'

'Well that's me off the hook,' Byrne turned away with relief. 'Merle will have told her everything already.'

'Do you think they saw a tall dark handsome stranger coming?'

'They almost certainly heard me. Fink got very overexcited barking at a woman he saw peering in through this window as I recall.' He looked across at her thoughtfully. 'She had feathers in her hair and looked rather like you.'

She blushed, wondering if it would be far too nosey to ask what the documents he was collecting had been.

But he had already read her mind faster than Madame Merle: 'The Deeds to Nevermore.'

'You own Nevermore Farm?' she gasped.

He propped himself on the sill of the solicitor's window. 'It came up for auction a few months ago; I bought it on a whim.'

'But you were so unhappy there.'

'I loved the land; it was my sanctuary. I want to knock down the old house and build something new. A holiday home for us, maybe. It deserves to be a happy place. Now let's go shopping.' He stood up. 'If I can buy a house on a whim, I can buy you a new frock.'

'Just something simple,' Legs insisted as she followed him back across the lane to Shh. 'You really don't have to splash out.'

'I insist. We are about to make a very big splash after all.'

Cici's spider's leg lashes performed a series of high kicks when she saw her young client returning to her emporium with a man in possession of a black Amex.

'I am all yours!' she announced orgasmically, turning the sign to closed and flicking the lock.

Byrne swallowed in terror and glanced at Legs who gave him an 'I told you so' look and resigned herself to being heavily accessorised. She was, however, determined to forfeit the fascinator and take the lingerie option this time.

Over an hour later, Legs and Byrne were finally released from Shh with more bulging carrier bags and boxes under their arms than the Beckhams coming out of Corso Como.

'You really, really didn't have to buy me so much.' Legs was embarrassed that the idle *Pretty Woman* fantasy she'd harboured in Dublin had become hardcore WAG shopping in Farcombe. As the door pinged closed behind them, she was sure she could hear Cici already on the phone booking a holiday.

'I really, really didn't have any choice,' Byrne laughed. 'That woman is terrifying.'

Legs reached up to remove the fascinator from her head. 'Tomorrow's crowds will be a breeze compared to her.'

'Let's not think about it.' He swallowed uncomfortably. 'We have a party to enjoy. Your friend Daisy seems to have invited half the village. She's even asked Poppy, I gather.'

'Poppy refuses to go to any parties except her own.'

Byrne gave her a shrewd smile. 'You might be surprised. She was looking through her turban collection when I popped in on the way here.'

'Oh God, how can we possibly make tomorrow work?' She was gripped by sudden nerves.

'It has to.' He let the bags and boxes fall from his arms as he wrapped her in a tight hug and kissed her thoroughly. 'It just has to.'

Chapter 55

As the barbecue sizzled and a bonfire roared in Spycove's clifftop garden, the sun set over the sea with such a splendid blaze of reds and oranges that the coastline seemed to be in flames, the rocks red as hot lava, the woods glowing like a forest fire and the sea itself a shimmering sheet of molten tin.

Legs sat beside Nico toasting fat marshmallows on the bonfire, watching Byrne talk to Will with great animation as they shared an adjacent log swigging wine from plastic cups, both men laughing uproariously as they flew through subjects like two running partners passing fast-moving landscapes at the same speed, able to keep perfect pace. Suddenly, she was reminded of her father and Nigel Foulkes.

'We used to do this as kids,' she told Nico, lifting her sizzling marshmallow to blow on it, 'me, your mum and Daisy.'

'You were all really close, weren't you?'

She nodded, glancing past the flames to where she could see her sister looking out to sea, talking quietly to another guest whose blond hair was cast brightest copper red in the setting sun. 'And Francis.'

He and Hector had rolled in about half an hour ago blootered from the pub, like a pair of naughty schoolboys on the rampage. Taking a detour on the way home, they'd clearly decided to gate-crash the Spycove barbecue, reeling around in an unruly fashion demanding to meet Gordon Lapis, and driving Daisy demented as she tried to stop them stumbling into the bonfire or off the cliff. It was no-nonsense Ros who'd taken charge of them both, helping Daisy to furnish them with piles of food and soft drinks to soak up and dilute the alcohol from a day in the pub, then posting Hector and his bassoon on a log with two chaperones to keep him busy while she took Francis to one side to listen to him reeling off reams of poetic quotes and ranting about his heartbreak.

Now, standing on the sunset-soaked decking alongside Francis, Ros had nothing but sympathy for her sister's spurned first love. 'My heart has been so badly broken, too.'

She shot her ex-husband's fireside log a martyred look over her shoulder and edged closer to Francis, who was woozily pronouncing that Will was a louse for abandoning her, an intellectual sell-out and a buffoon for becoming a house husband. Ros couldn't agree more. He launched into Milton again, staring out to sea, as noble as the Cristo Redentor overlooking Rio de Janeiro's harbour. Admiring his profile and remembering how much she'd secretly adored him as a girl, Ros was soon finishing the quotes that Francis was too drunk to recall.

Meanwhile, Hector played a lot of bum notes and showed no signs of sobering up, his loud voice still slurred as he tilted between his two companions like a wild-blown dinghy between sturdy boardwalks. 'The young have no sense of dignity,' he was saying now. 'Look at us. All friends. All forgiven. All forgotten.'

Dorian North gave him the benefit of his charming, diffident smile and topped up Hector's drink with his own home-made Dandelion and Burdock which nobody in the North family would ever drink because it led to vile wind and turned your pee green. On Hector's far side, Lucy smiled dreamily, sketch pad on her knee as she captured moments from the evening in soft pencil and charcoal.

'The young have no sense of what it means to be a part of our generation.' Hector was trending youth as a theme. 'We found free love in the seventies, got rich in the eighties, paid the price for both in the nineties, got naughty again in the noughties and now we're like teenagers once more, swapping truths round a campfire and occasionally kissing each other after lights out.'

'You certainly haven't lost your boyish outlook,' Dorian said with measured cool, handing Hector an undercooked chicken drumstick then watching with satisfaction as he ripped into it between drafts of burdock.

'We've known each other how many years now?' Hector threw his chicken bone into the fire and accepted another, along with a top-up of green pee juice. 'Twenty? Thirty? All water under the bridge for us, isn't it?'

'Indeed,' agreed Dorian and reached for a bowl of red eyed chillies he'd picked up from Will and Daisy's prep table which he now offered to Hector. 'Sun dried tomato?'

'Marvellous.' He scooped up a handful and shovelled them in his mouth, chilli seeds flying out as he talked. 'You're a good man, Dorian. Only wish old Poppy were so forgiving,' he sighed. 'She's been behaving mighty oddly this week. Mighty oddly. Think she might be having a fling herself. Gosh, those tomatoes are punchy.' Blowing out through his lips, he drained his glass.

'It might help if you paid her a few compliments,' Lucy murmured, looking lovingly across at her husband. On her lap was a magnificent depiction of his profile, drawn in the style of a Greek god.

'You must make her realise how much you love her,' Dorian agreed, gazing adoringly back as he topped up the now-gasping Hector's glass with more wind-inducing Dandelion and Burdock.

'Appreciate your differences.' Lucy patted his back as he started to splutter.

Now Dorian handed him a handkerchief to mop the tears running down his face. 'Embrace what you share.'

'Forgive.' Lucy looked gratefully at her husband who winked back and offered her a chilli.

'Forgive what?' Hector lamented, eyes streaming. 'Poppy is a bloody saint for putting up with my escapades. I could hardly blame her for wanting a fling. But I will kill the cussed cad if she is!'

On cue there was loud, whining putter as Poppy appeared at the wheel of Édith's bright green Beetle, her stepdaughter white-faced in the passenger's seat. Travelling at high speed, they slid to a halt just beyond Spycove's gates with the aid of a forsythia bush. Poppy cut the engine, patted the steering wheel and laughed delightedly. She was dressed in bright purple harem pants and a scarlet bat-winged top, her neat bob accessorised with a small sequinned pink disk from which colourful plumage sprouted. Legs recognised it straight away; she owned an identical one herself.

When Édith opened the bonnet of the car, it was crammed full of her stepmother's turbans.

'I am going to burn these tonight!' Poppy announced rapturously to the crowd around her. 'From now on, I am embracing the fascinator!'

Hector had leaped up and reeled to her side, bassoon aloft, mouth aflame with chilli after-blast. 'My darling you look as beautiful as I have ever known you. I love you!'

Poppy looked thrilled. 'I know that, you silly oaf. Now play me a tune. I have been reborn; tonight is my baptism of fire!'

Hector lifted his bassoon to his foaming lips and then lowered it again, eyes tortured. 'Are you having a bloody fling?' he thundered, mopping his weeping eyes on his broad shoulders.

'No!' She selected a red velvet toque that was pure Lillie Langtry and hurled it towards the flames.

'Good!'

As she lobbed more turbans onto the flames, he accompanied her by playing the solo from the Firebird suite.

On a nearby log, Lucy and Dorian moved together, sliding their arms around one another as they watched the bright headgear flying past them at speed.

'Well she's certainly having a bit of a fling tonight,' Lucy pointed out cheerfully.

'I'd forgotten how much they shout,' Dorian sighed. 'I suppose it comes from sharing such a big house. No wonder poor Francis has no volume control.' He cocked his head in the direction of the decking where poetry being recited very loudly to a rapt audience of one.

Lucy regarded Francis and her elder daughter thoughtfully. 'I haven't seen Ros looking this happy in a long time, have you?'

On an adjacent log to his maternal grandparents, Nico was devouring his fifth marshmallow and telling his aunt how excited he was to be seeing Gordon Lapis tomorrow. 'I think he'll be really dark and mysterious, like Edward Cullen. Am I right, Legs? Legs? Hellooo!' He waved his marshmallow toasting stick in front of her face, making her jump.

'Sorry.' She dragged her eyes away from watching a familiar redhead who had emerged from the back of Édith's car to help with the turban-tossing.

'Does Gordon look like Edward Cullen?'

'Yes, he does a bit,' looking around her, she realised that Byrne was missing from the fireside. She searched the garden for him with her eyes but he wasn't there.

'Bet you fancy him.'

'I do a bit.'

'I am never falling in love. It's for gross old people.'

'Ptolemy and Purple fall in love,' she pointed out, lifting up to stare over the fire. No Byrne.

'He'll suffer,' Nico predicted.

'I think he does somewhat.' Legs craned round to scan the parked cars.

'Don't tell me what happens. I'm so near the end. Purple is so cool sticking up for Ptolemy like that.'

'Told you. It happens to the best of us. Love.' She was raking back and forth across the garden with her eyes now, panic rising.

'I can't believe you've still not got me a signed book,' Nico said in a small voice. Then, seeing his aunt's anxious expression, he smiled and made light of it. 'I'm sure he's really busy.'

'I'll get you a signed book,' she promised vaguely.

'Tonight?'

'I can try. I don't have a copy with me, but I can—'

'Wait there!' He leaped up and raced into the house.

Within a minute, the hardback of *Raven's Curse* crashed down on her lap like a breezeblock. The bookmark was still poking out about three quarters of the way through, she noticed.

Nico thrust a pen at her, 'It's Dad's best "novelist" fountain pen – Daisy bought it for him. Please don't lose it.'

'I'll put it in my tent for safekeeping,' she laughed, standing up. 'And I'll get Gordon to sign the book later, I promise.'

'Is he staying nearby?'

Legs hugged the book to her chest and stared at the fire for a moment, its flames turning extraordinary colours as they guzzled up the beads and sequins on Poppy's turban collection. 'He's very close,' she breathed.

As she trailed towards her tent, eyes still looking everywhere for Byrne, she spotted Kizzy and Édith walking arm in arm to the viewing platform over the cove to look out at the sky which had turned richest violet shot through with orange now the sun had dropped behind the horizon.

Then she heard a dog bark in the woods. Still clutching the book, she ran between the trees, twisting, ducking and jumping to avoid trunks, branches and undergrowth.

He was perching on the lover's seat branches of the Tree of Secrets, carving something into the bark. Hearing a twig snap under one of her feet, he looked down.

'You found me,' he laughed. 'It was going to be a surprise, but it's almost done now. Come on up.' He reached down his hand.

Leaving the book by the trunk's base, she climbed to settle on the other lover's branch arm and read the initials he'd carved in a big, wonky heart.

'AN, JB, JL, PF, GL.' She smiled as she counted them up, squinting to read the last two which weren't quite finished. 'JJ and JO?'

'Jimmy Jimee and Julie Ocean.'

'Of course,' she laughed. 'There are certainly a lot of us in this relationship.'

'The more identities, the bigger the heart.' He tapped his graffiti with his knife before stooping to finish it off with a few final deft cuts.

'Everybody should change their name at least once in life,' she agreed, tilting her head to watch. 'You have a lot more alter egos than me.'

'You are going to change your name very soon,' he reminded her.

She looked across at him apprehensively, and he turned to kiss her firmly on the mouth. 'At the altar, when you marry me and my many egos.'

'Allegra Byrne-Kelly-Finch-Jimee-Lapis would be hell to fit on a debit card,' she joked nervously.

'Not Lapis,' he shook his head. 'He's not the marrying kind.'

'Who says?'

'I'm still in control of him, remember?' he said, then smiled apologetically. 'At least I am tonight.'

'I want to marry Gordon too,' Legs insisted. Using the fingers of her right hand to encircle the heavy gold band still trapped on her left ring finger, she gave an almighty tug and let out a cry of surprise as the signet ring came loose straight away and slipped into her palm, like Excalibur released from the rock.

'What are you doing?' Byrne laughed as she slipped the ring onto his little finger.

'Marrying Gordon before it's too late.' She stretched across to kiss him. 'Congratulations. You just kissed the bride.'

'He'll run away with another woman,' he warned her before kissing her again, so long and hard she almost fell out of the tree.

'For one night with Gordon, I think it's worth that risk,' she said breathlessly.

Byrne admired the ring, peering at its monogram again in the near darkness. 'P'.

'It's silent,' Legs reminded him, 'P as in . . .'

They both stared at each other in the darkness for a very long time, saying nothing. Then they laughed, stretching forwards until their lips connected and they kissed for as long as their breath and the branches under them could hold out. It was a very long time.

'Passion,' Legs laughed when they finally broke apart. 'P as in passion. Not very silent in our case.'

He flicked open his knife to carve a P inside the wonky bark heart. 'This is my first love letter.'

She admired it through the shadows.

'And P's for Poppy of course.'

'That's a P for Passion killer,' she grumbled. Suddenly remembering Nico's book in the undergrowth, she scrabbled down from the tree to pick it up and got the pen from her pockets before flicking to the title page. 'You can add your graffiti tag to this. Can you dedicate it to Nico?'

As he jumped down alongside her, she clutched the heavy book to her chest for a moment in dawning realisation. 'This might be the last Gordon Lapis book you ever sign.'

His voice was shot through with pure relief as he reached out for it. 'Such a shame Gordon's chronic arthritis will mean that he can never inscribe another novel after this,' he sighed, resting the book in the crook of one arm and leaning back against the tree to write the inscription, dark eyes wide in the fading light.

When he closed the book with a slam and handed it to her, that big, blazing hearth gaze locked onto hers. 'It's not too late to change your mind, you know.'

'About what?'

'I told you I'd give you plenty of chances to run away. But this might be your last one.'

'I'm not going anywhere.'

He cupped her face in his hands. 'I love you.'

'Grime poo.' She stared back in the darkness, knowing those bright eyes would light the way wherever they went.

She leaned into him, loving his lips on hers, the way kissing him always made the air around her go mountaintop thin. Then, as their kisses grew more urgent and excited, she found herself flying along a thrilling zig-zag black run ski-slope on the side of that mountain, her body coursed through with adrenalin, powerless to stop the momentum pulling her ever-faster towards the delicious blue lake of nudity and plunging pleasure that she knew lay at the bottom.

Still clutched in her arms, Gordon Lapis's huge hardback was jabbing her hard in the ribs now. Byrne reached out to take it and cast it to one side, but Legs clung on tight, knowing Nico would never forgive her for throwing his precious book around in the undergrowth.

'Just hold that thought!' She pressed a final kiss to his mouth. 'Wait there *one* minute!' She turned to race back to the garden with the book, almost crashing into Poppy who was picking her way carefully in the opposite direction with a huge floodlight in one hand and a small trinket box in the other. 'There you both are! I've been looking for Jamie everywhere.' Pointing her light blindingly in his face, she stepped towards him. 'It's about the *you know what*. I found it when I was clearing out my turban drawers. I told you I still had it.'

'What's the "you know what"?' Legs asked.

'Nothing you need to worry about,' Byrne reassured her, putting an arm on her back and steering her away from the tree. 'Slight change of plan tomorrow, that's all. You go and make a boy very happy. We'll be back out in a minute.' He leaned across to kiss her on the cheek, whispering, 'We'll take up where we just left off later.'

As Legs reluctantly trailed away, she distinctly heard Poppy say in a stage whisper, 'Are you sure about this, Jamie? What if Legs lets us down? Look at what she did to Francis.'

'She won't let me down,' he insisted darkly.

Nico was absolutely ecstatic to receive his book back, freshly signed by Gordon Lapis.

'Is he in the *woods*?' he whispered in amazement, having marked his aunt's movements closely since entrusting her with his precious possession.

'Gordon has a very good chauffeur,' she said vaguely. 'He can be somewhere at the drop of a hat when he needs to be.'

Nico was far too wise to be fobbed off with that sort of nonsense, but he was too busy reading the personal inscription to protest. 'Oh wow, oh wow oh wow oh wow. I so love you, Legs! This is just the Best. Thing. Ever.'

'What's he written?'

'*To dear Nico. May Ptolemy Finch and Purple inspire you to live for the moment as they have me. You will never regret it. Welcome to my family. Your very good friend and kinsman, Gordon Lapis.*' He read it, his voice shaking. Then he smiled and whooped. '*P.s. Your aunt's really hot.*'

Legs blushed crimson, pressing cool fingers to her hot cheeks. 'He never said that!'

'You're right.' Nico stretched up to kiss her. 'I made that bit up. Thanks, Legs. You're the best!'

When Byrne rejoined Legs at the fireside, he found her perched between Kizzy and Édith, three exquisite Witches of Eastwick faces illuminated by flames.

'I know we share a father,' Kizzy looked up at him tearfully, her green eyes like rusting copper verdigris in the firelight. Her elbows rested on skinny knees, her chin resting on entwined fingers with knuckles as white as chalk. 'I *promise* I'll not make a big thing of it. I know you think I'm a bit over the top, but I really won't do anything to embarrass you. You can trust me. You see, Poppy already told me about Brooke last week and Liz told me about it again last night. Now Legs has told me for a third time, only this time I actually know you know too, which is a real relief. I'm not sure I'd be very good at handling this on my own.'

'Me neither.' He stayed very still.

'And I haven't made a big fuss at all.'

'Me neither.'

'But I'd quite like to. At some point. When we're both ready.'

'Me too.'

There was an awkward pause. Catching each other's eyes over Kizzy's head, Legs and Édith took control of the situation. Slotting an arm each beneath Kizzy's elbows, they stood up as one, lifting her along with them until she was standing directly in front of Byrne.

They needed no greater cue than that, as they drew together into a warm, tight hug, pulling their lovers in with them.

On the far side of the crackling fire, Hector serenaded them all with 'Stranger on the Shore'. Beyond that, a sonorous voice could just be made out reciting 'At The Word Farewell'.

'Oh God, my brother's moved onto Thomas Hardy,' Édith

652

snarled quietly. 'Sorry Legs, but the sooner he gets a new girlfriend the better.'

Hearing her own sister's soft descant echoing the verse, Legs decided he was making a pretty good start.

Bursting apart from their impromptu rugby scrum of new sibling love and old sibling rivalry, the foursome settled back beside the fire and shared out the last of a bottle of rosé and a tube of Pringles.

'This has been the most amazing year of my life,' Kizzy laughed, curling up to Édith. 'Nothing would surprise me any more. If Gordon Lapis steps up on stage tomorrow and turns out to be that basset hound, I'll hardly bat an eye.'

Sitting statuesquely in front of them and drooling for a Pringle Fink let out a long, greedy whine that was almost human.

Byrne looked across at at Legs, dark eyes blazing. 'Now why didn't we think of that?'

The bonfire still glowed and sputtered in Spycove's clifftop garden, long after the barbecue had been extinguished and the party dispersed. Byrne and Legs shared a log seat in front of it, drawing in its heat.

They had the garden to themselves now. The guests were all gone. Daisy had long-since crashed into bed exhausted; Ros was in her tent in the woods listening to choral music; Will was in the house reading *Ptolemy Finch and the Raven's Curse* to Nico in the watchtower room, not because he needed to be read to these days, but because they were both desperate to know what happened at the end.

'They won't be happy when they find out Ptolemy's fate,' she sighed, hugging her arms around him.

'How can you be sure?' he breathed into her shoulder before kissing it. 'You haven't read the end.'

'I know what happens.'

'Do you now?' Resting his cheek against hers, he lifted his hand

and examined the monogrammed signet ring on his little finger, turning it round one circuit as it gleamed dimly in the last of the firelight. 'Stay there. I have something for you.' Leaving a kiss glowing warm on her cheek, he walked across the dew-soaked grass to his car and started searching around inside.

Legs gazed into the glowing embers of the fire, her heart thrumming faster as she dared to wonder if he was planning to carry on the conversation they'd had in the woods about changing her name.

But when he returned, he was carrying a leather document wallet. Settling down beside her, he reached into it and pulled out a neat sheaf of printed A4 which he handed to her, holding his torch over it.

She read the first few lines. 'This is *Raven's Curse*.'

'Read on a bit.'

Legs did, one hand flying to her mouth, 'You've rewritten the end of the book!'

Switching off the torch, he looked up at the sky where every autumn star was trying to outshine its neighbour. 'You were right when you said second thoughts can be as original as first ones, like second love and second chances.'

'And new beginnings,' she laughed.

'There's a new endgame.' He pressed his thumb to the happy tears springing from her eyes. 'Meet me on the shore.'

'We did that last time.'

'No we didn't. We never got that far. Meet me on the shore. Promise?'

'I promise.' She put her hands over his, not understanding, but he silenced her with a kiss before she could ask for an explanation.

As his lips found hers, that delicious mountaintop kiss burst through her. This time, as she skied down the black run, there was nothing to stop her plunging into clear blue water. Already ripping off each other's clothes, they raced into the tent where they rolled and wriggled all over the new end.

Chapter 56

Legs, Ros, Daisy and their families joined the crowds on the hill that had been nicknamed 'Gordon's Green' in front of the big screen television the following morning to watch the action live from the library in Farcombe Hall. There was a carnival atmosphere in the park with hundreds of fans dressed up as Ptolemy, Purple and other characters from the books, home-made banners everywhere, and picnics galore. Television crews from all over the world were prowling around getting footage, presenters perfecting their scripts and talking into fluffy-topped microphones.

The big screens were flashing up endless EuroArts TV promos, along with clips from the Ptolemy Finch movies and interviews with a seemingly unending stream of celebrities whose favourite books starred the little white-haired soothsayer.

Then suddenly the crowd fell silent and Legs looked up to see Francis's face on screen. God, but he was handsome, Legs realised distractedly. He was born for celluloid.

'Er . . . hi . . . thanks for watching . . . er . . .' Unfortunately he wasn't as naturally gifted a broadcast speaker as he was a looker, his voice as flat as the screen. He looked down, clearly fumbling for his script.

Thinking he was Gordon Lapis, the crowd started to shriek and whoop.

Thinking exactly the same, Daisy and her huge pregnancy bump practically rolled on top of Legs. 'Why didn't you tell me it was Francis? You must have known!'

Legs was too dumbfounded to react. This hadn't been in her script at all.

'I – er – my father was going to say this, but unfortunately he's got a touch of – er – food poisoning today, so it's down to me,' Francis droned, sounding like Prince Harry forced to stand in for Charles at an anti-Nazi organic gardeners convention. 'I just want to thank you all for coming here today on behalf of the Protheroe family and all, erm, involved with the Farcombe Festival, and I am delighted to take this, um, opportunity to announce a new – er – charitable project which my father has spearheaded called, erm—' he looked at his script and visibly winced. 'The Hector Protheroe Foundation for the Promotion of Popular Culture, which will be solely dedicated to art made by the masses for the masses. The charity's patron, Gordon Lapis, will be with you all shortly, speaking with Falabella Morestrops – I mean Parallella Frostmops. You know who I mean. Thank you.' He dived off screen to raucous cheers from the park, largely because he'd mentioned that Gordon was up next; few cared for news of rebel philanthropist Hector's latest kindness. In their minds, he'd already been Sir Hector for years.

But for his original little princesses, the king's crown had just been hurled to the hungry crowd, and not before time.

Daisy and her bump were still on board Legs and almost asphyxiating her now. 'Please tell me this is a weird dream?'

Legs was laughing too much to speak. This was Byrne's revenge, she was certain. How he'd swung it she wasn't sure, but she so loved him for it. Where was he? She looked around the park, but saw only a sea of eager faces looking up at the screen in eager anticipation. Turning back to watch it too, she saw a reality TV star describing Ptolemy as her 'main man' for the third time on the pre-recorded loop. This was art by the masses for the masses, she realised giddily, Gordon was the people's storyteller. The atmosphere around her was supercharged.

The big screen yielded no new excitements as the interview loop was repeated, along with movie clips and cover shots. As time wore on, there were a couple of shots of the library, which got everybody wildly excited before they realised it was just the crew setting up camera angles. The BBC's premier arts presenter, a bewitchingly erudite blonde in oyster cashmere, appeared to riotous cheers to record a few trailers and links for the upcoming live broadcast. Then the recorded loop restarted and everyone groaned good-naturedly.

But beneath the pageantry and cheer, the crowds were growing restless. Thousands of Ptolemy Finch tomes were clutched in eager hands, but Legs wouldn't be surprised to see a pyre of *Raven's Curses* soon forming as high as the hill they were sitting on ready to be incinerated. Rumour had started to spread that he wouldn't be signing books. Mutters of dissent were everywhere, particularly given the small fortune Francis Protheroe had charged them all for the privilege of being there in the first place, a profit now assumed to be going straight into Lapis's already swollen pockets. The love–hate pendulum for Gordon kept swinging one way and then the other.

For one ten-year-old boy, it was all one way. Nico was hopelessly overexcited at the prospect of seeing his hero's creator, and such was his total faith in Gordon that he believed Ptolemy would come to life again in the next book, a conviction he shared with a lot of the crowd around him.

'I can't believe you're not in there with Gordon, Legs,' he exclaimed for the fifth or sixth time. 'He trusts you so much. He's always emailing you.'

'Gordon has a big support team surrounding him, and anyway I don't work for Fellows Howlett any more,' Legs reminded him, glancing round. 'And keep your voice down.'

'Where's that new chap of yours?' asked Lucy, who was wearing her increasingly crumpled straw hat, tied round with a jaunty purple silk scarf to mark the occasion.

'He's just seeing off an old friend,' Legs said in a shaky voice, looking away.

He should be back by now, surely? He'd slipped away half an hour ago saying he was going to try to have a quick word with Poppy and he was still gone. Things weren't going according to plan at all.

She told her family she was going to brave the portaloos and checked out the hall instead, looking for a way in, but there were security guards everywhere. Every door was heavily guarded, along with the sea passage. Only those in possession of one of the sacred access-all-areas wristbands could get in. She had nothing, not even a bangle.

Back on Gordon's Green, she slumped down next to Will who put an arm around her shoulders. 'You're looking very wan, darling.'

She mustered a weak smile, watching as they re-ran another Ptolemy Finch movie clip on the big screen. 'Just worried Gordon might be having second thoughts.'

'Nonsense, he's an old pro at this publicity lark. I'm taking notes. And I have the perfect thing to cheer you up.' He reached into his backpack and pulled out a freshly printed page. 'See what you think of that. It's the synopsis of the novel that will make my fortune; incredibly moving stuff, with lots of middle class angst and dead children, and no Swedish detectives, although I have sneaked in a few vampires.'

'Thanks. I look forward to it,' Legs took it distractedly, glancing down at the page before her eyes returned to the big screen twirling Gordon's book jackets around.

'At least read the title,' Will's ego was brutally wounded.

She looked down again, and then let out a snort of surprised laughter: '*George Samson and the Magic Mousetrap*. It's a children's book, Will.'

He nodded eagerly, 'Think *Alice in Wonderland* with a boy hero; I was going to call it *George in Googleland*, but I thought I might have legal difficulties. It's going to be about a boy who escapes into an imaginative world on his dad's laptop by clicking a little icon he's found hidden in the logo of a popular internet search engine.'

'Sounds promising,' she humoured, but she was already distracted again by the big screen where the erudite blond presenter was sharing a joke with the sound engineer. Then the picture abruptly cut to the twirling books once more and the crowd around her groaned.

'The end's going to be the hardest bit,' Will was saying. 'I can't decide whether the computer should crash and reboot while George is in there or there should be a terrible virus . . .'

Suddenly Legs stopped listening. Byrne had written a new ending. A 'new endgame' Byrne had said. That's what he had been delivering to Poppy, she realised. How stupid of her not to realise it. But where was he now?

She gazed unseeing at the screen on which a picture of the cover of *Raven's Curse* seemed to be spinning ever-faster. To appease the crowds, the production team had started a countdown which flashed up on screen. Three minutes to go.

She looked around the parkland frantically, but there was no sign of Byrne.

The crowd were joining in the countdown now, clapping in time as they chanted the ever-decreasing seconds. Legs felt as though her life was being wished away as they got down to two minutes and then one. Where was Byrne? Where *was* he? This wasn't what they had agreed. Was he going to reveal himself as Gordon after all, without telling her? Had he been duped? He couldn't abandon her like this.

When the BBC's bewitching presenter reappeared on screen, this time to be cued into her live broadcast, there was such whooping and cheering all around Legs, it was impossible to tell at first what she was saying, although her smiling face indicated that all was well and Gordon Lapis was indeed in the building. Legs tried to remember what Byrne had been wearing. Nothing smart. Just jeans and a T-shirt.

As the camera panned out to reveal the figure seated beside the presenter, she recognised his clothes and her heart felt as though it was going to explode. His huge furnace eyes seemed to be burning holes straight through the screens at her. It felt as though he was looking only at her, trying to speak to her with just those amazing, silent eyes. They'd tricked him, she realised furiously. Conrad had tricked him into revealing his true identity after all.

But then the camera panned out further and she gasped as she saw Poppy alongside him. Resplendent in lilac crushed velvet, she was sporting a white fascinator of such feathery, sequinned brilliance that she looked as though she had a firework exploding from her head.

She was already talking, her deep sensual voice stilling the crowd as she started to tell a story that nobody dared interrupt. It was what Poppy had always done best:

'My name is Poppy Protheroe, but you know me better as Gordon Lapis.'

There was a collective gasp in the park so loud it seemed to suck the clouds overhead lower and pull the screen closer. Poppy had always had a way of dominating a space, however big, so that it felt like an intimate confessional:

'I am sorry that I have kept my identity a secret for so long, but I have been trying very hard to protect the person I care about most, and by association, the one you care about most. Ptolemy Finch is based on my son, Jamie. I know our story will be exposed many times over in coming days and weeks, and so I hope I may tell it first, simply and honestly. I went out of Jamie's life when he was just a boy, and have regretted that loss every day since. Ptolemy is that little boy I lost. This summer he came back into my life, and he is sitting here beside me.

'By the time that Jamie and I were reunited, *the Raven's Curse* had already been written. To those of you – and there are many – who I have upset by what happens in that novel, I think I should explain that I have had a change of heart, a total change of heart.

'There is now an alternative end. It will be live on my website by the end of today, and I will be reading it aloud throughout the course of this week here at Farcombe Festival. But first, Jamie has joined me here on camera for a very special reason. He is an intensely private person, but he's aware that all our lives will be under the spotlight now, and he wants to make a very public statement which will give many of you an idea of why Ptolemy deserves a new beginning.'

The camera honed in on Byrne and his huge, intense eyes, staring at the camera.

He had none of his mother's articulacy. He was tongue-tied and hoarse-voiced, intensely awkward and desperate to be done, like a hostage victim at gunpoint making a tape for his family back home. He would have made a disastrous media personality. But for this one-off appearance, this very handsome, very honest, very private man made himself an instant star with just six words coughed out at speed:

'Allegra. *Gráim thú*. Marry me.'

All at once the Farcombe parkland seemed to ignite with shared delight.

Legs let out a squeak of excitement, which was quite lost amongst the cheering and clapping around her. On all sides, people were demanding to know who 'Allegra Grime Poo' was, the real life Purple.

'How do I answer?' Legs wailed in sudden panicked realisation. 'How can I give him an answer?'

Her voice was drowned out by the crowd as they all whooped and shouted at the big screen, which showed one last lingering shot of Byrne's intense, blazing eyes before cutting to the spinning *Raven's Curse* cover again.

But one person standing nearby had heard exactly what Legs was saying. Immobile amid the frenzied animation, tufty hair on end, Will was gaping at her in amazement. 'It's *you*!'

Voice too choked with emotion to speak, tears of happiness already streaming, she could do nothing but nod. On the screen, the book jackets were twirling about like playing cards between an unseen magician's fingers as a commercial break was counted out.

'You dark horse!' Will laughed as he watched her spinning around in total, overexcited bewilderment.

'No,' she finally found her voice as she laughed, 'I'm a Heavenly Pony, trust me.'

He turned to shout at Daisy. 'It's *Legs*!'

Legs stopped spinning, trying to think what to do. 'He said to meet him on the shore,' she remembered, pressing her palms to her hot face. 'I have to get to the cove. He'll be going down the sea passage, I just know it.'

'Then run!' Will laughed, gathering her into a bolstering hug. 'Gallop as fast as you can, little pony. The world will want to know your answer.'

They heard a wail of anguish behind them that made Will drop Legs like a stone.

'Daisy!' He spun round.

His wife was squatting on the picnic blanket between the homemade quiches and her daughters' plastic tea set, waters breaking like a flash tide across the tartan check.

'It's coming!' she screamed. 'The baby is coming. And, man alive, is it in a hurry!'

'Oh shit.' Legs wavered in an animated dance between birthing friend and unanswered proposal.

'Go!' Daisy wailed, Will already at her side and talking to the local ambulance service from his mobile. 'Go, Legs, go, go!'

Legs didn't need telling twice.

She battled through the crowds, darting and diving, faster and faster as they thinned out where the parkland gave way to woodland. In she dived through the cool columns of willow and alder, pounding along the shadowed avenues, feet spring-loaded on the spongy paths of leaves and moss around the perimeter of the lake then into the darker shadows of the ancient oaks. Bursting out into sunlight again, the sea ahead of her, she crashed through the bracken to Gull Point and on towards the cliff path, slithering and tripping as the ground began to fall away from under her and she leaned back, hand out to balance herself against the rocks.

As she rounded the first hairpin turn in the steep, narrow track, she saw him emerging onto the beach, hair lifted from his face by the sharp sea breeze, those intense eyes creasing against the sunlight as he looked out to the horizon before turning to see her there.

She felt such love burst through her chest, she expected petals and confetti to steam out between her buttons like a magic trick at any moment. She put on a burst of speed, flying around the next hairpin, feet slipping in her haste. As she did so, the path seemed to crumble from under her, great lumps of rock dropping away so that she felt for a second as though she was running in mid-air, still ten yards above the stony beach.

'Arghhh!' She flung her arms out desperately, catching onto a twisted branch of whitebeam that was bravely growing out of the cliff side. There she dangled, trying not to whimper.

Byrne was at the base of the cliff in seconds, dark eyes blazing up at her.

'Are you holding on tight?' he called as he started to climb.

'Very, very tight,' she assured him.

He appeared alongside her, breathing hard with the effort.

'The answer's yes by the way.'

'Good.' He beamed across at her happily. 'Now we just have to figure out how to get you down so that I can kiss you.'

Epilogue

Text message received 09/09 11.57 WILL HERBERT: Baby boy! 8lbs exactly. Nigel Ptolemy Herbert, to be known as Toll. Mother and baby doing fine. Did you say yes?

Text message received 12/09 18.10 CONRAD KNIGHT: Secret safe. Gordon proving a superstar. Kizzy gone to work for Hector Protheroe Foundation; have a new assistant called Jean who will never threaten glass ceiling. Renewing vows with Madeleine. Live long and prosper.
P.s. Miss your flirting.

Text message received 30/09 21.33 NICHOLAS HERBERT: I have a girlfriend! She's called Violet (so almost Purple) and in my class. She's v good at Wii games. Mum quoting poetry all the time and acting weird.

Email sent 28/11 13.55
From: Gordon Lapis
   To: Allegra North
   Re: Sculpture

Allegra,
I am preparing a statue to celebrate your wedding, which I suggest should be erected in your honour on a stone plinth at the highest point of the field that is now known as Gordon's Green. I should like to unveil it personally at the next Farcombe Festival.

My son seems surprisingly resistant to this very important work of art, which will depict you both in the act of creating my grandchild and will give great pleasure to the many visitors who now flock to the site.

Please do your utmost to talk him round.

Gordon

P.s. Have bought red Mini. Very speedy. Will give you a spin next time you're here.

 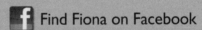